THE PAWNEE INCIDENT

A Novel by

Ira Bex

Order this book online at www.trafford.com
or email orders@trafford.com

Most Trafford titles are also available at major online book retailers.

CLASSIFICATION: Fiction

GENERAL: Mystery Western Adventure

Print information available on the last page.

ISBN: 978-1-4251-0411-5 (sc)
ISBN: 978-1-4907-8458-8 (hc)
ISBN: 978-1-4269-1388-4 (e)

Trafford rev. 09/19/2017

www.trafford.com

North America & international
toll-free: 1 888 232 4444 (USA & Canada)
fax: 812 355 4082

About the Author

Ira Bex is one of four pen names used by this knock about writer, Ron B. Williams, who also writes as K. Ardith and R. Ruby. In Australia over the past sixty years he has been an itinerant worker, boundary rider, rodeo rough rider, road navvy, stage-actor, film and TV-stuntman, Hospital Orderly and Medical Purchasing Officer. This man has traveled a wide percentage of the world in the course of his writing career writing, making television documentaries etc; most of his works has only seen the light of day in Pacific/Asia area, and the Southern Hemisphere regions of our world, but now we have a rare chance to experience the skills this writer has honed over the years through, blood, sweat and tears.
Under the name of Ron B. Williams he had been a member of the Australian Writers Guild for thirty-eight years.

TV Writing Credits: *It's Not a Dog's Life.* A documentary for the Dog Squad of the Victoria Police
Travelogue: *Welcome To Our World - South America.*
It's A Great Life - Introduction to life in the Australian Scouting Ass.

Contact: Williams39@optusnet.com.au

About the Story

It's 1867—the United States is gripped in yet another new battle after that of the Civil War years, auguring in a whole new era and folks are struggling to come to terms with peace and trying to rise out of the economical depression brought about by the devastation of war. Survival is with the opportunist and the need to make a quick dollar is high on the agenda and the methods pounced on are not always legal and many shady characters lie in wait for the ignorant and unsophisticated.

Frank Cotter is a drunken washed up journalist, who is thrown a lifeline by his friend of the pre-war period, opportunist Dr. Lester Lomax. Cotter realizes this could be his last and only chance to redeem himself and regain some measure of respectability and health. Lomax was aware of the scribe's sink to the bottom of the social keg and this was his reason for helping the man; however, Cotter's ruled that the ex-newspaperman dry out and endeavor to remodel himself into the man he once was.

Dr. Lomax heads a business syndicate in Junction City who are offering the Pawnee people on the government reservation the chance of a lifetime, in the form of an elixir developed by him, which the doctor claims will save the Pawnee from annihilation by the white man's illnesses such as smallpox etcetera that is spreading throughout their community.

The Department of Indian Affairs in Washington DC has their suspicions about Lomax and his syndicate being a bunch of con merchants and has them under investigation by the Army. Cotter's task, to convince the US Government and the general public by the power of the pen, that Lomax and cronies aren't the bad boys' bureaucracy thinks they' re con men, out to bleed the Pawnee dry of their gold, with false claims of this cure-all. Washington had forbad Lomax to experiment with the drug on the Indians but he clandestinely went ahead with his treatment of the indigenous folk with his unproven medicine, that in some cases brought about crippling, grotesque results to that of the human body. The Pawnee took matters into their own hands and a wild bunch of Pawnee rebels raided Junction City, where the innocent folk paid the price — leaving the air full of fear that an Indian War was on the boil — the Army stationed a day's ride from the town looked the city's only salvation. Even the might of the powerful Cattleman's Association who normally ruled the district with an iron fist knew they were inadequate to the task of keeping the peace.

Cotter's life took a dramatic turn when he boarded the stage west—headed for the harsh frontier where he would witness first hand its untamed lifestyle before he even arrived in the so-called tame Junction City. It was as if an unknown hand had turned on a faucet and its flow unstoppable. Upon arrival in the burgh Cotter was greeted with news of the accidental death of Lester Lomax which now clearly left him stranded, he can't accept the benefactor's accident as being just that, and has the feeling that there is something not quite right about the set-up and is not ready to accept things as they look on the surface as that of the good citizens and the law of Junction City. He sets about to find the truth and unwittingly opens a can of worms — notwithstanding the fact that he finds himself drawn to the lovely stage actress and ward of Lomax's, Miss Pearl Courtney. But we must ask the question, how genuine is her charm towards Cotter?

There is many a diamondback snake hidden in the long grass waiting a chance to strike the unwary and who will be next is the big question?

Frank Cotter never comprehended what was in store for him and just how large a mystery awaited him when he reached his destination. Army investigators were instrumental in unseating Cotter from his wagon of sobriety, in their efforts to collect evidence against Lomax's good name as they once more drew Cotter back into the alcoholic world he had abandoned out of respect and memory of his benefactor. Once more he was plagued with delirium tremens and haunting ghosts —

even though he knew the dead were under less than six feet of dirt. The town's body count began to climb like a stairway to the sky and no one knew who was to blame for it and why!

The truth of these mysteries came to one man out of the blue and yet he wasn't in a position to deal with it until he had no choice in the matter for events took their own turn and that man was none other than the drunken scribe Frank Cotter…

I

TWENTY-FIVE MILES WEST of Kansas City a restless column of buzzards were making lazy circles in the air-thermal of a clear Spring sky — not a good sign for neither man nor beast. Clearly the vultures were bidding their time for some life form to expire and then they would be able to gorge themselves on whatever fate had bestowed on them.

Joe Hunt — the stagecoach driver was glad the scavengers where to the left of his route, for if there was trouble in that direction he and his passengers would be well out of it. But the phenomenon humored him and broke his otherwise boring drive. Joe did not bother to point out the gliding buzzards to Elisha Fosby riding gunshot; Fosby had his own eyes and power of deduction. Another five miles would see the stage pull into the way station for an overnight break and a change of team.

The interior of the coach catered for six passengers but on this journey there were only five passengers — all males — out of Kansas City on this day and Joe had made it his business to get a line on the customers as per his curious mind dictated. There was a short-ass freelance drummer for the Colt and Winchester firearm companies, who went by the name of Whitney Dragoon — Joe had carried him before and Hunt knew the man was no tenderfoot in the ways of the west. Dragoon, this time round was now sporting a Van Dyke piece of fuzz on his dial and Joe had to admit that it suited the man — it made him a stronger looking character and he gathered that back in St Louis where Dragoon hailed from, that this sort of fuzz must be all the rage; Joe was certain that Whitney Dragoon didn't have it the last time he was out West.

Sitting alongside Dragoon was a new face to Joe Hunt — a stout ruddy faced carpetbagger who dressed more tenderfoot than Dragoon and was as much out of place here as a square peg in a round hole. He went by the name of Chas Morgan and had taken to carrying bottled water with a marble stopper and had two flasks of rye whiskey which he kept to himself. Joe suspected that he had a derringer or some such weapon hidden away on him somewhere, for he looked a sneaky cuss. Morgan had a handlebar mustache which was flecked with gray and stained with nicotine though he hadn't seen him with a cigarette in his mouth since he came aboard, that didn't mean to say that he wasn't having a puff or two down their inside the coach. Joe hoped he wasn't bothering the rest of the passengers if he was.

Across from Morgan sat another Easterner all the way from New York — his name Cotter — Frank Cotter. By all accounts he was a newspaperman whose claim to fame was that he was supposed to have written a couple of books about some important people of the known world — and was reported to be a great friend of the well known frontier Doctor, Dr. Lester Lomax who spent his time amongst the Pawnee Indians trying to help them cope with chicken pox, measles and Mumps — all presents passed on to them via the white man. Joe had no idea how the doctor and the newspaperman come to be connected.

This feller wasn't packing a gun as per usual of all tenderfoots coming West, but Joe knew that he would either have to come to look the part of a man wedded to Ma West and her ways or he'd be crushed underfoot — the West was no place for cry babies, mused Hunt.

Last but by no means least, was Father Lorimar of the Catholic faith. He was clean-shaven, and wore a black ensemble with a mahogany crucifix dangling on a silver chain from around his neck. The crucifix swung free over his heart. He wore a flat brimmed hat with a smooth crown and a loose chinstrap. He clutched a bible forever in his right hand when he didn't have his nose in it — because he was no stranger to the west he wore a Colt .44 in a holster on his right hip with the hickory handgrip butt facing forward so that he could bring the gun into play with his left-handed cross draw — just how quick the Preacher was, Joe had no idea whether or not the man was competent with his hand-gun. But being a man of God, Hunt doubted whether any baddies would stoop low enough and push the envelope into the realm of such an unknown territory.

Fosby nudged Joe with his Winchester, drawing the driver's attention to the fact that the station was at last in sight. Fosby must have known that Joe's mind was elsewhere. Hunt responded to the message and cracked his whip loudly over the heads of his six strong team of horseflesh who had become a bit complacent at this point of the haul. That overhead sound of the bullwhip awaked past memories in the horse's childlike brain of its sting, and as one they leaned harder into the harness — thus there was every chance that the Concord stage would reach the compound of the way station a skip and a hop before dusk.

Like his team mate, Fosby, was looking forward to that ex-army cot which awaited them up ahead — he knew that Joe was especially looking forward to a spell, for Joe's butt had been bumping along on the horsehair box-seat for double the usual distance a teamster has to endure, and he was beginning to feel the effects of the extra drive.

The fact that Hunt and his wife needed the extra money to make ends meet was the catalyst for his torture. Come early morning would see him set off for Lawrence where he would take over the driver's chores on the stage from Topeka along with its commuters — which had earlier set out for Junction City en route for Kansas City and all points, East.

The Concord wheeled into the forecourt of the station at a gallop— with a strong leg and equally strong hands and arms of any stagecoach driver worth his salt, Joe rammed the full weight of his thickset body on the foot-brake lever and locked the front wheels into a skid, while hauling backwards with all the strength he could muster from his shoulders and back muscles so that all six beasts of burden felt the bite of their bits and thus hunched their backs back into the harness straps to bring the vehicle to a stop in front of the building's porch steps — where their trailing dust cloud overtook them.

The lanky Fosby was out of the box like a man with his ass ablaze, using the iron footrest and the iron tire of the coach's front left-side wheel and hub as his ladder to the ground.

Two ostlers were already waiting out in the court-yard; each man grabbed a lead-horse by the bridle to ensure they came to a standstill and held it. Joe didn't allow the weight of his body on the reins to back off until he was sure that the Mexican lads had a firm hold. Then he dropped the ribbons over the side of the coach where a roustabout took possession of them.

Elisha opened the coach door and the passengers filed out down to the ground, all showing a bit of travel stiffness and upon getting their bearings, strolled the four strides it took to make the distance to the porch steps.

"You'll only need hand luggage — the rest will be safe on the stage," Elisha Fosby informed them, "Unless you've got valuables you wanna keep wif ya."

Jesse Bowman came out of the station house to welcome the overnight guests from the Concord with a seemingly winning personality, but in reality it was as false as a phony silver dollar, Bowman knew that unless they were the stage-line's regulars he would more than likely never set eyes on them again once they departed the premises.

Bowman had once been part owner of the coach line and a teamster, but had lost his share in the company at the turn of a deck of cards in Kansas City's Hard Rock Saloon. These days he carried a bit of a chip about on his shoulder which he wasn't backwards in coming forwards to dump on those about him, especially whenever the company's books turned a profit from the previous financial year's audit.

Today his handlebar mustache was untrimmed and the ends, unwaxed. Two-days of stubble stood out on his face and looked like a skin-rash of blackheads under his nose.

"This way folks..." Jesse indicated the open front door of the building — "Jist go right through out the back where you'll find dishes an' water to rid yerself of that goddamn trail dust...'

The passengers filed on through save for Fosby, who in the shade of the porch made use of his hunting knife and cut himself a wad of chewing tobacco from a plug he had been tooting in his vest-pocket and munched away on same while collecting his rifle and shoved off for the station house, where he made a beeline to the bar and unloaded the weapon of its live metallic cartridge rounds.

This was in accordance with Bowman's unwritten rules that no loaded firearms were permitted in the building — not since his nine-year-old boy, Gene, had lost an arm when he caught a stray bullet from a couple of drunk cowboys who decided to sort out their differences with a shootout. The boy might well have died as a result of his injury from a stray slug had not Dr. Lomax been on hand to do the necessary.

These days both hot headed cowboys resided out the back of the station in a patch of waste ground, their unmarked graves as per courtesy of Bowman whose frontier marksmanship — brought an end to their stupidity.

From that day forth, guns were not really welcome under Bowman's roof but were tolerated because they were part and parcel to one's survival here in the west.

Gene was embarrassed, having lost an arm at such an early stage in his life and kept the stump out of sight as much as possible.

Under the sailcloth roof of the back yard lean-to, the coach passengers gathered at a waist high bench where four tin washing basins and three gray speckled, slightly battered enamel coated jugs, furnished the folks intent on having a rinse with water and bars of homemade soap rested on bread plates, which were substituted for soap dishes; towels hung on wooden pegs driven into the adobe wall behind the bench.

The gun-salesman and the priest were old hands at this chore and pushed their way forward to get at the ablution facilities. Coats and celluloid cuffs and collars were removed by all, and hung on spare wall pegs as Chas Morgan and Frank Cotter followed the lead of Father Lorimar and Whitney Dragoon. Cotter ended up next to the priest at the bench and noticed that the preacher had not removed his gun, or its live ammunition. He queried this, as he realized that he was still wearing his Derby and removed it so that it would not get splattered with soapsuds.

Father Lorimar explained as he lathered his hands with soap — strong with caustic soda: "In this country a wise man looks to his own safety, regardless of Bowman's attitude towards loaded guns. You never know when yer going to come across a deadly snake — and I'm not talkin' of the slither kind — one's gotta be on guard against the two legged kind who reckon that a man of the cloth and tenderfoots, are always easy pickings — but a fast draw soon sorts the chickens from the roosters."

"You don't shoot them?" Frank Cotter asked incredulously as his wet soap slipped from his grip and splashed into the basin, which sent him on a fishing trip.

Lorimar rinsed his face and neck free of lather before answering the inquisitive man's question. With his face half buried in a hand towel which was clearly second-hand, the priest said: "…it came to that a few times but when most stand-over merchants see how quick my iron clears leather, they generally don't wanna push the issue; they're afraid I might be able to shoot too straight for 'em.

"It pays to keep their sort thinkin' that a-way…" The Priest stepped back to allow Cotter to get at a dry towel.

Twelve minutes later Frank Cotter, the priest and the drummer were ready to return to the main building of the station through the open back door, the men now paid more attention to their surroundings, such as the fact that the main building had two large rooms on either side of a hallway lined with hessian and covered with a sepia colored wall-paper.

These rooms were the passengers sleeping quarters and that of the Bowmans. Any women on board the stage doss in with the family while the men shared the only other room; it was obvious that the stable-hands slept out in the loft over the stables with the animal stock.

The hallway opened into a restaurant-bar like situation, in which there was a counter set before a stacked shelving of mixed goods, such as blankets, camping equipment and provisions which included a display of new and second-hand rifles and hand-guns and ammunition as well as a couple of small kegs of black gunpowder.

Built in a wall made up of river washed stones and plaster was a big open fireplace with plow sheer iron plate for grilling food and heating a couple of cast-iron pots and kettles — their exterior blackened with soot.

The fire was fed with anything combustible, such as dry animal dung, chopped wood or saplings and greasy rags, which had at one time been useful wearing apparel.

A t-shaped table and church pews were the furnishings of the eatery section; the table being spotlessly clean was kept that way by Mrs. Bowman's never ending supply of elbow grease.

The floor consisted of smooth hard packed ochre clay, which was only taken over by the plank flooring of the porch at the front door's threshold.

When Chas Morgan came in from the lean-to he found that his traveling partners had settled themselves down at the table and save for Father Lorimar, were engaged in a friendly game of cards with a deck which had certainly seen better days.

The priest sat apart from the card-players with his nose buried in his bible. Morgan came across and stood behind Joe Hunt who was engrossed in the game, from where Morgan took up a positioned so that he could see the reins-man's cards and the play. Frank Cotter was sitting next to Elisha Fosby and began writing up his daily diary.

Bowman was leaning on the corner of the counter reading a Chicago newspaper, which had come in on Hunt's stage — though already four days old it didn't bother Jesse, it was still all news to him. Mrs. Bowman was busy restocking the shelves with canned peaches that had arrived aboard the same coach from their supplier in Kansas City

"Where's Mr. Dragoon — the gun-salesman?" asked Cotter as he took a break from his scribbling.

Lorimar did not so much, as look up from the Scriptures; Answered Frank for no one else made a move to. "Strolling; He tells me it's a thing he indulges in prior to supper…"

"It's growing dark out there," Frank stated as he took in the failing light through the entrance, "— he might get lost as the night settles in …?" The priest shrugged and went on with his reading.

Bowman had overheard the men and straight off realized that the stranger could be right about the passenger. This prompted the station master to enquire about where Gene was, for it was their lad's evening task to fire up the exterior lamps which were hanging by the bails on six inch nails sunken it the porch posts.

"It time he got his lamps, lit…" Bowman folded away the newspaper.

"Give the kid a break," Thelma Bowman told her husband, "haven't you noticed he's had loose bowels since that jackrabbit stew we had fer lunch?"

Jesse frowned, "If that's the case —I hope you've no plan ter serve the leftover to our guests at supper…?" Bowman directed.

"Jesse Bowman," Thelma's hands went to her hips, she felt like throwing a nearby can of peaches at her husband's head. "— do you think I've feathers fer brains or sumthin'? I sent the rest of the stew down to the Mexican boys for their supper — I'm plannin' grilled steaks an' hash browns," she sneered, "if that's up to your likin', Your Highness?"

Gene Bowman, appeared in the room from the direction of the hallway, he had clearly been somewhere out in the yard. He was your typical shoeless kid with straight auburn hair like his Mom's, cut, basin style. He wore a gingham shirt and knee patched denim bib and brace overalls, which had faded a dusty hue —they had been his daily wardrobe for the past six days.

Upon sighting the lad his father transferred his attention to the boy. "C'mon, son…" Jesse said in a tone like that of a Master to his apprentice, "Get some lights about the place!"

The one-armed boy said naught but immediately went about the room collecting the unlit kerosene lamps and placed them in a line along the counter's surface and then brought a gray galvanized paraffin tin with a spout from storage and set about filling each lamp's tank with fuel.

"Don't forget ter light the porch hurricane lamp — we've got that Dragoon guy sashayin' about outside, he'll likely need a guide-light ter find his way in…" Bowman said, as he took the newspaper up to the dining table and left it there for any interested party.

The boy nodded.

Joe Hunt drew the cards towards him from where the other players had deposited them. "…What say you, Mister Newspaperman, join the drummer here and me, and Elisha in a game of cards with a little wager on the side ter make it interestin'?" He arched his eyebrows in Frank Cotter's direction—who had by this time pocketed his diary and pencil.

"Good idea, I'll be in that until supper's served…" Frank glanced up at the still standing, Mr. Morgan. "—you and the driver against me and Mister Fosby."

Chas Morgan did not need to be asked twice. He took up his position on the old pew next to Hunt, with a pat to the man's shoulder. "…Between us, we'll skin these pair alive, hey?"

"That remains to be seen, Mr. Morgan," Fosby slung in his direction, "I play a pretty mean hand when a few *pesos* might be won." Elisha reached across the table to the card deck Joe had built before him and placed the deck down on the surface of the table midway between then.

"If it's me backing the scribe against you, Joe, I'll cut first ter see who deals?" Fosby helped himself to a cut and kept the results hidden up against his shirt-front.

"That's awright be me," said Joe Hunt, "I've already shuffled the deck." He made his cut, followed by Drummer Morgan who copied

Fosby's example with the cards, there was barely enough cards left for Frank to make his selection. He took a peep at what he had drawn, but kept just as pokerfaced as the rest of them.

Hunt showed his card first, it was a Seven of Clubs. Chas Morgan flashed his card, a Three of Hearts. Then Frank showed his card to the company, a Queen of Diamonds. Then Fosby came to the fore with a King of Spades. One and all, throwing in their cards following this, and Elisha Fosby prepared the loose cards to take on the deal. Hunt looked across the table towards Frank and asked, casually, "Is it true you're a friend of Doc Lomax, Mister Cotter?"

Frank nodded, "Yeah, why? — you don't approve?"

The reins-man shrugged. It mattered not to him one way or the other.

This caused Elisha to call down the dining room to Thelma and Jesse who were together near the open fire. "Hey, this feller here is a friend of you pal, Doc Lomax!"

"Huh, that so?" asked Bowman as he looked the scribe over.

"Doc Lomax is a pretty famous sort of guy out this part of the woods," Joe informed Cotter and all else that might be eavesdropping on their conversation. "He made himself quiet a pal of the redskins too, out Junction City way. In fact wuz yore very friend who saved young Gene Bowman's life when he got shot — 'twas better the kid lost an arm than his damn life, as wuz the signs in the coffee granules. Doc's known ter have saved many a darn redskin's life too, frum the pox and influenza," Joe

Hunt broke off as Mr. and Mrs. Bowman now approached the folks at the table, their interest now focused on the Easterner. Gene was now outside on the porch attending to the lamps.

"You haven't been West before, I take it?" asked Jesse of Cotter.

"That's, right," answered Frank. "I've not been any farther West of New York than Uniontown, Pennsylvania. I was a newspaper editor there, for almost a year. I got to know Lester Lomax in New York in his student days when I was a cub reporter.

"We lost track of each other for a while during the civil war, where he went to dig out gunshot and set bones. I went Boston way and joined the arrogant social set where I filled my days chasing after foxes with hounds and Mark Potter. We founded *The Boston Star* newspaper—

which floundered after a run of only three years. By which time I learned that Lomax had gone out west and I went on to bum my way around the journalistic world and became a whiskey soak, in the bargain…" Cotter picked up his cards and fashioned them into a lady's hand fan.

"Lester got to hear of me being on skid-row, this knowledge, prompted him to offer me a job to come West and write a book on the work he is doing for the Indians."

"Why a book?" asked Chad Morgan.

Cotter frowned at his hand.

"—Lester believes the government isn't doing the right thing by the Indians. He believes a book exposing the truth of what's going on out here with the Indian Nations will embarrass the government back east, on the world's stage; So much so, that they'll have to take a much more careful way in how they handle the Indian way of life, which is steadily but surely, being destroyed." Cotter threw in three cards and called on his entitled, replacements.

"Me an' my family have no time fer any heathen Indians," Fosby informed Frank. "…They hit a wagon train my Uncle and his family were with, thirteen-years-ago —wiped 'em all out an' took every goddamn scalp they could lay blade on."

"Which reminds me," Joe Hunt declared. "I saw a column of vultures on the wing about two miles Norwest of here; anyone frum here check it out?" Hunt looked in Bowman's direction as though the man ought to know the answer. Jesse was letting the question pass and Thelma Bowman went off to prepare supper.

Young Gene had sidled up to his Pa by this, having finished his lamp chore and put in his two-cent's worth.

"Those buzzards have been ridin' those thermals since round ten o'clock this mornin'. Whatever's a-dyin' yonder, is sure taken a piece of time ter kick the bucket, but she'd be all over me now."

Jesse looked down at the boy with the look of a man who wished the kid would be seen but not heard in adult conversation. "For yore information, son; I sent Pablo over yonder ter see what wuz attractin' the goddamn scavengers. He reported ter me that it wuz a dyin' mustang who must've broke its neck when it somehow fell into an eight-foot deep, arroyo. He left her there fer the buzzards ter feed off. Satisfied, with yuh answer, Mr. Hunt? " he ended, curtly.

Whitney Dragoon came in from the direction of the porch and the early dark of night. He went straight down to the bare top counter and without tossing a glance in the direction of those folks settling into a game of Blackjack he raised his voice to impose himself and his wishes on the stationmaster.

"What's the chance of a feller gettin' some of yore rot-gut firewater you reckons whiskey, Mister Bowman?" Dragoon lent heavily on the counter with his right-elbow as Jesse, went behind the counter and from a hidden shelf under the bar he produced a bottle a product of his own still.

"Let's make up a pot worth playin' fer," suggested Hunt.

"Sounds reasonable to me," agreed Morgan.

"I'll go along with that," Cotter said as he fished change out the pocket of his brocade waistcoat and put it in front of him on the coarse surface of the table.

"You can count me in on that, score…" Fosby said, amicably. "— I've never been considered a Cattle Baron but I can manage a wee sumthin'."

Elisha began shuffling the deck and when he thought the cards had been mixed enough he dealt them out around to those in the game. It did not turn out to be too bad a deal for the players as cards fall, but at the close of play the kitty went to Chas Morgan.

Then as they made ready to start the next hand there was the sound and rush of arrival horsemen from outside — the noise caught everyone's attention, though it did not hold up the start of the serving of the next hand. The riders could be heard talking loudly amongst themselves as they hitched their horses to the porch-posts outside. The animals began to settle and the new arrivals were led into the station by Matt Flynn, the ramrod of the Box & Bar Ranch, owned by Kit Barr, located six miles south of the stage station. Flynn was accompanied by three cowhands, all had spent the day in the saddle working their asses off, and they had dropped by for a charge of the Bowman's rot-gut before returning to their bunkhouse; where at first light they would begin their routine all over again, except, for another visit to the station, they would be too work tired for that.

They were typical of their type and wore cattle punchers' rigs right down to the Cuban heels of their boots. Flynn had been in the Civil

War and came through it unscathed; eager to settle-down, had joined Kit Barr's spread where he made a nice enough niche for himself as foreman. He had been self-supporting since his early teens, as was often the case with many western lads who were either orphaned by the pattern of life or abandoned by their folks who could ill-afford to support them.

Trailing Flynn into the building was Moe Malthouse, a Canadian, whom had come south of the border to avoid a confrontation with a couple of Mounties whom were on his case for the stabbing to death of a prospector. He had been living and working south for the past four years and hoped that when things were quiet for him back in Canada, he might return. He was built like a Lumberjack across the shoulders but had never been drawn to it and was in truth a drifter. Moe wore a sheathed hunting knife and a Peacemaker — which looked all a part of him.

The next two through the open doorway was Texas Kid and "Rocky" Boyd — the Kid was also known as "Tex", and had been too young to fight in the war but back-shot a Yankee trooper just for the experience. Draped over his shoulder was the headless body of a rattler he had shot earlier that day, why he had souvenired it was anyone's guess.

"Rocky" Boyd was a middle-aged, ex-Army enlisted-man and once the war was over he returned to ranch work. Both the Kid and Boyd were two men it paid to be friends with. Not that one would readily race up and embrace them as such.

Whitney Dragoon read these blow-ins like a book and took his drink up to the others at the table and played the spectator; taking a seat next to the Priest. The cow-punchers came up to the bar and pushed the ostlers out of their way. The Mexicans took their drinks and went outside under the awning of the porch, to keep the peace and spend time with the sound of crickets.

Bowman produced two more bottles and stood them next to the one Dragoon had taken first pull from. He followed this with some shot-glasses and the boys from the Box & Bar filled their glasses. Gene came down to have a closer look at the dead snake and somewhat puzzled by why the cowboy was hanging onto it.

When Tex realized the boy was there gawking at the reptile over his shoulder he suddenly pulled the snake from his body and thrust the raw end of the rattle-snake at the kid's face, the boy, reeled back in fear, then realizing he had the boy's number, Tex chased the frightened lad around the room with the dead snake until the boy ran outside through the front door and lost himself in the dark as a shield from his pursuer.

Tex thought it was the joke of the century — no one else did… Though they said naught except for Jesse Bowman, as the Texas Kid returned with the dead reptile still in his hand.

"Don't you ever do that to **our** kid; I won't have it; he's been through enough in his short life!" Bowman said with piercing eyes. Thelma left her cooking to go off and fetch the young boy. The look she gave Tex in passing said it all — she would scratch his eyes out the next time he came at something so stupid.

"You better face it, Tex. You were way out of line," said Flynn.

"Rubbish."

"I reckon it would be best fer all concerned if you fellers had ya drinks and moseyed along fer the night," Jesse Bowman suggested with meaning.

"Ooh, I was lookin' forward ter one of that longhorn steaks yore wife's a broilin'?" said Boyd.

"Ferget it," said Flynn. "Our welcome's worn out fer tonight. Jist let's have our drinks and head off in the direction of the ranch."

"OK," said Malthouse. "Anythin' you say, Matt. C'mon lads, drink up!" Moe Malthouse led by example and the others followed suit. They left to mount their horses, and even by this, Mrs. Bowman had not been able to coax her son back in the building until the ranch-hands had ridden off into the night, in the direction of Kit Barr's place.

The passengers down to a man knew they were in for a shocking night; when they discovered their sleeping quarters were playing host to bed bugs and fleas. But they had no choice other than to bear it until breakfast time.

Thelma Bowman was aware of what the overnight guests had to endure, for the family were caught up with the same problem and she had been doing her devil best to rid the premises of the pests, with little success; so she made up for the passengers' near sleepless night by seeing that they all had a mighty good serve of rolled oats, pancakes — and for their break along the way to Lawrence, she baked some biscuits and wrapped them in cloth in an effort to try and hold in some of their warmth along the way.

Upon leaving the warm comfort of the dining room and stepping out on the porch, the Lawrence bound passengers were greeted by a morning so cold that hoarfrost covered the ground in considerable patches.

The Mexicans had obviously been up quite early and been busy, for the Concord was hooked up to the team which would drag the stage through to its next destination. Vaporized steam poured from their nostrils with every breath, caused through having been led out from their warm barn.

Both Hunt and Fosby had rugged themselves up to withstand the cold, Hunt was moving along from horse to horse, checking that their harnesses had been done just right so as there would be no chafing of the animals. Elisha Fosby was in the process of dismounting from the driving box, having gone aboard to store his rifle in the legroom of the box. He clambered down and opened the door of the vehicle for the customers in preparation for their boarding.

The passengers hurried into the coach as if they all believed that once inside they would find the warmth they were leaving behind at the stage-station, but were in for a reality shock, once they were inside — where they quickly wrapped their shoulders and legs in the heavy Indian blankets, provided.

The Butterfield stage had been underway for only a few minutes when Dragoon produced a bottle of liquor from his person, which he had no doubt purchased from Bowman for the journey. The pity of it was, that it was plainly a concoction he made up and passed off as ***whiskey*** — and was only accepted as such in desperation, especially by those with a serious drinking problem, though in this case, Dragoon was an exception to the rule.

"Hey fellers; got a little sumthin' which'll start a fire in your belly and chase away Mr. Jack Frost!" Whitney took care of the corkage and a sample swig — before proffering it around to the guys on board. His facial reaction to the swig only served to undermine his good intentions. "…***Holy shit!*** That must have half a ton of chili powder per fluid ounce in it!!" He turned to the Priest with smarting eyes. "— My apologies, Father; but she's hot enough ter melt the inlaid gold frum St. Peter's dome at the Vatican!"

"Apology, accepted…" Father Lorimar said, as he reached for the bottle, wiped the vessel's mouth with his hand and lifted the bottle to his nose for a sniff before pressing it to his lips and took a swallow.

"That'll chase out any devils you've got stalkin' about in ya soul," Whitney Dragoon commented in a voice that was slightly off key to that of its usual timbre. He owed this to the bite of his swig.

Lorimar tried to tempt Cotter into participating in a drink, but Frank knew Bowman's so-called whiskey wasn't for him, particularly after seeing the effect it had on these pair of takers, so he wisely reneged — a taste of that potion clearly would set him back in the battle of routing his system of this dependence on alcohol; he passed it back to Dragoon who replaced the cork stopper in the neck of the bottle.

Chas Morgan came to light with a shiny metal whiskey flask from his inside coat pocket.

"Better a Devil you know," Morgan stated as he unscrewed the flask and poured a dram into its screw top that doubled as a nip. "—Than the Devil we don't, huh?" Chas recalled Frank Cotter saying he was on the wagon and having just witnessed him renege the offer of Whitney Dragoon's, supply, made no offer to the scribe but returned the flask to his coat's pocket where he carried a hidden Derringer pistol.

"I'll see whether Hunt or Fosby wants a nip to warm their gizzards," said the gun-salesman, as he rose from the passengers' seat and found it a struggle to hold his balance against the swaying of the stagecoach. He made it to the communication hatch up behind Frank's head, which wobbled on his neck like someone suffering with palsy.

Dragoon could not seem to make the sound of his knuckles heard against the sliding hatch, by those outside, so he gave the idea away and reclaimed his seat, where he went ahead and fished out a cheroot, then lit it from a match he struck on the stiffened, canvas, window-shade. As he torched the end of his cigar and puffed it into life he explained to Cotter that in about another hour or so, the stage would be pulling off the road to Lawrence to spell the team in the shade of some cottonwood trees.

While here they would take a coffee break and thus give the passengers a chance to stretch their legs.

"…We can also put Bowman's liquor to a more practical use, too. It makes a good liniment, and will do wonders for our insect bites of last night… When I came through here last, the Bowman's had a mosquito plague on their hands and Jesse Bowman issued us passengers all a bottle of his drinkin' potion ter use on the bites."

"You know why that is?" said Father Lorimar, "because it **is** liniment; didn't you know?"

Dragoon frowned in the Priest's direction and thought about it; while doing so the Preacher calmly lent in Dragoon's direction and to all their surprises, relieved Dragoon of his cheroot — dropped the remains of the cigar on the floor of the Concord and crushed the life out of it with the sole of his boot.

"Oh, and in case you haven't noticed, *I* don't smoke…" Then sitting back on the bench seat, he added: "***and I*** don't wish to be subjected to the burn off of your filthy habits; if you can't dispose of the smoke from your mucus lined lungs other than in my face then you force me to take the only action left open to me."

The salesman fought to regain his composure, "Hey, h-h-hold on th-there… Lorimar! Where the hell's yer Christian charity? If *you* weren't wearin' that damn collar back-ter-front—I'd have your guts fer garters. Are you fergettin' that a Christen's s'posed ter turn the other cheek!"

The Priest fixed Dragoon with a sardonic smile and said, "…Seems you haven't been paying too much attention to things around you, son. Haven't you noticed that this is one priest that's taken to wearing his own hardware? That should tell you that I'm no chicken-livered Christian … This here ***man*** doesn't turn the other cheek. Get it? "

"What sort of Bible drummer are you?"

Lorimar crossed his legs under the blanket.

"I'm a breed of Christianity that's determined to survive and bring Christian civility to the West and make it last — even if it means usin' sledgehammer tactics ter drive it home so it'll last well, after I've long gone!"

Whitney Dragoon slipped into silent cogitation as he weighed up Lorimar's words. Cotter was obliged to look at the Priest, anew.

Then Lorimar took in how Cotter was regarding him and questioned him about it. "Why you lookin' at me like that?" he demanded of the man.

Frank carefully measured his words as he answered the man.

"I don't know when I last met a man quite like you before."

"Well don't let it give you gray-hairs," Lorimar licked his dry lips, and then continued. "If you plan on staying out in this territory fer any length of time, you'd be wise ter take on the ways of this growing land an' you could start by throwin' away some of them city clothes and airs to begin with.

"Take ter wearing a pistol and make it look like you know what it's all about. Otherwise, you being a tenderfoot will find yourself gettin' walked all over. Don't act like a snob an go out an' buy yourself a gleaming new fire-arm; buy one which looks like it's had some work in its days. "

"I realize you're trying to be helpful, Father. But although I have a job to go to when I step off this stage, I've no idea how long it will last *or if* I really wanna make the west my home,' Confessed Cotter to the Priest.

Lorimar looked Cotter deep in the eye… "You don't have ter tell me where you're at. It's in your eyes. I can see you've got a heap of fences to mend before you can start ter begin to paint your life anew.

"The thing is, we've all gotta pay the ferryman at sometime in our lives an' it isn't cheap. Drink hasn't been your only downfall…" Lorimar pointed out. "Adultery would be high on your list, and it's a wonder some husband hasn't come a-huntin' you with a gun before this. You see, you've got the brand of a philanderer there for all ter see if someone's lookin'… Have you been checked out fer consumption? "

"My lungs are a bit weak and wheezy at night. The last Doctor I saw recommended a dry climate — so Lester's job offer, came at a good time," Cotter dug out his fob-watch, and after checking the time, gave it a couple of winds before slipping it away.

"But you were right on about being threatened with a pistol or two from a few cuckold husbands — I got away with it only 'cause I made it a rule to never carry arms… I wouldn't know how to fire a pistol if my life depended on it — I'd more than likely shoot myself in the foot or something.

"I've heard there are two kinds of handguns as such. A single-action and a double action ... I've no idea whether one type is better than the other — it's because of this   limited knowledge of guns, I've never bothered to learn about handling them. Be no point to it, really ... My weapon has always been the pen — which has proven to be, mightier than the sword in its time."

The Priest looked sidelong at Cotter.

"If you run in to trouble out here, you'll need much more than a pen, son. Even the Bible is just made up of paper sheets and you can't expect to use it as a shield, there's been many a preacher has died finding out the truth in that."

The silent gun salesman felt that the Priest had left the door open for him to come in with his two cents, worth. "You're misleading our Mister Cotter there a bit Reverend, even though your advice is well meanin'. No man ought to put his life in the trust of a second-hand pistol. You've no idea how the previous owner looked after the jolly, thing. It might've been mistreated from day one and could be hankerin' ter blow up in yer face or take yer hand right off!"

"And you're looking at this gun business purely from the angle of a salesman, Mister Dragoon," said Lorimar. "...The man's jist explained that he knows naught about firearms, so he doesn't want some hothead tryin' him out in a drawing contest, 'cause he has a nice, new shiny gun. He needs ter give the impression that he's old material and not fresh off the stage frum Windy City. The best way to achieve that is to be rigged himself out with a gun and holster that has a bit of weathered look about it — and thus gives any hard-cases who are out ter make a name for themselves, food for thought. "

"Maybe Father Lorimar has somethin' there," said Morgan. "...He's tryin' to git Cotter to be a chameleon, blend into the surroundings..." then to Dragoon, said. "You know what a ***chameleon*** is, don't ya, Dragoon?"

Sarcastically, "'Course I know — D'you think I'm ignorant?"

Morgan now turned his attention to the Priest.

"So, goin' by all your talk about guns and things — how does one know, them guns *you're* packing — aren't a couple of phony pieces?"

Whitney Dragoon sat back and folded his arms across his chest and directed a look across at Lorimar which clearly read: "Now what've you got tuh say about that?"

"Hmm… That's fer me ter know and fer you and every other critter, to find out. Bear this in mind, if you're money's backing the wrong pony — you'll very likely end up under some sod on Boot Hill! "

Then Lorimar drew his .44-40 from his holster with almost unbelievable speed and cocked back the hammer in the one motion; the gun's muzzle coming to rest hard up against Morgan's ribcage.

The color drained from everyone's face, save for that of the Priest's. The interior of the atmosphere in the Concord was suddenly highly charged and tensed. After a suitable pause and, having made his point, Lorimar eased the weight off the frightened man's chest and slowly withdrew until the revolver's muzzle cleared Morgan.

"I'm gonna ease the hammer down nice an' slow," Father Lorimar informed the clammy Morgan. "Don't be silly to try anything with that toy you've got inside of your coat, Mr. Morgan — 'cause you might jist end up with a hole in yer that the famous Doctor Lomax, can't patch."

Then without warning Father Lorimar turned to Frank Cotter and proffered the .44 towards him. Frank shrunk back from the pistol as if it was something most disgusting.

"This, my friend, is a single action Colt. You cock the hammer back and squeeze the trigger to shoot — which is almost as good as having what is known as a 'hair-trigger'. "

He carefully holstered the Colt as he went on. "This sort of Colt isn't as safe as the double action Colt in some respects. A double-action Colt takes more strength to pull the trigger for it has to push the striking-hammer right back until it slips free and can begin its fall towards the percussion cap of the brass cartridge, it also, at the same time turns the rotatable chamber and brings the bullet in the cylinder up in line for the hammer's pin to strike the cap.

"However, the slightly slower action allows the shooter to consider if he wants to hit his target or pull the shot so that it goes astray — but each gun has its own particularities an' no one can judge exactly when it's gonna allow the hammer ter drop. That right, Dragoon? "

"Why bother asking me, Father," Whitney said sulkily, "— you seem to reckon you're an expert in *all* matters."

"There's no need to talk like that to Father Lorimar," Cotter pointed out.

"I'll talk the way I choose as long as I've got this strapped, on." Dragoon said as he moved the blanket and coat aside, exposing his holster and six-gun.

Frank Cotter backed off alarmed at just how touchy folks were becoming, he put it all down to the lack of sleep everyone had experienced last night and looked towards the Priest for support. Cotter was sure the man of the cloth would be able to make folks take a breather with their emotions.

Lorimar smiled coolly in Dragoon's direction. "...It appears to me that we're **all** a bit caustic today due to lack of sleep last night? Let's just all take ten, to cool off for a spell, before sumthin' silly, happens."

"I'll go along with, that," said Chas Morgan who realized that he was a contributing factor to the situation which had sprung up out of nowhere.

By the time the stage reached the rest area on the trail, those inside the coach had gone silent and each sat there rocking to the movement of the vehicle and mulling over their own thoughts in their own little world.

Joe Hunt was glad to bring the six-horse work team to a halt in the shade of four cottonwoods... by this time the hard work of keeping the team at a canter and on the road to Lawrence had made him hot enough to peel off his winter-wear while Elisha Fosby was still dressed very much the way he had been when they pulled out of Bowman's place.

Fosby climbed down from the box on his side of the coach while Hunt tied the reins to the foot-brake's lever before following suit — only in his case he went down along the line of horses to check on the leading nag, a mare in blinders who seemed to be making hard work out of her job.

Joe did not want the mare breaking down on him in harness. Fosby opened the coach door for the men to alight and saw the firm grouchy looks on the passengers' faces and gathered that they were not too friendly at the moment; but he said naught and went about the chore of going to the Concord's boot and getting out the gear to make up the coffee and produced Thelma Bowman's wrapped biscuits.

When Joe had done with checking over the horses and harness-wear, he came round to the old remains of a dead campfire, situated two yards out from the base of a healthy cottonwood near which there had been left some chopped dry wood, cut by previous folks, whom had used the area as a lay-by. Joe set about getting a fire on the way as the moody passenger walked about, stretching their legs.

He wondered what had brought on their sour mood, but was certain he didn't want any part of it. However, by the time everyone had had their coffees and biscuits, the passengers' disposition was much more pleasant towards each other and this certainly made the Butterfield staff happy, only thing was, that Joe Hunt knew that he was heading for problems if he continued on with his suspect, mare.

"I'm thinkin' of cuttin' loose the right-hand side lead mare, Elisha…" Joe told his colleague.

"Why so?" Forsby, drawled.

"I think she's developin' trouble with her offside foreleg an' if I keep her in harness she might breakdown, altogether. Best I drop her from the team and set her free; she might even end-up wanderin' back to Bowman's."

"But won't that effect the work of the rest of the team?" asked Elisha as he poured the coffee dregs from his tin cup, over an ant struggling across the ground with the crumb of a biscuit.

"I'll swap one of the middle horses over into her place — their rhythm will be off for a while, but it'll all come together in the end — we'll lose a bit of time but that can't be helped," Joe glanced in the direction of the team who were standing patiently in the shade, unknown that they were the topic of conversation.

A short distance away concealed in the nearby brush was a party of Indians, whom had taken off the day before from a reservation without permission. One or two of the tribe could speak the white man's tongue — and were already thinking of scoring the horse due to be abandoned by Hunt. It cared not to them, that the mare was some else's property; they would just wait until the coast was clear and then hopped in for their chop.

2

STRUCTURALLY THE TOWN of Lawrence was still booming in its own way, as the Kansas City stage passengers saw for themselves in the Wednesday's dusk. The Concord passed four buildings under-construction on the outskirts of town — two on either side of the road leading towards the town's center — viewed for the first time they appeared to have reached the same point of development, as if in a race for completion; the skeletal frames were being clad with unpainted clapboard, like a spreading cancer.

It took the five team stagecoach, six beats to pass the building site, and then it was hemmed in by a row of business premises which made up Main Street and ran out of steam at the other end of town, past the rockery which doubled as a roundabout at the intersection of Main and Hoedown Streets — roughly the town center.

Main Street was a conglomerate of buildings, mostly single story, double fronted, timber and clapboard buildings with corrugated iron awnings extending out over raised boardwalks — the harmony of these timber business establishments were broken by solid looking adobe dwellings which had been introduced by adventurous Mexicans years before Lawrence ever looked like becoming a town — most of the structures had a post and rail tie rack out front, which could accommodate six hacks or working ponies side-by-side.

Some buildings were already preparing for nightfall and had paraffin or kerosene lamps alight behind their window-frames, and as could be seen, only the affluent were able to afford windowpanes as most of the window apertures were enclosed with wax paper tacked to them, as a means of keeping the elements at bay.

As the Concord approached the Main and Hoedown intersection, Joe breathed easily for the first time since being forced to dump the mare at the cottonwood trees after the morning's spell. Like every buckboard, wagonette, wagon, coach and mounted horseman turning

22

out of Main Street into Hoedown — it was a case of one and all, using the rockery, which played host to a selection of prickly pears and blooming wild flowers as a roundabout. Getting a five-team coach round the rockery into Hoedown Street was an awkward nuisance, as far as a maneuver went; for Butterfield's stage office-cum-waiting room and warehouse, occupied the west elbow of the street block; with all loading and unloading being performed in the quieter and less frequented, Hoedown Street.

Nero Malley is manager of the Butterfield depot here in Lawrence, and stood outside the depot — under the veranda's awning, looking down Main Street at the approaching vehicle. He had been a worried man ever since it became apparent that the stage was late, something rather unusual with Joe Hunt being the reins-man. Hunt prided himself on the fact that only two things would delay him on his runs that was God and a goddamn tempest. As the coach neared the intersection Malley noted that the team was running one horse down and this gave him his answer for the coach being late. Clearly, the Concord had been involved in some sort of mishap for which he would need to make an official report to head office, as if he didn't have enough on his mind...

Over on the north corner of the intersection was the Lawrence Courthouse its impressive double-fronted façade made of chiseled basalt blocks while the rest of the building's structure was made from durable adobe with a shingled roof, it also housed the town jail which was run by Sheriff Jock Robeson, a Scotsman, whose claim to fame, was that he had gained his past experience in law by working with the **Pinkerton Detective Agency.** He had to work on trying to obliterate his Scottish burr and had been pretty good at it; for he had been one of Pinkerton's special undercover-agent on several cases for the government during the Civil War and a Scottish brogue could have been his undoing.

Robeson, too, was out the front under the veranda of the courthouse when the Concord hove into sight — his deputy, Bud Reed by his side. Both men had been pestered earlier by Malley with his concern that the Kansas City stage was over-due. Malley had wanted Robeson to send his deputy out along the trail to see whether there was any sign of the coach. Neither man really wanted to make, what they reckoned would be an unnecessary ride for Malley was known to be too ready to kick off a storm in a teacup, as had just been proven.

Bud bid the Sheriff goodbye as he went off in the direction of **THE HEART OF DIAMONDS SALOON** across the way and Sheriff Robeson returned to his office at the back of him for he felt naked on the streets without his pistols which he had left hanging on a peg, driven into the adobe wall of his office. Besides he had a summons to prepare for deputy Letterman to act on. Letterman was Bud Reed's underling and got issued the dirty chores of office as part of his on-the-job training.

The saloon always put up the stage-line's passengers who would stay overnight before continuing on the next day's stage to Junction City. The syndicate which owned and operated the saloon, boasted that they ran the most honest gambling house outside Kansas City and that their upstairs sleeping-quarters were free of fleas and serviced daily for customer-comfort, and peace of mind.

Directly opposite the stage depot on Main Street was *The Phillips Emporium*, which could supply everything from needle and thread to the latest curios from Europe as well as guns and ammunition.

The booking clerk, Issy Cantor, hurried from the counter out through the warehouse to the loading dock, just as Hunt brought the team to a stop near the raised boards of the sidewalk. He went out to be of assistance to any females whom might have been travelling on the stage — for the company had no means to forward a passenger manifest ahead of the coaches' arrival. When he realized that company was only hauling male passengers, he went back inside to the counter at a trot for he didn't wish to get caught up manhandling heavy baggage — physical work was not for dear Issy.

The Depot's ostlers came out of the stage-line's stables to take care of the horses, as Joe handed down the leather ribbons to the one who came down the horse line to the vehicle and reached up for them — as his stable mate took hold of the lead horses by the nose strap of their bridles.

Elisha climbed down from the driving box on his side of the stage nearest to the sidewalk, and opened the coach door for Frank Cotter to alight, followed by Father Lorimar, Dragoon Chas Morgan. Men from the warehouse went to the rear of the coach and began and unloading passenger luggage which had been tagged so that they could sort out the owners' baggage, which they spread along the edge of the boardwalk for transporting inside… Another young man appeared from the warehouse and climb to the roof of the stage and untied a canvas dust-cover which covered a couple of war bags and some pine boxes, all held fixed in place by a rope the gauge of a lariat. A forth youth appeared on the boardwalk near the coach, ready to help the feller on top of the stage as he commenced to hand the luggage down to him.

Fosby led the passengers through the warehouse to the waiting room and the ticketing counter, where Issy fussed unnecessarily with some paperwork Nero Malley met the passengers and welcomes them to Lawrence; he recognized Father Lorimar and warmly shook his hand.

"I thought we'd seen the last of you, Father, when you took off back east?"

"I'm afraid I've disappointed you then, Mr. Malley," said Lorimar. "But I was offered another diocese, which I declined. I'm a man who'd feel naked without my pig-irons," He slapped the palm of his right hand against the gun-holster strapped to his side. The folks from the stage gathered about as they waited for their luggage to be brought in from the street.

Malley caught Fosby's eye as the man left the passengers to wait for their baggage and went towards the staff rest room next door to the manager's office. "How come you've lost a horse, Elisha?"

"That's sumthin' you'll have ter discuss with Joe, he ought ter be in a moment —" Fosby stepped up on to an empty Boston chair where he could see everyone in the room and everyone could see him. "OK," he called to the passengers just in from the Kansas City stage. **"...Those people leavin' us here can collect their baggage and move out. Them that's goin' through ter J.C. — that's Junction City on tomorrow's stage, c'n grab yuh bags and follow me across the intersection outside to the THE HEART OF DIAMONDS SALOON ..."** At this point Fosby lowered his vice as he went on with his spiel. "The line's booked bed'n breakfast fer you as part of the service; but we didn't cover you for yore drinks and gamblin' habits.

"In the mornin' you'll be boarding about eight an' headin' fer J.C., wif a new crew. Me an' the driver will be returnin' ter Kansas City about the same time with a new company of passengers, *we expect.* We 'ope you enjoyed yore journey wif us an' that you'll enjoy good health an' wealth in the comin', future." Having made that announcement Fosby stepped down from his perch.

Nero Malley grabbed him by the elbow and as Fosby paused, Malley leaned over and said in his ear, "What was that all about, ***"we expect"***, business, Elisha? "

"Well, we have started back ter Kansas City befer ter-day wif an empty, stage!" said Fosby. "And it ain't no pleasure havin' 'orses fartin' in yer face fer no good, reason."

"I reckon yer being uppity. Tell Joe I wanna see him in my office before he makes a bolt for the saloon bar of the Diamonds, " Nero released Elisha's arm and set off in the direction of his office suite. By now the luggage had been transferred to the interior of the depot and the passengers got ready to collect their stuff, Joe Hunt came in from Hoedown street and went blind at the change of light but because he knew the interior of the depot like the back of his hand, he was able to head towards the staff room, knowing full well that he would have regained his sight by the time he was at the door. Elisha waylaid him.

"You've gotta see Malley in his office before you do anythin' else — that comes straight frum the 'orse's mouth."

"All right ... I'll go see what's got his whiskers in a knot," said Joe as he went round behind Father Lorimar and Frank Cotter on his way to fill the depot manager's order.

"Remember what I told you about fitting in out here," said the Priest to Cotter. "Get rid of the lemon you've got on yer skull — the Derby's not a hat for the West."

"What he's sayin' is right Mr. Cotter..." interjected Fosby who turned to the priest. "We've fixed you up with a room of yore own across at the saloon — the company figured you'd appreciate the privacy."

"That's mighty thoughtful of Butterfield, Fosby; but I've overnight accommodation fixed up here in town, already; I'll be stayin' with relatives, my sister and her husband, in fact. He is one of this town's two realtors. "

"Oh, OK then... Jist make sure you gets here in the mornin' on time fer the stage.'

"My brother-in-law will certainly see to that!"

Joe settled in the chair before Nero Malley's desk — over the shoulder of Nero seated in the swivel desk chair, Joe could see through the window out on to the Street in the growing dark, he could see someone had already lighted the street's gas lamp across the way. "What went wrong that you lost a horse, Joe — I assume that's the reason you're late?"

Joe nodded. "… I cut a lead mare out of the team 'coz she looked like she wuz going, lame. You can send someone down to round her up if she doesn't make it back to Bowman's place. She's near the cottonwoods were we take our mornin', break, she won't wonder far I shouldn't think."

"It's been a long day for you, Joe," said Nero.

"That's no exaggeration," Joe set to work trying to ease the crick in his neck as he spoke. "Darn glad ter git me ass off that drivin' seat. It's been a few years now, since I've had such a hectic drive."

Malley lifted the lace doily clear of the water carafe on his desk and poured himself a glass of water which was from the well in the backyard near the stables, then produced a small pink pill the size of a shirt button and washed it down. "… I'm sorry but I have to be the bearer of bad news, we, the company, are gonna have to prevail on you to take tomorrow's stage through to Junction City — we'll pay you double of course! "

"You must be kidding. My wife will have kittens if I don't come back to Kansas City with the return, stage.' Joe leant forward with his elbows on his knees. "…You do realize that means I'll be away from home and extra week and a half. How come Ben Armstrong's not makin' the return trip?"

"He's a very sick man. He only barely made it here as it was. We got Doc Borge to take a look at 'im — he had us rush Armstrong down to his surgery and might have tar operated on the poor coot — reckons he has a case of appendices — if they burst is could mean curtains for Armstrong."

"Hmm, that's bad."

Malley nodded. "… It is."

"Look, I wanna help you and the company out, but my wife will worry her heart out if I don't come back with the Kansas City stage. She'll be worried ter Hell that I've been shot in a hold-up or sumthin'!" Joe brought out the makings for a cigarette and shook out a measure of ready-rubbed tobacco into the cupped palm of his hand and used his teeth to grasp hold of tobacco pouch draw-strings to close off the pouch and put it down on the edge of Malley's desk. Then with his free hand he went ahead and found his brown cigarette papers in his right breast pocket of his shirt and skillfully extracted one from the collection…

"I know that," Malley said as he focused on Joe making the smoke. "…But you being here in town leaves me no choice as to whom I c'n use as a substituted driver to step into the hole, left by Armstrong's malaise.

"I'm in a **real** bind. The JC chapter of the Cattlemen's Association have a strongbox, booked to go out on tomorrows stage, marked **urgent**, I wouldn't trust their stuff with anyone other than an experienced and trustworthy, driver – and in this case, that's you." Joe considered the situation he had walked into as he went ahead and licked the gum side of the paper and glued it down, thus completing the cigarette cylinder he was responsible for. "…Awright … I'll force meself ter do you this favor but don't go expectin' miracles as far as speed goes; I'm already stiff an' sore and could do wif a good night's sleep and a bit of free time away from the reins. Don't be surprised if when I git here in the mornin' I'm like a bear wif a sore head — so be warned!"

"You do this chore for me and the company, Joe Hunt, and you could come here stark naked and I won't chastise you,' Malley told him, please that the weight had been lifted from his shoulders, though he never had any idea of the discomfort Joe's shoulders and back muscles were giving him right at this moment.

Frank Cotter's chosen Stetson was dark-chocolate in color with a matching leather headband with brass studs crimped into its tooled fashion design. As he continued to scrutinize his image in the emporium's looking glass, he admitted to himself that the new hat had done wonders for his appearance and gave him a more masculine look, which he knew, wasn't wasted on him.

Driven more by sales commission than anything else, the sales-clerk, Clancy Crowe, did his best to get Cotter to be even more adventurous and set himself out in the typical fashion dress of the West. Even tried to press him into buying a gunslinger design pistol set, with Mother of Pearl hand-grips, and when he got nowhere there, he stooped to trying to talking him into buying a 'sneak pistol', one which could be hidden on his person without detection from observers.

But he was right behind the eight ball for starters. For Crowe had no idea that Frank's wallet was on the slim-side and that Cotter had an aversion of firearms of any type. In the end he could see that the customer had dug in his heels and accepted his loss.

Cotter was happy with his choice for it matched his light colored chocolate flock coat with its dark lapels and pocket-patches and broad gold cravat with its stick-pin against his red-wine shirt and matching waistcoat and pantaloons, the laces of his boots where hidden with spats.

The emporium had opened its doors to the public for trading at 7.30 A.M. Frank had made a beeline for the store with his war bags, straight after an early breakfast of bison steak and eggs to purchase a hat which would cope with the country's bold sun and especially a new stick of shaving soap. Though why he bothered to buy the soap caused him to wonder for he had to rely on a barber's steady hand with a cut-throat razor to do his shaving, his hands still shook too much as a result of his previous binge drinking, to be safe with a razor.

Elisha Fosby was not a happy man this morning, for upon reporting to work he had been informed that he alone would be returning to Kansas City with the stage as its driver and security guard. He had no idea of the changes before this, because last night while he enjoyed a few drinks and a bit of gambling at the saloon tables, Joe Hunt had gone straight to bed and was in a dead sleep when Fosby and the others finally came upstairs to bed.

Upon entering the depot's waiting room Cotter found it nice and warm, someone had come in extra early and lit up the potbelly stove in the center of the room, so that any early birds could benefit from its warmth, especially those here to purchase passage on the service lines or board the stages for Kansas City and Junction City.

Father Lorimar's keenness to be on his way showed by the fact that he was there standing over the stove smoking a cigarette looking out towards Main Street — he had no baggage nearby so one could assume that it had already been checked in by the booking clerk, Cantor. Lorimar introduced his brother-in-law to Cotter and both gave their approval of Cotter's choice of a new hat, though the priest still voiced his opinion that he wasn't in favor of the newspaperman's spats. The priest also questioned Cotter as to why he had not taken his advice about acquiring a pistol.

"You already know where I stand on that subject, Father Lorimar; you shan't convert me on that score as long as you can stand square on your two legs..."

So it was left that they would agree to disagree on the subject of guns.

Whitney Dragoon arrived in plenty of time to book his bags aboard, and it was evident that they would get away on time.

Cantor was as busy as a honeybee; he looked as though he had not left the depot building all night. He was edgy about the strongbox; it was as though he had caught the same flu on the subject that Malley was infected with. It worried him whether or not the feller riding shotgun on today's stage was up to the task of protecting that which would soon be in his charge, Sam Korda had only signed on with the Butterfield company a couple of months ago. He looked every bit of a man who might know how to handle such a job if he got into a rough situation and it was rumored that he had a notch or two to his gun.

Korda was a solid bodied feller with a face set off with a bushy pair of muttonchops the color of coal. Maybe if you looked close you might see the odd strand of gray, but if there, they weren't noticeable. He had dressed for work with a flannel shirt under a bum-length coarse coat with a rusty colored bandanna about his neck. He had a high-crown Stetson which was a smoky black color and broken-in cord trousers which were tucked into a pair of chisel-toed Mexican leather calf length boots, scuffed from used. He had a pair of Colts on his hips and the company supplied him with a shotgun and cartridges loaded with buckshot for the journey. He was out on the loading dock watching the warehouse navvy load the stage. Joe Hunt hadn't turned up as yet; maybe he was still having breakfast at the saloon. He and Korda had only met in passing through the depot so one couldn't say they were that well aquatinted.

The stage had been under way already for twenty-minutes and the horses had settled into a steady rhythm that was guaranteed to gobble up the miles; this allowed the overworked Joe Hunt a chance to relax and let the team have its head and simply follow the trail lay out before them…

Another forty minutes into their journey and both men had from time to time had a glance back behind them on the road, and to their surprise, saw thunder clouds miles away behind them working themselves up into a pledge of stormy weather, but there was naught they could do about it, they had no control over nature. Both men could only share their concern about the weather and hope that it was possible for them to get to the next stage station before the developing storms were able to overtake them.

Lightning, thunder and hailstones would make life very hard for the reins-man of this or any other vehicle caught in the grip of such a storm, horses were easily spooked in bad weather for no matter how many storms they went through it always put the fear of Hell into them.

"We got our oilskins wif us, Sam?" Joe asked. "I reckon we'll need' 'em before the day's out."

"They're up here somewhere amongst this lot of junk," Korda said, referring to the tied-down baggage hemmed in by the Concord's roof rack Without being prompted Korda placed the shotgun on the floor of the box and turned about so that he might climb up and search through the top load of the stage, in the hope of locating their wet weather gear. He found the oilskins and sou'westers for the two of them, but as he made his way back to his place in the box with them, Sam Korda decided that the sou'wester wasn't for him, he'd stay with his Stetson for it had served him well enough in wet weather on the cattle ranges. Once back in position, he handed Hunt his share of the protective gear; the reins-man took it quickly and scrunching it all up, sat atop of it on the seat. Korda slipped awkwardly into the arms of his oilskin and hauled it up and about him.

"Want, I should take the reins fer a while, Joe?"

"Yes. I'd be much obliged, Sam," Hunt answered. "You had some practice at handlin' a six-horse team…?"

"Wouldn't suggest it, if I wasn't able too," Sam said as he held out his hands for the leather ribbons.

"That makes you pretty indispensable ter me," Hunt told the guard as Sam Korda relieved him of the leathers so that he could climb into his oilskin. Meanwhile the far off cumulus clouds back towards Lawrence continued to muster themselves together like a massive herd of plains buffalo which the Indian had found imperative to their way of life.

"This stage is damn cumbersome ter handle, Joe, don't be too long fussin' wif yerself," Korda called as Joe settled down in the box and got ready to take back control of the Concord's team. He too, hadn't bothered with the sou'wester...

"You can hand me the ribbons, now!" Joe took back the leathers and Korda reached down on the floor of the box and picked up his shotgun and settled back in his seat alongside Hunt. "...The stage feels awright ter me, 'cause I'm used of the reins," Joe told his sidekick. "What's nigglin' at me is that I don't know how watertight she'll be in the wet. Our passengers might cop a wet ass if the storms back yonder overtake us."

One of the lead horses stumbled and its head went down, Joe had to pull very hard on the reins to make sure the animal got its head up, otherwise, the workhorse would be down on the knees of its forelegs and with the trailing horses ramming into it from the rear, they would be in trouble!

"That wuz close," Korda admitted, as he realized what could have just happened but was only avoided by the skill of a top reins-man such as Joe Hunt. "— We were almost in the soup that a-time!"

"That's fer sure. You know what would've happened if I never got that cayuse head up in time?" Joe said.

"Sure do. We'd've had a pile up an' horses could've been hurt an' harnesses wrecked all out here in the middle of nowhere... Jist be lovely with a storm bearin' down on us an' all!" expounded Korda.

"You c'n say ***that*** again, Korda."

Joe's statement was topped off with the sound of a distant thunder peal from the direction of Lawrence; both men turned and took a look behind them over their shoulders. The clouds had come together in a long, high bank above the horizon and had begun to change their color texture ... They were gray in part and snow-white in others and elsewhere, they could be seen turning a dark purple, not a healthy sign and both men wondered what speed the wind at the back of them was traveling, they had no idea that by their present day's measuring devices, the velocity of the wind could not be measured, such as its speed.

"Hell," cried Korda, "we ain't in fer a picnic my son!' Both men about-faced and Joe urged the team of horses to pick up the pace.

"…I've seen weather like that before, and I don't like it," Joe told Korda.

Sam Korda agreed "— it's the kind of shit that harbors goddamn twisters in my book!"

"I c'n tell yuh Sam, I don't want any part of 'em, twisters. I've lived through three tornadoes an' that's plenty enough fer me! "

Sam Korda slid from the seat down slightly below the dashboard so that he was now crouched before the communication hatch under the seat and upon opening the hatch looked in on the passengers who were completely ignorant of what was brewing outside. Sam brought them up to date and alarm showed in the faces of the city slickers; save for the priest who said to Sam, "…All we can do is take what the Good Lord hits us with, Mr. Korda."

"If the heavens open up before we reach the stage station or a twister comes through, we could be in serious trouble," Korda warned. "Remember, we ain't magicians an' we'll have ter live wif what we get!" With that, Korda slid the hatch shut and retook his position up alongside Hunt. "… We aren't gonna make the station before that weather catches up wif us, are we, Joey? "

Joe shook his head. "Not unless these horses sprout wings — look how fast that weather's closed in since you last had a look…?" Korda didn't like what he saw.

Heading towards the moving stage was a vicious looking storm; the clouds were like towering canyon walls with cloudy draws big enough to hide ten longhorn herds of cattle traveling the Chisholm Trail all at the same time. Back behind the storm's front there came the report of a thunderclap which sounded like a cannon shot.

"God!" Korda hollered, "If that bastard had been right over the top of us, we'd have been deafened…" Now ahead of the storm-front came a stiff wind pushing all before it, especially anything which was not a firm fixture. Within moments it was gale force winds that they found themselves caught up in, their hats were torn off and lost to the prairie as dry tumble weeds of landslide bolder size and wooden pail size raced down pass either side of the Concord which swayed much more alarmingly as the vehicle took the full brunt of the wind-gusts. "— We won't be gettin' ter Spring Wells before we cop a dousin', that I can say wif confidence," said Korda.

A Few minutes later they had a wall of clouds towering right over the top of them and the storm's squall injected fear and terror into the team as heavy raindrops began to pelt at the men on top of the vehicle, the horses felt trapped and hindered by their harness. The daylight changed quickly into that of twilight and the transformation threw all horse sense aside — Joe had his hands full in simply trying to keep the frustrated animals on course with the trail. Dragoon stuck his head out of the coach window frame and his hat leapt from his head, hit the ground on the very thin edge of the brim, and bowled away like a unicycle as the wind propelled it over the stunted prairie vegetation or forced it to pirouette like a ballerina before continuing on its way. The rain saturated his hair in seconds and he had the message passed down inside the coach that they were just about in the middle of a tempest.

Then the hail came and at first it belted the Concord with ice the size of wheat grains and accumulated on patches of ground so tightly packed that its gathering looked like snow instead of hail; but right on the tail of these small grains came hailstones that were exactly that, stones in various sizes — some the size of pool balls which hit man and animals alike, with bruising force and bounced across the terrain like small, spent cannon balls. Overhead the thunder exploded like a cannon fuselage and wild dazzling lightning lit the broiling clouds and forked its way to earth. The trail quickly turned to mud which adhered to the iron tires of the coach like thick volcanic lava… Joe hauled the horses to a halt but in their terror they wanted to continue on and he finally had to risk getting down out of the driving box and snap a chain to the driver's side front wheel around the spoke; but even then the horses were too afraid to give in and they slowly dragged the vehicle along in the sticky mud until their strength gave out. Meanwhile, because the stage was only barely moving, Korda climbed down and got inside with the passengers to avoid being stoned, but Hunt had to stay outside and walk with the coach holding the reins in his paws, just in case the team got a second wind and decided to bolt for it.

Once the horses were spent and it was no longer possible for the exhausted animals to move the Concord, Joe, too, climbed inside to get out of the weather for now the hailstones only came in short bursts and had diminished in size to that of Roman marbles.

"Otto Lehmann's station is gonna look like paradise after this experience," Sam Korda told the passengers who sat waiting for the storms to pass. Meanwhile Joe's bruises began to come to life. He had a cut eyebrow and two lovely black-eyes due to the hailstones, for he had been hit mighty hard on the bridge of his nose, which accounted for his pair of eye bruises.

"When the rain and hail eases off a wee bit more, we all ought set about collecting any dead wood lying about and light ourselves a warming fire in the middle of the road," Lorimar suggested. Everyone agreed it would be a good idea because it was just about freezing with all the ice lying about. But not all good ideas are applicable, the hailstones dropped away in an hour or so to become torrential rain, helped along by gale-force winds which continued to batter the cumbersome vehicle.

"This isn't doing anyone any goddamn' good," said the battered and bruised Joe Hunt after a while. "… I'm gonna get back on top an' put the team ter work. We won't travel fast but every step the team takes will be takin' us that bit closer to the way station where we'll find some decent comforts." He opened the door and if it were at all possible, colder air found its way inside. "— are you wif *me,* Korda?" he called back over his shoulder as he slammed the door shut after him.

Sam Korda much preferred to stay in the coach with the passengers but knew that it wasn't fair to leave Joe up there in the box alone to suffer the elements; so he hauled his ass out of the vehicle through the other door near where he was sitting and joined the stage-driver up top, just as Hunt was in the process of taking possession of the reins. The wind and rain combined together in a raucous din and left the Butterfield employees in no doubt, they were nuts to be out here trying to fight against nature's elements.

The wind's force threatened to lift both of them off the coach like yesterday's newspaper and blow them across the plains like darn tumbleweeds. Sam grabbed a coiled lariat from the floor of the driving box; a spare rope was always kept handy onboard for necessary use.

"… This wind's gonna be dangerous Joe, we oughta rope ourselves to this darn critter fer our own safety – so's no one'll git hauled orf in this harlot of a gale?!"

"I reckon yer right," Joe answered, wisely as Sam paid some rope out to him. Both men wrapped the lariat twice round their waists and tied it off on either side of the luggage rail on the Concord according to each man's position. By now the down trodden horses had lifted their hanging heads for they realized that for them it was back to work and they leaned as one into their harnesses to commence the stage to roll forward as Joe hollered: **"GEE-UP!"**

The horses had managed to raise an acceptable trot and the vehicle rattled along through the squishy mud and rode over lumps of slowly melting hailstones, now half the size of pool-room balls. Worst of all, the squalling rain and wind had not so much as taken a breather from the time they had retaken their seats back up over the horses' rumps.

"…The German's stage station will be one haven we folks'll be glad ter reach," Korda yelled above the storm towards Joe.

"That's fer sure," Joe concurred as he joined in and turned their conversation into a yelling match to beat the howling wind. "…Otto Lehmann still wif his squaw-woman?"

"Halona? Ya; and his four half-bred off-springs…" Korda reminded Hunt.

"Do you know the Nor' Indian meanin' of his squaw's name?" Hunt yelled in Korda's nearside ear. Korda shook his head – he hadn't bothered to take onboard much Indian in his days – he considered them as far as people went, a bunch of has-beens now the Anglos and Latinos had collective power over them.

"It means "fortunate" – though ya can't say bein' hooked up wif old Lehmann's brought her any *fortune!* … Say, Lehmann's oldest bastard must be school age, now?" Joe surmised. His voice box was feeling the strain of making himself heard over the elements.

"Evident you ain't been this part of the run fer a while, Joe!"

Hunt nodded, **"But that don't cancel out that I've put me time in more than this fer west… I used ter hang out at Fort Stockton and Comanche Creek, sewin' me wild oats."**

The German, Otto Lehmann, Butterfield's station manager stood on the veranda watching the heavy rain and wind tormenting the establishment with vigor. Already the clay courtyard, worn low by the shod hooves and iron tires of heavy Concord coaches, had been turned into a lake of muddy water. Half a dozen tumbleweeds out on the open prairie bowled and bounced along with the wind on a journey to no-where.

Otto turned towards the windmill some 100-yards away, and marveled at the speed the vanes were being spun — they were a blur as they faced into the stiff wind and the bullet-like raindrops that collided with them, were smashing to molecules so fast that they became a fine mist hovering in the circumference of the outer edge of the blades; he had never before witnessed anything like it, nor had Halona, his chubby Indian woman whom, by this stage of her breeding cycle had given Otto three daughters and a son — they too watch the spectacle and heard the metallic howl of the vanes which had they ***known,*** sounded like that of a Banshee on the prowl.

The Lehmann kids wore clothing generally handed out to refugees in a crisis, but were ignorant of the fact — because in fact — the Lehmann household looked pretty much like what they were, poor, and illiterate folk. Otto's once blonde hair and bushy Santa-like beard, were now stained almost orange from the nicotine of the man's years of walking in the smoke of his homegrown tobacco. It had been years since both his hair and beard had been clipped. He was fifty but his wild look made him look older than his years.

Today he had rigged himself out in a flannel open-neck shirt, which could barely accommodate his well-developed biceps, and a pair of grubby, khaki, cotton drill trousers — which he's tucked into his old calf-length boots. A pair of adjustable leather suspenders held up his pants and he had thick legs like bollards on a pier.

Just about now, a tall tree down near the corral became a casualty of the storm and was uprooted with a resounding cry as the wind completed its extraction — the tree toppled over and partially flattened the post and rail fence of the otherwise empty corral — the surrounding area down there now resembled marshlands. None of the work animals were at risk, for the family had rounded them up and locked them in the barn.

The sound of the tree coming down and exposing its roots to the world brought Matt Flynn, Texas Kid and Moe Malthouse out onto the veranda. Their presence in this part of the world had to be a mystery, for they ought to have been back on Kit Barr's ranch waiting for the storm to abate, so that they could attend to their chores and any storm damage.

"…Told you ages ago that there tree wuz dangerous, Otto," Flynn said, taking off his hat and running his fingers round the sweatband of his Stetson. Malthouse stood by chewing his cud on a chunk of tobacco he's bitten from the plug he held in his hand. It had every indication of being a fresh plug of jaw tobacco and so it ought to have been, as the Canadian had only recently purchased it from Otto's shelf stock.

Tex stood there and secretly eyed-off Lehmann's squaw as he had been doing ever since the trio had arrived. Chunky women appealed to him sexually as too did black womenfolk, it mattered not to him whether they had calved to another bull or if they had the face of a Moose; he desired their raw, primitive aura, though he knew and understood that to a lot of white men they didn't appeal. Tex knew deep down that he wouldn't make a pass at the squaw for the German guy looked hotheaded enough to rip the arms out of a man's sockets.

"Vell no more worries fer you on that score, Mister Flynn," Otto pointed out to the ramrod. "…Must be two winter's worth of burnin' wood now lyin' down there — vot you reckon, Malthouse?"

"Don't go askin' me about trees, Otto. I ain't done any lumberjackin' in my life! Not   every Canadian's or has been a tree-jockey." Moe Malthouse said after spitting a stream of tobacco juice into the mini lake of rainwater, where it sank with the seeming weight of a pebble.

Then without a warning, out a-ways from the homestead what seemed like a ball of feathers come rolling pass and *Halona* realized right off that it was one of her free-range laying hens. The squaw came to life with a piece of speedy action that belied her demeanor, she moved with the agility of a lithe Indian maiden, she ran forward on the balls of her feet with full stride and upon coming to the end of the veranda she leapt clear off the building like a wild turkey attempting flight and sailed out a yard and a half before gravity took possession of her, touching muddy ground on the run, leaving her moccasins behind in the process as she went on to catch up to the tumbling hen and swept the bird up by hand while on the move without losing her grip on the hen; she had enough nous not to try and turn back towards the house for with her weight and speed she would slip over on the slippery surface of the ground and end up covered in gooey mud from head to toe … She carried on ahead until she has lost enough speed and momentum to eased herself to a stop with her prize pullet in her hand; the children cried with glee at their Mom's success. Returning to the sanctuary of the veranda, the squaw now realized that the pair of them was wringing wet.

"Zhat hen's for the cooker, woman —" Otto told his de facto as she caught her breath. "It's in shock and von't live ter drop, any more eggs!"

Without any backchat to Lehmann, the squaw went directly inside and set about preparing the bird for the pot. The children followed their Mom in awe as the wind and rain seemed to pick up, the stage station's building, although already vibrating to the force of the gale gave a woeful groan which no one missed as it warned to one and all that it might leave its tree-stump foundations. Then without warning the wind dropped to an eerie silence surrounded the station's immediate area, but the rain continued to beat down… Lehmann and his customers were about to go inside when they were all witness to the sight of a giant twister forming on the distant horizon in the southeast caught their attention. They knew they weren't in any danger from it as the Tornado was five miles away and heading away from them with the speed of an express locomotive, but it was certainly going to be a danger to the animals on the open plains, sucking them up into its eye and bring them an untimely end.

Then a coyote dam with two pups came in from the east, the rains has obviously flooded her den which she had made in the lee of a once, dry wash, and now she and her family were homeless. They must have been attracted to the human settlement. Tex drew his revolver and had a couple of shots at them, to see if he could hit one of the pups with a bullet, he missed a trailing pup he was going for, but not by much, still, his shots were wasted.

"Let an expert show you how it's done, Tex…" Moe drew his six-shot pistol and fired off a shot at the same coyote pup — his shot was also ineffective.

Matt tapped Moe on the wrist. "Don't waste the lead, pal. They're already outa range."

"Flynn's, right Moe. Zhere a good ninety yards away, now!"

Malthouse and Tex knew Flynn and Otto were right, the coyotes were certainly out of pistol range, so Tex angrily shoved his gun home in its holster.

"Come inzide an' I'll buy youse a drink while I've still got a roof on the place," Otto made for the doorway, Flynn, Moe and the Texas Kid followed without argument, especially as there was a freebee on the slate. Compared to Bowman's liquor, the German's stuff was like ambrosia — only because his product came from a reputable source. And since he had offered to do the buying, these boys weren't going to pass such an offer up.

Halona sent the eldest girl outside to retrieve her muddy moccasins, which she instructed her to put near the heath of the open fire to dry. The rain abated and only the wind came back to carry on harassing the station and the out buildings of Spring Wells.

While uncorking a fresh bottle of bourbon, Otto, noticed that his woman was beginning to make lunch and as he got down four shot glasses from the shelf at the back of him he asked the cowboys to join the family in their midday meal. Malthouse and Flynn readily accepted the invitation as they watch the Hun dust off the glasses from either accumulated dust or fly spots.

"What's fer grub?" Moe asked, as if it **really** mattered to him.

"Uh-huh, a mix of Whiteman's cookin' and a bit of tribal cookin' " Otto paused to rub his gut which had never been the proportion it now was, he had only filled out like this since he began bedding Halona and sampling her Indian culinary. Halona had been the best investment he had made since swapping his old Spencer rifle for her with her tribe. "Yew mightn't find our food thet over appertizin' — but it sure as Hell tames the worms inside ya guts …"

"And if you ain't got worms?" Tex asked.

"I thought everyone 'ad worms frum time ter time?" said Otto.

"Nay… 'Ts not so," said Moe.

Otto frowned and then said: "In zhat case it'll give 'em to you!" He grinned and saluted them with his bourbon and downed it in one quick swallow.

Malthouse and Flynn looked at the German like two men lost in a real conundrum. But the Kid had lost interest in the conversation his mind was fanaticizing, about how he would like to bore it up the squaw's ass.

Then without so much as a prior warning a trap-door in the floor was eased open and the black head of a wide-eyed Negro appear, as if it had risen up from the very bowls of the Under World. This was in fact the unofficial patriarch of the two, poor Negro families who now worked for Lehmann and lived below ground in the   storage-cum-storm cellar. The civil war of some years back had left them destitute and it was only through the German's kindness that they have survived thus far.

The crinkly gray-haired man had come up stairs with food to be prepared for his tribe's midday meal, although normally they worked through until supper time before eating the next of their two-day-a-meal rations, but the fearsome storms had curtailed today's chores save for those of maybe hooking up a fresh team to the expected stage if it made its way through and weather permitting, would continue on its way. But in weather such as this, that was asking the impossible.

The Butterfield stage-team had no respite from the wild gale, even though the humans had taken time out and been able to gather themselves together in the Concord. Now roped to the stage, like a pair of donkeys; Joe and Korda realized that the time spent inside the vehicle with the passengers out of the elements had in fact *left* both the Butterfield men wishing they were elsewhere other than out here.

The dark   plumb clouds over head, were certainly charged with an enormous amount of static-electricity which began a frightful light show as white and blue shots of lightning lit up the cloudy drawers and others earthed themselves to any highpoint of the land's terrain; whether it be a dried out knurled greasewood or brittle tumble-weed still rooted to the dirt for some reason, all became targets and were blown apart in a shower of sparks and left a smoldering mess — for lightning did not appear to strike in the same place, twice.

Hunt's fear was that at any time a lightning strike might go for the iron shoes of the horses, such a rare strike, but quite possible would kill the beast targeted, stone dead in its harness — all the man could do was hope and pray it wouldn't happen. Korda knew that forcing the stock on under such conditions was cruel, but he realized that forcing them forward as Joe Hunt was continuing to do was the only answer out here on the open range. Sam also knew that Hunt was in the same soup-bowl as he, and that the icy wind was chilling him all the way through to the bones. *Surely there could not be too much farther to go before they reached the stage-station,* thought Korda...

The horses were almost out on their hooves, but nonetheless, they were the first of this motley crew to sense the odor of humans coming from the direction of Lehmann's station, for the wind had done a complete about face and was coming directly into their faces. The team pricked up their ears, as the smell jogged their memories that warm stables and fodder might be just around the next couple of bends.

Just where the animals got their reserve from only God could know, but they certainly picked up their heels — they did not require the guiding hand of man to swing them away from the worn trail to Junction City, they instinctively took to the branch trail which took all travelers that quarter mile in to Lehmann's way station.

Lehmann's household came out and gathered under the awning of the station's veranda to check on the storm-damage, the Negroes from the cellar mixed in with them, everyone was afraid that if a tornado came through and hit the homestead they would all be homeless in an instant, for who knew exactly when the next wave of hellish weather might come through and tear the homestead from its foundations?

The children of the outpost were the first to sight the Concord coming along the trail headed towards the turn off into the way-station. Full-blooded Negro kids and half-cast White kids cheered for joy at the sight, as the coach now lumbered towards the station building and its mini lake of muddy water, now fetlock deep...

The coach team splashed its way into the small dam that had formed in the ground's depression and came to a ready halt in the murky rainwater. The animals looked to anyone's eye with a bit of sense —

that they were incapable of going any farther, such was their fatigue. The Negro men moved into action without question, they moved lithely across the veranda's decking on bare feet and dropped off its edge to the mud, which squished, between their toes as they made their way towards the horses and grasped the Flemish breed by their bridle'n bit. They were, to a man, versed in the handling of horses, for being former plantation slaves meant they were a skilled labor force.

Joe Hunt sagged there in his seat and allowed the reins to fall from his stiff, hooked fingers; his hands began to shake uncontrollably as a result of their hours of labor. There was no-way he would be able to force his fingers to work nimbly enough to untie the knot of the cow-rope on his side of the wrought-iron roof-rack which secured both him and Korda in position.

Whitney Dragoon twisted the coach-door handle and threw the door open wide, but baulked at its threshold when he saw the less than calm pool of water below in the depression; there was no way to ascertain its depth and he had no intentions of subjecting his precious footwear to that of the unknown? The other passengers on board knew not the reason for his hesitation and were keen to be anywhere else other than the interior of the stage.

Otto addressed the perplexed Dragoon, who clearly did not know which way to turn.

"Vait there, sir..." Lehmann turned to his son. "— Get some empty soapboxes from zhar cellar!" The kid eagerly went off to fulfill his father's command and he wasn't alone, for the siblings of both races wanted in on the act and chore, they ran in to the homestead and down to the cellar.

"...The soapboxes will act as duckboards ter get you from the Concord to zhar veranda steps," Lehmann explained with his hands shoved deep down in his pockets.

Tired though he was, Joe Hunt recognized the cowhands, Flynn, Malthouse and Texas Kid standing there in the group of folks gathered under the awning. It puzzled him as to how they got there and why they were there, when he knew they were employed by the Barr spread. Korda had put his rifle aside in the Concord's driving box and rubbed his hands together to get the blood circulating so that he might attack the rope's knot on his side of the roof-rack. But to his frustration he was unable to make any headway with it, wet with the rain, the knot simply would not give.

Mrs. Lehmann solved the problem. Without considering the matter for any great length, the squaw drew her hunting knife from its sheath at her waist and threw the weapon with dead accuracy at the stage near where Korda was struggling with the rope. The knife ***thunked*** point-first into the vehicle's woodwork where it wedged fast in the grain of the wood, the knife just suddenly appear there as if it were some stage-trick by a magician — the woman's action shocked Sam Korda— who nonetheless recovered his repose as he realized such a threatening instrument had gotten there, he freed the embedded knife from its tight wedge and set about cutting their anchor-rope.

Otto paid no heed to the falling rain as he reacted to the surprise he got at seeing the stage was being driven by none other than his old knock-a-bout pal from yesteryear, Joe Hunt. Otto came out from under the veranda and stepped down into the pool as though it never existed and trudged his way towards the stage, craning his neck to see round Korda's body to get a better picture of the exhausted, Hunt. "…Though 'tis nice ter zee you, Hunt, you look a drowned rat, man!" Lehmann said, informatively. "— how many moons now, since we did some jawin' over a hill a beans?"

Joe's mouth looked exactly like the slash of a Bowie Knife in his pale face. "G-g-give me some breathin' space, Otto, I'm plum tuckered out, man — someone's gonna help me down off this contraption, or I'll fall an' bust me guts."

"Abner an' Cyrus — forgit the hosses fer a bit and help that White feller down — take 'im inside and get 'im ter bed!" The Negro stable-hands left what they were doing and came a running. Meanwhile Otto scrambled under the coach tree and came up on Joe's side of the stage, and climbed up via the front wheel's hub to start helping Hunt, it was now obvious that he was as weak as a new born kitten and no doubt squamish.

Korda knew he was expected to help, but he only had enough strength in himself to make it down from the coach into the rainwater pond, and staggering like a drunk he made his way over to the veranda and gave the squaw back her knife, he thanked her with his eyes for he was too worn out for words. Then he sank down on an upturned wooden pail, which became a dearly needed seat for the shaky man...

It was only when seated, he paid attention to Flynn and his saddle pals, whom he clearly knew from sometime before. Moe had a shot of bourbon still in his paw and passed it to Korda. "Here, git this zin ya, you need it more'n I does," Moe told him. Sam took it without a word and downed the liquor in the one gulp, as two kids came out the front door with two pine boxes apiece — then still more children followed them each with a soapbox.

A Negro woman about 25-years-old or so directed the children to place the boxes in a single line from the end of the veranda on the ground across to just below the bottom step of the Concord. Tex silently appraised her as a likely bed-partner and quickly removed his hat and toyed with it in front of his fly-buttons so as to hide his swelling manhood. The passengers then took advantage of the temporary path, which led to the first of the two steps at the foot of the porch.

Between Otto and his staff they got the weakened driver down from the rig and across under the veranda as hail the size of apricots began falling out of the clouds —the storm lashed horses threw their heads and hunched their backs in an effort to avoid being struck. Lehmann turned to a lean, barefoot, naked headed Negro — who had been left holding onto a halter.

"Get zoes hosses and the stage undercover of the barn before they're beaten to a pulp an' the stage, wreck, Isaac!" he hollered. And as the man responded to his instructions, Lehmann turned to the children now in a group of their own and said: "I haven't zeen hail out zis vay shat big since a-fore any of you wuz born, D'you know?"

Flynn came and knelt beside Hunt and took in the man's condition. Hunt looked winded as though he had been thrown from a bronco.

"...These men need a bunk and plenty of rest," Matt reported to those around him. With that Matt Flynn, Father Lorimar and Tex, grabbed a piece of Joe and carried him inside; Tex knew if he got his mind off the colored ass nearby his member would stop having a mind of its own — Cotter and Dragoon and the others were left to bring up the rear, save for the squaw and the colored womenfolk... Korda and Malthouse paused a while out under the awning, they seemed to be taken in by the fall of the hailstones which were laying the stage station's vegetable garden to waste, at the side of the homestead — along with a bedraggled scarecrow. No, their minds weren't as interested in nature's destructive power as they outwardly seemed — their minds were working at something more lucrative, such as lining their pockets with what was in the stage strongbox destined for Junction City and out the corner of their eyes, they watch the Negroes steer the stagecoach into the red barn.

"They put the strongbox on board, Sam?" Moe asked, in a hoarse bourbon oiled voice.

Korda nodded. "Sure. What about Flynn and the Texan? Are they comfortable with the situation?"

"They ain't here fer the good of their health — jist their wealth!" the Canadian grinned, with an encouraging pat on Sam's shoulder.

Nodding, Sam told Malthouse: "Watch yer hands Malthouse; we're gotta appear to be casual acquaintances so no over friendly gestures … I don't reckon we should make our play jist yet, awhile… I need some rest befer hittin' any trail at a gallop."

"Awright. I c'n see yore point. Anyhow the country's too waterlogged fer a fast getaway — our hosses would need ter have web feet ter cross the mud flats an' flooded arroyos. You take yuh spell an' after that, we'll make our play fer the strongbox." Moe Malthouse said as he stepped round the stagecoach guard in the direction of the way station's open doorway.

"C'mon Korda, best we git our hides inside before someone gits curious about us layin' back in the harness …"

Korda gave Moe the right to enter the homestead first so no one would realize they were jawing away like one time war buddies.

By the morning the gale had blown itself out along with the rain, all Mister Weather Man left behind was a sky full of gray, lead-like clouds which looked destine to begin a fragmenting process — by noon the spring sun was in a position to work on drying out the wet terrain, and evaporate the pooled water in the landscapes depressions.

Hunt was on the road to recovery but certainly looked too weak to be up trying to drive a strong team of six horses. The poor man had slept late in any case and, when he did awake, Otto urged him to spend the remainder of the day on his back. There wasn't a muscle in his body, which wasn't screaming out for relief.

To get out of the house and away from Lehmann and the stage passengers, so they might hang-out together, the ranch hands went down to the barn where their horses were stalled and began working on their nags with a currycombs and dry scrubbing brushes. The three men made sure they were alone and could talk freely as they worked on their ponies. Finally, Matt Flynn said to Moe, "…Does yore friend Sam Korda knows I'm working in with you lot?"

Moe nodded, then stooped down low enough to pass under his mare's head and crossed over to Flynn. Then in a low voice said, "…Jist one thing though, he don't want us ter start anythin' for a day at least. He doesn't feel fit enough ter start racin' all over the countryside with a posse on his ginger…"

The Texas Kid joined the ramrod and the Canadian, his mitt held a dry scrubbing brush he had been using on his gelding in lieu of a curry-comb.

"…Mebbe a couple of day's rest will see us right what d'you reckon, Matt?" Malthouse suggested.

"Dunno. It'll all hinge on Joe Hunt's reaction an' what ideas he has about the stagecoach goin' on ter Junction City — Joe's a wiry old cuss — can't see 'im bein' too ready ter stay around makin' love to a cot fer too long," Matt said, "Don't ferget I've thrown away a damn lot ter hook up wif you *hombres* on this caper. Once we pull it off — my name'll be *Mudd* in this part of the country fer ever and a day. It ain't gonna take a genius ter figger out who wuz in on the robbery," He knocked the horse comb on the wooden rail to clear it of flea eggs and went back to curry-combing his cayuse. "The very fact we jist up an' vamoosed from our jobs'll be like an arrow-head pointing in our direction."

A free-range laying hen belonging to Lehmann's woman came scratching amongst the floor litter at the Kid's ankle of his boot and the young feller ignored it for a while as he said, "We don't have ter worry 'bout Rocky Boyd pointin' any posse in our direction, he'll keep his lips buttoned if he knows what good fer 'im; besides, he always hankered for ya foreman's job, Matt, and'll be lickin' Kit's ass-hole tar git his saddle on it, Matt."

Matt nodded, and returned the currycomb to his horse's hide while Tex laid a boot into the hen at his foot and sent her flying with flapping wings, through the air accompanied with a painful squawk. As the bird began to settle to foraging where the velocity of the kick had deposited, her, Flynn warned his partners. "But if I know Sheriff Robeson in Lawrence, I'm sure of one thing, that the ex-Pinkerton will come after us like a kid after pancakes an' maple syrup, jist ter prove his worth; he'd lead a posse ter Hell an' back if he thought it would make 'im a hero.

"That's why we've gotta take care there's no spilt blood on this job— we've gotta really, really be careful, there's no injuries or deaths…" Flynn pointed out. "You, Kid, don't let yore trigger finger git out of control, understand?"

"I'll be fine, Matt, jist so long as no one on that stage pulls a Colt on us; then I'll use this gat I paid forty dollars fer for what it was invented fer…" said the Kid as he slapped his side holster with the palm of his free hand for emphases, and returned to the care of his horse which every cowboy with any sense between his ears, needed no encouraging for. Malthouse pocketed his currycomb and began checking the shoes of his horse. He checked the forelegs then as he moved down along the side of his cayuse towards the rear, the trio cowhands heard noise which telegraphed to the threesome that they had the company of a fellow human near at at hand — it alarmed them as one, their guilty minds shrouded them like the cloak worn by Dracula. The threesome were sure that the noise had come from the horse stalls down on the right — they waited a moment longer to see if something more was forthcoming.

Nothing.

The trio were suspicious, and stood like statues in New York's Stuyvesant Park, not a sound was made — meanwhile their horses causally ate from the mangers as if the cowpunchers weren't there.

The Texas Kid couldn't contain himself any longer and to maintain the prevailing silence, slowly and silently eased himself away from his Cayuse and out of the stall — a questioning look crossed faces of Flynn and Malthouse, they focused on Texas Kid … Who gestured that they ought to go on talking, while he, had a quiet, look about the barn.

Matt cleared his throat, and then continued talking.

"…Anyway, Moe, I feel damn sorry about all the storm damage done ter Mrs. Lehmann's cabbage-patch — I took a stroll around there this mornin' an' the whole year's plantin's been flattened by hailstones and flooded by the rains." His words lacked any real genuine feeling, and would not fool anyone overhearing him, his heart was in it.

Moe took over when Matt paused for he had run out of words off the top of his head. Malthouse was no more convincing, but at least he made the effort. "Aahh, but she's a tough old bird that squaw. I reckon with her green-thumb she'll knock it back in shape and the Butterfield stage passengers will be soon gettin' fresh vegetables wif their, soups."

The Kid reckoned by now that he was onto whoever was hiding there near a pile of hay. He paused, Flynn and the Canadian's jawing was just a lot of hot air but to maybe it would still serve a purpose; Gradually his ears tuned in to the barn's ambient sounds and deciphered which was natural to the environment and that which was a dead giveaway they had a spy in their midst — the quick, heavy breathing of someone trying unsuccessfully to stifle any noise; which for someone on the spot was neigh impossible…

The Texas Kid set himself mentally as well as physically for the task ahead which was to jump his quarry and pin the snooper until his partners were able to come to his aid —The Kid hurdled the low haystack and almost landed unexpectedly right on top of the most frightened Negress he had ever encountered — *Abner Mambosa's woman,* **Ruth…** they rolled entangled across the barn floor until they were stopped by coming up against the wheel of the Concord — with the Texan on top of Ruth's torso — their eyes locked together, his, full of determined bastardry and her's of fear, fear for her life…

Moe and Flynn were quickly on hand to help The Kid, and were astonished by whom they had caught snooping on them.

The Texas Kid held Ruth by the throat and cut off the scream she was trying to mustering, and that was all she could do, try, he held her with a firm grip, he knew he could not afford to let a sound escape her thick lubra-like lips. But even as he straddled the woman her musky odor began to set his passion afire.

Time and motion froze as each tried to come to terms with the situation. The woman knew her position was dangerous and like a cornered beast of the jungle, tried to get out from under the White man, who seemed intent on two things — to keep her helpless by pressure of his strength alone — even if it meant he had to strangle the very life and breathe out of her…

Her cotton dress had hiked up her long shapely legs to mid-thigh and it gave her a wanton, sexy look, even with the whites of her Google-eyed almost fluorescent under the   current lighting conditions. The three men could literally smell her sexuality and it stirred each of them. This was the kind of situation that more often than not turned to a pack rape and murder for the weaker sex — Flynn knew this was wrong and that they were in **real trouble.** He turned his eyes from her and center on things around them. He saw a nearby wicker basket and a number of newly gathered eggs which has been spilt from it, luckily none had broken and this was obviously the reason for the frightened woman being here in the barn.

Malthouse licked his dry lips as he comprehended their situation and realized that time was slipping by — already the bitch needed air and the Kid was seeing that she wasn't going to get any of that. ***Christ, was he not going ahead and surely strangling the Negro? Yes, he was throttling her, he had no alternative!*** Flynn drew his eyes away from the free-range eggs on the barn floor and back to the distorted face of the dying woman… ***What are we gonna do?*** But he made no move to force the Texan atop of the weakling — to give the woman air.

Struggle though she might, Rose knew she was fighting a losing battle and that her position was hopeless, she made one last effort to break free of her captor which proved fruitless and with an audible sigh slipped into unconsciousness…

The Texan felt her body go limp beneath him but instinct told him that she wasn't dead, only unconscious. *Should he ease the pressure off in his hands?* His wrists ached and he was surprised to learn that it was not easy to strangle the life out of someone, especially a goddamn Negro.

"What are we gonna do?" The horny cowpoke asked of no one in particular.

They all knew what they would have to do, but no one wanted to voice it.

"— do I go ahead and finish the job, or is one of you goin' ter take over…?" He slowly rose to his feet and stepped back from the sprawled semiconscious black woman. It was clear that if something else was not done, no follow up made that she would begin to regain consciousness.

"We can't leave her alive, Flynn…" Malthouse told Matt as though he, Matt Flynn, were now in charge of things.

"OK. So if we go ahead an' kill the bitch how long d'you think it's gonna be until she's missed, fellers?" Matt looked from The Kid to Moe and back again as if they had all the answers: "Mebbe; Half-an-hour or so at the most. Lehmann and the blacks will organize a search fer her, and even if we were ter hide her body so as it isn't found, everyone will come under suspicion — no one jis' vanishes inter thin air."

While the cowboys had been caught up in discussing the woman's position, Rose had come to and her brain was sharp enough to fully understand her situation. She knew she had to act quickly. Without a pause she smartly regained her bare feet and made to rush away, like a doe in flight, but the desperadoes were fast to cut-off her escape and she never made it more than one-and-one-half yards clear of the back of the Concord before Moe and the Kid had brought her to ground and it became a darn free-for-all until the defenseless woman was brought to heel.

In the battle Moe had drawn his Bowie from its sheath and drove it home in her back, up between the ribs, and, within a matter of a minute she was deceased and like it or not, they had a body on their hands to hide. It also looked as if the Cattlemen's strongbox was safe and its contents beyond being purloined… The thing now, was what they could possibly do with the dead woman's body.

"Shoot," Matt breathed hoarsely as he realized that he was one of a partnership of three, now holding a dead body. Then for no other reason than the fact that it was there with them in the barn, the smell of manure, stale horse piss and straw assaulted his nostrils "— In God's name what have we done?! "

"…It wuz an accident, Matt, an accident," Moe whined.

"Where in Christ's name *did* that knife come frum?" the Texan wheezed.

"Hold it," said Matt with a raised hand; "Let *me think*… This roots our plan ter grab the strongbox as of now, I thought it was understood thar wuz to be no killings let alone a woman, black or white ——"

"What are ya tryin' to say, that *I* planned this mess at our feet?" said the Canadian.

"No," Flynn answered, "But all the same, we're all washed up and all that's left fer us three ter do is, skedaddle!" Flynn swung away and hurried off to make ready his Cayuse for the ride of his life. Flynn had instantly realized that everything was falling apart and that woman's body could lead right to a hemp necktie for the lot of them.

"Hey," cried the Texan youth. "Aren't ya gonna give a hand to stash this black piece of ass? Flynn, yew jist gonna leave it ter us?"

Flynn wasn't shilly-shallying about – already he was in the midst of spreading his saddle-blanket on his roan's back, when Moe approached him. "Tex is right 'bout the gooliwog – she'll have to be hid somewhere so no one'll stumble over her…"

"Hey, I jist got me an idea where we can stash the nigger!" said Tex. "It most likely won't keep anyone frum findin' her fer ever and a day; but it may give us some time up our sleeves ter make a getaway…"

Matt paused in saddling his gelding. "OK," said Flynn, "we're all ears, Kid."

"We'll make a nook in that hayrick over in the corner of the barn and shove it in there an' surround it with a few bales of hay…" the youth look from one to the other for their approval – almost holding his breath.

The two older hands knew that it wasn't going to be the perfect solution but it would at least buy them time and time was important at this moment. Flynn and the Kid left their jobs with the horses for the time and concentrated their efforts into stowing the corpse. Flynn mined a niche in the hayrick while the other pair collected the body and carried it to the hideout.

Malthouse and the Texan arrived at the mouth of nook with the limp body between. They placed it on the hard-packed dirt floor while they caught their wind.

"While I've been workin' here, I've been thinking, Moe…"

"Have ya, and what's it been all about, Matt?"

"I reckon the way I bolted fer me horse to make my getaway must've got you worryin' about Sam Korda's skin, now that this incident we're all involved wif has gone pear shaped, right?" said the ramrod.

The Canadian nodded. "I don't like to run out on any man if that's what yer mean."

"That's fine," continued Flynn, "I don't know what came over me. But in truth we gotta think about our skins in all this an' I think it would be acceptable if when we've got this body stored; me and the Kid mounted up and ride out, so we can be sure of bein' in place when the stage reaches the Marbles.

"Now if the body happens ter be found before the stage pulls out of Lehmann's way-station, the folks within smellin' distance will assume that me and the young feller are the culprits and by you staying behind and boardin' the coach no one'll suspect a hair on yuh head; so when you join the stage you'll be welcome as one of the fold. Both you an' Korda should be both in the clear after that, an' you'll be well placed to back me an' Tex here, in the eventual holdup..." The ramrod watched Malthouse closely to see how his ideas went down – the Canadian seemed to buy it by what Flynn could tell.

"In other words, I play Mister Innocent?" said Malthouse.

Matt Flynn nodded.

"I like the idea," said the Texan, then turning to Flynn the Kid added for Malthouse's benefit: "Bein' aboard the coach'll put 'im in position ter put Korda wise on the change of plans." The ramrod nodded that the Kid was correct.

"What about me hoss?' asked Moe. "If'n I'm onboard the coach what'll happen to my mount?"

"We'll cart her along wif us," said the Texan.

"I don't see that as a very good idea," said Flynn. "Moe c'n hitch his cayuse to the stage and let it be towed … then it's right on hand if'n he needs it in a hurry."

"And what's Sam Korda gonna do about a ride after we've hit the stage and are in flight?" asked Moe.

"That'll remain the same as wuz previously arranged – he can ride a nag from the stage team of horses!" Flynn pointed out. "Hey, what are you lookin' through the cracks in the wall for, Tex?"

"Checkin' ter see we ain't got any more surprises in store comin' down from the homestead; she's all clear," said the Kid.

So the trio set to work getting the dead woman hid away in the cubbyhole of the hayrick, after which they built a wall of hay bales across the front of the nook and thus it was truly camouflaged, unless someone decided to go poking around the place. Malthouse nodded his approval at their completed work then turned on his Cuban heels and set off upland towards the station house. The ramrod nudged the Texan in the ribs to get the kid's attention as the young feller was still caught up inspecting their straw-wall.

"We better finish saddling our mounts – we'll do Malthouse's too so he won't needed to be bothered with the chore!" said Flynn

Buckling up the cinch belt of his saddle, Matt said: "Although I've not ever been on the owl-hoot trial, I realize it's gonna require a lot of sacrifices if we're to get away wif our little gamble.

"My brain tells me, that if the four of us stick together in a group there's more chance of being run ter ground by the authorities. So when we're on the run we best split up – in fact, I reckon it's a ***must.***"

"As fer as I'm concerned that goes wifout sayin'," said the Kid as he went ahead and re-checked that his saddle-bags were securely hitched to his pony.

"You sound like you've had some experience on the outlaw trail, Kid…?" Matt remarked as he began checking the length of his saddle's stirrup straps.

"I've spent a season or two there in my short life," he lied as he shook his water canteen and learned it was still full, this made it clear to him that he could hang it on his saddle horn.

"If everything goes off right at the Marbles an' we pull off this robbery successfully, where are you headed?" Flynn asked.

"Mexico until the heat dies. What about you, Matt?"

"I'll head off ter Joplin, Missouri — I wuz bred in that neck of the land an' might still have some kinfolk there who'll hide me until things go quiet. How you gonna manage down Mexico way, Yankee money isn't readily accepted that side of the border?"

"I plan ter live like a peon and spend as little of my share of the strongbox as possible, until I'm able ter come back home." The Kid paused to watch Flynn check that his saddle was tight. Then the Kid grabbed the reins of his own mount and circled it around until she was facing towards the big open barn doors, near the Concord where he swung up into the saddle. The ramrod tied Moe's horse to a timber rail in the barn and then turned his mount around so that it too was facing the open doors, then put his left-boot up in the stirrup and hauled himself aboard.

The Kid put spur to horseflesh and his cow pony vaulted forward, out into the sunlight — he quickly looked to see if there was anyone close by, and was pleased that the nearest person was some Negroes working on the broken corral fence. Back in the rear of the Kid, came Flynn out into the light of day and without waiting until his eyes adjust themselves full to the exterior light, he did something totally unexpected, he dropped the reins of his mount and hauled his six-gun from its holster and shot the young Texan in the back, his target was not a difficult shot because the Kid was only four yards ahead of him.

The shot knocked the young man clean out of his saddle with the body-weight wholly on one boot-sole he was twisted backwards so that he was facing the way he had come. He hit the ground with a dazed puzzled expression on his face to that of someone whom had been thrown from a bucking bronco — next he realized that Matt was somehow standing high above him as he fought to gain the wind which had been knocked from his lungs and was impossible to recapture.

Abner and his workmate heard the unexpected shot of the gun from the direction of somewhere near the barn — they whirled in the direction of the sound and saw the figure of a person lying sprawled on its back with a horse that had been frightened out of its wits, fleeing towards the open plain. A cowboy was on another horse, towing yet another cow pony, a yard back from the person lying motionless on the ground. The fellow in the saddle began to dismount as Abner and his assistant dropped tools and started to run in the direction of the men down near the barn.

Suddenly Abner's brain flashed him a message, *what if that feller up yonder has the urge to add more notches to his gun tally…?* The thought put the brakes on Abner's rush to reach the scene and he eased up, allowing his co-worker to take on the lead.

By now, Abner had recognized the dismounted horseman as that of the ramrod from some ranch north of the station and an occasional associate of Master Lehmann. The Negro slowed to a walk as he focused on the ramrod, which had strolled up to the body on the damp ground and stood there inspecting the aftermath of his back shooting act. The assassin could see that the Texan's spirit was no longer a part of this world and therefore shoved his Colt home in its holster.

The Negroes arrived almost together but wisely came to a halt just out of Flynn's vision, he knew they were present for he could hear the panting of their breaths and the stale odor of their bodies, but all the same his eyes did not leave the body of the Texas Kid for a few long moments; Then slowly he turned slightly in the direction of the homestead and saw the eyes of the two nearby Negro males, were full of questions but too afraid to bring them to the fore.

You can't figure out these white men, thought Abner to himself. *No wonder The Good Book says that* all *men's sinners.*

Lehmann and his squaw were the first folk to appear outside the house on the veranda with anxious looks painted on their faces, then came, Malthouse and at either side of his hips came two of Lehmann's kids with innocent blank faces — they were hanging so close to the cowboy that they could smell the fine oil from his pistols. Behind Moe, came an anxious Sam Korda.

The Squaw ordered the half-cast children to stay put in her native tongue — these children had learnt from their mother and their Teutonic father that you don't argue the point with them if you don't want a harsh hand to the side of your face. For a moment both the squaw and the Hun took in the scene down the yard near the barn and set off towards it, alone at first until his squaw decided to join him and came forward at double time.

Abner shrugged in the direction of Otto who arrived at the location of the shooting with just as many goddamn questions etched into his face as the two Negroes. The body lay where it had fallen on the ground near a tuff of wild grass. Flynn backed up a little and gathered the dangling reins in his left-hand, his horse jerked its head and the sudden movement ran through the length of the ramrod's body as he firmed his grasp of the reins.

Out on the flats, the Kid's gun-shy horse was slowing to a trot, now anyone's property, free for the taking.

"Vhot's happened, Flynn?"

"Obvious, ain't it? I kilt Texas Kid," Flynn said, blandly.

"How, come?" Otto said without a trace of accent; meanwhile the Hun's de facto continued across the damp ground and came to a stop, a couple of feet away from the scuffed soles of the Texan's boots.

Halona noticed that the dead man's eyes were only half closed and that a fly had landed on the eyelashes of its left eye and was busy quenching its thirst from fluid of the man's lifeless eye.

Halona could hear her man's voice in the background: "— yesterday I would've thought you pair were friends? Zhen ter day you've blasted a hole in him that could stable a mule!"

"I wuz corralled inter them circumstances by the stupid, Kid —" said Flynn by way of setting the record straight. "… You don't know it yet, but the Texan turned into a rogue killer. He got hold of a darkie woman down in yore barn an' I guess he thought she wuz his fer the takin'. That part I'm not exactly sure about but I do know one thing led to another and he kilt her. I think it wuz wif a knife. I wuz back there in the horse stalls and had ter make me presence, known.

"Before I knew it, he got the darn drop on me wif his goddamn shootin' iron and frum then on I seemed ter have no choice but ter run wif what he said. He made me saddle up the horses so he could make a dash fer it; it wuz clear ter me that I wuz now a hostage an' once the murder come ter light, I'd be thought ter be part of it, 'coz I had gone orf wif him.

"He made me help 'im hide the body back there in the barn in the hayrick but all the time I waited me chance ter make a move, 'coz the fool hadn't collect my piece and I knew an opportunity might come my way sooner or later ter get out of this fix, and it did…" Matt glanced down at the body as if expecting it to contradict him, but there was no hope of that. Then he continued: "Mebbe this Negrah of yores should go in the barn and see if he can recognize the dame — he might know who she belongs, too?"

The Negro looked keen to follow up Matt's suggestion and looked all set to go with Lehmann.

Otto shook his head. "No. Vait here, Abner — I'll look inter it…" He moved off towards the barn. Abner moved to follow Lehmann but Halona deliberately blocked his way — there was enough death to be seen out here without seeking the sight of more. "Vhere's the body, Flynn?"

"Hold on…" Flynn handed the reins of his roan to the squaw. "—I'd better show you," he set off after Otto.

Meanwhile, Abner knew there was no ignoring the sting in his eyes, which would soon have them, smarting. Abner had his own suspicions that Otto Lehmann would find Ruth was the one lying dead in the barn, for already the African/Americans were descending on the murder scene from their various places of work. Besides, he had been with Ruth when she told the squaw that she was going down to the barn in search of the free-range eggs.

Seeing the Negroes going down to where the Texan's body was, decided it for the stagecoach passengers and the stage line's staff, they all began to make their way down the yard over the ground softened by the recent passing storms. Even the children, black and white, joined the throng for they thought the whole business, amusing.

The only person not there was poor Joe Hunt; still, not well enough to leave his bunk so he had to wait until someone saw fit to give him the news of the young man's death, for he had clearly heard the gunshot from Matt Flynn's revolver.

Arriving at the hayrick, Flynn showed the Hun the body. Between them they lifted the dead woman from the niche and placed her on the floor. Otto examined her for signs of life and had to admit defeat, she had long expired.

"Who is the woman, Otto?"

"It's Abner's wife…" Lehmann rose from his knees with his eyes focused on Ruth's remains. 'This vill break Abner's heart — she's a dead as a…"

"Why d'ya think *I* filled that no-good saddle-bum's carcass wif lead when I had the chance?" Flynn said

"Hmm. Vell there's not much more we c'n do here, but zee zhat Fräu Manbosa gets a decent burial," Then without warning the Prussian seemed to turn schizophrenic, he snatched Flynn by the shirt-front so violently and shook him that the ranch foreman lost his Stetson. "—'Ow could you have let this 'appen — vhy not you do somethin' to save her — yer gun wasn't roped to yore holster!" He threw Flynn away as though he was some sort of filth he didn't want to soil his paws, with. He dropped his clench fists to his sides.

Matt Flynn was flummoxed by the Hun's response and immediately wondered if Lehmann had been having relationships with the woman on the side — but he brushed that thought from the blackboard of his mind, for Matt knew he had someone strong on his side to believe his flimsy tale, and of course that was Korda, mean time, he had to calm the German.

"...Are you loco, Otto? What could I 'ave dun...? That Texan guy only had ter squeeze the trigger of his Peacemaker and I've been partnerin' the darkie I'd jist seen him kilt — that killin' iron of his revolver would have made a hole in me the size of a rebel cannon-ball!" Matt exclaimed.

Under the circumstances, Otto had to accept that Flynn was speaking the goddamn truth.

"The thing is, Flynn, I never took you ter be a spineless coot — But as there's no law out here an' zee fact I run this station makes me the law, and, I have ter believe zhat the Kid got the drop on ya an' that youse locked horns over zhar woman's death —"

Matt interjected Otto, as he, Matt, stooped and collected his hat. "Once I reckon I had the drop on the Kid, I made 'im pay justice money fer shovin' a gat in my guts and knifin' the darkie — it's 'im goin' under the sod fer worm meat; the kid got away wif nuthin', Otto!"

When the pair made their exodus from the barn they were met by a subdue mob of stagecoach passengers, station staff, and families. The children by this time had been won over with curiosity, as they became part and parcel of the mob. But not before the kids were chased off by the Indian squaw.

"D'you want me ter explain things to the folks, Otto?" Flynn said, for it was obvious that Lehmann was still emotionally moved by the business back there in the barn. Flynn went on without Lehmann's permission. "... I believe the dead woman in the barn is the wife of a feller known around here as Abner Manbosa." He paused to look around the crown for he hardly knew anyone by name, especially the Negroes.

Abner ejected a loud mournful scream from his throat which was almost beast like, and rush towards the stables his wife's name on his lips, he was followed in his grief by his dark brethren, each knowing it was their duty to console and mourn the man's loss.

"What in God's name happened, Mister?" demanded Father Lorimar.

To the priest, Flynn said. "I jist kilt a feller … He butchered a woman back there in the barn wif a bowie knife — before I could stop 'im. The dead man at my feet, is known as The Texas Kid an' he worked fer me on Kit Barr's ranch; I wuz his foreman, Lehmann here c'n vouch fer me, he's known me these past three years.

"The Kid knew I saw what he done ter the black woman an' that I wuz a threat to his freedom, so he wuz forcing me at gunpoint ter go off wif him. I figured that when he had no further use fer me, I'd end up like the poor wretch in the barn, he'd kilt me like a steer — so when I saw me chance, it wuz either me or him —"

"Says, you…" Korda said, pushing his way to the front through the crowded gathering.

"Are **you** callin' me a liar? Listen Sam Korda — I jist kilt a man I once broke bread wif and that's left me feelin' pretty damn low…" Matt Flynn rested his hand on his revolver butt. "I don't need the likes of you actin' like a flea in me ear. The Texan critter wuz aiming to have me act the candidate fer a rope collar that weren't mine, you better not 'ave the same notion — best you be warned by what's lyin' on the ground, here! "

"Hey, back ya Cayuse off a length or two, Korda," Dragoon suggested. "After what that man's been through, he don't need a tongue lashin' from you!" Whitney Dragoon was breaking in a new hat he had purchased off the shelf from Otto Lehmann, a replacement for the one carried away by the storm.

Father Lorimar came forward and stood alongside Flynn.

"Everyone settle down apiece; c'mon, settle down…" Lorimar barked and then waited until he had almost total silence save for the keening of the mourners back there in the barn. "The first we've got to do is see that the dead get a respectful burial so they can start their journey to the Pearly Gates, whether or not they be; God fearing people or heathens."

Later that day, the suspect murderer and his victim were laid to rest by Father Lorimar. The Kid was placed in the ground with very little ceremony. While on the other hand Ruth was buried alongside the storm ravaged vegetable patch with a cairn to mark her resting-place.

Halona and Otto cleared away the remains of supper in the dining room cum store as a full moon climbed clear of the eastern horizon to begin its long journey across the starry night sky.

By this time Joe Hunt was up with the news of the day. A passing saddle-tramp had stopped in at Spring Wells for a brief rest, but when he realized that the bunks in the establishment were at a premium, he opted to hit the trail and ride on to the next way station where his chances of a bunk would be better — the tramp had a back problem and did not fancy the prospect of sleeping on hard ground. He purposely didn't mention the fact that he had obtained his chronic injury in a saloon brawl.

Lehmann prevailed on the rider to carry a message to Tony Lett's station about the stagecoach being delayed because of Hunt's storm injuries. The message also asks if word could be sent to Butterfield depot in Junction City and that the Cattlemen's Association strongbox is safe.

Otto also faithfully promised Hunt that the stagecoach would be ready to roll when Hunt felt up to it. Meantime he would see that the Concord was cleaned up and that once all the mud, inside and out had been removed the vehicle would look as though it had just come straight from the coach builders workshop.

Flynn signaled Korda that they needed to talk — he explained what was going on, he did not want to make their association obvious to the other coach passengers that Sam and him had business with one another and that he appreciated the man's hostility towards him — since the shooting — who knows, this friction between them might come in handy for later.

Both the Lehmann's were busy, and the children were on a four seated stool near the heath, scribbling on cartridge paper with pieces of charcoal for amusement.

The priest was off in a corner of the room at prayers.

Joe Hunt was at the rustic dinner-table playing Solitaire, and Dragoon had his sample case of new revolvers hot out from the factory on display at his end of the table, he was rubbing them down one by one with a piece of velvet. The pencil pusher was once more scribbling in his diary as per usual.

Flynn sidled up to Korda drinking alone at the counter. "We gotta find some place ter talk, Korda," Matt muttered out the side of his mouth.

Sam Korda fixed his eyes bitterly on his empty glass as he snarled: "Gimme a break… You've got nuthin' I wanna hear, Flynn." Then Korda slapped the flat of his hand down hard on the bar-top with such force that it precariously shook the pyramid of whiskey shot glasses stacked nearby and hollered to Otto for a fresh shot of rye. Otto Lehmann was there with him in a flash and topped up Sam's empty glass — at the same time his spare hand hovered dangerously close to the glass pyramid, "You vant a hit while I'm at it? " Otto asked Flynn.

Flynn, nodded as he squared up to the counter — Lehmann slapped a shot-glass down on the counter and poured liquor to its brim, corked the bottle and left it there in easy reach of the two men while he went off to make the non-drinkers a brew of hot java and his squaw sent her kids off to bed.

As soon as Matt thought it was safe to do so he said quietly to Korda. "Keep your voice down, I don't wanna draw any attention to our lug bashin'."

This drew a glare from Korda.

"I've gotta speak ter you alone. Meet me down near the windmill," said Matt. "You don't know the half of it about today's shootin', nor does Malthouse." Matt then swallowed his drink and strolled away in the direction of the front veranda, just before he stepped out he paused and gave himself a stretch, then stepped off into the night.

Korda turned his back to the counter and looked out over the room. Malthouse was jawing with Dragoon about the guns in the sample case. Dragoon's eyes were on the pistols and quickly Moe Malthouse caught Sam Korda's eye and indicated to him that he should follow after the ramrod.

Sam didn't know why, but decided to see what this ranch foreman was up too. Korda moved off in the direction of the building's backdoor, in the direction of the outhouse and because everyone was busy doing their own thing, he too, became a part of the exterior dark.

Two things Korda wanted answered. Was the knifing of the darkie The Texas Kid's work? And just what did this trigger-happy ex-foreman think he was playing at? After all, he was just a "Johnnie Come Lately" — ***in this robbery caper*** — here just to make up the numbers. Didn't this feller know that this hold-up was to be pulled off without any blood being spilt? Our friend, Flynn, wasn't backwards in coming forward in inviting somebody to have a dose of lead. Flynn must have realized that Malthouse riding as a cow-hand was only a cover, the same as Korda riding shotgun on the stage.

3

ONCE IN THE dark, Sam paused a moment or two to listen to the crickets as they fanned themselves. Other than that, nothing stirred. He raised his right hand until it brushed the butt of his Colt, and decided that the beast was better in his paw than in its holster so he drew the weapon clear of the leather and moved away from the shadow of the building which the moon was generating — as he move about on faltering feet the cricket nests he neared fell silent for their own safety until he had gone by, and then, they would resume their nocturnal activities.

Sam gave the garden patch and the burial site a wide birth but had forgotten all about the irrigation ditch and fell into it like a poor blind man with far too much noise to conceal his presence. The muddy sludge made a mess of his clothes and even topped his boots, during his floundering about he lost his hat and six-gun and realized that it was pointless from now on to try and be stealth-like in his approach to the clandestine meeting.

He hauled himself out of the channel and knew he would have to tolerate the discomfort of his wet gear to keep his meeting with the dangerous, Flynn.

The ramrod heard the muddy splash of someone going head-over-heels in the channel and could not help but grin at Korda's misfortune. Matt lent against one of the windmill's legs and lit himself a cigarette he had rolled earlier. It was plain by the slight vibrations shooting down the leg of the mill and into his body that the overhead vanes were catching enough air current to turn the pump's shaft.

Flynn drew heavily on his smoke and increased its glow in the night so that it would act as a guiding beacon for Korda's mixed up sense of direction. Sam headed for the windmill now guided by the sounds of the breeze driven blades and the glow of the cigarette ember — he ignored the moonlight altogether.

"You're a noisy cuss, Korda…" Matt Flynn told Sam as he approached. "You'd never survive a night-walk in Indian Territory. I guessed it wuz you wallowing about like a hog in a bog — Didja ferget the irrigation channel? "

"Forget that business," demanded Korda. "Just what the fuck angle are you playin' frum?' Korda dragged his wet shirt out over the waistband of his jeans and empty holster; then he caught sight of a wooden pail upside down on the ground near Flynn and made his way over to it, where he sat down and emptied the muck out of his boots. "—For someone who's come in on our business at the end of the day, you're very bloody uppity."

Matt Flynn took a draw on his brown smoke then said; "it's not what it looks."

"Says you," Sam was not happy climbing back into a wet pair of boots, and held the ramrod responsible.

"Jist you listen and learn sumthin, Korda. Yore buddies and I, wuz gum bashin' in the stalls as we tended to our hosses like respectable cowboys. Thinkin' we were alone we got gabbin' 'bout the robbery and that damn goddamn black Mammy wuz prowlin' about in the barn looking fer eggs — she heard too much and sumthin' had ter be done."

"So youse were all in on it then? You all had a hand in her murder?" Sam asked.

"Couldn't be helped…"

"Then how come you shot the Kid dead, explain that?"

"It wuz a spur of the moment, bit of action. Moe came up to the homestead to hitch a ride on the stagecoach and be near you. He's ter give you the nod and let you know that me and the Texan would hit the stage along the trail, before it got to the next way station. We had his hoss in tow fer him to ride after the robbery."

"What of me? What was I s'pose ter ride after we'd hit the stagecoach?"

"I believe you could've cut a nag out from the hoss team pullin' the coach."

"You're sure full of bright, ideas – I'll tell you that!"

"Will ya listen? After Moe went up to the homestead and we were saddlin' ter ride off, it hit me that when and if the darkie's body wuz found it would be me an' the Kid who everyone would think kilt the lass."

"So, who gives a shit? And how come you had ter back-shoot the Kid, hey? " Matt threw the remains of his smoke away. "…To clear my name of murder, that's how come. I sacrificed the Kid and I'd do it again, I don't want a posse hunting me for murder, Korda."

"So what's the story now? You seem ter have taken it all upon yerself ter start remodeling our plans?"

"We stick to hittin' the stagecoach for the strongbox. We won't need ter change the location from where youse plan ter makes the original hit, follow? "

Korda nodded.

"I'll head out across country tomorrow wif the hosses fer our getaway — if I make good time I'll be at the creek ahead of you and lay in wait. Hunt and the passengers won't know what's hit 'em. I've got ter help youse make sure this goes down wifout too much trouble, and then we split the spoils and go our own sweet ways. After this, my name will stink like the rotting carcass of a coyote — no one'll touch me wif a barge pole. "

"Huh. The lot of us'll be in that boat, Flynn."

"Right," said Flynn with a sigh. "Then let's git back inside before we're both missed…" He turned and went off through the garden back in the direction of the front veranda — Korda watched Flynn all the way back to the homestead with the light from the overhead, moon.

When Joe Hunt was led out onto the veranda to see the coach and how well it had been detailed, he found it a sight for his sore eyes. Korda had had a restless night of it. He knew that although this Flynn guy was on their side he couldn't get over that fact that he was a feller who could not be trusted, not a goddamn back-shooter, ever.

Halona called everyone to breakfast and they all filed back inside from the veranda to a wonderful breakfast for folks raised on frontier food.

It was while they were all gathered there at the table to eat, that Joe confessed that in truth he didn't feel that he was ready to drive just yet and would prevail on the Lehmann's for another day. This played right into the bandits' hands, for it would make certain that Matt Flynn would get to the robbery site well before the Concord.

"I've gotta make my way back to Kit Barr's ranch an' report ter him what's happened ter The Texas Kid, he'll need ter notify the man's family about his death," Flynn told Lehmann. "So I'd better mosey off down to the barn and grab everything I need and hit the trail..."

Malthouse and Korda knew what Flynn was really up too and that Kit Barr would never be seeing hide-nor-hare of Matt Flynn, again.

"Zoo, yore taking leave of my hospitality," Lehmann said as he poured Flynn another strong pannikin of java. "...In zhat case I'll get someone ter saddle yore cayuse."

"No, don't bother Otto. I prefer ter saddle my own bronco —"

"Hey man, it's all part of zhar service, Herr Flynn!" Otto pointed out as Flynn massacred the eggs on his plate that had been served sunny-side up — the broken egg yolks staining the crisp ham like a sauce.

"That could be so, Otto. But no one touches my gelding an' saddle equipment *but* me..." Matt grabbed a couple of sugar lumps and dropped them into his coffee. 'Besides, I'm claiming the Texan's mare, seeing as I wuz the one who drilled 'im and stopped 'im getting away wif murder!"

"Hold it..." Lehmann put his hot pot of java on the table and wiped his hands on his off-white apron.

"I'm zhar proprietor here an' that Texan feller owes me a few bucks — I'm entitle ter first claim of his things. The hoss stays where it is, Herr Flynn, in my barn!"

"I'm claiming his hoss and saddle, friend..."

"*Nein...*"

"That means "no" in German, Mr. Flynn," Frank Cotter informed the bemused cowboy.

"— Zhee hoss belongs tuh me by legal right," Otto was emphatic that the horse would stay at the way station. "Look, no one lays a hand on zhat hoss, **no one!**"

Korda looked up from his plate — things weren't going to plan. He and Moe had an interest in the Kid's horse but couldn't show their hand and they knew why Flynn was laying claim to the animal. Korda tried to help Flynn secure the horse. "C'mon Otto, let 'im have the lousy horse; you've got horses runnin' out of yore ears — what's one more goddamn horse ter you? "

"She's a broken in cow pony an' vorth good bucks from any cowpoke. Zhis is my business here Herr Korda an' you'd be good ter keep mouth out of it!" Lehmann folded his arms across his barrel chest and it was a sure sign that there would be no more discussion about it while they were all under his roof.

"OK, Otto. How much *dinero* did the Kid get into you for?' Flynn asked. 'I'll square up his slate!"

Lehmann shook his head. "The kid owed me zhar money, not you."

"Can't you see, Flynn just offered ter buy the man's IOUs off you?" Whitney Dragoon said as he pushed his empty plate to one side. "You get your money and he takes the horse off your hands. It's seems reasonable to me."

Otto shook his head. "No. I own zher hoss — it stays!"

Matt scowled and rose from the table and dropped a silver dollar in the place he had vacated, he crossed to collect his bedroll, which he had earlier lent against the wall around the corner of the doorframe. He left in the direction of the barn without a backward glance.

Down at the barn, Matt decided to leave Malthouse's mount for Moe to bring — maybe Moe would have the brains to hitch-tie it to the rear of the stage and allow it to be towed; He concentrated on saddling his own Cayuse and that of the Kid's — and went ahead to hitch the mare to the cantle of his saddle. Before mounting his roan he checked the loads in his pistols and that of The Texas Kids six-guns. No one had realized that Flynn had quietly claimed those without anyone noticing.

At first the mare did not like to be led and it slowed Flynn's departure from the barn as she kept trying to pull away; so when he finally rode out of the building he was greeted by a determined Hun waiting outside with a double barrel shotgun, both hammers cocked for action.

Flynn did a double take — both horses halted — even in their childlike brains they recognized a "no-go" zone.

"Now, you vosn't gonna steal my hoss, voss yuh Herr Flynn?" The German said with a knowing smile as he brought the shotgun to bear on the ramrod. I thought you voz above horse-stealin' my friend?"

Matt Flynn looked down on Lehmann for two beats.

"Both barrels from my Fräulein vill do you much harm, Herr Flynn. I believe you are gonna leave zhatt cow pony, behind, huh?"

"When you put it like that, Otto, I'm not gonna argue." Matt shrugged.

Assuming the Flynn was at last going to be reasonable; Otto took his finger off the first barrel's trigger and hooked it around the trigger-guard. Unaware that Flynn had come to the conclusion that his only hope of getting away with the Kid's mare would be to ride Lehmann down into the dirt, for he realized that if he made any suggestive moves towards his gun holster while the Hun had his finger on the trigger, he, Flynn, would be dead meat for buckshot wasn't something you laughed about.

Matt hit his roan's flanks with the rowels of both spurs and the gelding lunged forward without any pre-warning, a hard wall of horseflesh charged into Otto, firstly knocking aside the gun barrels as he tried to bring them to bear on the charging horse and turned fingers to thumbs and thumbs to fingers in their action to find a trigger, anyone of the pair would have been suffice at this range. The gelding hit Otto full on and knocked him off his feet like a cannonball, in the short time his body had defied gravity — the man and shotgun parted company, Otto was occupied with trying to break his fall… the left barrel discharged harmlessly when the brass shoulder plate of the gun's butt struck the way-station's yard.

Though Flynn's cowpony was slightly hampered by the drag of the mare it towed, it simply increased its effort for it was used to dragging uncooperative roped steers to the branding fire…

Lehmann found himself on his belly with his shotgun lying on its side just a couple of feet ahead of him, he knew it still had alive barrel which would come to his aid if he could reach the weapon in time before Flynn and the mounts were out of range; he went for the shotgun like a goddamn bayou alligator.

The bang of the shotgun discharging a barrel load upon striking the near dried ground, brought the Negro folks from under the homestead and Lehmann's squaw, along with the Priest and Whitney Dragoon out onto the porch — Dragoon had already come out armed for action and paused to take in the scene. The Catholic Priest saw Lehmann floundering towards the shotgun lying ahead of him on the ground and *clamped* a heavy hand on his six-gun ran forward and jumped off the veranda floor- boards to the ground, and run towards Lehmann — Father Lorimar's hand prevented his own gun from being bounced out of its holster.

The priest reached Lehmann, who was on both knees with the shotgun in his paws, but realization was already sinking in that the ramrod and the horses were out of his range. He looked like a circus dwarf balanced there breaking open the rifle's breech to clear the now useless barrel. For some reason he, Otto, would not face the truth and clawed a handful of buckshot cartridges from the apron pocket in his lap and with a shaky hand shoved one in the breech of a cleared barrel — he did not even bother to place the butt against his shoulder but fired the gun from his knees, the buckshot traveled above the flat surface of the land with just twenty-four inches, clearance.

In response to the Butterfield agent's blast in his direction, Flynn drew his Peacemaker and sent a slug back in Otto's direction for good measure but range was a problem for both men at this stage and all the ramrod's lead did was make Otto flinch. Realizing that Lehmann wasn't wounded in any shape or form, save for his pride, Lorimar squinted in Flynn's direction, then turned his attention in the direction of the veranda in time to see Dragoon drawing a bead on the foreman off in the distance. *There's no point in sending good lead after bad,* thought the priest.

"Save yuh lead my son — he's too far…!" called the Priest.

The Father's advice drew the reality of the situation to Dragoon and he gradually lowered his Colt. The ramrod was 125-yards away and Whitney knew 60 to 65-yards was the best his six-gun could reach. He returned his pistol to leather as Halona jumped from the veranda and jogged down the yard towards the priest and her man, Otto.

Flynn holstered his hand-gun and gathered up the reins of his mount for the gelding had decided to stop hauling his payload and faltered which was not any help for a man who had to have distance between him and his last location. He urged both animals on across the flats. He feared that Lehmann and the others back there at the way station might have enough horses at their disposal to organize themselves into a posse and come out after him. So, ignoring the stuff which was irritating him, such as the mane of his own mount brushing his face and that of the strain to his arm which held tight to the reins of the mare — it was the only way he could stop the drag of the reluctant mare braking free of the buckles on the back of his cantle for this spare horse would be needed in the hold-up, he pressed on south.

The priest, Lehmann and the squaw made their way back to the main house where the other passengers and Sam Korda had now joined Dragoon. Lehmann was walking with a noticeable

limp due to a torn ligament. Those on the veranda had plenty of questions but were too polite to press things, as it was clear the German was not in the right frame of mind to share their politeness with his fellow man.

"...Damn, zhat low-down hide of Flynn!" Otto yelled to his audience. "— Zhat critter von't vanter show up here anymore in my lifetime, I swear. Damn, damn, damn… what zher hell's happened with me knee? Feels like I've been hornet, stung…"

Matt was determined to lead anyone attempting to trail him a merry dance. So he kept heading south until he had crossed over the horizon and then set course anew for his true destination, west to Diamond Creek, where he would lie-low and wait for the Junction City stagecoach. He knew he was on course for Diamond Creek, when he hit the main road, where a dried out broken wagon wreck, had been abandoned some years ago; it now served as a landmark for many travelers.

The day Joe Hunt felt well enough to take to the reins once again, meant that they made a late start, for it wasn't until after breakfast that the teamster decided he was fit enough to take on a six horse team and an awkward looking Concord. It was more like 11:20 AM before the harness tracers were attached to the stagecoach and there was some thought given to the fact that maybe the coach ought not to leave until after midday. But Hunt felt he should get the stagecoach on its way before he began to lose his enthusiasm for the task.

Moe Malthouse had arranged to join the passengers and in the time he had to kill, took a stroll down to the barn and upon seeing his horse still stalled, gathered in a flash why the ramrod had left it behind. So he went back to the station house and talked the driver into allowing him to hitch his saddled horse to the back of the Concord — for he had told anyone interested at Lehmann's place, that he wasn't going to return to Kit Barr's ranch now that Matt Flynn had seemed to gone a bit mentally, strange.

Sam helped Joe board the stage and the man settled down like a professional, and took up the leather ribbons of the team — all the horses wore collars but only the two leaders wore blinders. Joe kicked off the brake-lever as the stagecoach passengers piled in with Frank Cotter making it his business to capture a window seat. When he heard the door slammed shut by one of the older niggers, Joe glanced around to make sure none of the children were likely to get trampled on once the stagecoach got underway, satisfied, Joe shook the reins and cracked his whip — the Flemish coach horses and mix breeds put their backs into it and got the heavy Concord rolling as Joe maneuvered the team around, in a wide arc and faced the vehicle in line with the short trail back to the main road; the horses all the time being urged to pick-up their hooves; meanwhile the Lehmann family and the Negroes stood by, waving them off.

Once the horses found their true coordination it took a bit of the strain away from Joe's tired arm muscles, but all the same Korda realized that Hunt wasn't as fit as he had made out earlier. They covered the first three miles pretty much in silence, then Sam said: "You're not really up to this, are you Joe?"

"What you mean, Korda?"

"Well you're forcing yore self ter push this crate along ter Junction City, that's what I reckon?"

"There's a job to do, and I've gotta git it dun, son, that's all."

"Mebbe you should've taken another twenty-four hours, spell?"

"Look, pal, I've got a wife back in Kansas City who is pining my where abouts and has no idea where I'm at or what I'm up too. I wanna git home to her as soon as I can, not here lookin' at cacti, cottonwoods and goddamn buzzards."

It was now pushing onto about two o'clock in the afternoon and as yet they hadn't reached Diamond Creek where it was planned to stop and take on some of the food the Squaw had prepared for their trip through to Lett's station. But Sam knew they were nearing, the creek. For up ahead, Korda could easily make out the broken down wagon;

but it was Joe who made mention of the abandoned vehicle with its broken spine.

"That's a new addition to the landscape since I last traveled this road," Hunt remarked as he spat phlegm in its direction.

"As best as I c'n recall, it's been abandon there fer two years," said Sam as he changed the Winchester from one hand to the other.

"You ain't been wif the company more'n six months; how d'you know how long that wrecks been lyin' there?" Hunt asked.

"Easy. I've been hauntin' this neck o' the woods fer four years, now. In fact, that thar wagon; was owned by a Mormon family en route ter Junction City.

"The story is they broke the rear axle an' the Mormon brother sold one of his two wives to a gang of road surveyors ter give 'em a wagon and supplies so they could reach Junction City."

"You're sayin' this Mormon critter, had **two wives,** Sam?"

Korda nodded. "Those Mormon fellers are allowed more'n one wife accordin' to their bible teachin'."

"Aahh, I bet Father Lorimar would have sumthin' ter say in his Sunday sermons 'bout that? Two goddamn wives, hey? Golly-gee! I'm having trouble feedin' and clothin', jist the one!"

"I can't 'ave a piece of that conversation, 'cause I never been married!" Sam said, ruefully. He pulled a plug of chewing tobacco from the breast pocket of his green and black plaid shirt and bit off a satisfying slug, and then returned the tobacco to the shirt.

"What sort of religion is it, which allows a feller ter keep two wives, anyhow, Sam?"

"Don't know. But it sure must allow a darn lot of wickedness ter flourish in, their bedrooms. Some Quaker feller told me on a ranch I wuz workin' one time… That it wasn't always that-a-way — seems that many of these church folk felt obliged ter do their bit fer the war an' the Mormons were first in the recruitin' line and in most of the major battles, their loss of life wuz very high — leavin' a lot of their womenfolk widowed wif families.

"The church boss, a joker named of Young, says that an angel of the Lord came to 'im in a dream and told him that all good Christen Mormon Brothers, had ter marry these widows and care fer their children like they wuz their own; that way the brothers would relieve

the church of the burden of caring fer the widow folk an' their young…
That the story this 'ere Quaker told."

Hunt wrinkled his nose as if absorbing a tainted smell. "…How
come this Quaker feller knows so much about this Mormon clan? Are
they kinda brotherly, kin?"

Sam shook his head, "No idea. The next church I'm likely tuh go'll
be when I'm in a pine box."

"You not a God-fearin' man, Sam?"

"I put it to yuh this way, Joe. There's more fun in bein' a sinner than
carryin' the church collection plate on any God given Sunday! I like a
drink, chasin' a dove or two, which ain't as pure as the driven snow.

"Every church I've ever heard of spreadin' the word or shinin' thar
Christen Light of Glory, is against all that. Are you in ter religion, Joe?"

A rattler came out of a bush on the side of the road and started
across their path between the rear horses and the stagecoach — the
front and rear wheels on Joe's side of the vehicle ran over the reptile's
body, the weight of the coach almost severed the snake in half and left
it twisting up in an agonizing death-throes.

"God sure didn't favor that feller, hey?" crowed Hunt with glee.
'That what he got fer bein' kinfolk wif Satan!"

"Weelll — I guess you've given me yer answer to my question," Sam
said as he looked back behind the moving coach at the dying rattlesnake
on the limestone surfaced road.

Meanwhile up ahead of the stagecoach at Diamond Creek, Flynn had
really settled in comfortably enough for someone living rough — he
had long ago unsaddled the horses and had them grazing on native
grass but hobbled so they could not wander too far from camp. He had
made camp mid-afternoon a day ago. He had bedded down in the shade
of two gray, water-smoothed boulders the size of most log cabins one
would find in the mountains. The rocks were so close together that with
a fertile imagination, they could look like a giant's bare buttocks… The
top of the boulders wore a wig like crown of dry lichen. His campsite
was shaded by a clump of cottonwoods at the foot of the rocks and was
within walking distance of the flowing *creek,* in his time here, Matt had

found a waterhole in which he had been able to bathe; there was a bit of debris lying about where others had camped about the place before.

He had taken use of the time he had on his hands by stripping down the rifles and oiling them. He had a Springfield and a Winchester and by pulling them apart was able to assess their condition, which was more than fair. Then he did likewise to the handguns. The idea was, that before the stagecoach arrived at the creek's ford, he'd break camp and have everything ready to go, horses well and truly ready for the task which lie ahead of them. Korda, Flynn's and Malthouse's, escape routes had been all figured out.

"Not too far to Diamond Creek now, Joe," said Korda,

"Hmm, yep, you're right there Sam — about fifteen minutes or so." Joe did some figuring in his head and shared the result with Sam. "After the rain an' tornados weather that's gone through, I expect ter see the creek runnin' a banker!"

"Don't know 'bout you, Joe, but my tummy could do with some of that food the squaw packed us before we left, Lehmann's. What about we eat up in the shade of the Devil's Marbles and rest the team apiece?"

"I might jist do that, feller. I reckon it's me needin' more of a spell than the goddamn, nags!"

Flynn saw the stagecoach coming from a long ways off — he had managed to scramble like a lizard to the lichen top of one of the boulders for that purpose of his exercise. To make the climb easier for himself he had taken his pistols off and his boots, relying on his socks to find purchase on the coarse surface of the boulder. Comfortable with what he saw, Matt turned around and made his way down feet first towards the ground at the base of the boulder, at times sliding on his hams and braking with his heels and hands every time his downward speed got too fast for safety as he skidded along with the curvature of the structure until he was safely on the ground near the waiting horses, thus he allowed the boulder to mask him and the cowponies from the approaching Concord.

Matt pulled on his boots and then buckled on his pistols, while silently praying to himself that Hunt would not get a yen to bivouac on the other side of Diamond Creek, he would have to rely on Korda to urge the Butterfield reins-man to take the break at the Devil's Marbles.

Joe reined in the team two yards short of the waters' edge where the creek gave every impression that it was still quite high; Joe stood up as tall as he could to see out over the water…

"What we stoppin' here fer, Joe?" Sam asked. It didn't suite things if Hunt took it into his head to stop here a while. He would have to try and think of a reason to encourage the man to take the stagecoach across the ford so as he and his partners would have the advantage of surprise and not the other way round.

"I wanna get some idea how swiftly the water's flowin' and how deep it's likely ter be."

"It looks high but I don't reckon it's too high for the coach and besides, I'd much rather we rest in the shade of those boulders over yonder, even if it means the passengers   might git their boots wet — thing'll dry out in a spell." The expression in Sam's face made Joe realize the maybe the guard had a point.

"Right, I'll warn the folks inside ter expect to see water flowing through under the Concord's doors…" Hunt sat down and called a warning to the passengers, then, not leaving it open for debate, he urged the team leaders into the stream.

They were only part way across the creek's ford when water began finding its way in through the crack at the bottom of the left door and the passengers began laughing at the stupidity of their situation as they lifted their boots clear of the water which flowed in one side of the coach and out through the other.

Most of the bods in the Concord were unaware that they were not going to be getting any refreshments once the stage had forded the creek, the only folks who really knew what was going on were the plants on board the coach, Moe and of course Sam Korda. The depth of the water at the crossing reached up as high as the underbelly of the work-team and Moe's cow-pony. But only for the odd bump or two, when the vehicle's tires struck a submerged boulder, the size of a day-old foal was there any suggestion of a troubled, fording. Soon they had left the creek aft of them and with the water that had taken lodgings inside the Concord cascading out onto dry land, the vehicle made its way towards the shade cast by the basalt Devil's Marbles and the cottonwoods.

Hunt rose from his high seat and stabbed the whip's handle butt-first into the whip-ring holder fixed to the Concord's superstructure and twirled the reins round the foot-brake lever. Gnats, which had been haunting the shade and sparse grass, set about exploring the horses, which had arrived on their patch. Both Joe Hunt and Sam Korda climbed down from their perch on either side of the coach — Korda making doubly sure that he brought the repeater rifle with him.

Passengers threw open both doors of the stagecoach, eager to stretch their legs and do whatever they could for the Butterfield stage-crew in preparing Lehmann's food for their body cravings.

Hunt realized that the passengers and Korda had things in hand and he turned and walked down the line of horses, carefully checking the harness-ware on the way until he was up at the front with the lead horses. He then pampered these fellers with a couple of lumps of sugar he had taken from the dining table jar, for this purpose.

Malthouse made straight for his Cayuse to check that she was capable and ready to stand up to a fast ride. He was satisfied by what he found; her wetness wouldn't prove to be any problems he believed. Whitney and Morgan went on a hunt for twigs, leaves and cottonwood off drops with which to make a fire so they could wash down what food the squaw had packed with a mug or two of java.

Father Lorimar removed his Stetson and began fanning himself with it while Cotter removed his celluloid shirt collar and copied the priest in his fanning operation, both staying in the shade out of the sun.

On the far side of the boulders, Matt Flynn could hear all the sounds of their activities and dialog. He only hoped that his horses did not get it into their heads to let the horses hauling the stage know they were nearby and could smell them. Otherwise *he* would lose any upper hand he had hoped to retain until he made his move at his own direction.

Korda rested the carbine up against the body of the Concord and collected a tarpaulin from the stagecoach boot and lugged it over to where he reckoned would be a good place to spread it out for them to picnic. But his mind wasn't actually on the job he had other thoughts dancing round in his head.

I hope I figured Flynn right about the fuss he made over the Kid's horse with Lehmann. I don't fancy ridin' a bareback teamster fer a couple of days; my ass would become red-raw. Thought Sam as he returned to the stage for the packed lunches and gazed about the area for signs that Flynn was about. *Not a sign, nor hair of the man. Hope he hasn't turned tail on me an' Malthouse, and left us ter fend for ourselves?*

The drummers managed to get a smoky fire going so they weren't all that useless to the cause. Moe had gone ahead and tied his mount to some nearby brush and was heading towards the campfire to make it look something a roustabout would be happy to put his brand on. The Priest and Frank Cotter came away from the stage and headed towards the spread out canvas sheet. *Aahh,* thought Korda. *Good…once I've got the whole company together in one spot, I and Moe will be able to control 'em and no one'll get hurt if they follow orders. Now, where the Hell has Joe Hunt got to?*

Sam soon had his answer to that, Joe had been checking the other line of horse on his way back up to the vehicle and was now hoofing it in the direction of the gathering. Sam trailed along a few yards behind the coach driver to the tarpaulin and set down the eats. He glanced at Malthouse and gave him the nod — Moe Malthouse returned the salute, unnoticed by the passengers.

Damn! Sam thought. *I've left the rifle back at the stage. Damn, now I mightn't get a chance ter get hold of it before we swing into action!*

"…Awright, I need everyone's attention." Sam called, his right paw now filled with a production of Colt's pig iron. The sight of finding themselves covered by a six-gun meant that the feller holding it was serious about getting their mindfulness. Cotter was the only man in the group who was lost at what was going on. But as luck had it, he did naught but stare.

Korda cocked his long barrel Peacemaker "— this is as far as we'll be travelin' together.' He straightened up. "…Moe, fetch my rifle over there near the stage…" This was the first anyone realized that they were in the middle of a hold-up and that Malthouse was in fact part of it. "Right," Moe said as he also drew on pig iron Pete for emphases. "I'll git the strongbox first if ya don't mind, Sammy." Malthouse jogged across to the stagecoach and climb up on to the roof rack where the box has been tied to the wrought iron railing, Moe untied the box and threw it down to the ground. Then he came down and picked up Korda's Winchester and came back to join his buddy. Meanwhile everyone else just stood or sat where they were in silence, when it had been realized what Korda's and Malthouse's intentions were.

"One thing we don't want ter day is **heroes,**" said Malthouse to the passengers and especially to Joe Hunt. For most people here would expect the Butterfield man to make some sort of effort to put a stop to the hold-up. But Joe just smoldered quietly away inwardly, which was just as well for it was now that Flynn rode in from around the boulder and no one was in any doubt that he was part and parcel of the operation. He reined in just behind the bandits with the spare horse.

"Howdy," Matt said by way of addressing the group — the only man to speak up was Father Lorimar.

"So, the devil's decided to show his hand?"

"No sermons Father, no sermons," Sam warned. "We ain't in the mood."

"Besides, today's not Sunday, accordin' tuh my calendar." Flynn added.

Moe Malthouse swung his pistol round and to the surprise of all, fired four shots at the two padlocks of the strongbox. One slug ricocheted off the box while the others smashed the locks apart. Then Moe quickly covered the ground separating him from the strongbox and stood over it, where upon he kicked its lid open. Korda went across to join Moe in collecting the goodies from the strongbox, Flynn took over the task of guarding the passengers standing about the tarpaulin. The coach horses were clearly getting a bit edgy as if they could **smell the tension** in the air.

Sam lifted six calico bags of silver dollars from the box and placed them on the dirt in two heaps of threes, a foraging ant got crushed to death in the process. Malthouse played Lucky Dip inside the open box and brought out shiny gold ingots. Then he looked up at Sam. "That's it, she's empty!" He arose to his feet. The two men then grabbed the moneybags and gold between them and came back to Flynn and their getaway mounts; They reached up and unbelted the flaps of the saddlebags on Flynn's gelding and the mare that once belong to the late Texan and stuffed their booty inside the pouches on either side of the horses…

Then Malthouse ran off towards his own pony tied to a bush and it was then, as Korda was about to mount the Texas Kid's mare that he realized there was a carbine already in the saddle-boot. He didn't need two rifles, so changed his mind about mounting for the moment and trotted over to the stagecoach and smashed the Winchester in to two, against the rear wheel of the Concord, then leaving the useless weapon in bits on the ground he came back and mounted the mare.

Now all three road agents were ready for the trail.

"Bear in mind, Flynn, no one gets short changed by me and you won't be the first…" Korda told the ramrod.

"I've always had faith in you an' Malthouse doing right by me," he lied.

"Then let's **move our asses** — we'll divvy up at Coyote Pass!" Korda suggested not ealizing he had made the terrible mistake of stating their direction.

It was then that Flynn thought he saw movement over in the Easterner's direction — Father Lorimar was going for his pistol and Flynn knew that the man was making an effort to stall their getaway — he swung his Colt to bear in the Priest's direction but the man was quick and his bullet passed so close to Flynn's earlobe that he felt its breeze.

Malthouse fired his six-gun from the saddle and the shot was as lethal as sin, it hit the Priest square in the chest, slamming his dead body backwards to the ground; the noise startled the already fidgety stage team, who weren't accustom to so much gun noisy and so they broke away in to full gallop and raced round the immediate area in a complete circle, kicking up to full speed — Joe Hunt acted fearlessly for he thought he had a chance to grab at the harness piece of a horse as they circled past him, Dragoon and Cotter jumped out of the way of the cumbersome vehicle as it bore down on them and Morgan stood there rooted to the spot.

Hunt tried once more to catch a hold on the Concord as it was about to pass his already sore, body — a gesture which was as much fool crazy in its own right, as that of the Priest trying to play a Lawman. Joe fell under the rear wheel of the heavy vehicle that did untold damage to his innards as it rode right over him.

While the desperadoes wheeled their mounts round to the east and raced off together through the ford, at about the same time the crazy horse's dragging the coach hit the trail in the direction of Lett's place, leaving the passengers and injured, stranded.

Dragoon came quickly to one knee and drew his fancy showpiece six-gun, he let loose at the decamping robbers, but the excited state he was in meant that his bullets went everywhere but where they were needed. The only positive effect his gun-noise had was to drive more fear into the Concord's horses.

Once through the creek the road agents swung their mounts in the direction of Coyote Pass…

Dragoon stood up and shoved his pistol back in its holster, worried to Hell what was to become of them. Cotter came up and joined him as he worked at brushing away the dust his frock coat had collected. Then a groan from Joe Hunt back there behind them, made the pair begin to think of someone else other than themselves, they rushed over to him, no one thought to go to the priest, for it was obvious that he was dead.

Joe knew he was hurt bad, even before he began coughing up blood, for his arms and legs were useless and he had been about long enough to know when a man was in serious trouble and the Angle of Death was hovering nearby. In his race to board the passing stage he had ended up out in the open, five to eight yards from any shade thrown by the trees and the monoliths. Morgan joined them and was still too stunned to be of any help, besides, the shock of everything had been too much for him and he had soiled his underwear.

Cotter squatted down beside Joe. "We've gotta do something for you Mr. Hunt…" Frank drew closer to the injured man so that talking wouldn't strain him so much. "You can't stay out here in the sun." Frank looked up at Whitney for support, but one could see in Dragoon's face he was a fish out of water, when it came to any knowledge of medicine.

"Listen… listen… you've gotta listen ter me!" pleaded the breathless victim of the runaway coach. "You… you tr-try movin' me and you'll break me apart." He gasped to the pair of them. "— I know w-w-what I'm talkin' about. Leave me be…"

"But we can't. The sun will cook you alive! " Frank told Joe.

"Let's bring the shade to him," suggested Chas Morgan. "We can use the tarpaulin back there, rig it up with some saplings and drape the canvas over them."

"He might have somethin', there." Whitney said.

Frank considered the suggestion and realized that it was better than nothing. "Fair enough, I'll come and give you a hand …"

The pair of them went off to collect the canvas sheet, while Whitney Dragoon set about fanning Joe's face with Joe's dusty hat which he had found lying nearby on the ground.

Chas and Frank mutually decided to check on Father Lorimar — blood from the man's fatal wound had already begun to soak into the dry dust. They paused and looked down into the glazed eyes of the dead priest.

"What a waste," Chas commented.

"Amen to that…" Cotter said. "I thought he would have been like the rest of us, ready to soil his long johns."

"That's true," said Chas Morgan. "Only thing is, I *did* the job."

Frank nodded. "Mr. Dragoon and I are quite aware of that, Morgan.

"But Hell, Father Lorimar ought to have known he was dealing with fellers who were pretty desperate?"

"I reckon being a man of the cloth, he felt it his duty, ter chastise a sinner — I don't know," Morgan added.

"There's nothing more we can do for him. C'mon, let's get this tarpaulin for Hunt…" Cotter moved away from the corpse and Chas followed the scribe a beat later; feeling guilty for having stayed longer with the dead Priest he made double time towards the canvas sheet, by-passing Cotter in the process he reached the object of their journey. And without hesitation, Morgan reach out to grab hold of the canvas and only realized at the last moment that there in the sun, sunning itself, was a rattle-snake that had obviously wriggled out of the brush, having been disturb by the noisy hold-up and its aftermath. Its camouflage worked to perfection and being surprised so abruptly the reptile did not have a chance to give its rattle a shake. It saw the man's hand with fingers spread apart as a threat and it struck at the hand with lightning speed and buried its deadly fangs into the web-skin between the butt of the hand's index finger and the thumb…

Morgan yanked his arm back with the snake attached and its poison glands already pumping like Morgan's frightened heart, injecting venom into his bloodstream as the reptile developed lockjaw. Morgan screamed in both fear and pain as he flung his arm about, trying to dislodge the viper, at first with little success, then instinctively the reptile's jaws relaxed their grip in preparation of renewing its bite — a mistake — for Morgan's waving arm dislodged the rattle-snake and sent it hurling through the atmosphere towards the brush from whence it had come…

The sight of Morgan under attack with the snake attached to his hand, completely startled Cotter — he had no idea how he could aid the man who was dancing in fear and apprehension before him.

Morgan's cries drew Dragoon's attention to his co-travelers who saw Morgan dancing like a madman with the snake attached to his hand — Dragoon vaulted to his feet and ran at full speed towards the pair, and hauled his six-gun clear, with no real plan of action — Morgan hurled the snake away from him as Dragoon shortened the distance between him and the drummer.

"Christ!!" Hollered Morgan, "Jesus fucking Christ!!!!" he swung his arm around as though it were giving him much pain.

"Hold still, Morgan," said Dragoon. "Let's have a look at the bite?"

Holding out his arm, which was shaking through shock, the watery eyed Morgan said to Cotter: "did ya see it? It was a fucking rattler that got me — I never saw the bastard until it had me! "

The punctured marks of the fangs were easy to see and there look to be a slimy wetness engulfing the area the top and bottom jaws of the snake had mouthed. Even the immediate tract of the bite had already begun to bruise. Morgan had gone as pale as a ghost, and the three men knew without speaking that if the reptile had been a rattler, of which they had no doubt, the bite would be fatal — no one here had the slightest idea how to treat snakebite.

"How you feeling at the moment?" said Dragoon.

Morgan frowned at the man.

"What d'you mean? Is it possible it weren't a goddamn rattler, I never heard its rattle before it struck!" said the fearful man as he looked from one to the other of his colleagues.

"It might not have been venomous — mebbe we all just thought it was a rattler,' Dragoon said, trying to waylay Morgan's fear.

Frank Cotter said nothing, but he had read somewhere that a rattlesnake didn't always warn its prey and he couldn't afford to say anything for he wasn't a hundred per cent sure of his facts about the reptile. He glanced into Morgan's eyes, but they told him nothing, the only change he saw in the man was the fact that his perspiration had increased to that of the rest of the passengers, but that could because of anxiety. Then without warning the feller's eyes turned upwards and he swooned before anyone could catch him. Once on the ground on his back, Morgan went into convulsions – the man's traveling companions realized they had their answers about whether or not the slithering creature was poisonous and there was no doubts whether or not the drummer would be cashing in his chips; the scribe and the gun-salesman realized just what a couple of useless men they'd allowed themselves to end up — inwardly they realized how an innocent man must feel when being led to the gallows to face his hangman.

It was this feeling of helplessness that drew them away from Morgan and back to the injured, Joe, who wanted to know what the commotion had been about; Frank took it upon himself to tell the coachman of Morgan's fate; while Cotter told the rein's man that forlorn tale Dragoon picked up Joe's discarded and somewhat battered, Stetson; and strolled off over to the creek and filled it from the water flow between a pair of half submerged stones the size of horse-saddles, but had the water level been as low as its regular flow these rocks would have been revealed to have been the size of a pair of lowboys.

On his return journey to Joe and Cotter from the creek, the firearms' drummer realized that Joe's hat was far from being water tight and he lost more of the precious liquid than he had envisaged – so used the leakage to help bring down the injured man's body temperature by guiding the hat so that the water fell onto the fellow's *forehead* and ran down either side of his head past the temple area and into the roots of his hair at his thinning hairline. Then he hunkered down alongside the sprawled man's left-shoulder and directed some of the cascading water between the man's parched lips – which sated his thirst, regardless of the fact that it might prove to be injurious to him.

Then the pair of gents decided amongst themselves that Joe Hunt could no longer remain out here in the sun; so they decided to take the risk that the snake had abandoned the immediate area and went off to collect the tarpaulin. Between them they dragged the canvas sheet across the ground over to where Joe occupied the balding grass patch of ground and arranged it like a kind of windbreak, so that it also cast some shade over the uppermost part of his body. They took it into account that as the sun traveled across the sky in the direction of the horizon the shadow would lengthen.

A strange noise had come onto the scene and when the men took stock of their surrounding they found to their dismay that a flock of vultures was gathering high over head. It caused them concern; again they were lost in what they ought to do, until Whitney came up with an idea.

"We haven't any idea where the stage and those horses may end up. They might've come to a stop a little ways down the road and it would be silly of us to be stranded up here when there's shelter and provision just a walk away…I might hike it down the road a piece an' see what I c'n find; if they are there and the stagecoach is OK, I'll come back here for you and Mr. Hunt, and we'll drive on down ter Lett's way station," explained Dragoon.

"Can you drive a horse team, Mister Dragoon?" asked Cotter.

"No. But then ya don't really know what yer capable of until you try."

Frank drew Whitney's attention to the circling buzzards.

"What about those up there?"

"I've seen 'em. They'll keep their distance as long as we've got someone walking round down here; they're a cowardly lot until they get mighty, hungry; and it's down ter survival of the fittest."

"What if you don't find the stage and the horses, what if they don't stop running until they reached the way station, Dragoon?"

"Then I shall continue on the road until I get to the station. But it'll be a thing in our favor if they do that. It'll wise the folks up that we're in serious trouble, and they'll send someone out lookin' for us! …That'll sure save *me* a long walk"

Whitney lifted his revolver from its holster.

"You better take this and a few bullets while I'm away…" Dragoon unbuckled the holster which had shells in the bullet loops.

"What will I need this for?" said Frank as he took the hardware.

"To keep them damn buzzards from the bodies of Morgan an' Father Lorimar. You're not going to do it with a handful of stones, ya know?"

"OK. But I haven't the foggiest idea how to fire the damn thing," Frank turned the six-gun about and looked at it from various angles.

"You at least know which end of a gun the bullet comes out of?" Dragoon said, sarcastically.

Cotter nodded.

"Give it back here a second…" Whitney took the handgun off Frank. "I'm gonna show you how ter go about emptying the spent cartridges and rearming the cylinders with fresh ammo.

"Watch close so you'll get the hang of it…"

Whitney Dragoon had been trudging on road to the way station, for an hour. This was to say he had covered between four or five miles. He carried spare water in Father Lorimar's Pilgrim hat with both hands so as not to lose it all, hopefully by sundown. Luckily he had chosen a hat which was very much watertight. He had filled the hat from the waters of Diamond Creek, just as he had done with Hunt's hat. But that was after he and the newspaperman had gathered the pair of corpses and placed them back close to Devil's Marbles — say about three or four yards out from their bases where the boulders reared up out of the ground.

It irritated Dragoon that he had not yet come across the stagecoach and its team of horseflesh. He had expected too, before this. He recalled how the Concord was careering off into the distance behind the frightened horses. He had expected it to flip over on its side, but it obviously hadn't, well, not this close to the Marbles.

Whitney had heard a few distant pistol shots from the direction of the creek, and wondered whether or not the tenderfoot was having much success in scaring off the ever hungry vultures; he had not been in any doubt — that they would make a move on the bodies sooner than later, and if by now, instead of two, there were three — taking into account Joe Hunt's critical condition, the buzzers would not hesitate about getting serious.

As Dragoon continued with his march, the heat of what was left in the day, added to his discomfort as it made his body send rivulets of perspiration down from under the sweatband of his hat to his shirt and coat collars. Though he was hot, he was but nowhere near bored. His arms were tired of carrying the hat by the brim with half a crown of water inside to weigh it down. He had been forced to stop and place the hat carefully on the road's surface to rest his arms, and was aware that the odd rest spells were eating into his travel time. He was irritated with himself that he was not making as good a time as he had hoped. The only encouragement he got during these spells was the evidence on the road's surface of the vehicle's tire marks left in the limestone dressing, some showed that the stagecoach had gone perilously close to rolling over— but clearly had regained its equilibrium and escaped disaster to date.

When dusk began closing in the gun-salesman's feet where the worse for wear, blisters were definitely going to be a problem for Dragoon and he started to actually pray, that he would come across the overturned stagecoach and there find the horses anchored to the wreck by their harnesses. If that were the case he would be willing to try and free a horse so as he might ride on to Lett's place and thus save his feet. But he did eventually come upon the wrecked coach but not until night was well and truly coming in and the situation was not as he had hoped; the vehicle had been abandoned, for the team had broken free of the Concord's hulk and continued with their fearful flight ...

The overturned vehicle was lying in the middle of the road and had been battered out of shape; the Concord's load had been strewn all around, when the stage had succumbed to the uncontrollable swaying of its baulk. He found his case of pistol samples and the guns had survived the crash without damage, but he wouldn't be able to use them for he had no more shells with him. He placed the case inside the vehicle so as not to lose them.

The hold-up trio reached Coyote Pass after dark. They were anxious to a man to make camp and divide the loot. They would not be able to hang out here long if they did not want a posse of law abiding citizens from the surrounding district to pick up their trail. They all realized that there was enough men back at Tony Lett's station to form such a posse, and would certainly do so once the events that had occurred at Devil's Marbles came to light; Lett and company wouldn't wait on the Law from Junction City to swing into action; they would be obliged to be pro-active simply by the mere fact that the company stage had been robbed so close to their base.

Korda attended to the horses. He unsaddled them and rubbed them down while they caught their wind after such a hard ride to the pass. Moe Malthouse got a campfire burning to give them some warmth and light to work with. Matt Flynn took it upon himself to climb up to one of the high points of Coyote Pass and watch for anyone riding their way with firebrands; so the riders could see the ground their mounts were treading along.

When Korda had finished his horse chores and picketed the horses, he collected all the saddlebags with the help of Malthouse and took them over near the fire where Moe had earlier spread out a horse blanket. They were in the process of collecting all the money and small gold ingots in the middle of the rug when Flynn joined them in the firelight with his carbine. He was the only one of the three men wearing spurs he sat down and began removing them after placing his Winchester on the blanket.

"…How is the split gonna workout?" Flynn asked as he also began removing his spurs from his boots.

"Let's see jist what we've got first," Malthouse stated as he emptied the canvas money bags one on top of the other in the center of the blanket; The gold took Korda's fancy and he collect an ingot just to feel its weight; for something so small, it was a surprise to him and it showed in his eyes. No one here had ever seen or felt the touch of gold before and they all had a sample.

"Six ingots, that enough for two a piece," Flynn commented.

Malthouse paused in what he was doing and looked across the rug at his now ex-foreman; "We have already worked out how the gold's gonna be split, Flynn. One for you ... three fer Korda an' two fer me! "

"That seems a little uneven. Originally I wuz under the impression that it was gonna be a four way split when the Kid was around; but wif him out of it, shouldn't it now go three ways?"

Korda turned to the ramrod. "Look, let's not go too over the top about this. You'll get an equal share of the cash. But the ingots go this way. I get three and Malthouse gets two. As I keep tellin' you yore a Johnny-come-lately; the only thing you're gonna get an equal share in is the cash."

"Jist remember Flynn … we ain't back out on the range no more an' you don't carry the status of being me boss," Malthouse told the ramrod. "You be thankful fer small mercies … git, it?"

Matt Flynn nodded. Now wasn't the time for a fall out that might end in blood being spilt, Flynn had made his bed and now would have to lie in it. Anyway, after tonight none of them would have to abide each other's company, they would all ride their own trail — hopefully never to meet again.

Once the loot had been sorted, the three bandits packed their quota of the robbery into their own saddlebags and rolled out their bed-rolls, as they readied themselves for bed. Flynn lay there at first looking up at the canopy of stars and realized just what a mess he had made of things by bothering to join up with these desperados, he couldn't imagine himself as being like the others, a desperado. But he was, and now would have to live with it, for he was the one who took the step on the outlaw path; no one twisted his arm.

Sam Korda's voice broke the silence. "You still awake, Malthouse?" he asked.

"…If I wasn't I am now," he acknowledged, "What's eatin ya, Sam?" Malthouse asked while lying there on his back, his head resting on his saddlebags to keep track of his ill-gotten gains one would suppose.

"You still intendin' ter head back to the safety of Canada?" Korda rose up on one elbow and looked in the Canadian's direction.

Moe sighed. "…Can't have it any other way. It's been a mighty long time now I've been south of the border; a man mightn't have any kinfolk even left alive up there when ya think about it. Why the interest, Sam?"

"I wuz wonderin' if you'd mind me joinin' yer for a while, that's all. This darn area is gonna be too hot fer the likes of me and I ain't fixed any permanent plans of where ter go."

"I'm happy with that if you are?" Moe said.

The pair of them settled down to sleep and Matt was glad for the peace and quiet so that he might be able to concentrate on his own shut-eye. All the same he was glad that Korda hadn't insisted on wanting to join him, he much preferred to travel alone.

Dragoon could not see the point of pushing on into the dark as if there was not going to be a bright moon in the bargain, he could very well wonder off the road and lose his way. That would not serve in anyone's favor, for the Tenderfoot and Joe Hunt back at the creek was depending on Whitney to bring them help.

He collected some nearby brush from the side of the road, which looked, like it had died in the drought like conditions of the surrounding country. It had died long ago and the recent rains certainly weren't going to revive it. The brittle shrubs played havoc with his tender hands, but nonetheless it had to be done. Whitney carried three armfuls of the prickly shrubs to the coach, and built them into a heap, two yards out from the overturned coach; so later he would be able to have a bonfire, which would be seen for miles around. He had to have something capable of keeping coyotes, mountain lions and wolverines at bay, for he had no weapons he could rely on, his revolver and small supply of ammunition was with Cotter.

Finally he set alight to the brush and sat down with his back resting against the grease stained front wheel hub and gazed into the dancing flames and listened to the crackling of the burning fuel and mused at the sparks which rose like fireflies on the fire's up draught … It was not too long before the brush fire had him completely mesmerized and combined with his tiring walk the man fell into a very deep sleep, even though there was good signs that the Moon was on the wing.

4

THE WAY STATION managed by Tony Lett with a crew of six men, Sid Rover, Rolf Lygon an ex-cowhand, "Pedro" Fuller — a white man who looked so Spanish that everyone who met him always took him for a Mexican, thus he was nicknamed, "Pedro" — and whether he liked it or not, had to live with it — in other words he had to put up or shut up. Then there was "Red" Mick, a red-haired and bearded Irishman who originally came from far away, Donegal, and Con Ruby— born an' bred in the land of Daniel Boone, plus a Mexican, Benito Cabanas.

The station stood a quarter of a mile off the road on a slight rise, its false front facing towards Junction City. The rise was purposely used for it gave a fair view of the surrounding land and was useful back when the Indians weren't as tame as they now were.

The main building was oblong in shape — two average rooms wide and six in depth. The structure consisted of two types of building materials — adobe brick walls with a corrugated, galvanized sheet roof and gutter to catch the rainwater which was channel to a tin water tank on a tank-stand on the leeward side of the building. Three chain lengths away in alignment with the water-tank was a huge barn with a corral at the rear alongside the corral is a blacksmith's forge so as running repairs can be made to any of the stagecoach rigging and horses, shoed.

At the rear of the homestead was a much smaller corral used for herding a mongrel breed of goats which were used to supply meat and milk, butter and cheese for the Butterfield passengers or passersby. The goats were turned out daily to scavenge food from the surrounding plain, and low branches of an avenue of cottonwoods — there was no fear of wandering Indians stealing the goats for some reason they shied away from their meat, but local Mexicans scratching out a living in the open land kept sheep and were keen on mutton and goat-meat — though their herds were the bane of the cattle industry but not much could be done about them as the Spanish settlers and their sheep were here first.

The station also had two wells, which seem to never run dry and with the big rainwater tank there was never a water shortage.

Tony Lett's age was hard to assess — he was certainly over the fifty year mark and maybe under seventy; with a wild, white head of hair down to his shoulders which was so white it looked akin to snow. He was thickset and his facial features indicated that he had lived life both rough and tough — the truth behind his once broken snout was the effect of having been hit in the face with the back of a horse's head 15-years ago, at a piece of old rope on the ground, no doubt thinking it a snake? Tony realized his broken nose added character to his dial and made men believe that he was a feller well able to use his fists, which came at a price by living with a sinus complaint.

Whether he had ever been married was one of life's mysteries. He dressed in the manner of most range men and only slapped his fancy pistols on whenever he reckoned it was necessary. His .45s had horn pistol grips and were holstered in a rather fancy gun-rig of tooled leather and shiny silver rivets. He rode a beautiful gelding which stood 16 hands and was the same color as his own hair. Some years ago he went a bit haywire and purchased an expensive Mexican saddle and bridle with riding cups instead of stirrups — these cups are similar to those of the U.S. Cavalry.

At the moment, he and the way station's cook, Sidney Rover, were in conversation. The cook was concerned about how much food he ought to cook up for the station's hands and the incoming passengers.

Rover was roughly the same age as Lett and had only ever been a ranch cook or chuck wagon hand on cattle droving trips. He wore and old Derby on his noggin' which only ever came off when he laid his head to rest on a pillow at night. The hat's brim had been in the wars when a burro had taken a fancy to it one day. Sid Rover had a peg leg like a Caribbean Buccaneer, which he claimed he had lost to cannon fire in the war and made himself out to be a war hero. He had in fact partially lost his limb when run-over by a locomotive up Chicago way only four years back — there was no way he had ever been in the war as he was not a young man when hostilities broke out between the North and the South. But nonetheless he glowed in his false glory and got away with it most of the time.

"…I think we've got a problem, Mr. Lett," Rover said as he approached Tony who was playing solitaire at a table that someone had made from bits and pieces of two other tables, that did not quite match. Lett was the only man here who decided what or when he would work — like now he was enjoying some leisure time, unlike the rest of the males about the place who had their set chores to be done every day.

"And what would that be, Sid?"

Lett and his colleagues weren't aware that the bachelor community had a constant odor about it of rancid butter. To those used of the smell it didn't register but it was the first thing

"— Peaches, canned peaches. I wuz gonna make us all a dessert of peaches'n custard ter sort of put the passengers in a good mood after fightin' their way through that darn storm."

Tony racked his cards.

"Don't worry 'bout that — they'll jist be lookin' fer a quick meal and hittin' the traces fer the last leg of their journey. I wouldn't be knocking myself out about doin' anythin' fancy fer 'em. Keep it simple is what I reckon." Lett stacked the cards in a neat deck like a practiced gambler.

Cotter had been sitting down now with the injured teamster for the past three hours. It was time that didn't drag for the newspaperman, for he was concerned for Hunt's wellbeing but felt his hands were tied because of his lack of medical knowledge or what to do for the pain wreaked man. Gee, how he wished Doctor Lester Lomax was on hand right at this moment.

Frank Cotter looked skyward and judged that nightfall was only minutes away. He wondered whether the stagecoach driver would make it through the night, if not, three dead bodies would surround him. Already the vultures had taken up their perches for the night in the trees down at the creek, he had been able to keep them at bay thus far but they were a rude lot and he knew they could sense that food to their liking was close at hand.

The few times he had tried to shoot a buzzard or two had simply been a waste of good lead slugs. The pistol had a kick to it, which surprised the pen pusher, and he had come close to being smashed in the face with the iron body structure of the six-gun. He wondered what was keeping Dragoon, the way the man had spoken the stagecoach wouldn't be far away, and yet he had been gone for hours. He did not feel happy about spending the night out here in the so-called frontier.

Cotter looked down at the pistol in his hand once more — it looked so big and cumbersome for his hand, the hand of a writer. He couldn't explain it but it was the weight of the weapon that amazed him. When other folk seemed to have them in their hands they moved about with them as freely as a child with a toy but in his hand, it makes him feel shockingly, awkward.

A beating of wings drew Cotter's attention off that of the gun. He glanced in the sound's direction which he found was in the direction of the Priest's body… a yard and a half away from the corpse, between him and the robbery scene a vulture had touchdown on the worn grass which was struggling to take advantage of the recent rains.

The creature only had hungry eyes for Lorimar's body.

Frank came to his feet as fast as humanly possible and with a roar in which he tried to imitate that of a wild cat he ran towards the buzzard, waving his arms as though he was trying his damnedest to become airborne — his actions startled the bird and in fear, it changed tack, and so had to struggle for its life to get airborne once more, once off the ground by eight or ten feet the bird of prey instinctively knew it was safe and went back into conserving energy for a later time.

The scribe saw a rock on the ground the size of a Spanish onion, and scooped it up and threw it after the climbing bird all in the one motion. But it never ever had any likelihood of striking its target and when its velocity was spent it fell to earth.

Joe opened his eyes and glanced about him, for a moment he most likely didn't know where he was, but realized the day was getting on. He tried to call for Cotter but his voice was much weaker than average.

"Cotter… Cotter — w-what's wrong?" Joe stammered in a soft ragged voice, which took a lot more out of him than he ever expected.

"It's nothing Joe — just the damn vultures making a nuisance of themselves." Frank came back to Hunt. "…It will be dark soon, they won't bother us then I guess."

"You can't do the impossible, son. They know no better. W-w-w-where did you get the gun?"

Frank glanced down at the pistol in his hand; he had forgotten he had it.

"It's one Whitney Dragoon left with me…"

"I see," Hunt murmured. Then paused for a long time as though that was all he could manage to say. Then he fired up again. "C-c-c-can you use it?"

Cotter shook his head, "Not, really."

"Where's Dragoon gone, son?"

"See whether he can get help from the way station. He's hopeful that the horses have run out of wind up the road apiece and that he can find them and bring the stagecoach back here for us. I don't reckon you should be doing all this talking — it's taking too much out of you, sir."

"Hmm. Me thinks you're worried about them buzzards gettin' into me and the Priest but you mustn't, we'll be good fer sumthin' in the long run, you'll see." It was obvious that Hunt wasn't aware about Morgan's death by snakebite and Frank decided to leave it that way.

"I'll make a fire — we'll need it, Joe."

"I don't need a fire, I'm hot enough as it is," Joe told Frank. "You make it fer yore self if you think you need it."

A silence now built up between the scribe and the teamster and already when Frank looked back towards the cadavers at the foot of the boulders he found he could hardly make them out. He put the pistol in the holster and placed it on the ground near the quiet coach driver and went off to find something to burn.

Finally Frank had an armful of brush and twigs which looked suitable to get a fire started, though he was ignorant as too the agricultural names of the foliage he had collected nor of its value to animals skeptical to a diet of the stuff, all he could sense was that it would burn and that's all he was concerned with. He began carrying it over in the direction of Joe Hunt, making sure where he placed a foot for fear of snakes, when in the near darkness ahead of him there was a might roar of a pistol shot and a quick flash of ignited gunpowder!

Shock, realization, and disillusionment shot through his whole body just as fast as the six-gun slug from Dragoon's gun had buried itself into Hunt's body and carried off what had remained of his life on this earth.

Cotter threw aside his motley collection of fire fuel and raced towards the suicide victim, whereby he tripped over his own clumsy feet and went sprawling on his face. He scrambled back up with a frightened sob from his throat and continued over to the decease… And realized by the light of the moon balanced on the east horizon that the feller had done himself in.

Frank's shoulders sagged and he stood there looking hopelessly lost, at Joe's corpse. He slowly lowered himself down and took the pistol from the limp claw like fingers of a man he knew had proved himself to be a resourceful and brave fellow, Cotter knew that this man had just displayed in a split-second, that he had more honor and braveness in his little finger than Cotter could ever hope to muster from his alcoholic dependent, shameful body and soul.

Cotter need a drink, but realized that all there was here was the greasy hat of Hunt's — which contained creek water that Dragoon had collected before his departure. He picked up the broken-in Stetson and took a swig—it tasted unlike any water he had ever sipped before and he got no real pleasure from it, but still it wet his whistle and that was better than naught. …*Now what am I gonna do for myself?* The scribe thought, *Maybe everyone will blame me for Hunt's death.*

Maybe they will say I ought to have had more sense than to have left a loaded gun within reach of a man in Hunt's condition…?My God, this is gonna be a long night for me. Surrounded by three dead men and alone in the wilderness, what kind of hole, have I landed myself in?

Dragoon's reawakening was a rude one to say the least. Before he had even come to full consciousness he was aware of a vile odor, which he tried to place but couldn't as the untraceable smell penetrated his dilated nostrils—it was accompanied with a panting warm airflow… He raised his heavy eyelids and found himself up close and personal to the face of a curious night-prowling coyote — the coyote and man received the shock of their lives, for the coyote dam had thought the creature before her was a dead. Dragoon almost dropped his bowels and bladder as one; his holler was completely and utterly involuntary. The coyote sprung backwards with all fours and wheel her body round to flee in the opposite direction before any of her paws had made contact with earth, its claws bit into the dirt for purchase, and having obtained same

— it fled into the protection of the night with the speed any greyhound would be proud of; the experience had left Whitney Dragoon in a fine layer of sweat which was being immediately absorbed by the touch of his underwear, save for that on his brow and his upper lip. His calves were taut like the pigskin of a drum and began pulsating in time with his rapid heartbeats… He rose awkwardly from his position and realized that his surrounding area was now bathed in moonlight and he puzzled about how long he had been asleep.

His encounter with the coyote made him decided that for safety he should try and make himself comfortable inside the stagecoach where it lay on the road. To his horror, Dragoon found he had upset his water supply in the pilgrim styled hat of the Priest's, and now he was out of water. But his only option open to him now was the stagecoach.

The only way he had of finding his way in, was to climb the underbelly of the Concord like climbing the side of a log shack and when a top of the vehicle, he lowered himself down through the doors open window-frame. He struck a match once inside as the thought that a rattler might have already taken shelter in it for the night went through his mind as he thought of Morgan's sudden and unexpected death. The interior proved to be clear and he was lucky to find a full canteen of water amongst the debris.

Well, here's a bit of luck, thought Dragoon, as he secured the canteen. He had the urge to sample it but knew that every drop of fresh water was to be treated like a bonus from here on out, so he put it aside, and set about trying to make himself comfort enough to get more much needed sleep before the morning.

Meantime, at Lett's place, the household were getting a little concerned for the stagecoach, it was expected to have reached the way station by this, certainly no more later than a little after sunset.

Red Mick and Rolf Lygon were sitting on a stool that had been originally made up in the station's smithy some years back, they had located it out under the porch awning and were smoking wild marijuana.

Lett came out from inside the station and taking Red's smoke from between his fingers said: "…How deep have you driven the new cesspit, Rolf?" He took a drag on Red's smoke while awaiting the ex-cowpuncher's answer, then handed the smoke back to Red.

"'Bout nine feet, Tony. How deep do you want me an' Benito ter go …?" Rolf was not fond of digging the necessary hole but the present outhouse was getting dangerously full and the new one had to be sunk some two-yards over to the right of the present one.

"Take her down ter twelve. It'll last longer before we'll need a new one," Tony turned and gazed down towards the main road to town.

"You get on well, workin' with the Mexican, Rolf." Red said as he took another pull on his smoke. Then as he continued to talk, the smoke deep within his lungs came out with his spoken words until his lungs had emptied. "Better than most of us wee folk, how come you can get 'im to work?"

"Ben's all right if ya willin' ter treat him as an equal, that's the trick I reckon," Rolf explained.

"Yeah — well that's somethin' I guess," said Tony as he swished his ponytail and turned round then stepped up to the cowboy and now helped himself to Rolf Lyon's smoke. Rolf didn't renege, but he wished if Lett wanted to smoke their smokes why didn't he roll one of his own, marijuana was laid on about the place as there was nothing else to do after a day's toiling than to sit back and smoke oneself silly, it was cool.

Pedro Fuller came outside with a mug of java in his paw. Referring to Sid Rover he said to Tony Lett: "…Cook's gettin' pissed orf the stage hasn't arrived, says his supper's gonna be ruined if they're any later."

"Hmm. Sid's right. They're sure draggin' the chain a bit. But I wouldn't be too worried going by that, not after what that saddle-bum said, who wuz through here with Lehmann's message, yesterday. Lett reached out and helped himself to Fuller's mug without asking. "— Joe got a pretty solid beatin' from the storm, give 'em another forty-minutes then we mebbe oughta start to worry." He took a swallow of Fuller's bitter coffee and handed it back to Pedro.

Sid approached the station house door on his thumping peg leg and standing under the lintel a huffing and a puffing said: "Did Fuller give you my message, Tony?"

Lett's nodded his answer.

"Then what's the story? Do we bugger up me supper for everyone or are youse fellers' cummin' in…?"

"You're worse than a mad mole, Sid. Honestly! All right, we'll be in shortly," Tony told him and nodded to the fellers to join him inside.

When the white men filed inside they found the Mexican, sitting down to supper after having served himself when he must have come in from out the back of the station. He wore the typical pajama like costume of the peon's and a battered wide brim straw hat covered his oily dark hair.

As Sid limped by on his way to the stove he whipped the sun damaged straw hat from Bentio Cabana's head and threw it on the floor. "…Hat's off at *my table* you peasant!"

Benito went on eating as though the gringo hadn't done a thing to him — food was his only pleasure out here with all these men. It took the place of a good senorita for there was a scarcity in the district at the best of times.

"Did you milk all the goats before you started on that hole, Benito?" Sid called from in front of the stove.

"Si, Benito does all **his** chores the gringos throw his way." He broke off a piece of stale oven baked bread; Sid had made three days ago and dipped it in the meat juice on his plate.

With supper over and the washing up done, the men sat around smoking in the dark, only because no one felt incline to light up the lamps; the glow of the smokes gave off enough light if one wasn't set on moving about.

"What are you thinkin' about Red over there in the dark?" asked Fuller from some- where across the room.

"Why pick on me?" said the Irishman.

" 'Coz you've always got sumthin' interstin' ter say," Pedro explained.

"If you must know my thought then, I was thinkin' of the dear green, green, fields of 'ome. And I'm so homesick I could puke! Satisfied, Pedro?"

Just then their quiet peaceful night was shattered with the arrival of the coach team which brought everyone to their feet.

"At last," cried Tony. **"The stage – it's here!"**

Everyone piled outside to greet the newly arrived company, but was struck dumb when they discovered a loose team of harnessed horses who had run themselves to a frazil and no stagecoach!

It didn't take a College graduate to figure out what had gone wrong. The animals were easily round-up as they could barely raise a trot. Everyone got together and took the spent horses out the back to the barn and bed them down, then made ready the station's covered wagon, placing aboard rations and things which could serve as medical supplies in a pinch — for they had no idea what might confronted them down the line. As an added precaution they made ready an extra team of horseflesh and as there wasn't a great deal of stock at Lett's the wagon's own team had to supported with mules; for the thought lingered in mind that the stagecoach *might* be OK to use when they came across it.

Lett and Rolf decided to take their own mounts along as neither horse had been exercised for a time and both men knew they could cover the ground between them and where the coach might have come to grief, faster than the mule hauling wagon would move.

The rescue party pulled out under a full moon under the watchful eyes of Rover who was to remain here in charge of the station. No one could hazard a guess how long the party would be away. The peg-leg cook waved them off in to the night, and then returned to the lamp lit interior, of the homestead.

With just the moon, stars and dead companions at hand – Frank Cotter felt decidedly uncomfortable and realized that this wasn't a night that gave him any promise of sleep; and come morning, he would have his hands full keeping the hungry vulture at bay from the bodies of the Priest and the drummer which they regarded as their food and there for the taking. That dead meat would be seen as that of a rare banquet – and members of the flock would give their very lives so that others might gorge themselves without thanks.

Dragoon awoke and decided that he was much too uncomfortable for any more sleep and taking the canteen with him he climbed out onto the up turned side of the stagecoach and down to the ground. Then he set off along the road for a bright moon lit his way and as the night had cooled he knew the brisk walk would keep him warm enough to survive the night.

It was Tony Lett's horse, which picked up the scent of the approaching Dragoon first — for his body odor was carried downwind on a breeze which had come in from the prairie on course for Junction City. At this time of the early morning Lett and Rolf were spelling their mounts by walking them side-by-side along the road, they were very close to being three-quarters of a mile ahead of the wagon for the mules had long ago lost their zest for moving faster than walking pace.

"We must be nearin' sumthin' that's not natural, notice how my hoss is tossing the head and sniffing the breeze?" Tony told Rolf Lygon.

"Each man c'n read his own cayuse, boss — mebbe you're right," Lygon agreed as he sat his saddle with his hands one on top of the other atop his pommel.

"She's not a hoss who takes kindly ter strangers," Tony added.

"No need ter tell me that,' Lygon said. "She gave me nip ter remember when I went in her stall to muck it out."

"You didn't say anythin' ter me about it?"

"I'm no sop ... I've been kicked and nipped a few times since I started ter hang around the odd Cayuse, before!"

"Then you should've turn the hoss out into a corral before goin' into a stall with a beast ya don't know," Tony offered without sympathy. "With this harlot," Lett ruffled her mane. "— She might've trampled you ter death."

"Generally I am more careful around strange horses," pointed out Rolf as he removed his Stetson with his hand and held it out away from his head as he formed his other hand's digits into a claw and raked his hair.

"It jist that cook, Sid Rover, led me ter believe yore Cayuse was far from bein' an ornery critter."

Tony laughed, then added: "...Now ya know better than to take that lyin' coots word fer anythin'!"

"Ya live an' learn," Rolf announced.

"Look, how about you drop back and see what's holding Pedro Fuller and them hinnies back…"

Rolf replaced his hat with a nod and upon remounting, wheeled his bay round and headed off back towards the wagon.

Five minutes later Tony Lett could make out the details of someone walking towards him along the center of the trail – from that distance he could not tell whom it was but figured that it would be either one of the Butterfield staff, or a passenger. Lett's spurred his horse on to an even faster clip, keen to be of help to the wanderer – and to know his story. Old Tony was not afraid of his horse stepping in a hole, for the moonlight was now almost as bright as that of a firebrand, and the road was straight and flat, like any ancient Roman highway, at this point.

Whitney saw the pale horse racing towards him down the road; it looked like a ghost horse without a rider for Lett's clothing was quite dark. Dragoon decided to save energy and let the horse come to him so he sat down and waited. Lett reined in when he was almost on top of Dragoon and the dust stirred up and left trailing behind by the horseman, swept up and passed them. Tony recognized Whitney Dragoon of old.

"What in tar nation are you doin' out here — it is Whitney Dragoon I'm addresin', right?" Tony asked, as he looked the man over in the moonlight and saw the canteen hanging over his shoulder with the Butterfield brand on it.

"Yep," Dragoon answered as he slipped the canteen from his shoulder and prepared to have a swig. Then the gun salesman sat down where he stood.

Lett dismounted and stood over the sitter holding the reins of his horse. The horse began shifting its weight from one leg to the other.

Without being prompted, Dragoon told Lett the whole shocking story about the events back at Diamond Creek and that the stagecoach was a smashed wreck back down the road about three to four miles, if not more.

"…So, that Sam Korda ***did*** turn out ter be a bad egg!" said Tony once he had the full story. "I never trusted the guy you know. He had a look about him, which said he was trouble."

The station manager and Dragoon rode tandem on Lett's horse back to the slow plodding wagon. On the way there, Lett asked if

Dragoon felt well enough to ride a horse alone back to the way station. He explained to the salesman that seeing as Hunt was so badly hurt he couldn't afford to leave him out in the open too long as the weather might kill him with the help of his injuries. So rather than take Dragoon back to the robbery site he'd get the cow-puncher he had working for him, to loan the salesman his horse, while they went on to Diamond Creek and he rode on to the stage station, so maybe he might catch up on some sleep.

Reluctantly, the cowboy loaned the stranger his cayuse and the wagon and Dragoon parted company. Dragoon, to be sure of getting hold of the cowpoke's horse falsely promised he would nurse the pony all the way back to the station, but once out of sight of the covered wagon and the would-be rescuers, Dragoon gave the horse a lacing with the reins and had her striding it out a little to dangerously for his own good but this time he had lady-luck riding with him and he stayed in the saddle and the pony stayed on its hooves.

Lett was still away ahead of the covered wagon as he approached the overturned stagecoach in the middle of the road. He reined in and trotted his mount in a circle round the vehicle and was not happy that it had been flipped over on its side, but it looked as if, it might be able to be salvaged. He dismounted and wrote a quick note to the crew back with the wagon and mules, instructing them not to mess with the Concord but to continue on after him to the survivors down at Diamond Creek.

5

HEN HE REMOUNTED and wheeled his mare round so that she was facing the direction he wanted her to go and let the toey bitch have her head, slobber was soon trailing back from the bit and colliding with his shirt-front but he was eager to get farther and farther away from the coach before needing to give the horse a spell… *Day light can't be far away,* thought Cotter as he looked about the immediate area; even though sleep had not been a priority throughout the night he had managed to keep his mind occupied. He was conscious of the vultures perched in the branches of the cottonwoods near to the boulders and that put them within easy reach of Father Lorimar and Chas Morgan's bodies — Frank knew what each and every one of them was planning to do, and it was not hard or pretty to imagine. He realized that to protect the three bodies from being attacked and gorged on, he would have to be on his toes.

The moon was now egg-yolk yellow, because of the sun, which though still well below the eastern horizon was yet able to reflex off the lunar surface of the dead planet.

As a newspaperman he had had some experience with dead bodies and knew that Mister Rigor Mortis had paid his visit to Joe Hunt and his pals and had moved on, as is always its policy. Frank forced himself to grasp Hunt by the wrists and drag his limp body back across the ground until he reached the base of the Devil's Marbles, where he maneuvered the body so that the three cadavers lay side-by-side and very much in line. Then he dragged the tarpaulin about so that he could cover all three stiffs and hide them from the eyes of the scavengers… *Maybe out of sight, out of mind,* thought the newspaperman.

Prior to first light Matt Flynn roused from his sleep and reckoned it was time to make a move if he and his party wanted to be in the saddle by first light. Matt sat up and saw that Korda and Malthouse were still in a dead sleep. He flung back his warm horse rug to face the brisk, fresh morning air and decided to hunt up some beef-jerky for breakfast. Korda and Malthouse still didn't make any moves as he dragged on his cold boots over his thick woolen socks.

"C'mon you pair of lay-a-bouts — we've gotta get some miles under our belts if we wanna keep ahead of any posses!" Matt bawled out at the slumbering bandits. Korda stirred and sat up, looking for his hat with one hand and scratching his head with the other. Moe Malthouse never moved a muscle. He was still comatose as if he had been hit over the head with a Smithy's hammer.

Korda crawled on hands and knees from his bed-roll across to Malthouse and endeavored to rouse the man who continued to remain unmoved and this caused Flynn to move swiftly across the campsite to have a look at the Canadian. "…I can't seem to wake him, Flynn; what d'you make of it?" Korda asked. From Flynn's standing point, it looked to the ramrod as though Moe Malthouse was lying there in his bedroll — dead, but how could this be? He seemed to be perfectly all right on turning in; he had never complained that he was feeling ill or anything."

"It sure looks to me as if the guy's dead."

"Impossible," Korda said as he gave Malthouse a vigorous shaking, "no one jist up and dies like that!" But the cowboy's body just shook lifelessly from the rough shaking Korda had subjected the lifeless cowboy too.

Malthouse certainly looked like a dead man, the ramrod came over and knelt down next to Korda — both men were worried.

"Could he have been bitten by somethin' poisonous?" Matt suggested as he began unwrapping Malthouse's inert body, "— it might've been anythin'— scorpion or a damn snake, who knows?" Both men began searching under the cowboy's clothing for signs of a reason for his apparent condition but nothing was discovered which could account for such an obvious demise; nothing, not even an insect or possible animal bite stood out on the man's skin. They gave up on Malthouse and accepted that he was as dead as a door nail. "What do you want to do about this, Korda?"

"Why ask me? I've never come across anythin' like this," Sam Korda exclaimed.

"I know one thing, its cost us a good jump on any posse that could be getting setup ter come after us — look, it will be sunup pretty shortly and we'll lose any advantage we might've had."

"So what do we do about Malthouse and his share of the robbery?" Korda asked like a man lost.

"That's obvious to me," Matt Flynn told his colleague.

Finally the morning sun's edge nudged its way out from behind the horizon and turned the sky a hot red, the colors at this point made it extremely difficult to work out whether one was witnessing a sunset or a sunrise. Cotter had no interest in the beauty of the day being hatched for his main concern was how he would be able to keep the buzzards in their place. He took advantage of the fact that the drowsy vultures had not realized that he had covered the bodies and would be at a loss where their store of food had disappeared too. He made his way down to the edge of the flowing creek and rinsed his face and hands in the cold water and in a sense it stimulated him and chased his own weariness off. Then he made his way back to the bodies at the base of the boulders to be on hand should the buzzards get curious.

The beauty of a sparkling morning sun on the waters' of Diamond Creek was wasted on Cotter — he missed seeing the reason for the creek being so named. Frank wanted to get the fire restarted so he would have something to chase the morning chill out of his system and was lucky to find a dry broken branch from the cottonwood lying on the ground and enough near dry foliage to act as kindling. He noisily broke the branch and twigs up with sharp cracks and groans and then built the more solid wood up over the leaves etc. That work ate up a bit of time and too many matches in his awkward attempt to try to get the fire on the go; He realized that he would soon be out of matches and that would certainly leave him with no fire, at last a match ignited and before it died Frank shoved its head in amongst the matchsticks of his past failures and though only a couple of them caught he had the sense to nurse the struggling flame and fed it dry mulch which began to smolder and shortly through the smoke-haze he detected a flame the size of his thumb, it was encouraging and showed promise — he had to fight his emotions which came from his irritated inner core, for if he bowed to its demand there was every chance he would blow the growth of a promising campfire and that would be a disaster … in the next passing minute the small flame grew in both strength and size and he was able to add dry twigs which he built into a pyre over the yellow and orange, smoky flame … as the fire continued to catch and burn so did the scribe's confidence in it — so much so that he was able to take in his surrounding beyond the duty of nurturing the blaze and it was then he noticed that he had left the gun and holster back out on the open ground where Joe had suicided and used this as an excuse to escape the fire's playful smoke. The leather-holster and firearm were warm to the touch, for they had been focused on by the first rays of the sun, which had penetrated the foliage of the willow trees down on the creek bank.

He buckled on the plain holster and was reminded of the six-gun's weight. Then three vultures left the cottonwoods and came in to land fifty yards away. They began moseying along like a farmer pacing out the length of a proposed plow furrow… they didn't fool Cotter — he knew what they were about. He pitched to take a shot at them; the cheekiest one appealed to Frank's fancy. Then he got to thinking, that maybe they were too far away to risk a shot and a waste of lead.

How can I get over the weight of this goddamn handgun? If I pause, holding the gun for any length of time to take aim my arm and wrist feel like they are going to fall off, he thought. *That's it! That's what I've got to do, steady the revolver on something… but what?*

Maybe the answer is if I go and sit with my back against the base of one of the boulders and raise my knees up together I could rest my hand and the gun on my kneecaps. It will support my hands and maybe steady my aim — it might be worth considering?

Frank went over to the covered bodies and took up his position against the cool rock with the six-gun resting in his hands on top of his knees. Once settled he decided that he would stay as still as possible so that he might fool the most boldest of the vultures to move in closer, meanwhile, while they were still a distance away he drew back the hammer of the Colt so that any noise the gun made when being cocked, would not unsettle the birds of prey.

He was as ready now as he would ever be.

The birds gradually moved in closer and closer, from fifty yards down to about twenty... *They'll need to be closer before I can risk taking a shot,* thought Frank. *Kill just one of these bastards might make the rest of them think twice about trying to outsmart me...*

The most aggressive of the birds was obviously the self-proclaimed chief of the flock He or she, came forward once more as another two buzzard glided in and settled on the ground behind the trio already in place. Then another four came in and took up a position behind them — they were building up their ground forces like an Army.

Frank, squinted his left eye and bent his head forward until he had the gun-barrel's front sight in focus and then he carefully adjusted the weapons angle until it was pointed at the buzzard before him, who was scratching at the ground with its right claws, all its weight balanced on its left leg, its wings were stretched out away from its body — just like Cotter had seen turkeys do at a turkey farm he had once visited.

Suddenly he heard a voice in his head. The voice sounded just like his pal's, Doctor Lester Lomax. Voices in his head he knew he should ignore, but sounding like the Doc's and that made him decide to listen to it, and follow its instructions.

...Don't jerk the trigger whatever ya do. Just increase the pull smoothly — let the gun do its job.

Then without warning — BANG!

The gun recoiled with the explosion of the shell in the chamber of its cylinder and its kick-back made the weapon hit him across the bridge of the nose, causing a split-second blackout — the smell of shell's ignited gunpowder filled his nostrils and drifted back around his head, it would have stung his eyeballs had they not been driven shut by the bruising kick of the gun.

Upon opening his watering eyes the scene before him had barely changed. The vultures at the back of their leader began to prepare for takeoff but the honcho of the group stood frozen in motion with its wings still extended away from its body, with not a feather out of place. Its partners wheeled back around and headed towards the willows on the creek bank...

CHRIST! — CHRIST — I've missed!!! Thought Cotter, as the muzzle smoke settled on his clothes and the exposed skin of his face.

Then without warning or change of attitude, the vulture toppled over backwards like a stuffed museum exhibit, its stiffened legs and talons, skywards.

"…I've-I've… I've killed it! I've killed it! …I've sh-shot it! I've killed the son of a bitch!!!! " Frank hollered with rising joy and somewhat disbelief. He rose quickly to his feet; his eyes open wide like a madman in frenzy.

"C'mon, c'mon, c'mon *you* bastards! Come and get yer medicine!!!" Frank Cotter shook his fist with the six-gun clamped securely in it at the rest of the flock of scavengers in the trees — using each word like a drumbeat — he felt he was almost ten-foot tall with his success. The ignorant birds, had they been able to reason properly, looked down on him with contempt as they knew he was in line for their next feast.

Excitedly he fired off another shell from the Peacemaker, which true to form went wild, a wasted shot — stray, useless lead, cut an aimless path through the atmosphere until its velocity was spent. The birds never shifted on their branches for protection; somehow they knew they were safe.

It was their attitude towards Frank that made him realize the fruitlessness of his actions, and accept that he was no marksman with Dragoon's gun he had just pulled off a fluke, nothing more and nothing less. But he was sure of one thing, the vultures were too cunning to try anything for a while yet, or toy with him while he had the pistol in his hand. Maybe things would change later when the deed of seeing the leader of the flock die had dissipated from their memory cells and sating their hunger became top priority.

Frank walked a respectable distance away round the back of the boulders with the Colt in his hand; to find a place where he could empty both bladder and bowels for there was no stopping the call of bodily functions, even in his desperate fix.

Tony Lett was allowing his horse the leisure of walking for a spell along the road towards Diamond Creek. He didn't want to knock all hell out of the mare as he had no idea whether or not conditions up at the distance trees and the pair of monoliths was such, that he'd have to ride hell for leather back to pick-up the wagon, aft of him.

Tony could only hope that Pedro Fuller and the crew had found his note attached to the stagecoach and not dilly-dallied about the thing but had made those mules lift their legs and tails as they come along after him. Lett decided he should put a rowel to his girl's flanks and in doing so; this put her into a good lope that would certainly make his arrival on the scene look as though he meant business. Even from this distance he could see that someone up ahead, was still alive and moving about there at the foot of the larger of the two boulders.

Cotter saw the distant rider was moving in his direction at an acceptable pace and glanced down at the canvas covered cadavers in his charge and spoke to them as though they were alive...

"Youse can rest easy now fellers, help's on the way." Cotter walked a short distance off to greet the approaching horseman whose mount had clearly worked up a sweat and her blood was high.

Lett urged his mare to work harder the closer he got to the feller standing out there in the open, even from his distance of a mile away now he could see the feller was a bit on the bedraggled side... By the time he was within hailing distance old Tony was riding like a pony express rider — the front brim of his work-wear Stetson pressed back up hard against its crown. He rode like he hadn't a second to waste — and hauled hard and laid back stiff legged in his riding cups, the open mouth of the white mare was tucked hard back into its neck muscles, slobber and froth escaping her mouth.

The elderly man dismount fast skidding on the soles and Cuban heels to a halt, nearly losing his footing for he had misjudged the gait with which the mare was traveling.

The free-reined mare continued on down towards the creek to quench its thirst. As the men moved towards each other; the white-haired feller swept his hat off and ruffled his hair with a free hand — Frank was never so pleased to see another human before in his life. But once they got the salutations out of the way, it was down to business. Frank led Tony over to have a look at the dead men under the tarpaulin, on the way he told Lett that Hunt had in fact suicided and that it had come about because of his stupidity.

Upon raising the canvas cover, both men were shocked to see that the three corpses were covered from head to toe with ants.

"…Hell, I've messed up again!" cried Cotter. **"I never thought anything about ants."** Tony knocked the edge of the canvas sheet from Cotter's hand so that it fell back down over the dead and the ants whom were starting to get agitated by being exposed to the extra light.

"This hurts ter see," explained Lett, "but there's nuthin' you could've done about it. I've known two of those hombres for a few years, 'specially Joe there. The Priest, mebbe three…" looking about Lett admitted, "You can pat yerself on the back — you've appeared to 'ave done a mighty job by the look a-things. I see you've accounted fer a goddamn buzzard out yonder? You a bit of a hand wif a sixer? "

With a shake of his head, the scribe said, "Far from it. I don't like guns and they don't like me…" he handed the revolver to Lett who shoved it in his waistband. Frank continued explaining. "That dead vulture was just a fluke, shot."

Nodding, Lett's changed the subject.

"I've gotta wagon a bit back down the road; with a couple of pallets in back, so you can bed down an' git a bit of rest on the way to the stage-station —you'll have ter share it with these bodies though … we can't leave 'em here.'

"OK … I'm easy with that."

"Fine," Tony look about for his white mare and to his delight saw that she had taken her fill of creek water and was ambling back towards them. "I expect you are starvin' like them there buzzard friends of yores; When did you last eat, Cotter?"

"Yesterday."

"Then you won't knock back a piece of jerky I've got in me saddlebag?"

The scribe nodded with a slight smile on his face. "…It will be like a King's feast!"

"When the boys git here wif the wagon, we'll cook you some proper grub ter hold you over. Sorry it's gonna have ter be a slow trip back to the station, but we'll be bringing the stagecoach along wif us. She's a bit worse fer ware after her batterin', but you understand I can't jist leave it out here ter rot and git vandalized by passin' travelers…"

"I understand Mr. Lett…it's a case of patience being a virtue?" Tony nodded, "Pretty much so. And goin' by what I hear, you've had a very eventful journey? "

"You could say that…" Frank took the jerky Tony unwrapped for him, and eyed it suspiciously.

"It's all right — jist gnaw away on it…"

Frank gestured with the beef in his hand. "Is this another one of the initiation ceremonies a tenderfoot gets in coming west? — if so, what I've gone through thus far will sure take some beating." He took a tentative bite and realized that this kind of food wasn't something you ate with the delicacy of a New York's high society café Sheik.

The first of his abandonments for the day — was that of talking with one's mouthful.

"What will happen to the road agents when and if the law catches up with them?"

"They'll git their deserts. They can't expect ter be given any quarter — they hit the Junction City cattle barons' strong box— they'll git no leniency if they get run ter ground… they've cut their own throats," Tony helped himself to some beef-jerky for he hadn't had a breakfast break since coming across the Concord. "Plus the Butterfield company will wanna piece of their asses, too." Tony brushed a fly off which had come in out of the sun to benefit from the shade his nose cast on his upper lip.

"Our company is already up against it with the intrusion of the railway headed fer Junction City — news of us losin' such a quantity of valued property might be the last straw fer Butterfield in these parts."

"Maybe things won't be that grim for your people Mr. Lett …? I just might be able to play a part in catching up with those robbing scoundrels." suggested Cotter.

Lett scanned the tenderfoot with an interested gaze — *yes… he would like to know how come this feller thinks he can be some help to the company.*

Frank went on: "…I'm a newspaperman. Not only do I specialize in writing for the news, but I do my own illustrations to go along with the articles."

"How's that gonna help the stage line?"

"Can I take it you are familiar with the Wanted fliers posted up in and around most Western Union offices and buildings?'

Tony nodded. He even had posted them on the inside wall of his way station.

"Well, for a bit of extra cash I've sketched a lot of them from witnesses' descriptions for the city police. When we get back to your place, I'll be pleased to sketch the likeness of the guys who robbed the stage and killed Father Lorimar— "

"*You* c'n do that?" Tony Lett interjected.

"All I'll need is a lead pencil or two and some cartridge paper…"

— "D'you reckons you could hold a pencil still enough ter draw a straight line?" Lett said. "I've noticed you get the shakes a bit and I know them signs of old."

"What are you on about, sir?"

"No offence, but you look as though you're headin' fer a bout of the Dee Tees. Ya see I know the signs of a man who lives and breathes booze."

"You read the signs?"

Lett, nodded. "What hope have you got in control of yore hands? You'd need a steady hand to sketch a real likeness of a man — me, I'm no artist and don't suffer frum the shakes, yet I couldn't draw even ter save my own life!"

"Did I not control my shakes well enough to shoot that fat vulture over the way? I reckon in crisis like this, where it means a chance to bring the killers of the Priest and Joe Hunt to the end of a rope, I can do it — just wait and see!

"I know how much Joe Hunt's widow-woman'll needs the sort of help yew claim yew can deliver, mark my words," stated Frank Cotter. "I understand how Hunt and the Priest died," said Tony as he loosened off this mare's cinch-strap. "But how did the other drummer on board the stage cash in his bank account?"

"Didn't Dragoon explain it to you?" Cotter asked.

Lett shook his head, "Jist said that the Priest had been gunned down by the critters pullin' the hold-up an' thet Joe was run over by the hoss team an' coach — me reckonin' is thet is thet the Dragoon feller figures Hunt could be still alive."

"Wish that he were and by the Hell he oughta be but for my carelessness. Hunt got it in his head that he was finished an' his end was slowly creeping up on him on wheels of pain. He got hold of

Dragoon's pistol and used it to suicide with. The other dead passenger is a drummer by the name of Chas Morgan. He got bitten by one of them there rattle-snakes — died too damn fast for any of us to try and save him, not that we knew how..."

Looking over his mare's rump up the road; Tony saw that the covered wagon was moving along with ease in their direction and judged, without saying aloud, that it would be with them in the next fifteen minutes.

Midnight had come and gone by the time the wagon arrived back at Lett's way station. A refreshed Dragoon was on hand to welcome the rescue party along with Sid Rover who had been working at keeping a once hot meal, warm. Cotter confessed that he got little sleep lying on the pallet next to three dead men.

The spare stagecoach team had hauled the Concord back to the station, which took the pressure off the mules pulling the wagon. The Concord had to travel slowly so as no more damage would be incurred, especially if there was the likelihood of a coachbuilder reworking the coach's body back into an acceptable shape.

The station's crew had gathered the entire luggage that had been strewn about the trail and stowed it aboard the wagon. They located Dragoon's sample case which he had placed inside the wreck before setting off in the night on foot. Rover fussed about and produced a meal for the tired men while they fed and stabled the horses and mules out in the barn and laid-out the dead on planks placed across carpenters' sawhorses.

Over the evening meal it was agreed that Frank Cotter would work on the drawings of the outlaws, commencing first thing in the morning when he rose from his long overdue sleep.

It was a late rise for most concerned at the Lett's station — Rolf and Benito went back to their digging of the cesspit and the others worked quietly at their regular chores around the station.

Rover reminded old Tony that there was a light-coach hidden away down in the back of the barn buried under loads of rubbish which might be in good enough condition to carry the Concord's passengers on to

Junction City. It had been made over in Europe for a mostly absentee landowner, a Lord no doubt, who had only ever spent six months out in the Americas in his whole time of ranch ownership. The coach was useless for the Wild West terrain, because it was too open for those onboard should it come under Indian attack — a thing which was never experienced and so whether it was true or not, was never proven.

The English Lord sold out of the ranching business and the coach was auctioned off with a lot of other useless ware he had shipped out from England and Europe.

A buyer for Butterfield thought the European built coach might be of some use to the stage line but the vehicle lacked appeal and was but down in the back of the barn.

Then Lett turned his energies into organizing getting the ugly looking French built coach ready for the last leg of the Butterfield's trade route to Junction City.

Cotter steeled himself away from the others so that he could work on the facial drawings of Matt Flynn, Moe Malthouse and Sam Korda. He addressed his chore with zest, determined that not a facial detail, as he remember it of the men, went unrecorded.

Just as Frank completed the final detail of the last sketch of the three holdup men, old Tony appeared at his elbow and looked the drawings over with the critical eyes of an unbiased critic. He was in a position to give a fair judgment of Frank's work, for he personally knew

Korda and had had a passing acquaintance with Flynn from time to time — over the years since the war. In Malthouse's case he only vaguely remembered the Canadian, but guessed as the newspaperman had been so true in the captured details of the other men's faces, that he could not be too far off with the Malthouse character.

"Tomorrow at sun-up, we'll have the replacement coach ready for J.C.," Lett said to Cotter. "…You best guard those drawings wif yore life, Son. There's gonna be a lotta people interested in those three faces."

"I hope so." Frank placed each sketch atop of the other and rolled them up to form a cylinder of cartridge paper.

"I have ter hand it to you, Sir. I never thought you could do it wif them hands of yores. It amazed me how every time you got near to a pencil the shakes jist vanished like the result of an Injun Medicine-man's, magic!"

Turning on the chair and looking up at old Tony, Frank said with arched eyebrows. "...It's a case of mind over matter — there's your answer."

The four team coach was ready for what it was worth and its two passengers, Dragoon and Cotter, stepped down out from under the station's awning, after having had a meal of which had hit the spot, prepared by the Sid Rover who had, as cook, had to be the first one out of bed.

He had a big role to fill today, for the peg leg cook was standing in as the company's coach-driver. As the man was lame, Tony had also ordered Rolf to ride shotgun and help Rover whenever he felt the feller needed it. Though the surrogate teamster was very adept at living with his prosthesis, no one wanted to see him take a fall. Once settled in the coach box with the leather ribbons in his dough soft hands, Rover gave the ex-cowpoke the job of "whip-cracker", for his out of practice hands were full enough with just the reins.

Whether it showed in Rolf's face or not, he was glad of the chance to get away from sinking the outhouse hole and cracked the stock whip with relish which set the team in motion with a jolt to the unsuspecting passengers ... The mismatched colored bunch of workhorses put their backs into the job ahead of them, the coach so unorthodox to this part of the country wheeled away, putting both dust and distance between it and the false-front of the station's homestead.

No one on the stage returned Tony Lett and Pedro Fuller's good-bye waves; they never even threw them a backward glance over their shoulders. The station's mongrel dog trotted after the rig for almost a mile, but gave up when it realized that no one had any interest in its company.

JUNCTION CITY at this time was only a city by name and looked much the same as many towns of the west that were considered, frontier towns. Towns might come and towns may go, there is no guarantee any one of them will last into the next century and already the newly open up land, had given birth to ghost-towns which had once been proud monuments to man's El Dorado.

Luckily for the folks making up the populace of J.C., their time had come in another era and things were coming into more prosperous times for the people, even though the war had interrupted and set back things, some of which had witnessed the deaths of one or two towns, and seen them abandoned where they stood or watched heartbroken as their cabins, shacks and business houses were torched and burned to ash, which eventually was carried away on prairie winds — leaving not a trace of their existence.

Lazarus Rollo had arrived in the fledgling community when it was just a gathering of disorderly rustic shacks… he had barely a cent to his name, but the man had natural organizing skills and from just a few mavericks he went from strength to strength and now held the powerful chairmanship of Junction City's local Cattlemen's Association and was ranked as a local Cattle Baron.

People were ready to kiss the ring on his hand because of the weight he wielded in the town and the generosity he dispensed to people who were hard up — but of course there was always strings attached. He even had the town Sheriff, Klem Boston in his paw — even the democratically elected town council was like a toy puppets under his controlling influence. They were in essence controlled by fear, fear of Rollo's muscle men that even help keep the sheriff in line, if the latter entertained any ideas of enforcing any laws that might conflict with those of their employer.

Rollo's henchmen were the Williams brothers, Harry and Reg. Though they weren't twins they dressed and looked the part in their range cloths and were fast on the draw if the occasion called for it, and packed a good mitt full of knuckles whenever a situation called for reinforcing things further without the drastic measure of gunplay. In other words they were Lazarus Rollo's backstops.

Doctor Lester Lomax had finally hung his shingle in Rollo's town after the war, but not before securing Baron Lazarus Rollo, OK; after convincing him that the town could support *two* doctors, for Doctor Hallway had been first on the scene. However, Lomax seemed to lean more to the research side of their medical profession, plus both men agreed that neither man could successful treat his own ills — besides Hallway was no longer a young man.

News had not reached Junction City of the Diamond Creek stagecoach robbery. What was worrying to fifty-four year-old Glenn Corbin, the stage depot manager, was that the stagecoach out of Kansas City was goddamn late on reaching town, and realized that it would have had something to do with the recent storms and mini tornadoes which had cut through the land — notwithstanding the fact that the stage was carrying a strong box laden with the Cattlemen's Associations funds in silver and some gold, the latter item personally belonged to Lazarus Rollo, Corbin felt personally responsible for it.

As the hours had ticked by, Glenn Corbin grew edgy, much like a cowboy forced to face the inevitable doctor's lancing a carbuncle on the ass! So by two o'clock in the afternoon he was at his wit's end. Nor did it help matters that Lazarus Rollo was now in his office with two lackeys breathing down his neck.

"…So what sort of corral are *you* runnin' here, Corbin?" Lazarus Rollo growled at the one-time city-slicker whom had come west for his health. "— Yore the so-called *manager* an' ought ter know where everyone of the Butterfield rigs is at the drop of a hat!"

The associates accompanying the Cattlemen's Association chairman were like Rollo in some respects, they too had once been mere cowpunchers whose fortunes had changed with time by being in the right place and at the right time. In truth they were only ever really going to be pseudo businessmen alongside the real thing such as Lazarus Rollo, and he and Corbin knew it.

Their homburg hats, celluloid collars and frock coats could never hide the fact that they were from a dirt poor background. Rollo was a horse of a different color, he was suited from birth for something greater than a cowpoke, and today's elevated status fitted him like a second skin.

"The whole town knows that the storms have washed out parts of the trail between the way stations —" Glenn Corbin said as he rose from his desk-chair — his high forehead breaking out in a cold sweat. "…The crew would be doin' its damnedest to make it through the impossible weather that's passed throughout the country!"

"OK," Rollo said thinly. "So have you dun anything specific about finding out its whereabouts status? Like sendin' someone out ter find out whether or not, they're nearing the town?"

"What's the point? They'll get here when they can…" Corbin offered the three stirrers a Havana cigar each from the supply he kept on his desk for high rolling business customers.

I've gotta sweeten these boys up, Butterfield needs their business now that damn railway construction is breathing down the company's neck… thought Corbin as he proffered the cigars around.

"All that'll confirm is that the stage is on its way — that isn't gonna make the thing sprout wings an' fly here any the quicker!"

Lazarus Rollo took the cigar on offer, he appreciated a ***good*** cigar, and his sidekicks joined him, for they too would take anything that's going for free. However no one in the room ever realized how renown these cigars and their logo would become in later years and took the offering as though being offered nothing more than a match. "Are you too tight ter spend a cracker in finding out an answer or two?" Rollo asked surly.

"That's not the point, Mr. Rollo." Corbin returned to his chair as he set the humidor back down on his orderly desktop and gestured for Rollo and company to fill the empty chairs before him. Continuing to stand, Rollo, began to inspect the craft work involved in the rolling of the Havana grown tobacco leaf. *I'm not gonna tell Corbin that I've gold riding in on that coach. Even though I suspect the bank might have taken it upon itself to notify him by express over the telegraph, and though I hate to admit it to anyone outside of me knowing what's in that shipment — knowledge like that's courting trouble when all and sundry learns the Association's business;* Lazarus thought to himself, but instead said for the benefit of those in the office: "That's a weak reason for not keepin' tabs on yore chess players. Its yore ***business*** to worry about any late coaches … I know fer sure that some Indians have wondered away from the reservation and ya know they can't be trusted not ter make trouble, even though lots of folks think we've tamed 'em."

"I realize that, so I reckon I'll have the Williams brothers ride out ter intercept the coach an' escort it in!' Rollo then bit the end from the cigar and spat it on the linoleum floor covering. Then while he went ahead to ignite the cigar's end with his own match; he did not offer a light to his business buddies, for they had already popped their cigars in their coat pockets for later.

"On behalf of the Butterfield Company, I shan't say "no" to such an offer," said the wide-eyed depot manager.

"OK," Rollo said. "…I'll have Harry and Reg get ready ter leave by three-fifteen, if the coach hasn't hit town."

Lazarus turned and gestured with his head for his colleagues to follow and he headed towards the office door. His entourage came to their feet like quick lightning and stalked out after their leader like lap dogs.

Glenn Corbin and the ticketing clerk, Roland James, were outside the depot building on the sidewalk when the brothers headed off. With them were Lazarus Rollo and Sheriff Boston. The later was not in a gleeful mood for Rollo had chewed strips off him for being too lackadaisical about the whereabouts of the late stage.

The rest of the town's main street population went about their business while the quartet concerned with Harry and Reg Williams' departure, looked on as they rode east-bound from the town.

The four men lost any real interest in the pair of horsemen as they rode beyond the town's precincts.

The ticketing clerk went inside to continue with other chores he had on his program, leaving Mr. Rollo, Sheriff Boston and Corbin to themselves.

"…I reckon yore panickin' fer naught, Mr. Rollo," Boston said as he drew a rolled cigarette, which he had wedged, between his helix and skull. "That stage crew will be bendin' over backwards ter bring their stage in. We've no idea if the trail's passable. "

"I'll vouch for that," said Corbin.

"I don't give a monkey's ass what you pair think," exclaimed Lazarus Rollo. "I find yore attitudes very slack ter say the least." Rollo turned to the gammy-legged Lawman.

"It should be yore men goin' out on that trail, not mine… Yore not doing much about earning ya keep, Boston."

"I reckon I do more'n my share fer you, boss." Boston said with a good dose of frankness. Then he strode off along the boardwalk in the uptown, direction. He paused en route to strike a match off the veranda-post of the awning. It was clear that he was on his way off to his office and jailhouse, which lay off the main street, in Ridge Road.

"When ya plan ter shut, fer the night?" Rollo asked Corbin, as he turned to face him.

"Not until your men bring the stage in. If I don't stay on duty, I'll see that the limey, Roland James does …" Corbin promised. Glenn Corbin knew this would satisfy the big man and that's why he suggested it.

Sid hauled the working nags to a stop and turned to Rolf.

"Do us a favor? Get down an' breakout the storm lanterns an' fire 'em up. Hang one frum the rear axle and one up here on the coachwork to the right of me shoulder." Rover saw the way the roustabout was eyeing him off, so he felt he should justify himself.

"It'll be dark soon. We don't know what traffic there's gonna be on the road and I don't want some sleepin' teamster allowing his team ter collide wif us. Does that make sense, cowboy?"

"I see ya point," Rolf said as he lay this scattergun aside and climbed down to set things up. The passengers took advantage of the break to leave the vehicle to stretch their stiff, legs and empty their bladders — the noise of falling piss stirred two of the vehicle's own team into committing the same action.…

It was while all this was going on that the Williams brothers showed up.

Sid wasn't too sure what to make of them because of the trouble the Butterfield Company had suffered back at Diamond Creek, so he snatched up the scatter-gun and trained it on the two riders.

"Ease up there, pard…" hollered Reg — in the failing light he hadn't realized that Sid and company were already static — he already knew his brother was on the brink of reaching for his Colt, prepared to trade shots with any fool stupid enough to pull a gun on them, Reg and his brother were the ones at a disadvantage; Williams continue in his normal level of voice, "We're from the Cattlemen's Association in Junction City!"

"Yew fellers from the Butterfield stage line?" Harry asked — for in the dim light no one was all that distinguishable.

"That we are," Dragoon answered — Rolf Lygon and Sid Rover made no effort to say anything. Whitney Dragoon eased his coat open, which would aid him if he had to reach for his pistol, quick like.

"Hell," Harry Williams said. "What sort of contraption would you call that gig?" he was bemused by the foreign looking coach, having *never* set eyes on anything like it before. Harry rested his palm on the front of his left thigh, out of view of the feller with the scattergun; it would be easy for him to start reaching for his Colt without Rover suspecting anything.

Everyone was leery with each other.

Sid knew he could count on Rolf Lygon if things got out of hand — if they were in fact dealing with would-be road agents. He knew Lygon to be a straight shot with his .44; he had watched the feller shoot up empty peach cans before today.

"Go ahead an' break out the storm lamps, Rolf. I reckon I've got things under control from where I sit…"

"You're not alone there, Sid," Dragoon told the peg leg man. Whitney carefully draped his palm over the pistol grips of his Colt but left it nose down in its holster. Frank Cotter joined in by producing an over-and-under barrel Derringer — this fire-arm Dragoon had forced on him in the coach from his sample case after leaving Lett's, just in case they did fall victim of another hold-up, or at least an attempt.

"Any chance you know the hides of these jaspers, Rover?" Dragoon queried. But before the cook could answer, Reg Williams' voice came through the evening light.

"That your voice I detect, Whitney Dragoon?"

"Sure is," answered the gun-salesman. "Who the hell are youse?"

"You should recognize us … the Williams' brothers," Reg said as he kneed his horse forward. "We work fer Mr. Lazarus Rollo …"

"Where here on town business fer Rollo," Harry told the audience. "So let's drop all this debatin' and get rollin' ter Junction City — we're ya official escort."

"Hmm, if'n that's true," said Sidney Rover. "Then that puts another coat of paint on things…" he lower the shotgun and his finger left the trigger. "…Mebbe when ya hear a few things you won't be two very happy pups I'm a-thinkin'!"

"What d'you mean?" Harry Williams asked.

"I mean that if'n you fellers are frum the Association and as *I* figger it — yore here ter make sure the strong box gits in ter town in one piece," said Rover. "Then ya done missed der the boat…"

"What are you mumbling about old man? We ain't here about any boats," snarled Reg.

"What Sid's tryin' ter tell you fellers is that ya too late to do yore job," Rolf added.

Reg looked directly at this brother. "Do you understand what these has-beens are talkin' about, Harry? 'Coz I can't even try ter make a duck's ass out of all their gab!"

Cotter came up the riders. "Excuse me, but maybe I can explain…"

"Explain away, tenderfoot," said Harry, rising in his stirrups to looking across the head of Reg's mount.

"The stage wuz robbed back at Diamond Creek," said Dragoon by way of interrupting the scribe. "To be precise, yesterday; that's why we're not in a regular stagecoach."

"Their Concord wuz wrecked in the hold-up and a couple of passengers and the driver were kilt," said Lygon. "That's why we're usin' that strange looking contraption back there, behind us." Rolf gestured back over his shoulder.

Had there been enough light the coach group would have saw the look of surprise which crossed the brothers' faces.

"These raiders," began Harry. "Any of yew see their faces; know who the fools might be?"

"One of the men involved was in the employ of the Butterfield stagecoach line…," Frank said. "… Rode 'Shotgun' … Some feller called —"

"Sam Korda?" Broke in Reg. "Sam Korda had a hand in *this* pie?!"

"Huh, that figures," muttered Harry. "Who else…?" He asked no one directly.

"A couple of men who worked for Kit Barr's ranch up near Lehmann's way-station," said Dragoon.

"Was Lehmann a party to it?" asked Harry working at getting the facts straight for Rollo and Sheriff Boston who would be like hounds after every drop of blood once they hit town.

"No," said Frank.

"No, jist a couple of ranch-hands ... two herders and the foreman off the Barr ranch — don't ask me his name, I'm a bit hazy 'bout it," said Whitney Dragoon.

"That would be "Flynn", *we* know 'im." Reg told his brother. "We can take him down if we ever front 'im."

"No one else got any idea who the other two cowhands were?" Harry asked.

"Yeah," answered Cotter. "One was a feller that went by the name of 'Texas Kid', but you don't have to worry too much about him."

"Why's that?" Harry questioned.

"His ramrod back shot 'im — he's dead as a smelly skunk and under the sod feeding the Earth worms."

"If'n, foreman Flynn wuz party to the robbery why d'yew figger he gunned this 'Kid' down?' Harry Williams demanded. He couldn't get Flynn's actions to sit square in his brain box by anyway he looked at it.

"Their pistol war was over the murder of an ex-slave woman," Rolf Lygon explained. "But you're questions best wait until we're all in Junction City and puttin' it before the sheriff — this here dog-talk is only delayin' things fer Rollo an' company — don't yew think ...?"

Harry made a sharp nod with his head, "Mebbe yer right, Lygon ..." Harry ordered the passengers and crew back to the stage and he and Reg wheeled their mounts about and rode up front to take the lead into town with the coach at their rear.

Meanwhile inside the coach Dragoon recovered the weapon he had issued to Cotter prior to the arrival of the Williams brothers. "— Shit, man, you were skaing on very thin ice back there!"

Frank Cotter's frown went unseen in the somber interior of the vehicle as he asked, 'What do you mean, exactly, Dragoon?"

"The way you was waving that Derringer about at Rollo's gunslingers — you coulda got shot dead by either one of those trigger happy guys. I thought you'd realize that Derringer wasn't *armed*? I'd be a fool ter place a loaded weapon in the hands of a City slicker! ... Those critters up front weren't too keen ter be **your** pal. My advice for you is ter keep ya distance frum 'em if you wanna stay healthy."

"I'll sure do that…" Frank Cotter promised as he sat back in his seat: "I wasn't born a hero."

"That s good, ter hear;" said Dragoon.

The late running coach arrived at the Junction City depot at 10.50 PM. The cattle town was generally early to bed and early to rise so had closed down for the night except for those concerned with the late arrival of the coach and those at the couple of saloons on Main Street, and Ma Kelly's clip-joint-cum-boarding house in Bryant Street — the second main street of the burgh, which ran parallel with Main, a street block deeper.

All the horseflesh in the company of the Butterfield service and the Williams' brother's mounts were hot and sweaty and glad to see trail's end. The boardwalk out front of the depot's shop front, had a welcoming crowd of onlookers; waiting there to orchestrate things and hear first-hand the tales of woe, Corbin, was flanking respectively by Sheriff Boston and of course an agitated Lazarus Rollo; who was backed by his two board associates, lackeys who had been with the man when he had paid the stagecoach manager an earlier visit. Added to the crowd's volume were a couple of stable-hands and the plain curious.

Rollo changed his attention to the men he had ordered to escort the stage to town. Harry and Reg were a bit farther up the street dismounting at a free hitching rail ahead of the coach team…

They don't look happy about somethin'; thought Rollo as he decided to swing towards them and see what news they had for him. The board lackeys followed their master while the Sheriff and Corbin cut loose from them and went forward, Corbin to open the vehicle's door on the sidewalk and the Sheriff to find out why the strange looking coach was being teamed by two irregulars such as Lygon, whom he knew of old and the peg-leg cook from Lett's end of the line.

Rolf hit the decking of the sidewalk first so that he could assist Sid down from the coachman's box at the rear of the turret, but it wasn't a job he had to pull off alone — men from the curious crowd on the boardwalk were quick and willing to lend a hand ... The Sheriff would have been party to the helpful gang but was pushed aside in the rush and like Lazarus wanted to know how the strongbox had faired through all the drama.

"...What's the story, boys?" Lazarus asked the brothers as they reached the sidewalk before him. He needed to know their side of things before pouncing on the coach crew.

"You tell him, Harry," said Reg as he brushed his brow.

"Tell me, what?" Rollo's eyes bored into Harry. Behind him the lackeys looked on blank faced. As Harry told Lazarus of the robbery and who were the perpetrators, the man's temperature rose like a child's hot-air balloon.

Back at the stage Sheriff Boston asked Lygon, "What's happened to the stage? ...Why the change of caboose an' where's the regular crew?" Roland James brushed past the Sheriff and the coach crew and hopped up in to the reins man's box.

"What are you lookin' fer sonny?" said Sid firmly.

"The strong-box, of course, dummy!" answered the Limey as it dawned on him that it wasn't up there. The fatigue of the day was telling on him, it had been a long day and it wasn't over yet.

"Unless yore a magician, you won't find her there or anywhere else on the vehicle," Sid informed the eager beaver.

Taking in, the expressions which now dominated both the town Sheriff, and Roland James. Rolf Lygon explained as the two passengers were led inside the depot by a red-faced Corbin,

"The stage wus robbed way back at Diamond Creek. I'll tell youse about it once we're in the office ..."

Meanwhile Rollo and his lap-dogs had received the Williams' report and they turned and headed back towards the vehicle at the edge of the sidewalk as the sheriff and his bunch made for the depot's administration office.

Corbin's office suite housed the passengers from the coach and Lazarus Rollo and his cohorts; it was here they all got the story of the robbery and those that were known to be involved. Meanwhile Roland James

and the stable-hands unloaded the customers' belongings and stored them in the waiting room for collection, then got the hideous looking vehicle off the street out of sight of the inquisitive night-owls on the prowl; The team was unharnessed, rubbed down and stabled.

The limey, under Corbin's prior instructions, had organized with the wives of the local Masonic Lodge to put on a light supper of finger food and coffee for the office congregation and on a signal from him, trundled it across the street from the temple to the depot and into the Butterfield's office suite. Then they made themselves scarce.

Sheriff Boston joined Rollo at the desktop to inspect the tenderfoot's drawings of the trio whom had pilfered the contents of the strongbox and the Chairman's personal valuables. The charcoal and graphite sketches executed by Doctor Lomax's friend were commendable, better than most Poster engravings Boston had experienced, for sometimes he had reckoned when face to face with a wanted man that the poster and the subject were barely alike. But here there would be no mistaking the faces of the wanted men; they were very close to being mirror-like.

Although caught up in the lively assembly of the office, Cotter was concerned as to why he had not been met by an anxious Lester Lomax and he certainly expected his doctor friend to come barging into the office to join them at any given moment. He wanted no part of the ladies' supper and only handled a china mug of their bitter coffee because he was throat dry and nervous, even though his drawings were being praised and credited paid to him.

Looking up from the curled sketches which had been weighed down and held reasonable flat with a couple of inkwells and the stage depot-manager's cigar humidifier, Korda and Flynn were known to Lazarus Rollo on sight but he was a bit hazy about Moe Malthouse. On the other hand, all three were known to Sheriff Boston as they'd been fined at times for either spiting on the sidewalk or breaking some other minor by law infringement of the town … Rollo continued: "…Well, you were certainly taken in by our Mister Sam Korda, Corbin? What a shocking case of misjudgment *you* made there, hey? Look what it's gonna cost you personally and the Butterfield company!"

That statement cut deep into Corbin and his slightly paled face reddened, not for the better — that was for sure. Lazarus turned his attention to Boston. "I expect *you* to get onto this business right away,

Boston. You'll have no objections about my boys riding along in yore posse?"

"Not at all – Mr. Rollo; we're dealin' wif killers here. I knew poor old Joe Hunt fer many a year and we can't let the death of that Father Lorimar go unchecked. We'll roll out wif all the extra men we can git…" the Sheriff had no truck about the Williams brothers being included in his bunch of riders for he realized that if they ever did catch up with the stage robbers Rollo wouldn't be wanting them to be a part of this cosmos and that he would expect them to be hung from the highest tree bough, once all the valuables taken had been recovered of course. Boston was sure that if and when was a shoot-out which looked inevitable, the brothers would be more than keen to earn their wages and do the shooting, and thus saving someone else worrying about gettin' blood on their hands.

Rollo turned to Harry and Reg who were down near the back wall of the room in front of a cold fire-grate no one had thought to fire up. "You two know what you'll be called on to do frum here on out. Clear yuh selves with Ma Kelly, I want no excuses, right?"

"Right," the brothers answered in unison.

Lazarus then told the Sheriff and Corbin of his intentions of getting in touch with the ex-Pinkerton from Lawrence, Sheriff Robeson. He felt it best to get a really experienced man on the asses of these fellers who thought they were going to get away with a small fortune at the expense of the Cattlemen's Association. Then because the town gossip in circulation at the moment had a piece to do with Doctor Lester Lomax's friend, Frank Cotter, Rollo felt he was now indebted to the man in a roundabout way, because of the sketches there on Corbin's desk; which would play a major part in bringing the right offenders to boot. He suggested that the Sheriff ought to break the news to the scribe as to why Doc. Lomax was not here to welcome him to town.

Well, thought Boston as his eyes fell on the scribe. *You're certainly one feller who's in fer a shock.*

"I guess before we go on any farther I s'pose now is as good of time as any — but I've some very special news fer you Mister Cotter…"

All eyes went in the newspaperman's direction as he became the sole focus of attention, pain began to show in the Sheriff's face and any one ignorant of the town news could have been forgiven thinking that the

Sheriff's old wounded leg was causing him pain. Boston continued: "—Yore friend and mine, Doctor Lomax, was involved in a recent accident, which caused his untimely death. We, the town that is, held his burial today, I'm sorry ter say."

"What?!" said the stranger in a strangled and somewhat uncomprehending voice. "Did I hear you, right? Y-y-you're saying that Lester, Lester Lomax is-is d-d-dead! "

"He's telling you the truth, sir…" said Corbin. The man was already busy pouring Frank a stiff whiskey. Glenn Corbin was one of the few people in Junction City who was unaware of Cotter's delicate condition where alcohol is concerned. "It was a shock to all who knew the good doctor —"

"When did this occur?" Frank said tightly.

"Thirty-six hours ago. We had to bury 'im this afternoon," said Boston.

Frank Cotter looked the Sheriff full on, "…You're a friend of Lester's you say…?"

Frank Cotter nodded. "That's right … An old friend."

"H'm, I guess in more ways than one I could claim the same title —" Sheriff Boston slapped the thigh of his slightly crippled limb. "If'n it weren't fer his fancy skill with the scalpel an' needle, I wouldn't be walkin' on a pair of legs. But that's not a story you need ter hear at this moment. I have to tell yuh sadly that Doc. Lomax had a fatal accident on the street and is well…"

By the time Sheriff Boston had finished filling in Cotter about the death of their mutual friend, Cotter was flummoxed. It was difficult to believe that a man as well educated as Lomax was, could be so stupid as to walk blindly out into the path of a heavily laden wagon and be run down like a child! But believe it or not — this was supposed to have been the substantiated fact of the matter.

With unashamed tears welling in his eyes, Cotter asked Sheriff Boston, "Why in God's name didn't you hold over Lester's funeral until I arrived?"

"We weren't sure when the stage was gonna make, it; or whether or not, you were on it! Lester, Lester wuz very frank about yew to me; Even he couldn't trust the fact that you might spend the money he sent you for a ticket, on booze!"

Cotter paused to moisten his lips. Oh, how much he wanted that drink there in Corbin's hand waiting there for him just to reach out for it. But out of respect for his now dead pal, he had, with difficulty, to brush its temptation aside. Yet another test to his will power?

"Well, what happens to me now? Seems I've neither a job nor a place to lay my head. I was supposed to be staying with Lester at his apartment — now I'm high an' dry like Noah's Ark on Mount Ararat!   I've been using Lester's money for traveling expenses as far as I can. I won't have enough to rent a room or buy a ticket out of this hole. Have you any ideas, Sheriff — maybe a bed in one of your empty cells, perhaps?"

Klem chewed his lower lip in thought a moment. Frank went on: "The least you townsfolk could have done was to hold the funeral over. That hurts me more than the shocking way you dropped the news of his death in my lap." Frank drew a hankie from his pocket and dried his eyes and cheeks.

Boston turned towards Lazarus Rollo. "This feller's in a real fix Mister Rollo ... By his drawin's have really fingered the hold-up men for us and that makes us beholdin' to him —, don't you think ... I mean ter say we know these feller's dials like that of a clock. He's helpin' the town and yew; don't yuh think we could figger out some ways ter help him through this? "

"Yore right," said Rollo. "And we will help the man in every way we can. I'm sure Ma Kelly won't object to our friend staying in the Doc's apartment above the surgery until the man finds his feet. In any case, I'll have a word to her an' see she does the right thing by Mr. Cotter..."

"There's one other little problem," cut in Cotter. "What am I gonna eat, pasteboard? Shelter is all right but I still have to feed the little man inside."

"That'll be no trouble," said Corbin. "The Butterfield Company will pick up yuh food tabs at any of the eat-houses in town. Jist tell 'em to send their bills ter us, care of me." Corbin wasn't doing Cotter any favors he knew that the company owed him and the silent Whitney Dragoon, compensation in kind was the order of the night here and

Lomax's death provide the company with the where with all for that payment to begin.

"Well, now that's settled, I'll mosey along back to the jail and collect the keys ter the Doc's., apartment ..." said Boston. Turning towards the Williams brothers, "...Mebbe yew two could give Mr. Cotter a hand, ter get himself and his luggage round ter Lomax's place; I'll be along shortly; I'm sure Mr. Rollo won't object to yuh helpin' the stranger, would you, Sir?" The last question was directed to the chairman, for Boston was well aware that the brothers wouldn't take any orders from him without Rollo's consent.

Boston was not wrong on that score. Harry and Reg were not ready to go out of their way to help anyone unless there was some sort of payment for them at the end of the line.

Rollo could read it in the brothers' faces that they weren't jumping over hurdles to readily to do the Sheriff's biding. So he said the words which were necessary to make them change their minds. "Sure, Reg an' Harry will only be too willing ter see that our Mr. Cotter gets safely to his destination, won't you boys?"

The two men's faces dropped and they gave the room a curt nod. *Another goddamn tenderfoot ter take up the town's valuable space,* thought Harry Williams.

I'll make things as awkward as I can fer this goddamn tenderfoot — he won't wanna over stay his welcome, thought Reg Williams, *Especially when he's sampled our warm lovin' care...*

Neither man appreciated playing "wet-nurse" to the tenderfoot whom they had not the slightest bit of liking for, however, they had to make a living in the manner that best suited their psychological makeup and these pair had found their nook — and were happily aware of it. Their situation was unique in the fact that they served two masters pretty much equally well — the Association's Chairman, Lazarus Rollo and the matriarch of Junction City's red-light and theater district, Ma Kelly, who had her fingers in more pies than cherries in a cherry-pie. When not carrying out Rollo's off colored business under the guise of the Cattlemen's Association, they earned a few extra bucks seeing would-be amorous drunks behaved themselves in Madam Kelly's house of business.

Reg and Harry smoked their cigarettes of Drum tobacco as they strolled along on either side of newspaperman. Looking at the three men head-on it was evident that Harry was the shorter of the two brothers, the glowing coal of their smokes established that because their jaw-lines weren't level. Harry was on the roadside of the scribe and Reg strode along on the building side of Cotter's left. Cotter was not in the mood for a cigarette, not that he smoked much anyhow. The brim of Frank's Stetson came to Harry's eye-line and to that of Reg's earlobe. They barely talked as they moved along to their destination through deserted streets the late hour governing the situation, their boot were the only sounds in the area as they clumped along the boardwalk, unexpectedly the sole of a boot scuffed a warped board and this altered the sound of the rhythm of their steps, but other than that, there was nothing significant about their foot-beats through the town.

Rollo was in the middle of explaining himself to Corbin and Sheriff Boston, in Corbin's office. "…When I leave here, regardless of the late hour I'm gonna head round to the Telegraph feller's house and drag him out of his cot. He owes me a favor or two, so he can open up that telegraph joint of his an' send a wire back up ter Lawrence to Sheriff Robeson, I want 'im in the saddle as soon as possible. Who knows; he might be able ter head 'em robbing bastards off if they come into his neck of the woods?"

"Will the Lawrence telegraph office have anyone up there to receive yuh 'gram, Mr. Rollo?" asked Corbin. "…I fear the office down that end of the line will be closed up like a Mausoleum."

"Gibbons, the telegrapher, can sort that out from this end," Lazarus fired up a Havana from the pocket of his frock coat, whether it was one of his own or Corbin's was of no consequence. "Boston, you'd better get on yuh way and fetch that key fer that Cotter feller — otherwise you'll have him freezin' his ass off waiting fer yuh!"

"Right," agreed Boston as he turned away from Corbin's desk and limped towards the exit of Corbin's suite. Sid Rover and Rolf Lygon had already departed to the rooms the Butterfield Company had on permanent booking with a nearby saloon, further along the town's main street.

It was Harry Williams who first saw the glow of a lamplight behind the upstairs curtains in the doctor's apartment over the darkened surgery.

What the devil's going on up there, the place should be in darkness, in partnership with the downstairs surgery? Harry thought. With his free arm he barred Cotter's way — they were now at the corner of Starr Street, Reg baulked — shooting his brother an inquiring look. All three men were now poised at the edge of the curb of the boardwalk.

"Hold it…" Harry warned, as he dropped the carpetbag belonging to Cotter, then said in a whisper to Reg, "D'you see what I see?" without taking his eyes from the window above the awning across from the street from them.

Reg glanced up at the late Lester Lomax apartment window in time to see the silhouette of a man's shadow travel left to right across the shade's screen. Like his brother, Reginald dropped what luggage of Cotter's he was hauling with a THUD, and said: "That's not kosher…" in a corresponding hushed voice. The sleepy Cotter looked from one cowboy to the next on either side of him. "…What *are* you pair on about?" he asked irritably.

The brothers *shushed* the tenderfoot who now became interested in the upstairs window too, which seem to have commandeered the Williams brother's full attention three beats ahead of him. Frank Cotter became just as tensed as his escort — the feeling seemed like an endemic.

"I reckon someone's tryin' ter loot the joint, so shut yuh trap, Cotter!" Reg told the startled scribe — then to Harry, said: "looks like we're gonna play lawman fer Boston?"

"Yep. It's gettin' quiet a habit these days," Harry said through clenched teeth as he eased the low-slung right-hand Colt, from the holster on his hip. Reg did likewise with his right-hand revolver.

"What's going on?" Cotter asked.

"Nuthin' fer you ter bother wif … If'n yew wanna be of help — jist gag yer lips," Harry said out the side of his mouth. "You wait here fer either Reg or me ter come for you."

"He's too exposed where he's standing, Harry," Reg spoke out the side of his mouth like an ex-con. "… Cotter, when we move, you back away frum the curb an' stay, wif yuh back hard up against the buildin' behind us and don't you make a sound until we give you the all clear."

Frank was wide awake by this and started to edge his way backward at a snail's pace towards the building at his rear. The brother's ditched their smokes as one — the ember tips of the cigarettes arched out and down onto the crushed limestone which had been packed and rolled smooth so that it looked much like the icing on a wedding cake. Harry led his brother off the sidewalk and as a pair; they jogged across Starr Street with their pistols at the ready.

The shop front poked Frank in his back when he had run out of reversing space. *Damn, hope I haven't put dust on the back of my frock coat*, he thought, as he came to a halt and watched the brothers come to a brief stop at the foot of the boardwalk across the way; the open ground between his side of the street and that of the curb opposite were bathed in bright moonlight, it made for a dark shadow under the veranda and the brother's carefully and noiselessly mounted the sidewalk and were almost lost from sight as they flattened their bodies up against the front of the surgery and looked east up along Starr Street; before edging their way quietly along the building front to the end, where there was a break between buildings and a wooden flight of outside stairs led to the walkup apartment over the surgery.

Frank glanced eastwards along the street and moved carefully forward along the edge of the building he had previously backed into, he did not realize it but he was moving on tiptoe, the left shoulder-pad of his coat occasionally brushing the lumber wall of the dark shop front alongside him.

Cotter moved along until he was opposite the stairs of the walk-up apartment across the street, and turned to see what the brothers were up too. He couldn't find a sign of them and realized that he had kept his eyes off the pair for far too long. Cotter now felt like he had been totally abandoned and wasn't sure what his next move should be. He checked the direction he had come and saw that his carpetbags were back there on the boardwalk where the brothers had dumped them… a check of his surroundings showed the area to be barren of any signs of life, save for his own. He now realized that he had broken out into a slight sweat. He was scared out here on the street alone. He went to the edge of the sidewalk and stepped down onto the ground and loped across the street and up onto the opposite sidewalk. Here he paused, he realized he was short of breath and it dawned on him that in the moonlight like this, he was exposed, and knew that he could be compromising the brothers if he continued to stand out like a lighthouse. The lamplight in the upstairs apartment was on the move once more and Frank backed away from the foot of the staircase and tilted his head back to see up the stairs to an overhead landing — the risers and landing appeared to be free of any clutter...

Maybe this is as far as one ought to go? Thought, Frank. *I might spoil things for the Williams boys.*

Then suddenly and without warning there was discernible commotion from up in the overhead living quarts of the building, furniture sounded as though it were being up ended and trashed and amongst the din was the sound of glass being shattered. But then, because of the desperation of the sound of a mêlée going on up above him, he found himself throwing caution to the wind and was involuntarily moving towards the newel, whatever was he thinking of? As he hesitantly started up the rises in the direction of the landing the sounds of brawling came to an abrupt end, but by this time he had reached the landing and froze completely at a loss at what he should do next. Cowardliness grouped at his body and he now wished that he had followed the tough boys' instructions which now seemed very wise in the wake of things...

The door ahead of him was pulled open and a dark figure of a man stood in the doorframe under the lintel — somehow Frank knew that the apparition wasn't one or either of the brothers — the moon's glow glinted on the metal gun-barrel of a hand-piece in the phantom's hand. Cotter's body had ceased up and he wondered if he would ever be able to move again ...The scribe was completely without protection, not even a ready tongue.

"Come in an' join your friends, Sir..." The shadow in the doorway said to Frank; Cotter knew that in fact it wasn't a matter of having choices. Reluctantly he came forward and as he neared the open door he found he could see into the room for someone else in there was firing up a candle holder, the flame protected by a frosted glass chimney — extra light was being supplied by the light of a coal-oil lamp already aflame and Frank could see the Williams brothers sitting morosely on a loose covered settee. Both men were completely disarmed and in a disheveled condition.

"What is this … W-who the duce, are you?" Cotter demanded from the man at the door still armed with a pistol. Frank noticed he wore a fawn colored Stetson with a rolled wide brim and high crown. He had a fringed sleeved suede jacket over a sailcloth rust colored shirt and a faded yellow bandanna. His moleskin trousers disappeared into the tops of a pair of mid-calf boots.

The pistol-packing gent ignored Cotter's question. "Join yuh friends over on the settee," he wave of his Navy Colt revolver in the direction of the brothers. Frank proceeded to the settee and noticed in passing that to his left was a dining table with a lace table-cloth spread over its surface and lying at an oblique angle were a couple of six-guns   which Frank thought he recognized to be those of Harry and Reg Williams? Beyond the table in the low light, Cotter noticed the apartment's kitchenette and a partially opened door into another room, which he assumed could be a bedroom. There was the distinct smell of floor wax and bare floorboards under foot, which had to have been once covered by the bunched up carpet square that had been forced into disarray by the brawl between the brothers and the would-be looters. Frank lowered himself down on the settee alongside Reg, and noticed that both brothers had lost their Stetsons in the rough-up, which had ensured prior to Cotter joining them; Frank's mind was filled with reams of questions.

"Who do you think you are?" Reg said as he wiped a blood smear from the corner of his mouth. Harry sat there glaring up at the doorman's accomplice who Frank now focused on for the first time.

This feller was much the same stamp as the fellow over at the open door that had now turned in their direction and stood with legs apart summing up the trio on the settee. The man Cotter concentrated on had the look about him of a trained solder, *though* he was dressed in denim jeans, which hung over the tops of his cowboy boot, plaid fleece-lined shirt and an open Levi waiter's style jacket with copper studs instead of buttons. He had a sage-green bandanna and a black Stetson, and what he could make out of the man's hair was that it was a sandy color; while his partner in crime, had the color shading of a brunette. He wore a light-tan gun-belt and holster and he too held a Navy Colt on the settee's boarders.

"We'll ask the questions," said the black hat guy as he drew back the hammer of his Colt. He stood about 5-foot 8 or 9-inches tall. This man had been the fellow responsible for restoring light to the room. "That right, Sir?" he said to the man back at the door, who, heeled the door to the landing closed as Frank turned back to him, and found him looking like a man meant to be in-charge of things. It was now that Frank noticed that this man's holster was akin to the type of holster an Army feller might wear, similar to the Government Issue the Canadian Mounties wore, too. In Cotter's book this marked him as an Army man.

To the three men on the settee the suede jacketed feller asked: "What's your connection to Lomax?"

No one seemed anxious to respond to the question at first. Then Harry found his voice. "...*That's* a question you pair of critters should be thrown answers at."

"Don't git smart with **us,**" snapped our friend under the black Stetson "You've tried it once ter night and look where it got you!"

"But it's **you gentlemen** who are the **intruders** here..." Cotter stated, "So how come you're trying to be so authoritative? What gives you the right?"

The guy in the fawn hat lowered the hammer on his weapon and holstered it in the black leather pouch at his hip with the flap. A man could not make a quick draw from one of those holsters and because the wearer was generally a man with authority he did not have to make such a move. He obviously did not feel threatened so long as he had his sidekick in the black hat covering the threesome on the settee. "Never mind that, just you **three drovers** tell me how you're tied in with *this* Lomax guy and where he is?"

"You folks mustn't be frum this territory or you'd know the answers to those questions, already," Harry told them as he lowered his arms. He had been holding them high ever since losing the upper hand to these two men.

"Why isn't the Doctor here at this time of the night ...?" asked the sandy-haired guy.

Before anyone could answer the question, the man in the buckskin jacket said curiously. "...You're not patients of the sawbones?"

Reg and Harry *gestured* with their heads that they weren't. Frank Cotter sat there unmoved, and in so doing became the one to interest the burglars.

"What about you there, tenderfoot, what's your connection to Lomax?"

"Business associate …" Frank answered.

"That'll do us," said the man in suede. "Do you know where your friend is right now?"

Cotter nodded. "I do, unfortunately; as also, do these gentlemen."

"Then, out wif it," said Black hat. "We're not gonna wait here 'til the cows come home!"

"Youse want him pretty bad, do yuh?" Reg asked. He got no objections when he lowered his arms. "Then yuh better invest in a couple of pick'n shovels. You'll find him under the sod up at Boot Hill."

"What crazy nonsense are you talking?" The suede jacketed guy asked.

"He's trying to tell you thick headed patsies that if you wanna do business with Doctor Lester Lomax, you're too late. He's dead and buried," said the mournful tenderfoot.

"Seriously?" the sidekick to the man in the buckskin jacket asked.

The man in buckskin thought, *If this proves to be true, then we've got a real conundrum on our hands!* The Army Captain and his Lieutenant glanced at each other both faced with a problem neither they, nor Washington had *ever* contemplated.

Sheriff Klem Boston limped east; downtown along Starr Street under the awnings of the town's thriving business section, now in darkness, in his hand he clutched the pig-iron door-key to Lomax's bachelor apartment. The heat of the Sheriff's hand gradually drove away the cold touch of the metal as his body-heat transferred from his flesh and blood into the instrument. There was a break in the street verandas from time to time and the bare ground or board sidewalk ahead of the lawman became illuminated by the pale moon overhead. Boston would have liked to move quicker than he could, for he knew that the doctor's tenderfoot friend would be cooling his heels on the upstairs' landing, waiting admittance and, that the Williams brothers would not be the friendliest company to spend time with…

As he neared the intersection of Bryan and Starr Streets he noticed something very out of place on the curb of the boardwalk ahead of him… Frank Cotter's abandoned carpetbags? He recognized them from the stage depot. Klem paused to give the luggage the once over and then he ran his eyes around the immediate area to find a reason for them being deserted here like this, for it did not make sense to him and in fact it alarmed him. The tenderfoot's baggage being left here on the sidewalk and no one about just did not ring right to Boston, his skin began to crawl, he pocketed the key to Ma Kelly's building and picked up the two carpetbags and placed them in against the building line so that someone wouldn't fall over them. Then he stepped down off the boardwalk and crossed the street to the other side, only he did this with caution, then on tiptoe he moved east along the sidewalk passing the front of the surgery until he came to the corner end of the building where the staircase stood back a yard or so from the building line. The tension built up in Boston – leaving him slightly short of breath; so he paused to get control of his breathing. Then he stepped round the corner, where he paused once more alongside the newel and looked up at the landing. From here he could see the reflection of a coal-oil lamp's illumination through the small glass ten-inch panes in the door-panel and the hum of voices, it all seemed very odd to Klem. He was sure he would feel more comfortable with a pistol in his hand. He slowly lifted his right hip long barrel Peacemaker from its holster and brought it up level with his nipple-line pointed away from his own lower jaw and cocked the weapon's hammer. The he proceeded to climb the stairs one riser at a time, with his stiff leg, climbing stairs was far more awkward for the Sheriff then forking a saddled horse, but these were things he couldn't avoid doing in his job from time to time. As he moved on and up, he did not like the tone of the muffled voices filtering through the thickness of the door. Klem recalled that there was one of these risers on staircase that had a distinctive creak to it, he knew that should he step on that darn thing it would act as a warning to those folks upstairs of his presence — for reason's he could not conceive, he wanted his arrival on the scene to come unheralded. But that idea nearly ended when the Doctor's half-feral cat which must have been up top of the landing became conscious of him as a stalking hunter and came racing down the staircase spitting like a cougar — it raced away and thankfully lost itself somewhere in the number of shadows cast by the moon. The fright it gave Boston in fact helped him enormously by actually making him over step the creaky riser, even though it made him, grab the banister with his free hand to steady himself in mid-step. He took another breather here as perspiration brought on by desperation, came to the fore. Then he forced himself on, and made it quietly to the apex of the stairs where the carpenter had joined it to the landing. At that point in time, the moon passed behind some clouds and the loss of moonlight killed the Sheriff's shadow which was being projected ahead of him onto the door of the apartment, however before there was this loss of light, Klem saw the stranger's body-bulk ahead of him beyond the door panes and something about the man's stance sent him a message he could not ignore. Carefully the sheriff eased the door open and peered in, round the form on the other side of the door and saw Cotter and the Williams boys sitting somewhat uncomfortable on the doctor's settee, and a feller wearing a black hat and a fistful of Colt was in the process of snarling in their direction. He needed no more jogging ... Klem wrenched the apartment door wide open and shoved the muzzle of his Peacemaker hard into the back of the buckskin jacket before him — the thrust of his revolver sent the man in suede forward rather violently — as though he had been booted in the ass! The man with the black hat who had a good grip of Samuel Colt, half turned in the Sheriff's direction at both the noise and seeing his partner propelled forward into the dining table caught him unawares.

"Freeze you sons of bitches!" growled Boston as he swung his revolver in the direction of the man standing over the folks on the settee. Boston needed no telling that he was now in-charge of things and felt a good deal of joy in the fact.

Experience had taught the Lieutenant to know when he was in a pretty hopeless position and his thumb eased the hammer of his Navy Colt down to rest on the shell's cap ... The man in the fawn hat would have tried to snatch at one of the two pistols on the tablecloth, belonging to the Williams boys but his impact with that of the table and the weight of the weapons sent them and the lace tablecloth sliding across what was left of the surface and over the edge of the piece of furniture to the floor out of reach...The man in the fringed jacket, instead, steadied the wobbly table and used this action to control his balance. The man under the black hat now facing Boston developed myopic eyes as he realized his world was hanging in the balance. Harry Williams needed no prompting to add to the change in the man's misfortune, he came up out of the settee as if his posterior had been sizzled by the hotplate of a potbelly stove, and snatched the Colt from black-hat's hand and now covered him. One could see the depletion in his demeanor as clear as day. Reg was half a second behind his brother in his action, the delay caused as he waited to check on his siblings movements, then he left Cotton alone on the settee while he went and regain possession of their own guns on the polished board floor.

"Who's gonna enlighten me with the facts …?" said Klem, as he drew his left-side revolver and cocked its hammer.

Frank thought the question had been directed to him, and as he began to rise from the settee, the Sheriff signaled him to stay sitting. Lomax's pal complied, but had no idea why Sheriff Boston wanted him to be the only man in the room, seated. Boston's motive had come from experience he did not what the lively looking feller in the fawn hat making a grab at the tenderfoot and using him as a body-shield and a bargaining tool for freedom.

"On the way here, Harry Williams and his brother saw lamp-light up in the apartment behind the shades," explained Cotter. "…they suspected thieves, I think. They left me downstairs while they came to investigate, but apparently these pair of would-be burglars outsmarted them, and my escort became their victims.

"I was at a loss, for I heard sounds of a brawl going on and then silence… I came up to learn just what was going on and found Mr. Rollo's men had been beaten and taken prisoners by these men who had 'em covered with a couple of handguns. They also grabbed me when I tried to sneak a peep at the scene…"

"Anyone know who they are or where they hail, frum — they're strangers ter me?" Klem said as he eyed the suede jacketed guy over, uncertain whether or not he or his black hated pal was willing to come to the fore with answers.

"We tried ter git the drop on 'em," said Reg, "— but they pounced on us as soon as we made it over the threshold of the apartment!"

"Well, what did you expect *us* ter do?" griped blackie. "You came bargin' up the stairs like a herd of rampaging caribou!"

The buckskin-jacketed man told them: "You're lucky we wanted you alive for we coulda four times over."

Klem turned on the buckskin feller. "So what's yer excuse fer bein' here on private property, **Mister,"** Klem looked around at the topsy-turvy condition of the room. "...an' turnin' the place over like looters?"

"You've got it all wrong, Sheriff," The man in fawn said as he removed his hat and ran his left-hand round the inside of its sweatband. "We've got business with your so-called Doctor Lomax — government business it so happens — and when we found the place empty, we decided to search the residence. We're quite **within our rights,** I might add ..."

"Oh, are you?" Frank Cotter said, sardonically.

"And so you jist came up here an' tore the Doc's place wide-open, right?" demanded Klem. "Wrong. Not in **my town,** you don't."

"That's right, Sheriff, put 'em in their place." Reg said as he once again wiped the corner of his mouth, freeing his marred face of any telltale sign of bleeding. "...You can't stroll inter our town an' go about bustin' in peoples' doors an' belting the shit out of law abidin' citizens!" This was a pretty magnanimous thing of Reg to say; when one considers the times the brothers have done similar things to others on the orders of Lazarus Rollo. His problem was really that this time the boot had been on the other foot, the brothers now knew what it was like to be on the wrong end of a hard set of knuckles, this was Cotter's guessed, and, Klem Boston knew it from past experience.

"You going to lock them up, Sheriff?" said the scribe. This earned him a few Brownie points with the Williams clan, but in no way made him a blood brother. "...they just can't go round burgling a dead man's home and assaulting the citizenry." His voice rang out emphatically.

Because the feller in black hat could see that they were being fenced in he gave his partner a glance then said. "Before you take things too far, Sheriff; we ought to have a private talk somewhere away frum present company...Before you make the biggest mistake of your life!"

The man in suede had also been clerking up their unhealthy position and decided to take up his partner's tack. "Mr. Lawman ... I know you aren't aware of it, but we are with the Army. We've been ordered here on Government business from Washington; on assignment for the Indian Affairs Bureau. You're Doctor Lomax —"

Boston interjected: "I c'n tells you men here'n'now … Yew aren't gonna fast-talk yuh way out of this! What I see is a couple of would-be smart, cookies standin' before me — you're under arrest as of the moment I crossed over the threshold, yew can git yuh asses uptown to my jailhouse, pronto!" Boston informed the offenders. Then he turned to the Williams boys. "You two see they git to the caboose in one piece —" Boston stepped aside for the brothers to march the prisoners out, and turning to Cotter asked: "D'yew reckon you can settle yerself in while I check what Doc. Lomax visitors had in mine?"

"I'm not useless; my belongings are still down there on the street," explained Cotter.

"OK. I'll help yuh wif 'em," he took on an apologetic tone. "I'm sorry about what's happened here tonight. But wif out paintin' yuh a rosy picture, life out here ain't anythin' like you're use of in the east. C'mon, we'll git yuh gear…" Klem Boston said as he glanced round the sitting room at the destruction of what Lomax normally kept as a tidy bachelor's pad. He would be in for another hour here before getting away; he couldn't leave this mess for just Cotter to straighten.

6

HE NEXT MORNING found Frank up reasonably early, his head was thick through lack of sleep and his brain cells were still coming to terms of not getting their regular income of alcoholic fluid through their tissues. He had found Lester's double bed quite comfortable and what sleep he did have was deep, though his bones ached slightly. A leftover from the vibrations of the European built coach. He dressed in the same clothes he had worn yesterday, this he did purposely as he didn't want to put on fresh, clothes until after he had found a public bathhouse and paid a visit to the local barber — he knew the bathhouse was owned and run by a Chinese family — Lester had filled him in on that score in one of the letters he had taken the time out of his busy schedule to write — so the man knew that although Junction City was considered to be part of the frontier it was not totally, primitive. But still before venturing out on to the streets Cotter rinsed the sleep from his eyes and doused his face with cold water from a heavy china basin filled with water from a nearby ewer — the pair of these utensils was on a washing stand in the bedroom along with a clean towel and cloth face washer, and carbolic homemade soap.

He stepped out under the porch landing and turned to shut and lock the apartment's door with the key Boston had given him, and realized this was impossibility for last night's intruders had ruined the latch when they broke in and up until just now, no one was aware of the damage. Over one arm he carried fresh clothes to change into once he had bathed and while settling them more securely on his arm he notice there on the stoop with him was a dirty saucer from which a cat was obviously fed from; but no sign of a moggy in sight. Frank decided to take a risk with not being able to secure the door; he hoped that the town folk respected the doctor enough not to come snooping around. He almost tripped over an empty saucer on the landing which had been placed a little too close to the doorstep, — clearly it was representative of a feeding bowl for someone's moggy, however there was no other evidence that a cat came with the doctor's residence. Frank wasn't keen to know this; he had no time for pets in his life now or in the immediate future.

Out on the street he stopped a passerby and got directions to the Chinese owned public bathhouse — a family business Lomax had written him about to express to Cotter that Junction City was not real primitive. But before bathing Frank wanted the services of a barber and when he got to Main Street the hairdresser's totem pole stood out in all its bright colors — it was in the opposite direction on Main to that of the bathhouse, in fact, it was across the street from the coach depot next door to the Masonic Temple, Frank set a course for the establishment at a brisk pace, and arrived to find the premises had not yet open for business. He decided to kill time by viewing the bottled lotions on display through the windowpane — being a tobacconist there was an array of smokers' paraphernalia laid out on a cloth surface, such as a variety of smoke pipes and cigarette holders, however the scribe's attention to this was interrupted by a woman wearing a smock and carrying a millet broom in her hands heading towards the front of the shop from the bottom of a staircase which connected to the building's upstairs' residence — Cotter backed away from the window as the woman paused to unlock the front door and step out onto the boardwalk where she smiled in Frank's direction and began sweeping up the dry muck of mud and manure which had been deposited by the town's pedestrians footwear. The keen sweeper was out to protect the wax linoleum floor she was so proud about — though its slippery surface had nearly brought a few folks undone.

Once the barber's wife had done with the sweeping she put away her broom and removed her linen apron she wore over her smock and went about her next chore which took her to the nearby butcher's shop which was just three doors down along the sidewalk. She purposely left the shop door open as her husband was due downstairs at any moment. The butcher always opened early and it was a wise move to be there before the flies discovered that his window frames were not glazed in.

On her return with a parcel of fresh meat the wife of the barber grew annoyed when she realized that husband, Andy McBride, had not as yet, set foot downstairs. How could their business venture work if customers were left out on the stoop while her man dilly-dallied, about? She bid the stranger to follow her inside and occupy one of the two barber chairs while she went up to the living quarters and sent her husband down to the shop with an acerbic tongue to spur him along.

Andy McBride descended the stairs with a casual air. He seemed to have just as much of the a city man lingering about him as did Frank Cotter — especially in his attire and grooming. Frank felt sure they were going to hit it off; already he had on a long white apron which stopped short of a hand's span from the tops of his ankles… He wore a celluloid shirt collar over pinstripe trousers and a candy stripe cotton shirt. McBride's Scottish heritage stood out with his wax tipped, mustache and orange-red hair, though he had not retained any accent because he was already a second generation, American.

"I hope you didn't mind me making myself, comfortable…?" Frank queried the barber as Andy drew near with a welcome smile and, at the same time snatched up a freshly laundered, starched drape — no doubt the work of the lady of the house.

"Not in the least!" McBride told him. "…May I take your hat, please; before we get started?" He took the scribe's Stetson and took it across to the wall at the back of them where there was a row of hat-pegs. "I'll leave it on the wall-peg behind us."

"Sorry, I should have thought of that for you," said Frank as he settled once more in the barber's chair.

"Are you new ter town?" Andy asked as he spread the drape out over his customer and tucked it in round the man's neck to prevent hair clippings working their way down in under his shirt collar.

"Yes; arrived on the late stage from Tony Lett's way station."

"Expect to be in town, long? …What'll it be Sir? " McBride came round the chair and stood before Frank with his back towards a wall bench and picture mirror — his tools of trade set out behind him on the bench surface, the deal boards covered with a linoleum strip which had been tacked to it. Bottles of lotions and hair-tonics stood back along the foot of the mirror and the unmistakable perfume of *Bay Rum* became apparent only when McBride stood before him in front of a folded stack of towels to one side of his equipment; where there was a bench top mentholated spirit stove, for heating water.

"I don't think so… Haircut an' shave will be fine," Frank answered, and then added, "Though for a time there I wasn't sure whether we were ever going to make it."

"Why…? D'you get harassed by those renegade Indians off the reservation?" McBride collected a stainless steel Mentholated Spirit bottle from a shelf inside the cupboard below the bench. He went ahead to fill the small spirit stove as they talked. "By the way, my name's Andy McBride, and you'd be…?" He put the kettle on to warm the water for Frank's shave.

"Frank Cotter —"

"Oooh, so you're Frank Cotter? I've heard about you from Doctor Lomax. He was quite proud about you coming to work here with him. Pity about the way things 'ave turned out, though." McBride turned his back on the bench and faced his customer in the chair. "Who'd've thought anything like that would happen to the poor Doc? — *That* accident sure took a lotta people by surprise." McBride picked up a comb and a pair of scissors and went around behind Cotter and began to snip away at the man's hair.

"No more than it did, me," Frank admitted. "My whole trip West has been dogged by misadventure and death!"

"I take it yuh referring to that there hold-up," Andy paused and gazed at Frank's image in the mirror.

"You know about that already?" he said incredulously.

"Yes. And so will the whole town by noon. You were gonna be Lester Lomax's public relations feller, weren't yuh? " McBride asked.

Frank nodded, then, felt that the feller might be wondering whether or not Frank could pay for this haircut and shave. "Don't worry; I can manage to pay for your services."

Andy returned to clipping Cotter's hair. "Oh, no, no look, I wasn't worried about that, no! It's just that you'd have got a real shock comin' this entire way ter find you pal dead and all? "

"That's for sure. Lester was gonna but me up until I found my feet, but that's all changed now. Sheriff Boston, the fellow with the stiff knee-joint? let me spend last night in Lester's rooms because the stage got in so late. I shall have to talk to Lester's landlady about staying on until I sort myself out. D'you knows this Ma Kelly, Andy?"

"Who doesn't? Ma's my landlady, too. Ma Kelly must own half of Junction City."

"What sort of rent does she change?"

"Why do you ask?" McBride went back to the bench and exchanged his comb and scissors for hair-clippers, then returned to working on the scruff of the scribe's neck.

"I expect she'll expect me to pay for the privilege of staying at Lester's — I know *I* would. Last night the doctor had some unexpected callers who broke into his apartment. I'll need to get the door-lock repaired."

"You had a break-in?"

"The Sheriff knows about it. We well-nigh, caught them in the act!"

"They couldn't've been locals. People here don't specialize in robbing the dead — did the sheriff deal with them?"

"Sheriff Boston got the Williams Brothers to march them off to the jailhouse. The apprehended guys claimed they were Army men working for Washington."

"How come the Williams brothers got involved with their arrest?"

"They were escorting me to Lester's place. The fellers caught by us said they were there to discuss something private with Lester and that it was Government business and would only discuss that part of it with Sheriff Boston in private. But Klem Boston wasn't having any of that baloney. Mind you, it was a weak excuse I might add. The least I can do is get the door fixed, do you know if anyone in a town this size can repair locks?"

"You might try the Russian Jew who owns the gun-shop. He's a gun and locksmith," McBride informed the scribe.

"Where will I find his place?"

"…Err he's practically next door to the stage depot. He's shop door face mine across the street — turn ya head a little and you'll be looking right at his place…"

During the course of his barbering, Frank got directions from McBride as to the location of the local cemetery — it turned out to be on the Dodge City side of town, a clear patch of ground with a knoll almost in its dead-center. Frank wanted to pay his respects to Lomax ASAP. However he was not able to make the locksmith his next port of call once spruced up, his hungry stomach demand a breakfast before all else. He got directions from a local man who was busy collecting horse droppings with a shovel and bagging it in the middle of the road when he got free of the barber's chair. Traffic was still light so conversing out in the open was not problematic.

"Excuse me, sir…" Frank asked the stranger who now looked somewhat embarrassed by being caught in the act of removing the manure which lay in deposits most of the way along the length of the street, particularly near the town's hitching rails and water troughs. "Sorry, to interfere with work, pal—but could you direct me to somewhere in town where one might be able to get an early meal?"

"Be my pleasure, stranger." He leant on the shovel handle and explained. "If ya wonderin' what I'm doin' this fer. The council pays me ter collect this shit to try an' beat the fly menace — but it's a never endin' job."

"I expect so." Frank said for he looked about at the amount of manure on the ground here and there.

"The town's got three diners," said the street cleaner. "…Two on Main Street and a third one around in Starr Street, going back uptown opposite the funeral directors. But the one you'll want is any one of the two on Main Street."

Frank didn't mind. He had gathered that the jailhouse was somewhere uptown and he knew he had to call in and see the sheriff, so the Main Street eatery won his vote. Cotter thanked the street cleaner for his help and set off uptown, taking in the town sites as he went. What he saw, Frank realized that the town showed a good deal of promise and in his own mind could see that Junction City was going to be a force to be reckoned with once the railway head made it across land to the town. He found the diner easily enough by the cooking odor escaping from its premises as he neared the establishment, and the moment he crossed the threshold he could detect the mouth-watering smells of oatmeal, flapjacks, eggs, and hash and rump steaks — the latter proved to be the size of a six-shooter and one certainly had to be famished to pull one of them on after a bowl of porridge etc. Folks could either eat at the counter or lay claim to anyone of the eight tables and chair settings as they became vacant from time to time, then there were also the three dinning booths along the picture window, which faced out onto the passing sidewalk. There were no such things as tablecloths and napkins, but if you were in luck, one might win the services of a waitress to lie on some cutlery before someone with a plate of food in their hands homed in on the vacancy from the counter. Arguments often erupted from time to time when two people had targeted the same piece of furniture. The diner's eating irons were mostly doled out with one's tin plate or soup bowl, if opting for the oatmeal special or a meat dish, any attempt at finesse was purely accidental.

The cashier was situated just inside the establishment off the sidewalk. Here one gave their order that could be gleaned from a menu written with chalk on a quarry slate propped on her desk. The matured woman would scribble down your order on a slip of paper — the cost tallied and had to be paid for even before your meal was processed. The order was then stabbed to a nearby spike, one on top of the others; a floating waitress would collect them from time to time for the cook out in the kitchen in a room at the back… Then the wait would begin. Displayed prominently behind the cashier on the wall were the house rules, which stipulated the following.

All firearms must be surrendered to the Cashier upon entry. Customers will be responsible for the cost of damage to Crockery etc,
No cussing or spitting — this means U …

The meal prices were reasonable by the standard of the day's prices, so Frank paid for a bowl of oatmeal and a plate of fried eggs sunny-side up and two hash browns with an unlimited supply of black coffee served free of charge with all meal orders. He joined in with a group of males standing shoulder to shoulder at the counter; some had already been served and were eating breakfast standing up, though their eyes were busy looking out from time to time for a table vacancy.

To Frank Cotter, those at the counter reminded him of feeding time at a piggery and he knew it would be difficult for him to become part of this mad circus longer than necessary. By the time his meal arrived, Frank had concluded that the reason it would appear that the customers tolerated this set-up, was because, they demanded none better or were accustom to the arrangement; but this certainly was not Frank Cotter's way of dealing with his meals, when and if he could afford them.

He finished his breakfast by washing it down with two mugs of tar-like java and stepped back from the counter, his place was smartly taken up by another hungry soul as he heeled round and wiped his lips on his last clean hanky and headed for the exit, outside he got directions from a street-urchin as to where he would find Boston's jailhouse. He was informed that it was on the corner of Ridge Road, which ran north and south across Starr Street, and ended at Main Street, forming a T intersection. The scribe strode off uptown towards his destination.

Boston was seated on a plank bench in the sun on the sidewalk out the front of the town jailhouse, watching folks as they passed and sipped occasionally from a pannikin of warm java; the raw smell of the black Brazilian beverage was tempting to Cotter's nostrils… The sun's angle was such at the moment, that the false front building's veranda awning barely shaded the front door and windows that flanked it. The windows themselves were glazed with foot-square amber tinted panes; under each window the town's council had placed a plank wooden bench. He also noticed that the sheriff had been reading the local newspaper and he thought about approaching the rag for a job — but the lawman's upcoming remarks over excited the scribe and any thoughts he had about the newspaper fled from his head. "— I see yuh've begun findin' yuh way around, awright?" said Boston as he picked up the paper from the plank making room for the scribe to join him.

Cotter stepped up from the unmade road to the sidewalk, ignoring the two risers there to benefit pedestrians and joined the Sheriff on the bench; "Yes," began the tenderfoot. "…I got a haircut'n shave from McBride and a counter breakfast at Werner's Diner." Frank crossed his legs as Klem pitched the coffee dregs from his drinking vessel into the dirt on the dusty ground, where the dry dirt soaked it up like blotting paper. "Next. I'm off to the cemetery to look up Lester's gravesite. Then I must square myself up with this Ma Kelly about staying in Lester's apartment!"

"You haven't caught up wif her yet?"

"Nah. Why you looking at me like that, Sheriff?"

"Well, then, ya in fer a surprise," said the Lawman.

"Why, has she got two heads?" Cotter frowned in Klem's direction.

Nothing out here in the west would surprise me, thought Frank.

"No. I won't spoil it fer ya. You jist wait until the time comes an' see what you make of her," Klem brushed a fly away from the corner of his right eye as he continued. "You won't have trouble findin' the grave — it's the only fresh one there at the moment. We've only got a temporary headboard, but I reckon the town council will come up with a marble or granite headstone fer 'im, eventually." Klem rose stiffly from the bench.

"Where'll I find Ma Kelly? I have no idea where she lives, Sheriff..."

"Easy — the most readily place ter find her will be her office 'round three this afternoon at the Royal," Sheriff Klem Boston said informatively.

"And where might that be?" sneered Cotter — his attitude arising out of the fact that Boston had spoken to him as if he were a local, and knew his way round Junction City.

But to leer like this at the Law only tended to put Frank off-side with Boston who decided to overlook the stance he'd adopted and went ahead dispensing the directions the stranger required. "Her theatre's in Starr Street, down from the intersection of Bryan an' Starr streets — mebbe a hundred yards down from the Doc's surgery on the opposite side of the street, you won't miss it; it's the only two story building on that side of the street."A middle-aged man eased his horse up to the hitching rail in front of the Jailhouse. The Sheriff and the man barely acknowledged each other as the feller went ahead and dismounted and tied his horse to the rail. The horseman looked just like any common dirt farmer here on business. He walked over the road at an angle towards the ironmonger's store.

Frank uncrossed his legs. "I wanna get the door lock repaired before I start sweet-talking Ma Kelly, otherwise I might start life off on the wrong side of her..."

"Then, the gunsmith's the feller fer that," the Sheriff told him.

"So McBride says. I'll look the Russian up. Tell me, those guys who did the break-in last night; are they *really* Army feller's? "

"Didn't bother ter find out. In my book they were more trouble than a gnat. I kicked their hides' outa here before breakfast."

"You let 'em go...!"

Klem nodded. "I couldn't see the point of holdin' 'em. If I keep a prisoner here over night I'm beholdin' ter give 'em breakfast a-for

I turns 'em loose. If'n I git rid of 'em before sun-up I don't have ter supply 'em grub. The cost of a mornin' meal means me using my petty cash frum the council; they don't give this here man, carte blanche in that department. Once I paid fer a prisoner's grub an' I had ter screw the council treasurer's arm up his back ter git reimbursed, no more of that, crap!"

The scribe was not overjoyed to hear what the Sheriff had just told him. But he was coming to terms with the way things worked out here in the west and it made him more determined to get back east as soon as he could see his way clear. He rose from the bench, and pointing south of town asked, "Does this Ridge Road go through to Starr Street, Sheriff?"

"Mmm. Yes. At Starr you turn to yore right which faces you in the direction of Dodge City; then follow ya nose to the end of town. No one can ever miss Boot Hill it stands out like a beacon. I doubt that there'll be anyone up there this time of day, the grave-diggers only work contract and I'm not aware of there being any funerals due today. But they are the guys ter be seein' if'n you wanna find any special grave..."

The burial ground covered 10 acres and was on a slight grade just clear of the town's outskirts. It had once been covered in unbroken plains' grass and a sprinkling of sage. But today grave mounds were popping up here and there like houses — houses of the dead. Almost center of the acreage stood a knoll, which on a larger scale some day in the future would be reminiscent of a ground littered with the bodies of Custer and his men.

As suggested by Boston, none of the grave-diggers were on hand to guide him to the grave he wanted. But he found it easily enough. Only thing was that out in the open he and the area were being buffeted by a gusty wind because of the land's openness.

Frank was glad to see that people had braved the wind to pay homage to his friend's memory as the evidence of floral wreaths etc., were still there on display. A youngish woman in mourning dress and shawl was making her way down the bank in his direction — she carried a furled parasol — this he noticed as she passed, Frank glanced at her and her eyes were red from crying, she wiped her nose with an Irish linen hanky. But paid no heed to Cotter as she went by, it wasn't easy for Frank to dismiss her — for he was keen to know about her, and learn of her relationship with his late friend. But etiquette prevailed, and he would have to wait until they had been properly introduced to one another before approaching the lass.

Paying attention to where he was headed he noticed up ahead of him two businessmen were standing near the grave, their attire made them obvious and as he drew near, they showed signs of nervousness. Not wanting to be of a disturbance to the gentlemen Frank focused on three vases of fresh flowers, their bases having been pressed down into the still soft earth of the grave mound… Frank felt a miser for not having come up here with something ornamental. He found himself standing at the foot of the grave and raised his eyes to view the men down at the other end of the dirt mound, which was approximately the size of a pool table.

He wondered whether these men had been tending Lester's grave or whether the flower arrangements were the work of the departing young woman.

Cotter cleared his throat and asked: "Is this…?"

"Doctor Lomax," said one of the businessmen as he moved away from the headboard and came down alongside the grave towards Frank with an extended hand. "Yes. I am Monty Hill and my associate is Jonas Bevan. We're business affiliates of the late Doctor; and you are…?"

Frank proffered his hand. "I'm Frank Cotter, a close friend. I knew nothing about any of this business until I got to town late last night. God it knocked the wind out of my sails, I can tell you. Did Lester ever mention my name and that I was due in town, Mr. Hill?" Cotter addressed his question to both men at once.

Hill nodded as he took Frank's hand. "…Lester was looking forward to your arrival and *we* too working with you, Jonas and I are part, or were part of Lester's syndicate."

"Then in fact I would've been in your employ had things worked out differently?" Frank suggested.

Monty Hill and Jonas Bevan nodded.

"We're delighted to finally make your acquaintance Mister Cotter…" Jonas edged closer so that they too could shake hands. Jonas was watery-eyed and looked somewhat childlike for a man somewhere close to his sixties.

"What was the nature of your business with my buddy?" Frank asked rather bluntly. And as Bevan and Hill prepared to fill Frank in, Frank gazed over the grave — which plainly had been steadily upgraded as Junction City's signs of permanency had come into being. The older part of the cemetery was typical of a regular "Boot Hill", where gunfighters had certainly died with their boots on —were laid to rest without too much ceremony — there were too many graves here of young children — lives cut short as a result of measles, influenza, pox etc.

"Varied," Jonas Bevan was heard to say as Frank once more became aware of them as the man turned to Hill in continuance of answering Cotter's question. "— wouldn't you say, Monty?"

Hill agreed with yet another nod. "There is no doubt in my book that Doctor Lomax was a great man in his field, and the world will come to realize this one day.

"He must be the man of this century — not just because of the unselfish work he's been doing for this country's Native American people and their clans, but for the benefit of the whole of mankind! Lester was into everything, possible!" At this point, Hill drew the gravesite visitors' attention to the fresh timber headboard, purely by body-language, which Frank already knew was only a temporary measure, until the stonemason or someone with equal skills had the chance to sculpture and inscribe a headstone worthy of the man's contribution to society. But at this stage one did not know who was in such a position to order the installation of such luxury. A gust of wind across the open land almost lifted Frank's Stetson from his head and to ruin its attempt he was forced to quickly grab at the hat's brim and anchor it there.

"In Lester's mail to me back East," Frank begun. "Lester wanted me to help him in his struggle, seems he was having Government trouble with Washington; they wouldn't take the results of his medical discoveries as being viable. He said that in his opinion there were people in Washington who were continually undermining the results of his research and that they had an ulterior motive for this..."

"Don't we know it," said Hill.

"Our main stumbling block in the government was with the Indian Affairs Bureau," said Jonas Bevan. "Especially when they got to learn that the good doctor was treating the sick natives with a degree of success.

"They didn't want this, they were banking on the Indian Nations bein' wiped off the face of the land by the very diseases coming from us white men. It was a cheap type of genocide an' Doctor Lomax was knocking it in the head by his research!"

"They ordered him to cease treating the Indians for pox etcetera," Hill told Frank "That's why he wanted you to come west and write about their corrupt tactics. He couldn't continue his work and battle the government on another front."

"So where do you two come into it?" Frank said.

"That's an easy question to answer," Monty Hill said. "The doc was the brains of the organization and we, Bevan and I, were the money men. Research is an expensive business and we went out and found the finance the doctor needed."

"It's regrettable that I wasn't here before the burial took place," Cotter told them. "I was only hours away."

"Yes. But no one knew that," Jonas said. **"We** weren't even certain you were on the way, or that you were even going to take up Lester's offer. Don't forget you have a drinking problem, friend. No one can be certain what a man in your condition's likely ter do. Sorry."

Frank nodded. He knew that what Jonas Bevan had just said was true.

"Did you gentlemen hear about last night's episode around at Lester's place when I arrived?" Frank asked.

"Are you takin' about the visit you had from those government men?" Hill said.

"You know about that?" asked the bewildered scribe.

"We **know,"** Jonas nodded. "Sheriff Boston told us this mornin'. We saw him sitting on the seat outside his office."

"I'm not happy about him," Frank told the men. "He barely held them overnight and let 'em go early this morning. They gave the Williams brothers a going over: the brothers were escorting me around to Lester's place when they found them ransacking Lester's quarters. Boston ought to have charged them with assault against the brothers or if not them, me; plus breaking and entering. Least of all, he could have check that they were who they said they were!

"Boston told me very little about Lester's accident and how it came about. No, I'm not too taken with that guy — I can tell you." Frank turned away from the grave and it was obvious that he was going to return to town. "Well, that does me for having a job to come too."

Bevan and Hill fell into step on either side of the newspaperman as they started down the side of the knoll. "You say these government fellers beat up on Lazarus Rollo's men?" Monty asked.

Frank nodded. "I expected it to be me, next."

"That surprises me," said Monty Hill thoughtfully. "Those Williams boys have a reputation in this town of being pretty tough, hombres —"

"Not by last night's efforts they weren't. Those two blue-bellies whipped their asses… I think the three of us can thank our lucky stars that Sheriff Boston came along when he did. He an' his friend, Mr. Colt sorted out those so-called Army slobs."

"One thing… Dear Lester Lomax is now out of harms-way as far he's concerned with the Army." Monty pointed out.

"True. Lester maybe dead, but no one's going to shit on his name while I'm alive," Frank told his new found partners as they strolled back to town with him. A distance ahead of them walking along the edge of the road was the young woman with the shawl and parasol. A cowboy headed for Dodge on horseback, lopped pass the young lady and gave her a nod. "Who's that woman up ahead …?"

"Why do you ask?" said the watery-eyed Bevan.

"Just curious; I got the impression that she was up at Lester's gravesite with you two?"

"She was there," said Monty, "but not with *us.*"

"I'm wonderin' just what her connection was with Lester?"

"What makes you think there's a connection?" said Bevan.

"A feeling: nothin' more. Anyway, Lester's death has left me high an' dry, but I'm dammed if I'm gonna leave this town without seeing to his best interests. Can I count on you two?" Cotter enquired.

"Certainly," said Hill. "However I must put it to you that Jonas Bevan and I are in a rather awkward position in this town —"

"To some degree, our hands are tied in what *we* do," Jonas leveled with Cotter.

"What d'you mean? Why do you have to keep your heads down?"

"It's to do with the authorities," Monty said as he patted his solar plexus and gave a burp. "We can give you sound advice, but it would have to be in secret … we just can't come out and declare our hands!"

"In my case that'll be a lost cause," Frank told the pair as he once more focused on the young lady up ahead. She was now trailing the left curb on Starr Street as she continued to move east.

"You're still showing some interest in that piece of calico ahead?" said Monty, indicating Lomax's female visitor from the cemetery.

"Does it bother you?" Frank looked directly at the man.

"That young lady is a sort of Ward, of Lester's." Jonas said.

"Does that mean, 'hands off'?"

"You interpret it anyway you will," answered Bevan.

"…Then if she's supposed to be "Lester's Ward", maybe I should know something about her. Such as whom she is and where she fits into things?"

"She's not your worry, Mr. Cotter." Hill told him. "Lester has taken care of all her needs."

"All right, maybe he has — but I'd still like to know a bit about her, such as her name at the very least?"

Bevan came to life after what had seemed a spell in the wilderness. "…Her name is Miss Pearl Courtney — she's an actress performing at The Theater Royal in Ma Kelly's latest piece of city culture."

"Satisfied?" Hill asked. But somehow he managed to make the question sound acerbic.

Frank shot Hill a server look, letting the man know that he was not keen on the sound he had added to the forgone question. Mister Hill shifted his shoulders in an uncomfortable gesture.

Cotter decided to add more to his obvious discomfort. "As you two might imagine, I'm pretty much in the dark about Lester's accident; do either of you know anyone who can give me some details of exactly what happened? And ***don't*** tell me to go to Boston!" Frank said sharply. "I've already heard what he's had to say, he can only go on what peoples' reports, such as witnesses have told him, and I'm not into that; as a newspaperman I would like to hear from the witnesses myself who were on the spot when it happened, 'cause things have ways of getting twisted as they're passed from one recipient to the next." Ahead of Doctor Lomax's group of friends appeared a snake from under the right-hand sidewalk, it made its way diagonally across the dirt road, the trio watched with surprise as it slithered across their path and disappeared under the boardwalk. But the men were too engrossed in their conversation to break off and make comment. "…I can't understand why Lester didn't see or hear the wagon coming. I never knew him to be hard of hearing."

"The Doc., wasn't," Jonas Bevan said and Monty Hill shook his head in agreement as though he was aware that Cotter was now gazing in his direction, Frank looked from one to the other of Lester's business partners. But it was Bevan who ended up with the scribe's overall attention when he went on to add: "— you see Monty and I, were there with Doctor Lomax when he was run down, in fact, Monty almost went under the wagon with Lester…"

"You guys witnessed the accident?!" Frank was incredulous — he came to a sudden halt right there on the street. The abruptness of Cotter's reaction was such that Hill and Bevan couldn't stay with him and they continued on for another two paces before they too could pause in their progress, and half turned back to face the surprised scribe who upon mastering his shock and masked the *suspicion* he now held for these two men — *maybe these pair of characters should be bundled in with the opinion I have of Sheriff Boston,* thought Cotter.

Both Bevan and Hill had momentarily forgotten that Cotter was unacquainted with the accepted facts of Lester's accident. But dawn upon them it soon did, it was Hill who took it on himself to explain what the scribe needed to know.

"Jonas 'n I were with Lester when the wagon seemed to come out of nowhere and bowled the lad over!"

"Hold on," Frank gestured with the index fingers of his both hands at the pair of waistcoats before him; his hands and fingers were like those of a child using his hands like, two pistols. "— **Lemme** get this straight… You jokers were there on the spot when Lester got knocked over? "

They nodded.

"We were vistin' with Lester in his walk-up…" Bevan started to explain but was cut short when Monty Hill took over the narration.

"We went to Lester's apartment on business. He, Lester, was about to pay a house call on one of his patients when we arrived so we had to postpone our meetin'. But as we were now in the process of setting up a fresh meetin', we accompanied him downstairs to the street. The Doc and I walked together and Jonas here — followed; the staircase isn't wide enough ter manage three people…"

"I know that," said Frank.

"OK, so when we reached the ground we slowed to allow Jonas ter join us, then we turned left and headed down towards the corner of Starr and Bryan Streets —"

"Passing the surgery," chipped in Bevan.

"Let me tell it," Hill snapped at the smaller man, who dropped his lip. Hill returned to Frank. "Lester then went ahead of us, 'cause he had to collect his black bag.

We waited outside for him on the sidewalk. By the time he came back with his bag, me an' Jonas had ambled along to the corner of the boardwalk under the veranda and waited there chewing the fat. I think I might've lit up a cheroot — I can't rightly remember that part so don't hold me to it. Anyhow, Doc joins us and we kinda took up our conversation frum where we left it. Then suddenly Doc sees our company lawyer, Don Stroughton, across the north side of the intersection, and hails him. Then as if being caught up in a whole new wave of inspiration, Lester makes a shushing gesture with his free hand and swings down the steps of the veranda to the dirt road an' the loaded wagon was on top of him in a flash…!

"It was Lester's mistake, not the poor wagon driver's; Lester should've looked before stepping off — you can't jest stop moving horseflesh in the bat of an eye!" Hill's look was one of begging Frank Cotter to realize the wagon driver's position. "The workhorses drove poor Lester hard into the dirt like a bit of landfill," Bevan remarked. "I was so close to everything that I actually saw the sickenin' sight!"

"Do you mind," growled Hill. This was now the point when the relived images in Jonas Bevan's mind took over, and drained him of any further words on the subject. Hill then forged on: "The driver jumped down from his vehicle and secured his team of four, while Jonas and I went round to the rear of the wagon where Lester's body was lying in the dirt — it was ghastly. Then by this, we were joined by a badly shaken Don Stroughton, the lawyer was already blaming himself for what had happened to Lester — I an' Jonas had no thought of where any blame could be laid! We couldn't leave Lester there, bleeding … so the four of us lifted him from the ground and took him over and laid him out on the sidewalk in the shade…"

"Four of you moved, Lester?" Frank frowned. "I thought you said that for a moment there, there was only you two and the lawyer. Did the wagon driver give you lot some help? "

"No. He was still with his nervy team," said Bevan.

"Well mebbe there wasn't four of us, could have been my mistake! You've gotta realize we were all in a panic … if I remember right though, the wagon driver ran off to get Lester the town's other doctor — Doc Hallway, he has a surgery four or five doors along from the corner of Ridge Road."

"I don't know much about sawbones working, but I reckon that Lester was already dead when we stretched him out of the sidewalk," Jonas said. "But no, he was still wif us … But all the same he must've realized he wuz short on time."

"Yeah, that's right!" Monty Hill agreed. "… And do you know who his last thoughts were for mister Cotter? — *You!*"

"Me?" The sound of surprise stood out in Frank's voice. Cotter could barely hold back his tears which were threatening to gush forth — which to a drunk, comes much too easily and was as damn near hurtful as having to admit to folks, that one **was a drunk.** Yet here we have a man, apparently aware that he is nearing the end, and yet like a true Christen — was quiet prepared to give a washed up, whiskey soaked writer — his last thoughts.

"The way Sheriff Boston understands it, Lester died instantly," blurted out the scribe before he could check himself. "So, what-what were my friend's dying w-w-words?"

Bevan removed his bowler and raked his thinning hair with his fingers like a comb. "I can't recall his exact words. But because he must've sensed his approachin' death, he was a worryin' about how he wuz lettin' you down, and leaving you stranded… He said without him at your side, this wouldn't be your type of country."

Hill thought Jonas was putting Lester's words in a much too complicated, manner. "He made it our responsibility ter sees that you get back east without too much trouble or delay. We've got the power to order that company funds be used to purchase you a return ticket, east."

Frank nodded. He certainly did not want to be here in Junction City without Lester, either. Here in this town he was most definitely a fish out of water.

Monty Hill once more broke into Frank's line of thought.

"Jest so there's no mistakes, or misunderstanding. Doctor Lomax lived long enough to make his last wishes about your security and welfare before witnesses quite clear. Our dear friend took his last breath in the arms of his colleague, Doctor Hallway."

"I can tell you feller's one thing…" said Cotter.

"What's that?" asked Jonas Bevan.

"I'm not leaving here before they hold Lester's Inquest," Frank reported, unexpectedly.

"Inquest," chorused Hill and Bevan like they had never heard of the word.

"Yes. Surely they are going to hold one?"

"That'll be in the Sheriff's hands," Hill frowned.

"But there hasn't been any suggestion of one," said Bevan, his tone of voice showed that maybe he might have missed something going on around him.

Hill shook his head. "Why would there need to be an Inquest? Everything is all above board."

"Maybe so," Frank said. "But legally in deaths like this back east, they hold an Inquest into accidental death to ascertain where the blame lies, if any, might rest…"

"Look," said Bevan. "Let's continue this discussion out of this blazin' sun — I'm cooking out here!"

The three men began to head off in the direction of the nearby covered sidewalk. So while in transit Monty said: "…But we can't blame the wagon driver for any of this, it was entirely Lester's own fault."

"Well I must say this, Hill. For a joker who s'posed to be a business associated and friend of the decease, you're not pitching Lester any bouquets by a stance like that about this accident!"

"Mebbe … But you can't hide the truth, son. It's there plain fer all ter see."

"OK," Frank said with another nod. "But before I go packing I wanna talk with Lester's Attorney. Where does he hang out?" again Frank had thrown them an open question for any man to answer.

Jonas made a play to answer the man who seemed hell bent on trying to make the business of Lester's death a monumental event. "He's outa town at the present on business down in Dodge City — might be away a week or two."

"That's mighty convenient," noted Frank. "I take it he did the right thing by Lester and showed up at the funeral?"

Doc Lester's partners, nodded.

"Who else was there besides you folks?"

"Sheriff Boston, Doc Hallway — err — must've been about twenty-five people I'd reckon," said Monty.

Bevan nodded his head in agreement.

"What about that gal in the shawl with the parasol?" Frank's eyes bored into Hill.

"Yes, she was there; I shouldn't bother her. She's taking the Doctor's accident quiet painfully. She carried a torch for her benefactor and with good reason. It would be wise to let her be — that's my advice," said Monty Hill as he produced a couple of cheroots from the inside breast pocket of his blazer.

"I'm not worried about her. It's Lester's reputation I'm concerned about," Cotter told them as they resumed their journey along the covered sidewalk. Frank had his bearings, and knew that Lester's apartment was somewhere up ahead.

The boardwalk broke off abruptly at the end of the building alignment they were passing, leaving a six-foot space between buildings; it was the entrance to another one of the town's alleyways, which ran all the way through to Main Street. The sidewalk resumed once more and went all the way along Bryan Street intersection and beyond.

Bevan and Hill paused at the alley entrance and Frank got the distinct impression that the two want to leave him here and make use of the alley to reach Main Street. "Before you two go — can I have your home address?" asked Cotter as he moved out of the way of a woman passing along the boardwalk in the uptown direction.

Hill nodded. "We share a room at Ma Kelly's boarding house on Bryan Street, number forty."

"Ma Kelly? Is there not a damn thing in this town that that woman doesn't own," exclaimed Frank.

Both Hill and, Bevan grinned.

"I'll put it to you this way… What Ma Kelly doesn't own, the Cattlemen's Association sure does. But outside of that, anythin' neither those two own business-wise, isn't worth a plug nickel!" Hill and Bevan gave Frank a slight wave as they turned away from him and he, likewise, moved off in the direction of his temporary dwelling and the intersection where Dr. Lester Lomax met an untimely death.

Upon arrival at the corners of Bryan and Starr Streets, Frank paused to survey the area for now it had a much different meaning to him than being that of just a street corner in Junction City. Unknown to Frank, this was the accepted demarcation line between upper and lower end of town. He stood there on the sidewalk and tried to picture how the accident might have happened. The built-up area continued on pass the late doctor's corner surgery for six allotments on the left-hand side and nine on the right-hand side, then, the street seemed to peter out. There wasn't anything he could learn here, so he checked to see that it was safe to cross the intersection and, strode over to the surgery's veranda awning, and turned east to move along the building and pass the surgery entrance until he arrived at the end of the building line; and turned in off the boardwalk to mount the stairs to the apartment's landing.

It was here; he experienced a surprise that was totally unexpected … On the landing above him he saw a tradesman in the process of repair the euchred door-lock. In fact, as Frank came up the stairs he now saw that the tradesman had finished the repair and installation of the whole mechanism and was working with a screwdriver on the very last holding screw which attached it to the door. The man did not break rhythm in his task, but unless the man was deaf he had to know that Cotter was below him on the stairs.

Frank's guessed correctly that the man working ahead of him in the flock coat had to be the Russian gunsmith McBride and the Sheriff had told him about, for he had the carriage of a man of the Baltic States. There was no denying that he was Jewish, for he had a thick beard with very sparsely strands of gray through it and dangling down out from under the brim of his smoky colored Homburg were the long curls of religious hair were synonymous with that of an Orthodox Jew — being a onetime New Yorker he had become reasonably familiar with their culture—the fellows hat served two purposes, one religious, and the other to ward off sunstroke.

"…Hi," said Frank to the man who had an assortment of tools laid out on an eighteen inch calico sheet at his feet; which covered the weathered decking of the landing. "You're a welcome surprise. I was planning on tracking you down to repair that very thing you've been working on — I'm Frank Cotter a living-in friend of Doctor Lomax!"

The Russian nodded. Then drop to one knee with the screwdriver in his hand and deposited the tool on the calico along with his other instruments of trade and commenced wrapping up his tools. "I verk out who yew are…I fix zar lock for Ma Kelly," he said as he squinted at the Gentile.

"So I see… I was going to get you to do exactly *that,*" Frank told the Russian as he nodded towards the door.

"Ma Kelly orders me to fix zar lock quick and Aaron Yolson jumps to her ladyship's command. Ma Kelly is not a 'appy vermen wit yew my friend," He picked up his parcel of tools and rose from the floor of the landing.

"Did you know my friend, Doctor Lomax?"

"Not good. No …" The Russian was itching to be on his way and Frank realized this. "Zee town respect 'im very much, he clever zawbones an' quite zar entrepreneur."

"What do you mean, Sir?"

"He wuz as yew zay, involved witt many zings — a bit of zhis an' a bit of zat."

"That's why he brought me out here. Apparently he felt some folks, especially the government, were misunderstanding his motives for what he's been doing. The Doctor was gonna charged me with the job bringing his actions before the public for scrutiny … He hoped that together, we would kick-start the government into accepting its responsibilies towards the Indians!" While speaking from the heart, Frank realized that he was sounding like a political zealot.

Then from the bottom of the stairway he heard a slow sarcastic handclap from an uninvited audience of two. Cotter and the Russian gunsmith glanced down to the street below, the audience was non-other than the two men whom had busted up the doctor's apartment in their hunt for whatever it was they felt they were entitle, too.

Frank focused on the two men who were standing about a yard away from the newel of the stairway, just in off the boardwalk around the corner from Doctor Lomax's surgery; behind them, across the street in the background were the shop-fronts and a water-trough. Cotter's stance was uncomfortable so he lowered his leg from the upper riser and planted it next to his other leg.

"What in God's name do you want here?" Frank gruffly, demanded.

The feller in the black Stetson ignored Cotter's question, but said mordantly to his buckskin clad pal. "…Shall I find the man a soapbox, Captain Roscoe?"

Roscoe smirked up in Frank's direction. "It would seem a good idea, — but this town doesn't have a square for clown's to perform in!" The burglar's acerbity hit its target area and Frank took the bait, came down the staircase with abandonment to eyeball these fellers.

The Army men stood their ground for they had the numbers and Frank realized this to his better judgment, as his shoulder brushed passed the newel; Cotter put on the brakes and only just stopped short of chest-butting the Captain. " … Army or no Army, it's time you explained yourselves!"

Roscoe glared right into Cotter's smarting eyes. "Happy to do just that, friend. When, *you* take ya moush frum *my face* …!" There was not a scintillation of any joy for anyone in the man's eyes.

Frank stood his ground for at least another beat. Then reluctantly and through cowardliness, gave in — and moved back a step. "…The trouble with you Army types; is that you think your own shit doesn't stink!"

"That's better," said Captain Roscoe in reference to the fact that Cotter had backed down. "We need ter talk, so let us find ourselves some neutral and friendly, ground," suggested Roscoe.

"I reckon I know jest the place," said Briggs. "The saloon on Main Street…"

"One second," Frank said, and turned back to the Russian Jew. "Please leave the bill, under the door. I'll get back to you."

"No need Mister Couther … Ma Kelly has already taken care of zee matter."

"No, I shall talk to her about it —"

"C'mon, you can work it out later," interrupted Roscoe. "We've got things more important to speak about concerning your pal, Lomax!"

Frank turned to the two Army men at the back of him. "...If anyone ought to be paying for that repair, it should be you folk—you busted it."

"Yes, OK. I will talk to my superiors about payin' the Jew's account as a gesture of 'Good Will', you can't moan about the fairness of that?"

"Besides, our little chat might be in your friend's best interest — in the long run," Briggs said.

He has a point, thought Cotter.

Lieutenant Briggs took his companions down Bryan Street to Main Street, then up Main Street in the direction of Ridge Road, to a saloon on the same side of the street as that of the Barbershop and Chinese owned Bath House. Here in all its glory stood **The Sorrel Saloon.** Frank recalled that he had caught sight of the liquor house when he made his way uptown en route to the diner, earlier today. As they neared the saloon's entrance the house barkeeper chased a mongrel stray mutt off the premises — the dog raced to safety from under the bat-wing doors. The mutt had no doubt come into the liquor den for a free handout and for its troubles, got sent on its way with the promise of a taste of boot-leather.

The saloon's batwing doors were left flapping by the return of the barkeeper to his duties. Briggs was the first to hit the wood-louver batwing doors and lead them into the barroom. The lumber floor of the bar was covered with a thick layer of timber mill sawdust, in some places it was lumpy and in others, the boot traffic had spread it so thin that the boards beneath, showed through. The bar was constructed out of timber and had a white-gray veined marble top while its facing had been paneled with something resembling a walnut type of wood. Rising up out of the sawdust about 6-inches, before, where the counter met the floor, was a brass foot-rail that ran the whole length of the bar. Down the end of the room, facing towards the street, was a small stage only 10-inches high: Center stage was an upright piano, which had been covered with a loose throw-over cloth. There was no one in the room who looked remotely like a piano-player; of the eight tables and chair, one was in use — a couple of cowboys sat one table-setting drinking the saloon's rotgut and, playing Monte with gambling chips standing in for money.

Captain Roscoe led Cotter to a vacant table close to the bar and sat down. Roscoe took the chair with his back to the bar while Lt. Briggs passed on to the counter to order their drinks without consulting either man of their preference. Frank settled on a chair, the street entrance to his back, a painted fallen dove in the employ of the establishment entered the bar from a side door down near the stage. Her high-heel shoes made no noise on the sawdust as she approached the new comers and gave them the once over to check if they were worth her time to fleece, if not, she'd return to her hideaway beyond the door from whence she had come. The perfume of her powdered wig was the only hint of her presence.

Lt. Briggs returned from the bar with bottle of imported whiskey and three shot glasses; he sat down on one of the empty chairs and placed the already open bottle in the center of the table, within easy reach of everyone. Then he doled out the drinking vessels, while Captain Roscoe gave the bottle a quick check to see that no one had taken a slug out of it before they had taken possession of what the government had paid for. He didn't want to be paying money for watered down whiskey. Frank licked his lips in anticipation — even though his conscience warned him against touching the grog.

Captain Roscoe poured a round of drinks for them by way of commencing proceedings, "…So tell us, what's your association with Doctor Lomax, Cotter?"

"Whoa. Whoa. Whoa…I thought we were here to hear your explanation for acting like a couple of bowery sneak thieves, and taking apart a dead man's abode?" Frank said as his blood pressure shot up a couple of notches. "Instead you wanna know the insides of a duck's ass!" Absentmindedly and from monkey trained experience, he palmed the a whiskey glass which was clearly for him and held it in a hand that could very readily be changed into a fighter's fist within a brief second if it was warranted.

"What's with the feisty attitude, Cotter? Wait till you know a few truths before yuh get hot under the collar! … Let's all take five … have a drop of liquor — get the starch outa our collars … relax …" having said that, Roscoe and Briggs, saluted the newspaperman with their glasses, and threw their shots of whiskey down their throats like ninety percent of the saloon world's population — Frank Cotter looked on with narrowing eyes.

"Well, c'mon, what's holdin' you back?" snapped Lt. Briggs when he and Captain Roscoe realized that the city scrivener was holding back.

"Do yuh really wanna know?"

"Look, we're here ter clear the air between us," said Roscoe. "Your attitude thus far doesn't seem so frum yore corner of the ring?."

"Before we start drinking our heads off, you explain to me — how come you two got out of Boston's jail so damn quick?"

"What d'you mean?" Asked Briggs as he picked up the bottle and refilled their empty glasses.

"Yes ... What do you mean?" Roscoe finished his drink and licked his lips with the tip of his tongue.

"You jokers tore up Lester's place looking for something, you whipped the ass off two of the town's citizens and put the shakes up my spine ... Jest for breaking in and assault ought to have gotten you locked up for at least a couple, of months! Yet here you are, walking around the town as large as life. How come you bought yourselves out of jail, is the local sheriff that easily corruptible?"

"Who says *"we"* bought ourselves out of Boston's caboose...?" Briggs asked.

"Sheriff Boston was using his head and not making a mountain out of a mole hill, when he set us free. You don't know too much about people, Cotter—you really thought he was gonna lock us up and throw away the key over that business in Lomax's apartment? ... Hell man, he has his own issues with those two cowboys who were escortin' you." Roscoe told Frank.

A grin broke out on Brigg's face. "Boston never entertained the idea of ever jailin' us fer bruising those fellers faces a bit; he's been waitin' fer someone ter come along an do that to 'em on his behalf —"

"In fact," Roscoe said, "I reckon if we'd've asked for a "kick back" for doing him *the favor,* he might have slung us a few bucks. But that's not our style."

"You guys are pretty damn smug about all this; I'll say that for you..." Cotter finally tossed his drink down in utter disgust and in so doing, committed the biggest sin any alcoholic could hope to do, especially for one whom had been on the "wagon" for a short time as long as Frank Cotter.

That one drink was to be his undoing and fall from grace.

"OK," said Captain Roscoe. "…Lieutenant Briggs and I were sent here to Junction City on special assignment from Washington"

"An' what you're gonna hear at this table cannot go any further, understand?" interjected Briggs.

"Cut the crap an' get to the chase," snapped Cotter as he reached for the bottle to refill his glass, setting his own course on a journey to Hell. "It's can't be that serious to excuse you in defile my pal's name." He peered hard at his drinking associates as if trying to read their inner souls.

"Do you know much about the work Doctor Lomax was doing?" Roscoe asked.

In truth, Cotter didn't. He was relying on Lester to put him in the picture once he got here. He felt slightly embarrassed that perhaps these two men were more up with Lester's business than he. He took the bottle by the neck and poured another three fingers of delicious whiskey as he admitted his short coming… "We've only had contact with one another through letters over the past three months. Before that, it's been years since we were in contact. Besides there is only so much one can spell out in a letter."

"Then you **don't** really know what Lomax was doing with his time?" suggested the army lieutenant.

"Again, with the third degree…?" It hadn't yet dawned on Frank that he was back drinking like his old self. "You policemen are all tarred with the same brush…"

Already the drink was burning its way through his body, opening up the healing scars of his liver and brain cells. *"I don't like* ***Policeman!"***

"We're not police," Captain Roscoe pointed out to Cotter.

"That's right…" He threw his drink down the hatch. Already the first hit of alcohol was taking hold of his thinking and he, Frank, did not recognize the signs.

"Ooh, yes out here in the uncivilized wilderness they're known as either Marshals or Sheriffs—my tenderfoot mistake, but I'll learn in time, won't I?!" he said with bitter sarcasm and went for the bottle again.

Christ this is good stuff; it is giving me just the backbone I need to stand up to these motherfuckers! Frank, thought.

Roscoe and Briggs were witnessing the effect the whiskey was having on the scribe. It wasn't something they had expected; both men knew now how easy it was going to be to loosen this man's tongue. Continue with this tack, and who knows just what they might learn about Lomax and his activities with the Indians. Both could see that alcohol was this City Slicker's downfall and as dangerous to the man as any potent poison, but all the same they recharged the drunk's glass with one drink on top of the other and set out to drained his mind of all the knowledge that they thought they might need from this, their treasure trove.

"So tell me…?" Frank raised his glass once again and held it there like a well versed lush, his true colors steadily rising to the fore. "Just what is it you and the government are tryin' ter pin on, Lester?" He took a sip of his whiskey-crutch before going on. "… Now he's dead and defenseless you could pin anything on him because he can't speak up for himself, can he?"

Roscoe said, "Washington knows the dirty little game Lomax 'n' his pals have been playing at with the Pawnees…" the Captain could read in the drunk's eyes that Cotter wasn't going to believe what he was about to say but still continued for he wanted to hit one of Frank Cotter's raw nerves— "his rouge crew were bent on selling 'em a bill of goods, two-bit snake-oil as a cure for the ills that were driving 'em and their kids, to early graves…"

"That's **a lie!**" snarled Cotter and almost without warning he threw a round-house fist in the direction of Roscoe's head and had it ever connected would have knocked the Army Captain out of his chair. But Lt Briggs had sensed what was building up in the drunk's mind though almost a split second too late, he moved with lightning speed and deflected the dangerous course of Cotter's clenched fist from its intended target, then followed up with a rock-hard counter punch to Cotter's temple region which laid him out like a log on the barroom floor!

Then apologetically said to his brother in arms: "Sorry about that, Captain Roscoe. I should have been more on my toes when dealin' with a drunk!" Frank overheard Lieutenant muttering somewhere in the background but in his stunned condition it meant very little to him.

"We'd better tidy him up," Roscoe suggested.

The Army lads came round the table and lifted the dazed newspaperman still on the chair up and sat him down at the cheap timber table. The whiskey bottle had fallen over on its side and rolled over near the table's edge and halted, the liquor lapped in freefall from the bottle's mouth, down onto the absorbable dry sawdust … Briggs quickly ended this episode of spillage by standing the vessel upright, then quickly poured Frank a reviver and got it into him like a toddler being taught to drink from a cup.

"C'mon …Git this inter yuh—you need it!" Briggs ordered the stupefied man, and like a zombie, Frank swallowed it as though it were nectar from the Gods. So within the next few moments, he invariably blacked out.

Cotter awoke in Lester's bed — as far as he was concerned, he had spent the night in it upon his arrival in Junction City. He felt basically uncomfortable and his clothes were a crumpled mess. The room was dark and he had a hangover the size of those new-fangled steam locomotives … His head felt as though it were in a carpenter's vice.

On the bedside table a lamp had been left burning with a very low flame and Cotter decided to leave it that way, for he was afraid that any increase in the brightness of the light might toy with the pain of the swelling in each of his orbs. Then suddenly he was gripped with the sudden need for a drink and he started shivering involuntary, yet he was not feeling cold, instead it felt as though he had tiny worms trapped beneath his layers of skin and it was as if they were struggling to break through the dividing layers so that the separated colonies, might become one … His own intelligence told him it was the Demon Drink, sinking her sharp claws back into his innards after having been ejected and denied for the past weeks. In his mind he knew he had wronged himself in so doing, had wronged his dear friend, Lester Lomax … His mixed feelings were darting in many different directions at once and these too were a torture just as great as that which his body was suffering. He could no more explain these mental explorations the teeny scraps of decency and obligation that had clung there to the walls of his inner kernel somehow made their presence known. His conscience told him that while he still lived, he had something to finish — at all costs he had to be the White Knight and purify the name and reputation of Lomax, he couldn't do it from a sickbed nor from the inside of a whiskey bottle.

He tried to rise and found this a monumental ask. His repeated efforts turned his head and guts inside out — he'd never before suffered such a harrowing ordeal. By the time he was able to finally sit upright for any length of time, his bedclothes, that had been tucked up under his chin were wet with smelly vomit; He obviously had more tenacity than he'd ever given himself credit for— he finally managed to stay up in a sitting position and eventually was able to dangle his legs over the side of the bed, though he doubted he had the strength to leave its security— in his lifetime. But he decided against his better judgment that the bit had to be taken between his teeth and wriggled his butt over to the edge of the mattress; until he was at a point whereby any form of balance was beyond his control and so he crashed heavily to the floorboards with a resounding thump! He had no idea how long he was lying there helpless on the loose floor coverings, eventually the cold of the night made him attempt to struggle to his pair of unstable legs and he fell down once more, and so, like a boxing mug without any sense to know when to stay down for his own wellbeing, he hauled himself up with the aid of the bed frame and stood there swaying in the dark like an elephant sways to assist its circulation, and in so doing, kept his very own on the move. He did not need this explained to him he knew he had fallen off the wagon after weeks on the straight and narrow.

Doctors back east had warned him that if he ever allowed himself to backtrack on the course of cure he had adopted, he would most certainly be doomed. *Could he prove them wrong?* He asked himself. *By God he had to prove them wrong, or die in the process!*

Ignoring the risks involved, he decided to fight on and did a sterling job to stagger across the gloomy room to the china basin and ewer of rinsing water. Instinct, was the only force driving him now. He emptied the cool water from the ewer over his head and through his hair — rinsing away the smelly perspiration that had broken out on his skin across his skull amongst the strands of matted hair; but it seemed to do little for him. In reality it must have done him some good — somewhere off in the distance he could hear the faint sounds of music … if not music, then his mind was going on him. He willed himself to concentrate on the sound … he listened intently and was able to discern the sounds rhythm, and it's direction — he assumed it to be coming from the theatre-restaurant further along Starr street. He tuned the music out, for he knew his next port of call would be the wardrobe, but first he had to rest awhile here at the lowboy, while he composed himself; he had no idea how long he waited on outstretched arms in front of that piece of furniture but he felt that it must have been some time. Then he pushed off for the wardrobe and by the time he had reached the point of no return, wished to high heaven he had not pulled on the journey, he felt that he was on the brink of passing out, but he was truly grateful when he got to his destination and could rest up once more. He was fighting for breath when he got there, and in the poor light tottered first to the lowboy for a fresh shirt and underwear. He and opened, one of the doors and sunk down on its floor amongst the clothes, half in and half out of the 'robe. He became nauseous once more and feared that he was going to vomit in the wardrobe over the clothes. Finally he felt well enough to back out of the 'robe and struggle to his feet. Then he reached up and dragged down one of his empty carpetbags and forced it open and stuffed fresh clothes into it, he could not have a bath without climbing into clean gear — he had this compulsion that he had to get over to Main Street and the bathhouse — whether he had it in him to make it that far he would never know.

Much like a blind man he followed the wall of the room along to where it met the doorway and felt his way out into the dark parlor. He paused for a much needed rest at the threshold of the parlor-cum-dining room. The moon emphasized the whereabouts of the apartment's door and landing to the stairs. Frank lurched with his bag into the parlor and crashed into the kitchen table after only making a yard or so in the direction of the door. He took advantage of the table to take the weight of the carpetbag and its contents off him. He hung his spinning head, which was twirling like a gaudily painted wooden toy-top that brings so much joy to children, unfortunately for him, this whirling sensation was no joy, and it was accompanied with a sluggishness that threatened to withdraw all balance from him ... With the carpetbag in one hand he forced himself away from the table and over to the door where he wrestled it open and stumbled out onto the landing, almost blind with body damnation, he fell to his knees and incurred abrasions to both knees and balanced there with his forehead against the cool wooden balustrade, which was instantly like someone holding an ice-pack to him.

It seemed almost like an hour before his head and stomach was calm enough for him to try to regain his feet. Then he staggered over to the head of the staircase and stood swaying there while he wondered whether or not he should try to negotiate the steps — they looked dangerously steep to him from up here. It was a daunting task and no one knew better than he, that one mistake and it could cost him his life in a death fall to the ground below, even if he were to survive he would not get off scot-free, skin and bones would be the cost of his fool-hardy venture. He knew he would need both hands for the descent, so he threw the carpetbag down to the bottom of the stairs. He very carefully moved from the landing — taking it one step at a time, using both hands, one over the other to steady himself against the banister. When Frank could see that he was within an arm's length of the stairs he began to breathe a sigh of relief; he rested with his side up against the newel and bent at the knees to reach down and slowly picked up his 'bag but just bending forward to get a grip on the utility sent the inside of his head spinning and he had to stand there and wait until it subsided before pondering his next move.

Clutching the 'bag to him, Frank shuffled slowly forward out onto the boardwalk and while on the move kept himself at it for fear that if once he stopped for needy rest he would never be able to get himself back in motion … down over the edge of the sidewalk he stepped with added caution, the impact of reaching the road's surface jarred through his entire body but none the less he still plowed on across the expanse of the leveled off limestone where he finally reach the opposite sidewalk. He used his free hand to help haul himself up to the boardwalk and turning left, he continued to totter along the weathered boards to the corner where he had to once more step down onto the dirt surface of the street and cross it to the far side and then turn right and start along the sidewalk in the direction of Main Street. He realized at this point that his battle to stay on his feet was going to take a far greater effort, than he had bargained for. His body odor, was worse than that of a Polecat's and he knew he was not only offensive to himself but to any stranger crossing his path, he'd find it an awkward situation to come under their scrutiny every again… So far his prayers of not meeting up with anyone had been answered, there was just the occasional saddle-horse tied up to a hitching rail left in negligence by its errant owner; he was relieved that this part of Junction City seemed deserted ... This meant that his fall from grace might pass unnoticed and no one other than those Army bums would know he had fallen off the wagon — he doubted they would spread the word. Just then, Cotter passed a darkened doorway of a business premises and who should step out from the darkness right into his path was ***Father Lorimar!!***

This checked Cotter's stride and he grouped for something to say to the man who stood there before him as large as life!

"…Surprised to see me, mister Cotter?" The Catholic Priest asked as Frank backed off from the apparition. "Don't be scared, I'm not gonna hurt you."

"Y-y-you're d-d-dead!" Cotter blabbed in a hoarse voice.

"Am I? Um, never thought of it like *that*… "Lorimar struck a match off the edge of his thumb, it flared into life and then he torched a freshly rolled cigarette which simply just appeared there between his lips.

"You're not a g-ghost — I'm — I'm a practical thinker; I don't believe you're a ghost!" Cotter went on quickly, the words almost spilling out on top of each other.

"OK, so you're the clever one … you tell me what I am, then, huh?" Lorimar blew smoke in Cotter's direction.

"I saw you shot down in that robbery with my own eyes —" Frank's voice faded away on him until it was just a whisper: "— you c-c-can't be alive!!!"

"Who can say or know what you believe you saw? You're known to be a drunken lush and not an ounce of good to anyone. Look at the state you're in … You — a man who is the only one in the world who can clear Lester Lomax's name an' yet you foul the very air around you. Pull yerself together and begin to act like a man with conviction! "

Frank went to push the Priest away from him, but suddenly there was no one there! He turned to the darkened doorway from whence the man had appeared and there was nothing, not a living soul … He turned and checked the immediate area about him but found it still just as desolated as it had been before Lorimar seemed to have appeared on the scene. Cotter sobbed and sobered as one, he was now convinced that his ruined brain cells were playing tricks on him. *Surely the dead Priest hadn't appeared to him out of the night like some biblical angel, as though he had been chosen for a cause? I've gotta get away from here!* Frank Cotter tried to compose himself as now sober his faltering steps had vanished and he rushed on towards Main Street, pausing only to look back over his shoulder down Bryan Street at a ghost-town like street, lit only in Luna light. His experience had shaken him to the core.

Upon arriving at the bathhouse the owner wholeheartedly refused to let the putrid smelling man in to use the facilities — the Asian sincerely believing it would be disrespectful to their other clientele who paid good money to use the washrooms. The Asian and his Cathay brethren gathered together and put their shoulders to the heavy wooden door in order to bar Cotter's show of force, to enter their establishment.

Attracted by the din and shouting coming from just down beyond The Sorrel Saloon, Sheriff Boston clumped along the boardwalk with the best pace he could muster out of his gammy leg. Nearing the ruckus Klem drew his six-gun and at about the same time he realized, in the light of a wall lamp, that it was Doctor Lomax's buddy, caught up in a rowdy quarrel with the Asians over something … Boston slipped his pistol back into its holster as he neared the bathhouse door, which had just been forced, closed in Cotter's face.

"What seems ter be the trouble here, Frank?" Boston caught the ripe smell of Cotter's body-odor, as the man swung in Klem's direction. He would have commented on the smell coming from the man, but thought this highly unethical. "Yuh cuttin' it a bit fine ter want a bath; they don't run a twenty-four hour service, here." The sheriff's wary eyes ran over Cotter from head to knees — he was shocked to see the state of the man's dress—it would be criminal not to allow the man a chance to tidy himself up and be more presentable looking.

"I n-need a damn good clean up, badly!" Cotter said with his new husky, croaky voice. His breath smelt no better than his wardrobe looked and Boston had to turn his face away from the newspaperman to escape the foul smell.

"I can tell that! Awright, I'll get you a bath but first I wanna know where the Hell you've been these past three days…" Klem pawed his six-gun once again as he prepared to utilize the weapon as a substitute for a door-knocker …

"What d'you mean—by this "three days" business? … I don't know what **the Christ** yuh talking about, Boston," exclaimed Cotter. Klem frowned over his shoulder at the scribe, "What are *you* jawin' 'bout? You gone loco? I'm not speaking darn Pawnee! You've been missing frum round the town. I've been worried about you…" Boston began bashing the door's panel with the Colt's butt. He was determined to get some reaction from those inside, or batter the studded door to pieces. A short time later the face of a thickset Chinaman appeared at the Judas-hole…

Frank was busy trying to make sense of just what the Sheriff was on about, he could clearly remember being at the saloon on Main Street with Captain Roscoe and Lieutenant Briggs. He had no reason to make any secret about that…

"Go away — go away—go home…" But upon the bathhouse owner getting the panel of the Judas hole open and seeing who the noisy feller was it became a tune of differing notes. "Aahh—Sheriff Boston!" the Oriental fellow said, making a very poor attempt at appearing surprised. "Wot yew want? …We close, no service now, you and friend come back when morning sun kisses Junction City —" The man on the other side of the wooden barrier made to close-up.

"Don't you **dare** attempt to close that door in my face, Hung-Lee!" the lawman's strident reached through to the Asian and the half closed hatch door froze in motion. "This feller at the back of me, needs ter take a bath, urgently … Now git this goddamn door **open** or I'll bust it in an' bust yore ass and yore kinfolk all the way back ter China!"

"Zorry, no hot water — you come back when sun up!"

"Out of the question my little Chinese friend…" Sheriff Boston cocked his Colt and pointed it in the Chinaman's face. "If I pull this damn trigger it will send a slug right through this door into yore guts which no doctor would be able tar fix for ya, and we don't want that, do we Hung-Lee?"

Hung-lee knew the Sheriff was serious about the threat and leaving the Judas-hole open he went on to open up the main door and as Klem holstered his weapon he said: "At a boy, now you go boil up some water an' I'll sit wif Mister Cotter while he bathes…" Boston informed the Chow as Cotter crowed into the establishment almost on top of Hung-Lee in case there was a change of action and minds.

The hot water was impossible for Frank to sit in, so he had to squat over its surface like child squats over a commode when doing a job. The zinc bath contained water a foot deep, made cloudy by the homemade soap that the bathhouse provided, a soap heavy with carbolic which produced very poor suds. The smelly newspaperman washed and sponged the upper part of his body very thoroughly, while waiting for the water to cool enough for him to lower his privates into it without scalding them.

The sheriff sat on a low wooden oriental bath-stool back from the tub so as not to get splashed, while the City boy carried on with his ablutions. "How long you been drunk fer this round?" Klem asked as he fished a smoke out the breast pocket of his gingham shirt and stuck it between his lips. "—you shouldn't drink if it makes this kinda mess of you, Cotter." Boston had a row of ten vesta matches shoved in his hatband, and after some fumbling, got himself one and struck alight off the sole of his boot and lit-up the cigarette roll in his mouth. "—Lomax told me about you an' the piss …"

Cotter gingerly lowered himself into the water for he did not want to boil his gonads. He soaked the face-washer in the water and without squeezing off the excess slapped himself in the face with it, then pressing hard he slowly dragged it down his face, the heat from the cloth penetrated his skin and aching facial muscles. He could feel its drag on his whiskers.

"…I wonder if you might fetch my razor over there in my carpetbag." Cotter asked the Sheriff. Klem dropped his spent match on the wet floorboards of the bathing cubicle and went over and dug out the man's shaving gear. Meanwhile, Frank held out both his arms at nipple-height and saw what he feared— the shakes. It would be dangerous for him to try using a straight razor with those mitts; as Boston approached the tub, Frank begged the man to do him the honors, and shave off his three-day beard.

Boston found the bath soap was pretty useless at generating a respectable lather, but Cotter wasn't in a position to complain, it was a case of like it or lump it.

"Yew better come down to the jailhouse after this—I'll cook you a slab of steer an' 'tatters. Yew look mighty starved ter me; you need sumthin' heavy in yuh guts if you can hold it down…"

Sheriff Boston was only a campfire cook at the best of times, but the jailhouse potbelly stove did him proud. As the much refreshed news-reporter sat down on a stool borrowed from one of the two empty cells at the back of the lockup, he was handed a tin plate with a juicy semi-raw steak still sizzling amid chopped potatoes that were later to be known as "Potato Wedges". Cotter's hands were shaking and he had trouble for a while there, keeping a grip on the dull stainless steel cutlery. He had to willingly admit to himself that this was the worst he had ever been after a drinking spree; never before had he ever suffered any form of what every drunk will surely one day witness, the delirium tremens … He knew without a doubt that Father Lorimar had been a figment of his imagination triggered by alcohol, and yet it was a source of amazement to him that the whole episode had appeared to be **so real.** But real or not, the feller had made Frank take further steps about cleaning up his act; especially if he tended to work for the name of Doctor Lomax.

Klem watched Cotter struggling to eat and keep the plate on his knees and not lose it on the floor. It was no fun to see an educated man like Frank Cotter in such a state and he began to understand why Lomax must have felt duty bound to help his old friend.

Lomax had explained to Klem Boston about Cotter's drink problem and that he was trying to break the grip it had on him; that's why he had taken it upon himself to bring the guy west to work for him. As far as Boston could see it was in the man's nature to help folks less fortunate than he. Hence, his pro bono work with the wretched injun.

Frank rose from his stool with his now empty plate, he crossed the room to deposit it and the utensils on the Sheriff's desk, but it took him a moment to find a spot for them; at least his innards started to feel like something belonging to a human.

"Feelin' OK, now?" Klem asked by way of checking on his charge.

Frank nodded. "It's amazing the difference a bit of food makes…"

"Now all you need is sleep," Klem told Frank.

"Rubbish!" Sheriff Boston snapped at the tenderfoot as one of his deputies came in off the street. "—what you've had fer the past three days or so, no one can call sleep!"

Frank noted the deputy was a sloppy, lazy, walker as he ambled towards them from the jail building's entrance. He came through the wicket in the balustrade dividing the Sheriff's office area from any would-be customers who clearly had to remain on their side of the fence if here on business and not arrest. The Deputy's star was pinned to the outside of his dark-chocolate calf vest. When he removed his hat, which was a Stetson, similar to Klem Boston's and Cotter's, he revealed a growth of ill kept, un-groomed hair. Then he hung his hat on his pistol's trigger hammer by its chinstrap, where it remained clinging like a trained fruit bat.

"Evenin', Sheriff?"

"Howdy, Ben…" Boston caught the wicket with his hand and held it open. "Yore jest in time ter hold the fort down, while I walk this feller back ter Doc Lomax's place," Klem signaled Frank to pass him his hat for Cotter was closest to it. Frank passed Klem's Stetson to the Deputy who passed it over to the Sheriff. By now the Sheriff was vigorously rubbing his bad leg…"This here is Frank Cotter, the Doc's friend out frum the East — I told yuh about 'im?

"Frank, this here's Ben Lexmon." Both men shook hands.

Lexmon was about twenty-five and wore a light tan shirt under his cowhide vest which he had tucked into a pair of moleskin trousers, the legs of which disappeared into the tops of a pair of low-topped peewee cowboy boots. His boot's uppers were dusty from patrolling the streets. His boot's Cuban style heels elevated him slightly higher than his actual height — his footwear was in common usage by folks of most cattle regions. Buckled to his waist was a tooled, polished leather gunfighter's rig, his tied-down holsters were weighed down with a pair of Schofield Smith & Wesson.

To Cotter, Benjamin Lexmon looked the type of man one wouldn't want to be on the wrong side of… Frank didn't warm to him as well as he did to Klem Boston—maybe because Boston came across as not such a threatening man as that of Ben Lexmon. Klem and Frank headed across to the street door as Lexmon took over the Sheriff's Colonial swivel chair.

"Hell!" exclaimed Frank, "I've left my carpetbag back at the bathhouse!" Cotter could feel some sort of movement in his stomach as it made certain adjustments to accommodate the beefsteak and potatoes he had consumed and wondered whether he was going to be forced to throw-up, as he closed the jailhouse door behind him.

"…Don't worry, Frank. It'll be as safe as a bank wif the Chinese—I'll fetch it fer you sometime on the 'morrow," Boston set off along Ridge Road, in the direction of Starr Street. After passing only four properties, the boardwalk cut out and they continued on over a limestone path, which someone had partially covered with a single plank of lumber for folks to walk on when the surrounding ground was muddy and wet from rain. Klem walked beside the tenderfoot on the dirt for the timber wasn't wide enough to take two people, abreast. The sidewalk continued on like this for the length of five planks, all butted end-to-end until they abruptly run out; then it was back on the dirt, they trudged pass the fronts of four single-fronted cottages, the first and forth clapboard cottages were the only ones fenced in with white pickets.

The newspaperman's tummy was setting itself up to embarrass him, and there was naught he could do about it. He bolted off the pathway and only just made it to an empty hitching rail, where he held on for grim death as he retched and threw up on the soft dirt, once hard clay, which had been broke and softened by the calcified hooves of horses when tethered to the rail. Klem waited patiently until Frank's vomiting episode had past and Cotter stood there in the moonlight waiting to catch his breath.

"…Who got you started back on the whiskey?" asked the lawman, as he drew two brown paper rolled cylinders of tobacco from the pocket of his jeans. "Before Lomax's accident, he told me that you were at least making an effort ter keep as far away from the booze as possible…"

Frank turned round and rested his lower back against the tie-rail and crossed his gusseted elastic sided boots at the ankle, he had no choice but to accept the feeling of sweat breaking out over him as he took Boston's offer of a smoke. "Was my being a drunk that obvious to you?"

Boston pushed his hat back higher on his forehead. "…In this job one experiences pretty much everythin' in time. But the truth is, Lester laid it all out on the line about you ter me. He wanted ter make sure that you were saved frum yore self if things got too tough fer you. He geared up other folks here in town, ter promise watch over you, when he weren't about.

"—so who wos it led you astray?" Klem found one of the Vesta matches in his hatband, and struck it on the rail at his side, then went ahead to torch their cigarettes, he tossed the spent match into a council provided water trough. Klem knew that drunks were always on the lookout for a reason to get back on the sauce and offered him a line.

"Wus it Doc's sudden, death?"

Cotter thought: *Whom am I trying to kid? I could use that as an excuse but the fact is I'm weak and am an utter disgrace to Lester who was working hard at trying to do the right thing by me... The least I can do now is try and do, the right thing by his memory. Got to get a grip of myself before it is too late — a man shouldn't've touched anything those Army jokers shoved my way.*

Finally Cotter tried to answer the Sheriff as best he could. "I dunno. Maybe that had something to do with it, or maybe deep down I wanted to break out — who knows? I guess my mind is falling apart with all this grog I've punished it with over the years?

"On my way up to that Chinese bathhouse, I ran into Father Lorimar, well not him exactly, but his ghost. He talked to me just like I'm here talking to *you...*" Frank tapped his index finger to his left temple. "Now, even to me that is absolute lunacy! I haven't believed in ghosts since my days of believing in the "tooth fairy".

"The last thing I can remember … is that I went off to a saloon with them Army fellers you failed to lockup for busting into Lester's apartment. Maybe you ought to explain why you allowed them to waltz off into the morning, Sheriff? And now, as I talk, I am getting some foggy images of, of, of winding up down some dirty back alley an-and maybe — I'm not a hundred percent sure — but I woke up an' found this mongrel dog pissing in my face — the acid from its urine burnt the shit out of my eyes and, and I g-g-guess I must have passed out.

"…Then I've got this hazy memory or was it a dream? Of some fellers I think one was Monty Hill and his partner, Bevan, looking down at me from on high with pity and sadness. Then they seemed to-to-to stand aside and Lester was there looking at me with the Kind of compassion one might expect from a Savior. But this couldn't have been so, 'coz I know poor Lomax is dead, six-foot under the earth… I blacked out or something at that-that point…"

Klem blew smoke from his cigarette up in the direction of the stars. "I'm sure it's not the first time a feller in yore condition has seen stuff that jest isn't there? Take that business wif the dead Priest, huh?

"Bevan an' Hill? Now them we do know ter be real; and they did have somethin' going on the side wif the good doctor — but that wos their business, naught ter do wif me!"

While Frank was giving what the Sheriff said some thought, an irritated voice came out of the night from the open window of a nearby cottage. "Hey, you guys **go do** yore natterin' someplace else, some folks have ter go ter work in the mornin'!"

Frank caught Klem grinning in the moonlight and the pair of them nodded and thought it a wise move to amble on. They crossed to the far side of the dirt street and up a high step to the boardwalk. Frank was incline to give the Sheriff a hand up, but the man was too quick for him, Boston had had years of practice on how to manage with his leg, they proceeded on, now only two building lots to go before reaching Starr Street. Frank could not help christening the boardwalk with a veneer of steak and potatoes and so once more they had to take five — until Frank felt well enough to continue. But while waiting for that to come about they continued with their conversation.

"I guess you would be expectin' an explanation as ter why I let those so-called West Pointers go. But I c'n tell you here and now—yore not gonna git one. But frum my point of view I can't figger out why they'd go ter all the trouble they did ter haul you orf to a saloon and fill you full of piss!" Boston looked hard at Cotter. "…Were they tryin' ter pump you fer information about the Doc, not that I c'n see it doing 'em or their cause much good now he's dead. Are you sure it jest wasn't one more of yer drunken fantasies?" Klem hawked out a dollop of thick mucus and shot it across the sidewalk onto the hard packed limestone cover on the road's virgin landfall surface which caught Frank unawares, he dry-retched and transferred it into a burp…

Sheriff Boston stood at the bottom of the stairway and watched the suffering drunkard climb the multi-risers, a few of them creaked with the climber's weight but weren't in danger of collapsing.

Reaching the landing Cotter emitted a sigh of relief. Curled up on the apartment's coir doormat was a furry black cat that got out of his way as he approached the unlocked door and upon getting it opened, crossed the threshold. Klem Boston swung away from the newel and headed off back to the jailhouse.

When I cross paths wif those Army gents, thought the Sheriff — *they're gonna git a piece of my mind or I'm not Klem Boston! Fancy fellers in their position offerin' a recovering drunk the very poison he's addicted too? They might've killed the poor guy…Let's hope that tenderfoot is made of stronger stuff an' can beat this damn fall from grace!* Boston, hoped.

Frank struck a match and saw his way safely over to the kitchen table where a coal-oil lamp sat waiting to be fired up in the center of its expanse. He took off his Stetson and placed it on the tablecloth alongside the lamp's thick glass moldered reservoir, half-full with fuel, it was already disturbed by the vibration of the jar of him colliding with the table's edge. He eventually managed to raise the chimney glass and ignite the soaked wicked before the match had burnt down too close to his finger and thumb. Then he shook the life out of the *Vest's* flame and adjusted the wick to rid it apex of the oily smoke, which would quickly blacken the glass with soot if left unchecked … Then he went and sat heavily on a Windsor side chair, which groaned under his weight and stifled another burp.

For no apparent reason the flickering flame behind the chimney became a fixation to him and even without realizing it he was soon staring deeply into the dancing flame … its hypnotic rhythm had a soothing effect on his nauseous stomach, unwittingly he began to drift off into a deep trance … his heavy head dropping forward until his lower jaw rested on his upper body's manubrium bone.

Cotter had no idea how long he had slept balanced as he was; he impetuously awoke with a start! Looked about, he discovered he'd now inherited a crick in his neck, while at the same time he comprehend that the wick's flame had burnt down dangerously low and was on the verge of snuffing out. He twirled the adjustment to wind up more wick, this action saved the life of the flame, and hence the illumination …

Oh, wouldn't Ma Kelly love that, me, burning down her whole building?! The dangers of a neglected flame had been driven home to him as far back as he could remember... He rose stiffly from the chair and stood over the chimney, then blew the flame out; the exertion of which made his head spin and he swayed like a tree being put under stress of a passing gust of wind. Then once more flopped down on the chair so as to not suffer the loss of balance and end up on the floor with a cracked, skull.

While sitting there he chides himself for his stupidity and reckoned he had better start on the untidy mess he had left in the bedroom. His short walk was paired with a shocking headache and he didn't relish the thought of the necessary labor he knew he had ahead of him. He entered the dim room and crossed to the west wall where a window with the shade drawn, faced out over looking Bryan street. He raised the sunshade and what sky he could see, revealed that a new day was approaching, even though he was turned away from whence the sun rose... his eyes worked overtime in the room's gloom and yet he somehow knew it had been treated to a thorough cleaning in his absence — the bedclothes and linen had been all changed and straightened up — it was as though the room had not been used for days! The air was now heavy with the odor of Lilac!

How?

Who would have done such a sterling job? It now dawned on the man that some **Good Samaritan** had certainly exceeded themselves beyond all limits. Like an unthankful oaf, he went through the apartment to see if anything might have been taken, maybe something import, but then it dawned on him that he hadn't yet aquatinted himself with the place and would have no idea whether or not anything had been lifted by whomever had been pussyfooting about the billet.

Something soft and furry brushed against his legs and he glanced down to see the black stray cat rubbing itself gently against the leg of his trousers. It began purring —as if wanting to be adopted, but Cotter had no inner space for such an option.

"Hey how the shit did you get in? Hey, enough of that..." and nudged the animal away with enough pressure in his movement that it would get the message. *What the hell's the matter with a ma, standing here taking to a dumb animal? Hell, what further proof do I need to damn convince myself that my mind is on the wing? First I'm talking to ghosts and now damn animals!* Frank stooped down and scooped the feline up in his hands and looked into its black face, in this light there was no way of seeing its features, but the touch of fur gave him a comforting feeling. The cat, like a miniature panther, made no effort to squirm free but snuggled in against his chest and rubbed its purring cheek against him. This was a good indication that the creature wasn't feral— it was used of the human touch.

Regardless of that, Frank didn't want to become responsible for something now at this point in his life that would be an encumbrances to him — no sir. He carried the purring cat from the bedroom, across the parlor and out on the landing; he lowered the moggy at the top of the stairway so that it might choose to make its own way to the street below, then as he turned away to signify to the freed animal that it was no longer wanted Frank caught sight of the pet's feeding bowel — he understood the utility's importance and that it looked as though it too had always lived up here. He wondered about it... *Had the cat been Lester's houseguest?*

The cat descended the staircase to the street below, instinctively knowing that it would have to start fending for itself — at least for the time being.

Looking about the kitchen area of the apartment from just inside the door, Frank developed a strong need for a drink, but not that of the Adam's ale type, the firewater, kind. He shuddered as if a spirit had walked over his grave.

Hell, he only needed a nip, a nip to get him through the day or the monkey on his back would drive him to distraction!

It was the sound of music from the nearby theater, which had been following its usual program of plying trade from sunset to sunrise, which penetrated his subconscious. Aahh, yes Ma Kelly's theater was just along the street. Maybe now would be as good a time as any, to make her acquaintance...

Upon arriving at the entrance of the establishment, Frank encountered the Williams brothers. This was a surprise, for it was crystal-clear that they were working here and Frank Cotter felt all mixed up — he was under the impression that the pair work exclusively for Lazarus Rollo, the Chairman of the Cattlemen's Association.

"Well, well, well, well — if it isn't Mister Tenderfoot the pen-pusher!" Reg Williams pointed out to his brother unnecessarily, the latter raised his eyebrows. The fading bruising on his cheek brought the memory of the brothers' run-in with Captain Roscoe and Lieutenant Briggs… Harry gave the new arrival the once over as he ditched the remains of a cheroot butt out on the road, a feral canine came out of nowhere its fur damp with overnight dew, and sniffed a moment at the butt before ascertaining that it wasn't something edible, and wondered off into where some dark shadows were now struggling to remain alive as the day's ever brightening sun still hung short of the distant eastern horizon.

To Frank, there was something familiar about the stray mutt, but he didn't know what — Harry Williams grabbed his full attention.

"…Need one ask what yuh doin' here? We've plenty of female company waiting ter do you proud, ***Mister Cotter!* "** He said sarcastically. Harry moved clear of the doorway so that Cotter might pass on if he so desired.

"They got a bar in there?" the scribe asked, and as if his question was a cue for the orchestra somewhere still out of sight, the musicians struck up their variety of wind, string and percussion instruments.

"Jist beyond the curtains — is the doorway ter paradise!" Reg grinned mischievously.

"Inside you'll find ***all*** Junction City's got ter offer by way of ***sin an' culture.*** There's live theater an' buckets of booze, local and imported … And the lovely open thighs of thar best She Devils outside on Kansas City — the pick is yores! Harry Williams informed Cotter with an ever broadening grin — if it were at all possible, than any brother could produce.

Nodding Frank stepped over the threshold around the curtain into the building, where he promised himself only that one, quick drink, just to get him through the next couple of hours.

7

THE SIGHT BEFORE Cotter was quite unexpected. Here was a combination of a city styled saloon with fancy paneling and mirrors which made the place look a Million Dollars ... slightly off center to this layout was a delightful theater with plush seats on a sloping floor that ran towards the stage, the orchestra pit and the proscenium with front and back stalls, seating. It was difficult to imagine one wasn't at a theater in the heart of New York or Chicago.

Either side of the stage was a couple of doors that led deeper into the building; one was marked *Stages* and the other, **La femes.** A smartly dressed youth in a bellhop's uniform approached Frank, for the man looked quite lost.

"...I hope you weren't expectin' to catch a performance of our current play sir...?" the bellhop asked. Frank looked at him blankly as the youth continued: "The players won't be performing until 8 PM tonight. Maybe you'd like one of these in the mean time..." he proffered one of a handful of *playbills* he had with him.

Frank took up the offer, but right now, Mister Frank Cotter, was more interested in the establishment's bar and its shelving contents by way of hard liquor rather than the grease-painted faces of some second-rate Thespians. "...Excuse me," said Frank as he glanced away from the bellhop and sort an easy path through the theater section to the busy saloon bar. In transit to his destination he spotted the familiar faces of the Captain Roscoe and Lieutenant Briggs at the bar with drinks in their hands; suddenly a dazzling white colored rope was there right across his path — it baulked him; it separating the saloon from the playhouse section. Here a man dressed in tails stood on the other side of the rope, which was fastened to a heavy, highly polished stainless steel, waist-high pole. Without question he unclipped the rope and allowed the scribe to pass through the barrier and refastened the rope back to the pole once he had gone by. As he made his way to the bar he glanced down at the playbill. The play was obviously a drama if one were to put stock in its title: **Rebel in Our Midst** — a play by K. Ardith.

The program read: *To-nite's play is presented with the following cast:*

MARSHALL BALLANTYNE	Mr. David Hyde
CPT. MILLER	Mr. Simon Eddey
MRS. PENNY FRASER	Miss Elspeth Hopgood
MISS BESSE LANE (spy)	Miss Pearl Courtney

This told the scribe what he wanted to know—he closed the playbill and without expecting it, Cotter found himself strolling up to the bar, where there was an open   space between two customers and, he caught the eye of one of the five bartenders and gave his order.

So much for the man being set to get himself together, as vowed only a short time ago… Lieutenant Briggs had been watching the scribe's progress from the time he had come pass the rope. "Get a load of this, Capt.'s…"

Roscoe turned and looked up from his drink and spied Frank Cotter as he neared the bar and began giving his drink order to the barman. "That guy's still alive?" Captain Roscoe remarked in amazement.

"Wonder what accounts fer his late arrival on the scene, Sir?" said Briggs as he got rid of his empty glass on the bar's zinc bar-top behind him without looking.

"No idea. But the effect those drinks we loaded him with, ought to 'ave made a darn corpse out of him," said Roscoe, not knowing how near to the bone he was. The two men watched the unsuspecting soul as he spoke further to the bartender; they were too far away to have any hope of hearing what was being said.

"Excuse me a moment…" Frank said to the bartender who was just about to bolt off to serve another customer as he deposited Cotter's drink on the bar before him. The bartender pause with a raised eyebrow that indicated to scribe that Frank had his attention. "— do you have any idea if a Miss Courtney would be still on the premises? And if so, where I might find her, it's most important."

The man grinned across the bar at Cotter. "Most fellers who wanna see the gals working in this place, consider their business wif them, ***important*** if you get what I mean…" Frank didn't but that was no matter.

"She might be still hangin' around but I ain't seen her since the play finished about eleven last night. If you go out through the door marked **Stags** you might find someone back there who could help ya. But a word in ya shell-like ear… Miss Courtney doesn't work the customers and you might get yuh face slapped in the bargain!" Cotter picked up his shot of liquor and headed towards the door. He ever gave any thought to the fact that calling on any so-called lady at this hour was certainly out of order.

"Look, Captain Roscoe," said Briggs excitedly as he once more called the Captain's attention to Cotter as Doctor Lomax's pal moved in the direction of the door at the side of the stage. "— I'll be stuffed; he's off in search fer some hairy crutch at this time of the day!"

Curiously, Roscoe muttered. "Briggs, you don't suppose that booze we poured into Cotter has done him **more good** — than harm?"

Briggs considered the situation a moment, then, said: "… I wouldn't say he looked an oil paintin' going by his facial color, would you?"

Upon shutting the door behind him, Cotter found himself in a whole New World. To his right there was a short flight of stairs which led to the wings of the stage and from where he stood he could see that the backstage area was still well lit up and he could see a range of windlasses here and there, some painted scenery from the current stage production and some of past shows, and drapes of long stage curtains which disappeared up high out of sight into darkness. Clearly, the backstage was deserted, a long corridor ran from the doorway down the length of the building to the back, where there was obviously some sort of foyer and from here he could see the newel of another staircase, this indicated to Frank that that stairway would connect to the upstairs area of the building. With his drink in hand, he moved down the passage to the foyer where he found it had been converted to an open office and across from the staircase out of sight from anyone using the passageway, against a wall was a leather four-seated sofa.

Sitting here was an over-weight, red-haired lass, very seductively dressed and was obviously a lady of the night. Her dull bored face, sparked into life upon Frank entering the lobby.

"…Hullo love; you lookin' fer dear little ol' me?" The fallen dove almost squealed as she came off the sofa with surprising speed and joined him in the doorway.

"W-would you be Ma Kelly by any chance?" said Frank, for he had no idea what to expect Ma Kelly to look like.

"Hell no darlin' – you've got the wrong kitten. I'm dear, desirable, **Red Bubbles...** Surely you've heard of Bubbles and her specialties?"

Cotter was embarrassed by her pawing, and wanted to back away. "— err actually I'm looking for Miss Pearl Courtney and I guess Ma Kelly."

Bubbles realized right off that this was going to be another customer to slip through her fingers, and took a step back, looked the scribe up and down then went back and flopped down on the sofa with the sound of displacing air.

"You're wastin' yuh time chasing after dear sweet, Pearl." Bubbles told the stranger. "And you must be a stranger in town Mr. Tenderfoot? Otherwise you'd know that **Miss Pearl Courtney** is outa bounds ter the guys, and has been ever since she sashayed in ter Junction City wif her tight little ass."

Frank nodded. "D'you knows how I can get in touch with Miss Courtney? I've got some serious business matters with her..."

"Of course I know how she can be got in touch wif. Right this very minute she is tucked up in her bedroom upstairs catching her beauty sleep."

"She lives here, in this goddamn place?!" Cotter's voice betrayed his surprise and shock, which came about because he had put two and two together about The Theater Royal.

"Don't *you* go gettin' the wrong idea about *our* Miss Courtney!" came a mature woman's voice from near the bottom of the staircase. Bubbles closed shop and Cotter swung in the direction of the voice, he knew the moment he set eyes on the voice's owner, that it had to be none other than Ma Kelly. He turn to face her and watched as she descended the last three steps and made her way across the lobby to take up her seat behind the desk.

"Maybe I ought to introduce myself before we go any farther," said Frank.

"Oh, it's a bit late for that Mr. Cotter," Ma told him with a wave of her jeweled forearm. "I know all I need to know about you and your relationship with Doctor Lomax!"

"…Then you have the advantage," responded Frank as he approached the front of her desk and stood before her.

"I always try to have that in my business…" she turned to Bubbles. "You can call it a night, Red."

Red Bubbles nodded, and readily rose from the sofa and marched across the lobby, then began mounting the stairs, leaving the smell of cheap cologne in her wake.

"So, I guess I owe you a very big thank you for letting me stay over there in Lester's place. I'm sorry about the broken lock, you've got to let me pay for its repair," Frank said as he began to raise the drink from waist high towards his mouth. However Ma Kelly was fast coming off her posterior out of her desk-chair, she swiped the glass of liquor from Cotter's hand, the shot-glass and its whiskey went hurling through the air and crashed onto the carpet runner of the fifth riser of the nearby staircase, completely empty, it came to an abrupt stop still in one piece, Frank Cotter was flummoxed!

Retaking her chair Ma snapped at the newspaperman. "—you've already had quiet enough of that shit!"

"What the —"

"Quiet and open yuh, ears!" Ma Kelly hollered at him — then continued in a more civilized tone. "I'm allowing you ter stay in that apartment only until you can get that goddamn ass of yours aboard a stage back east. Without Lester Lomax here in town, you're as welcome as a goddamn tornado. The Sheriff an' the unofficial King of this town, Lazarus Rollo, have made it plain to me that unless I look after you I shall have trouble keepin' and my other business ventures, as a going concern if I wanna stay in this town and reap the benefits of the incoming railway. So you, sonny Jim, do what's expected of you.

"You may not realize it man, but you are damn lucky to be alive! If it wasn't for Monty Hill, Jonas Bevan and that Limey, James, you'd be up there in a sod on Boot Hill alongside your friend, Lomax. Do I make myself clear?"

"What do you mean?"

"What do *I mean? … I mean* you owe it to them fellers' fer finding you on that vacant allotment when they did. You looked as though you had spent a day or two inside a pickle jar in the sun. Those boys brought you back to my place and we nursed you back to reasonable health. We kept you hid away so no one outside our select group knew where you were. Not even the Sheriff.

"When we reckoned you were well enough to survive, we shipped you off back to Lester's apartment. If I catch you trying to touch another drop of liquor while you're in town I'll personally have yuh guts for gaiters!" Ma stood up and turned around and collected a fur wrap, from a clothes tree alongside her heavy iron Pittsburgh safe. It was an item Frank recognized from the pay room of one of the newspaper rags he had worked.

"Come on now, make yourself useful and walk me an' my son home to bed."

"Bed?— it's almost daylight! Where do you live, exactly Mrs. Kelly?"

"My apartment is diagonally opposite Doctor's surgery." She came out from around her desk and went over to where the upstairs banister joined the newel and gave it a wrap with her knuckles, in less than a minute Ma Kelly's Mongoloid child appeared on the stairs and made his way down to the lobby and where Cotter waited, he became more cautious with each step. "…Mister Cotter, I'd like you to meet Peter, my son." It was plain that Peter was no child he was either in his very late teens or if not, mid-twenties.

But most people could read by his body-language that he had not left his childhood realm as he ought to have. "You remember Mr. Cotter don't you Peter? He was that very sick man, in the room next to Pearl Courtney? She helped Mommy and the girls look after Mr. Cotter and made him all better."

"I must've been in a pretty bad way," said Frank. "I can't recall any of what you have told me Mrs. Kelly. Not a thing."

She nodded, "I don't expect you would. But Pete here will soon remember, won't you dear …?" Her son nodded — his movements were exaggerated.

"And Pearl, err, Miss Courtney, she saw me in that condition?"

Ma Kelly began to help Peter on with a coat as she nodded in answer to Cotter's question; "And while yuh in town you can refer to me as 'Ma Kelly' the same as the rest of the town folks, does. I wuz never the marryin' kind and this here wee feller of mine, wuz God's little joke on me —I guess you might say.

"Pete's a fine boy and you'll find his heart is always in the right place … C'mon Pete, leave the coat alone for Mommy you'll find it's cold this early —and stop playing with your fly or I'll cut yuh finger off!"

"Tell me, Ma … when's the best time to catch Miss Pearl Courtney. I want to have a talk to her about a few things, seeing as she was Lester's Ward."

"Who told you that? Pearl being Lester's Ward?" asked Ma Kelly.

Her question caused Frank to frown. "I think it was either Hill or Bevan — not sure now I come to think of it …" Ma and Peter set off along the long corridor in the direction towards the playhouse with Cotter on their tails. When they entered the theater-cum-saloon the place lacked any sight of patrons, save for the night shift cleaners who continued on with their chores to refurbish the establishment for the expected parade of customers they knew would likely pass through its doors — the owner and her troupe made their way directly to the front exit, Harry and Reg were at the door leading out onto the sidewalk and when Harry saw them approaching he came forward.

"You ready to be escort home, Ma?" asked Harry.

"Mister Cotter is going to do the honors, Harold, aren't you kind sir?" Ms. Kelly said with a turn of her head in the scribe's direction.

"So it seems, seeing as we're heading pretty much the same direction." Harry Williams looked put out.

"I've balanced the books a little earlier and the takings are safe and sound in the Pittsburgh. So, we'll jist amble along and I'll leave it to you and yuh brother ter work-out who's gonna work late…" Ma turned her son round to face in the uptown direction and it was as though she had released him from a dog-chain — Peter took off like a colt hungry for its freedom. "By the way, Reg, I'm running those stables of mine for profit, if you ride any more of my fillies without buyin' a saddle, it'll come out of yuh wages. Do we understand one another?"

Williams nodded without a word, and watch their departure with narrow, bitter eyes. *I'd like ter see that old bat take a fall and skin her bloody fat knees!* Reg thought as he went inside. *…She's sure to get robbed some night and I'll make damn sure I'm slow ter respond. Maybe Harry an' I ought to arrange it — what an idea!*

The old gal waddled along the sidewalk with Cotter by her side. Peter was in the middle of the plank sidewalk, delighting in the noise his stomping on the boardwalk made. He found a loose board and gave it a punishing, trying to no doubt break through it to the ground below, but the failed effort soon tired him of that, and he ran off further ahead of them until he came to a water-trough for livestock. He climbed up into the trough and stood there in water in his ankle-high boots and began stamping his feet, water was sent everywhere about the area in a half-yard radius and sloshed out over the sides of the trough onto the ground. Peter continued to enjoy himself in this way while Frank and Ma Kelly caught him up.

"…Without your generosity I'd be dead on my feet, that's for sure," Cotter told the fat woman. Ahead of them on the street, was the late doctor's black cat, the sun had just tipped the eastern horizon at the back of them and the first of the sun's rays reflected off the high gable roof of the surgery's building, it was going to be a glorious morning.

Ma shot the city slicker an askance look, then added: "You ought not to be too ready with your "thanks" Mr. Cotter. You haven't been hit with any of my bills, yet. I'm not going out of pocket for Aaron Yolson's services!"

Frank knew that things were looking too good to be true; his face took on a more countenance expression. Having notice the change which her words had made to the newspaperman as well as that of his body language now coming to the fore, Ma Kelly knew she had been taken rather seriously, even though that was not what she wanted — in reality she got a kick out of turning much of life's hardships into a joke, as was the case here. She had no intentions of charging Cotter any rent, as Lester always kept his rent in advance, prior to his untimely death. Besides, there were no prospective tenants on the immediate horizon. Better to have this easterner there than leave the building empty so that squatters wouldn't be able to commandeer the place. Ma decided to let the poor feller off the hook.

"Hey, ***c'mon*** big boy — I'm only kiddin' yuh!" Kelly dug Frank in the ribs so he would understand that she was only joshing with him. Frank then experienced the best laugh at himself than he had had in ages especially when he realized what he must have looked like with a hound dog expression all over his face.

"You're a devil of a woman, Ma Kelly! Having a poor feller like me on for the duration... So, these ideas folks have *of you* being as tough as nails, aren't all that true, hey? "

Grinning she said: "Oh, I have my moments Mister Cotter — I have my moments."

Suddenly the panther-like black cat dashed into view from its hiding place, a recessed doorway of the shop directly opposite the exterior staircase to Lomax apartment, the cat's

fur coloring became a perfect camouflage as the animal became invisible, once it found the last vestiges of the night cling in areas where the new day's light had not reached.

Neither commented on the illusion but continued along the sidewalk to draw alongside the trough of water and Peter — "Are you feeling any better now you're on your feet, Cotter …?

"Pete … you get out ***now***." Ma Kelly snapped at her son and went back to her conversation with Cotter. While Peter Kelly became quickly disappointed looking, and ran the short length of the trough before being forced to hurdle out of it to land with a crashing on the boardwalk a yard or so ahead of the couple. "…I'm sorry I got so mad at you about your drink, but now is the worst possible time you could touch the stuff!"

He nodded. "I know that now — but I needed it to steady my nervous before meeting Miss Pearl Courtney. I don't know what I was thinking, expecting her to be still working and on her feet at that hour. I just wasn't thinking straight."

"Boozy Frank has gotta watch out for that."

Cotter nodded. They had come to the end of the boardwalk on the corner of Bryan and Starr Streets. Frank wasn't sure how much further he was expected to go with the *Madam,* Peter was across the road under the awning of the corner building, Ma Kelly's own private apartment was perched on top of the ground flood business house and the intersection. Peter by now had found a new interest, he was bemused by an abandoned dog's turd on the boardwalk and as the moments went by he became more taken by its shape and texture, so much so, that he looked ready to squat down and explore it with his fingers...

"Call in at the theater later today and you'll be able to catch up with Pearl, it might be a good idea if you two do meet — **Pete!**" Ma

Kelly called to her boy. "...**touch that with those *hands*** and Mommy'll break every goddamn bone in your fingers!" The retard backed off with eyes still fixed on the animal feces. Ma knew her son, and immediately had no problems with accepting that he would listen to her. No disobedience, here.

"Right," said Frank. "I'll take your advice, Ma."

"And where did you meet up wif Messrs. Hill and Bevan?" asked the hotelier.

Frank began toying with the knot of his cravat as he answered Ma's question.

"Up at Lester's gravesite: That is also where I saw Miss Pearl Courtney *my* mystery woman.

"Heck, Hill an' Bevan is a couple of characters, it's plain what they are about..." But before he could add more, Ma sharply cut him short.

"They ***were friends*** of your Doctor Lomax—" she reminded Cotter.

"Yes. They made sure of telling me that. Business partners I believe — in whatever it was they were in with him; they are part of a syndicate. His moneymen I believe? However, I've not mixed with Lester in some time, I can tell you, they weren't his type. They strike me to be a pair of faggots, are they not?"

Ma nodded and her two chins took the shock wave with ease. "... Does it matter?" Her facial expression confirmed to Frank that his suspicions were well founded.

"Not to me," shrugged Cotter. "The way I see it, they'll play no part in my life once I've shaken the dust of this town from the soles of my boots. It's just that being a onetime newspaper man I'm curious about things. Like the way Lester died. Accidents are a part of life from time to time, and some even amount to a few unfathomable mysteries, strange as it may seem, I have this growing feeling that in Lester's case that is what we have here, a mystery of sorts. There is something about my friend's accident that sticks in my craw."

Ma sighed. "...Mebbe. But one reality I can put to yuh and it'll do you good to know and remember. You owe your life ter Hill and Bevan."

"So I understand."

"Then show 'em some respect and gratitude!"

Cotter nodded. "Yes — you are right, sorry."

"That's more like it. Now you'll have ter excuse me but it's getting near our bedtime… c'mon Pete; bedtime."

Peter turn around to face down Bryan Street's sidewalk, in the direction of Main Street. Then like a school kid, skipped along the sidewalk until he came to an open doorway which led from the building to Bryan Street's sidewalk and disappeared through the aperture which obviously led to a flight of stairs that climbed all the way up to the next floor level, in essence served as both the entrance and back door of the above, self-contained, apartment. As yet unknown to Cotter this was where Ma Kelly and her Mongolian son lived, virtually overlooking the intersection of Starr and Bryan Streets. So when Frank allowed his eyes to scan the building line, he now realized where Madam Kelly dwelt.

"So that's where you live?" Frank said as he gestured with his head to Ma's lodgings.

"That's correct. Right overlooking the intersection where dear Lester lost his life," she admitted, with a growing sadness that she did not even wish to deny or cover up.

"Does the intersection experience many accidents a year? — I realize that not all of them would be fatalities, like Lester's," said Frank.

"That's true. Not unless folks start ridin' blind mules or horses. No. That's the only real serious accident I can recall being there since I've been in Junction City. I had   that piece of land over there where the surgery now stands, built it from scratch. It was a weed chocked lot for ages."

"You weren't around when Lester had his accident, by any chance?"

"Why, do you wanna know?" Ma Kelly said with interest.

"Well by what I've managed to put together about the accident, the intersection was just about crawling with people, witnesses. It's purported that Lester's own attorney called out to him from somewhere across the street and this contributed greatly to the accident, especially when Lester made a spur of the moment decision to dash across the street in his direction — bang, this loaded wagon was there and on top of him before anyone seemed to have seen it!"

"Even doctor Lester," said Ma Kelly.

"Yeah — even Doc Lester. He apparently was walking out with Hill and Bevan, who are all now prime witnesses to the mess."

"I went very close to see it too, you know?" Ma Kelly announced as she began to look about for her wayward son. He had returned to the street when his mother hadn't arrived to open the door to their apartment and was now straddled an empty tie-rail outside a building in Bryan street, he was making like he was on a wooden pony. Having satisfied herself of his whereabouts she continued: "…I wuz out in my kitchen, surrounded by all the noise going on around me, when suddenly I sensed this strange over bearing quiet, a dead silence. I sensed something bad had happened out on the street, I ran into our parlor, its window overlooks the intersection, jest as Lester's parlor window does…"

Frank felt obliged to encourage her. "What did you see?"

"Well, I never saw the actual incident, per se, but the aftermath. The wagon had come to a halt in the middle of the intersection, and people were hurrying to this figure of a man lying on the ground protrudin' halfway out from beneath the back of the wagon. People were rushing towards the person, whom I didn't at the time know, wuz Lester. I saw Bevan and Hill and recognized Lester's lawyer in the thick of it. Some folks were gathering about the wagon driver who wuz walking around frantically in circles, wringing his hands and hollering for a Doctor! By now Lester's friends had started to get organized and were preparin' ter carry him over under the awning of his veranda outside the surgery… when they got there I knew they'd be out of sight from me because of the angle —"

Cotter cut in. "You see, I can't get around the fact that in all this, there doesn't appear to be a single, independent witness," Frank pointed out. "Everyone in some way is an associate of Lester — either a friend or a business affiliate. That fact alone seems to give it a surreal suspicious atmosphere, in my book…"

"That's not true about there not being an independent witness," Ma Kelly added. "Although I did my best ter get down stairs ter see what I might be able to do; I saw someone else helpin' Lester's friends. He had taken Lester's head an' shoulders so they might keep the body straight and level — I saw it from my window before fetching a towel for the bleeding…"

"Poor Lester," muttered Frank Cotter as he visualized the scene. "So as he was being conveyed from the road to the sidewalk, he had no idea his very life was ticking away!"

"What's that you say?" Ma Kelly asked.

"That Lester only had at the most a few minutes left to live — and still he tried to deal with matters he knew were vital to other peoples' lives."

"How, do you work that out?" asked Ma Kelly with a curiously.

"Why that's what Bevan and Monty Hill led me to believe, they swear he was conscious and functioning quite well, though he had no idea his life was ebbing away!" Frank Cotter focused on the mature woman's features.

"I don't understand," she said, barely above a whisper. "No, No, No — that's impossible!" responded Ma, "How could anyone believe that Lomax was still alive, after being bowled over like that?" She shuddered at the very thought of it. "— I wuz at my window trying ter figure the quickest and safest way down to them— I'm no ballerina, an' most of the time I move like a beached whale! I can't afford to have a goddamn tumble down my stairs, I've got Pete to think of ... but as long as I live and breathe, I tell you I saw five men transport our dear friend over to the sidewalk, an' they were most certainly carrying a dead man!"

"Now *I am* confused," Frank looked across the empty intersection at where the fatal accident had taken place. He could not have expected to see anything still there in the dirt, which would indicate the exact spot. Instead saw a very small bird the size of a cotton-reel pecking in the dirt, its breed was unknown to him, and it flew off just as Ma Kelly began to speak, it was as though the sound of her voice had alarmed it ...

Kelly shook her head. "...What would be the purpose? Boston had enough people who witnessed the accident. The whole thing was nothing more than a nasty accident. I and a lot of the others went back to our own places and only bothered about takin' care of business."

"Did you, or would you recognize this feller in the brown, again?"

"I think not. He didn't at any time look up in my direction. When I got downstairs, he had gone. He wuz nuthin' special, jest an ordinary looking feller ter me—I didn't pay him any heed, Lester wuz my main, worry!"

Frank's brow was getting clammy... he raised his hat slightly so it would catch some of the morning breeze moving through the intersection. He had no idea if his clamminess was due to his growing tension or was his body crying out for another fix of alcohol. "Maybe you should tell the Sheriff what you've just been telling me…"

"And your point, **being…?**"

"Well, it might assist the inquiry into Lester's death, I think." Cotter pointed out to her.

"Inquiry? Why, what'd be the good of an *Inquiry?* It all looks straight up an' down ter me. Besides, I don't reckon Klem Boston's gonna force an Inquiry and cause the Government to send out a special judge to hear the case before the regular circuit judge comes through."

"Whether you reckon there should or should not be an Inquiry held into Lester's death is beside the point."

"Do you think Sheriff Boston will be ordering one? I don't. I think he's happy with things they way they are. He's the man who would have ter set that ball rolling."

"And you don't think he will?" Cotter asked.

Ma Kelly shook her head.

"Well, Ma, I can tell you, *I for one* will be pushing for such an Inquiry whether Mister Sheriff Klem Boston likes it or not—an Inquiry brings closure to matters such as this and *I* wanna see 'closure', even if it mean a bit of serious law management for a change on Boston's part."

"Mister Cotter—" she sounded like she was lecturing a person with the same intellect as that of her son. "Back east I realize folks do things with a bit more finesse than we folks here might. But then you've got Judges and Attorneys the size of a tribe it makes it so much easier. Here, we have to wait months for a judge to hear to our legal business, an' I fer one, can understand Sheriff Boston's approach when it is an accident that's as open and shut as this. Look, if I thought it needed rising I'd've mentioned this fifth feller to Klem. Should it turn out that Boston is gonna call and inquiry, I'll come forward to verify the existence of this feller in brown — though I can't see it being any good, as he can't be identified."

"Aahh, but wouldn't it be civilized to have an open inquiry? … Who knows, he might even come forward himself if town gossip reaches his ears? Just knowing he exists, puts another slant on things. Back there you said that Lester appeared to be already dead, then how was it he was able to make certain stipulations about the welfare of myself and Miss Courtney?"

"I don't know, I'm no Greek Oracle" Ma Kelly retorted.

"Right…" Cotter's shoulders, slumped. "Look I've kept you away from your bed long enough, you must be worn out after such a long night?" suggested Cotter.

"That's for sure… even you with your conditions still needs plenty of bed time, if you want to get back on top of this alcoholic business…" They began to prepare to go their separate ways but as Ma Kelly left she reminded Frank not to forget to get in touch with Miss Courtney. "We run three performances of the play tomorrow, oh, that's today, my mistake. There is a matinee, around two P.M. and two performances during the night. I suggest you see her at the end of her performances of the night shift, that way if you have an upsetting meeting — it won't affect her work."

"I'll go along with anything you suggest, Ma'am. Anything for a quiet life, 'bye…"

"Yes, goodbye — Pete, c'mon, bed…" She called to her son who still played happily on the tie-rail.

Frank turned toward the surgery across the street, but before stepping down from the sidewalk he checked to make sure it was clear to cross the dirt road, for he was only too conscious that this part of Junction City had proved to be a dangerous part of town. As he strode out for the sidewalk steps ahead of him he glanced back over his shoulder to his right and saw that a Milliner's occupied the ground floor under Ma Kelly's apartment. Then, before he realized it, Frank was in the act of mounting the very steps which Lester had no doubt descended, on his unrealized appointment with destiny. Here he paused and studied the undressed boardwalk, was he doing this out of respect for the memory of his dear friend or was he being morbid, and in truth looking for some blood stain left behind where his friend's bleeding cadaver might have rested?

Cotter shoved both hands down inside the side pockets of his frock coat and in the bottom of his left-hand pocket found an old pre-rolled cigarette that had been there for some time. Even some of the dry tobacco had fallen out either end, but it was still worthy of smoking. He put it in his mouth and found the one only match there, in the same pocket. He crossed to the window of the Lomax's surgery and struck the match on the glass pane and torched the end of his smoke. At the same time he peeped in through the glass and studied the surgery's waiting room and the medical equipment he could see there in, gathering dust.

From where he stood there was very little to see and his warm breath began to manufacture condensation on the pane that could have used a feather-duster on it to remove some of the street dust which had settled over its surface.

The interior of the waiting room looked too spooky to hold Frank's interest and he made his way east along Starr Street until he came to the end of the building and turned in and safely ditching what was left of his smoke he carefully climbed the outside stairs. The angle of the staircase reminded him of the sloping side of an Egyptian pyramid he had once climbed when he was in a much better physical condition than he was today. As he began the climb he knew it was going to be beyond him to reach the landing in the one trek. He gave himself credit for being foolhardy enough to have made the effort to come down them in the first place when he came to in the bedroom. It showed him just how dangerous a life he had been leading since alcohol had taken over his body and soul.

*Just take it one step at a time…*He told himself as he followed his mind's thinking. The moment he began to feel light-headed he paused and looked east out at the new the new day that had to mature more before it could claim the title. Eventually well enough to push on, he took it even damn easier, and was glad when he reached the landing where he paused and looked out over the nearby rooftops while he continued to recover from what felt like altitude sickness. He lowered his eyes to the false front façades of the buildings on the same side of the street as The Theater Royal, he let his eyes descend even more and finally they focused on the damp boards of the sidewalk, the result of being exposed to the night's dew — owing to the broken gaps in the almost continuous veranda awnings. In a still dark recess, the doorway of a vacant shop, opposite the water trough where Peter Kelly had taken a spontaneous footbath— Frank sensed there was someone lurking in its dingy interior. This was weird, because he hadn't seen or heard anyone out there on the street. But then again, it might be one of those so-called Army spies keeping tabs on him. If so, he hoped that the spy caught himself a dose of pneumonia in the process of his clandestine activities. Frank crossed the landing and drew open the unlocked door and slipped into the apartment, which proved to be a few nicely welcomed degrees warmer than outside, he owed this to the dying fire left in the grate of the Benjamin Franklin, stove.

He dumped his hat on the table and discovered that the candle in the holder had been left alight and had burnt down to within half an inch of its base, the rim was full to nearly over flowing with tallow, it was in the act of solidifying.

Frank took hold of the candle's holder and took it and what remained of the candle with him into the bed room, where he fired up the remainder of what was left of the wick of the candle-butt and undressed by its lamination; the fresh nightshirt he had selected, reeked of camphor… a perfume he was well accustom too — since his nursery days; he buried himself within the cover of Lester's bed, rightly assuming that he would drift away into a much welcomed, slumber.

When Cotter woke from his dreamless sleep it was quite dark in the bedroom and he did not have the slighted idea how long he had slept. He was conscious that it must have been one hell of a long doze though. He carefully climbed from the bed and went to douse himself in the washing basin, the water he had left there was stale smelling from his last lot of ablutions. His nightshirt's weight was a nuisance to him as he padded back across the room on his bare feet in the direction of the parlor and stubbed his toe on the foot-leg of the bed in passing, his fault; because he realized that he ought to have got a candle or lamp going before traipsing about the apartment. He was sure he had lifted a flap of skin on his small toe and he might end up having to wrap it with a clean piece of toe rag…But nonetheless, knowing this didn't stop him from cussing himself for his stupidity.

In the parlor he found the room being lighted from a clear easterly moon, its pale light washed in through the east windows and half-glassed door, all, which faced out onto the landing. He was thankful that the windows and door were draped with lace Café curtains or the apartment's dining area and sitting room would have been blacked out. He got a lamp going and examined the damage he had done to his toe. It was not a pretty sight but for now he would have to grin and bear it. He tidied up the wound to his foot and wrapped the toe as promised with rag then took the risk of getting dressed without so much as a rinse, for he had to go and meet this Miss Pearl Courtney as he had promised Ma Kelly. He found Lester's toilet water and wet his face and behind his ears quite liberally with it, brushed his "nest-like" hair into a reasonable state for he was sure in the presence of a Lady he would be expected to remove his hat. He found the playbill and checked it out once more before leaving for the theater, then set off…

The same bellhop as before had ushered Cotter backstage through the door signed *"Stags"* and led him up the steps that led to the right wing of the stage. It was quite obvious that he was acting on the directions of Ma Kelly; otherwise no member of the public would have been privileged to this taste of theater life. The actors, prior to the stage curtain having been lowered, had frozen in their movements like life-like statues and held their poses without blinking until the curtain had become a barrier between them and their audience. Then seeming without any signal, all the still-life Thespians came to life and stepped completely out of their stage character; this transformation also transferred itself to the backstage theater hands who moved swiftly into action as they, in surprising silence flocked on stage and began dismantling unwanted flats and hauling in the next set and stage props.

As providence would have it, Pearl Courtney made her exit to the very wing where Frank Cotter waited. As she approached him Frank could see that she was pretty much bathed in perspiration and certainly looked as thirsty as she must have felt. She made a beeline to a canvas water-bag hanging on a wall peg not far from Cotter. Pearl poured herself a liberal amount of water into a tin mug that had been attached to the vessel with platted string. The entire town's water, had a slightly brackish taste but it was eventually acceptable after one had been on it a month.

Stage riggers ducked in and around the actors who either went to a nearby skip for a costume change or grabbed a quick bite to eat from a food hamper spread out on a nearby picnic table in an out of the way corner, though off-stage space was pretty cramped as the scribe learned. Meanwhile, the players were individually praying to themselves that they wouldn't lose the mood he or she had set-up with the audience out there across the foot-lamps; for if this mood wasn't sustainable, then the players had failed, in their craft and they had been sweating their dear hearts out for nothing. This is why the stagehands' and their skill at striking a set and getting another up in its place with lightning speed was so essential.

"Miss Pearl Courtney…?" Frank asked on approach.

The actress turned in his direction — Cotter thought he saw a smidgen of recognition register in the young woman's eyes, maybe she did recognize him from their passing up at Boot Hill; but she straightaway masked the emotion as only one could expect from an actor with any class, and looked at Cotter quite blankly.

"— Frank Cotter, perhaps you've heard of me?" He said to allow her time to maybe reconsider her non-committal attitude. Then added: "…I'm a friend or *was* a friend of Doctor Lester Lomax."

"Oh, I see…" Her voice still held its stage projection quality about it.

Frank continued on, his voice held at one's normal pitch and hopped that it would encourage her to speak in a normal voice, though having never encountered the young lady before, did not know whether once she had developed a "stage voice" could revert back to that of the normal populous.

"Thirty seconds!" called the Stage-manager from his overseer's chair in the wings. The stage call would have only been heard by those behind the theater's fire curtain, to ensure some form of backstage privacy for actors and stagehands alike.

It was clear that Miss Pearl Courtney did not wish to be dealing with him at the moment, and hissed for him to come backstage after the third and last act, then right on cue she made her stage entrance. But Frank had already made up his mind that he was not going to be played like a trout — he planted his feet firmly on the floor and was determined to stay put until all this play-acting was through for the night.

Finally, as the woman spy, Miss Courtney was put to death before a Northern Army firing squad, and then her limp body was carried shoulder-high from the stage by a couple of two bit-players. Where once in the wings the pallbearers lowered her to her feet and moved off to take their curtain call.

Discovering Cotter still backstage sent her off looking for the stage manager to inform him that she wasn't in a position to take any curtain calls, tonight. It was easy to see in her face that she was angry about being forced into this position by the scribe playing at his own game. But at least now she was talking in a voice short of using her stage voice and she was at least proving to be human. The newspaperman could feel himself growing pesky with Lester's ward, and he made no bones about letting it show through in his demeanor, even though he was forced to trail her deep backstage to a steep 10-foot set of stairs which led down below stage level to the theater's dressing rooms — which housed five long low-ceiling rooms, two of them had been fitted out to serve as dressing rooms for the cast; they remained housed the costume department etc. This theater did not cater for a star system, all players or dancers were forced to dress and rest off-stage in rooms which were simply designed to their gender by the simple wording of *Ladies* or *Gentlemen* on the appropriate door. Pearl pushed open her door and entered a room large enough in length to accommodate at least a dozen people. Here Frank noted two cane woven costume skips and a vanity set of drawers, the latter was where the actress or performer might apply her make-up. Although the lids were shut down on both clothing skips, one skip had the bodice of a dress caught halfway in it.

Courtney grudgingly offered Frank a seat on a milkmaid's stool while she went and sat in a rattan chair before her vanity mirror. Cotter had to get the hang of sitting on the three-legged stool before he felt safe. Alone in the room with a female stranger made Cotter feel slightly ill at ease while Miss Courtney seemed reasonable relaxed. A couple of kerosene lamps were already a light on the chest before the mirror and these afforded her to make use of the oval looking glass as she prepared to remove her greasepaint with an oily face cream.

Seated with trepidation on the stool, Frank said: "...I must say that I enjoyed the play, Miss Courtney — you were *very* good. As a newspaperman, I did a stint as a theater critique, so I know what I'm speaking about..." Pearl surprised the scribe when she suddenly pulled off her stage-wig, for Frank had taken it for granted that he had been looking at her own hair, but now her own locks had been exposed he much   preferred the real thing to the false wig she used for her stage work. Once recovered from the shock he continued. "I expect that Ma Kelly told you I would be calling on you sometime today? Lester and I have been friends for nigh on twenty years..."

"I see. Well, Lester never talked about his friends to me," she lied, but Frank had no way of knowing this. She leant down and opened a cupboard level with her own shank. Inside was a bottle of unopened bourbon, Pearl set it down amongst here stage grease-paint sticks and powders on top of her vanity. "Would you like a drink?"

The thought of bourbon was very tempting, but he already had enough regrets as to how readily he had yield to the ugly side of liquor. On the spur of the moment he decided to test his willpower and made a concerted effort at holding the monster at bay.

"I'll pass if you don't mind," he told her with a wave of his hand.

"I don't mind. It was a present from an admirer but I would much prefer to sell it back to Ma Kelly, anyway." Pearl Courtney informed Cotter. "Mom Kelly pays her legitimate actors the bare minimum … Why did you wish to see me, Mr. Cotter?" She returned to working on what make-up she had left on her face.

"I wanted to get to know a little bit more about Lester and his activities…" he watched her wipe the last of what was left of the face-cream and make-up from her face, using a clean piece of rag. *H'm. I must change that toe rag of mine on my toe before bed,* he thought. "— In part he has become somewhat of a stranger to me."

"Lester's dead, or haven't you heard?" she said, trying to be sardonic towards Cotter. "So what more is there one can say? Everything he stood for **and did** is now all in the past tense."

"Look. I got the impression that he somehow become pretty close to you? Closer, than most guardians … Were you quite fond of Lester — he was quite a remarkable rogue as *I* remember him?" The rooms below the stage felt a bit on the close side for Cotter, he produced a hanky with which to wipe his brow — he did not realize it yet but his clamminess was another symptom of his body's need for alcohol.

Pearl frowned in Cotter's direction. "Why ask me something like that? That's not something **you'd ask** a stranger… and we are **strangers,** Mr. Cotter. Besides, I've hardly started to live life. I don't know how one would interpret my feelings towards Lester…All I know is, that when I heard of Lester's death — something inside me died along with him — and I wished I had died, too!"

Frank lost all confidence sitting on the stool and rose to stand with feet apart but found he was swaying slightly for no accountable, reason. "I met two of Lester's friends up at the cemetery… Monty Hill, Jonas Bevan. How well do you know them? They claim to be Lester's business associates, but failed to mention what their business was, exactly. Have you any ideas on that?" *I hope she cannot tell that I know things she may not want me to know. This is a test I must apply to her to ascertain how genuine she is…*

"No, I know very little about them."

Frank looked at Pearl suspiciously. "I find that hard to believe. The three of you were up at Lester's grave side when I showed up," he exclaimed. "And I might add those gentlemen, struck me to be a couple of strange coves. I, for the life of *me,* can't see them being Lester's type. Are they Southerners?"

She shook her head. "…I know whom you mean — Southerners? Who knows? And now the war's over aren't we supposed to be prepared to bury the hatchet?" she let go a shudder that was barely susceptible; but it projected the impression to Frank that she wasn't too keen on the pair. *Why so?* He thought, but could not think of an answer.

Courtney went on, "According to all reports, they were with Lester at the time of his accident. They claim to be carrying out Lester's last wishes and gave me an envelope of money. It was appreciated, especially as Lester's death just came out of the blue!"

Looking over Pearl's shoulder at her reflection in the looking glass, Frank said: "For a man in the throes of death, Lester must've proved himself a remarkable fellow; so clear headed that he remembered his fellow man. He instructed the Southerners to look out for me, too. This all suggests that he couldn't have been in all that much pain at the time. But Ma Kelly's account of the incident refutes pretty much what they said and acted as if their claims are impossible."

Pearl's brow furrowed like a farmer's field. "What did she say?"

"She told me the man she saw after being run over by the loaded wagon was most certainly dead! He was in no position to issue out any instructions to anyone. Even his features were crushed in the accident so badly that according to her, his brains were almost hanging out —"

"Just suppose there was an Inquiry held tomorrow, how do you think, it would turn out?" asked Lester's ward.

"Stop it! Please Stop it!!" Pearl screamed at Cotter's reflection. "Stop such horrible talk— I beseech you!!!"

Cotter blinked his eyes uncontrollably as a result of Peal's hysterical reaction for a few moments, as he focused on their reflection in the looking-glass, and then stepped back.

Pearl clearly made an effort to get control of her outburst and succeeding, continued: "I had a talk to Doctor Hallway later, and he told me that Lester was quite lucid for a dying man, and ***that*** struck him as being unconventional..." Courtney turned her rattan chair to face Cotter, her back now to the oval mirror.

"You've spoken to this Doctor Hallway?" asked Frank in amazement as he wiped his hanky across his chin.

"Yes," Pearl nodded. She went on to study Cotter's features and realized just how ill at ease he appeared, and in fact how pale his face had become just since their arrival in the dressing room. *This Cotter feller doesn't look too healthy, in fact, if he keeps going on like this he may very well need the services of a Doctor* — she thought, but said: "Hallway knew Lester well. He treated Lester whenever the need arose. In fact, when the accident occurred the doctor wasn't far away and was able to attend to Lester almost immediately, so I'm told."

The more I hear about this damn accident the more jumbled up the facts seem to be, Thought Frank. *I've got Ma Kelly on one hand saying that Lester was dead and it looked in some ways to her that he would have died instantly according to his injuries. Then I have two people who no one disputes, who were right there when it happened and they say that Lester was conscious enough to issues out orders, his doctor, says he was lucid. Someone has got things very badly wrong somehow. How very bloody strange?*

"This accident of Lester's has got me so confused I honestly can't think, straight." Frank confessed to Pearl Courtney. "And you were right when you shouted me down a while back there. I owe you an apology for being such an inconsiderate fool! ...I've no excuse, none at all. It's just the accident doesn't sit right with me!"

Courtney turned back to the mirror and checked herself over, saying, "So to ***you,*** the accident sounds, fishy?"

He sighted. "In some ways, yes; the only way to really sort the whole thing out would be for an Inquiry into the whole thing. But that's only my opinion."

"That is not gonna happen," said Pearl as she pushed back her chair and upon standing and turned to Frank, no doubt studying his features.

"So Ma Kelly explained to me," Frank muttered with a shrug and stepped out of Pearl's way, allowing her a clear passage toward the door. He fell into step alongside her.

"Do you understand the reason no one wants an Inquiry?" Pearl said.

"Yes. Out here the law is just too lazy to instigate it. Seems to me to be a very poor excuse; But then I reckon this Sheriff Boston is a pretty poor excuse for a lawman in my humble opinion, anyway. As long as I spend time in this town it is gonna eat at me that Lester never got a fair shake…"

"I'm no soothsayer, plus, I wasn't there when Lester met his Waterloo. But in more ways than one, it sure smells as though some meat has gone off, somewhere. Maybe, maybe I'm trying to make something out of nothing, who knows? "said Frank as they made their way back to the corridor which in turn led to both the auditorium and the reception lobby of the high-class brothel, Frank realized that he had not got as much out of Miss Pearl Courtney as he had hoped, and that maybe she was much shrewder than he gave the lady credit for.

"Are you settled in at Lester's place, what's it been – close to a week now since you arrived, right?" Pearl said this suddenly.

Frank nodded, "That's about right."

"I was being naughty with you in my dressing room. Lester did explain everything about your coming and what type of work you would be doing for him."

Frank jumped in on her. "You're more informed about things than I am, that's for certain."

"Yes, but only because I'm a part of this town, remember?" Pearl nodded. "You don't appear to realize what you've been through yourself, do you?"

"What do you mean?"

"You don't know that you have been pretty near to death yourself the last few days, do you? You were found a living mess on a vacant block of land where your drinking pals had left you to die –"

"What are you on about, Ma'am?" the Easterner asked, his face projecting bewilderment from every pore.

"Ma Kelly and the gals practically brought you back from near death. You were nursed back to health by a group of us in secret up there in Lester's apartment – Ma, Ruby and I spoon-fed you gallons of broth to help you pull out of your delirium. I hope you appreciate all what we've done for you? ”

"You are telling me, that you gals were my Guardian Angels?" asked the tenderfoot

"That's, right, Mister Big City Man." She said as her eyes looked about to shed a tear or two – but she controlled herself with some effort.

Frank felt enormously indebted to them and said: "Let me put it to you this way. If I had half a million, no, say a million dollars, I'd give the lot to all you womenfolk – every red cent of it, truly. But then, I haven't even got a lousy hundred buck!"

Pearl laughed out loud, her first real laugh since Lester's death. "Let me say this, if I had a hundred bucks, I **would** feel like a Millionaire!"

"Hey, wouldn't we all?" beamed Frank. "Being serious for a moment, can you give me any idea why the United States Government would be so interested in Lester and his affairs, that they'd send a couple of strong-arm chums 'round to breaking into his private apartment?

"Seems that his dear friends in Washington – put this Captain Roscoe and Lieutenant Briggs up to it; something to do, about Lester's business dealings with the Indians in the area, by what I've worked out for myself!"

"Whatever Lester was doing for the Pawnee Indians and the others of the county were for their own good. He never bothered trying to explain the medical side of his life to me because he knew it was all beyond my understanding. But whatever it was he was trying to do for them, cost a lot of money to develop and that is where those two strange Southerners come in. They had the means of getting the money Lester needed. Do you think those Army men found what they were looking for?"

Frank shook his head. "Whatever it was they were after – I reckon they drew a blank. That's just my feeling, otherwise they wouldn't have done what they did to me, nor would they still be hanging around Junction City. You wouldn't have any idea what they are after, would you, Pearl, err, I mean Miss Courtney?"

She shook her head, "No."

"Now it's my turn to ask you a question, d'you mind?"

"Just ask away…" Frank told her.

"Lester allowed me to leave a few things up there in his wardrobes, things which would grow legs and move away of their own accord if they were kept here in my room. Do you understand?"

Cotter nodded. He too had had that experience before, himself.

"Would you mind if I came and collected them sometime, I don't feel that I have a right to leave them there any more now that Lester's, well, you know…"She waved a hand.

"That's up to you. But they can stay there if you like, it means nothing to me!"

"No, not while those two men from Washington are on the loose. I'd feel safer if they were with me."

Frank and Pearl entered the hallway and together they headed to the foyer of the brothel, it seemed second nature to Pearl Courtney, not because she was employed as a fallen dove, for this wasn't at all true, but because she roomed in the upstairs' quarters.

"Have you eaten as, yet?" Pearl asked Frank

"Not anything you could call worth-while…"

"That's settled then, let me buy you dinner out front?"

"Shouldn't the boot be on the other foot?" Frank said.

Pearl smiled and said, "It would be if you were a man of means, but we know you're not. No come and join some of the cast out front, Mom picks up the tab for us as long as we are bringing in the crowds…" They changed direction and headed off for the front of house but Frank was puzzled, why out of all the people he knew in this town, they all referred to Madam Kelly as "Ma", and yet Pearl called her "Mom", strange. Was Pearl much closer to Ma Kelly than anyone might expect? Who could swear on a stack of bibles that Ma Kelly had only ever slipped up once and given birth to only one child in her days as a pro – Frank had to pull himself together, surely this was the stupid wanderings of a mind which had absorbed far too much alcohol – he must get back on track or he'll certainly be a candidate for the mad-house and then he'd never be in a position to clear Lester Lomax's name.

After dinner with the cast and crew of the play, Frank agreed to Pearl's request that she come back to Lester's apartment with him and start collecting some of her property. By now it was apparent to Frank that Pearl and Lester had been living together in Lester's rented apartment and that since the fatal accident, she had moved back in at Ma Kelly's place.

Arriving at the entrance door of the Theater Royal, on their exit, they found the Williams brothers dealing with an inebriated cowhand who wanted entry. But Ma's rules were law here and one of her rules was that no one loaded with liquor set foot in the place without first handing over their firearms and this rowdy feller wasn't having a bar of that idea. With their hands full of the cowboy it allowed Miss Courtney and Frank Cotter to slip out without a pause and make their way off along the sidewalk in the direction of Lester Lomax's apartment.

Pearl didn't hesitate when crossing the threshold of her decease's lover's apartment ahead of Frank, coming here to care for Cotter had cured her of any phobias she had at first harbored. She went straight to the dining table as she removed her shawl, draping it over the back of a Windsor chair. She then slipped her hand into a concealed pocket of her dress and produced a box of matches and singled one out for the task of lighting up the oil lamp on the table. With one hand she replaced the chimney and shook out the match in the other.

Frank joined her at the table with his Stetson in hand and deposited it on the furniture next to the lamp. Meanwhile Miss Courtney scanned the parlor as though it was a home she was returning to after a long absence.

"…Are you all right Miss Courtney?" Frank said as he could read the sadness in the frame of her body. Then he went to the kitchen bench with a built-in dish sink, where a candleholder sat on the sink's wing, holding a candlestick, half the length of its original height. The candleholder's saucer base held a small collection of spent Vesta matches lying on its lip — matches which had served their purpose of firing up the candlewick on previous occasions. He lighted the candle with one of his own matches, explaining that the room could do with the added illumination. The sash cord window overlooking Bryan and Starr Streets' intersection was in the far wall behind them now and its high angle view of the unlit streets was that of an oblique angle. Turning with the candleholder in his hand towards Miss Courtney, Frank, with his back now to the sink, said "…Although I've never had the chance to see Lester in these surroundings, I feel it's still full of his presence."

"Oh, I agree — it's as if he has only just left this very room a few moments ago!" Pearl seemed to have taken root to the carpet square like a sapling. Frank, with the candleholder still in his hand went down to the sash window and drew the drapes.

"I'll light up a few more parlor lamps to give the place a decent bit of ambiance," Frank told Pearl reflectively.

"Fine," she muttered.

"Strange you should mention that about Lester's presence," Frank went on. He raised another lamp's chimney and torched its wick to life with the flame from the candle he carried. "I've experienced the very same thing — once I imagined that he was close by, staring into my face. That tells you just how strong a personality the man had."

Pearl nodded, and said: "That's eerie," Then she went up to the street window, where she opened the edge of the curtain's drop and took a sad reflective look down at the intersection now bathed in the moonlight. There was nothing of any real interest to see accept the shadowy false-fronted lumber buildings which hours ago had taken on the appearance of a ghost town. Cotter heard Pearl mutter, "…Down there – that's where my future died along with Lester."

Frank came across the room and joined her in the view. "Hmm — mine too in a sense…" Frank whispered hoarsely.

Pearl allowed the drape to settle back in place and turned to Cotter with a face shadowed in wonder, Cotter felt he had to explain himself. "My life's been a mess for far too long now, Lester threw me a lifeline when he invited me to Junction City. This town and our work here were to be a whole new beginning for me. Without Lester who knows how much longer I can survive? "

"You knew Lester before coming here?" said Frank.

It was clear that Pearl didn't want to discuss that subject and said: "If you'll allow me to pass, I'll see about brewing us some coffee … I'm sure we could both do with a cup." She pushed pass Frank and went over to the cast-iron cooking range where she checked the kettle's weight to tell whether it had enough water in it for the task ahead. It did. Then she checked the firebox which Pearl found had been set with kindling and old newspapers and only needed being fired up and the flue opened to create a draw needed to set off a cooking fire. Frank came to the kitchen cabinet next to the sink and brought down cups and saucers for the table while Pearl lit another of her own matches. Frank did not know his way round Lester's kitchen, where Pearl Courtney was the reverse; it was she who got out the coffee caddy and the gray speckled enamel coffeepot. Then she spooned ground java in to the vessel.

"How strong do you like your coffee, Mr. Cotter?"

"As it comes will be fine!"

"Oh, that's how Lester and I used to take ours, too!" She informed Frank as she returned to the grate and went through the job of adding a small chopped log to the blazing kindling therein, knowing full well that it would take and establish a healthy fire to bring the kettle's water to the boil and warm the combined dinning and sitting room areas. Then she shoved her hands down deep into her skirt that stopped three inches short of her elbows. These clandestine pockets could hold all manner of womanly things, thus they were quite useful.

"…I think while we're trapped here waiting for the water to heat up, I might just slip into the bedroom and gather a few things together from the wardrobe, d'you mind …?" Lester's ward inquired. Because Lester was the civilized Doctor from the East, he made sure that he created a comfortable lifestyle for himself and any likely guests, ample knick-knacks and decent practical crockery were his own personal stocks — as Pearl had lived here for a time she knew every corner of the abode like the pages of a play's script.

Frank nodded his approval to her request and as he rose to his feet he hooked onto the candleholder's handle and in unison the couple moved towards the dark bedroom that began to liven up into mobile shadows as they entered the room along with the dull light of the candle.

Cotter headed across to the bedside table near the headboard and used the candle to light the kerosene lamp and so add more illuminations to the room which thankfully now smelt appropriately enough to be acceptable to visitors … in the meantime Pearl went along the wall separating parlor-kitchen, from the boudoir to the second of the two wardrobes and there began to pile garments single-handedly on to her free arm, one article on top of the other.

Frank placed the candleholder on the washing stand and sat on the side of the bed as Pearl then closed the wardrobe and came across and placed her bundle of clothes on the end of the bed about arm's length away from him, then she went to the lowboy and picked up a six-by-four inch studio photograph of her and Lester in an oval rosewood frame — an article Frank hadn't before noticed. She studied the photo for a moment, as she no doubt recalled her memory of the day it was taken, then, with a sad sigh, she pressed it to her bosom and took it across to the clothes on the bed and placed it on top of the pile.

"May, I?" Frank said as he reached over and took the rosewood picture frame from the topmost dress — Pearl shrugged. Frank looked at the smartly dressed couple depicted on the photosensitive pasteboard … they certainly looked like a couple suited to each other and took a wonderful photo, together.

This was Frank's most recent sight of Lester in years and he felt pretty dismal knowing he would never see the light that shone in Lester's eyes the last time they were together as buddies. "…It's hard to imagine that a man with so much to give is now lying dead under six foot of earth," Cotter said forlornly as he put the frame back on top of the mound of clothing and looked up in search of Pearl Courtney, whom he discovered had returned to the lowboy and was gazing at her dim image in the mirror, clearly judging her outward appearance — *Oh Gawd my hair looks a mess,* she thought — *I look the typical war waif?…*Pearl spontaneously reached down and drew open one of the top drawers, where she knew a hairbrush was located and lowered her eyes to focus on what she was doing; but something down there in the drawer gave her a start and her response was that of someone seeing a **ghost!** … She paled as she backed off from the furniture and slammed the drawer shut with nothing short of fury, and in so doing, said. "…I think that kettle will have boiled by now," Miss Courtney told Frank in a tone of voice that was curt, as she started for the parlor. Frank jumped up off the bed and collected the photograph and garments in doing so and went out to join her in the parlor-cum-kitchen. He placed Pearl's stuff down on the dining table far enough away so that it would not be in their way while they had their coffee.

Frank wondered what it was Miss Courtney had glimpsed in the drawer of the lowboy which had clearly upset her. Was it another personal thing that meant something only to her and Lester? He decided that whatever it was, it was none of his business and sat down in the chair he had earlier occupied.

"...I expect that Lester has a lot of things he needs to keep private. Does he have a safe or something somewhere around the apartment for keeping his private papers and things?" Frank asked Miss Courtney, assuming that perhaps he ought to avoid the drawers in the lowboy, though he had not as yet gone delving about the suite.

"Lester has a sort of safe down below in his surgery where he keeps anything personal — I'll show it to you after we've had our coffee," Pearl said in a sulky tone as she poured steaming hot water from the kettle into the coffeepot on top of the ground coffee beans she's spooned in prior to adding the water.

"Did you know that Lester had a bit of a sweet-tooth? … He, he, was into this new idea of putting cane sugar in his coffee — have you tried it?" she put the kettle down out of the way and shut the hinged lid of the coffeepot.

"Naah can't say I have — though it is getting popular back east," Frank informed Pearl. "He just about converted me until his accident. But since then I've gone back to having it the old way— Black." Then she surprised Frank by going to the kitchen cabinet and returning with a bowl of brown sugar, Frank had only seen it on the odd occasions before coming west. "Care to try a pinch?"

Frank took the bowel in his hands and scrutinized its contents. The porous sugar granules had adhered together because of condensation and being stored away out of the light… "I don't expect it will be any worse than one mixing whiskey in their brew," He remarked. Then when he took his eyes off the sugar he found that Pearl was just sitting there somewhere off in another sphere of her mind. She sat there staring down into her coffee — possibly still upset by what she had clamped her eyes on back there in the bedroom's lowboy drawer. Frank continued to eye her off but was unaware that he was doing so. What was obvious to him was that Lester's ward was carrying about a lot of excess emotional baggage with her, and he certainly understood all about that.

But then on second thought he might be reading her all wrong; after all, she had a heavy, demanding rôle in that play…

Maybe we ought to forget Lester's safe for tonight? After all, she's been alone with me up here for a bit and that will not do her reputation any good, seeing as she was with a stranger and no chaperone. Cotter thought.

"Sssooo. Did you find everything you were after?" Frank asked, and then quickly added: "...I'm not trying to be nosy, mind you, Miss Courtney."

"No, that's all right. We, Lester and I, had just simply drawn very close over time. Lester tried to get me to move in here, and I practically did. But I always had my own room over at the theater. Lester saw to it that word got round town that I was still as pure as the driven, snow – he was aware how tongues tend to wag," This time she shot Frank a wicked smile. By now both of them had drain their cups.

"OK. In that case to keep your reputation intact — I should be getting you home with your things. I fear much more time here with me tonight will be compromising enough!" Frank pushed his chair back from the table and together they rose and stacked the china coffee cups and saucers in the kitchen sink.

Pearl and Frank stepped out onto the upstairs' landing with an equal share of what was to be carried up to the theater over their arms, the garments were being carried with care as neither wanted to over wrinkle them. Frank checked that the door to Lester's suite was fastened, but Pearl Courtney explained it wasn't necessary in this town, the only light-fingered people one might encounter were the Pawnees, and they hardly came into Junction City, the reservation seemed to suit them.

Upon reaching ground level, the miniature Black Panther met them; it was hungry for food and badgered the couple all the way across and up the street until they had almost arrived at The Theater Royal.

"Take no notice of the cat," Frank told Pearl Courtney. "It's been hanging around me for a free hand out, which it won't be getting — I don't wanna encourage it, though I think Lester might've been giving it a bit here and there."

"Well *you* should," Pearl said sulkily. "It's Lester's. He named him *Blackie.* I drop him off the odd table scraps when I think of it."

The cat ran off diagonally across Starr Street under an empty hitching rack and water trough, then sprang with ease up onto the sidewalk and disappeared in to the dark well of a recessed vacant shop's doorway. "C'mon, let's get you home — that cat's feral enough to find a field mouse ..." Cotter said, setting off east towards Junction City's den of iniquity.

Outside the theater-cum-brothel, the Williams brothers were chewing the fat with one of Ma Kelly's ladies of the night. Like Bubbles, she too had a pair of hindquarters like that of a brood mare; she even had Red Bubbles' flirtatious nature.

"What are you doing off the chain, Ruby?" Pearl asked in a friendly manner. Frank rightly realized that this gal was one whom had helped bring him back from the depths of despair. "You know Mom doesn't like her talent fraternizing with the hired help!"

"I'm samplin' some fresh air — there's none in there..." Ruby informed Pearl Courtney with a shrug in the direction of The Theater Royal's door. Harry Williams lit a cheroot and handed it to her, even though she hadn't indicated that she wanted one or even needed one.

"And where do you think you're goin'...?" Reg said to Frank Cotter.

"I'm giving Miss Courtney a hand with her things she's collected from Doctor Lomax's, apartment." Frank told Reg and gestured with the clothing over his arm.

"Listen, **Mister,** this town has **"rules"**... An' when the theater and restaurant's closed as it is now, only men wiv the price of a woman set foot inside. Get it, tenderfoot?" Reg said, looking down his nose at Cotter.

Frank nodded at Reg Williams. But down deep inside he would have liked to put the hard case in his place. Williams hadn't been softened up much by his hiding from the Army men. Gee, how Frank wished *he* had the guts to stamp his elastic-sided boot down on the instep of the bouncer. But then again, he would have to expect a punch or two in the face in retaliation.

Pearl realized that the scribe would be out of place mixing it with these pair of smart-ass cowboys and that they in turn would be in their element knocking the sawdust out of the Tenderfoot, for these men always worked in pairs. Once was enough to be beaten by them — wisely one didn't come back for seconds.

"I can manage from here, Mister Cotter, thank you kindly for your generous help — Ruby can give me a hand upstairs." The prostitute knew that the Courtney gal was trying to avoid a nasty situation, so she stepped in and took the garments off Frank's arm. Between them they hurried away with the clothes and didn't look back.

Frank Cotter got the message and reluctantly faded off in to the night in the direction of Doctor Lomax's apartment.

8

AT 2.10 P.M., Sheriff Jock Robson and Deputy Bud Reed arrived in Junction City from Lawrence in response to Lazarus Rollo's telegram on the robbery of his strongbox from the Butterfield stagecoach at Diamond Creek. The pair made their way straight up Main Street to Ridge Road through a town, which was in the throes of recovering from its customary lunchtime sluggishness. The lawmen's geldings sensed they were nearing journey's end and the saddle-weary horsemen could feel it in the strides of their beasts.

They eased their mounts up to the hitching rail outside Sheriff Boston's jailhouse, and even as they prepared to dismount, their thirsty horses were nudging inwards towards the water-trough and lowering their long necks to quench their thirst.

Reed dropped first from the saddles to the ground, and tied his horse to the rail. Sheriff Robeson took a moment to spit the tobacco from his mouth before swinging down. Meanwhile, Reed hitched his saddle's left stirrup to the saddle-horn and reached under the saddle skirt to get at the double cinch straps and loosen them off for the benefit of his well serving horse. No one appeared to open the building's front door;

This indicated to the visiting Sheriff that no one had been watching the street from the office. This didn't alarm Jock Robeson at all, for Boston would not have been expecting him as late in the week as this, no doubt knowing that the Chairman of the Cattlemen's Association had sent off a telegram for him to join in the search for the riders responsible for the offence at Diamond Creek.

Lazarus, Boston and company would have expected Jock to drop everything and high tail it down here like a Bat out of Hell! But Robeson had other things to take care of in his own patch, before he could just up and leave Lawrence in the hands of his able deputies.

Robeson knew that Boston was Lazarus Rollo's man, otherwise he would not have been holding the town's sheriff's position, but Jock knew that the town's unofficial king, Rollo, must have his reasons for calling on his services, for he was quite aware of the role the Williams brothers played in the Chairman's control of the town, they weren't just there for their looks. So it bugged him as to why he wanted both the ex-Pinkerton detective and his deputy, Bud Reed. He wondered whether it was because at one time Reed had been Boston's deputy and it was rumored that Reed and Boston hadn't seen eye to eye.

Word of the stagecoach robbery had spread fast and wide. The executors had not gone to any great lengths to hide their identity, nor could they for the fact was apparent that this had been an inside job. Robeson assumed that he had been called in and would be offered a private commission to work for the Association to hunt down these Owl-hooters and recover the gold and see that they faced justice. But not wanting Boston's nose put out of joint, Jock had called in on the local law.

Jock and Bud entered the Sheriff's Office just two steps apart. Robeson went across to the gate in the wooden polished fence, which divided the office and the cells from the public. The jails were way back, deep in the room. A rickety flight of stairs ran up alongside the right wall of the building's interior to an open loft, where the living quarters had been squeezed in under the gable roof, for the structure had no ceiling; this space was usually where the jail's keeper roosted, when the cells had someone in residence for more than an overnight's stay.

"Sheriff Robeson and Deputy Reed!" exclaimed Deputy Ben Lexmon who was in the midst of mopping the floor, on the town side of the banister. He submerged the head of the mop in the bucket of soapy water and cresol mixture, and left it soaking there. "You were expected a few days ago," He told the men. "Mister Rollo has been chewin' his fingernails down to the quick worrying as ter why youse ain't put in some kind of appearance!" Lexmon hefted the bucket and mop up from the floor and lugged them off to hide them out of sight in the storage closet. Then he returned to the wall where his gun rig hung on a wall peg and buckled it on. He now looked like a man who could mean business and not a lackey.

"Where's ye boss, Lad?" asked the robust Scotsman as he dragged out Sheriff Boston's office chair and planted himself down on it, facing Ben, whom by this time of the day had won himself a five o'clock shadow. Meanwhile a thirsty Reed had gone over to a couple of gourds handing by leather thongs on a peg … He helped himself to one, then filled it with fresh water from a Mexican clay water cooler which reposed on an iron leg stand. He brought a drink back with him for Jock at Boston's desk.

"He ain't showed ter day, yet. C'n I help yuh?" Lexmon was a fan of Robeson's the moment he learned of Jock Robeson's Pinkerton reputation. To Ben Lexmon, Jock was the essential Lawman, in more ways than one. Lexmon surely hopped that the Scotsman did not see him as just another jailhouse lackey.

"This ain't nuthin' special, Deputy; jist a courtesy call," Reed said while Jock took a gulp of water from the leaking gourd his Deputy had given him.

"Rollo sent for us —" continued Robeson as he removed the drinking vessel from his lips and sat there with it in his hand, ignoring the drips of water that dropped into the lap of his Levi's. "I just did not want tuh barge in on Klem's territory without he knows what's goin' on," Jock then drank the gourd dry...

Both men had plenty of signs about them to show that they had rode across a good piece of country without protection from dust and sun.

"Well, sir, that's mighty neighborly of you Mister Robeson... Yeah, yuh right, Sheriff Boston might misinterpret things an' sour over it apiece. I can tell you that he don't like bein' bypassed if there's sumthin' on the nose in our county — all due respect ter you, Sheriff Robeson." He ended this bout of dialog by rubbing an itchy corner of his eye with the knuckle of his hand.

Jock handed the gourd to Ben, he told Lexmon: "I'd be feelin' that way meself if the boot wuz on the, t'other foot. Thanks fer yuh time. Tell Klem I'll do me best to catch up with him before we hit the trail." Then he screwed his head round to Reed and said: "Let's mosey down town to this Rollo joker's office."

They filed out to Ridge Road. Ben had a quick look around the jail from where he stood near the desk and then returned the gourd back to its place, and then went off to hunt up Sheriff Boston. He mused that he would see if Klem were down the bathhouse having a free bath on the Chows.

Lazarus Rollo stood with his back to the window of his office on the second floor of the Cattlemen's Association Building on Main Street. The ground floor walls of the building were made of cut stone blocks, while the upper floor had been constructed from lumber and clapboards as the quarry from where they had been getting their stone had been exhausted; the builders were lucky that they got enough material to complete the first floor before it gave out.

With hands clasped behind his back, Lazarus addressed the two lawmen sitting across the mahogany desk from him in the Chesterfield club chairs. These were companion chairs to the sofa back against the wall. The pair facing the imposing Rollo had already heard how the Association wished to hire Robeson's expensive services in the hunt for the missing gold, and the desperate perpetrators whom had claimed two lives.

"Are you aware that if I take on this assignment it will be at the cost of my position as Sheriff of Lawrence?" Jock explained. "…I can't play the fiddle for two masters — it isn't fair to either party." Jock rose from the Chesterfield to get the kinks out of his knees.

Bud wondered whether or not he was expected to stand, too. He did not want to appear disrespectful to his superior in front of witnesses.

"That's understood. But I suspect it will only be a temporary setback and I should think that when the case is over that you will be able to return to yore post as Sheriff of Lawrence — surely the councilors of Lawrence would not let a man such as yore self slip through their fingers?

"But should the unthinkable happen, I'm sure I could persuade our board to pay you a regular salary until something suitable comes along — which in yore case shouldn't be too long!" said Rollo, sticking his neck out on the block, having already decided that the ex-detective had to be in on the hunt for this ramrod, Flynn, and the Butterfield guard. "Then, in that case you've got a deal," said the Scotsman. Jock turned and looked down at Bud Reed. "While I'm out of circulation, I'll press the Lawrence council to put you in as temp' Sheriff — 'twill be good experience for you."

"That's great by me," Buddy beamed.

"Just a minute, Robeson; I sent for both of you to work this case as a team. When Reed worked for Klem Boston I could see he had potential. I envisaged him as being yore side-kick?" Lazarus Rollo said.

The Scotsman turned to the Chairman. "How many stagecoaches were robbed, Mister Rollo?"

"What do you mean?" Rollo frowned. "One, you know that as well as I!"

"Then you'll only need the expertise of one ex-Pinkerton agent," Jock said to him.

Lazarus Rollo looked dumbfounded.

Jock said without pause. "I can't do much now; my horse needs to rest up. Meanwhile I'll need to talk to the passengers still in town who were on the coach. Who've we got?"

Working off the top of his head, Rollo said: "…There's only two. A feller called Dragoon, a regular. He sells guns in this area for the Colt and Winchester arms manufacturers. And some newspaperman who was to begin work here but now finds himself, jobless.

"He's pretty damn good with a pencil and did a couple of freehand sketches of the robbers." Lazarus picked up the drawings of the perpetrators that were laying spread out on his desk.

Robeson and Reed both craned their necks in the direction of the sketches done by the tenderfoot. Jock was going to commit them to memory. *They look very good,* thought Jock. — *But just how reliable are they?* Then he asked: "How sure can we be that these hand-sketched portraits are a good likeness?" Robeson passed the drawings to Reed. He in turn took a good hard long look at them.

A smile appeared on the Chairman's face that traveled right through to the inner most reaches of his eyes.

"I know this guy, Flynn," said Bud Reed. "That there drawing is as good as you would git of the feller if you were lookin' right at 'im. If this pen pusher can draw Flynn's mug so lifelike, I'd wager that's a darn good drawin' of his partner in crime! "

Rollo flowed back into the conversation. "I showed these drawings to my employees, the Williams brothers, they know the other feller, Korda. They vouch that Korda's picture is lifelike, too."

Jock nodded. "I've a question for you Mister Rollo…"

Rollo glanced at the Sheriff from Lawrence, expectantly.

"Why didn't you drop this job in Klem Boston's lap? It would've cost ye a lot less ter have him bring them in than its gonna cost. It's well known that Klem and the Williams brothers cover your ass in this neck of the woods!" Jock wrinkled his forehead under his widow's peak.

Nodding his head of well-groomed hair, Rollo asked: "What we say in this room stays here, right?"

Jock nodded and all three knew it went without saying. But as far as Lazarus Rollo was concerned, Bud Reed's opinion was unimportant to him.

"I've left Sheriff Boston out of this because he mightn't prove to be as judicial or persistent as the likes of you. He, with his crippled leg; can be a drawback and we, that are the Association, and the town council, only keep him where he is with a vote of sympathy…"

Personally, I've always found Boston a good man. He's done a lot for the Association's Chairman in the past, some of which was pretty questionable at times and showed himself ter have too close of an affiliation with Mister Lazarus Rollo, so I can't see what he has ter be squealing about! Thought Robinson, — I may've been too quick in agreeing to leave Boston ignorant of how Rollo thinks about him. Hmmm, I might have to think again about how I'll handle that part of our agreement… "Right," the Scotsman said aloud. "— Reed and I better skedaddle if we wanna get non dormitory rooms at The Palomino Guest House on Main…"

The room's trio had to go through a bit of social nodding and hand-shaking before Jock and Buddy got clear of the office, with the understanding that the Cattlemen's Association would pick-up the tab for their rooms and the boarding of their horses at the livery stable, down near the stage depot.

Once the pair of lawman had stowed away their gear they went along to the bathhouse and spent time on ridding their bodies of ingrain trail dust and body-odor, after which they paid another visit to Junction City's jailhouse, this time Klem was on   deck and Lexmon was out doing a patrol of the town. Boston expected Robeson to call on him once he knew the Lawrence lawmen were in town; he offered to buy them supper down at the diner on Main, meanwhile, Klem produced a deck of used cards from one of the desk drawers of his keyhole desk, and the three of them played a couple of friendly hands of poker. During the course of these games, Jock opened up and told Klem what he was doing here in town. He also unloaded the fact that Rollo and the council looked upon him, Klem, as being pretty much a second-class Lawman, but he broke it to Boston in the nicest possible way.

Surprise, surprise — Klem didn't give a stuff about Lazarus Rollo's opinion of him as a lawman, nor that of the council — he knew he could still do his duty and facedown most hotheaded drunks with a gun in their hand, in this town. Present company accepted, Klem held little fear that no one in the place could hold a candle to him on that score other than the Williams boys.

Doctor Lomax's attorney, Donald Stoughton, returned from Dodge in his surrey after having completed some court business and called on Frank Cotter the moment he learned about him being in town — which was about fifteen minutes after placing his carriage and mare in the hands of the folks at the livery stable.

Don Stroughton was much the same age as the late Lomax and Cotter. Stroughton was a sharp-eyed even featured man who looked just as much at home on the range as he did behind the business desk of his office. He had several Stetsons in his wardrobe and right now he had on his powder blue hat over a city-made suit which was protected by a beige duster. He kept himself well barbered, hair neatly trimmed and his thin mustache shaped so that not a hair was out of line. When out of his office he was prone to gray cloth business suites worn with the coat open to show off his satin waistcoats. Under the coat's vest he wore a white shirt with a string tie just below his Adam's apple. He made no attempt at hiding his shoulder holster, which packed a .38 Smith, and Wesson. However, when in court he kept his suit-coat buttoned, out of respect for the courts.

"Did you hear who has hit town, Mister Stroughton?" said the stable-hand as he took charge of the lawyer's surrey.

"Nope," Donald Stroughton said with interest in his eyes as he heaved his baggage from the surrey "Doc Lomax's tenderfoot friend frum back east." The stable-hand took the mare's reins and toyed with them while waiting for the attorney to attend to his luggage and court papers.

"Have you set eyes on him?" Stroughton stooped over and picked up his gear. The mare shook her head to rid herself from an annoying fly and slobber from its mouth, showered the stable-hand.

Used to these sorts of shower it therefore did not faze the fellow who went on in answer to the attorney's question. "…Only from a distance — he looks a shoddy bastard, and, doesn't have that friendly look of the late Doctor Lomax. He's also been knocked off balance by the Doc's death I might tell ya."

"I expect he would," said the lawyer with a nod.

The ostler continued: "Also, there wuz a bit of a ruckus over at the Doc's place the night he got in, too. He an' the Williams brothers caught a couple of fellers in the apartment tryin' ter Do a bit of poaching …" Hearing this interested the lawyer. The stable-hand went on: "Yeah. But before you git it into yuh head that they trounced the fellers doing the burglin' the boot wuz on the other foot — Reg and Harry copped a serve. Turns out the looters were government men in the Army frum Washington."

"How, d'you know that?" the Attorney questioned.

"I don't rightly know that part of the story, but that's the gossip going round town," said the stable-hand as he dropped the reins and moved down alongside the mare on his side to the front of the vehicle, near the surrey's dash-wall. "Boston got in on the act and arrested the Washington fellers but later let 'em go. Then later they wuz seen drinkin' wif the tenderfoot and then the three of 'em vanished fer a couple a days. Rumor has it, these fellers frum Washington are tryin' ter find some papers belongin' to the Doc, so some important folks in Washington cam make use of 'em in a legal case against the Doc's good name."

"Thanks for the information, Merriam." Don said thoughtfully. "Do me a favor…?"

Merriam nodded.

"Take my things over to my chambers for me. Tell Mrs. McBride. I've gone off to look up Lomax's city friend, and I'll catch up with her later."

Stroughton left the livery stable building by a side door, which opened out, into an alley that ran all the way through to Starr Street. He was keen to make the newspaperman's acquaintance and hurried along the alley pass the very piece of waste ground, where the Frank

Cotter had lain in a drunken stupor for over 48-hours before being found. At the end of the alleyway, Don turned right and stepped up onto the boardwalk which ran in the uptown direction along and under the overhanging balcony of Ma Kelly's *Theater Royal,* he continued to make his way along the sidewalk, at the same time focusing on the staircase to Lomax's suite, which from his point of view placed it on the opposite side of Starr Street. He noticed that Lester's black cat was stalking an English sparrow as the bird pecked at something in the dirt. But the lawyer's hurried approach alarmed the sparrow and it took to the air and left a dejected feline in its wake. The cat then took refuge in the stove's wood-heap under the stairs.

The identity of the man who answered Stoughton's knock on the door really didn't need to be confirmed. He looked too much at home not to be Francis Cotter.

Health wise, the lawyer thought the man looked quite seedy. In the man's hand was a damask tea towel, the man had clearly been drying some dishes.

"Frank Cotter, I presume?" Stroughton said with raised brows.

Cotter nodded. "...And who might you be?" asked Cotter for he had no idea of who the joker before him was.

"Donald Stroughton, may I come in?"

"Oh, sure, sure, sure — don't mind me, I'm tidying up—C'mon, come in—care for a cup of coffee; it's fresh?"

The man nodded as he crossed the threshold and removed his hat as he went across the waxed floor, leaving a trail of dusty footprints on the boards until his footwear hit the carpet.

The attorney sat on the sofa that Lester always kept covered with an Indian blanket that had been woven as a gift by some squaw out on the reservation. The furniture was the very piece that had managed to come through the rough fight unscathed between the Williams brothers and the two army men.

"...I just got in from Dodge and came straight over here." The lawyer placed his Stetson on his lap and undid his duster and suit-coat for comfort; he was already breaking out in a film of perspiration from his hastily made detour.

Frank caught sight of the man's armory that was never meant to be a hidden commodity. Cotter went over and collected the china cups and saucers he had washed and had been previously used by him and Pearl. The Attorney continued: "I expect you've got some questions about Lester's terrible accident...?"

"Have I ever—and I hope you're just the man who can give me some sensible answers on the subject." Frank picked up the coffeepot, using the tea towel as a potholder. He transported the enamelware to the table where he placed it down on top of the breadboard so as not to scorch the tabletop beneath the tablecloth. "— how in God's name, could Lester have been so careless?" Cotter began filling the cups as the lawyer rose from the sofa, and leaving his hat behind, he crossed to the table and drew a chair out to use. In the mean time, before beginning to pour a second cup Cotter aligned the pouring spout above the empty cup, which stood beside the full vessel of beverage.

"It was just — just one of those stupid things that happens from time to time, really ... I mean when I called out to Lester..." the lawyer broke off, then went on: "You do know most of the details by now, I guess?"

Frank nodded. "As best as anyone can get to know of something like this, second-hand. But I'm keen to hear your story."

Donald Stroughton nodded, and then went on. "I was on an errand, wasn't expecting to see Lester or the others who were with him if it comes to that. I only called out to acknowledge him, but when he saw me he suddenly bolt down off the sidewalk in my direction. He didn't even see the wagon and the wagon's teamster couldn't avoid Lester, the horses were on top of him before anyone could react. It, it, w-was shocking the way it happened—it knocked everyone for a goddamn loop!"

Don drew the cup, which was intended for him across the table cloth as Frank returned the coffeepot to the flat pig-iron stovetop.

"So then the damage was done and over within a matter of seconds, eh?" Cotter sat down in the Windsor chair that had earlier been warmed by Miss Courtney's posterior, but had long ago, cooled.

Donald nodded, then added, "Lester's death has dumped you right in the middle of limbo, right, Frank?" He paused with his cup of brew having raised it to his lips and blew on the surface of the liquid to lower its temperature. It's radiant heat acting as a warning to the man that it was too hot for his mouth. "I can call you, ***Frank?***"

"Frank's fine. Had things gone to plan without this accident, we most likely would have been working together. But now that Lester has gone, this sort of washes me up with Junction City. I guess I'll be off back east once I've rested up from the journey. It has been a pretty harassing time for me in more ways than one!"

"I guess you're referring to the trouble you walked into here at the apartment?"

"You know about that fiasco?"

"It's the talk of the town… A stable-hand around at the livery told me about it the moment I hit town. As Lester's attorney I shall have to sort this business out with Boston— can't allow that kind of thing to go on in the town, we're supposed to be starting to get civilized out here, why, we've got the railway heading in this direction…"

"That'll bring you and the town its own set of problems. Some folks might even come to curse the day the railway came, but that business of this invasion of Lester's suite isn't the only thing that has not made the west very welcome to me. Coming here the stage was held up by road bandits and we were robbed at gunpoint."

"You were!" This was news too to the Attorney.

"Three people died as a result of the robbery, too." Frank went on to tell Stroughton about that miss-adventure, and how he had drawn sketches of the offenders for the town's law officer and the Cattlemen's Association chairman, Lazarus Rollo. "…those drawings of mine will put the lever of the hangman's scaffold in the hand of the Hangman, and a rope round the necks of those uncivilized killers!"

"H'm. After your experiences, I can quite understand your desire to head east. But as you know, Lester's death has left his business affairs in tatters and it is going to take some sorting out. As one of his oldest friend, maybe you should stay on a while and help with ironing them out; maybe there is some necessary background of the Doctor's, you can help us out with?"

"Don't worry I intend staying around a while yet. There are a few things I have learned about Lester's death that don't please me." Frank told the lawyer with raised eyebrows.

"What d'you mean?" Donald asked.

"Well, for one thing, I have heard that there doesn't look to be as if an inquiry is going to be held into Lester's accident and why Washington sent two Army-men here to search Lester's belongings … No, there are too many questions that need to be answered!"

"That's very interesting to hear about Washington's interest in our affairs. But go back a couple of paces to Lester's accident business. It's quite well known, there's no need for an Inquiry. There are quite enough witnesses to testify that what happened was an accident. There's, *me!*"

"Then how do you account for the discrepancies in the story of Lester's accident between witnesses…?" Frank said.

"I'm not sure I follow you?"

"Then maybe *this* will jog yuh memory? What has become of the fifth fellow who helped you jokers to carry Lester over onto the sidewalk from the road?"

"What are you on about, Frank? … I don't follow you and your thinking!"

"I happen to know that there was a fifth man there at that accident and if there is ever going to be an inquiry into Lester's incident, he will need to come forward."

"Rubbish! Face up to it Frank, there is no need for the expense of an inquiry and I for one will oppose it." Donald Stroughton was most serious about that, too. You could read it in his face. "What crackpot put that notion into your head?" He took a sip of his java.

"…Someone you would know pretty well I should, say. —" Frank said as he paused and looked across the rim of his cup at Lawyer Stroughton. "Ma Kelly, and *I doubt* you could consider her a "crackpot" as you so quaintly put it!"

Stroughton thought the possibilities over and recalled that Ma Kelly did come on the scene not long after the incident and had with her a towel or something, intent on trying to be some help as he recalled. "Yeah, she was there at some point. But, but — *I don't* recall this feller you say she remembers. Things were very hectic, and who can say what was and wasn't happening at the time? Ma could've easily made a mistake…"

Frank shook his head and lowered his drinking vessel to its saucer. "I don't reckon so. Aaawhat I've seen of her, she has a pretty sharp brain and I'm inclined to take what she told me was gospel. If she says this extra guy was there, then he would have had to have been. You see Donald, it is things like that which scream out loud an' clear that Lester's case needs clearing up with an inquiry."

"If what you say is true and it can be authenticated by Ma Kelly, then I too would start pushing Sheriff Boston for an *Inquiry.*"

"Do you know Ma, well?" Frank asked. The Attorney nodded. "Then maybe you should have a yarn to her and then you just might learn something."

The Attorney had been thirsty when he hit town and the rush to get to Lomax's apartment had made quenching it the second most important thing he had to do, after first meeting up with Lester's friend from back east. Donald swirled the last quarter of his beverage round in the lower part of his cup to mix up the dregs as he spoke. "—I'll put that at the top of my list of things to do, the moment after I've cleaned up."

"Good, that's the sort of thing I like to hear," said Frank, and he looked that little bit happier. "And while you are at it, try to get to the bottom of it with Sheriff Boston, how come he let those blue-bellies out of the can so soon after committing their act of Breaking and Entering — they should be jailed for a year or two by law!"

"I think I did hear somewhere that they were in and out of jail like a cowboy in an' out of a whore's piss flaps. I certainly wish I was on hand when all this took place," confessed the lawyer.

"Boston should have held these so-called army fellers behind bars much longer than he opted for. We had no proof that they were who they said they were, neither of them was in uniform and they were reluctant to produce any form of identity. One of them was wearing an army flap-top holster." Frank nervously drummed the finger pads of his right-hand on the table as he waited to hear what Stroughton had to say about that.

"You know why Lester wanted you out here? It was because of the hassles and oppositions to his research with and for the Indians, coming out of Washington. Your main function was to write newspaper articles that would inform the reading public how insincere Washington was about supporting his important and valuable work; not only for the Indians, but also for mankind in general. I shouldn't be surprised if those army men weren't working hand in glove with the Indian Affairs Department, and if so, I reckon I know what they would be after for Washington!"

"What's that?" said Cotter.

"…They would've been sent here to obtain the Doctor's research formulas by hook or by crook. They wouldn't have known about Lester's sudden death but I bet when they got here and heard all about it they would have seen it as manna from Heaven. They would have spotted the man's death and burial as open slather for them to raid the apartment, and most likely the surgery looking for these formulas which would all vanish into the ether once they reached Washington. Could you do me the favor of an inventory of Lester's belonging and private papers for me, it'll save me a lot of work and allow me time to run these Army guys to ground and sound them out."

Frank nodded. *Sure, going through Lester's stuff would give him something worthwhile to do — stop him being more bored than he was at the moment,* thought Cotter. Then aloud he said: "I don't know whether or not Roscoe and Briggs are still in town. Hopefully they have departed for Washington and get themselves a grilling for daring to sally the Army's name via a criminal act."

"That sounds more like wishful thinking on your part, Frank."

"I guess so. But if they are still in Junction City I don't reckon you'll have to go looking for 'em. Once they know your affiliation with Lester, I feel damn sure they will pay you a visit or two; if that happens, be very careful of them. I don't know how much Lester told you about me, but I'm trying to dry myself out — kick the booze, since he, Lester, held out a helping hand to me.

"I don't wanna let him down and I owe it to his memory to get my act together so there'll be something to show for the help he's offered me. I had done a fair job of it too, until those two guys pulled the rug out from under me. Whether it was intentional or not, I don't know — maybe they were just lucky, I hope I can find a bit more reserve to haul myself back on the wagon, I'd sure like to give it a try."

"Tell you what..." said Stroughton. "If they are in town and come bothering you again, point 'em in my direction," He put his now empty cup back on the saucer and rose smoothly off the Windsor and slid it back towards, the table. "You make a damn good cup of coffee, Frank, I'll say that fer you." Lawyer Stroughton went over to the sofa and picked up his hat, and carrying it with both hands, was about to head towards the parlor door which faced out onto the landing.

"Before you clear off, where's yuh office, Don?"

"D'you knows the Masonic Hall and Temple's located on Main Street?"

Cotter nodded. "Opposite the stage, depot…"

"Correct. My shingle's hanging from the overhead awning above the sidewalk outside my front door. It's a four room place, two up an' two down — you can't miss it. OK, I'll be off and let you get started on that inventory … anymore questions you've got, please don't fail to ask me, I'm ready ter help all I can … 'Bye for now."

"Oh, yes, there is one more thing—"

"And that is?"

"Indians," the one word spilt from Frank's lips. The word puzzled our lawyer friend. Realizing the attorney wasn't *following him.* Frank continued. "… everyone tells me how Lester was very involved with the natives of the area, but d'you know that since I have been here in Junction City I've not clamped eyes on one! Don't they ever come into town for any sort of reason?"

"Hardly—everything they need is on the reservation. The Government supplies 'em even bullets for their hunting rifles. It's a costly business for the Government looking after the Indians. That's why most politicians would like to see them all die off. And what better way to see that happen than when a tribe gets infected with white man's diseases. That's the reason they didn't want to help Lester with his research. Someone back there in Washington wants to get their hands on the Doctor's formulas, to prevent the manufacture of a medicine that will cure these ills that are decimating the Pawnees in this area."

Frank nodded, satisfied by Donald Stroughton's answer. "Yeah… OK, well I'll catch you soon."

Alone, Cotter went and found himself some writing paper and a sharp graphite pencil. His mind working on two levels, he began making an inventory and at the same time he thought about more questions he might ask Lester's attorney. And he must remember to look up another person too, Doctor Hallway.

The first room Cotter began making notes on was the bedroom. He opened the drapes and raised the sunshade and the sash window to allow fresh air and light into the room—then just as he was about to start there was a knock at the landing door. Annoyed by the interruption, Frank laid aside the pencil and the writing tablet and strolled out in to the parlor… but even before he got to the door he could see who it was through the café curtains and glass panes. His visitors were the dread of his life, Roscoe and Briggs … *Now what do these pair want?* Thought Cotter as he wrenched opened the door.

"All right — what's on your minds?" He made a point of leaning on the doorjamb to block their way and he was determined to stand firm.

"We're still got some jawin' ter do," said the Lieutenant, "So d'you mind if the Captain and I come in for a while?" Roscoe stood there on the doormat, looking as though the end of the world was neigh. Briggs stepped round the captain and drove Cotter backwards into the room, Roscoe followed on the man's heels as though he had every right to be headed where he intended to go. Briggs spun Frank round and forced Cotter's arm up his back between the shoulder blades — the pain was excruciating and he did not even get the chance to dig his toes in, Lt. Briggs marched him over to the table and dragged out the chair Stroughton had recently occupied and thrust him heavily down onto it at the table's edge.

"Who the hell do you think you're pushing about?" Frank demanded, in the voice of a man who's realized that against these pair he did not have a leg to stand on. The intruders took command of the other empty chairs at the table, Captain Roscoe and his lieutenant removed their hats and dumped them in the center of the furniture—they weren't about to be going anywhere until they had the answers they obviously came for.

"This time we're playing for keeps!" Roscoe snapped as Lt. Briggs pulled his Colt and pointed the bore at Frank's throat across the table, its butt resting steadily on the tablecloth, his trigger finger right where it would do the most good. Frank Cotter, like any man caught in his position he went as pale as bed-linen and moisture welled from the pores of his forehead.

"Play along with us and you won't get a wrap over the knuckles — get smart and it might buy you a slug for yore corner, right?" Briggs, the seasoned campaigner, held the heavy handgun like a toy. In this crazy moment all Frank could think about was how deceptive the weight of a six-gun was in reality.

Massaging his shoulder joint, Frank said, "— I don't know what you jokers expect from me, but ya going about getting it the wrong way."

"That's possible," Captain Roscoe said. "Experience doesn't grow on trees, we just have to feel our way through this sort of thing as we go; there's no written manual on how one gets answers to certain questions. I get no joy out of going about things this way either, but we've a job to do an' we'll work our way through it until we think we have got what we want."

"So, what sort of friendship did you and Lomax share?" Briggs asked, his pistol muzzle steadily pointed at Cotter's body mass. Cotter's eyes betrayed his discomfort as he focused on the weapon's barrel.

"…Quite a long one," Frank told them as he went back to rub the area of his muscles that were as painful as any "Chinese Burn" he had experienced back in his school-yard days?".

"That would have been back, east?" Roscoe put his forearms parallel on the table and entwined his fingers.

Cotter nodded. "We were at college together, he was drawn to medicine and I, to teaching. But through different turns of events, I ended up in the newspaper business and Lester continued on with medicine. Our paths went their separate ways and we lost contact until the war. We found ourselves on the same side, him patching up the wounded and dying, and me … I wrote copy on the war for the *New York Tribunal.*

"At war's end we again went off in different directions until our trails somehow converged. By then, much water had passed under the bridge and Lester reckoned his future was out west… We again lost contact and I moved into a new phase of my life, some of it worthy of distinction and other parts, not so… In some weird way we found our niche in life. Mine was in the bottom of a whiskey bottle and his … Trying to find some way of doing the impossible, curing those affected by sickness or disease."

"Lomax sounds quite ***the*** do-gooder," Roscoe said with a sarcastic sneer.

"He had a heart, yes. Is there something improper about that in your book?" Frank found that his arm's discomfort which had been caused by the lieutenant's strong-arm tactics was beginning to come good and so he stopped rubbing his shoulder, instead he looked from one, to the other of the men, he tried to read their thoughts which proved utterly impossible. Cotter had no special gifts such as being a so-called psychic.

"Where do you fit into the scheme of things?" Roscoe asked but from habit he made it sound like an order.

"What d'you mean?" Frank Cotter focused on the Captain, though he was no more comfortable about the gun being aimed in his direction. He could feel a deep rumble in his gullet and thought that perhaps he might have to make a rush to the commode in the bedroom for the outhouse was down stairs in the yard. Now, that would be damn embarrassing.

"Your doctor friend began making up some sort of concoction which he claimed would combat the illnesses we white men are accused of bringing to the New World, such as Whooping cough, et cetera.

"Without anyone's permission in the Government, Lomax began experimenting on the local Pawnee population, here. He ignored the fact that the Indian Affairs Department didn't want him to trial his stuff on anyone until it had been proved safe — there are some folks in the department who were pretty skeptical about Lomax's claims as to how good it was. And when it's all said and done, they have the responsibility of our Native Americans health and survival. He did not wait for that permission from the Bureau before going ahead with his experiments; That is why he's in trouble with the Government."

"—Not ter mention the horror his phony medicine visited upon the poor helpless underdogs when it backfired on certain individuals," Chipped in Briggs. "This medicine he was makin' up, killed orf more Injuns than it cured and those, who did survive, have been left cripples. Even heathens don't deserve the treatment he handed out to 'em! "

"Now hold on a minute," Cotter turned on Lt. Briggs. "You don't know what you're talking about —"

"Try me!" snapped Briggs; Roscoe gestured for both men to lower their voices.

"Why do you thing Lester brought me into the picture?" Frank said, demanding an answer from both or either one of them at the table. But they never offered up any answer to the question, so Cotter went on:

"I happen to *know* Lester tried to make the short-sighted people in both the Government and the Indian Affairs Department, see reason and allow him to try his medicine on the Indians — his view being that trial and error would eventually save the day — but no, they stalled and all the time people, women and children, were, and are dying!

"Lester was aware he has friends in the government who have faith in what he was attempting to do, and sure, his detractors — but he couldn't afford the luxury to wait until things sorted themselves out. He wrote me his government friends were outnumbered in the game of politics and so he took the bull by the horns and went ahead with his experimental medicines on the Indians, right or wrong; he had to prove his theories one way or the other. I was employed to write the truth of what he was up against behind the scenes in our government and that there were certain people in high places who saw the disease and pestilence as a means to an end with our Indian problem, to some, the Indian is nothing more than a pest. The annihilation of the Indian peoples would save a certain element in the Government getting blood on their hands, they'd not have to even dream of running a covert genocide program.

"With my penmanship I was charged with the duty of exposing the Government conspiracy. Lester wanted Mister and Missus America to know the truth of the situation." Most of what the scribe had just said was supposition.

"What alcoholic brain cells are activatin' yore mind? You truly can't believe that?" Captain Roscoe asked.

"I do," said Frank with a nod. The expression in his face showed that he did in fact believe all of what he had just said. "… I know for a fact, that his syrup was first tried on white children and that it appeared to work. I do believe that Lester was the type of man who would not condone giving anything to anyone which would be detrimental to them." To anyone other than Roscoe and Briggs the scribe sounded sincere – it's amazing were man's brain draws its ready beliefs.

Captain Roscoe placed his hands, clasped together under his jaw. "You believe this? ***Really believe this?***"

"Yes."

"Then more fool you!" said Briggs bitterly.

"Our job was to come here and git a-hold of all the copies Lomax has on his 'cough remedy' as the Doctor called it. We were to arrest him and take him all the way back to Washington for a full investigation and a possible, trial.

"The politicians know Lomax had been treating the Pawnee tribe out at the local reservation. He's not been treating them as any act of martyrdom, but for every ounce of gold they can drop into his upturned hat. ***Your Doctor Lomax*** and his fellow partners in this sham are raking in a fortune; whilst at the same time his snake oil is turning once healthy individuals into twisted cripples, physically and mentally!"

"Lies … **filthy lies,**" Frank sat back in his chair. "— I don't believe you." Cotter folded his arms across his chest. He came across as a stubborn child.

"Oh, it can be easily proved — if you want," Lt. Briggs said as he eased the hammer of his Navy Colt down softly onto the cap of the shell in the chamber aligned with the gun's breech..

Frank countered. "Uh, it would need to be very strong proof before you could persuade me that Lester Lomax was born to be a cruel swindler. Understand this … in the past I've lived with the man and witnessed his undying compassion for the unfortunate folk in this world. He's not the type to make his fortune off the backs of people in misery!"

"Says, you…" Roscoe sneered. "Have you not heard of gold fever? Gold changes a man; it's been known to draw out the hidden streak of evil in people who at first seemed void of such shortcomings. Your friend, your Doctor Lomax was as much in love with **G-O-L-D** and all that goes with it, as the next. Even though you're good for nuthin' friend seems to have come to a fitting end, we still need and want, his recipe for that snake oil. Have you any ideas where he might've stashed it?"

Frank's face did not telegraph the scribe's inner thoughts, but it struck him that the only likely place Lester might keep papers of such high value would be in the safe, the knowledge of its existence Frank had learned from Pearl, which Lester had down stairs, somewhere in his surgery. Cotter made sure that he would not hint of its existence, to these pair of cruel bastards. Pearl was the only one he knew who knew the whereabouts of the safe and no way would he let these polecats anywhere near its contents. They were over stepping their mark and he knew that this time he had them for assault and that Boston would have to act on his charge and follow through with it, now that Donald Stroughton was back in town.

"Think about it? How would I know where things are kept? If for instance I accidentally came across it, how would I know what it was? I'm not scientifically minded, and besides, Lester would've written it in ***Latin*** — I wouldn't know Latin from a plug nickel…and if I did get my mitts on it, you'd be the last people I would give it to!"

This made it certain to the Army boys that they would stand a better chance of finding what they were looking for somewhere in the apartment — there had to be a hideaway in some nook or cranny and they would stand a better chance of its discovery if they turned the place over with the scribe somewhere out of action — after all, he would only run to Sheriff Boston once they started their dirty work…

Lieutenant Briggs stood up and as quick as a flash, and totally unexpected, butt-stroke the newspaperman across the table from him. The single blow from the soldier's substitute cosh snuffed Cotter out like a candle — even Captain Roscoe was taken aback!

"Sorry, Sir, but that drunken sod's only gonna be a hindrance. Now we can search the place wifout a bowel blockage ter hamper us!" said Briggs with a sardonic grin.

"Now **I know** why I picked you for this assignment. I'll hit the bedroom and you finish off in here what we started, days' ago. If nothing shows up, we'll go over the surgery downstairs from top ter bottom!"

Briggs nodded. "But first, could you give me a hand ter lay this drunk out on the carpet? He might do a header from the chair an' break his neck…"

"We could be so lucky," said his captain, as they took the unconscious Cotter between them off the chair and began to stretch him out on the carpet. "— Hope you didn't tap him too hard?"

The was a sound of a "gasp" from the direction of the apartment's entrance, the Army men glanced in the sound's direction and there in the open doorway to the landing, was Ma Kelly's overgrown child and both men felt momentarily like a child too, both caught with their hands in the cookie jar!

There before them stood a young man his normally almond eyes now wide like saucers, a colored pinwheel in his fat fingered left hand — the toy's wheel was as big as a wild sunflower — both men realized that the person gazing at them was the Down syndrome being of whorehouse owner, Ma Kelly.

Recovering his composure first, Roscoe asked: "Who are you?"

Peter Kelly stood there in the doorway not knowing what to make of it, seeing these two strangers holding the sleeping Mr. Cotter between them. For some reason Peter's mind sent a warning through his body that something here was amiss.

"Who are you...? – W-what d'you want here?" Captain Roscoe's questions were not in keeping with this lad's world; they were too complicated for Peter to respond too at first. But then he found his voice.

"Peter," Peter shouted at the quizmaster. "Peter, Peter, Peter — Peter K-K-Kelly … P-P-P-Peter K-K- Kelly — Peter Kelly…" Then he began swinging his arm with the pinwheel in it, back and forth across his tubby body, creating a draught which spun the colored paste propeller clockwise and anticlockwise depending on whether the pinwheel's stick handle, was thrust forwards or pulled back.

It took a moment or two before either soldier understood the significance of the situation and realized that this had to be handled with diplomacy.

"Peter … Peter," Roscoe spoke tenderly to the retard until he caught his short-term attention. "Peter, **I think** your mother is looking for you," Roscoe looked in Briggs' direction for a sign of approval as to whether or not this was the right way to handle a person of this ilk. But Briggs was not in a position to help, like the captain he too lacked any experience in handling these types of people. Realizing he was on his own in this, Roscoe took the risk and continued: "Peter, yore Mommy wants you; I can hear her calling, quick, go see what she wants!"

Peter paused to listen for his mother's voice…

Peter can't hear Mommy calling? Mommy no wants Peter. This man he very bad liar… Peter no like these men they hurt Doctor Lomax's friend he shouldn't sleep like that, me think these men make him sleep when he should be awake…He not going to tell lies he going to tell man Mommy no calling Peter…

"Peter no hear mommy call — you liar man!" Peter exclaimed.

"Oh, yes she is," said Lt. Briggs.

"Peter no hear mommy," pouted the lad. "You no like Peter. You no like to play with Peter like Doctor Lomax." He lowered the pinwheel down alongside his thigh.

"You no friend of Peter, Peter no like you, you bad, bad, bad men …" Standing there in the doorway, Peter's eyes went once more to the unconscious Cotter who was showing no signs of coming to.

Roscoe tried a new approach. "Peter is right. Yes, we are bad men, very, very bad men — if Peter doesn't go home this bad man will chop

Peter up into little pieces and cook you up in a cooking pot on the big stove. Then when we know you are cooked up nice n' tender, then we're gonna slice you up and eat you for supper and there will be no more, Peter, see! "

"That's right," chimed in Briggs as he licked his lips with a hungry snarl on his face. "And no more will Peter's mommy see her little boy!"

Peter shook his head slowly from side to side…

"Peter will be all gone, down inside the bad man's tummy!" Captain Roscoe added. This was too much for Peter Kelly; he turned and fled down the side stairs to the street below, screaming like he had finally lost his marbles..

Now free of the curious eyes of the Madam's son the men from Washington went straight into searching the apartment with no hindrance likely from the unconscious Frank Cotter.

Regaining consciousness for Frank Cotter was akin to waking from a heavy sleep. He was aware that he had been lying on his back looking up at the ceiling of a room — *Aaahh yes, the ceiling of the apartment's parlor, that's what I'm looking at!* Frank thought. He could feel also that he was lying on carpet, and, in fact that he was experiencing yet another hangover, his limbs were sluggish and he had a shocking migraine. He listened to learn whether or not he still had company, or if in fact he was now alone.

There was nothing for him to hear.

He was surrounded with the emptiness of a still dwelling as it reacted to the changing temperature. He rolled over onto his hands and knees, and then crawled across the floor to the table and with the combination of table-leg and those of a Windsor chair; he managed to get to his feet, where he swayed like a pencil pine in the breeze for a moment until he was sure he had his balance… He recalled that he had been with Roscoe and Briggs and that Lt. Briggs had done something to him, but what he could not remember.

It was not the first time he had resurfaced from a blackout — plenty of alcohol had made him almost accustom to that, but it was not something he enjoyed. He found his way across to the stove where the coffeepot sat atop of the hotplate which was dead cold. He tested the "pot's" weight to learn whether it was empty or what. He judged it to be half-full. He awkwardly knocked off its lid and guzzled down the lukewarm java that lay within, even the dregs — these brought on a coughing spell which came to an end, after it had run its course.

He returned to the table and while on the move, explored the swelling that engulfed his temple region with his finger tips — it was too tender to toy with. He made his way into the bedroom and examined himself in the mirror on top of the lowboy, the whole side of his face was slightly distorted, and in surveying the room he saw that it looked as if a mini tornado had gone through it. As he scanned things his brain made him think about how these damn Army jokers seem to be always chewing him up and spitting him out at will. He decided to head off down to the Sheriff and swear out a complaint and force the country hick to do something serious, about them … He must get himself along to Doc Hallway and let him see if he can fix his head with vinegar and brown paper! But first he had to make himself presentable for the public, Frank came upon Dragoon's pearl-handle Derringer, which the man had loaned to him, he thought that Dragoon had taken it back and could not recall how he had come by it. He slipped it into the side pocket of his trousers. He would pull it on them blue-bellies if they crossed his path before he got to the sheriff. Passing through the parlor he could not but help notice the army's handiwork; things in the room had been strewn about.

Cotter realized that it was imperative he get to Boston's place as soon as possible before those army bandits got out of town—once out on the street he'd wave someone down with a buggy to carry him to the Sheriff's Office for he didn't believe it possible he'd make it there quickly enough by use of shank's pony. The black cat came out from hiding in amongst the woodpile under the stairs, and followed Cotter until it realized it had reached the outer limit of its territory where it broke off shadowing Cotter and went home.

Deputy Ben Lexmon was just leaving the jailhouse when Frank arrived and because of the contusion — he, Lexmon, almost didn't realize who it was. Boston was still in the office, entertaining Sheriff Robeson and Bud Reed.

"This feller will interest you, Jock," said Boston with a nod as Frank approached the divider fence. "— He's the joker who wrote up the report of the robbery and sketched the mugs of the bushwhackers who did all the shootin'!

"Mister Cotter, I'd like you ter meet Sheriff Robeson frum Lawrence, county. The Cattlemen's Association has put 'im in charge of the stage holdup," Klem said by way of introduction and explanation.

Boston, Robeson and Reed were sitting round Klem's desk in a half circle in captain's chairs, all relaxed. Jock rose for the occasion and his chair's vertical spindles and runs creaked with relief as the tall thickset Scot proffered a hand pretty much the size of a church bible.

"Pleased it is I am to meet you, sir."

"Likewise," Frank said as he thought; *now that's what I would call a Sheriff.*

Reed gave the tenderfoot the once over and found it a bit amusing to see a city dude wearing one of them stupid hats they call a Derby. He didn't know that Cotter possessed a Stetson but had mislaid it somewhere in Lomax apartment. The distorted face of Cotter's did nothing for him in a hat such as a "Bowler".

"Say," said Klem. "That's a real dandy hat yuh wearin' there, man!"

"It's what they call a 'Bowler'," Jock informed his ignorant companions.

"I've never seen you wearing that hat, before, Frank…?" Klem pointed out, he much preferred to see Cotter in the Stetson, but kept quiet about it.

"Couldn't locate my new hat, so fell back on this thing as a standby…"

"It looks like one of them fancy things folks put under their bed at night, to avoid a visit to the outhouse in the dark!" Bud Reed said. "What brings you down this part of town, friend?" Boston asked as he now realized that the side of Frank's face was swollen as if hit by a Queen bee. He suspected that maybe Frank had got on the wrong side of a cowhand, well, you would if you were wearing that stupid Bowler, thing.

"You remember those two army fellers who claim they were with the Indian Affairs Department, Klem?"

"Don't tell me, you've had another run in wiv 'em?!"

Cotter nodded. "They came back to Lester's place and finished off that search they started before. That joker … the young one, clobbered me with something and left me senseless — they ransack the apartment. I don't know if they work the surgery over — didn't think to check."

"They're dead set on getting something that the Doc has—even if it means going ter jail, for. I dunno, it has me buffaloed all this damn business with those two guys," Klem got up and went and collected his hat from a nearby peg near the drinking Goudas.

"C'mon, we'll have a look in a couple of saloons and see what they have ter say for 'emselves."

"I know what they want," Frank said to Klem as the man limped back to him. Boston shot the tenderfoot an inquiring look. "They're after the formula for Lester's serum, he's been using on the Pawnees. D'you knows anything about it, Sheriff?"

"Can't say's I do," He strapped on his gun-belt and check the right-hand side gun's revolving cylinder for ammunition. It was fully loaded to his satisfaction.

"I hope you are going to arrest them this time — not give them a tap across the knuckles like before, Sheriff?"

"I know my job, Sonny-Jim!"

"I'm more than ready to swear out a complaint of assault this time around as well as 'Invasion of Property'!" Frank told Boston.

"We shall see how it plays out, first." Klem warned.

"Far be it for me to meddle in your affairs, Klem, but sounds like you're goin' to need to take a firm hand with these Army types — or they'll have yuh losing face in yer own croft!" Robeson warned Boston.

"I know that — they won't git away wiv anythin', they've over stepped *my mark* this time. I tend ter give a feller a bit of latitude until I reckon they have gone too far, as is the case here…" Klem Boston opened the gate of the wicket and joined Frank Cotter on the other side of the divider, uninvited, both Reed and Robeson were clearly coming along for the ride. "— The Army don't run *my* town an' they are gonna learn it," then to Frank. "Do you know where they hang out?"

Frank shrugged. "Sorry."

"They won't be hard to find, not Army blokes," said the Scot

"They are not in uniform, not these fellers," said Klem. Then Boston turned to Cotter. "…How's yore head standin' up? You are feelin' groggy, it seems ter me?"

"I've suffered worse with some hangovers. No. I'll hold up."

"Mebbe so," said Jock. "If I wuz you. I'd get myself to a sawbones and let 'im check you over. That's some swelling you are carryin', sir."

"Sheriff Robeson's right," Deputy Reed added.

"You take off ter Doctor Hallway and we three jaspers will search for those king-hittin' sidewinders." Klem ordered. And to be truthful, Frank knew the man was right.

They were more than capable of haulin' Briggs and his friend in. "Leave it to us to bring those army lads to task," Jock said as he loosened the Colt in his left-hand holster.

Cotter lay on his stomach on Hallway's examination couch while the man carefully scrutinized the swelling. "H'm. That's a sizeable contusion you have there ... it's indicative of having been given a blow by an iron object or something in that nature. Sore, isn't mister Cotter?"

Hallway had been the first medico to put his shingle in Junction City and proudly boasted that he had delivered most of the young scallywags that raced about the town on ponies or young colts.

"You fingering the swelling like that, doesn't make wearing it much better," said the grouchy Cotter.

"Sorry. But it is the only way I've got of having to tell whether or not you've got bone damage under the skin." The doctor stepped back to allow Frank room to work round into a sitting position, at the same time the doctor removed his own smock. Frank maneuvered into position so that he could drop his legs over the side of the couch.

Klem and present company had walked Frank to Hallway's surgery and left him there while they went off looking for Captain Roscoe and the Lieutenant.

"I can't do much for you but order you to bed. And when I say 'bed' I mean, *bed*. Only get up for meals. I can give you something for the headaches but I don't know how well they work, 'coz I've not had to take 'em, they are some new type of pills."

"That's fine by me. I'm a bit of a sook. By the way, I've been looking into Lester's accident and folks have been telling me Doctor, that it was you who attended Lester when he got knocked down by that wagon... "

The Doctor frowned, and then raked his gray hair with the fingers of his free hand. "What has it got to do with you if I did?"

"Didn't you recognize my name when I gave it to you on arrival? I'm Lester's friend from —"

"*I know* who you are — Lester told me about you … over coffee. But my question still stands, what has Lester's accident got to do with you?" Hallway sat back in the Captain's chair and crossed his hands in his lap and waited for his answer.

"I think because of that, that's reason enough to be entitling me to details about Lester's life in Junction City, and especially his accident? Which until to date; no one seems very keen to say much about it to me." Frank began to put on his socks and boots, as he looked quizzically at his late friend's medico.

"I see," murmured Hallway. "To begin with, if you have any questions relating to Lester's death, and in particular the accident details … you ought to get them from the Sheriff. I was only Lester's colleague and medical adviser, that's all."

"That makes it **more** the reason I want to talk to you, the fact that you were perhaps, in some ways — his confidant." Frank sat up straight now that his hosiery and footwear were in place.

The doctor put a pellet of "breath freshener" in his mouth before continuing, thoughtfully.

"Well as far as things went it was just a terrible accident. The poor fellow just stepped down off the sidewalk right into the path of an oncoming wagon — and was killed — all in the blink of an eye. He was dead when I arrived — look, is there any point to this? It'll all be in the Sheriff's report, get him to let you have a copy of it if you're so interested."

Both men sat there for a moment just staring blankly at each other. Then Frank gave a slight shake of his head and said: "She's a darn weird town, this."

"What makes you say that, Cotter?" The doctor looked as though he was getting on the defensive against any criticism of Junction City from an outsider.

"Boston never made any offer to let me see a report. Yes, I shall ask to see it. However if he refuses I can't do **that much** about it. If this was back east I could have gone to the Inquiry and got the same information by just sitting in. But most people I talk to about an 'Inquiry' into Lester's accident, keep indicating that there seems little possibility of there being one. In the East, most accidents are always looked into from the legal aspects of things —"

"But you are forgetting, sir, this is not New York or Washington, this is practically still a frontier and why should the courts out here allow themselves to get clogged to the gills with a lot of legal rubbish? People here want to get on with their lives — the past war wasn't any help to the majority of folks and they'd be viewing this sort of inquiry as clogging up the court's works; when there are property matters n' water right that need sortin' out."

"Forgive me Doctor for saying this — but you spoke that more like a money grabbing, Attorney that a concerned citizen."

"Well, maybe I'm in the wrong profession — who gives a shit?!" He snarled.

"For one; me: I'd like to know more of the details surrounding this incident involving Lester."

Hallway's face broke into a sardonic smile. "You strike me to be a person with a morbid attitude towards thing?"

"Maybe… But ***is it*** gonna hurt you to humor my morose tastes, Doctor? Of course not, so please draw me a mental picture of the scene and who was there at the accident."

Doctor Hallway wet his lips and then began to reminisce at Cotter's request. "…Let's see. There were four of Lester's friends on hand."

Frank frowned, ***"Four. Are you sure?"***

"Positive," said the Doctor, cocking his head to one side as he thought about it. "Yes, definitely four. Why d'you question that?"

Frank's mind had started to grab at any detail that presented itself as not ringing true or quite right, maybe he was grasping at straws to build a mountain out of a Mole hill; he was working without a plan — just taking a hunch as it came through to him.

"You say he was dead when you reached him, right? …So, what kind of injuries did he sustain which could have brought about instant death? And in your opinion, since being injured, could he have been conscious for even a short time?" Frank's eyes betrayed his excitement. He was like a hunting mountain lion that had gotten the scent of its prey.

"What are you trying to imply?" Hallway said his breath now sweet from the throat lozenge.

"When Lester was being moved from the dirt-road to the sidewalk near the front of his surgery, some people at the scene — friends of Lester's, said he was conscious and lucid. He even spoke to them about my future, how do you account for that?"

"…Anything is possible," said Hallway truthfully.

"So how about, pain? It would've been pretty unbearable, wouldn't it?" Frank now crossed to the chair and sat on it, the chair was located near the examination couch. The doctor opened his desk drawer and withdrew a four by four beige cardboard box with a lift off lid, even from Frank's point-of-view he too, could see that it held a quantity of pills; they were like red-pepper berries.

Frank continued. "— in the few minutes Lester might have had left, could he been capable of conducting any form of business arrangements?"

Doctor Hallway was certainly thrown a puzzle here by Cotter, and he could not understand where the man was coming from.

Cotter saw that the doctor was completely baffled by his question and felt he had to explain himself. "His business partners claim he instructed them to sort things out for me in particular, now that he had apparently realized that death was overtaking him."

The doctor gathered a number of the red-berries from the paste-paper box and put them on his desk, some stayed where he had put them while three or four of them, rolled a short distance away from the nest and came to rest in the furniture's grain.

Hallway replaced the lid of the box and returned the pills to the desk drawer. "I can't make that sort of judgment," the doctor eventually said. "I wasn't there …" The doctor left his hand in the draw a moment longer to collect a small white round cardboard box, it seemed obvious that this smaller box, which looked similar to a doll's hat-box, was a container for the pills the doctor had prescribed for the scribe. As the medico transferred the pills from his desk to the interior of the small doll's hatbox he explained: "People are all different — I can only limit my opinion to the cause of death. There isn't any other evidence to suggest I change that."

"Could it have been more than just a simple accident?" Frank said as he watched the doctor write with a quill, the directions for use of the red pills on the top of the slip on lid, of the pillbox.

"Suppose Lester didn't just step-down and out in front of the wagon — what if someone gave him a helping hand out in front of that vehicle? Something planned, like a push or something?" Cotter stood up and held out his hand for the pillbox.

Hallway passed the box of pills over to his patient, who in turn slipped them into a side pocket of his pantaloons. "You know young man, whether Lomax was pushed, fell, or slipped into the path of that heavy wagon — the resulting injuries incurred to the head would have been the same. The man's face was unrecognizable … his facial bones had been crushed in by the wagon's combined weight; I wouldn't have known 'im, save for his clothes and body statue.

"You are saying, folks say Lester spoke to those around him?" asked the doctor. Frank nodded. "Then if that were the case … I don't know how they would have **understood** a word he said. His jaw was dislocated on top of his other head injuries …I reckon he was dead by the time I got on the scene but mebbe he wuz alive when he wuz carried from the road so only those with him would know if'n it wuz possible fer him ter speak. I see you're favoring your arm, d'you want me to have a look at it while you are here?" The Doctor was referring to the torture Briggs had served up to the scribe.

"No, it'll be OK. A feller gave me a bit of a sprain on purpose, it should be fine in a day or so; but thanks…" Frank went for his billfold. His finances were getting low and he did not know whether or not he had enough to pay the doctor.

"Those pills for the headaches, will work on the pain for your arm, too." Hallway informed Cotter.

"Look, I'm a bit short of cash at the moment —" Frank confessed as he opened up the billfold and showed the medico how light on the billfold was for money. "— can you bill me for this visit?"

"Sure. Just don't for get to pay a man before you leave town," Doctor Hallway said with a grin.

Captain Roscoe and Lieutenant Briggs were found in a card game by the three lawmen at *The Sorrel Saloon,* which the army lads had favored as their habitat.

"That's 'em," said Klem as his party stepped through the batwing doors and round a false wall, there to shield passing pedestrian traffic from the shameful, world of alcohol, gamblers and women of doubtful repute. As it was nearing vespers, the bar-gals were a little thin on the ground. Boston led the trio over the pine sawdust covered floor, as the bar's pianist, a pale faced Frenchman who had long ago abandoned **Gay Paree,** began tickling the ivories.

Junction City's Sheriff and his back-up stationed themselves round the table and allowed a couple of hands to be played before stepping in. The Captain and the Lieutenant knew that Boston wasn't here for his health, but they tried to ignore the crippled lawman, who they assumed was here alone. But they soon learned otherwise when the present card-hand had been completed, for as Briggs was in the process of dragging in the cards for his deal, Boston came to life and made his play to arrest the accused. Taking it for granted that these two men were Army. Boston was actually saving taxpayers' money by arresting them, for it was more than likely their gambling spree was to be covered as part of their found. That is of course, if they were really Army personnel.

"Roscoe and Briggs …" said Boston in an authoritative tone. The addressed men looked up in the Sheriff's direction. Briggs froze; Captain Roscoe calmly removed a half-smoked Cheroot from between his lips and placed it on the flat lip of an ashtray, which clearly had been in use for some time. The other players in the game knew that their session with their new acquaintances in town was up and, began to reach for the "house-chips" on the table's rustic surface.

"Let's begin wiv you fellers handing over yore guns, nice an' casual-like. But first, if it isn't askin' *you* too much; and wiv-out any backchat, ease away from the table an' stand at attention…" Boston demanded. "Now that last part I'm sure you've had plenty of practice at, especially if you are who youse reckon you are…?"

Roscoe spoke more to the ashtray than to the Sheriff. "—I won't bother asking you what you think your game is, Sheriff. But do you get a kick outa making a damn fool of yourself?

"Remember what happened the last time you tried to slam us in the guardhouse — it'll only turn into a repeat performance this time around, you'll be paying a **penalty** you'll never expect. You're gonna learn that a civilian doesn't stand a chance against the Army. "

"That aside — I'm a-waitin' fer you to start movin' yore pair of asses," it was plain to one and all, that Boston wasn't fazed by Roscoe's lip. Roscoe looked across the table at who was willing to take the sheriff on; he had that look there in his eyes. Roscoe indicated to his subordinate not to make a play, but to comply with the sheriff for the time being. Roscoe was unarmed, as it was he had left his army issue Colt back at Ma Kelly's boarding house along with his flapped holster.

"Realize this, Boston…" said Roscoe as he had somehow twigged that the Sheriff seemed a little too confident for someone here alone to arrest an armed man. "Because you've got reinforcements we will comply…" He then addressed Briggs who was most puzzled by his Captain's reaction. But his attitude soon became very clear to him when the officer indicated that out of range of his vision, the sheriff had company. "— humor the **cripple,** Lieutenant."

Both suspects rose from the table, the backs of their knees ferried the chairs at their rear away from the table, leaving furrows in the sawdust.

"Sheriff Boston doesn't need reinforcements," said the Lawrence lawman, his Scottish brogue which he normal went to pains to conceal was allowed full rein.

"Umm, easy tuh see where your sentiments lay, Scottie…" Captain Roscoe had already noted the Silver Star on Robeson's vest. The engravings etched into the metal also showed that this lawman was from another county and was therefore out of his jurisdiction.

"Aye, that's trew lad. So don't you and your friend push yuh luck? Let us all act like gentlemen and mosey uptown to the jailhouse like dear old friends." Jock pulled his pistol and cocked the hammer, holding it on, while without prompting, Deputy Buddy Reed came forward and relieved Briggs of his pig iron. Reed shoved the .45 behind the buckle of his gun-belt.

The saloon was all quiet through this part of the performance, the Frenchy had turned away from the keyboard of the upright piano to what was a piece of live theater that had captivated the bar-room.

However once the lawmen had departed from the premises with their prisons, life resumed in the den of sin and the Frenchman went back to encouraging a jolly tune from the honky-tonk piano and chase away the air of gloom left behind by the administrators of law and order. The guys whom had been playing with the strangers resumed their game when two young cowhands, who seemed only too willing to treat their hard-earned money with contempt, or could it, have been foolhardiness, joined them?

Outside on the boardwalk, Klem instructed the arrestees to walk up along an imaginary centerline in the dirt of Main Street, while he and his associates followed hard on their heels. Klem was experienced in the ways of desperate men, he knew that had they stuck to the sidewalk amongst the interspersed pedestrians, it could afford his prisoners the chance to breakaway and flee the clutches of the law, because it would be too risky to send hot-lead after them in a crowd, dense or not.

"D'you knows why I'm doing this?" Klem said to Roscoe with his six-gun aimed at the small of the captain's back as they moved up the street.

"I know why you think you have to do it," Roscoe said over his shoulder. "You reckon yuh holding up the town laws. But, you have got it all wrong, *again.* Truthfully — you're as dumb as an obstinate Mule —'

"— we're the "good guys" here," Lt. Briggs butted in, "but you haven't got the brains ter recognize it!"

"I s'pose burglarizing someone's home an' gettin' violent wiv an innocent man is the Army's way of goin' about business, eh?" to emphasize his point, Klem jabbed Roscoe hard with the blunt tip of his weapon's muzzle. Roscoe felt like turning on the Sheriff, cripple or not and laying into him with fists he had hardened in brine; but he knew it would be best for his cause to take the humiliation in his stride — his time would come. But in fairness to this hick, he decided to give it one more try to get through to the stubborn Boston, in the hope he could get the man to see things Washington's way.

"What we've been doing may seem unorthodox to you, Sheriff. But our rôle in all this is to find evidence, which will expose Lomax for the cruel, low-down rat, he was. His death cheated a lot of hard working and sufferin' folks out of a justice they deserve," Then to Briggs he said: "Isn't that true, lieutenant?"

"Yes sir, very true." Briggs said.

"Hmm, is it not trew you've found no such evidence?" Jock asked.

"Luck hasn't favored us thus far." Roscoe admitted. "But we're certain it will be found somewhere in the doctor's place. All we need is ter get our hand on is the copy of the recipe Lomax uses for his syrup and the Government will have him! Then the government scientists will analyze jist what goes into that damn concoction which is so detrimental to peoples' health.

"Lomax was nuthin' more but a thieving con man and that feller he brought out here from the east, is coated with the same brush of paint!"

Soon they had turned off Main Street into Ridge Road and as they angled their way across in the direction of the jailhouse Klem said: "Well, here we are boys—Home sweet 'ome." Boston bypassed his prisoners and shouldered open the office door and waved the soldiers through. "Yeah gonna be here for a while this time so make yuhselves comfortable!"

The lawmen ushered the reluctant prisoners through the gate in the divider and down the back of the room to the iron barred cells; meanwhile, Klem grabbed the bailing wire ring that held the keys from amongst the stationary and other items on his clattered desk and wanted notices—which would eventually find their way on to veranda posts about the town the, crim's' notoriety had been written into criminal history the moment they had either gunned someone down or committed a crime against State or County. When Boston came through to lock up the county guests, he found that Reed and Robeson were patting the blue-bellies down to make sure they didn't have anything hidden on their person which could be used as a deadly or offensive weapon.

It was almost suppertime when Frank called on Attorney Stroughton. The lawyer had turned out to find himself a meal and to ask Cotter to join him — they headed for the diner in the uptown direction for both men were familiar with its fare. The Doctor had wrapped a bandage round Frank's head much like a sweatband and thus it was not possible, for him to wear his bowler, which he now carried. Stroughton made no comment about the hat carrying business, but wanted to know how come Frank was so bruised up and hurt bad enough that he had to have his head bandaged.

Frank relayed his mournful tale as they tread the boards up in the direction of Ridge Road. Because Donald knew Frank to be a recovering alcoholic, he had assumed that the man had fallen and was too embarrassed to tell the truth about it. At first, Donald thought that the city slicker had been telling a tall tale about how he had come by his injuries. However, by the time they had reached the diner he had accepted Frank's story and realized that when he crossed trails with those Army bods, he would need to be very weary and on *his* guard.

These guys from Washington are out to try and pin all the dirt they can on Lomax and they will try to target me now they know of his death, seeing as I am the man's lawyer! Donald Stroughton thought.

Donald, like almost everyone else entering the diner, save for the Sheriff and his men, checked his .38 in with the Cashier while waiting for a table to become free. Cotter had forgotten to do likewise because he had completely lost any memory about Dragoon's Derringer.

The attorney quickly led Frank to a table that had become vacant over near the picture window that looked out onto the street and the passing town's folk. They had to wait a few moments before a surly, stumpy waitress wiped the table over with a damp cloth, taking with it the remains of the last customer's meal, evidence that he or she hadn't had any table manners. Stoughton opened up their conversation with: "Look, allow me to say here an' now, that any friend of Lester's will be a friend will be a friend of mine – and I say that with all sincerity!"

Smiling, Frank said: "And that goes double for me. However, will you still feel the same when I tell you Counselor; I've not yet even begun that inventory you asked for?"

"That's not a very good start to things, Frank…" said the lawyer with a smile, "but when you get around to it I'm sure it will be fine."

Hill and Bevan entered the diner and fronted up for the establishment's counter service as table settings were scarce. While waiting for attention Monty Hill allowed his eyes to do a tour of duty over the faces of the surrounding customers and spotted Cotter and

Donald Stroughton. He whispered in Bevan's ear, then leaving his partner at the counter, Hill approached the lawyer and scribe with a deep serious look on his face.

Frank, read in the man's face that he was out to make conversation with them — and noticed that Hill was focusing on Stroughton rather than him.

"Hello Counselor and you too Mister Cotter…" The change in the scribe's appearance now that he was focused on the man, really alarmed Hill and before he could put a stop to his forwardness he blurted out to Cotter: "What's been happening to you – someone bury a hatchet in yore skull?"

"It looks a bit like it I guess Mr. Hill…"

"Oh, for God's sake drop that **"Mister",** business – Monty's just fine, "Mr. Hill's" too formal for friends of the late Doctor. So what's been done to you?

"If'n, that's not too rude a question?" However before he could get to hear and details on the subject he waved for Bevan to come across and join them – on the way through the room Bevan collected a couple of chairs which had become available at a table; It was clear by the obvious reactions by some waiting customers in the room whom had been holding out for an empty table, that they didn't appreciate his actions – they went and complained to the Cashier who was completely flustered by Bevan's conduct; by this time the chairs were being warmed by Hill and Bevan's posteriors. Now Frank understood why no guns were allowed in the place in a frontier town like Junction City – blood would most likely have been spilt over this had so hot-head been armed. The offended customers stormed out in a huff.

Frank went on to explain he had caught up with Ma Kelly and she had put him wise as too how he owed his own life to Bevan and Hill for what they had done for him – the two men brushed all that business aside with words to the effect: "We have done the same for a Black fellow if we found him in your position…"

"Now it seems that I'm indebted to sawbones Hallway, for patching up my noodle, thanks to the Army. Ma also told me her version of Lester's accident; she had a bird's eye view of the intersection from her upstairs' window, apparently. Ma Kelly watched as Lester was carried off the road onto the sidewalk outside his surgery…"

"I didn't know she saw anything," Donald told Monty and Jonas without being asked. "I thought she was a post accident spectator who came down to lend a hand!"

"No, she didn't see Lester get actually rundown," Frank went on to explain to the men but did not understand why; it just gushed from him before he had given it any thought. "She saw you folk carry Lester off the road."

"Did she?" said a puzzled Jonas Bevan, as he looked around the table at Hill and Stroughton. "But then after any accident there's a darn lot of confusion."

"And no two people seem ter see things the same way," Stroughton said. "I come across it a lot in our courts."

"That seems to be the case here. Ma Kelly tells me that there were five men all up, who carried the dying Lester over to the boardwalk. Yet when I was at Doc Hallway's today, he saw things slightly different. His memory of events differs to that of Lester's landlady. He's certain that only four fellers did Lester the honor conveying him from the point of impact to the sidewalk."

"How would he know?" said the lawyer, "he didn't get to the scene of the accident until Lester had been laid out on the boardwalk!" Donald's dialog was brought to a stop because of the arrival of a waitress with a serving tray holding their meals. Hill sorted the meal orders out for her while she stood sullenly by. Once she had departed, Donald Stroughton lent in and said: "Right. Now for everyone's benefit I'll throw in my version of what happened. I'm the one here who feels really shocked about the whole mess. For if *I* hadn't called out to Lester when I did, I reckon he would still be alive and probably sharing our table this very minute. It was me who called out to him … I was simply acknowledging the fact that I had seen him — I didn't expect him to come bounding down the steps and out in front of that wagon, like he did! Christ! Even I didn't see the wagon coming!

"Maybe if *I'd* been the one to start out across the road instead of Lester, things would've been completely different — I'd've most likely seen the damn wagon. Every time I think about it, I blame myself, I really do. I've never witnessed a man killed as simple as that," confessed the Counselor.

"All the same," said Frank. "I can't help feeling in my water that there's something about that accident that doesn't sit right. Look, I know you're all friends of Lester's and business associates in some way or another, but I must be forthright with the lot of you about this here accident — no matter whom *I* offend."

"You're damn right there is!" Don exclaimed.

Surprised to find a ready partner to his theory, made Frank view the lawyer in a different light. "Aaahh, so I've a co-partner sitting at the table?"

Donald Stroughton shrugged, "The whole **bizarre** thing beggar's disbelief. To have a life end on a street …"

"Is that all you mean?" Frank said, incredulously.

"What else did you think I meant?" Don asked as he paused with his fork halfway towards his mouth, the instrument covered in mash potato.

"Doesn't the identity of the fifth man who helped carry Lester's body, interest you? He just upped and vanished like some Genie off the face of the earth!" Frank said as he viewed the Attorney's opinion and found it incredible.

"I can't see where you are tryin' ter go with this, mister Cotter?" Jonas Bevan said.

"Then open your eyes, little man — **open your eyes!**" Frank snarled at him. "He just being there means that we have an independent witness to the whole shebang! He might very well have a much clearer picture of things than anyone of *you*."

"I think you're making too much of this "witness" business," Hill said. "Anyway, what do we need particular witnesses for? There ain't gonna be no inquiry, and if there were, *we* have more than enough people to support what happened. There's Counselor Stroughton, Jonas Bevan, the wagon driver and me — how many more would you expect, Cotter?"

"Because with an accident inquiry held, it looks much cleaner on the court records if you have "Independent Witnesses", you jokers are all either personal friends to Lester or business affiliates…" Frank Cotter pointed out to them. "Surely as a man of the law, you can see what I mean, Donald?"

"I know what Frank is driving at," Donald said to both the puzzled Hill and Bevan. Then he turned on Frank. "But it is not going to happen — if it does, it will be over my dead body!"

"Are you afraid that if this fifth feller turns up and an inquiry is held, that he might say something, detrimental?" Frank said to Stroughton's face.

"Listen to **me,** and I'll tell you why we don't need an inquiry into Lester's death…" Don looked fiercely across the table at Frank and Frank could see that Hill and Bevan were a party to Stroughton's feelings towards him. "Your beloved desire for an inquiry will achieve nothing. Not a thing! We're all aware that the Government's out to destroy Lester's good name and standing in the community of Junction City. As long as Lester Lomax is headline news, the more the Indian Affairs Bureau will want to show him up as a lowlife, swine." The Lawyer paused, so, as what he had just said would have time to sink in. He continued when he thought ample time had elapsed: "— *we* can't let them do that. After all, no one more than the people here at this table, knows that there are people in Washington who simply hate Lester's guts; for the changes his research might likely make to the world that we live in today. Jealous people in Washington are afraid to face the fact that out of Lester's success would come, personal wealth to Lester and those associated with Lester's enterprise. No one better than he knew, and understood about the hidden corruption at government levels. You, Cotter, were to be his sword in all this, which's why he wanted you on board. But what's done is done and should now be left that way — we should just concentrate with getting on with things. Besides, the wagon driver, Dunne is hurting enough over this and may never fully get over it."

"Lomax is dead an' buried," said Monty Hill. "I say let it stay that way."

"And you should forget this fifth man caper," added Jonas Bevan to Frank. "He's a will-o'-the-wisp, a figment of an aging woman's imagination," Bevan turned his attention to Monty Hill. "Do you remember ever seeing this so-called other guy, Monty?"

Hill shook his head. "I can't say I did… But then again, it was all utter chaos after the accident."

Donald Stroughton said to Cotter, "Let me put this to you. If Ma Kelly thinks she has anything to add to the details Sheriff Boston has taken down on the accident already, she is the one who ought to go to him with it. Next time I see her, I'll tell her that!"

"Ma has her own reasons why she doesn't want to get involved and upset certain people in this town and I can see her position as things stand," said Frank. "But the reason I should like her to come forward, is because she's the type of woman who wouldn't be easily flustered in the surroundings of a court — she wouldn't stand for any browbeating. I think its worthwhile taking her account of the existence of there being a fifth feller.

"And as far as the teamster who was driving the wagon goes, I can understand how cut-up he must be feeling — but I too, have things to struggle through. The only way to solve 'em is to have a wide open and shut closure to Lester's accident."

The rest of the meal was eaten in silence as everyone seated at this window table struggled with their own thoughts. Frank's food craving had migrated elsewhere.

When supper had finally run its course and Stroughton's party had taken leave of the Werner's Diner, save for Hill and Bevan who could not escape a dressing down from the manager-cum-cook about their queue jumping, the lads under the hammer followed Cotter and the attorney out onto the sidewalk with their respective tails between their legs; here the four men came upon an impoverished Mexican working the boardwalk's passersby with his homemade Spanish style guitar and gravel voice. There was no doubt that he could hold a pretty fair tune as he strummed away Flamingo style. His upturned straw sombrero on the weathered boards only held a few coins— certainly not enough there to buy the blind fellow his next meal.

Donald Stroughton paused at the hat, where he fished in his pocket for some change and came up with a few bits and dropped them in the straw well of the sombrero, joining the coins already there. His gesture encouraged Bevan and Hill to add to their donations, but Frank stalled, for he had no idea how long he was going to need what small amount of cash he had, so he held back.

The sightless troubadour was none the wiser as to who had come forth with alms in passing and whom had not. The singer's jet-black hair was plastered over a balding scalp and his complexion of mustard-brown skin was as smooth as that of a baby's, all added to one's conception of what a "greaser", and should look like, even down to his thin, drooping mustache, which seemed almost false and ready to fall from his upper lip if the twist of his face went the wrong way.

"…Are there many beggars in the town, Counselor?" Frank said as he thought: *How long is it gonna be before I'm out here or somewhere else, begging for my next meal?*

"Not too many," he led his combo over to the edge of the sidewalk opposite a tie-rack that held two saddled mules and three cow ponies. The Mules stood like statues without moving so much as a hair, but the horse shuffled about a bit as though lazy flies from the manure just below their rear fetlocks were troubling them. "…A few Pawnees come in from the reservation from time to time and try their hand at it, but most folks simply ignore them."

"That's because they have the government to look after 'em, haven't they?" Hill said into the hanky he was using to wipe his nose. Bevan had read Don's thoughts about partaking of an after supper cigar and readied a Vesta for the occasion. The awning post he struck it from was marked by the scuffs of other men's previous firing up, attempts.

Puffing his long, fat cigar into life from the proffered match flame, the lawyer went on: "…The Mex has been in town along time, before Hill and Bevan were here, to ever get the dust of Junction City on their leather uppers. So, what's on the cards for tonight, boys? Feel like coming upstairs for a friendly game at my place?" His offer was made to all and sundry in the small group. Hill reneged and Bevan followed suit, Frank wondered if Jonas ever decided things for himself without first noting what Monty Hill intended. Hill maintained that they were going round to *The Theatre Royal* to enjoy some of Junction City's culture; it was going to be the second dose of the play Pearl was in. Frank felt he ought to call on Boston and see what progress he had made about the Army thugs, and hoped that he might find them warming the cots of Junction City's cells, as promised. Then Don suggested to the faggots that they keep an eye on the wagon driver if they came across him in the saloon section of Ma Kelly's establishment.

"The town's rife with rumor that the shock of the accident has turned Dunne to the grog and that is bad for **his** business… What's bad for his business, is gonna be bad for **everyone** in the long run. Look, let's have a meeting in my office tomorrow morning and we can sort a few things out which need straightening — that invitation is extended to you too, Frank."

Cotter nodded an "OK" to the meeting, besides he wanted to meet the wagon driver. "Dunne is the name of the guy who drove the wagon?" Frank asked; Donald nodded as he blew cigar smoke over the heads of the animals tethered at the hitching rack. The faggots looked at each other as they agreed with the meeting and broke away from Frank and Stroughton, and went off in the downtown direction amongst the pedestrian flow of traffic.

"Something's puzzling me, Don."

"And that is?" The attorney knocked the growing ash from the tip of his cigar.

"Why are you so concerned about Dunne's welfare? How do you and the others tie in with him?" Frank looked at Lester's lawyer and ignored the two cowhands who arrived at the hitching rack to collect the mare and the gelding that had been tied up with, the Mules.

Stroughton was busy thinking about how best to go about explaining certain facts about Lester's complicated business life. For complicated it was.

"…It's like this. I'm the business lawyer for Lester in various ventures he had set up. For instance, Lester was in partnership with Dunne in the freight-line." Learning this, was a surprise to Frank Cotter — *what the Hell is going on in this town?*

Lester was rundown and killed by his own business partner? That's damn too extraordinary for words!!!

"I see you're overwhelmed to hear that?" said the Attorney. "Yes, Lester was Dunne's silent partner in the freight-line, the silent aspect of the arrangement was Lester's idea. It was the Doc's good name with the bank that secured the loan to set Dunne up. Lomax, Hill and Bevan formed a cartel that was to distribute Lester's medical discovery throughout the nation, once it had gained government approval — they all stood a good chance to make a lot of money, it would've been like owning your own money printer.

"Lester had friends in Washington who realized that the Indian Affairs Bureau was pussyfooting around while someone inside the Bureau put out feelers for a cut of the action — for they could see the millions that were likely to be made. But Lester, Hill and Co., backed away. I don't know how true it was, but word began to surface that some of the Indians, adults and children whom Lester had treated with his discovery were left in pretty poor shape. How? I don't know. The formula for the "mixture" is a closely guarded secret, and there are those in the Government who want to get their hands on it, hence your Army friends. They wanna get the formula to the government scientists so they can find out just what's in the brew —"

Frank cut in. "And thereby placing the Government in a position to squeeze Lester and his business cronies out of the equation!"

Nodding, Don agreed with the scribe. "—you're catching on. Now before that accident, Lester made a will; it's back there in my office safe right at this very minute. Tomorrow, I'm gonna open that sealed document in front of all of us in my chambers. I'm sure you will be interested in being there for the reading?"

"Wild horse couldn't keep me away from that one!"

"That's what I thought," said Attorney Stroughton as he threw the remains of his cigar down on the ground amongst the hooves of the mules. An obliging Hinny stomped it out — as though it had been trained to perform such a trick. At that moment Doctor Hallway approached Frank and Donald from the direction of Ridge Road, it became apparent that he was heading to supper at Werner's Diner whose front entrance was just beyond them at the back of their shoulders.

"Hello, hello, hello…" He paused to give Cotter the once over. "Evenin' Don, evenin' Mister Cotter. I see you two have finally caught up with each other?" Hallway said, stating the obvious. The doctor casually drop back a step to let some change fall into the Mexican's hat; then he stepped back up to the lawyer and the scribe.

"I thought I told you that, Doctor?" said Frank.

"Mebbe you did Mr. Cotter. But sometimes a man my age forgets the odd one or two things — you two, taken supper already …?"

The pair nodded, this deflated the medico for he was after some stimulating company along with his supper. "When did you roll in from Dodge, Don?"

"About, tenish." The Attorney said as though making a report to the Doctor as if he were Judge and Jury.

Hallway brushed off a gnat in search of a landing site.

"Cotter tells me you had to patch him up?" Stroughton said.

"Yes…" Hallway glanced in the direction of his patient. "Saliently, Cotter doesn't follow a doctor's orders. He ought to be in bed, resting!"

"Then I'll see that he gets where he belongs, Doctor. I'm for an early night — beginning tuh feel more than a bit trail weary myself, now that you've mentioned 'bed'."

"I wanna call on Boston before I turn in, don't you remember me saying, so, Don?" Frank reminded the lawyer.

"You can do that any time friend; Boston's not a traveling man… " Stroughton told Lomax's friend. "I'll walk you back to Lester's place."

"I'm not a **child** —"Frank stubbornly point out.

"That doesn't stop one from acting like one! Bed, *now* … as soon as possible," The Doctor turned to Counselor Stroughton. "And can I rely on you to see that he stays put?" Stroughton nodded.

"Well then gentlemen, Good night to the both of you…" The sawbones wheeled away from them and headed over across the planks of the sidewalk to the diner's open door and the mixed smells of cooking aroma.

Stroughton turned and headed downtown with Cotter tagging along, for the moment both men were occupied with their own thoughts.

I wonder if Lester knew what he was doing, when he decided to bring this goddamn drunk west and mix him up in our business affairs. Stroughton, thought. *I can't see any justification for it! I can't help but think that Cotter is a dangerous liability to our whole organization…*

They saw some boys unwrapping packets of fireworks and both knew that there was going to be trouble in store for folks with livestock, be it horses, dogs or what-have-you. Frank went on to sum-up this Lawyer feller. *I fear Lester's Attorney doesn't like me, much. Even though I've accepted him with an open mind, he had already made his mind up about me, and I don't reckon she's all that favorable — that's for damn sure … I bet a hundred bucks that Lester has told the whole damn territory about my coming and that I was the Crown Prince of the lushes! If so, that was damn cruel of him — that's not the actions of a man set on trying to get me back on my feet, so as I can once more stand up and be counted…*

"I want you to be straight with me, Don —" Frank said as they made it to the corner of Bryan and Main Streets. "Is there no one in the county Lester hasn't told about my trouble with the bottle?"

Don could hear the bitter tone in Cotter's voice as they were both forced to duck under a low hanging copper lamp attached to an angle beam beneath the corrugated iron of the overhead awning. Stroughton felt compelled to placate the disturbed man.

"Lester was your friend, Cotter. His bringing you west was his way of throwing you a lifeline. Lester had friends in all sorts of places, as you must well know. He knew what you had been reduced too ... living on rotgut and lyin' drunk in filthy whore- houses. "Anyone he ever told about your short-comings was for a reason, so that they might help keep you sober. Your sort, has to be guarded against yourselves, there wasn't anything malicious in him towards you..." Stroughton indicated to Frank that they should cross to the other side of Bryan Street to be on the sidewalk which crossed Starr Street on the same corner of Lomax's surgery — when they finally reached the corners of Starr and Bryan Streets, Stroughton paused and explained. "I'll leave you here, Cotter. D'you thinks you are capable of handling the stairs alone, or do you want a hand?"

"I can manage from here." He told Don. "What time shall I report to your chambers in the morning?"

"Any time after nine, or so ... You look after yourself and get a good night's sleep!" Then the two parted, Frank crossing empty Starr Street to climb the stairway up the eastern side of the building, while Stroughton continued along the sidewalk, past the theater to the alleyway that ran right through to Main Street.

Moving like a Panther out from beneath the staircase the black cat came to meet Frank upon his approach to the building. Cotter relented, and knelt down and patted the cat between its ears; the feline creature began purring affectionately as if it had already comprehended that this man was her new master... Then suddenly both cat and man were startled by the sound of Sheriff Robeson's voice from the dark beyond Cotter's left shoulder.

"Evening, Mister Cotter." Frank moved almost as quickly as the cat, as he came upright and whirled in the direction of the voice. To his utter surprise he discovered the Scotsman and his Deputy standing there at the edge of the sidewalk on the surgery side of the street.

"Sheriff Robeson," said Frank in a shaken voice as he came to a halt before the tall brawny fellow.

"That's right, Lad. Glad I caught up with yuh. We thought you'd like ter know that Sheriff Boston, Reed an' I, have got your Washington friends in custody for assaultin' ye …" Hearing this, brought forth a long overdue smile to the City Slicker's sore face. "Aaahh, Aye — thought that would bring a smile to yer face," Robeson turned to his Deputy. "Now didn't I tell you Reed, this young feller would think it were Christmas when he heard the news …?"

"You sure did, Sheriff!" Buddy Reed confirmed his boss's statement with a grin to equal that of the assault victim.

"Well, it is good to know that Sheriff Boston can be as good as his word. Now I shall breathe that little bit easier tonight for a change."

"Now, one good turn, deserves another. So could ye see yuh way clear of doing *us,* a favor?" Robeson asked.

"If it's in my power …"

"I need ter know every small detail you c'n tell me about the robbery. Things like who said what and who done what? I know about the shootout at the German's line station — Deputy an' I heard about it on the way through here ter Junction City…"

"Right," said Cotter as he backtracked in his memory. "First. Let's use these steps for a pew, Sheriff; I've been on my legs too long today. That brain rattle hasn't left me a hundred percent…"

"How thoughtless of me," Robeson gestured towards the risers of the steps. "Be our guest." The black cat had by this time taken up a position at the top of the landing and regarded the humans below with a look of contempt.

In retrospect the lawmen's faces had taken on a mantle of that of a Priest in the Catholic or Orthodox Faith, waiting to hear a sinner's confession…

9

S EEMINGLY SATISFIED WITH what Frank was to tell them, the law officers bid him adieu. They explained that their next chore for friend Sheriff Boston was to call at Werner's Diner and pick up supper for Klem and his prisoners.   Frank paused on the steps for a while after they had gone to enjoy the evening breeze, then he hauled himself up by the banister and trudged up the remaining steps to the landing where he stood before the apartment door and went in search of the door key, while at the same time, twisting the doorknob with his free hand. To his dismay he found that the door had been left unlocked! Cotter was sure he had closed and locked the door before leaving, he could not be sure that Roscoe and Briggs wouldn't return and he was not going to make getting back in the apartment easy for them. They might be in jail at the present but who can count on how long that will last. If they were who they say they are, and Stroughton doesn't seem to doubt it, that Washington will pull strings for Boston to free them. But just in case someone was secreted inside, Frank recalled that he still had the Derringer at hand and took it from his pocket and cocked its hammer.

What little light there was at this time of the early evening seeped into the parlor from the street window overlooking the intersection of Lester's death ...

Cotter's eyes scanned the gloom from where he stood framed in the doorway and to his disbelieving eyes saw that the apartment had been tidied up to some degree, he easily recalled that he had not been up to doing any straightening up before his departure from the premises and the mere fact that something's had been moved about and rearranged in his absence, filled him with apprehension. ***Careful Cotter, something's not quite right here…Hmm, looks like a Good Samaritan has visited me — or is there danger lurking here!*** Cotter brought the Derringer up so that it was only a matter of pointing the muzzle in the direction

269

of its target should he be confronted by any foe. He strained his ears for any sounds that might be foreign in this setting outside of that which usually impregnated the apartment ...

Nothing; but he took solace in the fact that at last he was acting responsibly like a cautious westerner. After a few moments he was ready to accept the reality of his position and that he and only he, was here in the apartment. He heeled the door shut behind him and crossed to the table and placed the Derby and Derringer, still cocked, on the damask cloth near the center of the dinner table, next to the table-lamp and worked on getting it fired up. Once the lamp was underway, he was better able to take in the full extent of the room, and in so doing, discovered that the whole parlor at least — was now shipshape. With the lamp in his hand he went forward to the doorway of the bedroom and from his position under the lintel, saw too that it had been made orderly. He returned to the dining table where he sat down on a chair and ran his fingers, through his hair, baffled as to who would have been so thoughtful to have come here and tidy up.

How the hell's-bells am I gonna cope to sort out this mystery surrounding Lester's accident? — What I need is a damn good drink! Oh yes, I know, it cannot be anything alcoholic, I'm not that dumb! What about your promise to Lester? Shut up! I know what I promised to his memory and I am going to keep it!

Cotter got up from the table and went over to the Benjamin Franklin cooking range and opened the firebox, it was almost half full of cold gray ashes from the spent fire. He took up the fire tools and the empty coalscuttle and scrapped the ashes from the firebox into the scuttle. From the nearby wood box at the side of the stove he found kindling and an old newspaper and some logs and set about building a small stove size pyre inside the firebox — it was something for him to do... *I might as well light the works and boil up some water to make a pot of coffee.* This he did, and while the logs were being set alight by the burning kindling, he went through his pockets until he had located the small pill-box Hallway had given him, he realized that with all which had been going on he had forgotten all about his migraine; but now with the box of pills in the palm of his hand, it returned with vengeance. He paused to admire the neat handwriting on the surface of the lid, it instructed him to take two pills per day... one in the morning and one before bed, or whenever the headache was present. He removed the lid as he sat down at the table and inspected the red pills, which truly looked like berries from some kind of bush — he rattled the box and then selected one from the middle of the gathering and put it on the table — it reacted like an outlaw and tried to gain its freedom by rolling over towards the edge of the table, but Frank's reaction was too quick for it.

After a cup of strong bitter coffee and playing Doctor to himself, he took two pills to begin with, a total departure from the instructions laid down by the doctor, he took himself off to bed, within three minutes he was riding aboard the comfortable soft clouds of sleep.

He woke where he expected to be, on Lester's bed. He felt fine and lying there in the dark he could hear the mute sounds of music coming up the street from the theater. After a few minutes of lying in the dark he concluded that sleep was now like his appetite, off miles away. He rose from the bed, deciding to take in some culture. In the kitchen he found enough warm water with which to rinse his face and hands. The head-bandage had come off while he slept, and the image of himself in the looking glass, gave him the idea he could get away without wearing it, though his bruising stood out like a sore-thumb. He put on one of Lester's coats for a change of color and then went in search for his Stetson, but found that to be a bad joke; however he found a hat which he assumed might have been one of Lomax's field hats — it was a high top, lemon squeezer.

"What brings you back, Tenderfoot?" Harry Williams asked Frank as he approached the entrance. Williams noticed the bruising, curiosity kicked in, but he held back on it for a few moments while he stroked the tails of his bandanna.

It seemed to Cotter that Williams was working the door alone, tonight.

"You may recall I missed a major part of the play, the last time I was here?"

Harry nodded. "I remember, but it'll cost you full price…" Frank nodded that he was OK with that, and began looking for change for the female cashier in the ticket box. But Harry simply *had to* know about the bruising. "What 'appened to yuh head…? D'you gets a kicking frum a hinny?" asked Harry as he leaned up against the ticket window with the seat pricing tacked on the wall in hand written script, behind him.

To-nite.
Stalls 50c.
Back Stalls 15c.

"I had my own run-in with our burglar-friends; they paid Doctor Lomax apartment another call… Like you two, I came off second best." Frank reported to Harry.

Without allowing it to show in his face, Harry was pleased to see that the scribe had got something for his corner. However, Williams said: "They got lucky the first time round wif me and me brother — next time, I c'n assures you it'll be another hand wif a fresh deck of cards!"

"Should there be a 'next time', you'll have to wait in line," Frank told Williams as he placed coins on the window ledge. Harry Williams raised his brow skywards as he wondered what the Tenderfoot was on about.

Cotter explained. "— Sheriff Boston has slapped 'em in the lockup for assaulting me and messing up the apartment. They sure seem pretty determined to mess up Lester's place. It seems as though they have a lead on something which belongs to Lester they just have to get their hands on!"

"I didn't know that civilian peace officers were allowed ter lockup, any Army men?" Harry suggested.

"Do you believe their claim that they are Government men, Williams? They might be just pulling the wool over our eyes — they've done nothing to prove that they are who they say they are, working for the Indian Affairs Department. Why haven't they produced papers to that effect? " Frank collected his ticket the cashier had left for him on the ledge.

"Oh," said Harry, "another thing. Ma Kelly has her hooks out for you. So before you get into the show, mebbe you'd better pay her a visit. Wouldn't hurt ter upset yuh landlady. You do know the way to her office?"

Frank nodded and knew that Harry was just being his sarcastic self. Cotter ducked round the heavy door curtain into the theater-cum-saloon.

The seating for the play wasn't in great demand as yet, but the same could not be said for the saloon bar and restaurant area. They were playing host to a crowd that looked typical of a Saturday night outing. Ma's banker would be pleased. *Maybe it is Saturday night,* thought Frank for he had lost count of the days since hitting Junction City. He made his way to her office which was established long ago in the foyer of her cat-house, where she could keep control over her gals — so she could chuck them a bonus.

Ma regarded Frank with pursed cherry red lips, and then said as she mentally noted his bruise: "So, the rumor round Junction City's true — you're back on the sauce, again?"

"You don't think I got this by being fallen down drunk, surely?" He made sure he kept his fingertips away from the tender tissue, even though he gestured towards the bruising.

"You tell me," Ma said as she reached for her smoldering cheroot in the nearby alabaster ashtray …

"I wouldn't willingly go back to the bottle. So how come you heard so quickly I was flat out on my back?" Frank scratched the lob of his itchy left ear with care.

Ma took a last puff of her cigar and crushed it out in the ashtray as she said: "Peter came and told me that you were acting kinda like a dead man. Peter's taken a shine to you I might add, in his world that's a pretty honorable position. Peter doesn't take to too many people, I can tell yuh.

"Peter liked Lester a lot, 'cause Lester had time for him — Lester an' you are akin in that respect, the way you've both taken to Peter and the way Peter has taken to you. Peter especially went over to the apartment to show you his new toy, which we picked out from a Seers' Chicago mail-order catalog… He came upon you drunk on the parlor floor. When it sank in, his heart wuz broken...

"It took me hours ter get any sense out of the boy! I went across to see what I could do, but you'd come to I guess, and wandered off ter some saloon in search of another bottle — you were too cunning to head this way for fear of what I'd do to you, hey?"

"Where is Peter, now?" Frank said as Ma hauled herself up out of her chair and came round to his side of the desk.

"Upstairs restin' in a spare room; He's very disappointed in you, Frank, very." Kelly examined the bruises for herself at close range. "My son has moods swings which he hasn't much control over like normal folk. When he closes down in one of his moods, you can't get anything out of him; he won't open up until he is good an' ready. That's why it took him hours ter come and tell me 'bout you. This tells me it is too late to be of much help to you in Lester's name. I know that Peter dramatizes things, but nonetheless, I wuz worried about you, especially when I found a spot of dry blood on the carpet."

"I'm glad to hear that someone's worried about my welfare. Did, did Peter mention anything about my unwanted visitors, two men who were bashing me about — for that is what caused this mess to my face!"

Ma shook her head: "Nope. Are they the same two critters that pushed you off the sobriety wagon?" Frank nodded slightly, but with the inside of his head it wasn't something he would be anxious to repeat, even having Hallway's pills inside him.

"The same two guys who gave me an' Harry a pasting?" said Reg as he descended the curved staircase and leant up against the newel across from the Tenderfoot.

"The very pair." Frank confirmed. Ma Kelly wondered what Reg had been doing upstairs. She hoped he hadn't been ignoring her previous warning to him about leaving her gals alone and paying for their services instead of demanding free saddle time.

"When next me an' Harry get a chance," said Reg, "We'll collect you and you can have a look in on how we take our revenge on those pair. I tell you, it won't be a pretty sight. Harry and me; don't like leavin' unsettled, scores."

Frank produced Whitney Dragoon's Derringer. "Don't worry, Williams … If I see them first, I'll frighten the daylight out of them with this!"

"You can forget that toy. That's a woman's play thing and won't do anyone much damage unless you shoot 'em at ***point blank,*** range," Reg came forward and took the gun carefully from Frank's hand, Williams examined it like an expert.

"What d'you mean by 'point blank'?" Frank said.

"What Reg means, friend —" Ma began by way of explaining. "— is that you can't use that lightweight gun unless yuh no more than a yard away from your target when you fire it!"

"Now that's jist the toy I need," muttered a nimble looking young female from over on the Chesterfield. Frank had not noticed her sitting there before. "I could holler to me customers, "awright boys — youse pay up first before yuh touch the merchandise," And if they refuse, I'll whip out me little pistol an' shoot one of their balls, off! "

"Oh yes…" said Reg, "and where you gonna hide it? You c'n see through everythin' you wear and that's precious little, Hester!"

"My pouch isn't jest fer ferrets, Reg. That Derringer's jest the item fer a working gal's pouch! " Hester exclaimed.

It took Reg a second to think about that, then he answered: *"Yore* pouch, mebbe — you've got the biggest in the 'ouse!"

"You should know – you've explored it enough!" Hester snapped. Reg Williams' face glared at her blackly.

"Touché," exclaimed Ma Kelly with a grin the size of a barn — even Frank had to risk a smile at that one. Ma said: "See Reg — bordello women have tongues like a viper an' you shouldn't play outside your league."

Frank retrieved the light firearm from Williams and stowed it away in his hip pocket. "Oh, and while I think about it Ma … thanks for tidying up the mess in my apartment. I might have to decide making you my wife; 'cause if you decide to bill me for all this, I'll end up bankrupt."

Ma frowned. "What your meaning, Cotter…? Make sense, will you?"

"I'm talking about you making that messed up apartment, shipshape!" Frank begun to look puzzled. "You did tidy it up, didn't you, Ma?"

"No way… Ma Kelly cleans up for no one other than her Peter," she told the Tenderfoot, "You've got yourself another Fairy Godmother — and I'm betting it's Pearl Courtney. Mebbe it's her you should be thanking?"

"Does Miss Pearl Courtney have a key to Lester's apartment?"

"It's possible. Lester appeared to have both trust and faith in Pearl. Their affection for each other ran to going deeper than just holding hands," Hester said.

Ma returned to her desk and found herself a fresh cheroot in its drawer.

"That's true," said Reg when he saw that Frank doubted Hester's word on the subject. "They tried ter keep it quiet, but things in this town have a way gettin' public. Everyone knew what wuz going on!

"Even you, Ma, thought that Pearl wuz a-wash wif hidden talents, that she couldn't make use of on the stage. Admit it Ma, you reckoned she lacked sense turning tricks fer nothin' for Lomax!"

"You're as thick as an elephant's hide, Williams!" Ma turned to Cotter with her unlit cheroot, and continued: "Forget what Reg says, he's got sand fer brains!"

"It's almost gone and forgotten. But I know you are a shrewd businesswoman. It would be only natural for you to always be on the lookout for a fresh jewel in your jewel case!"

"My God!," came Pearl Courtney's surprised voice from the high curvature of the stairs — it was certain to one and all, that Courtney had got an earful of the conversation; all eyes focused on her, as she made her entrance and continued with her descent of the rusty colored floor covering of the staircase. She was already in costume for the play, but as yet had not attended to applying her greasepaint. From her height on the risers, she had a full view of the anteroom and those in it, especially the bruised contusions of Cotter's face. Seeing this obliterated her shock about how folks in the town were talking about her behind her back.

"W-w-what, what happened to you, Mister Cotter?" she made it quickly to the newel alongside Reg Williams.

"Someone kissed me with a lump of pig-iron in Lester's apartment. Naturally, he wasn't an invited guest. Doc Hallway patched me up and reckons I'll be as good as new in a few days!" Frank took a step backwards for he though the way Pearl stepped forward once more that she was going to caress the injury and he anticipated and feared the pain it might create. But she held her distance and scrutinized the bruising from where she stood. Williams waited at the back of her with his hands clasped in front of his fly.

With doe-like eyes Pearl said: "You mean you were **attacked**!"

Frank nodded glumly. "…Yeah," he answered. Then went on to try and make light of it. "Not by any Indians, thanks to God."

"Shouldn't you be resting or something?" Pearl asked. "Look, I might be as folks say, 'a Tenderfoot', but that doesn't mean I am made of porcelain. C'mon, just to show you how fit I am, I'll walk you to your dressing room, Miss Courtney…"

Frank offered the actress his arm and together they set off down along the hallway to the stage wings. The moment the couple was out of earshot, Ma snarled at Reg Williams who went red of face.

"You are a rat bag, Williams! Telling that reporter feller I'd tried to recruit Pearl Courtney for my stable of gals… Can't you read people? That feller's smitten with her!" Ma Kelly picked up her ashtray and threw it at him, but she was no shakes when it came to throwing objects at anyone and she missed Reg by a mile, and the off target throw was partly meant not to connect, though Reg still shied away from it. "— Learn ter button yuh lips about what goes on behind the scenes here, or you and yuh brother can find somewhere else ter do your moonlightin'. You know Lazarus Rollo, only allows ya ter work here, coz through you brothers, he knows my every business move before I make it!!!"

Reg hooded his brow. There it was now, all out in the open. So Ma Kelly knew all along that they were reporting all her business to the Chairman of the Cattlemen's Association.

"You'll realize, two can play the same game," Ma added.

Pearl composed herself before her dressing room mirror on her stool and began applying her make-up. "What are you doing here at the theater, anyway?"

Frank sat on the lid of a laundry skip. "Came to see the part of your play I missed out on," He transferred the little pistol from the hip pocket of his trousers to the inside pocket of Lester's coat.

"Are you going to tell me what happened to you?" Pearl asked with genuine concern on her face. She applied face cream to her skin to set up a basis for the greasepaint. While waiting for it to soak in she prepared herself to hear about Frank Cotter's misadventure.

"Do you *really* want to know?"

"I asked, didn't I?" She had a carbide lamp used by miners; clamped to the top of her looking glass this practically made her face, shadow free.

"Those men from Washington came down on me again. They are defiantly after something belonging to Lester and think I might know what it *is* and *where it is!*"

"Now you too, are accepting that these thugs are from Washington?"

"Mainly because Lester's attorney seems to have accepted that they are who they say they are!"

"You've seen Donald Stroughton? He's back from Dodge City, then?" asked Pearl.

Frank nodded. "As a matter of fact he has seen me twice since he got back to town. He hurried around to the apartment to introduce himself and this evening we had dinner at Werner's diner with Hill and that Bevan, feller…" Frank drew his hand lightly across his partly closed mouth. "Tomorrow morning I have a meeting with the lawyer and Lester's partners … There, I'll get to meet the driver of the wagon. Did you know that this Dunne guy and Lester were in this freight business together?"

Pearl nodded.

"Then how come you didn't mention it before?"

"I never thought of it — too upset about things I guess," she told Cotter and then began working on her face.

"Apparently Lester has made a last will and testimony before his fatal accident. Stroughton has it in his safe and is gonna break it out when we've all gathered at his chambers. Should prove to be interesting reading, what do you reckon Miss Pearl?"

She shrugged her shoulders. "Whatever. I told you before; Lester could be very secretive when he wanted … Aren't you afraid these thugs might come after you again?"

"I think that will be very hard to do now that Boston has them behind bars. Where, he ought to have kept them, the first time round."

Pearl began applying greasepaint to her forehead, ***"Behind Bars? What d'you mean? "***

"Klem Boston arrested them earlier today while I was seeing Doc Hallway. I've had them charged with assault, so they won't get out of jail this time in a hurry. A thought just struck me, what if what those men are after is there in Lester's safe in the surgery. You said he was keeping papers there of yours, too. Maybe they are under everyone's nose…?"

"Lester wrote a lot of his scientific research work in Latin. We wouldn't know what we had in our hands, even if we do dig it up," Pearl Courtney confessed. "It might be a good thing all round if we never turn up his formulas for this elixir — it's only wanted now by those to condemn his soul. I don't care if this formula never turns up!"

"I'm not sure it is gonna be that easy, Pearl, err I mean Miss Courtney, sorry..." the scribe apologized for his indiscretion.

"Pearl is all right, Mister Cotter. I don't stand on ceremony with someone I consider a friend."

"So how about you call me, Frank?"

"My pleasure…" she began applying eyeliner. "What did you mean when you said it still wasn't going to be easy for Lester, even if they, the government, never get hold of his papers of the formula?"

"I fear that that Washington will manufacture enough evidence against Lester, to squarely crucify him in the eyes of the public ... It's just my opinion." Cotter rose from the skip and came up behind Pearl's chair.

"Maybe Lester's accident is not as it seems, either. I have had this feeling all along that it or something about it isn't quite right. Even you've caught *my* fever, only you've tried to be more vocal about it. I couldn't afford to be because I have to live in this town, where as you can kiss the place goodbye at the drop of a hat."

Cotter regarded the actress for a moment before telling her: "The only people, who ought to feel guilty in this, are people with something to hide. I feel you're in the clear but there are others who mightn't be. Maybe the trouble is *me*… Maybe in coming here I was expecting too much — something which couldn't be delivered? I know I am having trouble coming to terms with my friend's death. And as if that isn't enough, I've been towed to the stoop of death's door by alcohol — bashed over the head with a gun ... I'm sorry, but I'm afraid that none of this has made Frank Cotter a very happy, guy!

"I have never been fond of the dregs the Army attracts to its ranks — recent history hasn't done anything to change that belief. I don't intend being in Junction City longer than I must, but before I go I would like to see the town hold an Inquiry into Lester's accident. Clear it up once and for all! I can't wait for tomorrow to come face to face with the teamster who was driving the wagon that hit Lester!"

"And what do you hope to achieve by it?" Pearl asked. She was growing melancholy and did not relish beginning tonight's performance. She knew she was going to have a night of bad concentration and would have to rely heavily on her prompt. "What I've seen of Dunne since the accident, he's taking Lester's death very hard and you forcing yourself onto him will only drive him deeper into the doldrums."

"If the teamster's on the level, he shouldn't be afraid of me. What harm can I do him? None — not a stitch. But he might be able to clear something up for me, he may be able to put a face to the fifth man who helped at the accident, and then went missing. For some unfathomable reason everyone else at the accident has conveniently deleted him from their memory." Cotter drew his watch from his vest. "...and if I intend seeing this play from the start to finish, I'll best be getting out to front of house!"

"Didn't you get enough of it the other night?" Courtney said as she set about changing her footwear to that of the play's character.

"Remember, I only caught Acts Two and Three of the play..."

Cotter was ushered to his seat and on looking about the auditorium was encouraged by the swell of the audience. The folds in the burgundy stage curtains look   like solid giant columns of marble that seem to rise up and up, until they disappeared into the proscenium. Cotter's focus was drawn to the four piece combo in the orchestra pit who was entertaining the waiting patrons with gay musical numbers, quite a change for people used to hearing the bellows of steers and cows. A change of rhythm in the music acted as a wake-up call to the shuffling audience that the play was about to commence, the murmur of the theater crowd dropped away to naught as the stage curtains parted smartly to reveal the stage set, off-stage the theater hands were as busy as slaves at their windless as the outdoor garden setting generated its mood, the audience had been transported somewhere in the southern states, possibly Alabama. The stage props consisted of a shady Magnolia tree in the throes of dropping the odd blossom; Miss Courtney playing the part as Miss Besse Lane occupied a garden bench beneath the tree. Lane was busy doing needlework and a white man, poorly made up to represent a Negro slave, approached her from the wings...

The end of Act One drew a good response from the audience, a number of the people rose from their upholstered theater seats to stretch their legs and cheer the performance of the players. Some of the folks on their feet made a rush in the direction of the bar. Frank thought of going backstage to pay Pearl his respects, but then doubted that there would be enough time, so decided on having a quick glass of sarsaparilla from a bartender not bothered by what the patrons threw down their throats, just so long as it added to Ma Kelly's income. Without direction the barkeep chipped off small lumps of ice from a larger block, the size of which would require the use of a man's two hands to manipulate; these off-cuts of ice he added to Frank's drink.

Ma Kelly owned the only ice-works in Junction City that supplied ice to the town's other saloons and a few households whom had the newfangled ice boxes that were becoming the trend back east. Frank got these tidbits of information from the few householders whom had the newfangled ice boxes that were becoming the trend back east. Frank got these tidbits of information from the barman who prepared his drink. The chips of freezing water had small air-bubbles trapped within its formation — their freedom could only be assured as the small chips melted in the warmth that surrounded them.

Regardless of the drink's temperature, Frank skoaled the 10-ounces of root-beer, only now realizing how parched he had become during the play's first act. Cotter signaled the same barman from a distance, for a refill and while waiting for the busy man to cater to his needs, he felt a light tap of someone's finger on his shoulder. The man responsible for the familiarity, pressed in on the bar, looking this stranger over, Cotter realized that they were very much the same age and almost the same stature — but it was obvious that this man was far more stronger than the newspaperman, their different lines of work had nurtured that. The rude fellow was dressed in clobber that was indicative of a man tied into some form of manual labor. From top to toe the new comer wore a flat-crown sweat stained beige Stetson, a loose thong chin-strap dangled from close to the outside of the hat's crown down, either side of his jaw-line and under his chin, to his Adam's Apple. His cheeks were rough with a three day-old beard and his complexion had a dull unkempt look about it. Parting his hazel eyes was an aquiline nose with brows that crossed his face in one almost straight line. It was unknown to Cotter whether the guy had a full head of brown hair or if in fact he was balding, the hat played hide and seek with that bit of information. He had a dusty black bandanna which disappeared into his red shirt open collar. The breast pockets were stuffed full, one with a drawstring pouch of tobacco and the other with a plug of chewing tobacco, he wore the shirt tucked into a pair of moleskin trousers, which he had slipped into an old pair of Calvary boots. He stood so close that one could not avoid his body odor, a combination of moldy bread and vinegar.

"I hear yore lookin' fer me, Cotter?" he leaned heavily with one elbow on the zinc top of the bar and regarded Lester's friend with eyes seeming to float on the effects of booze.

Frank knew all about this, but before Cotter could get his voice into gear the man answered his own question, "I'm Sean Dunne," he murmured with a scowl in the scribe's direction.

"I sure am," admitted Cotter as he offered the man his hand. "—You've been a missing link since I hit town..." Dunne looked down at the proffered hand and it took him a moment to decide whether or not to take up the offer or not; Then with a "what the Hell does it matter" look, he took the scribe's hand in a firm grip.

"Sorry I ain't been around but I've been tryin' ter run a business — it's been hard ter keep going, since Lester's accident. I'm trying ter keep the wheels of industry turnin' if you know what I mean?" Frank nodded that he understood where the teamster was coming from. A barman closed in and Sean ordered tequila from the man before he reached their area. The bar hop went away to fill Dunne's order. Frank commenced their conversation, "It has been a nasty business with Lester; his death has left a few of us in a damn big hole, Sean — I can call you 'Sean' I take it?" Cotter asked. "My handle's Frank ... by the way."

Dunne nodded that no one here had to stand on ceremony. "I've got a battle on me hands with all the worry over this accident..." The barkeep arrived with Sean Dunne's *tequila,* he left it on the bar without waiting for payment and Sean noticed the surprise look that crossed the scribe's face, so he explained that Ma Kelly allowed him to run a slate.

"And how long have you been drinking tequila ...? **That's** gut poison." Frank pointed out.

"I'm a bundle of nerves since Lester's accident — it's the only stuff that seems ter settle 'em," Dunne explained. "Night's the worse time. I keep seein' Lester as he stepped down off them sidewalks steps — right in to the path of me wagon, over, and over, time an' time again! The whole episode prowls round in my head like some Indian demon, leaving me no peace." Dunne downed his shot of spirits in the one gulp with trembling hands and slapped the empty glass down on the zinc bar, with the body language of a man demanding a refill!

Nodding at the empty glass, Frank said: "Take it from me, you won't find any solace in that shit! I've been down that road..." Frank made a gesture with his sarsaparilla towards Sean's shot glass as it was snatched away by another barkeep for a recharge.

"Mebbe you're right, but ter me this is the only good thing ter come out of Mexico!"

"You won't think that once it's got its claws into you. Just wait until it makes you start to see the real phantoms of your mind. You'll get scared shitless and wish you'd never been born!

"One time I found myself floundering in a cesspool of human excreta, riddled with worms and leeches; it was trying to suck me down into its very bowels, like quicksand. The smell would make a gutless whore, vomit! … That's just one of the many horrors I can relate to you off the top of my head, and the more —"

"HALT, RIGHT THERE…!" Dunne cried and covered his ears with the palms of both hands, "I don't wanna hear it — I don't wanna hear anymore — I've got me own *torments* ter sleep wiv!"

"Don't get me wrong, Dunne. I'm trying to make you see that tequila isn't a friend you trust!"

"Don't **you dare** to lecture me — don't walk into my life tryin' ter act the goddamn Savoir! Lester told us all about you, you can't preach ter me! Yore a drunk from the soles of yer boots, up!"

"I'm not that weak that it'll get its claws in ter me. It's a medicine, and I use it as such!" Sean Dunne shouted. All the folks within a yard's distance had tuned into the scribe and teamster's discourse.

Frank had to make the feller see sense; he had been there and done that… He ignored his embarrassment and told the man straight: "We **all** think that," He paused and took a sip of his soft-drink and then continued: "I'm just trying to advise you. You don't wanna listen, then, you are welcome to your own Hell. But promise me one thing?"

"What." The word was said begrudgingly.

"Before you've lost yourself in your own swill, I wanna hear your story about Lester's accident."

"Go fight a grizzly! I've had it wiv Lester's accident right up ter here!" He drew the edge of his hand across his throat like the slash of a knife blade. Frank could see that if he pursued the matter, Dunne might turn violent; and he had no desire to tangle with the man.

To the nearby barman who was scrutinizing them, Frank said, "Give the man another shot of cactus juice on me!"

The barkeep jumped to it, anything to quiet the pair down; otherwise the Williams brothers would be called in to eject the two of them and that could very well lead to something more serious. "All everyone in this town seems to want to do is leave yours truly out in the cold. Maybe having a damn good talk about this whole messy business would ease your mind, Sean. Have you thought of that?

"Ma Kelly nearly saw the whole incident from her apartment window overlooking the intersection…but what she seems to have witnessed, doesn't gel with what the rest of those connected to the accident; doesn't quite match with what some folks says took place. All I want is the truth, no more, no less."

The haggard faced teamster snatched the fresh glass of tequila from the bar and then toyed with it for a bit in his thick callous fingers and after a while muttered. "…W-what does she think she saw, then?"

"She missed the actual business of Lester being breasted by the horses. She saw you jump down off your vehicle, and race back to Lester's body on the ground where you were joined by the others, Hill, Bevan and Attorney Stroughton. She saw five of you pick Lester up and carry him over and place the Doctor on the sidewalk near his surgery … by then she's managed to find a clean towel and make her way as best she could with her bulk, downstairs and out to the intersection where the others had laid the doctor out…"

Dunne raised his glass slowly up to just below his nostrils and sniffed the cacti juice and said: "…Huh, there you are then…she's got it all wrong!"

Frowning, Cotter asked: "How so?"

"If I recall rightly … me an' the Attorney got to Lester 'bout the same time. I took hold of the left leg I think it wuz and Stroughton, he, he grabbed the right leg. Monty Hill and Jonas Bevan took Lester's arms an' I went back ter look after me team; they had enough help ter move the Doc without me. Where did this fifth feller come into the paintin'?"

"According to Ma Kelly — he took care of Lester's head. Carried it like a melon in his hands, I imagine!" Frank suggested. "She seems to think he was a passerby who stepped in to lend a hand on the spur of the moment, I don't know."

Dunne shook his head, the loose chin-strap swayed back and forth beneath the stubble of his chin. "I dunno. You dunno because you weren't there. I can't recall there bein' anyone holdin' Lester's head. All I reckon that concerned us at the time wuz gettin' Lester up out of the dirt somewhere clean."

"Who was it fetched Doctor Hallway?" Frank asked.

Again Sean Dunne shook his head. "…We were busy wiv Lomax. I can't say who got Hallway — he just appeared there with his medical bag, though there wuz little he could do."

"Sean, I heard at one point that it was you who went off in search of the sawbones, yet you say you were there with Lester … that being true, maybe it was this that fifth fellow, who Ma Kelly claims was there?"

"Yuh damn irritatin' *me* … what is it wiv you an' this fifth feller, business! All the time you wanna know about 'im!" Sean Dunne threw down his drink to annoyance; it must have tasted nasty for he pulled a face as it slid down his throat to his upper stomach.

"The reason I'm prepared to believe in the existence of this joker, is because Ma Kelly says he was there. She's an astute businesswoman and would have no reason in the world to make something up like that! In fact, if you like we could see the woman together and see what she has to say to you, face to face? Maybe in the excitement you overlooked the guy's presence?"

H ARRY WILLIAMS AND the youth whom had seated Cotter for the first performance of ***The Royal's*** play, passed through the bar and into the restaurant section of the saloon and back again, each shaking a Swiss cow-bell to draw the audience back to the theatre for the second act. But more important business was going to make it a non-event as far as Frank was concerned; he and Dunne were instead — heading towards the door of the bordello.

In the anteroom Frank and Sean found Reg Williams using the third step up from the floor as a seat, he was bored and sat there with both elbows on his knees with his hands hanging limply, fingertips towards the carpet. Ma Kelly had a tin cash box open on her desk where she tallied up a gathering of banknotes and bank-scripts, save for those customers of her's whom had paid for services with gold bucks and silver eagle dollars, any currency was welcome in Ma's establishments, excepting for the now valueless Confederacy lucre. It had clearly been a busy night for the girls in Cotter's absence.

The Chesterfields were not at this time warming any pussies, so either some customer had found the play not to their liking or the liquor and menu shelved for a later time. Peter had left his nursery blocks in disarray and was tossing colored gambling chips in the air and awkwardly trying to catch them — the "click" of the discs as they met in either midair or on the carpet was like a dancer's castanets to the young man's ears — he was impervious to Cotter and Dunne's arrival.

Pausing with paw full of banknotes in her hand, Ma Kelly peered with interest at the two men who now came to a halt before her desk. Frank knew there was no need for any preamble, so he came right to the point.

"...As you can see, Ma, I've finally caught up with Sean Dunne. I wonder if you could tell this feller what you told me about Lester's accident; it might straighten out the confusion that has been growing about the incident. He refuses to listen to me and accept that you saw a fifth man at the site of the accident…"

"This visit ain't my idea, Ma. This here friend of Lester's shanghaied me frum the bar. He's all fired up like a darn Pinkerton detective as you can see!" Dunne said, shamefaced with the effect of the tequila in his belly. Then suddenly he recalled that he was wearing his hat in the presence of a female and whipped it off and held the Stetson in front of his pelvis. "— I've err, no-no idea why he wants ter play the rôle of a Lawman, that's Klem Boston's rig ter flog I would've thought?"

It was plain to all that being brought before Ma like this had unsettled the teamster; already those around could see that he had become clammy.

"It's all right, Sean." Ma told him in the tone with which she would generally use when talking to Peter. Then she swung her eyes in Cotter's direction, by then they were as hard and cold as two ice blocks. "— are you tryin' ter get me hung or sumthin'?"

"What d'you mean?" Frank was genuinely puzzled.

"I thought I made it clear to *you,* I want no part of this accident business. If I reckon I'd had anything to add to what has occurred, then I'd be the one who'd waltz along to Boston and kick up my heels!

"I'm not a woman who allows her word to be questioned by jist any Tom, Dick or Harry!" Williams, upon hearing his brother's name mentioned — began to pay more interest in what Ma and the two men were discussing. Ma continued, now addressing both Dunne and Cotter: "Before I set off for the intersection with that towel, I was certain I saw five men pick Lester up an' lug him across to the sidewalk… the fifth feller was kind of supportin' the Doctor's neck; Now what happened to the fifth guy in certain I saw five men pick Lester up an' lug him across to the sidewalk… the fifth feller was kind of supportin' the Doctor's neck; Now what happened to the fifth guy in the end, I can't say nor *do I* damn well care! …It's no use asking me ter put a face to him — ter me he wuz jist someone out of the crowd, a stranger whom I'd never set eyes on before that time nor since —"

"But being that close to him, you must've seen his face?" Frank said forcefully, like a lawyer pressing home a vital point in a court case.

"*I* explained all this *to you* before, mister Cotter," Ma said heavily. "*My* concern was for the doctor. All, all, all I can recall about him wuz that he wore a wide brim Stetson and it wuz angled so that it seemed to mask most of his face… and come ter think of it, I only say him through my upstairs' window — he'd gone by the time I got down on the street."

"But you're sure there ***was a*** fifth, man?" Frank demanded.

Frowning in Cotter's direction, Ma said sarcastically: "Have I got a **Mongolian** for a son?" Her question left nothing more to be said about the sincerity of her belief. So with that, Frank Cotter and the teamster excused themselves and adjourned to the bar room…

On the way there, Sean said: "I dunno — I still reckon that woman has her knittin' needles, crossed. We'd've known if there was a stranger in our midst…"

"Which ever way you cut it, I'd sure like to know what he saw of the accident. I can't see Lester charging out in front of an oncoming wagon — maybe he got a helping hand … copped a push or maybe he slipped off the steps into your path? I can't rest until I understand more about what happened."

Cotters wrenched open the door into the bar. Dunne stepped over the threshold. "I've told everyone who will listen how I believed it happened, Hell I have been living with this nightmare ever since, let me tell yew it's no picnic. I wish someone could give me an answer of why it happened at all? … It was as if he wuz pushed in front of my wagon by the hand of fate!"

"Uh, if he was "pushed", it would have to have been by someone on the sidewalk and if that were in anyway true, it would paint a very dark picture for Messes Hill and Bevan."

"Frankly I can recall everything about those last few seconds before my team knocked Lester down and my wheels crushed the life outa him." They reached the bar, which was now a little less crowded, and Frank ordered a root beer and let the teamster order, his own poison. "I was on my way along the Street from our warehouse wiv two pianos for the mercantile store on Main Street.

"One wuz an upright piano — the other, one of them baby grand pianos, plus some odds an' ends. The Grand had been ordered in especially fer Mister Lazarus Rollo's pretty wife. I must've been hauling almost a ton in weight, if it wuz an ounce!

"Next thing, Lester is there on the road, dead in front of me team! Jist a-for the first pair hit him, Lester turns ter me and looks me right in the eyes wiv a look of horror an' fear — then he wuz gone, out of sight, under the hooves of the whole team! I felt the bump of the wagon as the goddamn iron-tires of me bogey-wheels must've went over the top of 'im! I swear, I could hear the crunch of bone as I reined the whole lock, stock an' barrel to a stop." It shook Dunne hard to make that verbal statement. It was his own personal horror, which as he said, haunted his dark nights when peaceful sleep should have been a priority. Frank patted the teamster on his hunched shoulders and lo and behold, bid him to get a shot of liquor into him. Placing the empty shot-glass back on the bar for a refill, Sean Dunne went on now without any prompting.

"Now you answer me sumthin' Mister Cotter. W-what diff' would it 've made if there were jest four or five fellers ter remove Lester off the road out of that dirt? It wouldn't've altered the final outcome would it? He'd have stilt wound up in that damn cemetery?"

"Sorry, Sean, I'm not a clairvoyant. Oh, by the way — before I forget. Stroughton has called a meeting for tomorrow morning in his office. He wants to discuss Lester's business interests, so you will certainly need to be there... even I was invited to attend. So make sure you make it!"

By the time Frank resumed his seat in the theater, act two had finished and the third act was about to begin. He was therefore able to compare this part of the play with that which he has seen before, though tonight's performance seemed to be a bit flat. However, the audience gave it the thumbs up.

After the final curtain, Cotter called backstage all prepared to lie through his teeth if Miss Pearl Courtney did not steer clear of calling for his review of tonight's lackluster performance. Thankfully, Pearl did not ask his opinion, and Frank therefore did not linger too long, as he wanted to take full advantage of being let off the hook.

Captain Roscoe was sitting on the edge of his cell bunk when the appreciative smell of a cooked meal reached his nostrils. Supper for the prisoners had been delivered from the diner by none other than Deputy Reed, the out of town law officer. Roscoe rose and moved over in the direction of the cell bars his shadow, Briggs, was not far behind.

Meanwhile the Scotsman, Jock Robeson, rested his butt up against the office divider.   The prisoners watched with hunger as they saw the meal for them had come in a Dutch oven along with the utensils needed for serving out the diner's stew, enough for the four of them. The Werner cook had also sent along an oval loaf of sourdough wrapped up in a red and white check tea towel. This Klem broke apart with his unwashed hands and placed a lump of dough on the edge of the inmates' plates. And rolled a couple of after dinner brown paper smokes, these, Roscoe suspected would be for the trio of law officers, him and lieutenant Briggs thought how much better they would feel with, a cigarette between their lips, but their makings had been confiscated along with their money belts and weapons.

Prisoners' rights were pretty grim and had gotten grimmer since the war, this came about as a result of the amount of PoWs whom had managed to escape, and play merry hell on the poor sodbusters and their kin.

"Boy! What I would give fer a cigarette right now, Captain," Briggs mused, his thoughts in line with those of his C.O.

"Yeah, I know how you feel…" Roscoe said with longing. "Forget about a smoke and be thankful we're at least bein' fed some decent chow. That's more important."

Deputy Reed collected the tin plates for the county boarders after Boston had placed a spoon into the full-body stew, and accompanied Reed down to the cells with the key and instructed the inmates to back off from the door area, which they did. Reed slipped in and placed the food on a small rustic stool that could barely accommodate the utensils. As Reed backed out he thought how lucky the prisoners were to be getting such a tasty meal, he could hardly wait to get back to try his own serve.

"Have you notified the Army authorities that you've got us locked up?" Roscoe inquired of his jailer.

Boston locked the cell. "—Been done." He lied. *I've got no proof they are Army people and they haven't come forth with any identity in line with that so, as far as I'm concerned you mugs can stay where you are…* thought Klem.

"We thought you ought to have had a response from them by this?" said Briggs as the captain crossed to the stool and collected both plates and came back to the lieutenant. Both men then went to their respective cots, one on each side of the cell.

"You'll get put in the picture when something worthwhile happens," Turning to follow Deputy Reed back up to the office section, Boston added: "But you've done the crime, so be prepared ter do yuh time, even if you be war heroes!"

Briggs accidentally dropped his lump of sourdough on the coarse, undressed floor boards of the cell, while retrieving it, he realized that if things came to the worse, they could execute an escape by lifting the warped boards under the window of the rear wall where the adobe wall and the floor met, then maybe dig their way out through the earth for he was sure that the structure hadn't been built upon what one could seriously consider to be building foundations. The speed of the dig needed to achieve such a means of escape would be the catalyst. The lieutenant came over to his C.O., and explained the possibility of what they could or might attempt.

"Good man —" This pleased Captain Roscoe and confirmed to him that he had made the correct choice in Briggs. "But let's leave it for now and give headquarters a chance to do their thing. The Government won't let this hick-town Sheriff, lock us up an' throw away the key!" "That's if they know about our situation, Sir." Briggs dipped his sourdough in the gravy of his stew. "We've got no proof that Washington knows what's happened to us — I don't have much faith in that Boston feller."

"Relax a bit and enjoy the stew, I'm confident that "Hop-a-long" Boston will be foolish enough to do the right, thing." The captain sampled his stew. "…You know, this stew ain't half bad — I'm gonna miss it when I get a new assignment…"

Later, Boston sent Deputy Lexmon down to the cell to collect the prisoners' eating utensils. Klem was sure that they would have finished supper by this. In the meanwhile Sheriff Robeson and his deputy had left the local law officers and went off to pay a visit to the oriental bathhouse for that which Junction City was becoming famous for. As Lexmon locked the cell, the Army officer asked if it would be stretching the bounds of friendship for him and his subordinate to regain possession of their tobacco and cigarette papers and a match or two. "… After all, it's very monotonous to have naught to do but pace the cell."

Lexmon did not want to be watching over a couple of prisoners all night, just for the hell of it they would keep him up on his feet riding herd over them with superficial wants et cetera. He had an inviting cot awaiting him upstairs on the mezzanine floor over the cells. He turned and hollered to the sheriff. "Sheriff Boston… Is it awright fer these fellers ter have their makin's back? "

To help the sheriff consider things in their favor, prisoner Roscoe called: **"…*I* promise we won't set the place a-fire, Sheriff!"**

Boston grabbed their stuff and took it down to the cell, passing his deputy on the way. "You won't wanna try…"warned Klem as he limped up to the bars and passed Roscoe a tobacco pouch, along with shop bought cigarette papers. "I'm what some people call a "sadistic bastard", when I've a mind tuh apply myself to it, so don't push yore luck. But you can at least answer me sumthin' Roscoe?"

Roscoe took the goods proffered to him. "I'll try." Roscoe passed the tobacco and papers over his shoulder to Lt. Briggs, who all but snatched then from his colleague's hand and, took them over to one of the cots and began rolling a couple of cigarettes as if bring them into existence was a life saving chore.

"I'll suppose fer a moment that you are who you claim ter be. So what is it that Washington has in their craw against the late, Doc Lomax an' this Cotter feller, anyway?" Klem planted his boots firmly on the floor and folded his arms across his chest, awaiting a reasonable answer.

After considering Boston's question, Roscoe commenced to answer it in a way, which would be favorable to their position behind bars. "The Army has got nuthin' against Mister Cotter — it's jist that he *will* insist on getting in the way of our duty.

You wanna know why the Army seems tuh be hounding Lomax, even though he's boarding up there on Boot Hill?

"Yore dear Doctor Lomax; is a cruel goddamn con-artist of the worst kind!"

Now, that's totally unbelievable, thought Klem — his disbelief showing in his face.

Roscoe then played another card to see if this would make the lawman see the light. "Look, Sheriff... I don't know what you and this town have against the army, or why you are so protective of the Doctor and his reputation. But only if **you people** got to know, and, understand the real man behind the façade he's built round himself, as we in the Government have, you'd be shocked beyond belief.

"Your doctor claims to have developed an elixir that will save mankind from the rigors of disease such as whooping cough, croup, pox and influenza. He's been illegally treating the poor ignorant Pawnee Indians with phony medicine and charging 'em for the privilege in payment with **gold-dust**, under the guise that he's protecting them from illnesses, us whites has infected them with.

"Lomax and his business partners are robbing the poor devils blind, turning those he treats with his "snake oil" into crippled, slobbering imbeciles. The Government scientists wanna get hold of his formula ter find out what's in it — and ter see if they can come up wif an antidote to treat Lomax's victims ... Well, that's about the size of it. "

Sheriff Boston gripped a cell bar with one hand and rested the other on the butt of his holstered six-gun. "We in Junction City have heard such rumors," Klem lied to Roscoe, he was getting plenty of practice at this chore. "Though as fer as we know, that's all it is, rumor. I owe Doc Lomax as much as anyone in this town. If he says he can produce sumthin' ter combat these illnesses, then I fer one is ready ter believe him. Coz after all, who am I ter argue wif him?

"He told me on more than one occasion that he thought he had found a key which would turn the scientific world on its ear! But he reckons the government had refused him permission ter try it out on people who need it most. Some six months ago, he told me he had friends in Washington who knew why the government has refused ter allow him to test his mixture on the Pawnee people. It was because there's s'pose ter be a conspiracy within the Indian Affairs Department ter stall off his discovery until the Native Americans have been so decimated by white man's diseases, there won't be enough of 'em left for the bureau ter worry over." The lieutenant, who had been quietly listening to Boston while making up a supply of cigarettes, dropped his chore and Lieutenant Briggs said: "Fer someone who claims ter know so little, you sure had a mighty lot of manure ter spread jist now."

"The Doc an' I did our piece of jawin' frum time to time. But all the same, I try ter keep well away frum politics and his field. If he wuz meddlin' with the health of the Indians, I'm sure the Indian agent, Warner, would've said sumthin' ter me and I'd have ter act on it, friend or no friend. Now we come ter this Tenderfoot you keep messin' wiv. I happen ter know he wuz s'pose ter be a pretty good newspaperman in his day, until he became a drunkard. Lester Lomax wuz gonna put his talents ter use exposing the government's fraudulent actions to the public, but Doc's unexpected death has changed all that..." Boston focused his attention on the soldiers. "—you've dun untold damage ter that man when you threw 'im in to a whiskey pond, wifout a lifeline. An' ter later belt him over the head wiv pig iron Colt — could've given him brain damage.

"Have any idea how hard you struck 'im? I'll tell yuh. Next time I know of you ter use a pistol like that on someone, I'll break yer bloody arms fer yews!"

Briggs showed no remorse or fear in his body fiber after what Klem Boston had told him about Cotter's drink problem, for he had no time for drunks. His sister in Dodge City had married a wife-beating drunkard of a cowpoke.

But Briggs solved his sister's problem; he had taken furlough owed him and arrived in Dodge at the dead of night were he hid out in the town for a few days, waiting for the right moment to gun-down his brother-in-law, in a dark secluded alley—as the critter made his way home, from a whore's nest. No one had ever suspected him of his in-law's murder as far as he knew, and no one ever would. Better his sister became a widow than serve out her married life to a gutless swine.

But what interested Briggs at this moment were not the domestic problems of his sister, right now he was compelled to help his Captain get the government's message across to this Sheriff.

"If you'd seen the results of your so-called good doctor's miracle cure, and what its done ter folks, you'd spew!" Briggs told Boston. "They're nuthin' more than that of the livin' dead!"

Roscoe butted it. "We know what we speak of — we've seen the results of Lomax's so-called 'miracle cure'. The down-side of all this rubbish is the fact that the Injuns don't understand the value of gold in the white man's world, and this allows Lomax and his cohorts ter get away with tons of the stuff! They'll come out of this, very rich men ... perhaps some of the richest men the world has ever seen! Just think about it?"

"You spin a pretty good yarn, soldier. But I don't believe a word of it. The Lomax I know, wuz a man wiv a heart of gold for suffering men," The Sheriff was now joined by Lexmon; it was evident that he was going off elsewhere.

"OK. Then allow me to put something else to you, Sheriff," Roscoe said as he took a cigarette now being offered to him by Briggs. "You let Briggs take you out to the reservation and see the living mess that's out there what this Warner feller has been hiding from you and the people around here.

"Then once you've seen with yore own eyes the living hell we've seen, you won't be able ter ignore the reality of it." Pausing, Roscoe took a light from the match Briggs was holding out for him. "— I'll wait here alone as yore hostage, ain't that fair? Take Sheriff Robeson and his deputy as witnesses, they strike me ter be honest men."

"Do yuh reckon there might be somethin' in what they claim, Sheriff?" Lexmon said, for he found it interesting what the prisoners had to say.

"I don't know. I don't know..." Klem chewed on his lower lip for a moment. "I have a damn lotta doubts now you've spilled yore guts ter me, Roscoe. Doubts I wouldn't have if you owl-hooters weren't tied in wiv the government!"

"Aaah, so now you are willing to believe who we say we are?" Briggs said with the confidence reserved for men of medicine and law.

"He didn't say that," said Lexmon to the prisoners.

"I admit, you've got me interest, and I've half a mind ter mosey out to the Chickadee reservation and see what Warner might be hindin' out there. I'll have ter think about it fer a while..." Boston wandered away from the cell up towards his desk, heavy in thought.

"You two make sure you butt-out them smokes properly when yuh finish wiv 'em," Lexmon warned the prisoners. Then he went to join Klem.

Sheriff Robeson flung the jailhouse entrance door open as he made an enthusiastic entrance, with Lazarus Rollo on his heels. Robeson had his blood up and the Chairman of the Cattlemen's Association looked chasten. Rollo looked as if he had gotten too big, for his boots and had to wear it. Bringing up the rear was Corbin the stage depot's manager; he looked nonplus in life's endeavor.

"I do not like for my words ter be question, Mister Rollo!" The Scotsman said as he came through the gate of the divider with a full head of steam like a Mississippi paddle steamer at full throttle. Sheriff Robeson paused at the Sheriff Boston's desk.

"… I only wanted to know who you've spoken with, Dragoon or Cotter, that's no reason to blow yore stack!" Rollo wailed.

"Cast yuh eyes over yonder," Jock Robeson waved an arm in the direction of the cells. The prisoners came to the iron fussed bars of the cell. They looked on the gathering with concern at those in the outer office. Boston hauled himself up out of his captain's style chair with eyes as big as horse apples. "— What d'you see?" growled Robeson.

"Two men, two men behind bars," Rollo stated, what else was there to say?

"An' what does it make 'em, boys…?" Robeson demanded of Rollo through clenched teeth.

Rollo said, doggedly: "Prisoners?"

"That's right Laddie; Prisoners!" Robeson said as though he might be the one man in the room who was learning a whole new language. "Now tell me, sir — why do ya think in *the entire* town they might be boardin' with Sheriff Boston?"

"You're suggesting that those might be part of the gang who robbed the stage?" Corbin asked.

"Let me put it to ye this way. I've spoken ter Cotter and in less than an hour these two men are here, behind bars! That means I'm makin' headway and I'm makin' headway because, *I* ask the questions, not *you* Rollo; or Corbin —" Jock hooked his thumbs in his cartridge belt.

Lazarus Rollo said: **"*We don't*** expect wonders, Mister Robeson," Rollo gestured with his hands like someone facing a man with a loaded gun in his hands. "I was wrong to question you about what you have done about earnin' yore money — please accept my apology and Mister Corbin's, sir!"

"Hey," cried the puzzled stage depot manager. "What have *I* got to apologize about?"

"Will someone please tell me what is going on here?" Klem demanded. "This does happen ter be *my jailhouse!*"

"Later, later," said Jock with a wink in Boston's and Lexmon's direction. "I'll see yuh before you turn in," Robeson then ushered Rollo, Corbin and Reed outside.

"What do you suppose that wuz all about?" Lexmon asked his boss now they were away from the prisoners.

Still focused on the door, Boston slightly shook his head and muttered: "They say a genius is only a hare's breath away frum madness. Blowed if I know what ter make of all that!"

"For the answer, I guess we will have ter wait to hear frum, Robeson…" Klem's deputy suggested.

"Jist remember son, that's the guy *you* admire." Klem reminded Lexmon as he returned to his chair.

Cotter was one of the last people to leave the theater, save for its staff. This time he took a new tack to that of his usual course back home to Lester's apartment. Normally he would walk down Starr Street towards the corner building to almost opposite the Doctor's surgery and cross here, taking him across the street in line with the bottom of the staircase that went up the east side of the two story building, and thus to the apartment. Tonight he walked straight out from under the canopy of the theater's marquee and across to the boardwalk on the same side of the surgery so that he was across the road from the water trough that Peter Kelly had paddled in the morning he walked Ma and her son home.

As he neared the doctor's building, Frank pondered with the idea of bringing the black cat inside with him, he did not want it disturbing his sleep out there on the landing as it howled and meowed to be let in. By this time he judged that the cat had prowled about enough tonight stalking the odd mouse, rat or squirrel before seeking the benefit of the cozy apartment. As Frank approached home, he espied Lester's cat come out from somewhere near the wood stack under the stairs with its ears pricked and searching out the various night sounds, it made its way to the edge of the sidewalk and came to a halt. The mini panther checked the street was safe to cross and then dived from the boardwalk down to the road awash with moonlight, and disappeared in the dark foreboding recess of a doorway opposite the staircase. It was as if the cat were on a mission. Had Frank witnessed something he wasn't supposed to? But all the same Cotter did not break stride. Then as he neared the open ground that led from the sidewalk to the stairs and lay in line with the dark doorway of the building opposite, Frank stopped and called to the cat, but the feline had other stubborn ideas, and purred, and rubbed its body up against a pair of familiar trouser legs whose presence was camouflaged by the surrounding Darkness; the cat was well accustom to the feel of the material that had been missing from its lifestyle for the past week or so.

From where Frank Cotter stood near the weathered and chipped edge of the boardwalk, he could hear the cat's purring in the still, quiet night — someone had to be standing over there in the dark, otherwise the cat would have come trotting across to him, someone or something was adamant that they would not reveal their *mien,* Frank knew that right across the street from him in that doorway were the ghosts' of the night — his spine tingled and he got annoyed that the black cat, preferred the mysterious somebody concealed over yonder and for what purpose?

Fear prevented Frank from taking the bit between his teeth and charging across the limestone topped road for a confrontation with whom or what was lurking in the shadows… He might be assaulted or even murdered in this lonely location if he put a foot wrong. Standing his ground Cotter tried to force his eyes beyond their capacity and depth of field to no avail. Fearfully, he glanced around to see if there was anyone else on the street; but he had to accept that he was alone with his fears and no one on hand to give him a boost of confidence.

The cat had no intentions of leaving that which was there in the dark for Frank's company. *So then,* thought Cotter *…cat can learn a lesson — the landing will have to do you tonight!*

However, Cotter was determined to let that which was concealed in the recessed doorway know, he or she was there. *The gun; the Derringer*

— I'll let them know I mean business…"Who's there…?" Frank asked in a voice which betrayed his lack of confidence.

No response.

He tried again: "I know you're there — show yourself?"

Again there was no reaction from the dark recessed doorway.

"I'm armed I'll have you know… I've got a handgun — c'mon, come out … be warned, I'm prepared to shoot if I must — I'm not in the mood for stupid games!"

The spook hidden in the doorway kept its eyes on Cotter, while slowly and silently reaching behind its back it noiselessly opened the door on to an even darker interior, and then slunk backwards into the black shroud at its rear and carefully closed the door without noise to the street, where it sheltered in the darkness for its own health and safety.

The cat, now finding itself alone in the doorway recess, turned its attention to Cotter and moved out into the open — where it made a short, silent jump, from the boardwalk to the surface of the street and trotted nonchalantly across to Cotter, whose warm hand was transferring some of the heat it possessed into the cold metal of the pistol. The cat paused slightly in its stride to set itself for the small spring that would be required to carry it upward to the sidewalk… Frank ignored the arrival of the feline and focused on the dark doorway.

…If that bastard hiding over there in the doorway makes a break for it, I'll send a bullet right up his ass, that'll teach him to go about terrorizing, people!

But nothing happened and because of that Frank turned away from the street and made his way to the staircase, the frustrated black cat now in tow. However Frank could not get his mind off the thought that someone was definitely concealing themselves across in that doorway.

I bet whoever was hiding over there across the street — thought Cotter, *if anyone ever was there, I'd whack a dime down with any bookie that it was one of those Smart-ass Army Joes who'd wangled their way out of Boston's jail. Gad yuh can't believe anything anyone tells you these days… that Sheriff from Lawrence said that Klem Boston might be able to hold them for a while, but looks as though the ass has fallen out of that jug…*

Peter Kelly opened his eyes and at the same time the marvel of sound came to his ears, he lie in the rumpled bedclothes on the iron spring bed. He could hear the late morning life going on in the town outside his window on the street. Generally, Pete was an early riser, but today, he knew he had slept late. He threw aside the covers and swung up from the mattress, his bare feet hitting the cold floor; but that did not bother him one bit. With legs stiff from lack of movement, he made his way to the curtained window. He drew one side of the sunshade away from the window's edge and looked down to the sidewalk under the awnings of the buildings opposite — people were up and going about their business. Now it struck young Kelly that the upstairs apartment was just, so quiet, no sounds of his mother preparing oatmeal cakes in the kitchen for them; as should have been the case. *Should that worry me?* Peter thought. But that thought quickly departed his mind as he realized an itchy feeling down there between his legs under the flannel nightshirt where his limp *Dickey* hung... Pete lifted the hem of his stripe nightshirt to look at his *Dickey* to see what was making it itch. Peter liked window. He drew one side of the sunshade away from the window's edge and looked down to the sidewalk under the awnings of the buildings opposite — people were up and going about their business. Now it struck young Kelly that the upstairs apartment was just, so quiet, no sounds of his mother preparing oatmeal cakes in the kitchen for them; as should have been the case. *Should that worry me?* Peter thought. But that thought quickly departed his mind as he realized an itchy feeling down there between his legs under the flannel nightshirt where his limp *Dickey* hung... Pete lifted the hem of his stripe nightshirt to look at his *Dickey* to see what was making it itch. Peter liked looking at his *Dickey,* particularly when it was swollen and stiff and it seemed to be pleading to be touched — but Peter knew his Mommy didn't like him touching his privates as she called them, and today they didn't want to be touched either. Peter had to be careful when he played with his *Dickey* 'cause his mother was serious when she forbid him to toy with it — she caught him one day at it and she gave him the mother of a beating with a willow switch. He never wanted to go through that again, so he made especially sure he was alone when *Dickey* wanted to play.   He dropped the shirt and felt its hem brush against his mid-shins as he turned to get his carpet slippers from under the bed, for Mom had another one of her rules, and that was he wasn't allowed to walk about bare feet, she said it marked the wax floorboards of the apartment.

I know what I shall do, thought Peter. — *I will go to Mommy's room and give her a big hug, a surprise, she will like that!*

He crept to his bedroom door on tiptoe; his legs were losing their stiffness. He eased open the varnished wood door to the parlor and crept out into the room; the apartment was a mirror copy of Lester's save for the richer quality of furnishings and their placement. The same contractor had built this building and the one across the intersection that Doctor Lomax had occupied.

Peter paused before his mother's bedroom door and quietly twisted the porcelain doorknob to withdraw the lock's tongue so that he might thrust the door wide open and rush in and jump on top of his sleeping mother, but first he had to make sure she was asleep in bed. From under the lintel he looked into the room, the sunshade and heavy curtains were drawn and this wasn't in any way out of the ordinary. He could see the hulk of his mother as she lie asleep on her side, facing away from him, this was good — it meant that he could rush across the room and jump right up on her, and land with all his weight. He chortled quietly to himself and dashed forward with lightning speed across the room, in a flash he became airborne – like a bird in flight, then without warning he came down and landed heavily on his mother like a sack of potatoes, screaming with glee!

But in the semidarkness of the room, with all its feminine attributes aside, the room held a shocking and horrible secret! Now the gory secret was revealed! The messy bloody sight shocked and blurred the edges of acceptability in his small narrow mind, he saw so much, so quickly that confusion surfaced as did instinct, the latter took charge of Peter's reaction, dumbly for a few seconds he sat atop of his mother and viewed her dead body… blood from her slit throat had spilt from her jugular in copious amounts onto her pillows and bed linen.

Peter wanted to get her help because he knew people shouldn't bleed like she had bled. But he could not move at first. Then suddenly he had an excess rush of energy and he leaped away from the horrible sight on the bed. He hit the floor hard on his posterior and to his horror saw that he had his mother's blood over the hem of his nightshirt and his palms and fingers — so much blood, to Peter it spoke of death and dying and he knew he had to get **HELP** — *HE HAD TO GET HIS MOTHER HELP, BUT FROM WHOM? Doctor Lomax, Oh where now is Doctor Lomax?*

He scrambled to his feet and ran screaming from the room towards the stairs that led to the street below. He went down the stairs three at a time and found himself out on the crowed sidewalk amongst the pedestrian traffic; People reeled away from him with shock at the sight of blood on his hands and on his nightshirt! Not knowing what to do, the lad was soon disorientated to that of what could be consider by his standard of orientation — those that knew the boy/man by sight, would believed that he had finally lost it, he ran in ever widening circles round the middle of the intersection; within less than a minute he was highly distraught and incoherent, all he wanted was someone to stop and listen, someone to get his mother help, someone who knew what must be done in a situation like he had found his mother!

Two mounted ranch-hands were holding their horses in check from breaking into a trot as they came along Starr Street in the morning traffic from the direction of Boot Hill and saw this oversized kid rush out into the intersection a short ways ahead of them, he was screaming and racing around in the center of the road covered in a bloody nightshirt!

The approaching horsemen were now too close to the crazy fellow and were afraid of their horses being spooked by all this carry-on. The ranch-hand on a piebald, and the only one of the cowboys wearing chaps, could see that the troubled citizen was in danger of being rundown by a horse or carriage—the only thing for it was to bring the critter to ground, he spurred his cow pony into a lope … it carried him within easy range of the nightshirt to make it easy for him to bulldog the guy, who was obviously a loose cannon and had bats in his head.

The pair was soon entangled, engaged in a serious wrestling match — the surrounding folks were aghast, meanwhile, the cowboy's partner — had dropped from his mount and gone to the aid of his friend, now we have two men trying to overpower Peter, who only wanted someone, anyone, to come along with him to help his bleeding mother! Cries were heard for the services of the Sheriff and or his deputies…A passerby on Bryan Street, the main street side, of the intersection, took to Ma Kelly's stairway, determined to fetch Ma and get her to come and get control of her wayward idiot.

But he in fact became the person destined to discover her body and the same horror Peter had been subjected too amid the bedding, life in Junction City had taken change of direction that no one could ever have foreseen.

Whitney Dragoon had been heading towards Bryan Street along the sidewalk, which ran smack bang up to the Lomax, surgery. He saw the commotion was caused by a trio of wrestlers out there in the intersection and bunch of rubbernecks looking on in shock, ogling the action. Dragoon recognized that one of the three was Ma Kelly's son even at this distance, the rag-tag youth was somehow starting to get the better of the cowboys. But somehow the blood-stained nightshirt signaled to the gun salesman that the youth was the one who needed being brought under control, buttons were already ripped from the ranch-hands' work-shirts. With a surprising flow of sympathy for the Kelly youth, he, Dragoon went forward into the mêlée before the youth hurt the cowboys or the other way round. This commotion even brought Frank downstairs on to the street, to the corner of the thoroughfare. Now for all he knew, Cotter might be standing on the very boards on which Lester's body had been placed. The sidewalk here at this point was almost two feet, above the ground; and upon digesting the disturbance saw Dragoon was in the thick of it. He wondered how this could be. Then in the scuffle he conceived the Kelly youth in a blood stained nightshirt. *Were these roughneck cowboys attacking Ma's son? Had they already injured him?* These thoughts shot through Cotter's mind, and before he realized it he had left the safety of the boardwalk and was heading in the direction of the youth who had suddenly collapsed in a tearful, exhausted heap at the feet of Dragoon. The ranch-hands also realized at once that all fight had left the grief stricken youth and they curbed their enthusiasm and went in search of their loose mounts while Dragoon and Cotter tried to comfort the town loony, which was now on his knees before Cotter, whimpering like an abandoned puppy, with arms wrapped round Frank's knees.

"What the devil's going on?" Frank Cotter asked no one in particular.

"The half-wit's gone loco," Whitney answered, seemingly stating the observable. The gun salesman leant forward and eased the youth's grip on Frank's legs, then Frank joined Dragoon and together they lifted the barefooted youth to his shaky legs. Peter kept his head bowed and began blabbering incoherently to Cotter and Dragoon; both men were at a complete loss to understand Ma's son.

The cow-hand who had bulldogged Peter to the ground, returned with his horse and began to explain to the men who were comforting the youth what had caused such a wild struggle. "…The idjit wuz out on the street — hollerin' like a female bear on, heat, blood all over his goddamn nightshirt!" The range-rider began to readjust his bandanna that had ended up screw whiff.

"Hey, everyone —" someone at the back of the dispersing crowd called. "Make way for Brewer!"

A conservative looking citizen pushed his way forward to join the muster surrounding Peter Kelly, the newspaper scribe and the gun salesman, Dragoon. "The Kelly feller is gonna be in the hot box be the look of it," Brewer went on. He had to speak around the unlit stodgy clenched between his lips by his teeth. "— The darn idjit has sliced his Mom's throat open while she slept — can yew believe!"

"What are you talkin' about, Brewer? — this poor sod here, wouldn't 'urt a fly…" said another cowboy as all eyes turned on the sniveling, Kelly youth.

"Say's you, Brody," cried another voice from the crowd. The fellow now been identified had lost the protection of being incognito and went back in his shell.

"— I have seen the body, it's there in the front bedroom where he left it; all covered in blood… By Gawd look at the blood on his nightshirt — 'ow d'ya think that got there?" Brewer sounded off.

"Has anyone gone fer Boston?" A woman's voice said from mid-crowd, its timber painted a mind's eye picture of a hatchet-faced woman. "He's gotta sort *this out* — that's what we pay him grub-money, fer!"

"Sheriff!" the cry went up from the mob. "Someone fetch thar Sheriff!"

"I think someone's on to that, already," Brewer announced for all to hear.

Frank held his hand up. "Settle down; settle down — some folks are getting over excited. Look at the state poor Kelly's in? "

"How about we take the poor feller somewhere, quiet?" Dragoon suggested to the scribe. "That's what I figure he needs right now!" Frank searched his pockets for the key to Lester's surgery. It was the first place that sprang to mind right now…

Success, he had the key. Dragoon, Cotter and Brody, who had regained some backbone, shepherded the zombie-like Kelly over to the sidewalk, up the steps to the boardwalk, where they paused in front of the timber and glass cream door of the surgery, Frank unlocked the place — the need for the rooms to be aired rushed at them with a strong smell of ether and formaldehyde fighting to make an escape.

"Shouldn't someone git Hallway down ter check on Ma Kelly? She mightn't be dead," said Brody. "After all, Brewer's no sawbones."

"She's counted her last silver eagle; you can take it from me!" Brewer said emphatically, this earmarked the fact that he had tailed the men with Peter under their wing into the room. It also notified the sticky beaks on their heels that Ma was most definitely a candidate for Boot Hill.

There wasn't an examination couch per se in Lomax's ground floor surgery, but there was in fact a divan with a bolster that the trio had no trouble getting the weak-minded youth to lie down on — Frank found a clean folded bed sheet nearby that smelt strongly of neoprene and covered the trembling youth, for even though Cotter was far from ever being a medico, he realized that the mentally retarded lad was being pressed almost beyond his limit.

"Comfortable, Pete…?" Frank enquired as he looked down into the eyes of a tortured soul. Alas, he could see that his question hadn't got through to the distraught adolescent-like mind, nor would it ever have gotten through to the inner depth of his mind under normal circumstances. The shuffle of feet behind him caused Frank to turn towards the open door and here he found that total strangers were edging their way into the surgery; Cotter wasn't going to have this, he growled at them to back off. It was a reluctant crowd of Junction City's citizens that obeyed him, but they did back away. A water cistern was on hand in the corner of the room fitted with a faucet — Frank tried the water-storage tank and found it was far from empty and half filled a clean laboratory flat-bottom flask

— it was all he could see, suitable as a substitute tumbler. Before returning to the divan, he sampled the water to make sure that it was not stale. It proved satisfactory. Frank took the flask over to Peter and lowered it to his parched lips; the youth drank like a man whom had been rescued after being lost at sea for a week without water. Pausing to force Peter to have a spell, Frank asked the gun salesman where he had been for almost a week. Dragoon explained that he had been doing the rounds of the surrounding homesteads, seeking orders for guns and ammunition.

"How come, Yolson doesn't object to you taking his trade?"

"I'm not stupid; I see he gets his cut. I hired a mare from the livery stable; man she was a horse and a half! She wanted ter head for every stallion in sight — a real hussy. D'you knows that I could've sold that piece I loaned you three times over, to the ranchers' wives! Have you got the derringer handy?"

Frank fished the pristine Derringer from his gray, silk fronted vest, which he wore over his shirt, and handed it to Whitney. "…Thanks. If I hang 'round this town much longer I might have to invest in one of those."

Dragoon took the small-bore pistol and gave it the once over; it showed no signs of wear or misuse. This pleased the salesman because it meant he could still get the factory price for it. "You've looked after it, pretty well?"

Frank gave Peter another dose of water from the laboratory vessel. "What do you reckon I am? ***Heavy handed, Luke?*** Had to nurse it like a new baby — how do I know it isn't going to be the one you sell me?"

"You're really thinking of buying a firearm?"

"The idea is growing on me. In this neck of the woods, one seems to need to look out for one's own safety." Frank took the flask away from Peter.

Hungry for the odd extra dollar, Whitney suggested to the scribe that he might think about something with a heavier caliber… something more in line and fitting a man out here in the west.

"I might entertain your suggestion if I were planning to put down some roots, here. But the east is definitely my habitat, back there, there's not much use for a six-gun… a man would look a goose with a Navy Colt strapped to his waist as he walked the streets of New York." Cotter pointed out.

"The Derringer's a good little pocket gun, a deterrent good enough to put shivers up an' down the old spine when yuh on the wrong end of it; it will scare off a street thug armed with a cosh or a blade — but it's certainly not the widow makin' kind.

"The bore's not big enough fer one thing, however, it's easy to conceal! Ask any cardsharp who's been caught making a switch when Aces High, are on the agenda."

"I know what yuh getting at, Whitney."

"I'll put it to you this way, you want a gun, then don't bypass me, I'll cut you a good deal!"

"What about, Yolson? — leaving him stranded on this one?"

"This is personal, not business!" Whitney confessed. Deputy Ben Lexmon came in from the street. He looked wide-eyed and confused. "Where's Pete Kelly?" He had not seen the youth on the divan because of Frank and Whitney's frames masking him. Whitney and Cotter stood aside so that the deputy could see him.

Peter was shivering as if half buried in a snowdrift. Lexmon approached them. "What happened?" Lexmon read the situation for what it was; and realized that he would not need to pull his gun.

Frank looked for, and found Brody was still here. He indicated Brody to Lexmon. "He's the one who would seem to have the answer to that,"

Nodding, Brody stepped forward. "Me an' my pard' were riding along Starr Street towards the intersection where Doc Lomax had his accident. When this here feller comes out on to the road, screamin' and a-hollerin' blue murder! He wos like a goddamn headless chicken! He would've scared the livin' be-Jesus out of our hosses if he wos let go on… So me an' Kenny Dugan bulldogged him right there and afore you could say "Pick yore ass", we realize he is in his nightshirt — wifout a stitch on underneath and covered in all this blood like a slaughter man! That's all I c'n say, Mister Deputy."

"Where's Dugan?" Lexmon asked.

"Outside I figger—lookin' ter our hosses," Brody told the lawman.

"The boss will wanna talk ter the both of ya, so don't git lost."

"Right," Brody answered. He had already figured out that he and his partner were a couple of very important fellers for a change and were going to enjoy every bit of this moment

Ben Lexmon gave Dragoon the once over.

"I helped wiv the boy. I'm Whitney Dra —"

"I know who you are," snapped the Deputy. "Go ahead, say ya piece!" '

"OK," began Whitney. "Well I sees Pete Kelly in this brawl with these two cowhands and I, knowing he's a simpleton, I'm afraid they might hurt 'im, so I threw in my ten cents worth and tried to calm the young guy down. After a bit, it wuz sort of realized that he had blood all over the hem of his nightshirt and hands — someone must've run upstairs to his Mom's place —"

"— Brewer it wos, Stan Brewer, you know him Deputy?" Brody remarked as he copied the deputy's example of overriding Dragoon. He went on to glanced round the room in search of the outspoken man.

"People have been sayin' Ma's had her throat cut?" Lexmon asked inconsiderately in the presence of her son. The audience in the surgery nodded like a gathering of marionettes

"That's the size of it as we understand things at the moment," Cotter said as he moved to a table that Lester had in the past, used as his desk. It was partially littered with the late Doctor's files. Frank deposited the laboratory flask in a clearing amongst the paraphernalia...

"The young feller wuz hollerin' and carrying on like a mad thing, on the forth of Jew-lie," Whitney finally got in.

Looking Peter Kelly over, Lexmon could not but help remark: "Hell, this man did never think that Peter had a streak of violence in 'im... always saw him as a damn weak, insipid sort of feller. But this shows that we can all hide a rattlesnake inside our hide."

"Are you gonna be in charge of the case?" Frank wanted to know. He was worried that poor Pete might not get the sympathy he somehow thought the kid deserved — now that folks were warming to the fact that he was a dangerous, killer.

"No. Klem Boston an' even Sheriff Robeson are over yonder in Ma's bedroom, seeing things fer themselves..." Lexmon move over closer to Peter and could see that the youth had retreated back inside himself; which sent a shiver down the Deputy's spine. "This kid's Mom really dotted on 'im — an' this is the way he thanks her. Some folks in town said Ma ought to have sent him off somewhere back east... where people like him is cared for; now look what it's come to?"

The grim-faced Sheriffs entered. They had been across to view the body of the bordello owner in her deathbed. They pause above the Arabian style divan and Ben Lexmon move out to give them room.

"How you doin' there, Pete …?" Klem asked softly with his doe-like eyes reflecting the sadness he felt for both mother and son. Boston reached down towards the youth, who was just like a person whom had allowed 'emselves to be hypnotized by one of them traveling hypnotist showman. Boston stroke the simpleton's cheek then continued. "Seems like we gotta have us a talk son; a ***real serious*** talk. Do you feel up to it? … Do you know what has happened to Mommy, Pete?"

It took about two minutes before Peter seemed to find it in him to recognize the kind Sheriff looking down on him. Yes, he knew the Sheriff. Now he began to realize that this horrible nightmare he found himself in the centre of might stop, if anyone could put a stop to the horror of his day it would be Sheriff Boston, Sheriff Boston was a very good friend of his mother, this he knew for a fact.

Peter slowly brought his left hand out from under the sheet; he was unaware that his fingers were sticky with the drying blood of his mother. He took the Sheriff's hand; the one Klem had used to stroke his cheek. He drew it down towards his mouth and kissed the man's hand like one would go about kissing the hand of a Bishop.

Klem Boston had had very little experience with that of any retarded beings, but this show of affection and trust almost brought Boston to tears, tears because he knew that he would have to deal with the youth on a detached legal plain, because of what this poor innocent had done to his Mom. Klem wished he were somewhere else, far removed from this tragedy.

"What's the matter?" Jock said. He could afford to be less emotional for this wasn't his town and these were not his people. Yet he too, felt that by law this poor young innocent creature would learn that in these cases the law is cold, hard and unrelenting. "Has the devil in hell got your tongue?" he asked the youth whose eyes came across and focused on the Scotsman. Glancing around to those near at hand, Jock asked: "Can he speak for himself?" '

"Look," said Boston. "Let me see if I can coax the story out of him, alone. He might open up to me if there is jist me and 'im."

Realizing and accepting the value in that, most of the onlookers removed themselves out of the room on to the boardwalk. Only Klem and Jock stayed in close proximity to the be- wildered — Pete Kelly. Jock was prepared to be just a silent witness of what was going to be said, if anything. Frank drew the door shut after leaving the surgery and by now most of the crowd had decided to go back about their business as they had gleaned enough information to start their own bush telegraph. The day's sun was getting a bit of a bite in it and had now angled in the sky so that its light washed away any shade from the awnings, on this side of Starr Street.

"Smoke?" suggested Whitney to Frank as he pulled his tobacco and cigarette papers from his coat. Frank decided to pass and it was just at this time that Pearl Courtney arrived on the scene, her normally pretty face was plagued with apprehension, and she had heard the rumor of Ma's death via the town's grapevine.

"Isn't this an unbelievable, mess?" Miss Courtney said as she came to a stop near Cotter, she had come from the direction of *The Royal..*

"It's a calamity, all right..." Frank mopped his brow with one of Lester's pressed hankies. "It is gonna be a big shock, for the whole town."

"You mean the ***county!***" exclaimed Deputy Lexmon, now over near the veranda post.

"It has all the makings of a Greek tragedy!" Pearl Courtney pointed out.

"That's true enough," then it hit Frank that he had an appointment to keep at Stroughton's office around on Main Street. "Good God, I'm to be around at the attorney's office!

"Peter's back there in the surgery with Sheriff Boston — trying to sort fact out from fiction. I think the boy needs to be with someone he knows and can trust, not with a lot of aliens — c'n you help by staying close at hand with the poor fellow...? He needs no one rousting him too much to try and get at the truth. It has got to be done with plenty of sympathy, not bullying..." The scribe told both Courtney and Dragoon.

"I thought the same. That's why I'm here with the blessing of Ma's gals from The Royal. Some of them would have been here, but when they walk the streets of Junction City, they get cursed by the town's upstanding church loving women, and it doesn't make for a pretty scene…" she did not spell it out and had no need too, for these same high and mighty womenfolk had her in their sights as well. "Do you know the exact circum stances of what has gone on? Has anything been done about mother Kelly's body?" Pearl removed one of her white gloves from her delicate hand.

"She'll be the responsibility of Messes Churcher and Hodder, funeral directors," Lexmon informed the actress. "—knowing 'em, they'll be on the ball with this one! Heck, I wonder who is gonna end up wiv all Ma's cash and bank accounts. That idjit in there don't know nuthin' frum nuthin'! If there's any relative an' she's got a will, it'll go to them. That right, Cotter?" said the deputy. Showing he only considered himself a layman, when even he came to the law.

"I guess," Frank responded.

"What'll happen to Peter?" asked Miss Courtney as worry lines, foreign to her brow, furrowed deeper.

"The idjit will certainly git sent off back east ter some sort of sanatorium, after this — I'd reckon!," suggested Ben Lexmon. "Can't very well hang an idjit fer murder, can ya? … Wouldn't be humane?"

Frank nodded, but even he had his doubts how things would work in these cases. "Hmm. Look Mister Lexmon, could I ask you a favor?" The deputy frowned in the scribe's direction. Frank continued: "Could you drop referring to Peter Kelly as an "idiot"? He had no control over the situation he was born into." Lexmon took it to heart and realized how it looked to Cotter and was suitably embarrassed. Then Frank turned to Pearl. "I'll leave you with these keys if you don't mind. One's for the upstairs apartment and the other locks the surgery. If Klem and Robeson get finished with Peter before I get back, please lock the place up for me," Cotter broke away from them and returned to the apartment to collect his frock coat and Stetson. When he re-emerged from the apartment and came down stairs Dragoon stopped him.

"I won't hold you up because I know you are in a hurry. But d'you mind if I do something about your hat? You look like a damn Quaker with that broad, flat brim and hilltop crown…" Without license, Whitney removed Frank's hat and rolled the left and right side of the brim tightly in his hands so that when let go, it remained slightly curled. Then he put a dint in the crown so that it took on the shape of being a flat top of a rocky mesa. Then he passed it back to Cotter for his approval. It certainly did not look daggy anymore. Cotter settled it back on his lush head of hair that was just beginning to take on the odd gray spec of hair, but even this turned back to its own natural color with an application of liquid hair tonic.

"There now," said Dragoon with approval. "Now that makes ya look like a Westerner — it suits you, too. OK now, get off to yuh meeting and me an' Miss Courtney will watch out fer that sad feller in the surgery."

Frank moved swiftly across the street in to Bryan Street in the direction of Main Street. There were people out on the sidewalk making conversation, no doubt their topic was that of the death of the town's foremost businesswoman and the accusation that her own son had done her in. Frank avoided that side of Bryan Street where he had experienced the dead Priest's apparition — there was enough reminder of death in the air today for him.

Two eight-year-old street-urchins, wearing bib an' brace overalls and no footwear, raced up the middle of Bryan Street, in the direction of the intersection, unaware that they had missed all the excitement they had come to see. Their ignorance to the sudden death and its permanence at their age allowed them to view the drama in a lighter light; their goal was to join the ranks on rumormongers, finding out what the drama was all about and spread the story about the town; making them heroes of the hour. They weren't aware that the local newspaper reporter had already gathered all the useful stuff he'd need to write up his report, they were also unconscious that the Tenderfoot passing them on their left, had actually been caught up in the events, that now lingered in the back of Cotter's mind and would from time to time, reappear with his thoughts of Junction City and Lester Lomax.

Following Stroughton's directions — Cotter homed in on the attorney's shop-front office, there to his surprise he found the Barber's wife in the role of office receptionist. Seeing a friendly face he knew — was like running into an old friend, this went along ways to relaxing Frank, somewhat.

The homely looking woman showed Cotter through to the lawyer's inner office, where the attorney was already entertaining Sean Dunne —Dunne was still wearing the same clothes he had on the night before.

It was imprinted in his face that here was a man doomed to join the ranks of that private club, Drunks Inc. It was quite evident

Dunne was not going to heed Cotter's warning about drink. There were distinct signs on his beardless face of the work of an unsteady hand that had maneuvered a straight razor awkwardly about his jaw line and the area between his top lip and under the nose. As Frank settled in a vacant chair, the receptionist returned to the outer office and closed the door in her wake.

"We're just about to have some java —" Donald informed Frank as he waved his hand in the direction of a Sterling silver coffee set on a salver, the whole lot had been placed on Stroughton's office credenza. "…Would you care to join us?"

After the recent morning event, Frank quite liked the idea. "Sure, why not?" Donald twisted his chair towards the credenza and sorted out three cups and saucers of fine china, and commenced pouring the coffees from the pot with a thick handle. "Have you heard the dreadful news about Ma Kelly? Sean here only just arrived with the story." The lawyer's eyes were focused on the stream of hot beverage as it filled the first eggshell china cup, someone in some far off place had decorated the coffee cups and saucers with an artwork of thorny steam roses — the brewed coffee beans released its odor to the whole room, overriding the office smells of glue paste and paper. The three men were already lusting for their caffeine fix.

Cotter nodded his thanks, as he took the saucer and cup of piping hot coffee the lawyer held out across the knee hold desk, relieved of this responsibility, the attorney went ahead to pour Dunne's drink. Frank unconsciously registered the fact that Donald Stroughton was ambidextrous. "Gosh, news travels fast in this town," Donald stated as he passed Dunne his cup of java. Cotter took the crockery in both hands and watched as the swirling liquid lost both speed and movement. Then he glanced in Sean's direction as the man took his beverage in both hands, too. Only Dunne's hands were shaking with the effects of last night's booze, some of the cup's contents spilt over into the saucer as the man's posterior made contact with the seat of his chair. Dunne took up the conversation as he blinked at the mishap. "— I heard about the killin' on my way downtown, its thar talk of the Junction. No need fer a newspaper here when these things happen!"

"Being a newspaperman, I shouldn't say Frank would agree with that remark, of Sean?" said Stroughton as both he and Frank Cotter watched Dunne take a tentative sip of the coffee.   Both men were thinking that the late night drinker might still slop more of his brew in his saucer, but he managed not to. Wrong though they were, it was a close call and both men did not miss it either.

Halfway through their first cup, Monty Hill and Jonas Bevan arrived and were ushered in by the barber's wife. So this meant that Attorney Stroughton had to go through the whole ritual of providing them with java. It was getting off to a slow start this morning, even though both men showed adequate signs that they had been rushing to get here and their blood pressure was above normal. Settling with their coffees, Monty asked: "Anyone heard about what happened to Ma Kelly?"

Don Stroughton, Dunne and Cotter nodded almost as one.

"Nasty — shocking," was Bevan's remark about the phenomenon.

"I hear folks are saying her boy is responsible," Monty said, "But *I* can't see *that* — not 'im!"

Frank glanced up from his hot drink to those in the room. He noticed that Bevan was looking over at Donald Stroughton like a lovesick sweetheart, but the attorney was not aware of it, he had his mind posted elsewhere. Monty Hill looked edgy, like someone nervously awaiting a late stagecoach while on the other hand Sean Dunne, looked green about the gills and it would be pretty true to assume that his coffee had turned his stomach — he even looked sweaty and was certainly a man suffering a hangover. Cotter well knew how the teamster would be suffering. Finally, putting aside Dunne's troubles, Frank said: "In regard to your question Mr. Hill, Junction City certainly has a taste for rumor and I can only suppose it is because of its isolation. With Ma Kelly's case it's true she seems to have met up with a violent death…" Here, he paused and lent forward in the direction of Stroughton's desk, and there deposited his saucer and cup, the latter, now empty, next to a combination of alabaster inkwells and pen rest, then sat back and went on. "I've got the son with me at Lester's place, I'm going to do my best to see he stays there until some sense has been made out of this shemozzle," Frank stated sincerely.

Stroughton came out of his chair and around the other side of his mahogany desk, his cup of cooling coffee still in his hand, his pinkie, crooked. "It is a situation that is gonna be a headache for me — I'm the Kelly's lawyer… Let us push on and get our business sorted…"

With the coffee paraphernalia cleared away by the receptionist, Stroughton swung into action and back at his desk he drew open the top left-hand drawer and extracted several thick buff colored envelopes. Each was sealed with a thin red taffeta ribbon and sealing wax.

"I've no idea which of these files one should open first —" Don stated as he looked up at his captivated audience as if expecting one of them to make a suggestion, but as none was forthcoming, Stroughton continued: "I haven't the slightest idea what's concealed here in, they were written up by Lester himself and privately sealed by him a week before his death and delivered into my hands; naturally *we* had no clue that in seven days' time, he would be deceased."

"It's a pity no one has a crystal ball that opens up a window on our destiny," Jonas Bevan said and no one in the office made any smart answer to that.

"When we were at dinner last night, you never mentioned anything about any of this?" Cotter said to Don. "You should have said something, at least..." There was now something about this shyster that made the newspaperman uncomfortable.

The Attorney swept the folks in his office with reptilian-like eyes and knew that Cotter's remarks could be suggesting to one and all, that he was a sly customer, so he tried to explain. "True. But then as far as I was aware, Lester Lomax had never set out a will as such. Hell, he wasn't a clairvoyant — if he were, he'd have been one of the first to do so, make a will, I mean. " Don selected the topmost envelope. He untied the ribbon and broke open the seal with the pointed blade of a letter opener. He lifted the envelope as though trying to gauge the weight of it its contents.

Monty Hill cleared his throat and commented: "They're reasonably thick envelopes?" No one bothered with answering the obvious.

Lawyer Stroughton placed the cartridge paper envelope down on top of the others, still there on the desk waiting to be opened. By now the observers had come to notice that the envelope's flap was also glued down; so Don had to once more retrieve the stiletto opener and carefully slit the flap open and shake out the envelope's contents. Which turned out to be a short note, again, written on cartridge paper, all this accounted for the envelope's thickness, included with the note was a bank-draft—the text written on both pieces of paper was most certainly Lester's hand. The attorney went ahead and picked up the note and read it in silently to one's self, his face was nonplus when he picked it up and did not change throughout the length of time it took him to read the script. Then he swapped from the note to that of the bank-draft and looked it over. Then to everyone's surprise passed both items across to Frank Cotter.

"For me...?" Cotter said as he took a second to get his hand in motion and tried to check the surprise in his face. He was completely disarmed.

"So it would seem. I'll go on and open the others while you familiarize yourself with the contents," Donald Stroughton began going through the same procedure with the next envelope. "—I'm sorry I jumped in and read the enclosed letter, Frank, but I thought those instructions might have applied to me. So maybe with the rest of these envelopes I should pass them on to whomever they've been addressed to, unopened."

Meanwhile Cotter went ahead to read what was obviously Lester's last piece of correspondence to him. "— excuse me interrupting," He said, "But in fairness to all here, I feel I ought to share Lester's epistle … That way no one will have cause to feel slighted or left out in any way—agreed?"

This suited the gathering, because they were all interested to know what business Lester had with the scribe. But as for the others, their vibes was not so open, anyone wanted to share their dealings with Cotter, but this made no difference to Frank's decision.

"So with your approval, I shall commence..." Cotter took a fresh breath and began reading aloud:

Dear Frank — if by chance you are presented with this envelope, it will mean that yours truly has come to an untimely end. Therefore, regretfully, I am not in a position to fulfill my promises and obligations to you. Thatbeing the case, I realize that once again you will feel life has let you down, but really, pal, it is I who have let you down and deeply feel for you. But whatever you do, swear you'll continue with the good fight we started out on together; that of standing shoulder to shoulder against the Demon drink. I know that if you continue along that path you will definitely beat it!

I know too many, if people other than you read this, it sounds prohibitionist, which we both know from our student days, I'm not. However in your case it is different and I'd be forced to turn in my grave if my death, becomes the catalyst of your return to the bottle and certain destruction. I feel on that score you won't let me down.

> *Enclosed is a check for the sum of Eight hundred dollars, which I urge you to use wisely. This should give you the steak needed to make a fresh start in your life, whether it be in Junction City or some other place of your choosing.*
>
> *Look on this as not the end of the road, but as a new beginning - one promise I know I can keep, and that if there is truly a 'Hereafter' we will be sure to meet...*
>
> *Your old chum, Lester Lomax, dated 11/6/1867.*

Frank slowly lowered the letter. Sighed, and moisturized his dry lips. On looking up Cotter saw with surprise, that tears had welled in Bevan's eyes at the reading.

This is not right, thought Frank. *Sure, I'm almost down to my bottom dollar, but I have been broke before and yet somehow I've managed to survive, even if I have spent the night in a gutter or the drunk tank of the odd jail ... but this, this can't even be considered a windfall — it is a handout, a goddamn handout I never earned a cent of!* Cotter felt like he was genuinely bleeding inside from an open wound.

Don cast his eyes around... Dunne, Bevan, Monty Hill as he tried to preempt whether or not they wanted the guts of their letters made public... it was impossible tell what each of them were thinking individually. So rather than put anyone's nose out of joint, the lawyer asked them if it would make it easier if he were to open each of the remaining letters and read them aloud.

Dunne said: "It sure looks ter me as if the Doc is trying ter be up-front wif everyone. Mister Cotter here wos ready ter be open about what the Doc is tryin' ter do fer 'im from the grave.

"I reckon in fairness ter all, we should all cop it the same way; After all, the man wos our partner in more ways than one..."

Bevan and Hill took a moment to adopt Dunne's proposal but finally nodded their agreement.

The Attorney opened the next envelope and read the contents, But considered that the time it would involve reading aloud each one added together, and the likely debates which would follow each one's reading Don suggested that in the interest of time, he quickly read them through and gives them a capsulated breakdown on his readings as he would see to it that each person here would be handed their own copy addressed to them and they could read it later.

This was then adopted as a done deal.

"Now this is most interesting... Lester wants all connected with the freight line to keep it in operation just as long as it can hold its own and meet the bank's loan and interest rates. This letter shows that Lester was confident that once the company turned the corner — investors will likely double their money before the Kansas Pacific Railroad is in position to put the firm out of business. The line's way behind schedule because of construction delays brought about before and during the war, by Confederate sympathizers.

"He suggests that as the warehouse landlord, I should take over his stocks in the company and be an equal partner — which I am quite prepared to do, if, of course the rest of you gentlemen are in agreement?"

Monty Hill, Bevan and Dunne were in accord with the late Doctor's idea. Frank said nothing, for he had naught to do with Lester's other business ventures. Frank had his worries about seemingly to benefit in a financial way from his friend's accident. He reflected on the fact that he had fallen off the wagon where the *Demon Drink* was concerned, and he was in fact struggling for a new toehold.

But now the attorney had come to the third letter, or file. Don Stroughton went carefully through the pages that from where Cotter sat, they appeared to be written in algebra, certainly something beyond his ken. Yes, it certainly looked like the script of a formula. The lawyer explained that it looked very much like the formula to Lester's wonder drug. In the attached notes Lomax admitted that to having used the Pawnee Indians as guinea pigs, and the success of his medicine might well turn its manufacturers into very wealthy and powerful men of commerce.

This is what the Army fellers were after; I bet a million, thought Frank. *They are so desperate to get their hands on that document in Stroughton's hands that they were prepared to bash me about with booze and gun-butts — yet all along it seems they were looking in the wrong location. Lester didn't keep the formula at his own premises, but here in the attorney safe, seemingly without Stroughton's knowledge. Again it seems that these three bods are joined at the hip in a business sense.*

Stroughton penetrated Cotter's daydream by his seemingly excited approach to the job at hand when he said: "…In accordance to this job Lester had handed me on a platter, I shall have to get busy and draw up a number of legal papers an' lodge 'em with the courts for the formation of our new syndicate." With an excited gleam in his eyes, the Attorney swept them over his would-be business associates.

Frank judged from his point-of-view that he was extremely keen on the legality of things and Frank felt he could see a greedy streak in the man. He did not like it. He noticed that Donald Stroughton had a way of drawing the trio of Hill, Dunne and Bevan into his line of thinking that he felt was unhealthy. He somehow felt a degree of safety by having been left out of things for he, Frank, would not stand for being led like a bull with a ring through its nose.

"Our enterprise will need a fresh, new name — however we can leave it stand for the time being, while we all give it some thought," Don Stroughton said with the eager sound of a money hungry man. It irked Cotter.

From where Hill sat, he could see the unmasked emotions that ranged across Cotter's face. He interrupted them correctly while yet to others would remain a complete mystery. Monty felt sure the ex-newspaperman was unappreciative of what Lester had bestowed on him. *Does the bum want more? I'll stick the knife in and give it a twist... a bit of torture and pain might make him a bit appreciative.* Though Hill.

"Hey," Hill said, making sure his tone was one of sympathy and not doused with a detectable ounce of bitter essence — "why so melancholy, Frank? You came inter Don's chambers as poor as a church mouse, and ya leaving with a small fortune!"

Like members of the Spanish Inquisition, all eyes turned on Frank and this made Cotter feel as though he owed them an answer.

"This bank-draft doesn't sit easy with me..." Frank gestured with the document towards Hill. "— Lester brought me out west to work for him as his Public Relations man; He knew I don't and won't take handouts from anyone, not even him!"

He knew this was not really true, but as these guys did not know him from a bar of soap, he knew he could make himself come across as a sanctimonious bastard. So he continued: "***This*** is nothing more than charity — a charity that has arisen out of a friend's untimely death. I'd feel a goddamn heel, accepting it, truly!"

"Don't you think you're letting **conscience** get in the way of **commonsense,** Cotter?" Stroughton said without even needing to understand the implications of the forgone dialog. "If I'd been aware that Lester had that sort of small change lying about, I'd've urged him to put it to better use, which would have made our bank manager, Lon

Parker, a happy man. Parker's had itchy palms ever since he allowed Lester that loan on the freight line. Lon's been dotting on every cent Lester has paid back.

"I'll wager when you present that bank-draft, Parker's jaw will drop all the way down to his gold watch-chain! Don't worry, if Lester hadn't met with his fatal accident —he'd have you earning every cent of those greenbacks…" Jonas Bevan silently envied Cotter's windfall and could not understand Cotter's hesitation in accepting the money.

Don continued: "I'm surprised of another thing, too. Why the devil did Lester not cut you in for a slice of his Indian medicine deal? But then, I s'pose this bank draft is his way of dealin' with you in place of that? You've come out of this show better than you went into it! "

"That money's yours, Cotter—so if it's gonna make you feel guilty about accepting it," exclaimed Monty Hill, "you c'n drop it in my lap… If it were me, why I'd fasten onto it with the fangs of a coyote—stop acting the role of a square peg in a round 'ole! "

Frank Cotter glanced down at the papers in his hand and thought. *If I wasn't a pauper, this money would be back on Stroughton's desk and I'd be outa this room. But the truth is, I owe at least something to Ma Kelley's estate for what she has done for me, and I do have debits still standing back east.*

OK. I'll accept it and split it down the middle with Miss Pearl Courtney, that way Lester's money would be helping two people. Yes. Lester would approve of that, that's for sure and that is what I shall do…

Frank sighed and looked up into the watchful eyes of Sean Dunne. They were void and unreadable. "What do you think, Sean? You must have an opinion, everyone else in the room does!"

"It's been your bank-draft since the moment Lester wrote it out along wif the instructions in that letter," said Dunne, "Its yore decision. But as ya askin' a man, here's what I reckon you should do. Take it and go back ter where you came from… There's nuthin' here fer you now that Doc's gone. Truthfully, yore presence irritates me—you keep tryin' ter make something more out of Doctor Lomax's death than there is.

"There ain't any fifth man mixed up in this accident business, Ma Kelly? She wuz wrong, she made a mistake. Now there's none here can argue that there wuz a fifth man now that she's been kilt… So that leaves you wiv naught," wound up Dunne.

Hmm, good point you've raised pal. Frank thought. *In my opinion, there is still that business of the fifth man to be sorted out to my satisfaction, regardless of what you say, Dunne. I can't and won't shake the dust of this cow town from my boots until I reckon I have got to the bottom of things. Already two things have happened in the last twenty-four hours I am not happy with. There was that mystery person hiding over in the dark doorway who wouldn't come out and show his face, that in itself might interest Sheriff Boston, who knows it might even tie in with Ma's murder? People are too ready to lay the blame of her death at Peter's feet. Besides, everyone knew she was loaded and took precautions where her wealth was concerned; hence her reason for keeping the Williams brothers on-hand.* Frank realized that the folks round him sat there with bated breath.

Frank said: "All right, you've sold me. But I warn you people, as long as I am here I am gonna push an' pull Boston to have a full inquiry into Lester's accident, no matter whose apple cart I upset in the process!

"So, at this point maybe I should take my leave and let you people get on with your plans…" Cotter grabbed his hat and made to rise from his chair, Donald Stroughton also rose and came round the desk to escort Cotter through to the outer office and then out onto the sidewalk. On the way he gave Frank directions to the bank further along Main Street.

"Exchange the bank-draft as quickly as possible. It would be wise to get Parker to open you up an account and only draw living expense from it as you require them. Carry too much money around in this burg is inviting a mugging, believe me. And I hope before long that you'll realize your pursuit of this so-called mystery man is nuthin' more than a bum-steer."

"I shall take your advice about that bank account, Don. But as far as forgetting all about that fifth man, you can forget it. I somehow know that if I spend enough time on him, he will show up, especially when word gets out that I'm after him. Now the bank is down this side of the street, near the Masonic Hall, right?" Frank said, confirming Stroughton's directions.

The lawyer nodded. He could see that now was not the time to argue with Cotter about his fanaticism of the fifth man and changed the subject for the time being. "And for a short cut back to your apartment, jist step out the bank and cross the street, that alleyway going up alongside the livery stable will take you through to Starr Street.

"Should Lon Parker be a bit hesitant about opening up an account for you, tell him I said I'd vouch for you, right?" Stroughton waited expectantly for Frank's answer.

Frank donned his hat and began to move away, "OK, OK, OK..." The Attorney shrugged, turned and entered his office without a backward, glance.

Following Parker's instructions, the bank teller, James Lygon, who looked your typical banker, in a three piece suit with detachable starched collar to his candy stripe shirt, set about counting out twenty-five single greenbacks and twenty-five silver dollar coins from his cash drawer for the bank's newest customer. Lon Parker stood nearby overseeing the transaction. Parker had set up the account personally in his office, but as he never kept any cash in his suite, it had to come from Lygon's drawer.

Franked double-checked the money counted out on the linoleum lined counter on his side of the grille. He placed the banknotes in his billfold and the silver in the right side pocket of his tailored pants, and then he set off towards the bank's front exit doors.

Once on the sidewalk he check for two things before crossing the street to the alley, one, that it was safe to make the short journey and that there were no men lurking about at the entrance of the laneway. Taking the short-cut via the alley made good sense, for once in Starr Street he only had to cross the roadway and walk down to the building containing Lester's apartment and surgery. Just before turning off the street to climb the side staircase, from his angle he found that he could see partly into Bryan street and there parked at the curb was the mortician's vehicle—the white silk side-curtains of the hearse were drawn, a good indication that Ma's body was within, awaiting transport to the director's morgue for embalming prior to her funeral.

Cotter decided to move further along the sidewalk to check on whether or not folks were still in the surgery. Looking in through the dusty window he saw that the place was empty, but all the same he tried the door to see if it was secure. Which it was, then he retraced his steps along the lonely street back to the staircase on the way he noticed that the tie rack on the other side of the street was not in use and the general area was quiet, save for an English sparrow perched on the edge of the water-trough sampling its water. An investigative stray fly buzzed in under the brim of his Stetson, forcing Frank to brushed it aside, as he began to mount the stairs to the apartment. As he made his way up the risers he noticed the smell of wood smoke in the air and glanced skyward towards the shingle roof where the stove's chimney pipe extended out into the open. The smoke of the apartment's cooking fire zigzagged into the air and dissipated some five feet above the muzzle of the chimney. By the time the scribe had reached the landing he found the door slightly ajar and the inviting aroma of corn beef, spuds and boiled cabbage announced that they were on the menu for today.

Frank entered the apartment to discover before him a most domestic scene, Miss Pearl Courtney was standing over the Ben Franklin stove wearing a full-front apron over her bodice for protection of her calico dress, her hair pulled back from her face and pinned in place, but alas, a few strands had escaped the capture and floated weightlessly in slow motion with her body movements, the heat from the hot-plate had produced shinny sheen of perspiration on her forehead, giving her a rather earthy appeal. Frank heeled the door shut after him and now took in Whitney Dragoon, who although lounging in one of the four Windsor table-chairs at the dinner table, he had his back to the main parlor area. Whitney signaled Frank, to keep the noise down; at the same time, pointing towards the Moorish type bedroom door. Dragoon's cutaway frock coat lay draped over the arm of the sofa but his corduroy waist-coat was fully buttoned, save for the missing two which had obviously been torn off in the struggle with Peter and company. A fresh gingham tablecloth had now replaced the previous one that had been covering the table since Frank's arrival in town, the reason for this was that the scribe had not made himself fully acquainted where all the linen supplies were kept. While crossing the room towards the table Frank had noticed that Whitney had removed his sidearm, the gun and holster attached to the cartridge belt, hung on a clothes' tree in the corner of the room along with the man's Stetson.

"—Not too much noise, Frank—" muttered Dragoon in a stage whisper. "Pete Kelly's asleep in yuh bed. Doc Hallway gave 'im sumthin' ter drink—a **real** "Mickey Finn", snuffed him out like a candle. The poor guy wuz in a real distraught mess after Boston got through with him, not that it was the Sheriff's fault, it's jist one of them things. Even a feller like Pete, must have some instinctive feelin's? Whatever the Doc's gave the youth to drink, dropped him like a ton of coal from a tip cart."

"What's the story, then?" Frank now part of the company, whispered.

"Miss Courtney will explain..." Dragoon answered as Pearl left the stove and joined the men over near the table. Cotter was still standing because he had not yet taken a seat. Frank threw his hat from where he stood over onto the sofa and drew out a chair to rest on near Dragoon. As the scribe sat down he noticed Pearl's sunbonnet at the far end of the deal table, next to the "A" frame lampshade.

Pearl began, but this time she did not bother to whisper and by not doing so, this would encourage the men to follow suit with their dialog. "First, no one was able to find a murder weapon. Doctor Hallway had taken a look at Ma's body and says that what must've been used on her was mighty sharp instrument ... maybe as sharp as a man's straight razor, at least.

"Pete wasn't in any shape to get much sense out of him," Pearl sat on the chair opposite Dragoon who was forced to straighten up to give Miss Courtney leg room under the table for her knees.

"Miss Pearl went to the surgery and sat wiv Pete while Robeson and Boston tried ter make sense out of the poor lad's jibberin'," explained Whitney. "No one knew what ter makes of the blood on the feller's nightshirt."

Pearl began to tell the salesman and the scribe what they had no idea of knowing, what took place in the surgery where the emotionally drained youth lay on the divan. "...Sheriff Robeson pointed out to Sheriff Boston that because of the scarcity of blood on the hem of the nightshirt and none on or about the upper-chest — that it probably wasn't Peter who slashed his Ma's throat. Robeson reckons the killer would have been sprayed with Ma's gore when it would have gushed from her jugular. Robeson made this assessment after he has drawn back the sheet someone had draped over Peter when he laid down on the divan. The blood was only on the hem and the buttocks of his nightshirt—if Peter had been the attacker, Robeson opined he should have had blood all over his chest —"

"Which was sensible thinking on his part, Frank," said Whitney as he thought aloud, and the others here could see his reasoning for that.

Pearl added. "Rather than see poor Peter locked up until this mess can be sorted out, I'm sorry, I keep thinking of him in the sense of a child!"

"Don't we all," said Cotter.

"Anyhow *I* put myself in to care for him until there's some sort of legal case — he can stay with me and the gals at The Royal when he comes to.

"Boston got rid of that horrible nightshirt for us, so Pete's dressed in some of your things until we can get into the Kelly's apartment. I hope you don't mind, Frank?"

"Only happy to help; One thing, my clothing will be a bit long in the legs and arms, not that it will matter." Frank said and truly felt that way. By now his appetite had come home to roost, he could not help but make mention of the food simmering on the stove alongside the coffeepot.

"Golly, I'd almost forgotten," Pearl smartly arose from the table and was now a bit flustered, she went for the crockery section of the kitchen cabinet for dinner plates and the coffee cups.

"It smells delicious!" Frank told her truthfully — even Whitney concurred with that. Going to the stove with a china platter and a long pronged fork, Pearl removed the corn beef from the boiler…

"If I were you pair I should wait until you've tried my cooking before making any comments," Pearl warned them. "—cooking isn't my forte!" She took the platter of beef over to the wing of the kitchen sink, and went back to the stove for a saucepan of boiled cabbage and potatoes, the latter two she strained off the hot water and then set about emptying these vegetables out on the side of the platter, steam from the hot food rose towards the ceiling. Once she had divested herself of the cooking utensils, she brought the platter to the table. In the meanwhile Frank had given his mealtime friends an account of the meeting held in Stroughton's office. He told them a white lie when it came to the bank-draft Lester had drawn up for him. He said that he had a bit of trouble getting the bank to convert the draft to hard cash for him but they were finally persuaded to make the conversion with Stroughton's interference but only on the proviso that he open an account with them. He withdrew fifty dollars in greenbacks and silver, leaving the remainder in the account, in accordance with Lester's wishes; he was to share the money equally with Miss Pearl Courtney. With that, Cotter produced the money from his pocket and billfold, which he placed on the tablecloth between him and Whitney.

Frank took the platter from Pearl and set about carving up the beef she had provided and served it out onto their respective plates. Meanwhile Pearl sat dumbfounded on her chair looking down upon the windfall that had come her way. *Lester's been more than generous with me with what Hill and Bevan gave me in the envelope, but now this – why, I don't know what to say!* She thought. Frank urged Pearl to select the money of her desire from one of the two small piles; Cotter made it clear that he did not mind either way what she chose. She selected the shiny silver eagle dollars, Cotter, only out of curiosity, asked why she had latched on to the silver coins.

"Silver dollars are readily accepted by most folks now that the war's over and besides, Yankee banknotes were too readily faked if one knew a feller with a good printing press and the correct color ink."

Having concluded their meal, the men sat backed and enjoyed a smoke while Pearl went off to check on Peter. Miss Courtney noted that he was still off in dreamland, though it was clear by the twitching of the nerves in his face that his sleep was a troubled one, but there was naught she could do for the youth that could ease his torment. She tucked in the bedding for he had made a mess of the top sheet and blanket. When she returned to the parlor she was surprised to find that the men had left the apartment without a word to her, but she discovered the note Frank had left on the table. It informed her that Whitney had gone off to book passage on the next stage heading out to Kansas City and that he, Cotter, had gone to have a talk with Sheriff Boston.

Pearl did not know about Frank's encounter last night on Starr Street, so had no idea that his main purpose for seeing the sheriff was to let him know about the episode, and that it might be connected in some way to Ma Kelly's murder.

At the jailhouse, the lawmen, Boston, Robeson and Deputy Bud Reed had been mulling over the facts of the apparent murder and had begun to nurture a few ideas of their own. However Klem Boston was still very much annoyed with Sheriff Robeson's performance in his office with the Chairman of the Cattlemen's Association, Mr. Rollo, and the stage line manager, Glenn Corbin. He could not understand for the life of him, what the motive was behind their invasion of his jail. Sure, he had gone along with Robeson's game, only because he knew Robeson well enough to guess that he must have an agenda as to why he went on like he did. But now, come Hell or High water he wanted an answer to flush away his bothersome feeling and clear his head, so that he could concentrate on the matter at hand, Ma's murder.

"Jock," Klem said by way of gaining the man's sole attention. Having succeeded he continued as Robeson's gray eyes centered on his face. "…I wanna know what thar hell wuz goin' on t'other night when you barged in here wif Rollo an' Corbin and then carried on as though me prisoners over yonder were bein' held on your account and biddin'."

"Oh, that!" said Robeson with a cock of his head, "Yuh, I guess that sort of threw you boy, but I was thankful by the way you played it by ear and helped me pull that wee stunt off. I was on my way home ter Kelly's boarding house, when those pair of Freemasons bumped into me an' Reed… You knew they were 'Masons, didn't yuh?" frowned Robeson.

"I've had my suspicions. They've got a strong lodge here in Junction City. But you go on wif what you wuz sayin'." Klem urged.

"So that smart-ass Chairman, sprags me about whether or not I'd contacted the stage passengers an' that fellow Corbin comes in on the act! Look, by this stage of things I'm dead tired; I wanna hit the goddamn hay! So I spun 'em a yarn that wasn't as convincing as I thought, they weren't convinced I was speaking the trewth… So I had ter bring them here and play out my dummy hand to the end, which, with your help — sold my case to 'em like it was gift wrapped frum Edinburgh Castle.

"All in all, I wos showin' those geezers that although I was engaged by them, that I run me own show. No one kicks my ass but me, Klem! So that's why the charade involvin' you and your, prisoners! Does that satisfy? " Drawing his dialog to an end his tongued darted out the corner of his mouth like a desert breed lizard.

*He's like a darn desert lizard…*thought Klem, *but all the same you can't fault his damn reasoning.* "Yeah — I only asked 'coz it wuz annoying the Christ outa me."

Then as if on cue, who should come bustling in through the front door of the jailhouse was Frank Cotter. He strolled up to the wicket, and halted with his Stetson in hand, real polite, like, his bruised face looking now more like a large birthmark and spread through it. He gave an unexpected burp as the corn beef and cabbage lunch repeated on him.

"Sorry about this gents—please excuse me. May I enter?" the scribe asked. Upon receiving a nod from Klem he pushed open the wicket and stepped in and up to the desk. "Since the discovery of Ma Kelly's body I had cause to think about a strange event that happened last night on my way home. Now it may not mean anything and then again it may mean something. But last night as I neared Lester's apartment I got this weird feeling that someone might have been stalking me in the dark. I called on them to come out into the open so that they might be seen, but instead they slunk away. Mind you, I warned them that I was armed and that if they got too fresh I wouldn't be afraid to shoot. What d'you folk reckon; is it worth something in line of what happened to the Kelly woman?"

Buddy Reed reckoned that the Tenderfoot looked a bit shameful with himself, and said so.

"Well, the more I think about the situation and what's happened since; I wish that I'd showed more guts than I did. Maybe if I had scared the guy off, Ma Kelly might be alive this minute, don't you think?"

"Hard to say," said Reed. Just then Lexmon came in from the street, he was surprised to find the scribe there with his law associates. He came through the wicket and unbuckled his guns then went across to hang them up.

"It most likely doesn't mean much, you were more than likely spooked by the moon, and its light can be tricky on the eyes." Sheriff Boston told the scribe. "I know ya worried about the boy in all this, Cotter. But I c'n put yore mind at ease and tell you that both Sheriff Robeson and I don't believe that poor Pete hacked into his Mom," Klem said as he looked to Robeson for back-up. The Lawrence law officer was ready and willing to give it.

"Then," Cotter looked from one lawman to the others, "d'you think it was a robbery gone wrong or something else?" Frank was beginning to feel relieved that in his position now, he couldn't be accused as being in some way responsible for her death, especially by his inaction.

"At the moment all we can do, lad, is **speculate.** Now that can be either a good thing or a bad thing." Jock Robeson said. "And no one will know that until either the killer is caught or comes forward and confesses."

"Well, we all know that there is little chance of the killer giving himself up, and confessing to the horrible crime," Cotter rubbed his jaw and to his soft hand it felt like sandpaper his whiskers reminded the scribe that he had not shaved so far today.

"Anythin's possible," pointed out Boston. "I c'n tell you that Ma Kelly didn't have any cash up in her apartment, last night; Williams told us she left it locked up in her safe."

"But it was known that she did take it home with her at times?" Frank said. "You don't think she smelt a rat, last night?"

"I dunno," Klem answered. "But Ma was aware that her takings were always like a bone to a hungry dog, and took precautions – hence the Williams guards. Besides, I don't believe in this stuff that people can read the future. However she never stuck to the same procedure when storing her haul. She reckoned inconsistency was self insurance; so as any owl-hooters wantin' her dinero would have ter work fer it before they got their foot in the door." Boston folded his arms across his chest.

"Ma's killer must feel a miserable cuss after going to all that trouble to come up empty handed," Jock stated. It looked as if he wanted to change locations and Deputy Reed sensed it, so he moved aside so that his boss might come forward and occupy his position within the range of the desk. "This presence you felt out there on the street, Cotter. Do you experience that sort of thing very often?"

Cotter shook his head.

"Pity ya so yellah Cotter." Roscoe hollered from the back of the room — "Might've saved the old slag's life!" It was only now that the people up at the top end of the room realized, the prisoners had been eavesdropping the whole time. Klem screwed in the direction of the cells. He wasn't real fond of Roscoe from day one; He never raised his voice so was not particularly concerned whether Roscoe and could hear him or not—"you count yore lucky stars I had ya locked up behind bars, or you would've been my first suspects."

"That's the type of typical thinking we know we can expect from you!" said Roscoe. Then he dropped his voice and added: "We can see that you've no idea which end is up and which end is down in this man's world," Then he turned his back on those in the office and addressed, Briggs. "This will end up your typical civilian cock-up, mark my words, Briggs! The Mongoloid doesn't have brains enough ter count— it took someone calculative and snake-like ter do the old tart in like that."

Boston moved down the room in the direction of the cells. "We already ruled the boy out as the murderer for ourselves, all on our lonesome —" Briggs came and joined his Commanding officer near the bars to listen for himself. Klem continued: "Fer yore information, by the time the lady's body wuz discovered the town had been an open book too long ter shut the place down. Folks mixed up in her killing, would've hightailed it long ago!"

"Don't do yore crying on our shoulders… Anyway, when you going ter open these bars and let us out? Surely you realize the charges yuh holding us on are weaker than water? You'll git in more trouble than you can handle out of this. Wake up to yore self and stop playin' things close to yore chest…" said Briggs.

"I plan ter let the circuit Judge take care of youse. Judge Wolfsohn, will decide whether I'm right or wrong. You jokers had better get used of sleepin' in my flea-ridden blankets apiece longer, unless our friend here, the guy you keep knocking about wantin' ter have you let out: What do you say, Cotter?" Boston stopped, half turned back towards the scribe. "You wanna drop the charges against these sidewinders, Cotter?"

Frank wanted revenge and for every second or minute they were behind bars, satisfied him. *These fallas destroyed my grip on the wagon and filled me full of rotgut… Cracked me on the skull and wrenched my arm up my back until it all but dislocate. No, damn 'em, until this Judge Wolfsohn comes on the scene.* "… Leave them stew there for the judge, is what I say!"

"Of course, that's what I've been considering," Boston glanced thoughtfully in Robeson's direction.

"Don't bring me into it," Robeson warned Klem. "They're your jailbirds—they claim they're working for the Government and are Army. That's your problem ter sort out. Tomorrow my deputy and I will be stirring dust as we head for Lawrence; we've been away from home too long. Besides, I've got a couple of killers to bring to justice, Flynn, Malthouse and Korda..." Jock nodded to Reed and Sheriff Boston. "As one lawman to another, I certainly wish you luck in finding Junction City's, murderer. Murder is a hard one to solve unless you've got reliable evidence and an eyewitness. Still, a confession can always be hoped for—otherwise you'll be left with an unsolved murder on yer books."

"You don't leave a man with any illusions, Robeson, I'll say that fer you..." Boston limped back over to the wicket and held it open for his colleagues. "Then wif a long ride starin' yew in the face—best youse try fer an early night. Don't know about yew but too much saddle work don't agree wiv me." The Lawrence visitors agreed with Klem, both men understood that forking a horse for him would be a drag. Trekking overland is irksome enough for anyone without a disability, for one in Klem's place it was an arduous at the best of times. Cotter joined the Sheriff and his deputy as they started to execute their egress with Boston in tow; the prisoner played yet another card.

"Cotter, before you slip away, can we talk turkey—its not gonna hurt anyone!" called Captain Roscoe.

Klem sighed, "— now what?"

"We don't wanna hear this, we'll be on our way," Robeson said and he and his deputy moved off so that Boston could close the door after them, then Klem and Frank, curious as goddamn chimpanzees, sauntered back through the wicket and down to the front of the cell.

When the Sheriff and the layman were standing before the prisoners, Roscoe went on. "We told you before there wos something you ought to see for yourself out there at the reservation. So why not do *you self* a favor an' do sumthin' right for a change? ...You're all getting too embroiled in this mess ter see yuh own lunacy. You can't see it, but it's you who's on the wrong trail, here.

"Whaddya' tryin' ter do? Throw away yuh career? Yore gonna end up pushin' the Army too far, Mister. Save ya hide, bring this dude out to the Pawnee reservation and let yuh own eyes judge the truth fer yuh selves? I told you before; I'll stay in the cell as yore hostage and Briggs will guide you out to the hell-hole …"

Klem said: "We're aquatinted well enough where the Indian reservation is, an' need no guidance frum Briggs. Look, if the Indian agent Warner wuz in trouble, I'd be the first person he'd come to fer help."

"You reckon?" Roscoe sneered. "Would *he* be so ready to call the likes of you in, if'n he knew he'd done the wrong thing by allowing Lomax to toy with the Pawnees' health without Government sanction? That's a crime and this Warner feller's well aware of it. The government's kept him fully informed of their views. He's been in on all this with yore friend from the very start!"

"What do you want us to look at?" Cotter said. He sounded like a man whom had heard the old drumbeat of salvation once too often.

"The Hellish curse Lomax has left in his wake!" Lieutenant Briggs said as he wrapped his fingers round the two-inch thick bars.

"You can see the damage the medicine Lomax knocked up and has done to the pagans… That's what you an' the Sheriff'll see!" Captain Roscoe said, forcefully.

"Frankly, I don't trust either of you," Klem admitted. "Look how you've gone about things in this town? You've broken into a dead man's apartment twice! You've assaulted this tenderfoot wiv a pistol—you could've kilt 'im! I reckon if I took you out to the reservation, you'd try an escape!"

Roscoe shook his head. "I won't need to do anything like that. Not the way you are performing your duty. I reckon it's only gonna be a matter of time before the fort sends out a patrol to learn what's been our fate, we've been out of contact far too long. We have to report in every so often to Washington and the Indian Affairs Department via Fort Hancock, and that hasn't been forthcoming. Besides, I've every faith in Lieutenant Briggs; he won't run out on me as long as I'm your hostage. If you think like that, then you are nuts!"

"Come on Sheriff, do yuh self a favor before it is too late," said Briggs as he brought back into the conversation. "Stick Deputy Lexmon in front of our cell with a fist-full of Colt aimed at my Captain's heart while you are away …"

"You guys are making it darn hard fer me ter refuse yore request!" Klem Boston stated as he felt that maybe he should pay Warner and his wife a visit and see what these army lap-dogs are pissing on about.

"I should hope so," Roscoe said. "I c'n tell you Sheriff, lives are dependent on you out there at that reservation."

Cotter could feel a shift in the lawman's attitude towards his prisoners, he was edging a wee bit in their favor and Frank knew he had to do something or say something, which would alter the change in tide. "Just supposing for a moment that you pair are working for the Indian Affairs folk, I reckon you are pretty damn dumb men for that positions you claim ter hold," the scribe said.

Boston turned in Cotter's direction. "Mebbe I should ride by Warner's place and see what he's up to," Klem drawled.

"You don't believe their shit, d'you?" Frank had no doubt that Boston was considering the jailbird's plea, even after what they had put him though and the muck with which they were trying, to smear Lester's good name.

"I don't know," muttered Klem. "Mebbe they're owed some consideration?"

"Do we have a deal, then?" Roscoe said as quickly as a striking rattler.

Klem turned to Cotter. "Whaddya, think?"

Such a question from Boston really infuriated the scribe. *What is wrong with peoples' thinking out in this part of the country?* Though Cotter. "What can I say? Are you gonna listen to me, Sheriff? I think you've half made up your mind already on this. But if you do intend to visit the reservation, you're not leaving me behind. I want to see things for myself before I'll be convinced by anything these two con artists say!" Cotter snapped venomously.

"Can you ride, Tenderfoot?" Lieutenant Briggs asked the newspaperman.

"Find me a quiet horse and I'll make it. It'll be interesting to see if your claims can stand up to any scrutiny." *Hell,* thought Frank. *I haven't been in a saddle for ages— this could turn into a sore day's ride for a man. Maybe Miss Pearl Courtney ought to come and see what these fellers are trying to accuse Lester of?* "Are there gonna be any restrictions who comes on this picnic?" Cotter directed his question to Boston.

"This won't be **any picnic,**" Lt. Briggs said.

"Who are you thinkin' of bringing along, Cotter...?" Klem asked. For he had no idea what was behind the Tenderfoot's question. Besides, he was debating with himself whether to ride out there on horseback and risk a few days of leg aches and cramps or grab a buckboard from the livery – maybe the lawyer would hire out his surrey?

"I was thinking Miss Courtney might like to be included in this outing,"

"It's not a place for a woman," Captain Roscoe pointed out.

"No," Briggs said, agreeing with his C.O. "— the sights in store out there are too vile for a woman!"

Ignoring the prisoners' protests, Cotter told the sheriff who was by now looking doubtful about Lester's ward being included in the phalanx. "…Let Miss Pearl make her own choice, Sheriff—she has as much right to be included in pretty much anything that is going to have a bearing on her future opinion of her guardian as anyone else. Besides, I've heard it rumored, that Lomax and Miss Courtney were stepping out together and that has to be worth something."

At 7 AM., Klem Boston's party and prisoner rode out of Junction City — the Sheriff had sworn in another couple of deputies for the occasion so that Cotter and Miss Pearl would feel more secure. Klem Boston had been forced to ride his 14-hands high Morgan bay mare; as Donald Stroughton would not hire out his surrey for reasons unexplained. Because of the Sheriff's disability, he had a saddle especially adapted for his needs but it still didn't make riding long distances easier for him. His right-stirrup-strap was extended to its full length to favor his stiff-straight leg, while the other stirrup strap had been adjusted to that of a rider with no physical shortcomings.

Miss Courtney had her own horse, a present to her from Lester only three months ago. It was a dignified Hackney gelding. Pearl cut an interesting figure in her riding habit, as befitting a lady, and rode sidesaddle on this occasion. Her stiff, short brim silk top-hat and insect netting attached to dissuade the flies, and though she carried a riding crop her horse did not need it, her riding hooks made her mount respond to the paces she required.

Frank had done his best to dress fittingly for the great outdoors. His Stetson Dragoon had reshaped for him sat proudly on his head.

To-day he wore a double breasted open-neck, light green shirt—his denim Levi jeans were slightly on the tight side because of their newness, but a day's wearing would soon stretch them into shape. The legs of his jeans were tucked into a pair of Alligator, peewee cowboy boots.

With Pearl's help, Frank had been able to hire a quiet toffee colored mare and saddle from the same livery stable as where Boston kept his horse, housed. But because Cotter was gun-shy, the rifle-boot of his saddle had been left empty.

Sheriff Boston did not bother to rope Briggs to the saddle of his Army horse. This was the first time that Klem had seen anything of the prisoners, which indicated that they were Army. The horse wore an unmistakable Government property brand, a pair of crossed Army sabers on its hide, under the letters 'U.S.', but all the same, Klem made sure that his prisoner rode dead ahead of him, and adjust his holster so that he could get at his Colt very quickly without hindrance should the Army Lieutenant take it into his head to make a run for it. As an added precaution, Boston made sure the part-time deputies hemmed in the blue-belly as if he and his horse were in a corral chute. It was with protest that he accepted the actress riding out to the reservation with them; his opinion hadn't changed since last night, when the outing had been arranged in detail.

Klem Boston forcing his hands into a pair of working gloves — told the riders on their shuffling, toey mounts: "C'mon folks, no more wastin' time… I wanna be well on the way before the sun gits that warm it starts cooking the hides of our mounts!"

With that, reins were tugged and spurs put to horseflesh and the mounted posse, cantered out of Ridge Road into Main Street, their progress causing Sean Dunne's freight wagon to yield way to them.

Dunne twisted on his seat to follow their progress with dilated eyes as they went down Main to the corner of Bryan Street and made a left turn so they could continue in the direction of the reservation. Meantime, now that the street ahead of Dunne was clear, he got his team of Clydesdales back on track and wondered where Sheriff Boston would be headed with an organized posse. *And what wos Miss Courtney and that city dude doing with them? By God, I hardly recognized Frank Cotter in his get up!* Dunne thought.

They had been in the saddle for maybe an hour and Frank was already feeling tight in the leg muscles, and began to understand what he was in for. His legs weren't used to something this wide between his thighs—horse riding is a breeze when you are in form but lack of such exercise will leave one sore. His horse was not keen to travel with a mob and dropped back, and back, and back until he realized he was being forced to swallow on the dust of the horse-party up ahead. To ensure he could get a dust-free ride he let his mount decide how far away from the other horses they would travel.

Courtney turned in her saddle to see where Frank and his horse had gotten too. Pearl was not comfortable with the fact that Cotter had fallen so far behind and wheeled her mount about and headed back in his direction. Her assessment of his situation was that the horse had realized it was lugging an inexperienced rider and decided to take advantage of it by being a lazy-heel on the job. When she arrived at her destination she wheeled her mount about and rode in close to the toffee horse and gave it a forceful slap with her crop, the horse livened up with the shock of the blow and took off after the bunch of riders up ahead, the tenderfoot was forced to hang on for dear life.

With a grin from ear to ear, Pearl took off after Cotter's mount until she caught up with them, then matching the livery stable horse's pace, she stayed with the scribe. To divert his apprehension from his fear of riding fast, he drew Pearl's attention to a depression out on the plain to their right. "See that depression out there on the prairie?"

Pearl knew what he had to be referring to, and nodded. "— D'you knows what caused it?"

"No," Pearl replied as she raised her hat's netting.

"Years ago… most likely before humans trod terra firma, an immense meteor landed out there—crashing into the Earth's crust. For thousands of years wind and rain had attacked the crater it left behind… Now in *our* time, it's nothing more than a depression that collects water. It must be a godsend for the rancher who owns that piece of land. It's a natural water basin and in dry times his cattle would never want for water."

"I thought you were a **newspaperman?**" Pearl Courtney questioned.

Frank frowned. "Whaddya' mean?"

"You talk like a College professor — not a reporter," Pearl exclaimed.

"In my job one has to do a lot of reading," Frank said with a smug smile. "Before I came west in some of my sober moments I read a magazine article or two about *that* phenomenon over yonder. What say before I head back east, we ride out and explore it —see what it's got to offer?" Frank instantly realized that he was trying to make a date with Lester's so-called, ward. Honestly, he could have bitten his tongue. *I shouldn't be into this! Not a lush like me! Dear Pearl's probably only being sociable in the first instance on account of Lester's memory,* he thought.

"If you want… but there's not much to see. Only a sinkhole, it drops down into an extensive network of caves, caverns and dangerous tunnels. It's a popular picnic spot for energetic town's folk; Lester and I have been out here exploring the place for our own satisfaction a couple of times." Pearl adjusted her hat—the interference set free a couple of long raven strands of hair, similar to the time back in Lomax's apartment when she cooked up the corn beef meal for him and Whitney.

Pearl continued. "It can be a treacherous place if you aren't careful. There are some stories of people vanishing in the underground down there, especially when, without warning thunderstorms hit the prairie— runs-offs of water drain down into those caves and have been known to wash folks to oblivion and certain death. You've got to pick your visiting times with care, ask anyone back in Junction City. That's what fascinated Lester about them—their mystery and danger."

"Knowing Lester the way I did, I can understand that about him," Cotter said, frankly. "Lester and I were like two peas in a pod in a lot of ways—though I must admit in some things he was a bit more reckless than, I. By the way any of the caves have stalagmites and stalactites growing in them?" Frank brushed a fly on the hunt for a landing site away from his cheek.

"Only the one underground chamber we knew of. You realize that it's a labyrinthine down there? Water rushes into the place from other sinkholes out on the plain, some not much bigger than a gopher hole, the water pressure in places is reputed to be like that of a water-cannon used on the work-face of mine quarries. You can be flushed along in the roaring waters of a water-chute," Pearl glanced forward to where the posse was, and realized now that they too had begun to lose more ground, it bothered her knowing Frank's mount was using him as a sucker.

"Under certain conditions," Frank said knowledgeably. "—Water has awesome power. That embedded meteorite was for the most part as hard as iron, yet over the centuries the outer layer of it succumb to wear an' tear of the forces… Ya know, maybe we should consider the weather factor and give it a miss?" Cotter had latched on to the fact about the violence of the flushing waters as a possible excuse to break the date with her if it looked like becoming a reality Pearl smiled in Frank's direction. *Gee,* she thought. *What he's saying has given me the heebie-jeebies — darned if I knew it was as dangerous! Still, I think this time of the year one would be quite unlucky to get a violent storm to get a decent run-off to wet the inside of the Pawnees' sacred, place. Frank should be able to at least say he paid the place a visit …*Thought the actress, for in her mind she did not see going out into the country alone with Cotter as a date.

"With the chances high on the cards that you won't be putting roots down in Junction City as planned, I think you should have a poke around down inside the meteor before you leave…" Miss Courtney told him. "It might give you some material to use when writing for a magazine or newspaper, I'll even put myself up as your guide, how does that sound?"

"Do you know your way about down under there?" He really wondered whether it would be worth such a risk. Frank managed to keep the fear out of his voice and off his face, he did know he suffered slightly with claustrophobia. Pearl's intuition told her that Cotter had something to hide and let it go at that.

"I can assure you, that if we come out here, we won't go too far in — only deep enough for you to get the ***feel*** of the place. It'll fill in the best part of a day from your calendar. Just the trip out and back. The Pawnee hold this freak of nature as a sacred site, and aren't too fond of white folks crawling about inside it…"

"Indigenous races all over the world are like that with any phenomenon they can't understand," Frank explained.

Pearl decided that she ought to enlighten Frank about how his hired horse is cunningly playing him for a sucker. "Look, I know you aren't too familiar in the ways of horses, but has it dawned on you yet that your horse is playing you for a ninny?"

"Whaddya' mean?"

"Look how far away the posse, is?"

"So," Frank said with a shrug as he looked in its direction.

"At the rate we're moving cowboy—that posse is going to meet us on the way back from the reservation! So I say, 'hang on to your britches'! " And with that she laid into his horse, with her crop, the shock the animal got sent it racing at full gallop after the posse who were lopping along. Frank would have lost his hat except the chinstrap snagged his nose and held it there long enough for him to grab it before it got away from him. Somehow he managed to stay in the saddle but he looked dangerously awkward on the mount. Courtney raked her hooks into her mount and set off after Cotter, ready to grab him by the seat of his jeans if he looked like being unseated.

Frank cussed to himself as he fully realized that the next couple of days he would have to eat standing up.

The Government Indian agent led the party across the compound to the infirmary—the 14-foot high building mounted on two-foot stumps was close to 40 foot long, the outside walls were clad with clapboards and the roof consisted of galvanized, corrugated iron sheeting. The lower ledge of the fanlight was four hands above the lintel. Three tall windows had been fitted in to the side walls of the infirmary spread out equal distances apart, the sash windows were fitted with Holland sunshades, each shade had been half lowered against the rays of the sun — there ought to have been window drapes too, which had been assigned to the hospice back in Washington and shipped west, but somewhere along the track had been purloined by someone who believed they were too good for the likes of redskins.

The long ward looked and sounded echoic, like a gymnasium, the odor of the sick —hung heavy in the air that reeked of stale vomit, feces and ammonia, the latter being the after math of urine. Two rows of iron hospital cots faced each other foot to foot across an aisle of undressed redwood floor boards; the beds were once as white as virgin snow in color, but were now off-white, chips and scratches destroyed the mint condition — this the result of mishandling when being moved about by the hands of the Indian staff whom had no understanding of how careful one ought to be with the white man's furnishings. Collected under the beds of the sick were fluffy balls of lint and wool from the gray army blankets used to cover the patients.

There was no apparent discrimination between age nor sex, children and adults, young or old, were all lumped in together. What's more, no one appeared to be responsible for the care of these unfortunates. These poor souls were in no man's land, with little or no chance of survival over the next few days it would appear—nature would determine their fate as it grabbed at the hearts of the posse—down to the last man, woman or child.

Briggs and a tubby 50-year-old, Jack Warner, led the Sheriff's party through the building, pausing here and there at the foot of the beds haphazardly. Under the grubby bedcovers of the present bed they had halted before, lingered a Pawnee child of no more than eight, at first it was unclear as to whether the neglected patient was male or female. With pleading fearful eyes, the mute being—looked at the white-eyes gathered about the bed.

"Remove the covers, Mr. Warner..."Briggs instructed in an authoritative tone. The agent wore a bucolic wardrobe, slouch hat, open-neck, plaid flannel shirt and a red and white spotted bandanna. His shirtsleeves were rolled up to the elbows of his masculine forearms. His insecurity showed in the fact that he wore corduroy pants with canvas and leather suspenders and a single holstered Navy Colt strapped round his waist. The legs of his trousers were stuffed into a pair of unpolished, dusty Cavalry boots. The agent moved reluctantly down along side of the bed towards the fearful child who, must have already guessed that she was about to be put on exhibition. Jake focused on the back of his hairy right-hand and the talon-like fingers grasping the edge of the blanket and filthy bed sheet. Then, back-pedaling down the bedside, to its foot, Warner, trailed the bedcovers with him... thus the Pawnee lass had her naked body exposed to the searching eyes of the white people, they had not been expecting the horrible sight that was now before them on the foul dirty mattress. Every joint of the child's limbs had become swollen, stiff and calcified in appearance. Toes and fingers were arthritic and curled back under themselves and the bones between the patient's joints had wasted away to look like twigs or young saplings. The putrid smell that arose from the body only added to the scent of muck in the air, each man, or in this case, the only woman, found before them an affront to their very upbringing.

There were only just two people who had control of their emotions, for they had already experienced the shocking horror this hospital ward possessed, and that of course was Briggs and Warner, but for the rest of them their stomachs were sickened, some slightly less than others because they had had their share of horrors of Indian fighting and therefore were more hardened.

Pearl felt totally ashamed of the humiliation of this helpless child and as the pity of her stomach stirred with queasiness, she took a furious grip of the bedding and flung them from where she stood back onto the child who because of her disabilities could not react or show thanks to the white squaw. Pearl spun away from the bed-end and placing a hand over her mouth, rushed down the ward to the doorway eyes wide as tears welled in them, she fought not to embarrass herself by throwing up along the floor of the aisle—only she knew that once beyond the door in fresh air she would revive.

"This child originally came down with measles," Briggs explained, and upon scanning the faces of the men, saw that he certainly had Cotter's attention. The tenderfoot was so pale that the reaction his face displayed, gave great satisfaction for Briggs to see — "now this here lot is the aftermath of yore friend, Doctor Lomax and his so-called medicine. If any of you need ter see more, then jist go to any bed you desire an' draw back the covers. "

"I fear you are getting a kick out of this!" Frank knew he too had to get outside; he could not stand any more of it. His own stomach signaled that it would soon be reacting biliously... He did not know how the others were feeling at this point, but he knew he should take Pearl's lead and headed for the outdoors. *It is still not too late,* he thought, while fighting to hold down his last meal.

"Look round you," said Jake Warner. "These are the failures of the Doc's treatment, save for those who have already died."

"Has there been any success on the doctor's part?" asked one of the men who had volunteered his services to the posse.

Warner admitted that there were some lucky patients whom had been treated successfully by the doctor and these successes are what kept the man at his work. Boston felt guilty in the presence of the patients about his well-being and speaking for the rest of the group, said, "…I think we've seen enough," *What is gonna be gained by suffering this stink anymore and looking at the misery of some poor soul who can't be helped by any of us!* Klem thought.

The posse started to trudge after Klem, whom had realized for there was nothing more to be had by forcing the party from Junction City to continue viewing these wrecks of humanity.

How the hell could Warner allow this to happen right under his nose and help keep it hidden from the public? To now know this, is shocking, and demoralizing. He and lots of others in the town held Doctor Lomax in such high esteem! What excuse is Warner gonna try and come up wiv? He has been as much a party to this as Lester. How am I gonna handle it? God, it wuz Lomax who saved me leg – without his help and medical skill I'd've been a another one legged cripple unable ter earn a livin' and left to rely on the charity of others! Thought Boston, he eyed the Indian Agent off, marching along the aisle to the ward's egress.

"Who is supposed to be caring and nursing those stricken children?" Pearl asked as she glanced at the faces of the men coming down the steps from the infirmary. Warner provided her with an answer to her question. Already Boston was now wrestling with the idea, of whether or not to arrest Warner and his wife on the spot. Then, concluded that if he did this what or who could he substituted them with, who in the town had the know-how to take charge of the reservation in their absence? No one came to mind and he decided to leave things stand as they were, until he had been in touch with Washington for guidance.

"The Pawnee squaws," Warner said in answer to Pearl Courtney's question. "But they can only do that when they are free of their own domestic works." He recognized what was in Klem Boston's heart with regard to him and feared that the half-crippled Sheriff might start throwing some muscle about.

"Who normally is in daily charge of running the hospital on the reservation?" Frank asked as he realized the mounting tension between the lawman and the Indian Agent.

"I officially oversee what goes on throughout the reservation," Warner tried to shrug off the grip Klem now had on him, but the Sheriff would have none of it, in fact, he hauled his revolver from its holster and covered the agent.

Warner blushed. "The injuns have many superstitions and so it makes it hard fer me to keep squaws fer the sick and ailing on the hospital floor. This mess the doc left behind could get me hung, and I know that!"

Cotter addressed the group as a whole. "The Lomax I knew was a very passionate and caring man. I ***can't believe*** for a second that if he saw how his medicine had effected even one poor soul like that kid we saw back there," Frank stabbed at the air in the direction of the hospital with his forefinger, "Why, he would have dropped all notion of carrying on with his experiments—no matter how much he believed he was on the right track!"

"Like I said before—the doc had his successes, too. That's why I threw in wif him against Washington," The agent said as he looked from face to face, Boston, Miss Courtney, and lastly, Cotter; He obviously did not care about what the rest of the party thought of him and his actions.

"But those poor children…!" Pearl said with anguish. Her normal color was returning and the perspiration on her brow under the brim of her hat was less and less, the result of her squeamish tummy beginning to settle.

"That's ter be expected," Briggs said. "I and Captain Roscoe had the same question and the captain put it ter Warner. He told us the reason fer that is because he worked on trying to save the young in preference to their parents."

"You've all gotta understand that Doctor Lomax couldn't figure out why the medicine clearly worked with some of his patients, it cured most of them of the scourge that struck 'em low but turned some of them into ugly horrible, specimens … He kept doing what he did ter try an' iron out the flaws… what more could yuh ask fer?" Warner said and it was clear that he might breakdown into tears at any time. He was growing so emotional. "Anyway, let's git outa this sun and into my office," He broke away from Boston and headed towards the admin' quarters.

Klem turned to nearby Shorty O'Neill, who was now regretting joining the posse. He had only signed on to raise a bit of money to feed his gambling habit. He had witnessed Sheriff Boston and Sheriff Robeson's arrest of the Army guys back in the saloon. Klem continued: "O'Neill, git the hosses watered before we start homeward."

"Sure thing, Klem..." O'Neill affirmed as he turned to some of the other men around and asked them to give him a hand down at the well.

The Sheriff, Miss Courtney, Cotter and Lieutenant Briggs followed the agent into the low squat, log building, the last to enter the barn-like room, closed the door behind him to keep out both the heat and flies.

The interior of the agency as one came through the door, revealed it to be the administration heart of the reservation. A rustic desk made from local wood was where Warner did all the official paperwork in the daily running of the place. On the wall behind the desk was a map of the local area and in an umbrella stand stood the Stars and Stripes, flag ... Passing the desk and heading deeper into the room you found yourself in a sutler's store with a collection of farming tools and hardware plus groceries which were stored along with Manchester goods ... There was a counter where items could be placed on and tallied up or even wrapped for carrying. There were a couple of open wooden barrels; one-held shovels and another had ax handles, at the front foot of the counter were pine boxes of unwashed dry-mud potatoes. Behind the counter attached to the log wall of the building was a rifle-rack that carried a number of single-shot lever action rifles. Repeating rifles could not be sold by law to reservation Indians for obvious reason, according to the Government of the day. Rifles were only allowed for hunting purposes. At the end of the counter was a stack of wooden crates piled five feet high. For the moment these items had gone unnoticed by the people from Junction City. The back of the room had an open doorway which gave access to the private living quarters of the overall structure where Mrs. Anne Warner ruled supreme. The floors throughout, were covered here and there with throw-down fur Indian rugs and some had even been used on the interior walls to hide the drab, bark-logs and lime mortar as well as hopefully stopping winter draughts that might be able to worm their way into the building through unseen openings between the logs.

Anne was only one or two-years older than Jake, but she was a fine figure of a woman. Warners had come from Knorr in the Black Hills part of the country, so mixing and working with Indians was not something new to her or Jake when he proposed marriage to her ten-years ago, telling Anne that he was going to take up the position of Indian Agent down this end of the country. Anne's folks had come from far across the sea, Holland, better known as The Netherlands, and were known as "The Dutch Lessweiner Family" and had established a successful cattle spread. Some say, Jake had been the Lessweiner's foreman, though these days he did not want to know anything about steers. Anne had snow-white hair; which she had maintained in a chignon style since she was 14 and free of her pigtails. To family and friends, she was simply known as "Snowy"

To-day Anne wore a pair of dungarees, a short-sleeve blouse with a French Collar and a pair of native moccasins. When her husband returned with the Sheriff and the towns' folk from the hospital, Snowy was in the sutler's section of the store taking inventory to keep her mind off her worries — now that the reservation's secret was out. She wondered what would become of her and her husband. She opened a pasteboard carton of canned peaches on the counter and began to tally its contents. Jake Warner did not even acknowledge her as he strode in with Boston and the others. Anne was trying to hide the fact that she was under pressure and nervous, she had been riding her husband for these past months, since the Indian Affairs Department had picked up on Doctor Lomax's clandestine treatment of the sick children as they had come down with chicken pox, et cetera… She had warned her hubby that he was stepping out of line by working hand-in-glove with the Doctor in this business. But no, he wouldn't pay any heed to her, Snowy.

Warner placed his hat down on a clear space of the desk's surface, its draught sent papers airborne and spiraling downwards likes feathers to the floor on the far side of the desk. Anne lowered her hand which held paperwork from the freight company to the counter-top and moved to the center of the sutler's section where she stood and watched her husband whirl round to face the Sheriff, Army Lieutenant, a stranger and the Thespian, Miss Pearl Courtney, whom Anne knew only by gossip spread about by the ladies of the Apostle Church Choir..

Briggs said to Warner's back, "— and that's the crime, treating people with flawed medication — using these Pawnees as his own personal Guinea-pigs!"

Warner was by now squarely facing the threesome he had in tow. "Mebbe we wos wrong in what we did, but Doc Lomax had his heart in the right place and I ain't gonna stand around and let folks kick dirt over his good name!" Jake said as he shoved both hands in the hip pockets of his jeans and shoved his chin forward. "…he wos not, and could not be as callous about the Indian's problems as the Affairs Department expected him ter be. *He hurt* so bad fer the Indians that even *I* could just about see 'im bleedin' inside. Look, he got no joy seein' those monsters his elixir created, but the successes, made it worth the anguish." Turning in the direction of the counter and his wife, Warner, removed his hands from the pockets of his jeans and headed into the sutler's section, a worried Anne followed him with her eyes. *What is Jake up too, now?* She thought.

Everyone's eyes were on the agent. He continued: "The Doc accidentally discovered that there was a way to relieve those sufferin' monsters of their pain…" Warner had come to a stop before an open deal box, with the words **BANNING'S WHISKEY** stenciled on it. A pinch-bar lay nearby and was responsible for the loosened boards. He removed the boards by hand and standing upright in the crate could be seen two rows of whiskey bottles protected by having been placed in straw sleeves. The agent removed a 26 fluid oz bottle from the crate and tore away the straw, letting it fall where it may.

Cotter stormed across to the crates, and snatched the bottle from the agent's hand. "…Isn't it illegal to keep whiskey on any Indian reservation?" hissed Cotter in the direction of both the Sheriff and Lt. Briggs, they nodded as one.

"But none of you understand," Anne cried in a weak attempt to side with her husband. "Doctor Lomax proved *beyond doubt* that it was the only thing that numbs their pain!"

"What Snowy says is right…" Warner said as he took the bottle out of Frank's hand and put it down on the counter. "All the poor ones sufferin' acute pain are to be kept in a state of drunkenness, blind as bats it is their only salvation, believe it or not."

"You can't be saying the same applies to children?" Pearl asked in a shocked voice.

Jake and Snowy nodded.

"It's the only humane thing we can do fer 'em," Warner pointed out in the hope that they would understand.

"This *is **criminal!***" Cotter blurted out. "— I find it unbelievable!"

"Much that surrounds *yore* Doctor Lomax is **unbelievable.**" Briggs remarked.

"Let me understand …" Pearl said. "You are telling us that the naked young squaw back there in the hospital ward, is *drunk?*"

"That's right," admitted Briggs. "From the time we sanctioned Warner to go on treatin' the sick using Doctor Lomax's methods."

"You and your Captain allow Warner to keep kids like her drunk!" said the dumb-founded Cotter.

Both Warner and Briggs nodded.

Turning to Pearl, Frank said, ***"I can't believe, this!"***

"You'd better," said Warner, "when the Captain n' Lt. Briggs first arrived here and saw what we were housing and the ongoing treatment we were doing in Lomax's name they were shocked!"

"Where *we,* ever!" Briggs admitted. "We ordered the Warners to halt their way of treating the patients in their care with alcohol, and in doing so we were unwittingly inflicting the poor wretches to a living hell!"

"When Mr. Briggs and his Captain saw what happened with their own eyes to the patients not being fed the whiskey as ordered by Doctor Lomax, they had a complete change of heart!" Missus Warner said.

"The whiskey had been certainly numbing their pain – so we had to allow the Warners to resume treating the survivors who hadn't come through the original treatment of Doctor Lomax's snake-oil!" said Briggs.

Pearl was as confused as Cotter and Boston, and no doubts the others here in the room. "You people accuse Lester of all sorts of horror," Miss Courtney said as she now focused on Briggs. "And yet you allow these people to practically force-feed young kids booze!"

"I know it sounds weird," Anne said to Pearl. "But by them being kept drunk, out of their minds, is the only way they can find peace." Snowy's eyes were pleading for understanding.

"The pain is so enormous that without the whiskey you would have to be merciful in the only other way possible," Jake Warner said. "And that's a bullet between the eyes!"

"Warner showed us that it works, otherwise Captain Roscoe would not have endorsed the treatment be continued."

"The pain is so enormous that without the whiskey you would have to be merciful in the only other way possible," Jake Warner said. "And that's a bullet between the eyes!"

"Well I do not see how a man of Lester's character, could be tied into any of this. If anything, Doctor Lomax was very much against alcohol and I could *never* imagine him authorizing hard liquor for a child ..." Pearl Courtney was most forthright in what she said.

"I must agree there with Miss Courtney," Frank said as he joined forces with the actress. "— No way, no way..." Cotter added.

Based on the looks Lt. Briggs was getting from the actress and the tenderfoot, he could see they still had their doubts about the opinion Washington had of Lomax and his business buddies. The lieutenant felt duty bound to make them see the light even if it was against their will. He dealt them another hand: "The purpose of this trip to the reservation to-day involving Sheriff Boston's, wuz to get a point through to 'im — you folks by rights shouldn't be here. We only allowed the Easterner to come because he's so tied in with Lomax that my Captain and I thought by him seein' the truth of the quack's actions would make him see sense..." Briggs focused on Miss Courtney. "— It wasn't my idea to bring yew into it Miss Courtney, it wuz purely supposed to have been men's business. It wuz Cotter who insisted that you be here...

"The two of you are here to **learn** a few facts along wif Boston — of which, you an' Cotter don't seem to wanna accept. Nuthin' c'n change what you saw out there in the hospice, lady, as horrible as it wuz — yore greedy Doctor Friend and his cronies brought it all about with their hunger to bleed these Indians dry of their gold.

The Pawnees had been conned into believin' that his Whiteman medicine was gonna protect 'em from plague — but they ended up getting far more'n they bargained fer.

"When Lomax approached the government about his idea of runnin' tests on the Pawnee community, congress gave it the thumbs down; but this didn't stop yore friend and his buddies — they went ahead behind everyone's back and things got right out of control until now it's reached this point!

"No one knows where it's gonna finish but I can tell yuh one thing, folks. In the end yore gonna have to face up to the facts along with the rest of this town, or be damned."

O'Neill poked his head round the door. "We're all ready out here Sheriff, when you are."

"Give us a minute," Klem said over his shoulder as he kept his eyes fixed on Briggs. O'Neill returned to the posse members outside with their mounts. They were keen to be away from this hell-hole.

Briggs continued: "Greed. And that greed you dick-head, was fer the love of **gold.** That's all this affair amounts too," the lieutenant jabbed a thumb in Warner's direction. "Lomax gave this lousy excuse fer a human-bein', twenty-five bucks fer every patient he okayed fer him to treat!"

"That true?" Klem asked the Warners.

"Yore not obliged ter say anything, Jake!" Snowy Anne said, before her husband could part his lips.

However, Warner went on all the same. "The Great George Washington an' his buddies wrote us a constitution fer the protection of all Americans, and I'm gonna cloak myself with it. That's all I've got ter say at this stage." Jake Warner then placed his hands defiantly on his hips.

"This isn't getting you and your cause anywhere, Lieutenant," Cotter told the experienced campaigner. "Sure, you have subjected Miss Courtney and me to a human tragedy: but how can you excuse not putting this man and his woman in chains for being a known party to such an adversity?

"People are all out after Lester's hide, but they are still in their job, here!" Cotter opined as he punctured the air with his finger.

"There's more sides ter this triangle than one," Briggs said. "They'll face justice in time, but right now we need someone ter over see the reservation; and he's experienced. The Indians are up in arms over this whole shebang and could take to the hills if the Indian Affairs Department does not handle it right. Warner can vouch for that fact. Have you noticed how few Pawnees there are around the place? The place is almost a ghost town because they have forsaken the area around the hospital as being haunted by the spirits of their dead. They've moved back to their old village site and no one knows what is cooking back there in their minds. This place is a goddamn powder keg and only needs a live match to torch things off and the whole box an' dice will become a blood bath!"

"I'm inclining to think like Mister Cotter," Pearl admitted. "This whole situation needs a "fall guy" and I believe you have selected Lester to be the one. Mister Warner is the one I see here who has a lot to answer for — and that is *his* incompetence. Washington, your Captain, and you, are trying to cover up his actions with pieces of official paper, you are all hiding Warner's part in this with the same pieces of paper!"

"You leave my husband be," Anne Warner hollered at Pearl Courtney. "The whole town knows that you an' Doctor Lomax were being a damn lot more friendly and cozy together than holding, hands!" Snowy Anne Warner poised as if she were about to rush at the actress. Cotter braced himself to cut her off if she did move in that direction. Meanwhile Lieutenant Briggs slumped with a sigh, as he realized that it would take a heavenly sign to open Cotter and Courtney's eyes.

"You're in a no win situation," Sheriff Boston pointed out. "You'll never convince some people that Doctor Lomax wuz a humbug!"

Lieutenant Brigg's hooded eyes came to bear on the Sheriff. "If I had you convinced, I'd consider that some sort of victory. Then you could set me and the Captain free ter get on with our jobs. I'm not too fussed about whether or not a city drunk and a woman of the theater believes in what the government, says."

"I've something more ter say, here —" said Anne Warner. "I want *this* fancy lady and the rest of yuh out of my house right now," she focused on Klem Boston. Sheriff, if you feel that my husband has done any wrong, as the Injun agent here, then you better call in a U.S. Marshal… Cause as a government employee, he's the only lawman he's answerable too!"

"I agree with Mrs. Warner there, Sheriff…" Cotter said. For he knew an outsider like a Marshal would be above suspicion and not likely to be corrupted by any money being slipped under the table. "Plus, I am sure that like me, Miss Pearl Courtney would rather be back in town as soon as possible, this whole trip has been a futile exercise as far as we're concerned…"

11

THE POSSE'S RETURN to Junction City began at a fast clip as the riders wish to reach town before dark, at least by twilight. It was only when the horses showed signs of tiring apiece that the gang slackened pace and settles into a steady lope. Briggs contented himself by riding in near silence as he was in a bitter mood and the thought of contemplating another night in Sheriff Boston's cell was not popular with him. He prayed and hoped that the Army would get the lead out of their ass, and bounce Sheriff Klem Boston's powers right out the window. *Why hadn't the Army come down hard on the hick with booth boots?* Was down there amongst this man's thought. Though, he did feel the Sheriff was now not as opposed in the belief that Lomax was such a white-haired boy, as others seem to think. *I'll tell the Captain what I think and mebbe he might be able ter work on Boston further?* Thought Lt. Briggs, *Anything was worth a try...*

It was a little after four in the afternoon when the posse started to nose its way into the north end of Bryan Street, heading for Main. Miss Courtney and Cotter were riding drag as per usual; with Cotter certainly looking forward to the end of to-day's ride. He was correct in assuming that he was the only one whom had earned a case of saddle-soreness. At the corners of Main and Bryan Streets, the scribe and the actress broke off from the bunch, as they headed to the livery and the rest of the posse went on up to the jailhouse where they'd be dismissed and paid off.

The Livery stable doors were still open for business and the pair walked their mounts into the lobby area under the wide lintel. Cotter reined the toffee mare to a stop with a tired sigh and somehow managed to dismount before Pearl, and so was able to grasp her mount's bridle while she dismounted with panache from her horse. Standing alongside her mare, she rearranged her skirts as a stable-hand appeared out of the gloom of the interior and took charge of the toffee mare, and another feller came up and led Miss Courtney's horse away to unsaddle and turn loose in the sandpit for a roll.

"What are your plans for the rest of the evening, Miss Pearl?" Frank inquired as he rubbed his tired lower back muscles and tried to figure out just how successful a hot soak in a tub would go to taking some of the sting out of his muscles.

"Busy," she answered brusquely. "I'm off up the alleyway to my room for a fresh change of clothes, and then a visit to the Chinese Bathhouse. Then it is back to the theater for a quick nap before show time…" She raised her hat's fly net and left it resting on the hat brim. "…How goes your legs, after that ride?"

"— I'll survive… Though there's no doubt I'll be looking for elbow room at the diner's counter for a few days, no table and chair for me," he confessed.

Pearl advised, "Take a long hot soak in a tub of suds with bath salts, that's about the best you can do for what ails your thigh muscles, Frank."

Frank Cotter could tell by the frequent use of his Christian name, Pearl Courtney was growing comfortable in his presence and he quite liked that idea. He valued the fact that their association was becoming less staid. Frank did the gentlemanly thing and took Pearl by the elbow and ushered her out of the building away from the aroma of chaff, manure, and stale horse piss — outside on the street they found the air much fresher, and paused to get their bearings.

Boston allowed his deputy to re-acquaint Briggs with Captain Roscoe behind bars, in the meantime Klem paid off the stand-in deputies from petty cash. The disbanded posse formed themselves into a queue and filed past with their hands out ready for the dollar each had been promised for their day's time. Boston knew that it would burn a hole in their trouser pockets before tomorrow's sun sank below the horizon. Then Klem enquired whether or not the prisoner had been any bother to Ben while he was away. "Has the Captain been a good little boy …?" Occasionally Boston liked to talk with tongue-in-cheek.

"You'd better follow me Sheriff..." was Lexmon's reply as he turned down the room in the direction of the two cells. " It has been a hot little town while you've been out socializin' at the reservation."

They moved deeper into the building and as the pair drew near to the cells, Boston noticed for the first time that the second cell was now housing a morose Pawnee buck, his arm in a sling which had been doctored with a splint. The Pawnee sat crossed legged on the broad plank flooring.

Boston studied the Indian buck for a few moments, and then Roscoe, who joined the sheriff in the mood which was setting in on him. The lieutenant strolled over to the bar-divider. Unlike the Sheriff, Briggs had been put in the picture history-wise, by Captain Roscoe, who had explained how the injured Pawnee buck had ended up in the cell alongside them.

Lexmon explained the presence of the Indian. "— Four bucks rode in here while you wiz away..." There was a tinge of pride to his voice, and as the story unrolled he had every right to his feelings. "They were full of fire water — rot-gut whiskey. There wiz no doubt they were wild an' mean, ready ter start their own private war ... Don't know where they got 'em from but they wiz armed with a couple of Sharps. They stopped off in front of Hallway's clinic, and began shootin' it full of holes; Folks on the street were terrified an' scattered fer fear of coppin' a stray slug —"

Captain Roscoe butted in: "— Deputy Lexmon and I heard the shooting from here and cries of a full blown, panic!" Not wanting to take away any of the man's glory he turned to Ben. "You tell yore boss what you did —" Then Roscoe quickly turned back to Boston before Lexmon could get a word in —– "this this man proved himself a **real** hero. If he was in the service — he'd've earned a medal for **courage under fire!"**

Boston's eyes widened in surprise and he looked on Lexmon in a new light. Ben was keen to blow his own trumpet and as Klem swung his eyes back to the buck, he realized that the feller was more like a cornered cougar than a wounded Indian.

"...The captain and I were doin' some jawin' and playing a few hands of cards through the cell bars ter pass the time. When the sound of rifle fire broke out down near Doc Hallway's place — but I had no idea it wuz his place being shot up! When we heard the screams an' cries of womenfolk — we knew I had one helluva shindig on me hands! I let Captain Roscoe loose ter back me up, as you must understand I didn't know, what I might be walking into … Once armed, we bolted in the direction of the ruckus; and run in ter a wall of folks runnin' up the street like goddamn Lucifer wuz on their ginger!

"Then we spot this wild bunch of Pawnees on horseback, millin' around in front of the Doc's, pepperin' the façade wiv hot lead! You know the old mule skinner, Judd Burnacre…?" Ben asked. Klem nodded, he knew the man well. "Well, he's hunkered down behind a water trough in front of Mullins' saddlers across the street from the four bucks — wiv his old peepers, he ain't hittin' a thing worth a damn — all he wuz doin' wuz putting a woodpecker out of business.

"Me and the Captain were forced ter hug the walls of the buildings as we advanced, using the recess doorways fer cover as we moved in ter range on the hell fired idjits! Roscoe, err, Captain Roscoe, an' me were hollerin' ter folks ter keep low and indoors!

"We could see there wuz no time fer a parley. So I opened fire an' my first shot knocked a critter off his pony — he were as dead as a doornail a-for he hit the dirt, he'd no more be stirrin' up any more shit fer Jake Warner! Captain Roscoe shot a hoss out frum under another drunken buck while my Winchester put paid ter a real raging' maniac! The fourth one wheeled his pony and comes racin' hell fer leather up the street, like his buck brother — he wuz as loco as a hive of bees! I had no choice. I wanted ter put a charge into him but the works jammed on me gun or I had a misfire… then I realized in the damn heat of the moment I'd come away wiv out my revolvers, I threw away the rifle and went after 'im on foot along the sidewalk and as his hoss drew alongside an empty hitchin' rail I angled over and leaped from the boardwalk to the cross-rail an' sprung from there in full-flight onto him and his mount, I swept the ugly cuss right off his bronco an' together we hit the dirt — wiv me lucky enough ter have the advantage, 'cause on landin' — that feller collected a broken arm. Hallway has since been here and tried ter patch him up a bit." Ben folded his arms across his chest to savor the expression on the Sheriff's dial.

Roscoe now added what he thought Lexmon had not covered about the skirmish. "The Indian horse I shot left the rider stranded an' unarmed on his knees in the street, but his boozed filled eyes sighted a rifle on the ground and he went for it; Having no idea whether or not it was working, I squeezed off a slug and caught him in the skull to be on the safe-side, I knew that hotshot had put him out of the equation."

Lexmon was now on a roll and returned to his story. "One of the first two bucks shot, wuz still alive, and while me and that buck there in the cell wuz going at it head-to-toe — the wounded brave makes it to his feet and is set on giving me something' fer my corner, he raised this Sharps to his shoulder… Well finally ol' Judd gets his eye in, jumps out frum behind the trough and drops 'im deader, than a week old dead rattler. And that's pretty much the whole story. Our local rag is going to run the full story on the attack and I bet a million ter one, that when the folks back east read about it, it'll make Junction City, famous!" Ben Lexmon said.

Klem shook his head. "You've got it wrong. The town won't get the fame or glory, but you will. All that Injuns' run-in will do fer us is paint the town wilder than ever. The town council won't like it, 'coz it'll drive away would-be settlers planning' ter head west, they'll think the Indian War has been rekindled. Anyway, how many folks got hurt in this brush wiv the Pawnee, Benny?"

"Two."

"Two! Hell and be damned," Hollered Boston. "That's two, to many! Have ya questioned the buck as ter what made 'em hit the pickle juice and attack the town?"

"No. I ain't game ter get close to 'im… I'm thinking I have used the best part of my luck wiv him in our punch-up. Jest look at the size of 'im? He must be as strong as a damn Buffalo and fuming like a volcano ready ter blow!" Deputy Lexmon said without exaggeration.

"Now he's starting' ter sober up I reckon he'd be like toying' wiv a cantankerous grizzly — nah going' tooth an' nail once wiv him wuz my quota, thank you very much!"

Klem judged that he might have to agree with Benny on his assessment. "Who got hurt — what wuz their wounds?"

"A mother an' a young, tyke! You'll want the details fer yore report, I guess?" opined the deputy. Boston nodded and glanced through the bars at the feller from the reservation — he tried to recall whether or not he knew the brave's face, but he looked no different than a whole lot of other bucks out there in his age group.

"I tried ter do some interrogation of him for you, Sheriff." Roscoe confessed, "But my Pawnee is a little rusty and I don't know what his English is like. He might be ignorant of jist playing it clever — it's always hard ter tell with these tribal people," Roscoe slipped a cigarette between his lips and ignited a match from the coarse surface of the bar in front of him. Then exhaling smoke from both nostrils towards the floor as he went on: "I think he might be willing to palaver with the Indian agent — he got that much through to me, all right."

"Uh—well someone has ter get to the bottom of all this," Boston coughed as a result of Roscoe's smoke. "… And that someone jist happens ter be me. Ben, ya might have ter grab a man or two frum the saloons ter ride over to Warner's, and bring him in? Like me he would've been unaware any of the tribe were orf reservation grounds."

"Wouldn't termorrow be more fittin', Sheriff?" Ben asked as he gave the matter the consideration it deserved, it was late in the day to be pounding hooves out to the reservation. It would mean trekking around in the dark and he gave away cow-punching because he didn't like riding herds at nights.

Scratching his right sideboard, the Sheriff pulled rank on Lexmon and his ideas. "I don't like the looks of that red feller in there. The longer we hang on ter him I figure his brethren, might bunch together and give us more trouble than we've already had. Warner's only one man an' when it comes down to it, he can't chain the tribe to the reservation if they didn't wanna stay there. Five bucks went walkabout last week an' haven't returned, but that's a matter fer Fort Hancock. Look at the hate, *that* buck has in his eyes towards us? I order you ter get Warner so we c'n git this rotten business squared away. And if ya see the sawbones en route — order 'im ter git his carcass up here ter me — now be off wiv yuh!"

Lexmon knew not to argue with Klem, so he went and put on his pistols and grabbed his Stetson from the wall up near Boston's desk. He paused to check the loads in the chambers and lit out.

Boston picked up the ring of fencing wire with the key to the cell-doors. Unthinkingly, Lexmon had left the key on the stool this side of the bars, it would have been the stool he had used to sit on when playing cards with the Army prisoner before the Indians had hit town. "…Looks like I'm ter be yore jailer fer tonight. I'll be on the mezzanine floor right over head — so don't plan on staying awake too late; I wanna catch some sleep." Boston then limped back up the jail suite to his desk and there unstrapped his Colts and put the guns in the third drawer on the right-hand side of the 10-year-old desk. Then it was paperwork time and Boston began to write up the day's reports with his supplied quill and ink.

Frank Cotter was none too keen about leaving the wooden tub, even though the water could only be gauged, as tepid. He knew that the Chinese-staff had tired of keeping his tub topped up with hot water. It was already full to over flowing on the cubicle's floor, and the remnants of carbolic soap made the wet boards as slippery as any iced over pond in a New England winter.

All the water from the ablution closets were tipped out onto the sloping floor-boards, and hence, they drained through to a hollow log channel that carried the bath waters outside to the backyard where it was collected in a three foot deep dam, and when required, the Chinese irrigated the vegetable patches of lettuce, cauliflower and a variety of root vegetables that were sold daily to the women folk of Junction City through the Asian green grocer.

Although Frank and Pearl had come to the bathhouse together after collecting their change of clothing, there was no question of unisex bathing. Pearl and Frank parted company in the lobby of the bathes and after her refreshing bath, stuck to her routine. The Chinese back-scrubber told Frank about the Indian raid on the town earlier that day. It sounded as though it had the makings of a good story for an eastern newspaper and wondered if the local news journal had any links with any eastern news outlets. This he would have to explore for there would be no point in trying to flog a news-story back east, if the greyhound had already left the box. He had an editor friend at 𝕿𝕳𝕰 𝕹𝕰𝖂 𝖄𝕺𝕽𝕶 𝕮𝕺𝖀𝕽𝕴𝕰𝕽; this friend knew that Cotter had taken up a position out west to start anew. So while soaking his tortured muscles, Cotter mentally began composing the article he intended drafting there amongst his gray cells housed in that cranium of his.

Finally free of the tub and dressed, Cotter paid for the services of the bathhouse. Then with a shortened stride owing to the stiffness in his legs, he set off down the sidewalk in the direction of Bryan Street, the odd lamppost had been fired up for the evening so he was comfortable with the idea that he wasn't likely to fall over and break a bone. He came upon Whitney Dragoon leaning on a veranda post smoking a cigarette at the curb outside a tailor shop.

"What yuh doing holding up the awning…?" Frank said as he drew to a stop with his riding clothes draped over his forearm — he was now dressed in a city-cut suit.

"Only that it wuz a shocking business those Indians hittin' the town like that," Whitney said, gravely.

Cotter shook his head. "Did you see or hear anything of it?"

"Me? … I wuz in a saloon when it happened! I know when ter keeps my head down! I buried my snout in a pint of draft beer… Anyway, it was over quick, like. We had some townies poke their heads up out of the burrows to see the end results," Dragoon ditched his cigarette butt. "Did yuh have an interesting day out with Miss Courtney?"

Looking deep into Dragoon's eyes Frank asked: "Are you keeping tabs on me?" While waiting to hear the salesman's answer to his question he fished in the pocket of his coat-vest and withdrew a couple of fresh cigarettes he had made up a day or two ago. He proffered his spare one to Whitney who did not need a second invitation to add another layer of nicotine to the lining of his lungs. "…I'm just on my way home to write up a version of today's Indian attack on the town, it might earn me a few bucks if I can get it in THE NEW YORK COURIER."

Dragoon supplied a fresh match and struck it off the coarse weathered veranda post he had been leaning on when Cotter came along.

"How yuh gonna write about something you didn't witness?" He held the flame of the match to the tip of Cotter's cigarette. "Hell, you weren't even in the burgh at the time!" The Vesta's glowing flame lit their faces as Frank was given the privilege of lighting up first, while Whitney Dragoon waited patiently for his answer, he put his unlit cigarette in his mouth to fire up from the same match. Cotter exhaled smoke through his nose, "Join me, and I'll explain…" Cotter said as he set the pace and they moved off side-by-side. "You see, it is all to do with one's imagination. I'll levy the story as though I were there, right in the thick of it… No one back east will have cause to question the validity of what I've written — they'll swallow it like soda pop on a summer's day…" Frank was not pleased by the way Dragoon seemed to be regarding him. "— Gawd man, it's only a story; it isn't as though someone is going to be physically hurt by it!"

"Well," said Whitney. "I guess you know *your business* better than me. How often does this go on in the newspaper world?"

"What do you mean?"

"This kind of lying… why I could never take something I now read in the 'papers seriously any more. I used ter reckon what they printed was the gospel!"

"Since the first newspaper appeared in print, the news has been tinkered with. During the war you did not think that the published casualty lists were authentic? Imagine how devastating the truth would be to the moral of soldiers' families' back home, or to the man in the field? The full truth never gets into print."

"But that's a bit immoral, ain't it?"

"Immoral? I s'pose so… But there's a word for what the war department needs from newspapers and it's a thing known as ***Propaganda*** — and if you don't know what that word means, look it up in a dictionary! Anyway, by the time my story sees the light of day in the east; it'll be more than a month old! So folks won't get that all worked up about the matter, will they?"

The salesman shrugged. He had no idea what folks in the east would do. "Oh, by the way… I have a booking on tomorrow's stage to Kansas City. If you want, Mebbe I could speed the delivery of yore story East by taking it part of the way with me, then posting it on — might save you some time…?" suggested Dragoon.

"Sounds good to me — I'm sure it would speed things up, rather than relying on the regular stage route. Tag along back to the apartment and I'll scribble the story down you can even act as my source of information which I'm sure will add to making it sound more bona fide."

"As you like," answered Whitney agreeably, their footfalls now matching one another. Bustling along the sidewalk towards them was Doc Hallway carrying his black leather sawbones' bag. He looked smart wearing gray twill cuff-less trousers with a charcoal stripe running down, lengthways — to his gleaming polished shoes, a thin veneer of dust was part and parcel to the town's strollers. Cotter also noted that the doctor wore a white waistcoat and an Ascot at his throat — his frockcoat in this light could have been black or maybe Navy Blue, where the sleeves ended, one could see detachable shirt-cuffs. His gray Stetson looked sharp with its flat brim and hill-like crown. He traveled like a man on a mission, Cotter, hailing him socially.

"Howdy there, Doctor…" Frank said as they neared, but reading Cotter's body-language, Hallway realized that the man was on for a chat, and that was out of the question at the moment; but he slowed stride as the distance between them shortened with each and every step. "— I heard some disgruntled patients visited you, today?" Cotter went on with a grin.

"Not now, man…" Doctor Hallway answered brusquely, "The Sheriff needs to see me." He made to go on but in the last moment, decided that this would appear too rude, so he paused; though his eagerness to continue with his summons gave him the jitters.

"I only need a moment," said Frank, pleading his case. So the sawbones caved in.

"I didn't know that Indians still attacked white settlements in this day an' age. I heard all about what happened to your surgery from the Asians up at the bathhouse. Is it true, Deputy Lexmon stopped the attack almost single-handed?"

Hallway nodded. "You could say that, yes."

"We're you in attendance at your clinic?" Cotter enquired.

"Of course; why do you ask, Cotter?"

"I've still got contacts in the newspaper industry back east — thought I might dispatch the town's story to THE NEW YORK COURIER. It's such an exciting event I might even get two articles out of it now I come to think of it. D'you think, Deputy Lexmon, would favor me with an interview — tell me how he saw things unfold?"

"That's up to him. But I can tell you he's not in town at the moment. He and a few fellers have gone off under orders of Boston ter fetch the Indian agent, Warner. Klem wants ter see if the Pawnee prisoner will explain his actions through Warner as interrupter … Seems the Pawnee prisoner has gone and developed himself a case of lock-jaw and won't explain himself. "

"Hmm," Cotter brushed away a mosquito that had no doubt been born and bred in the waters of the bathhouse storage pond. "— It's been said, that a couple people were caught in the gunfire. A young mother and her kid, a toddler?"

"That's unfortunately true," confirmed the medico. "I managed to help the wounded woman, but there wos nuthin' one could do fer the small boy — you win some, yuh lose some, that's the way of it in this medical business."

"How long d'you expect me ter wait around while you write this here two part story?" Dragoon asked; for he was thinking that the way things were shaping up, he would end up with a late night on his hands and it didn't suit him. "I wasn't plannin' on having a real late night with having ter face a long journey."

"I'll write it now that I'm all fired up and in the mood; but you don't have to stick about for the second half of the article. After all, they mightn't wanna two edition spread. I just thought that I'd get one ready, incase, and one from the town hero's angle would go over well," Cotter informed the man. "I will only prevail on you to get the first one away, that's all." Cotter informed his friend.

The doctor was eager to be on his way, so he reminded them that he was still there. "Well the Sheriff is waiting for me, I *must* be off. If you plan to write a second part though, you might like to include the family's point of view; it might be a good idea if you turn up at the funeral and make your acquaintance with the dead boy's kinfolk … Anyway, that's up to you. Good evening, Gentlemen," Hallway doffed his hat and abandoned both Dragoon and Cotter.

Returning to their business Frank said as they moved off. "That's not a bad angle the sawbones suggested… the emotional upheaval this boy's death will cause the family. I can easily write up the second installment after the funeral…"

"But you won't know that until you see what the family has ter say? They may not like having their private feelings spread all over the pages of an Eastern newspaper." Whitney said as he spat aside into the dry street drain.

"In the years I've been a newspaperman, I've not met a person who doesn't like being glorified in print. I can write pretty fast when need be and seeing a decent night's sleep's a concern to you, I'll write my dispatch and have it ready before the stage leaves tomorrow, how does that sound?" Frank watched Dragoon's response.

"Fine by me," said Whitney Dragoon. It was going to be a damn responsibility to be in-charge of his article before it went out on the regular service. He would have hated for it to become lost en route.

Cotter now in shirtsleeves, sat at the dinner table in the apartment writing furiously on loose sheets of onion paper. Frank decided that he would make up the attack of the Indian renegades from the point of view of someone lying undercover at the scene. But while laboring at his writing chore he had a re-think and decided to write the tale in three chapters. He would write the first installment just dealing with the shoot-out on Hallway's surgery and get it away via Dragoon. Then he would write the second part based on Deputy Lexmon's account of things and the third version would tell of the effects on the decease's family. Lexmon's version and the emotional family's article he'd jot down together and send them out by stage at a later date; He determined that, the most effective way of writing the story and this would make it an emotional tear-jerker. But the most important thing would have to be its title – it would have to have a commanding title for each of its chapters so he began with, ***The Pawnee Incident at Junction City…!***

Frank surfaced from what he thought had been a deep sleep, to discover that he wasn't as refreshed as he had expected. He felt drained of energy and had a shocking headache; he put it down to too much black coffee. Enough daylight was coming into the apartment from the bedroom window, so he knew he had been asleep but he couldn't recall having drawn his writing to a close or how he had made it in here to the bedroom. He had to admit that he felt befuddled …

Heavy-headed, he sat up and made what was a difficult journey for him from bed, to washing stand and poured cold water into the hand basin from the ewer — doused his face and hands and poured water through his hair. His actions were becoming a bit of a habit. He found a towel and dried his hair, face and hands in that order, as he made it back to the bed and stood there alongside it wrestling with his thoughts. He went through the routine of searching under the pillow for the derringer he had been given by Whitney, and then it dawned on him that he had returned the small pistol to Dragoon. Approaching the parlor, he had no trouble remembering how saddle-sore he felt, and he knew that it would be with him for a few more days, yet. He looked over at the dining table and saw his night's work, pages of written text and crumpled pages on the floor, which he had rejected as being beneath his standard. For some unexplainable reason he got the impression that someone had been in here snooping about! Walking on the balls of his feet he moved out onto the upstairs landing to see if anyone was hanging about down below — no one, he had gone through the torture of walking the extra steps for nothing. The black cat stirred from its cubbyhole in the woodpile under the stairs upon hearing Cotter's movement's overhead. It came into view and hoped that maybe this morning she would not have to resort to her stockpile of dead mice back in the logs cut to suit the stove. But again she found herself being ignored.

Cotter returned to the apartment and went across to the dining table and began checking through the papers; he had an unwritten law that he always left this finished writings, correlated, and the fact that he found two pages out of place, surely added to this uneasy feeling that he had not spent the entire night here, alone.

Frank, though still a stranger to Junction City, found the mortician's place of business almost mid-city on the left-hand side of Starr Street heading towards Boot Hill. Two hearses had been drawn up out the front of the premises and Cotter realized that he was none too early when he saw that both vehicles had already been loaded with their respective cargo.

One could not get the funerals mixed up as to whom was who, for the hearses casket sizes and quality were quite different. The vehicle bearing the smallest and cheaper quality of coffin had to belong to the victim who had died as a result of the Indian attack; the other hearse had a real-highly polished casket with ornate filigree workings on its lid and sides. The family of the deceased boy from the surgery incident were already waiting on the boardwalk out the front of the funeral parlor with a couple of older children, two boys in short pants that hung 2-inches below the knees, their loose long socks had slid down to their ankles in a heap atop of their laced-up boots. They wore collarless homemade shirts and battered straw hats. These were obviously brothers of the victim. A ten-year-old girl stood quietly nearby staring at her brother's coffin through the glass side of the hearse. Her frock had been converted to her size from an adult's, like the boys, she too wore lace-up boots. The mother of the family stood out not only for her pale complexion and distraught and neglected appearance, but also because of the chocker-like bandage that encircled her throat, clearly the work of Doctor Hallway. Apparently a bullet had either nicked her or gone clean through the throat with it having left little effect on her. Her husband was doing his best to appear almost unaffected by the death of the youngster, but on closer scrutiny one could see it was just a front, he masked this successfully by comforting his wife. The deceased's siblings were missing him but were already adapting to the extra bed space in the household.

Glancing once more back to the mother, Frank mused that she looked almost too young to have mothered a family of this size, but recalled that this was the way it was in the frontier settlements, daughters were married off when they reached childbearing age for a husband relieved the financial strain on frontier families who had the misfortune to have been blessed with several females in their midst.

Neighbors from either side of the family's rented cottage were here to lend their support, along with a number of Church members. Hallway was there with a woman of his own age and without knowing it officially, Cotter could safely assume that she was the Doctor's wife. The Doctor was more than likely here to see both the deceases off, but still kept a wary eye on his patient, the tyke's mother.

While Cotter had been soaking up the scene the second hearse, bearing Ma Kelly's casket had been shrouded with wreaths and silk ribbons of pink and black from people gathering to pay her their last respects. This was in contrast to that of the small white coffin in the front hearse that had only the one single long stem rose lying on the center of its bare lid. It rose looked so forlorn. Naturally Ma had the greater number of mourners which was made up from a cross-section of Junction City's community, even the puritans were here to see Ma off, though they kept to themselves on their part of the sidewalk on the opposite side of the street; talking in whispers and taking in Ma's known personal friends across the road. There sat cowboys on toey horses, dance-hall gals and cardsharps from opposite business houses and fun palaces, and of course there were Ma's working gals as well as the theater folk for the establishment had closed out of respect for its owner.

Stroughton was there with his fringed surrey and two gray mares. Riding up with the lawyer was Pearl Courtney who accompanied a phlegmatic Pete Kelly, whom folks looked on with curiosity. The surrey was festooned with black ribbon and bunting. Members of the **Theater Royal band** had arrived with their instruments and got down to tuning up straightaway so that they would be ready to give their rendition of the **Funeral March** to the cemetery.

Frank noted two fiddlers, a trumpeter, a clarinetist and a big bass drum, a weedy feller was toying with a button accordion and a round-faced, red cheeked band member who usually played cymbals was fingering a Jew's harp.

The funeral director, a gaunt morbid looking type, was common of those attracted to the profession, called the band to order and they commenced to line up behind, the child's hearse in front of Ma Kelly's conveyance. At the rear of Ma Kelly's hearse her working gals lined up three abreast and so did other folks whom wanted to be included in the march to Boot Hill. Frank opined that this was as good as any place for him and strolled in amongst the mourners and introduced himself around.   Then there was the mourning coach for the child's siblings and parents, how this mix-up occurred no one knew, for it ought to have been trailing their son's hearse. Behind this was the float from the town's ice works, which folks knew was one of Ma's business enterprises.

The Mayor and his wife arrived on foot, late for someone in his position. He was decked out with his mayoral gold chain; they ignored the other mourners and went forward up front and took up a position behind the band.

It then hit Attorney Stroughton that it would be a fitting gesture if Ma's band led the double funeral parade from the front, as then it would be seen as a mark of respect for the poor child whom had died in such tragic circumstances that had hit the town. Donald stepped down from his vehicle and made his way up to the mortician and explained the idea to him. The morbid fellow's face lit up and he beamed proudly and went into the action of re-organizing the band and correcting the location of the mourning coach and explained what was going on to the family. Then the band was encouraged by the funeral director to strike up the march and on his direction, stepped off as they followed him for the walk along the street to the cemetery. At the intersection of Starr and Ridge Road the procession was joined by the stiff-legged Sheriff Boston, Jake Warner and Ben Lexmon, all fell in step behind the Mayor. The Lawmen and the Indian Agent came unarmed in consideration for the dead.

At the cemetery the funerals parted at the direction of the mortician — with the band now leading Ma's hearse away to the right where the hole for her remains had been prepared. The family and its smaller procession moved to another section of Boot Hill where a much smaller hold had been broken open in the earth's surface. It was now that the mother of the young boy lost control of her emotions and her mournful wailing could be heard topping the band's music.

Preachers waited at both gravesites with their black covered Bibles in hand. The whole time Frank Cotter had been in the city he had never set eyes on any preacher, had they been hidden away like frogs under rocks? The feller officiating at Ma's interment; read a good sermon, one of the best, Cotter had experienced. But it was a waste on poor Peter; he had no more interest in it than watching a couple of flies trying to copulate on the brim's edge of the Attorney's Stetson. In fact the crows that haunted Boot Hill had more fascination for him than the grave side service. Already the horrible, gory sight of his murdered mother's body on her bed was fading from his simple mind. Three times, Pearl had to hush Peter when he got restless and rowdy. But thankfully, Ma Kelly's mourners had prepared themselves before hand to over look the feller's indiscretions.

Once the expensive casket had been lowered into the depths of the waiting hole, folks came forward and took up handfuls of soil and sprinkled it down onto the coffin in the meantime Stroughton and Pearl led Peter away to the attorney's surrey.

Cotter departed the scene for the burial site of the young child's grave, where a small group of folks were gathered. But his escape was capped off with an invitation for him to join Ma's mourners at a wake later in the day at the theater.

When Cotter thought it appropriate, he made himself known to the boy Lawson's parents and told them about the dispatch he had been writing for the newspaper back East. He told them how he would like their permission to include their views in the article about living and surviving out west. But as he talked with them he soon realized that they were poorly educated and did not really grasp the purpose of his proposal — but nonetheless they gave their permission for him to make the death of their son public.

Whitney Dragoon was nowhere in sight for he was most likely still preparing for his journey, surmised the scribe.

12

FINALLY BACK AT Lomax's apartment after the cemetery, Cotter check the final draft of his first installment of The Pawnee Incident, and it was with much satisfaction that he lay aside his wet pen and opened the door to find Sheriff Boston, Warner, the Indian Agent and Deputy Lexmon on the doormat.

"Hi." Klem said a little embarrassed looking. "We're going to Ma's wake and were wondering if you would like ter join us?"

"I was invited but I reckon I'll pass on it. I've been writing out a newspaper article on the Pawnee attack. Whitney Dragoon has offered to carry it for me on the stage. I was up very late last night working and I fear I'm too bushed for any wakes …"

"I never got the chance ter speak to you up at Boot Hill …" said Boston. "I wanted you to hear this from me. I have ter tell you, I reckon I'm gonna have ter let your Army thugs out. I can't hold 'em fer ever and a day on such flimsy charges; it would be worth more than my job is worth."

Frank's shoulders slumped. "…Maybe in that case I ought to look up the gunsmith and buy myself a pistol, for protection?"

"Do you no good if you can't shoot, Cotter!" Ben Lexmon pointed out.

"That's, true…" Warner agreed.

"I'm sure as long as I'm in Junction City, I'm gonna need some kind of protection…" He unbuttoned his shirt cuff and rolled it a couple of turns up his fore-arm; all three men were surprised as to how well developed the pen-pusher's forearm appeared.

"What are you about, Cotter?" Klem asked.

"This town of yours — lives by a rather peculiar code, don't you think…?"

"I'm not sure I follow you?" Boston frowned. This tenderfoot was a puzzle to him, make no doubt about it.

"OK. It is just that people in this town seem to pay folks surprise visits. Last night while I was a sleep, I am sure I had a prowler right here in the apartment — someone got in on the quiet, and went through some things I left out on the dining table."

"Anything taken…?" Lexmon asked.

"Not that I've establish. Either of you know who else in the town might wanna come sneaking about Lester's, place?"

"Haven't a clue," Boston answered with a shake of his head.

Cotter then added. "What if it was Ma's killer sizing me up?!"

"I doubt that," said Boston.

"But can you give me a guarantee?" Frank began rolling up his other shirt cuff. "Somehow I don't have your confidence, Sheriff. I would've blamed Roscoe and his pal for being in here last night, if I didn't know they were warming your jail cots."

"Look Cotter, I swear ter God that I never knew that Doctor Lomax was the basis of a government investigation," Klem told Cotter, his emotions reflected in his eyes. "…The more I learn about **my old pal,** the more I realize he wuz a man of mystery — no one can claim they really knew what made 'im tick."

Cotter cocked his brow in the Sheriff's direction. "Sounds to me as though you're not too sure where your allegiance ought to lie. May I be so bold as to remind you — you told me you owed the fact that you've still got your leg to Lester — that should account for something? "

"I know where my allegiance needs ter throw down its bed-roll, Cotter — and I don't need you ter remind me!" Barked the Sheriff — his eyes ablaze. "But ter change, the subject apiece. This Indian attack business … How can you write about somethin' you weren't a party too?"

"Does it matter? Don't tell me you wanna censor it before it goes out?" It now did not surprise Frank what went on in this town, censorship could easily be one of them.

"I'm concerned about what you might write and how yore words might hurt the town and the people in it, yes!" Klem said, and it sounded like if need be, he would pull the rug on out from under the story so's it won't see the light of day.

"And in that case, so am I!" Agent Warner added.

"Count me in!" Lexmon said. "How can yuh write about sumthin' you weren't here ter witness, Cotter? I sure would like ter hear that!"

Turning full on to Ben Lexmon, Cotter said: "Don't take everything so much to heart, feller. The way I've written up the event, you'll show up as the town hero to the people back east! People might offer you big money to come east and allow them to see you in the flesh and shake you by the hand — imagine you could end up writing your own meal, ticket!"

"Ya mean I could be another **Kit Carson?**" The notion Frank had put in the young man's head was a seed that did not fall on stony ground.

Cotter faced the deputy with a broad grin, "And all the wealth and fame that goes with it!"

"Lexmon might fair awright out of it, but not the town or its people," Boston pointed out.

"But certainly not, the Pawnee, I wager!" The Indian agent was referring to the Pawnee captive in Boston's jailhouse.

Turning on Warner, Frank said: "Where was yuh so-called **Indian concern,** when four wild, drunk Indians cut down a poor defenseless, little kiddy?"

Suddenly realizing he was now out on a limb, Warner said to Boston, "— if you don't need me anymore ter day Klem, I'll head back out to the reservation an' give the wake a miss, I can't stomach much more of this guy."

"Hmm, might be a good thing. It goes without sayin', it seems as though we've got some folks round here with a few hot gray cells in their head."

Warner turned and heading across to the stairs, without a backwards glance as he went ahead down the staircase carefully watching his footing—his face flashed red.

Lexmon was thinking about a new lifestyle that might be ahead for him.

"I'm sorry, Sheriff, but my story is going east, with or without your blessing. How it affects this town I'm not worried one iota; I don't hope to be here much longer, anyway… Just as soon as I have your assurance that you'll hold an Inquest into Lester's accident, and bring to life the fifth man who witnessed my pal's death on paper; I'll be off, outa here!

"And anyway," continue Frank. "Did you get anything worthwhile out of your Pawnee prisoner? I take it Warner tried his best to get through to him?"

"They talked," admitted Boston.

"I don't doubt it, but can you trust Warner to translate what was said, truthfully?"

"Captain Roscoe speaks some Pawnee and kept his ears twigged while Warner questioned the Redskin so we've got enough of an understandin' what brought the Pawnees ter town," Deputy Lexmon answered for his boss.

Then the sheriff took over. "Accordin' ter Warner, the buck reckons it's because of what Lomax and his medicine did to the Pawnee people, someone in this white man's town had to pay with a life fer a life. They view things this way. As a white-witch doctor brought the evil spirits to dwell in their *wickiups* and stalk their nation, so a white-witch doctor has ter pay with his blood, an' as Hallway wuz the only doctor left in town, so to them Indians he's a medicine man and, that made him their target."

Then Ben Lexmon said what the Sheriff didn't say. "It seems they, the Pawnees have guns hidden away somewhere in the honeycombed meteorite; he wouldn't give away its location—an' *we* reckon they might be planning another hit on the town."

"What'll happen to their dead?" asked the scribe.

"They've all been taken care of," said the Sheriff. "Sean Dunne has the job of freighting 'em back to the reservation so as to keep the peace we're allowing the Pawnees ter bury 'em accordin' ter Pawnee ritual; It seems these red fellers have enough hatred towards the folks in this town—ter begin more Indian wars, because of Lester's medicine."

Cotter felt he knew what might be hatching here. "Don't start trying to blame Lester for yesterday's mess; I shan't let you or this town make him a scapegoat, now he's not around to defend himself, *he* at least can count on me!"

"Hey, don't squeeze me into the same can of peaches as those who are against 'im," Boston gestured with his hands. "— I've got an open mind about the Doc, and I'll keep it that way until I see sumthin' that makes me look at him differently!"

"Just don't allow that redskin in your calaboose, to use his heathen tongue to malign a good man's reputation," Cotter exclaimed.

"Cotter, I heard what Warner said and what the Indian had ter say. I've spent half the night going over and over all the details I could gather…" Klem said "— and the more I think about it, I'm sure the poor kid that wuz kilt and his Mom wounded, weren't the victims of any lead their weapons spat out, they were too drunk an' couldn't hit the side of a barn wiv a handful of wheat. This is awkward ter say but there wuz only one person on that street that day who wuz firin' goddamn haywire an' that wuz the good intentioned, half-blind an' half-crazy Mule skinner. We're pretty sure if need be, we c'n prove it. You agree wiv me there?" Klem turned to Ben Lexmon. "— don't you, Ben?"

Ben nodded. "…He wuz jist as dangerous as them Injuns, that's fer sure! His loose bullets had me and the Captain crappin' in our pants… Any second we thought we were gonna catch a dose o' lead!"

"Doc hallway says in retrospect he suspects the slug that hit the kid might've been the result of Burnacre's wild shootin'." Klem added.

This brought about a pregnant pause over events taking place up there on the apartment landing. It was Frank who pruned any further growth. "I see — so that's, gonna be the old man's thanks for being civic minded enough to try and stop the marauders!" Cotter shook his head in utter disgust.

Hell an' be god, thought Boston quickly. *— I cannot let Cotter think we're gonna crucify the old geezer in lieu of the Indians! Yuh can't hang the poor feller fer tryin' ter do his civic duty — not now he's almost as much a hero as young Lexmon… That only opens more doors fer this Cotter feller ter use ter muddy further the town's reputation with those folks back east. It's me duty to our town ter set him a course he can't do any tackin' frum.*

"No one's pointin' the finger — yet," Klem Boston told Cotter. "Even if it were Burnacre's slug what did the damage… in the end there mebbe no point in shining a lamp on that part of things — best ter deem it an accidental death by a stray bullet frum an unknown source? But in any event we can't truthfully lay the death of the young in' at the feet of the bucks who hit town — their drunken spree most likely only resulted in damage ter some woodwork an' window glass."

"What you're saying might be true, Boston…" Cotter agreed. "But it's for sure that none of this would have happened, if the reservation wasn't awash with whiskey. Warner knew that whoever suggested he allow booze through those gates — was committing an illegal act. Capitol Hill's going to have a lot of egg on its face if it gets out! Guns and whiskey in the hands of those illiterate beings is a combination for a catastrophe. It's like handing out powder kegs ter school children on the Fourth of July…" Cotter produced his pocket-watch from his open waist-coat pocket, and checked the time. "All I'm a-askin' is that you be more responsible in yore thinkin' about what you write fer newspapers back east, Mr. Cotter. You should feel – as though you owe the town an' her citizens somethin'?" Boston questioned. "Think before you put pen ter paper about the damage yore newspaper stories can an' will do!"

"Sorry old chum, but as far as my story goes, things stay as they are." Cotter said with unmistakable finality in his voice. "…I've got Whitney Dragoon acting as my personal mailman; he claims he'll get my papers through quicker than me relying on the regular mail service," the scribe slipped his pocket watch away.

Boston and Lexmon realized that they had failed in their attempt to induce Frank Cotter to change his mind about his article for the sake of the town's standing. There was no more they could do short of robbing the newspaperman of his story and locking him up out of harm's way, being lawmen; robbery and illegally holding a man in jail was out of the question. They departed.

Frank Cotter took what he estimated to be the shortest way down to the stage depot, going via the alleyway where his cast aside and drunken form had laid and become a piss-stone for smart-ass cowboys and stray dogs, but alas, he arrived too late to catch the coach's departure. It was one of those times that a Butterfield stagecoach departed before schedule. This was depressing for Cotter, for it rose the question that the scribe's silver plated pocket watch was out of whack, but a check on the banjo wall clock in the depot's waiting room, proved that his watch was correct with local time.

Corbin, who happened to be standing in the open doorway of his office, saw Doctor Lomax's friend enter in a rush, plus the look of disappointment that infected his anxious face upon realizing that the stagecoach had already departed.

"Trouble, Mr. Cotter?" Glenn Corbin came forward.

"The stage — **it's gone?**" cried the disappointed scribe as he approached Corbin.

Corbin nodded saliently, proud of his staff's combined efforts, to see that this fact had been achieved. "— About seven minutes ago," stated Corbin as he glanced in the direction of the wall clock, and tallied up the present time against that of when he knew the stage had pulled away from the front sidewalk. "Were you after a ticket?" Corbin asked then realized that the scribe didn't have any baggage with him and he felt foolish.

"No. I wanted to catch, Whitney Dragoon!"

"Dragoon…? I can't recall him being amongst those on board… Was he up for departure?"

Cotter nodded and brought the envelope he held in his hand up into view. Frank had made up the envelope with brown parcel paper and paste made from flour and water.

"Sorry about that, but they got away a fraction ahead of time today — doesn't always happen, but there you are!" By now Corbin had joined the scribe at the front counter.

"So you people don't bother to run the line according to the published timetable?"

"This is the west, sir. Our coaches depart when all ticket holders are here — be it a bit early, or a bit late." Corbin shrugged.

"That's some way to run a stage depot," Frank said, sarcastically.

This City feller seems quite put out, thought Corbin. *Being a potential passenger would not be wise to have him off side… Best I explain to him the facts of our way of life he's yet to learn…* "Schedules are fine for you city folk. But fer us Westerners it don't follow. In the cities you've got hansom cabs, trains and steam tramcars going left, right and center. Out here it can be sometimes weeks between coaches; so we tend to cater to local demand — it sometimes isn't possible fer folks ter get here before departure time, so we in turn delay setting out until they get here and take up their seat. And then when all the ticket holders are lucky enough ter get here before leave time, and we've got our full accompaniment they get waved out. Here, that's the way we work it."

Frank shook his head. "What this neck of the woods needs is more order and discipline!"

Clasping his hands behind his rump with legs apart, Corbin said: "Sorry some of **our ways** don't fit in with yore city ideas, Cotter. When you decide to live here permanently, you'll have to get in step with *us,* and not expect us to fall in step with *you!*"

Looking upon Corbin with a hatchet face expression the scribe hoped it would be little him. Its effect was that it made the manager realize he had better show the scribe his better side in the future.

"If you'll be so kind as to wait a few moments, I'll endeavor to establish whether or not Mr. Dragoon ***did*** catch the stage!" He swung round to the counter where an open ledger which lay atop of the bench. He drew the book to him and turned it around to scan. "…Uh, here it is! Yes, your friend did make the stage —" Glenn Corbin tapped Reg James' handwritten notes with his forefinger. "It shows a tick has been made next to his name; your friend must be a Willow-the-Whips', he got pass my attention."

"Dammit!" Frank exclaimed and slapped the envelope down on the counter alongside the ledger with a noisy 'WHACK'.

Nodding in the direction of Cotter's letter, Corbin remarked: "Something special in there?"

"You could say that. Not that it matter much, now." Fishing in his pants pocket for change Cotter enquired how much it would cost to post; he didn't bother to ask when the next outgoing mail was due to leave, he just paid up and left it at that, he was so upset that the thought of a Western Union office down the way, didn't come to mind.

13

"Looks like i'm going to have a lot of time on my hands for the next few weeks," Pearl Courtney said to Frank over supper in the restaurant of The Royal Hotel-cum-bordello residence.

"How come …?" Frank paused with a piece of range beef on his fork, midway between his plate and mouth. He was just about to swallow the bit of masticated meat and spuds already on his tongue near the back of his throat.

"Don Stroughton, Ma Kelly's attorney, has decided to close the play for a while — he wants to work on her books for the revenue department for tax purposes. You knew he did her accounting, didn't you?"

"No, I didn't. What about her other activities? The bar, restaurant…? And not forgetting the bordello?" Cotters eyebrows jacked themselves up in the direction of the overhead, seraglio.

"Ma had her fingers in more pies, than enough in this town…" Pearl said as she cut off a slice of boiled pumpkin and forked it in her mouth; she chewed delicately with her mouth closed while Cotter chewed his food with fewer manners than the actress.

"So one keeps, learning." Frank lowered his eyes back to his plate.

"When it finally comes down to carving up her estate, many of her ventures will be euchred and folks put out of work. An example will be her profitable cathouse; it'll fall flat like a house of cards. It's too much a "red-face" business for an entrepreneur to consider, unless he or she's willing to ignore the acceptable business ventures to make money," frowned Miss Courtney.

Frank could not find it in him to feel much sorrow for Ma's prostitutes' position. "I don't think Ma's gals will suffer too much. They might have to move to another climate, but there's always a role for them in the mining and cattle towns west of St Louis," stated Frank.

"I'm in much the same position," Pearl took a sip of red wine then returned her stem glass to the linen tabletop. "… I seem to lose out all the way down the line. When Lester came into my life it was like a ray of sunshine and I can honestly say, I was riding the crest of a wave… Then look at what's happened since I lost Lester? Without him nothing will be the same for me.

"The closure of the play means the end of another phase of my life. I honestly don't believe it will re-open here, there's no venue suitable for a full-scale play in the area. My theater career's on very shaky ground. Only hope is to move back east to find work — it's hard enough convincing people that I am a legitimate actress and not a part-time prostitute.

"You saw Mrs. Warner's looked at me out there — at the reservation? I've never turned a "trick" in my life — but how's a gal gonna get people to believe it?"

"Don't worry about what other people, think…" Frank said as he broke a slice of bread in half over his bread and butter, plate.

"Anyway — are you busy tomorrow, Frank?"

"Why, what's the reason?" Frank frowned and for the first time Pearl realized that his hairline rode forward as his scalp tensed, Pearl had never noticed it before, *interesting.*

"At the funeral I told Don that you were interested in the sinkhole out on the prairie. He thought the three of us ought to a picnic there one day soon. It's a whole darn new experience in itself getting down and up the wall of the hole. You've got to be fit, are you fit, Frank?"

"That depends… you know I've been a grog-artist for a while so I don't know how I'll cope, but if a woman can overcome the difficulties out there to be faced, I'll make the effort too; If not, then I'm well an' truly past it."

Pearl shook her head with just the hint of a smile. "Don's free tomorrow and it's my roster day off, baby sitting Pete. We gals have been taking turns looking after his needs until he moves east to his Mom's family. They have offered to take the boy —"

"*Boy?*" Frank said.

"You know what I mean… It's hard to think of Peter in the same context as another man his age," Pearl said, as she explained her attitude towards her late bosses' son. Hardly anyone who knew Pete respected him as a man.

"Does the Kelly family understand about the feller, and that he's a Mongoloid? Do they understand that he needs special care, looking after him can be awkward?" Cotter pointed out as he picked up his stem glass of root beer.

"Stroughton's the one who has been in touch with them — I expect he's explained to the family the situation regarding, Pete." She now forked a mix of spuds and meat into her mouth.

Regarding his root beer like a glass of imported wine, Frank said: **"...I suspect** that they are going to be more interested in the wealth that goes along with him, than the person. It's to be hoped they won't abandon him once they've got their hands on Ma's money — they could turn out to be very mercenary people, *we* don't know? "

Pearl swallowed ahead of time, so that she might answer Cotter, "That's always a risk, I suppose. But then Pete's whole life in a way has been one **big** risk — and will be ... until that day he meets Our Maker.

"But let's get back to tomorrow's business," said Pearl as she guided the conversation around to where she wanted to operate from. "Don suggested that we trot out to the sinkhole with his surrey — I told him you are not the best saddle bum in the west —"

"Oh, thanks a lot!" Frank's voice told Pearl that he did not appreciate her heralding the low level of his riding skills, to the community at large.

"Well, it is true… anyway; we have to rope-climb and carry storm lamps with us for the caves, we can't exhaust you just in getting you out to the meteor site — not with all the work that's in store."

Cotter frowned. "Work…?"

"That's right," said Pearl, "there's plenty of cave walking and some climbing to be done; if you're gonna probe the interior of the meteor."

Don Stroughton chained the left-hand front wheel to the body of the vehicle while Frank, like the Attorney, now attired in outdoor clothes, unloaded the coils of rope and a couple of kerosene lamps. By the time the tenderfoot had done those few things, the lawyer had collected two nosebags of chaff and oats for the horses, these he knew, would keep them pacified while the men were underground.

The edge of the sinkhole that had become the launching place for those energetic enough to want to explore the paradigm, the men dropped their gear. Here some thoughtful individual had driven an iron stake into the hard rock, from which one might tie a rope and dangle it over the rim of the craggy precipice and carefully lower themselves down to the slab floor at the bottom.

Tying a drop-rope securely to the stake Stoughton noticed that Cotter was looking down into the depth of the crater with notable impressiveness at what he saw, the magazine he had read on the sinkhole before had never drawn a vivid enough picture of it for him; on that score, his imagination had let him down.

"…Surprising, isn't it?" Don tugged the rope he had knotted tightly about Cotter's waist to check its security. Then set about wrapping a rope round his waist and tying it off.

"Never imagined it would be like this… but then knowing Lester I should've. I find it hard to accept that Pearl was up too this? There must be more to those womanly looks than meets the eyes?"

Don nodded. "Too bad she couldn't make it," commented the lawyer. "I've a sneaky feeling she wanted to see your reaction when you were confronted with what's ahead of you…"

"Yeah…? Well that Kelly feller sure picked the wrong time to come down with a damn toothache! I was surprised to learn that Hallway is the town dentist as well, is there nothing he can't do?" Cotter moved back from the rim of the abyss about two-feet, he was afraid a wind-gust might suddenly come up and topple him over the edge.

Stroughton moved to the iron stake and satisfied himself that all was in readiness, and then he turned to the scribe… "Now we will put the second rope round you for lowering purposes. Put it around your chest and up under your arms. This is a safety-line in case I accidently lose my grip or for some reason, I can't hold you." The lawyer *helped* the scribe with the ropes; as it surely appeared that the lawyer was in some sort of hurry to get rolling.

"What's the hurry, Don?" Frank asked.

"This is only a day trip. It'll take us a while to get down inside the crater — then there's the time we'll be spending underground seeing the sights!" Don checked over the things Frank had brought down from the surrey and saw that the man had forgotten the water canteens. "You didn't bring the water along," said the Attorney in an accusing tone.

"Didn't, I...?" This surprised Cotter for **he had** meant to bring the both canteens. As both men had roped themselves up it would mean an awful waste of time to untie one or the other so they might retrieve their canteens.

"Don't worry about it..." Don sighed. "We'll make do, there's fresh water down there in the guts of the meteorite to survive on," Pointed out Stroughton who was an old hand at visiting the underground. He guided Frank towards the sinkhole's rim, for the man was as ready, as he would ever be. They approach the edge of the ledge, adrenaline rush through his body and already, he began to get a bit light-headed and shake as though suffering a hangover. He knew it was not through lack of grog in his system but wondered whether or not Donald Stroughton would realize it. Frank got down on his hands and knees and crawled closer to the stake and grasp hold of it tightly... then he backed himself out over the edge on the crater's rim until his shanks were suspended in space, his knees spilling lose shale down the long drop to the old floor of the hole, the echoes of the gravel bouncing on the slab below were like the short bursts of fusillade one hears from a rapped-firing Gatling-gun.

Nervously Cotter lowered himself away until Stroughton had his full weight, his confidence in the Lawyer grew fast when he could see that the man was strong enough to take his bodyweight and control its downwards motion as he departure from the safety of the ledge. He was only being held by the rope curled round the iron stake, which was firm and solidly anchored to the rock-ledge — he began to feel with the toes of his boots for the cliff face, but had no success at first — he found himself swing like a pendulum in the niche of a Grandfather's clock. But somehow he got control of his motion and altered the swing of his body from side to side to that of back and forth, eventually his boots found a foothold in the scabrous wall about four-feet down. The Attorney loomed partly out over the edge of the ledge and nodded to Frank that he was safe and to continue on downwards.

Well. Here goes nothing... thought Cotter as he lowered his eyes down to take in the toes of his boots and the drop beyond. He crouched and this took the top half of his body down to almost the same level as his ankles, and taking a hand-hold of the rough, broken cliff-face he felt Stroughton give him some slack on the ropes and he took another step down two-feet, his hands now taking the weight of his body until the toes of his boots found another toehold and then he repeated his previous action. Suddenly and without warning he lost his footing on the rock-face, it was now four-feet away from him! He found himself swing free, the cliff was out of reach of his hands and feet! It was then left to Donald to lower him away — all the way down to the lava base. He broke out in a sweat and wondered how he had let himself get talking into such a predicament. But before long his feet touched terra firma and he breathed a soft sigh of relief as the abnormal pressure of the pressure of the ropes eased.

With trembling hands he freed himself and before he could get to tell the attorney that he was free, the lawyer began his own descent, sending forth a shower of gravel too, as Frank had done, when he commenced to let go of the overhead ledge. Frank dodged the falling pebbles and had sense enough not to look up as the Attorney lowering himself into the sink hole, he realized that now wasn't the time to get one's eyes full of grit. But all the same the lawyer warned the city slicker about looking up. When Stroughton was safely down Frank came across and helped the man extract himself from his ropes where they dangled down into the hole from the iron stake above. Donald's ascent into the sinkhole was made more awkward than Frank's, because it had been left to him to bring along the lamps. As the pair of them took shelter from the sun in the shade of the far wall with the equipment, Frank asked: "Are *you* sure Miss Courtney could scramble up an' down that cliff-face, Don?"

"Like a mountain goat," he grinned. "You don't really know our Miss Courtney yet, my old son, no sir."

Looking about the crater from where they stood, Frank couldn't envisage religious Indians actually climbing down the walls of the sinkhole too readily; they must have had themselves another way of accessing the site to carry out their ceremonies, surely? He asked Stroughton.

"The Pawnee brave in Boston's jail is reputed to have told Warner that they had their weapons and ammunition hidden somewhere down here. But I can't see the likes of them hauling guns and things up and down the sides of these walls, can you? The Pawnees never climbed a darn step. It's well known that they have a secret entrance to this place and the caves within." He went on to shake out a couple of small cigars and returned the packet to his denim jacket's pocket; Frank needed no encouragement and supplied a match fired up for their cheroots. But when he took a drawer on his cigar, discovered that it had been flavored with rum by its maker, and did not know whether for a man on the wagon smoking, these cheroots was a good thing. But all the same, Cotter had not turned himself into a complete prude, nor did he ever wish too — so he carried on as they moved together in the direction of a six-foot high fissure in the crater's wall. "…Pearl tells me you've become a bit of a portent on this place, Frank?"

"I did some reading up on it back east," he avowed. They went under the arch of the fissure, with the Attorney taking the lead. "How many times you been down here, Don?" he said to the man's back.

"Five."

"And how many times did you go down with, Lester?"

"Three."

"Then I guess that also makes you some sort of authority on the place, too?"

"You might say that. It's a fantastic spot, but alas, very dangerous for the unwary. When it rains out on the Plains, all the water run-offs finds a way through what flaws there are in the ground, then it comes down the underground chutes and narrow water worn tunnels — for a short time they become gushin' rivers, capable of filling up every nook an' cranny… The power of the water in these floods can be very awesome and have been known to sweep thrill seekers to their deaths — by Gawd; you'd drown in a flash and ya remains could end up anywhere!

"It' a case that when yuh thinking of c'ming down here, you've gotta be damn sure the time is right… So welcome to one of the great wonders of our world!"

They continued to move beyond the entrance where the reflected daylight faded to insignificance and their lamps was all that stopped the pitch black darkness, engulfing them; now and then, there were times when the passage narrowed so much that one would brush both shoulders against either side of the passage — but they quite smooth, as if a cabinet maker had sanded them down with glass-paper.

"It's ungainly I know," Stroughton said in agreement with Cotter's unspoken thought. "The corridor widens a few steps farther on; and you'll find the going much more negotiable…"

"What is that odor we can smell, Don?"

"Coyote piss. Strong isn't it? We'll soon leave that behind, though."

"How the hell would a goddamn coyote get down here?" Frank cracked his shin but didn't let on to Stroughton; he also thought he might have broken the skin.

"Mebbe they found the same entrance the Pawnee use… OK, now here it opens out and we go down a steep grade, about ten or twelve feet. Careful you don't slip — I don't want you hurting yourself and have ter carry you out of here! This part of the cave will bottom out for a quarter of a mile," Don waited until Frank was breathing down his neck before starting downwards. Frank in turn, allowed Stroughton to get a start before treading cautiously after him, as he did not want to slip over and skittle the man and risk injuring his guide.

The lantern movement of the lawyer indicated that he had reached the lower level; Frank set off after him, dragging his free hand along the side wall of the cave for stability as he had no idea of the condition of the surface beneath the soles of his boots. By the time he had reached the Attorney his cheroot had gone out, but Don had smoked his down to a butt and while waiting for Frank, had dispensed it under heel and fired up another one, with the flame of the match he had used, he restarted the butt between Cotter's lips, together they stood and smoked as the lawyer parted on further information about the interior of the meteorite.

"…Ahead is a marvelous cavern. I liken it to a Petrified Forest, built entirely of stalagmites and stalactites! Once in there, let your imagination run wild, you can imagine all kinds of things… Dragons and careening stagecoaches fer example come to mind, they seem to loom out of the dark at you an' **I defy** anyone setting foot in there to come out and say they weren't fearful of being left behind by their mentor…" Stroughton broke away from Frank and headed up a steep damp grade and crossed the threshold of a cavern's entrance where he encountered the calcified wax-like rain forest. By the light of his own lamp; Frank looked down upon a smooth clean floor that looked as if it had only moments ago, had been washed down with bucketed water and then gone over with a squeegee. There was no sign of debris, not so much as a loose stone.

The Attorney's lamp was Frank's beacon to the crest of the incline and as he neared the peak of the rise he had just about ran out of steam and seeing Cotter's predicament, Donald Stroughton reached out and grabbed the city man by his shirt front and hauled him up the final half-yard and brought him to a halt, alongside him. The sight his eyes were subjected too within the range of the lamps was truly breath taking … Frank stood in awe at the sight now spread out before him. In the sepia glow of their lamps he saw completely joined stalactites and stalagmites reaching from the cavern's ceiling to the floor, or depending on the journey of one's eyes. There were some that only had half-an-inch to grow, then they would fuse together as one, some looked ivory in color and others looked like giant candles of wax that at times, had melted and cooled into flutes and Grecian columns, fit for a temple — dedicated to the Greek Gods of Mount Olympus: others had become imitations of fine Irish lace. The vastness of the chamber and its collective beauty was hypnotic and without equal. Within these walls and ceiling of the cave, one would have been able to house at least two hundred covered wagons parked head to tail.

Frank left Stroughton's side to wander with his lamp amongst the water and lime salt tree-like trunks and realized that if he made no move at all to push on, they would easily end up caught here by this special, all day! Stroughton could not allow that — for there was much more they had to feast their eyes on and explore before they ran out of time.

The lawyer cleared his throat by way of capturing Frank's attention.

"Come on," Frank said, "there's more **we must see…**" Cotter returned to his guide.

"— this is, unbelievable," He told Stroughton. Cotter spoke with a reverence generally reserved for a Godly Citadel. "— **All** I've read on this place did it not an ounce of justice!"

"True," Stroughton said with equal reverence as he too became caught up in the same spell as that of Cotter's. "It is truly a wax-like wonderland… Did you notice the Greek pillars? The one broken halfway up must be the result of an earth tremor." Both men focused on the columns surrounding them.

"They were broken off a long time ago," Cotter remarked, stating the obvious. "These formations grow very, very, slowly — shit, this place *is* **old!**" Donald nodded, but Frank did not see it, he was fascinated by the all over effect of the grotto.

"All right, now there are two more things I must show you before we head for home. That's **The Cathedral** as the locals call it and, ***Neptune's Pond.*** Thirsty…?" Stroughton asked, because he was getting a little that way himself.

Cotter nodded. "Yes."

"Hold out for five more minutes and we will be at the pond and you'll be able to curb your thirst with the sweetest water that's ever trickled down your throat…" The Lawyer spoke more like a water diviner trying to promote a deal for his services.

Moving along side by side, Frank wanted to know who named the underground features, but the Attorney couldn't answer that for him. Like Cotter, he had only read about the place until he and Lester got the opportunity to join a party of Junction City's citizens keen to set eyes on it for themselves, its many virtues being gleaned from the local Indians. As far as the Pawnees were concerned the fact that it was a sacred place of theirs meant that it was in effect taboo to the eyes of the white man. But knowledge of the taboos only stirred the curiosity of the white settlers. A couple of would-be heroes were washed away in underground floods when water from the prairie emptied down into the buried meteor and a Pawnee medicine-man told the town's folks through an interrupter, that the spirits were angry with the "white-eyes" for defiling sacred grounds, and this was their retribution and that they could expect more of the like.

The tunnel they were now moving through ran direction wise like a crescent.

"You say the Indians consider this sacred — however — I've not see any evidence to date to support that." Cotter opined.

"Oh, there is —" Stroughton said over his shoulder. "You will eventually see it…" Their tunnel switched sharply back on itself returning to its original course and the newspaperman was in no doubt that he had to write an account of today's experience. Abruptly his Stetson was swept from his head as he struck the crown of his skull on the tunnel's low-slung roof — he was forced to draw his head in like a turtle struggling to withdraw inside its shell for protection. By the time he took this evasive action the ceiling went suddenly from, a few inches of clearance space to three or more feet above his head and his gesture, of trying to avoid any further collisions with the ceiling was a fizzer.

"Have you any idea where we are?" Frank asked for he knew they were a long way from the entrance at the sinkhole, he could feel a lump building up under his hair from the crack he received on the head.

"Gettin' claustrophobic?" Stroughton questioned.

This was known to be part of the deal with some people who came down here.

"A little, I think… Don't know how your arm is Don, but mine is getting tired of lugging this damn lamp about!"

"Well it's not far now to the *Piazza* that's self-explanatory," said the lawyer. They continued on Indian file, for what seemed to Frank to be almost an hour's walk. It began to worry him that they had come so far down into the earth, and on top of this he had lost all sense of direction. It was now plain that they were making their way along a disused water chute, but wasn't sure when their course had changed and when they had linked up with it — unexpectedly they had come to the end of the run and it was like being inside the neck of a giant Champagne bottle. Squeezing their way out through its aperture, the pair dropped out one after the other down three feet onto the sloping floor of a wide open square, vast enough for a rancher to herd cattle in. It was an echo chamber and all sound, soft or loud, was intensified and thrown back at the source of its creation.

"We'll leave my lamp here as a marker and use yours to light us the rest of the way to the *Cathedral.*"

"Where's all this drinking water you promised?" Frank's thirst was such now that he was certain that he could polish off a pint of *aqua* without pausing for breath. "I'm as dry as a prairie chip!"

Donald Stroughton laughed out loud. "… Where did that come from? Am I witnessing a city slicker turnin', native?! "

"What are you on about, Counselor?"

"D'you know what a "Prairie chip", is?" He asked incredulously.

"Sure — it's the phrase I picked up from Whitney Dragoon. It's a sun dry lump of cow dung, I hear that cowboys chuck them on campfires, they help keep away mosquitoes, right?"

Shaking his head, Stroughton said: "Wonders will never cease. C'mon, this way to yuh water..." The two men set off with Cotter's lamp, traveling the slope of the Piazza's floor along the wall of the cavern, they went pass two water chutes about eight feet apart in the same wall, one was just waist high and the other at least a good seven feet above their heads.

Water was still trickling from their apertures which were no bigger in circumference than your normal dinner plate, the moss growing on the wall at this point shined and glittered like glass the whole way down to the floor and slowly trickled off in the direction the pair were taking.

"...Can you conceive," Don pointed out, "When these chutes are spewing water out under pressure, that they would be like darn water-cannons I've seen being used in gold mine quarries! " The counselor's description echoed about the square as his voice jogged Cotter's own mind into painting a clear mental picture, of the water-chutes just as a Stroughton had hinted to him, *No way would I like to find myself trapped down here under any circumstances!* Frank thought.

Eventually the counselor and the ex-newspaper scribe arrived at the water's edge of a wide, dark pond. Seeing the water under lamplight, Frank had not the slightest hope of fathoming out its depth. It might be just ankle deep or ten or more feet deep.

"Here's yore drinking water, Frank!" The resounding echo bounced of the surround iron space rock like a ricocheting bullet. "Here's yore drinking water, Frank! — Yore drinking water, Frank! — 'ore drinking water, Frank!" Frank's thirst dictated the man's next action. He removed his gloves and stuffed them through his pant's belt and eased himself down on one knee. He cupped his right-hand and dipped it in just below the surface...

The water was freezing cold to the touch! Cotter bent forward at the waist so that the upper portion of his body overhung the lapping edge of the pool, he ladled the icy water up and sucked it from the cup of his numbing palm — while the excess water escape back to the pond through his numb fingers that appeared to have adhered all into one, like a marine animal's swimming fin. Three times he scooped water from the pool which had the taste of pristine water laced with health giving minerals — but three dips of the frigid water was all he could handle, more would have been just self-torture to his hand.

The counselor swept his hat off onto the slab floor which they had tracked down to the pond's edge and he crouched a moment while he lowered the base of his hurricane lamp to the granite floor and then got down and laid flat-out on his stomach — his shoulders protruding forward out over the water... Then he lowered his open mouth to the water's surface and began siphoning up his fill like a camel taking water, the water temperature governed his intake and soon both men had had their fill.

Frank arose from his knee and shook the water from his fingers... Then he recovered his gloves and worked his hands into them, up to his wrists. "Would this be Neptune's pool? — This be Neptune's pool? — be Neptune's pool..."

Don, now upright dried his lips on the forearm of his sleeve and via a muffled voice, said: "Yuh on the money, Frank —" Then waving out across the pond, his voice level normal and unadulterated by echoes added: "Over there's the entrance to the Cathedral — three passages run parallel into the cavern...their wall thicknesses varying from five to eight feet.

"Each tunnel seems ter have chose its own course through the center of the honeycombed meteorite, I guess you would say where the strength of the water was able to find a weak point in its formation — the tunnels seem to have become interconnected with worn channels, some of which have small amounts of water trapped in 'em, while others have drained, dry..." The resounding echoes continued on in their desolate, irritating fashion... By the time Don had produced his flat-pack of cheroots; which in the meanwhile had been crashed slightly more flat by his body's weight while drinking. But this did not faze Cotter for he, thankfully took the cigar as he quite liked their liquor flavoring. Both men lighted their smokes with a degree of anticipated pleasure.

"...This pond — would it be permanent?" Cotter asked as he exhaled cigar smoke from his lungs.

The lawyer inhaled on his cheroot before answering. "So it seems. Every time I've been down, it's been here and at the same water- depth. There's a natural weir holding it back, but that's only until the next flooding; d'you knows this water is ten times healthier for us, than yuh general drinking water? "

"I suspect it might be..." opined Cotter.

"The spillway maintains the depth of the pool which is about shin deep —" Taking up the lamp Don walked out a yard into the water and stood there for Cotter to see that he had spoken the truth about the pool's depth. "C'mon in, the water's cold – almost like ice, but it won't freeze you!" Stroughton said as he turned and headed off across the pond and because he had the storm-lamp, Frank had to follow in his wake.

The freezing water had a numbing effect, and this proved to Cotter that the thickness of his boots provided no protection. "—we shan't spend too much time here," Donald told Frank. "I wanna get back ter Junction City before dark…" There was no hiding the tone of boredom that he was feeling, it had set in while they were making their way to the Piazza via the dysfunctional water chute, but until now he had managed to keep signs of it out of the timber of his voice – but not anymore.

They moved up out of the water and passed into one of the three tunnels that led into the vestibule of the so-called Cathedral, it was almost as overwhelming as the grotto in which the Petrified Forest grew wild amid the Greek temples and imaginative ruins.

Finally satisfied that the underground tour had won over Lester Lomax's friend, the city trained lawyer announced that it was time to turn tail and head for home, they departed the rock cathedral which the rushing waters had carved out of the softer stone than normal meteor iron-rock — and retraced their steps out to the pond and through it to the slab floor of the Piazza. They stamped the water off their boots on the rock floor, and upon locating their beacon ahead in the gloom, they made for the dysfunctional water chute — surrounded by their reverberations as they homed in on the storm lamp.

Frank picked up his lamp and crossed to the cavern's wall where the attorney hoisted him up to the mouth of the chute, accomplished by the lawyer forming a footing stirrup with his clasped hands. Cotter realized from prior acquaintance with the interior of the chute's space that it was unable to take the two men side by side, someone had to take the lead and this time it happened to be Cotter; Stroughton explained that when they reached a suitable part of the underground labyrinth they would swap positions with the more experienced of the pair leading them back to the crater. However until it was practical for them to make the switch, the scribe had to walk crouched like a stooped old man through the corridor of the time worn meteorite, it was awkwardly difficult for Frank, and he could hardly wait for the switch over to take place. But all good and bad things have an end, and so without regret, Cotter — finally surrendered the lead to Stroughton who readily led the way back to the fissure in the sinkhole's cliff-face.

By now the men were ready for another thirst-quencher and were looking forward to the water supply they had up in the surrey. Moving out into a hot sun, for the earlier shade had changed position owing to the movement of the sun, during the time they had moved from the crater — the sounds of their footwear on the harsh slab had a ring to that of shod horses. A lizard scurried away into a flourishing sage bush; the shrub had taken root in the lava floor's crack, others had formed through years of expansion and contraction of the lava brought about by many appearances of a blistering overhead sun.

"You look parched," Don said to the scribe as he removed his hat and held it at arm's length overhead, its projected circle of shade engulfing his face and with narrow eyes to control the glare; he scanned the cliff-face to check for the ropes hanging from the iron stake down the jagged wall.

"I am," avowed Cotter as he pushed his Stetson's sweatband up the forehead of his sweating brow backhandedly; and turned his hooded eyes in search of the ropes... both men focused on the iron stake above them and together they realized that it was naked as far as the existence of their ropes were concerned – their disappearance a baffling mystery!

"What's up?!" croaked the hoarse Attorney

"Where in God's name *are* the ropes?!" said Cotter as though it was the fault of Donald Stroughton.

"Someone's gotta be playing a prank on us — fer sure!" said Don as he ran his eyes along the ledge to where it petered out. There were no signs of any ropes!

"How come?" asked Frank as he came to the conclusion that they were stranded down here without ropes.

Don replaced his hat and started chewing his cud like a cow, he turned to look up at the wall behind them for some way up by hand and toeholds — but he ascertain none, as too did Cotter, for he realized what the actions of the lawyer were about.

Stroughton finally shook his head in despair as he realized their situation.

"Someone must be trying to playing tricks on us!" said the counselor. "No one ought ter be messing with our gear, that's for sure."

"Damn stupid sense of humor if you ask me. You don't think it might be the work of the Pawnees, Don?"

"Why do yuh say that?"

"Well, this place is important to them, spiritually. They might have had enough of white folks messing with it. After their raid on the town a few days ago, they might be making sure we're getting their smoke signal; A couple of bucks might've been here looking about and seeing the surrey and the ropes leading down into the sinkhole, they might have become damn irate; They could have taken our ropes to teach us to respect their spirit world." Cotter suggested.

"I hope you're wrong Cotter — *very* wrong!" With that he whirled round to face the cliff which most people scaled by rope and headed in its direction. Cotter trailed after him like a puppy.

"What are you proposing *we* do?" Cotter asked as he rushed along behind the Attorney, his Stetson did a back flip from his head; it bounced off his right shoulder blade to the iron-hard floor, and he left it for the time being.

"Looking ter see if'n they were thoughtful enough to drop us off a supply of water!" Stroughton said, but at the same time he realized how illogical this line of thinking, was; someone mischievous enough to snatch away their life-lines would not be that considerate.

"Forget it," snapped Cotter. "Even this tenderfoot knows, that Indians don't think along those lines! That's if it **was** a tribal native — they would be hoping no one will come looking for us until we have been boiled alive by that there sun's heat, dehydrated beyond help!"

Both men were now at the base of the cliff where the lawyer commenced his search, not a difficult task as most of the area was quite open, anything lying about would be easily noticed. "We're in serious trouble my friend if we can't get out of this here crater!" the counselor owned up. He slowly craned his head back as he made a careful study of the rock-face. It was plain no one would be climbing up out of this place very soon.

Noticing the way the lawyer was surveying the cliff, began to giving Cotter frightful ideas... "You aren't planning to have us try to climb out of here, surely, Don?" Still looking for some way they could better their position Stroughton said: "We just may have ter try and help ourselves. We will surely die waiting for someone to come looking for us."

"Have you considered the fact that the culprit behind this, could be up there watching our **every move?**" Frank had not forgotten his growing need for water. "There's only one way ter find out..." Donald Stroughton tilted his head back and putting his hands on either side of his face, divided by his nose, yelled: "Hey. Hey — c'mon — you've had ya fun. You've got us as jumpy as jackrabbits... Send the ropes down and we'll treat the whole damn episode as a joke!"

The lawyer got no response, even though they waited a respectable time to see if something might follow on from his plea with the unknown.

Silence ... Nothing.

Don wanted to offer a second inducement, but Frank vetoed his effort with a restraining touch to his hand. "I wouldn't waste your time... All this hollering is only making us look idiots and further drying our throats. If there was someone up there, the culprits would have long gone, thus handing us our fate..." Stroughton was certain of one thing that if they did not make their own luck they would both perish down here before being discovered. Even by the time Miss Courtney realized they'd not return to town and organized someone to come in search for them there's a good chance they'd be dead or near dead of thirst.

The scribe was no psychic, but he could easily see what he and the lawyer had to face together, injury or worse — death. "Don't try it Don... You only need to run out of steam, slip, or have a lump of rock break off in your hand and depending on how high you've scaled, you could do yourself a serious injury!"

Don took heed of Frank's words and dropped all notions of trying to make like a spider going up the cliff.

"Maybe we should move back inside the fissure and try to find that hidden passage the Pawnee have gotta be using – but I don't like the idea of doing a cold search with you tagging along. Might be best if I leave you here in the shade for I'm damned sure I'll make better time without you as a drag anchor."

Frank saw the sense of the lawyer's assumption and really wanted nothing more than to get out of here to safety – who knows there might even be a damn cougar hidden away down there and if that were the case he would rather hold ground here until Don fetched some sort of help — Just get ter hell out of here, will you? I wanna sleep in a nice soft bed tonight!" he grinned.

Don nodded and went off on his way deeper into the fissure; Cotter rose to his feet and watched as Stroughton moved away without a backward glance. Cotter leaned up against the rock wall with his ankles crossed and listened to the lawyer's progress as he nosily went off deeper into the network of underground tunnels as he tracked the barely discernible path of the coyote spoors.

Frank wished him God's speed and heavily hoped that the man would manage to fluke the whereabouts of the Pawnee's secret entrance to what one might term as the gateway to *Orpheus's Under-world*. It was then that Frank noticed an old dried out coyote's stool and prayed that this was a good omen in itself.

The lawyer discovered four tunnels that were new to him, the first three were a nuisance for between them, and all led to dead-ends or had partly caved in. These blanks consumed a lot of time that was vital to both Stroughton and Cotter making it to safety. He had a mishap which was totally unexpected, he fell down a steep bank, but a piece of quick reaction on his part saved the loss of both lanterns, one had its glass chimney broken in the fall and somehow lost a good amount of oil. Had the spare lamp not survived the man's head-over-heel's experience the attorney would have been in a lot more trouble than suffering just a few abrasions. He fired up the second lamp, and checked himself over in its light, and then he inspected his surrounds where he had finally lodged. He decided that the bank he had somersaulted down was an obstacle he ought not to pursue and instead, holding the lamp a high, he elected to proceed in the direction he now found himself facing. Ten slow minutes later his heart sank when he came to what seemed to be another dead-end.

The throw of the lamp's light was not terrific and weighed with disappointment he thought he had nothing to lose by crisscrossing the impenetrable barrier before him, in the faint hope that he might hit upon a fissure that would allow him to escape this natural imprisonment… He came upon a narrow rift and though it was a tight squeeze to make his way in, it turned out to be the exact escape route needed and before one could utter: "Jack Frost", Don found himself in yet another chamber which was the size of an Army warehouse. This looked promising — especially when he discovered Indian relics of pagan worship to their spirits and the Sun God. It was here he found a Prairie Schooner still loaded with repeater Winchester rifles and Sharps; there was also plenty of ammunition for all the weapons. The rifle boxes and the cartons of shells were marked with Government logos. This had to be where the bucks from the reservation had laid hands on their guns. Don toyed with the idea of grabbing a gun or two, but realized that if any of the tribe came back to the cache of weapons, someone might realized they've been tampered with, and come hunting for the intruder — getting out of this hell-hole was his main goal. Especially, now he was certain that he would have no trouble finding the exit from this chamber to the surface — three minutes later he strolled with ease from the cavern into an open box canyon, and though night had already fallen, he was able to get his bearings from the stars.

He believed himself to be some five miles north-west of the sinkhole as the crow flies and set off on foot, not knowing what the ground was like he had to cover. For the first time in a long while, Don began to worry about the fact that he was unarmed and therefore at a distinct disadvantage if he happened to run into any danger. He had left his shoulder-holster and pistol wrapped up in his jumper under the seat of the surrey — he hoped that whoever had removed the ropes had not been too particular about searching his vehicle or hurting the livestock.

Movement was all that kept the lawyer warm as he stumbled along some arroyos, one time he stepped into a gopher hole and there were times he even tripped over the occasional stone. Traveling time was poor, and he worried about how Cotter was making out…

With the onset of night Frank Cotter knew that he had to move as much as possible to ward off the cold and above all, occupy his mind. He did this by stepping out the distance of the sinkhole's floor. He learnt that the slab of bedrock had cracked in to three sections after cooling and assumed that this might actually be the outer layer of the partially buried meteorite.

Stroughton reached the surrey and his snoozing horses, just half an hour before the break of dawn. However, there was no rest for his tired feet, he had vital chores to perform even before alerting the scribe that he had made it safely out. He removed the feedbags from the grays' snouts and stowed them in on the floor of the surrey between the front and backbench seats. Then he removed his hat and filled the inside of its crown with water from both canteens and gave it to the thirsty horses. It wasn't much but it would at least give them some relief. When he reached the ledge overlooking the crater, the growing light made what had to be done a lot easier. The person responsible for hauling the ropes up out of the hole had been lazy for he or she had left the cow-ropes on the ground, just a couple of feet from the edge of the cliff, on the ledge. While preparing to get them ready to throw over the lip of the crater he was able discern the noise of Cotter's movements down there on the rock-slab, especially the heels of his footwear as he kept moving about to keep warm.

Frank was suddenly aware that there was someone up there on the rim, near the ledge. For a few brief moments he was anxious that it might be those responsible for their threatening position, "…Is that you, Don?" he called up with a nervous caution in his voice as he fumbled his way across to the foot of the cliff.

"Yep," Stroughton called down to the man in the pit.

"How long you been back?" Cotter stopped when he came to within a foot of the cliff's base and looked skyward, but could not make anyone out. A light fall of gravel rained down from up in the direction of the ledge and Frank closed his eyes for protection and blindly back off to a safe distance.

"About twenty minutes or so," the lawyer reported as he lowered the ropes down into the hole. "I have been tending to the horses so that once I have you up, we'll hit the trail! Are you OK down there?"

"Sure. Just a bit stiff from the cold," Frank confessed.

"I've sent the ropes over the side, tie 'em on you the way I did yesterday, can you remember?"

Cotter nodded, forgetting the man above couldn't see him. Frank caught hold of the ropes as they swung from side to side, after managing to time the swing he caught the ropes and tied himself up like an Alpine rock-climber. Satisfied that he had done the task to the best of his ability, Frank gave the rope a tug then stepped up to the rock face and fumbled to find a handhold to lever himself up when the counselor took in the slack and began the heavy haul — *Now the struggle to get up the rock face will be on in earnest…*thought Frank as he managed to get his first hold.

From the lawyer's end of things it proved to be a job and a half to haul the awkward tenderfoot up the side of the sinkhole until the crown of his hat appeared at the edge of the ledge near Stroughton's feet. Don dropped the roped from his gloved hands the moment the newspaperman grabbed a hold of the iron stake and dropped to his knees and leant out over the man and seized him by the upper portion of his body around the back of his shoulders and dragged the man over the lip of the ledge to a less dangerous position, there the pair lay sprawled on the ground panting for breadth from the strain they had inflicted on their lungs.

Stroughton broke their spell when he made the effort of being the first to their feet; once joined by the scribe, together they gathered up the equipment and started up the worn path to the surrey. "…Any sign as to whom was trying to play games with us, Don?" asked Cotter. But he did not really hold out much hope of that.

"Not a clue," answered the lawyer as he put the gear he was carrying aboard the surrey. Before doing likewise Frank picked up one of the canteens and was somewhat put out when he found it empty. He went for the other one and found it in the same condition.

"…Looks like they stole our water." Cotter suggested, disappointed by his discovery.

Stroughton went on to explain that he had given it to the horses before rescuing him from the hole. "…Their need's greater than ours — they're the ones who still have *work* to do; out here, a man's horse comes first because life depends on them." Now Frank understood the situation. And he also believed he understood the significance of the lawyer collecting his gun from under the seat of the surrey and strapping it on before looking to his safety. "One never knows, Frank, — **our friend or friends** may not have had their fill of games so I'll keep this handy," he said, slapping leather.

"Good idea," agreed Cotter. "I take it our first port of call when we hit town will be the diner?"

Don unchained the surrey's wheel and they climbed aboard, then Stroughton took up the reins as he vowed that not only would it be their first stop, for he could already smell the buttered toast sourdough and the aroma of java in which he intended to wallow in until his gut was ready to burst.

14

J ACK WARNER RETURNED from the reservation with official forms for Sheriff Boston to sign. When any Indian had to be dealt with by a white law officer the government bureaucracy had to have a hand in it. The agent looped his mount's reins round the sun-bleached hitch-rail out the front of Boston's jailhouse and entered by the street door. Klem and another deputy, Luke Mullen, were brewing coffee for themselves and their prisoners at the pot-belly stove … Upon seeing whom it was coming through the front door from the street, Mullen's left the sheriff at the stove and came forward to open the wicket for the feller who had to have been an early riser to be getting in to conduct business this early.

"Good mornin' Sheriff — Deputy Mullen?" said Warner by way of greeting.

"— Jake," Klem nodded. "I'd say you'd be on fer a mug of java, right?"

"You wouldn't be wrong, Klem… I've been warming saddle-leather since five this day," Warner crossed to the desk and dropped the forms there for signing, and then he came over to collect some warmth from the hot stove-iron. "— seein' as Lexmon wuz the arresting officer, he'll need ter fill in those forms. Where is he?"

"Down at the diner fetchin' our morning vittals have you eaten?" Klem handed the Indian Agent a clay mug of black java. Warner nodded his thanks as he took it.

"What sort of night did my brave have?" Jake allowed the heat from the pottery to seep through the leather of his riding gloves to his numb hands.

"I believe he was a nuisance to me other prisoners … At certain times throughout the night he began chanting like a goddamn Witch Doctor! I had ter come down here and bury me boot in his ass!"

"Sorry 'bout that Sheriff. Mebbe you should let me keep him out in the reservation's cell 'til Judge Wolfsohn blows in ter town?"

"No can do, Jake. He's facing' serious charges an' there is no two ways about it; that Injun's gonna swing — white man's justice is gonna prevail here. Don't worry it'll be all legally done, accordin' ter Judge Wolfsohn's instructions. In fact, I reckon the judge might even want ter supervise his hangin'!"

"I know Judge Wolfsohn of old — he will see he gits a square deal," The agent produced his gear from his person to build himself a cigarette. Boston watched the man and as his desire grew for a smoke he knew by etiquette that Warner would have to offer him and Mullen's one, too. Warner added: "It's the mood of the folks in the town and the surrounding district I worry about. There are still too many people round here who remember what it wuz like before the tribes hereabouts turned 'emselves in at the Chickadee Reservation."

"Tell me sumthin' I don't know? Luke here has already been hearing grumblin's that's a **real worry** ter me. Don't be surprised if the town starts to holler fer a lynching! I ain't ever been confronted with anything like that an' don't wann be…" Boston said as the agent passed him the cigarette makings as expected — he set about building himself a smoke from the agent's ready-rubbed tobacco.

"If we 'ave a lynch mob come our way — I'd bet me last dollar that the Williams brothers will be there in the thick of it — they hate the guts of any goddamn redskin, and that's a known fact!" said Deputy Mullen.

"If that is the growin' feeling, Klem… Mebbe you should warn the people out at the Army Fort about it?"

Boston broke off building his smoke — "I may have a stiff leg, Jake Warner, but don't underrate me none; I can still make a few lousy hotheads in my town toe the line… I'll git on top of it an' stay there 'til yore Indian friend finds himself on a mud stage ter Yuma prison fer his date wiv the rope — or I'll turn in my star!"

"Let's hope it don't come ter that, boss," Mullen's said.

"Are you sure you can handle the Williams, boys? We know they don't readily come ter heel for you; 'Coz they only feel amenable ter the late Ma Kelly and Mr. Rollo."

"True. They might think they can be a problem ter me," Klem admitted. He could not lie about the attitude of the brothers to him, for he knew it was a town ***whisper*** behind his back. Then he gestured to Warner and his deputy to draw near, then continuing in a whisper: "...This is fer your ears only. A lotta folks hereabouts think that when it comes ter the push the Williams brothers can best me. Wrong. I'm not above bushwhackin' them or any other clown when it come ter a showdown. "Low" is ***my middle*** name... Get me?"

Mullen's and Warner nodded in chorus. But all the same Warner knew that the thought of a lynching and trying to keep that very thought in a corral was no picnic. "I dunno," said Jake. "It's a big ask of a Sheriff an' a couple of town Deputies ter line up against a lynch mob..."

Returning his voice to its normal volume, Boston went on. "My trick is ter nip everythin' in the bud before it gits outa hand..." Klem passed the cigarette makings over to Mullen.   But right at that moment the actions in the jailhouse were augmented by a rowdy thunder of hooves outside on the street, clearly in front of the jailhouse which caused the trio, concern and questions. No one here had heard such a stampede of horse or cattle flesh come to a standstill so abruptly. It would prove to be the arrival of a Calvary patrol sent over from Fort Hancock to secure the release of Captain Roscoe and, his lieutenant from Junction City's jailhouse.

The door to the street was thrust open amid a heavy thump and scrape of Calvary boots upon the splintered boardwalk adjacent to the threshold and the flooring of the establishment.

The energetic force used on the door was such that it would have had to shorten the life-expectance of its hinges. A nutmeg haired, Sergeant O'Dowd was first through the door and came smartly to attention, as if now an extension of the door, his eyes focused straight ahead at the wall across from him; it was as though he had eyes that could see right through the adobe. He held his unsheathed saber in close alongside his stiff body, its sharp killing point directed to the ceiling. A beat later and with the casual action of a man in authority, a West Point Lieutenant crossed the threshold... He was, already in the process of tugging off his gauntlets while crossing the walk, to be this far into the process. His tunic protected from trail dust by a beige duster that stood open down the front. Inside the building he slipped his gloves under the leather belt of his tunic and paused for a moment to survey the office lobby and its baffled inmates.

Sheriff Boston was the first of the trio to snap out of their shocked. He moved forward towards the wicket with his mug of coffee in one hand and his freshly lighted cigarette between the fingers of his other...

"'Morning, Lieutenant?" said Klem as he recognized the officer's status from experienced associations, but not the face, it was new to Boston.

The West Point man focused beyond the sheriff's statue to the white prisoners in the cell at the back of the jail house.

"Sergeant O'Dowd!" He hollered without turning away from those in the room. The man he was seeking would have needed to be down at the end of some Parade Ground under normal circumstances to be spoken to with such, volume.

"Sir...!" responded the sergeant in kind as he executed a military style turn to his left and marched down to the room-divider and halted alongside his commanding officer with a tramp of boots. "Sergeant O'Dowd, reporting, Sir!"

The West Pointer indicated that he wished the sergeant to open the wicket for him so that he might pass from the lobby into the office proper. His subordinate opened the wicket and the officer passed through, making straight down the room towards the cells; O'Dowd moved in after the officer but did not follow him down to the men behind bars. Instead he came to a halt before Boston and lowered the point of his saber to the floor and there he stood once more stiffly to attention.

Klem and his companions were still recovering from the shock invasion of the troopers. The West Point officer stood before the men behind bars and gave them and the "once over". Captain Roscoe and Lieutenant Briggs were already straightening their attire — they rightly assume that their stay in the jailhouse was fast drawing to a close.

"Stand easy, sergeant..." said the West Point lieutenant over his shoulder to O'Dowd, but clicked his own boot heels together out of respect for the jailed Captain. Without taking his eyes off the now busy Roscoe, the West Pointer continued for Boston's benefit — "We've come under orders to relieve you of the Army personnel you are holding, Sheriff...

"O'Dowd, be so kind as to show the Sheriff our authority!"

The sergeant removed an envelope from a dispatch pouch on his tunic belt and handed the orders to Boston who had to place his cigarette in his mouth to gain a free hand, so as he could take possession of the envelope, which he carried over to the corner of his desk, where he deposited his coffee mug so that he might get at the contents of the unsealed envelope. He extracted the documents and unfolded them to scrutinize the written text. As he read and digested the documentation, ash developed on the end of his smoke and when he spoke it broke off and fell to the floor. "What's this all about?"

There were no doubt they were papers indicating that his prisons had to be hand over to the detachment upon arrival and that he was to be taken under guard to Fort Hancock — this last part made him feel as though he needed to use a lavatory.

The Lieutenant swung away from the cell bars and came back up towards the Sheriff. "Lieutenant Wilcox is my name as those papers have already explained our mission... (The Lieutenant's voice lowered so that it became more civil as he continued) I'm placing you under arrest, you and your Army prisoners are to return with me to Fort Hancock *post haste,* so let's waste no time and get mounted, Mister!" Wilcox said rather brusquely. "Free the prisoners and return to them any property you're holding!"

"Hold on a cotton pickin' second, *Lt. Wilcox — I'm* Sheriff of this town an' **no shave-tail** West Point cockatoo's gonna ride into "my town" and start by ridin' my ass around in a bloody circle!"

"—that's right," said Warner as he reached for the dispatch papers from Klem's hand to see for himself what the papers were all about.

"And who might *you* be?" Wilcox demanded.

"Warner. Jake Warner ... Indian Agent at Chickadee reservation."

"Then I suggest you take a more thorough look at the papers you're holdin'. You'll see that the Sheriff is under military arrest. Come, we're wasting time! You order that cell open and make ready to accompany me and my men, sheriff..."

Looking at the papers, Jake found the part of the document that gave the Lieutenant the authority to arrest Sheriff Boston, and cart him off to Fort Hancock in restraints, if need be. Warner showed the sheriff the part that read just that, and Boston's face turned gray.

"…It's not true, is it, boss?" asked Deputy Mullen. He had never heard of a Sheriff being arrested in his short time spent wearing a star.

Warner passed the papers across to the deputy to read. "Yes… it's true… see fer yore self."

Boston told the deputy to get the prisoners read then turned to the Lieutenant. "Look, you'll have ter bear wiv me I have my hoss stabled down the livery, if yuh expect me ter ride my own mount, out ter the fort…" Boston gave the cell key to his deputy who went off to free Roscoe and Briggs.

"You can ride double with O'Dowd down to the livery an' collect yuh horse!" The Lieutenant told the Sheriff. And within ten minutes they were on their way down to get the Sheriff his horse and to collect Roscoe and Biggs's mounts.

When Ben Lexmon got back to the jailhouse he queried with the Indian agent and deputy Mullen why he had seen the Sheriff riding doubled on a horse with a Calvary sergeant and an Army patrol riding off down Main Street.

Between them, Mullen and Warner explained what had happened in his absence.

"So I guess that leaves you in charge of the place, Ben," said Luke Mullen. "And that, makes you responsible fer our injun prisoner."

"How come Fort Hancock bought in to all this?" Ben Lexmon asked as he placed the hot breakfast from the diner on the desktop. "They didn't," said Warner. "They were only carrying out orders from Washington, I read 'em myself. As usual, the Army's timing is up ter putty. This couldn't have come at a worse time. This town is seethin' with hatred and ready ter blowup like a powder keg."

"Can the Army jist ride in to town and arrest its "Sheriff" like that?" said Lexmon to the agent. Like Mullen he did not know that such a thing was allowable.

Warner shook his head and said: "…I don't know enough about the law ter say one-way or the darn other, that's fer sure."

"Someone will have ter let the Mayor and town council know about Klem's arrest—it's all wrong in my book!" Luke stated.

"Yore right, and I'm gonna do sumthin' about it," said the Indian agent as he pushed his way through the wicket of the divider. "You men stay put; I'll fetch the Mayor and the councilors —!"

"In that case, you had better let Mr. Rollo know what's been going on in this town behind his back, too!" Lexmon pointed out. "Him and the council better take over runnin' the place!" Lexmon suggested.

"Yore second in line ter the boss — isn't that yore job?" asked Luke.

"Who says it's a job *I want.* I wanna keep as fer away from that position as I can at this time," Lexmon said clearly.

With the meteor crater three miles behind them and nothing more to be said, Stroughton busied himself with driving his grays, Cotter was soon rocked asleep by the movement of the surrey as they linked up with the road back to Junction City.

Swinging the surrey in a right hand arc and thus placing the morning sun slightly to their left, Don allowed the horses have their heads; the shade of the vehicle's roof would protect the occupants from sunburn.

Well, thought Donald. *Those damn buzzards will have to look elsewhere for their next meal, they are not gonna feed on my beauties!* He noticed some broken ground on the trail ahead and realized that crossing over it would give the surrey a decent jolt and surely awaken the snoozing Cotter …*After all, why should he sleep while I do all the work?*

The vehicle was jolted so hard that it almost pitched Cotter from the surrey and Don Stroughton had to grab the man by his shoulder to keep him aboard. "— Christ Almighty! What are you trying to do?" Frank cried as he woke with a start.

"I thought you could do with a bit of stimulation — yuh sleeping there like a goddamn Pawnee papoose! Keep me company; otherwise I shall fall asleep, too. I walked, half the night away and got no forty winks like some people I could name!" Stroughton sounded a bit caustic and Frank believed he owed it to the man to be more sociable. So Cotter kept the attorney entertained about his life as it was back east before he fell from being a "Good-time-Charlie" into that of a boozy lush — who spent more time in the city gutters than out of them… wine, women and song had all added to his downfall and Lester Lomax come on board as his savior. But now after all this time he felt like he was getting some purpose back into his life — as he settled on trying to make sure that his pal's accident was thoroughly looked into.

Looking askew in Cotter's direction Donald Stroughton said:

"— You are really going to sink your teething into trying to prove a ***fifth man*** was at the accident?"

"Yes — I believe Ma Kelly knew what she saw down there on that, street."

"OK then, let us be hypothetical for a moment ... say you find this missing witness; what will it prove? If this feller's truthful — there will be no more to add to what has already been covered. Surely you understand we've already raked over this ground before and got nowhere?"

"You're welcome to your view and I am welcome to mine ...!" Cotter pointed out, as the trail ran into the nor-west end of Bryan Street. "I'll stand you breakfast at the diner, Don… Seeing as you walked half the width of the county last night," Frank told Stroughton.

"You're on," Don eased the pair of grays back in their gait as they approached the intersection of Main and Bryan and wheeled right into Main and headed uptown to the diner.

The main breakfast crowed had already begun to welter as Donald nosed the grays into the hitch rack next to an empty concord buggy. Cotter alighted and stretched the stiffness out of his muscles. The lawyer slipped the bits from the horses' mouths and chained the front wheel; already the grays were lapping up the water from the slow leaking trough beneath the tie rail. Then the attorney and the scribe mounted the walk and went in to pay their respects to the Werner family business.

Frank felt like putting something heavy in his tummy, so he ordered a big, steaming bowl of oatmeal with hot cow's milk. The counselor ordered ham and eggs plus a couple of China mugs of coffee for the pair of them to sink. They thirstily downed their first mugs of java and smartly went back for refills from the urn on the counter — and as they approached their table the waitress came in from the kitchen with their breakfast.

"Excuse me, Mr. Stroughton —"she said as she placed their meal on the table.

"Yes?"

"There's been folks lookin' all over town for you this morning — did you know?"

Don shook his head but made no effort to explain the break in his morning routine.

"You are usually in for breakfast before this —" Then she looked at Cotter and added: "You're both late this morning?"

"Who's been askin' after me, Miss Olga?" Don fixed his eyes on the waitress as he dissected his ham into diced meat.

"The Mayor and the Indian agent." she said.

"H'm — that *is* heavy, Don," said Frank with tongue in cheek.

"Right, when I'm clear from here I'll look up His Honor!"

"They seemed anxious ter find yuh — I reckon it might have something ter do with the Army coming into town and arrestin' Sheriff Boston!" She then moved over to an empty table and begun to collect the soiled cutlery left behind by a satisfied customer.

Stroughton pushed his chair back from the table and went after the girl. "Whaddy mean?"

"Where have you been, Mr. Stroughton? Down some gopher hole?! … The Calvary rode in from Fort Hancock and arrested Boston fer locking up the Captain and Lieutenant in his jail — seems the arrest were all out of order or sumthin'. I never thought Sheriff Boston would arrest folks without good reason!"

"I *know* he wouldn't — not that guy," Don said emphatically. The attorney turned back to Cotter. "Something serious seems to have come up Frank — I'm heading to the jailhouse; do you wanna be in on it?"

"Thank God you've turned up, Counselor…" said the Mayor as Stroughton and Cotter moseyed through the door of the jail. The Mayor looked beside himself. He arose from Boston's desk where he was surrounded by Deputies Lexmon and Mullen and agent Jake Warner. On f the desk was a serving tray with the now cold breakfast that Lexmon had fetched from the diner for the prisoners and the Sheriff Boston.

Between Warner and Mullen, the story of the Sheriff's arrest got another airing. "The thing is," Ben Lexmon broke in on Deputy Mullen. "— This mess couldn't've come at a worse time. There is heavy talk flying about the town that folks wanna see this redskin of Warner's strung up quick, like, wivout a trial.

"Klem wanted ter get a handle on it all before it got out of hand. I've had my ear to the ground an' found out that the Williams brothers are the ones stirrin' the pot. You can say all you like 'bout Boston bein' a cripple and not really fit fer the job, but I believe he's the only man in this town with the know-how ter water down such a situation…" Ben Lexmon looked across at Stroughton to see if he had grasped the gravity of the problem facing the town.

"What d'you expect from Counselor Stroughton?" Cotter asked as he realized anything involving the Williams brothers was always going to be like a boil on one's ass.

The Mayor ignored the scribe but placed his hand on Stroughton's shoulder "We, that is me and the council — need ya ter try and sort this mess out with the Government through the Army at Fort Hancock. Surely there must be some legal way around this arrest? …It's an embarrassing situation for the council to deal with!" The town Mayor pointed out.

"When did all this happen?" said Don.

"About seven o'clock," said Mullen as most of the folks looked in his direction for the answer.

"They've had a good start on us by now," Don explained to his audience and then without making any noise about it the folks could see that the lawyer was tired. "If we set off after them we haven't a chance of over-taking the Army before they get to Hancock. In any case, it will mean a round trip to the fort and back…"

"Your surrey team won't be able to do a round trip to the fort, Don, you know that?" Cotter mention to the Attorney, even though the scribe hadn't ventured to that part of the county.

"Why would that be?" the Mayor frowned.

"Forget it — it's nothing to do with this. I must say here and now, I have never been involved with anything like what Boston has got himself caught up in…"

Stroughton disliked making such an admission; he did not like people knowing much about his law experiences.

"But you are gonna try and help?" asked the Mayor which was more a plea.

"Of course, yuh Honor…" *Okay. I can swap my grays with Ma Kelly's two Morgan's down at the livery,* thought Stoughton — *there is no way I'm not gonna be able to catch up with that patrol before it hits Hancock. So it's at the fort I'll have ter argue my case for Boston...I'll have to be on my toes up there as I won't be playing on my own home ground. Hmm, first before going or doing anything I'll have to have a bath at the Chinese. Hell, am I doomed never to get my head down on a pillow, again?*

"Do you plan to go it alone?" Cotter asked.

"Why? ... You wanna tag along...? —**you** realize — you're to blame for Boston being in this fix," Donald Stroughton pointed out. "If he hadn't locked that Captain and Lieutenant up on your behest — Boston would be right here with us and I would not have ter be racing all over the place to secure his freedom."

"Those men broke the law," pouted Cotter. "Had things worked out differently — *I* might have been dead too, at their hands!"

"Well, ***hooray*** fer that!" Don then turned to Warner and put on his Attorney's hat as he said: "You were here when Klem was arrested?"

"Right, yuh..."

"I better have you along with me as an independent witness, are you free to come?"

"As a breeze!" said the agent.

"I would join you, Don — but as the town is without a Sheriff I ought ter remain here..." the Mayor pointed out.

"Yes, you need to stay put — what's Mr. Rollo's view on this? I take it he has been filled in?" the lawyer asked. "I don't wanna be stepping on his toes in this mess."

"He wants you to handle it your way," said the Mayor.

The Attorney turned to Lexmon. "My surrey is outside the diner, the team's had a pretty rough time of it, so could you get someone to take them along to the livery for me, and get them to swap my team with Ma's Morgan's while Cotter and I stop off for a douche, at the Chinese?!"

"Mullen's can organize that," said Ben with a nod. "— I best stay here wiv Mr. Warner's Indian friend..."

"Right," said Deputy Mullen as he broke formation and made for the wicket.

Counselor Stroughton called after Mullen, "Ensure that the stable-hands harness the team up with their own harness they're used of wearing, they'll feel more comfortable and settled during the trip!" Mullen's waved back over his shoulder on exit, and the Attorney knew the deputy had understood his message.

Stroughton's surrey wheeled down Main Street with its fresh team and three passengers with a supply of provisions hastily thrown together for the occasion. The men all wore protective dusters over their clothes. The lawyer felt he must have missed his calling and should have been a teamster; he'd had reins in his mitts so much during the past forty-eight hours.

Ma's twin horses were a fine pair of high stepping beauties and Don could see no reason why they shouldn't make good time to Fort Hancock — they traveled past the skeletal timber frames of a couple of houses under construction on either side of the street — two domesticated dogs gave chased after the surrey for a 100-yards then gave the idea away once their master whistled them up; then before long the surrey broke free from civilization as it came to the eastern boundary of Junction City on course for Hancock.

Approaching a growth of cottonwoods, beyond which lay a dry wash they would need to cross, Stroughton decided to spell the horses over a coffee break. Warner built a quick campfire and the lawyer and scribe organized the java between them.

Later Cotter carried his tin mug of black, bitter java a little ways off from the fire to escape the smoke and stood there in the open, gazing into the distance at a girding flock of turkey buzzards. The Attorney left Warner back in the shade with the surrey and came out to join Frank.

"...I reckon I know what's eatin' you Frank?" Stroughton said as he drew to a halt alongside Lomax's pal.

Cotter looked sideway as the lawyer. "What?" — *How could **he** know what I'm **thinking**?* — Frank thought, still regarding the Counselor over the rim of his mug as took a sip.

"How close we both came to being buzzard, meat."

Looking squarely into the lawyer's eyes, he admitted, "It crossed my mind... I'd like to know who wanted us stranded out there and why?"

"It's as good a place as any, ter git rid of someone who's becoming a saddle-burr, I guess. We wouldn't have lasted much longer if I hadn't found that exit n' reached the surrey."

"I know that." Frank said as he continued to gaze at Stroughton.

The crafty lawyer could see that Cotter had a bunch of questions unasked hidden there in his eyes, and rightly knew that in time they would be put to him, but apparently the newspaperman doesn't feel it the right time or place for such questions.

Frank lost his thirst for what remained in his mug and cast aside the rest of his coffee, the two men set out back in the direction of the surrey and the campfire. . "How do you think you are going to make out with the Army business an' Klem? The Army seems to be playing serious games here like *our* would-be assailant!"

"It's no game, Cotter... The Army's acting for the government in this business and that means getting Boston out of their clutches won't be an easy task."

"True. I don't envy you your job. I've been thinking — what if the Army has a federal marshal waiting at the fort to take Klem's star from him? Have you given any thought to that?"

"I shouldn't think they would take things that far... We shall just have ter wait and see. You are pretty pessimistic, Cotter."

"A newspaper reporter gets to see the other side of the coin too often, Don. Like you attorneys. If the government removes Boston's star that makes him ineligible to wear a badge for the rest of his life!"

"Let's face that jump when we come to it. C'mon men, let's git the lead out of our ass — or we won't be at the fort before *taps.* Once they close the gates for the night they don't open 'em again until *reveille,* and I don't feel like sleeping in a crowded surrey!"

Warner got the message and threw the dregs of his java into the low fire, sending a shot of hissing steam on a journey to the sky. Jake arose and played "wife" by gathering together all the utensils left about from their break, with the intensions of loading them aboard the surrey. The Attorney and Doc. Lomax's friend had started towards the team who became alerted at their approach, the lawyer set about removing their nosebags while Cotter joined Warner, and handed him the tin mug he had been using so that he might pack it away in the hamper basket.

"Frank," said Donald to get the man's attention. "I have a spade aboard — could you do me the favor of burying our fire? We don't just walk off and leave a live campfire…" Frank nodded and after locating the shovel took it across to the fire, and began covering it with loose sand of the dry wash. But his actions were revealing of the fact that a shovel was a tool totally foreign to him, nonetheless he did the job.

Sam Korda was just two days ride from the Canadian border when he rode into Zeb Bosshart's isolated trading post. But still couldn't really accept the unexpected nor unexplainable death of Malthouse back at Coyote Pass. Sam Korda decided he would rest here for a time, for with his seared hand was incapable of holding a pistol or a rifle steady, and that was risky in itself, in a new country; no one knew what might befall them in these places.

He stayed on for ten whole days while his hand continued healing without the help of any so-called salve.   Korda wanted to be sure he could use the hand efficiently when he crossed over into Canada; he did not want to be carrying something with him, which would make him stand out and be remembered, he wanted to blend in to a community like a local. He knew in himself that he could have crossed the border long before he got to Bosshart's place, but had taken Flynn's advice and traveled in a zigzag course through the wilderness to cover his trail. However on the way — in a small dump of a town he came across called Rockwell, he spent some loose change on local moonshine and at his lonely campfire out in the woods, Korda drunk himself into a stupor and lapsed into a restless sleep; During which he somehow shoved his mitt into the open fire — it sobered him up all right, but left him in a pretty bad way. Cooking one's own flesh he could not recommend. With great difficulty he caught his mare and saddled her, and then he headed into Rockwell to see if they had a sawbones, of which he very much doubted. He was proved right. The folks of Rockwell survived or died from so-called home remedies like so many small towns and settlements. There wasn't even a known doctor within a hundred miles and that explained to Korda why the place had a sizable Cemetery.

And about now the poor folks of Rockwell realized that the stranger in their midst smelt of money, at least more money than the richest in this poor community. Realizing this, Sam Korda felt a growing discomfort within, especially the way the men folk started eyeing him off. Rockwell was a lawless town in this neck of the woods and who would bother about a stranger's sudden disappearance? But out in the forest timberlands he realized his hand was a problem and decided to head for Bosshart's Trading Post a renowned refuge for men on the dodge. Here he could sleep with a gun cocked in his good hand and rest up a while.

Right at this moment in time, Sam was the richest member his family ever known, but the ironic thing about it was, he couldn't spend up big like he wanted too without drawing attention to himself...not yet a while; otherwise the vultures of humanity would have no qualms about issuing him some lead pills. He wondered if Matt Flynn was making out any better.

The fugitive, for that is what he now was, had been held up at the trading post far too long for it to be healthy. Already the hang abouts were getting a little bit too friendly for his liking — he could not afford to waste any more time as he was now within reach of his goal. He decided to take a full bite of the cherry and go for broke to the nearby frontier border.

The day he decided to make his departure he was up before dawn to make his last minute preparations so that he might be in the saddle when dawn broke. It was still as awkward task as ever, for him to harness his cayuse, mostly with one hand. But finally he had mastered the chore and led his mount out from under the lean-to that Zeb Bosshart had allowed him to use for a stable and throw his bedroll down — the outpost had been fortified with a log wall in earlier days to keep marauding Indians at bay. Sam led his reluctant horse across the compound by the reins as the first curl of blue fire smoke rose from the cabin's stone chimney, thus indicating that Zeb or someone was up stoking the old fire back into life for the first meal for the day. Breakfast would be a busy meal here at the post because some fur-traders had drifted down from the mountains to escape last night's cold frost. They had thrown their bedrolls down wherever a space could be found in the trading post's store-cum-living room. The trappers were a motley lot — capable of anything, but then Korda was no angel.

A rooster suddenly crowed and scared Sam a little, because it had been totally unexpected. Had his blistered and scarred hand not been bandaged in strips of torn blanket he might have drawn on the rotten mongrel, he didn't want it announcing his departure — though a pistol-shot would wake the dead at this hour of the morning. He eased the pony to a stop before the wood pile, the logs were slick and snow white from last night's frost… he made use of the wood heap to climb up into the saddle, but had to be careful of slipping. He found the stirrup like a blind man and heaved himself aboard as the barrel-belly landlord opened the back door and threw the remains of last night's slop bucket out on the grass, its contents being food scraps and the family's overnight collection of urine.

Free-range fowls seem to come from everywhere as they sensed something for their empty gullets…

Bosshart was wearing a pair of Wellington boots, moleskin trousers and a plaid flannel, open-neck shirt. His uncombed hair was all spikes and a three-day-old beard adorned his cheeks. He had lived a hard life and it was all written there on his face. He looked a born bachelor but had in fact shacked up with a woman he took as his wife without the blessing of church or law — his common law wife had given birth to a dozen offspring but only a few survived to number five, the rest of the children had fallen victims to diphtheria, Indian kidnappings, wild bears, cougars or wolves. It was a hard country to try raising children in, and they either grew up with plenty of savvy or just didn't make it.

"Gettin' an early start, Mr. Cobb?" asked the loudmouth Zeb in his gravelly voice. It was always roughest first thing of a morning due to having hibernated for the pass ten hours.

He always spoke to people as if they were like him, half-deaf. It was for this reason Zeb had learnt to lip-read.

Sam settled in the saddle… Since arriving at the trading post he had adopted the name, Sam Cobb; For since being on the dodge he had used a few names other than his own, mostly the first name that popped into his head; he had been Sam Bucksmith, Sam Roach, Sam Lithgow and now, Sam Cobb — he had no intension of being know as that by the time he set up in Canada. His disguises had one flaw and that was for no accountable reason — his Christian name he never changed.

For a man of Jock Robeson's ilk, Sam's deception was not working — for Korda had no idea what sort of man was hot on his spoor.

Sam threw Zeb a curt nod. He did not want a fuss made over his departure. Cobb edged his mount towards the ever open gate of the old stockade, one that had not been closed in years and could not be closed now if want, because the wild grass had it good and choked. The horseman urged his mount to a trot but the animal was reluctant to respond for it had begun to like the freedom of not wearing a saddle in the time it had been stabled here, Sam had to give it a touch of his rowels to get the movement out of the lazy beast he required. There would be no speed made through these woods as the trees were only spitting distance apart, but once within the tree-line he would travel with the comfort in mind that his route would be camouflaged from prying eyes.

"…Hope yuh hand comes good soon, an' yuh have a good trip ter Canada." Zeb hollered after the departing rider and stepping backwards from the doorsill he closed the rustic door to his dwelling, so that the heat escaping from the heath would begin to warm up the interior.

Korda was not happy that Bosshart knew the destination of his ride, but could do naught about it — it was very clear where he would have to be heading, by the direction he took, from the gateway to the trees. He ought to have shown more cunning, Korda mentally castigated himself for his stupidity – he'd just have to live with it; Anyway Canada is a big country and he was sure he would soon lose himself in its wilds.

Inside the trading post with its log walls lined with cow and bear hides to keep the greater part of the cold winds on the right side of the structure, three trappers woke as Bosshart and his family roused and went about their work. A couple of Zeb's boys got into a roughhouse fistfight to welcome in their day, Zeb let them fight them out; it was just them losing skin that was needed to toughen them up. The money hungry trappers even bet on the outcome of the boy's fight amongst themselves; eventually the fight petered out and could only be assumed a "draw".

"Where's that feller, Cobb, this mornin'?" asked Porky Lowe. He wasn't called "Porky" for nothing.

"Hauled 'imself outa here an hour ago," Zeb told Lowe as he was joined at the plank table by an ornery Cass Bumstead. Cass had been practicing his own tailoring for years without hardly any improvement in his skill since day one, so, wardrobe-wise he left a lot to be desired.

"That Greek wild man, says he's loaded wif money — that true, Zeb?" Cass found another button loose on his heavy jacked and tore it off with anger and put it away in a pocket for reattaching. The trappers had all slept fully clothed under fur wraps and none had removed their boots and socks for over a week.

"Don't know, an' don't know how Spiro would know…" Zeb looked about the room for the man in question and asked curiously, "— where in the blazes has that mean mix got ter?"

"He slipped out ter track Cobb, don't you trouble yore self 'bout him," Lowe warned the trader as he removed a long bladed Bowie knife from its sheath and lightly touched its keen edge with the pad of his thumb. There was a meaning in his gesture and Zeb had no plans to do anything that would leave his family fatherless.

"Hey… I want no part of what you have brewin' in that wicked head of yore's. Jist leave me to my tradin' and family out of it!"

"Damn good ter sees a man — what knows his place…" Porky put away the knife. Him and his buddies were old-timers at this racket, Bosshart reckoned if the truth be known one could count their victims on two hands, and as to the whereabouts of their remains, was anyone's guess. It was even a guess whether or not all their victims had been truly cashed up at the time these mountain crazy butchers descended on them. In an about way, Zeb and his family did profit from the deaths, for the trappers spent all their money here at the trading post, it was their home away from home up in the mountains The feller they referred to as the Greek was a bit misleading — he was part Greek, part Indian and part French! This was no doubt a volatile cocktail, but with a   name like Spiro Malasis to his credit, everyone understood him to be Greek. As far as knife play went, he could leave

Porky and Cass for dead. He wore a black slouch hat with an Eagle's feather poked into the band. His upper body was covered by a chamois, fringed hunting jacket with Indian designs and colored beading. The lower part of his body was clothed with Indian leggings and redskin moccasins. In fact, this bunch of trappers all wore moccasins. Spiro choice of weapons was a Bowie knife; an old Peacemaker in a holster made from elk hide. None of the trappers had shaved proper in a long time so they all wore scruffy short beards which were kept that way by a pair of scissors they shared, all had head-lice and fleas and were scratching at themselves from time to time once their minds were not preoccupied with any work at hand.

Zeb watched Cass and Porky checked their pistols — these pair packed their faith into a couple of Dragoons apiece and a couple of Sharps rifles for deer or bear hunting. Zeb had been trying to interest the trader had been trying to get all three men to purchase the latest Winchesters, but because they reckon their armory suited *their* needs in the hunting game he couldn't persuade them to update and as a result he cursed their damn cheap asses! *Maybe someday it'll prove to be their funeral,* Zeb thought.

Spiro flung open the front door to the building and rushed in, his face, what you could see of outside his matted beard was livered — he had made an unscheduled return to urge his compatriots in crime, to move with yet more speed.

"What's the hurry, Malasis?" Bumpstead enquired.

"Yew wuz right, Cass — he's headed terwards the border – how much break yews gonna give this sucker?!" Spiro said, brusquely.

"It's fishin' time, Malasis — we play 'im like a mountain stream trout!" Porky answered — though deep down he felt like murdering their quarry, just for the Hell of killing.

Zeb knew these rummy men of old, he sneered in their general direction: "And what makes you reckon Cobb's worth wasting ya lead or time on?"

With hungry eyes the mongrel rats of humanity explained for the landlord's benefit: "I been a snoopin' in his kit — my eyes see **gold ingots** this big!" Spiro used his free hand to draw a shape in the air — no one but Malasis knew or realized he was over exaggerating their size with his sketch.

"Then why didn't you snatch 'em when yuh ha the chance?" said Zeb Bosshart, not realizing that it would have seemed the obvious thing to do — he asked the question as though, he were a learned man.

The Greek waved his arms about to encompass his brethren.

"Vee is one – we don't include traders in this part of our business!"

"Jist remember Bosshart, fer yer own health and the health of yer kin; if anyone comes a-lookin' fer this Cobb feller — the critter wuz never here." Lowe told the trader. "We respects yew and therefore we don't rob or kill anyone on yore door step —"

"And we aren't gonna start, now," said Cass Bumstead, over riding Lowe.

Zeb nodded. "Jist yew boys do me the honor of seein' his body or any part of it doesn't turn up; otherwise I'm the one who'll become suspect by the authorities as I'm the only trader fer miles in any direction," Bosshart pointed out to them as a reminder.

"Has any or our bodies surfaced in these woods?" said Spiro.

"Nope, but there's always a first," Zeb pointed out.

"Don't yew worry Bosshart," Malasis instructed, "no one will find this one, either!" The mix-blood turned to his feral pals. "C'mon — we don't want this Cobb critter gettin' swallowed up by the forest!" Malasis turned on his heel and trotted for the door with Cass on his tail and poor Porky, left to bring up the rear — they left the plank door wide open in their wake.

"Uncouth sons-of-bitches!" snarled Bosshart as he put himself out to go down the store and close the door after them.

Korda had been forced to make camp earlier than expected, the canopy and entangled limbs of the giant pines had been quick to shut out the dappled sunlight — once God had dipped the sun's angle to meet the hour of five…Sam was not keen to ride half-blind in the forest's gloom and risk endangering his mount to injury without good reason, as he had no idea that he was already the target of three men who ran hot and cold according to opportunity, for life was difficult enough at present with a crippled hand; though even now he was certain that had he found a sawbones back there at Rockwell, the feller would have recommended saying good-bye to the hand.

Here in this jungle forest, Sam Korda guessed that this was well stocked with feral game, skunks, squirrels, chimp monks, deer and brown bears. Though he himself had yet to sight both a deer or old man Grizzly; though he had seen evidence of their presence, the fresh dropping were undeniable proof that the latter was nearby and that signalled the end of hibernation for the brown grizzly. Sam had seen a man after he had been mauled, and it wasn't a pretty sight — he knew they were just as much a night-prowler as the other known nocturnal animals, such as the owl and friends who haunted the trees and undergrowth.

He luckily came upon a natural clearing that would maybe house seven covered wagons for a night's stopover, unhappily there wasn't any trace of free flowing water about, but Sam knew he could live with that for it wouldn't be too long a stretch between streams. He slid down off his horse and working mostly with one hand, struggled to unsaddle his cayuse then hitched it to a convenient sapling. The horse immediately sampled the brush as substitute grass that the forest floor lacked, as it was covered in thick layers of leaves, pine cones, and damp decaying natural mulch. Sam got down on his knees and cleared a small area of forest floor with the edge of his gloved hand about a half a yard in circumference, amidst the mulch he disturbed, Sam found signs of ash and carbonized twigs, the ruins of a long ago forest-fire that had at one time ravaged the mountains in its race to the top of the ridge, luckily for Bosshart and family, it was moving away from the trading post at the time. Here, after gathering forest debris and pine cones from hereabouts, he piled it in a mound which an hour or so later, he had convert into a campfire. Sam decided to kill time by unwrapping his bandaged hand to see what changes, if any, had occurred since yesterday…during which time Sam was struck by a cone from one of the overhead trees, a somewhat hazard of pine forests for the unwary, the blow had sufficient force behind it that he saw stars for a moment or two. Once his head had cleared he soon busied himself with   other thoughts other than feeling sorry for himself… *It hadn't been too awkward playing poker with the hillbilly trappers, now there was a bunch of crude slimy damn critters,* thought Korda. *They sure had that hungry killer look about 'em. They were a gang one had ter be sure of not turnin' yuh back on… Hmm, that's strange the cicadas have shut down like someone threw a blanket over 'em. Mebbe it is the presence of me horse; they'll probably start up their racket once they git used of him…*

Sam re-bandaged his hand and decided to start munching on some of the biscuits he had purchased from Missus Bosshart; and now it seemed that the cicadas had accepted him and his horse and went back to cooling off. A few minutes later when his fire was smoking less, Sam went over to his saddlebags for some beef jerky and sat near the fire gnawing on it occasionally to ward-off the uncomfortable pangs of hunger — he questioned himself whether or not he had done the right thing by not buying up more provisions for the trail, had he done so, it would have made his card-playing friends realize he had money and start giving them and the Bossharts some unhealthy ideas, he was no simpleton and knew that lonely scattered settlements could run their own book on life and not answer to law and order as there was barely anyone in these vicinities folks had to answer too. Later when it came time to settle down for the night in his bedroll, Sam could not put the thoughts of prowling bears completely out of his mind. So he bedded down with one-eye open and his six-iron cocked ready in his good hand. During the night in one of his waking hours he heard the stealth like sounds of a human moving through the underbrush — at first he thought it might have been an Indian from a local tribe, but later, the more he thought about it he was certain that it might have been one of the trappers from the trading post — Indians he recalled were fairly timid folk after dark. So Sam decided to sit up for what was left of the night, with his back against the bollard of a tree, he didn't wish to be caught napping by those shady misfits; out here they and *he* were answerable to no one.

The next morning Korda rolled out from under his horse blanket — though far from rested he knew he could face a day's traveling for he was so close to his destination he did not mind pushing himself. He brewed a pot of java and when he was through; he dumped the dregs on the fire, and then broke camp.

For the first hour he lead his horse up hill and when he look down through the trees behind him, he thought he saw the Greek trapper making a failed attempt to act like an Indian as he moved amongst the trees and brush for cover. Sam knew the man's partners wouldn't be far behind. He moved down alongside the horse and tightened its loosened cinch strap and hauled himself up into the saddle — the sounds of creaking leather no louder than soft groans and the rustle of his clothing as he maybe moved a forearm or twisted in his saddle now and again was all the ambient sounds within hearing and were of his own making, the brush and pines had thinned out some and he felt this was in his favor. He let the animal pick its own path, just so long as they were heading in the right direction he was happy. But after a while he had to brush her flanks every now and then with his spurs to keep her on the move as the horse seemed to want to stroll to a standstill and become one with its surroundings.

…This isn't good, thought Korda. *The fellers on my ass are out ter rob me blind of that I am sure! Let us hope there is too much timber and brush about for 'em ter try back-shootin' me out of the saddle…So how will they play it without things playing their tune? The edge is gonna be wif the feller who strikes the first blow. God, this is their country, so fer starters from their point of view, they have the benefits of taking him out pretty much in their favor. There is still too much timber for 'em ter git a decent shot, so I guess they will try stalk me out and then go ter work on me wif their knives — three against one, don't leave me much odds… Well, we will see about that…*

Just then Korda's mount passed under a low bough of a pine, low in the sense that by extending one's arms above the head a man could grasp the limb with both hands and as long as the horse kept on the move this same man might be able to haul, himself up into the tree, above. It would be a painful move for one with a damaged hand but then when your very life depends on pain, the latter is better to bear. He spurred the horse just before parting company with the saddle to keep the animal on the move after the saddle became weightless for Sam had grabbed a low over hanging bough. The pain in his hand was worse than he dreamed it would be but as he believed his life hung in the balance; he tried to ignore it and put up with the blood sweat and tears, as he first chinned the bough and with a full on effort, like a chimpanzee of a far off distant jungle in another land —— managed to scramble up into the overhead wood. Unbeknown to him he had momentarily gone back to man's Ape stage but nonetheless he achieved his aim and was soon standing on the bough and able to lean with his shoulder up against the tree trunk while he caught his breath and regained some of his energy. He flexed his sore hand for a few minutes not knowing whether this was a good or not for it; but all the time he was conscious that down there in the forest his pursuer would be pressing on. Neither the Greek trapper; or Korda had any idea how far ahead he was of his back-up; and as Sam planned to jump the guy — he had to pray that they were too far off to be of any use to the homicidal trapper.

"I've lost sight of the Greek half-cast," Bumstead reported hoarsely to Porky Lowe, when he caught up to his comrade crouching down on one knee alongside a big mountain red. Cass Bumpstead had his pistol ready in one hand and his Bowie in the other.

Looking at the clammy faced Cass, Porky pointed out: "He'll be OK, Cass — he tracks better alone. Why are yuh holdin' up here?"

"My stomach isn't good this mornin' — must've been Bosshart's rancid food," he suggested. "I feel like I'm 'bout ter heave up a bucket of bile!"

"You rest here an' I'll go up yonder ter give Spiro a hand wiv that cowboy. Come when yuh ready, two of us'll handle him awright..." Porky patted the nauseous trapper on the shoulder, and then pushed off after the Greek who had left a trail for any trapper worth his salt to follow.

The Greek/Indian, moved with extra caution when he realized he had lost sight of the cowpoke and the cayuse who were further up the hill amongst the trees... sure he knew roughly where they were; Spiro moved with the tracking skill his Black foot brethren had drummed into him... His ears were like those of a wolf and it began to bother him *at* he was now heard nothing from up ahead other than the sounds of the forest. If anything, he could most decidedly hear the sounds from downhill of his partners as they fought their way towards him. He edged forward with his eyes forever on the lookout, but nothing seemed the least bit out of kilter…

Sam balanced rock-still on the bough and waited for the man below to edge himself in position, which would be to his advantage when he launched himself out of the tree. He hoped and prayed that the old pine would not pick this time to drop a cone, for it would draw that mixed-bloods' attention right to his hiding place. Korda quietly filled his good hand with the weight of his pistol and steadied himself against the tree-trunk, with his good hand. His eyes were beginning to sting for he had not taken the opportunity to blink them, fearing that they might make noise enough to bounce off the man-hunter's eardrums, though at the time, he did not realize how ridiculous his thinking had become. Then there was no more time to cower and dally there on the bough for his quarry, the man-hunter had become the hunted and was drawing to a halt, right where Sam Korda needed him to be. Sam dropped off the bough and hurtled towards his prey like a massive bald eagle diving in the direction of its next meal. The tree sighed as the weight of the human became airborne — somehow the trapper became aware that danger was near and he whirled round with his businesslike Bowie at the ready to deliver a deadly blow to someone or something that would be about equal to his own height! … Sam's two-point landing made less noise and caused hardly any jarring to his ankles for all was absorbed by the leafy carpet and pine-needles of the forest, he landed crouched, this meant his head and shoulders were only waist high and not as Spiro expected, chest high — the turning man's awesome knifepoint thrust pass Sam's hat with a vicious hiss as it sliced the air. Sam started to rise, knowing that he had no alternative but to render the trapper powerless, whether by serious injury or death. Korda squeezed the revolver's trigger, no need to aim at this close range, shock of shocks — his gun did not respond — the expected shockwave of a discharging shell did not eventuate, the six-gun had failed to functioned, why? A glance at the rear housing of his gat showed that he had forgotten the basics, he hadn't cocked the hammer! Now if there was a chance, any chance of keeping the high ground — Korda had to act and act fast! He reacted on instinct — and thrust his hand with the 5-pound pistol at the face of his quarry, the gun-barrel now became a blunt instrument, his weapon of war — the surprised trapper took evasive action to avoid the hard, hurtful, barrel, zooming towards him with the forceful kick of a mule, the Greek's action had thrown himself off kilter, and although the gun-barrel's stabbing action missed the half-cast's head by merely a few inches, the momentum of his defensive move was a misbegotten mistake — for from his position he could not carry through with any successful action to counter that of his opponent's — before he could attempt to correct his mistake; Korda shove the unrelenting revolver in his face with such force, that it all but knocked him out. He could feel, but not see the fact that his body was collapsing towards the forest floor — *has someone cut my legs off at the knees?!* The Greek thought.

Both men were carried to ground as things continued in hand-to-hand combat. But the stage robber was determined to use any means to best his would-be killer, he shoved his burnt claw-like hand into the trapper's windpipe, obstructing any cried for help or sound escaping his throat that could alert those downhill that their partner as in dire trouble.

Korda clubbed Malasis a second time in the puss, making a further mess of his already broken nasal cartilage that in turn ceded him unconscious. Breathing heavily Korda awkwardly made it to his feet and looked down at the unconscious trapper while he caught his breath and made ready to correct his mistake of not cocking his revolver. He knew the others could not be far behind and wasn't sure he could get away with a shooting the trapper dead, so he legged it to shelter behind the trunk of a nearby big red, this, the very tree he had dropped unexpectedly out of the sky from; now he would play the waiting game.

Porky Lowe came upon the Greek sprawled on the forest's mulch and the shock of seeing the breed with his battered face mattered with blood and pine-needles brought him up short. Before advancing further to ascertain the man's condition, Lowe looked about to see if Malasis's attacker was at hand, and whether or not he was the one now in danger of being bushwhacked —*If I wuz **that feller**, I wouldn't be hangin back now I knows the score…*Thought Lowe, he brought his Dragoon up ready for action. He cocked an ear for the tell-tale sounds of someone crushing their way through the undergrowth — there was none …*Huh, mebbe I'm later than I think?* Lowe concluded. Just then, an ashen-faced Cass Bumpstead arrived and the Greek began coming out of his induced sleep. The breed's cohorts aided him in getting to his feet, but by the hell, he was in no condition to dance the polka… Lowe and Bumpstead had no inkling just how close they were to Sam Korda — only the thickness of a pine trunk separated the trappers from their intended prey, now unaware that they were his quarry.

There is no time ter play footsie wiv this lot! Sam thought as he brought his pistol up to arm's length, then stepped clear of the tree with the clear intension of dispensing death to the unwary. Was there the snap of a twig that maybe warned at least two of the party that they were about to be drygulched? Or was it their uncanny backwoodsman-ship that warned Bumstead and Lowe that they were in peril? Both men moved as one in an effort to preserve their grip on life but the gat in Sam Korda's hand was armed and ready, there was not going to be the same mistake this time, the first two lead missiles traveled far too quickly across the space that separated him from Porky Lowe — the target had no more time for anything but flinch before the impact the lead gave his body, the slug hit Lowe in the stomach atop of his bellybutton, and tore deep into the man's lard and crossed left through his body and left-lung, exiting his back where it punctured a tree-trunk to his rear, the tree began to bleed sap. All this happened as the shot's knock drove Lowe backwards in a limp-limbed flight, to crash lifelessly on the carpet of mulch with half-open eyes staring sightlessly up into the forest canopy of pine tree limbs.

Bumpstead got his Dragoon pistol up in an approximate line with Korda's frame and brought off a shaky shot at the cowpoke, the lead buried itself into the tree at Korda's elbow, the near miss did not shake Korda's aim, he fired over Spiro Malasis's shoulder as the groggy man staggered between him and Sam Korda's target — the reverberating gunshots only worsened the breed's dizziness — his mind was busy trying desperately to understand what was going on around him, and the pain of his smashed face…Korda's bullet took off Bumstead's right earlobe as he tried to spin away from the slug's wallop and cannoned into tangling brush, he tripped up, causing the loss of his handgun as he fell face down into a thorny bush.

Without any need for taking a second aim, Korda shot the breed in the small of the back, this lead deflected on its journey through the Greek's body which left an exit hole out the front of his chest near the right nipple! The sounds of Korda's three shot fusillade faded away into the wilderness, two out of the three trappers lay lifeless on the floor of the forest.

Bumpstead, having now regained his feet tried to back away from his killer with blood dripping onto his collar from his missing earlobe. "…P-please … please no-no more — I surrender— this wasn't my idea!" Cass cried out in desperation as he arrived at a place in the forest where there was nowhere for him to go.

"You're as much a player in this as those two buddies of yores," Korda delivered a killing head shot to Bumstead — death was instant. Sam now realized that his bad hand was bleeding through the gray Army blanket's bandage, but judged that it would be wise not to interfere with it. He also decided that there would not be any time to waste burying the dead — the forest animals could feast from their carcasses.

Sam then went off to find his wandering horse; it was easy to track the shod hoof marks of his mare to where it languished about 200-yards up the mountain when it realized it was on its lonesome… Clearly the horse had taken off through the trees once he started throwing hot lead about.

Korda could not afford to lose the horse now, for it carried his booty from the robbery in the saddlebags; he was certain the horse would not go far and had only fled the immediate area because it was skittish of gunfire, Korda found he had to track the mare further than expected, and felt uncomfortable on foot in bear country. Sam stopped to reload his six-gun and rammed the weapon deep into its stiff leather holster, so the gun would not be easily dislodged from its pouch as he hurried downhill, for his mount had changed the course of its tack — sometimes his pace got the better of him and he was in danger of losing his footing. To prevent this, he took snatch-holds of pine trunks and Aspen saplings in his descent.

Jock Robeson picked up Korda's trail in Rockwell and knew that if he was going to hog-tie this feller it would be best done before the robber crossed over in to Canada. He did not fancy the idea of trespassing in to a foreign country after quarry — he had been there and done that on a couple of Pinkerton cases and his experience was that the North-west Mounted Police did not approve of U.S. Law officers nor private detectives coming into their territory on business, uninvited; The Canadian Police wanted to do their own house cleaning and wanted to be sure that American outlaws got the message that they were not going to escape to freedom just by border hoping when it suited them. The Scotsman found Bosshart's trading post by directions given him by a lay-preacher in Rockwell. Jock was pleased that he had reached the old fortified post during daylight — he had encountered three grizzlies on the way in but fortunately for him they were a safe distance off and each going in the opposite direction, he had even heard a wolf or two baying in the woods somewhere out of sight. Camping rough in this area had no calling for him. It was that time of the season when bears had not long come out of hibernation and these big fellers were moody as they were governed by nagging bellies afire with hunger. These fellers and wolves you treated with respect or paid the price for your indiscretion.

The trading post's dog came out to meet Robeson and his horse — the bitch had a cunning grin on her face and Robeson spoke warmly and encouragingly to the canine — who without warning got around behind his mount and started menacing the gelding's fetlocks — his bay lashed out at its tormentor with a sharp kick, but the dog had experience behind it and managed to stay clear of the deadly hoof. The lawman wished he had known about the dog and would have come prepared with a couple of pocket-size stones to drive her away from the horse, but that was in itself pointless, wishing for something one hasn't got.

The Sheriff stepped down from his saddle and hitched the gelding to the tie-rack near the leaking wooden water trough, which could have been fixed with the interior being tarred — the dog made like a cougar and stalked in towards the man and horse as though it were undercover and not out in the clear forecourt of the post. Busy with slackening off the saddle girth so the tired horse could take the pleasure of blowing its belly, Jock kept an eye on the cowardly bitch and when she made a fresh dash at the bay's fetlock, Robeson acted swiftly and buried the toe of his boot in to the mutt's ribs with such force that the canine was thrown off course and continued on its way to take shelter under the elevated board floor of the porch — it peeped out from under the boards with a look that suggested that she wasn't finished with her tormenting tactics as yet.

Jock adjusted his revolver's holster and untied his bedroll from behind the cantle and slung the roll onto his left-shoulder, then dragged his Sharps from his saddle scabbard and mounted the walk-up porch with saddle stiff legs and kicked the door to the settler's open — nothing like plenty of noise to announce one's arrival, Jock thought. He strolled across the plank floor to a counter made of the same planks as that of the building's flooring but suspended on big beer kegs — the counter was almost clear save for a wicker basket of free-range eggs and some jars of sweetmeats, pickled onions in vinegar and gherkins — which Fiona Basshart had the chore of making up when stocks needed replacing.

The room displayed its settler's wares such as long and short handled shovels, Indian blankets, and pickaxes, ax heads and handles and a number of adzes as well as new and secondhand six-guns and hunting rifles. Replacement hickory tool handles were shoved end up in open cooper barrels, storm lanterns hung on six-inch nails driven in to the wall logs through animal hides. The shelving on the far side of the counter carried stumpy boxes of bullet cartridges, canned food, tin dinner plates, mugs, cutlery, Dutch ovens and bolts of cloth. A sign informed the reader that Bosshart made his own liquor that was sold by the dram. Off to the left was a sit-down eatery consisting of bucolic furniture, sleeping quarters were behind the diner, partitioned off with a tarpaulin on curtain rings and a running line. It was plain that everyone dossed down in here, whether you approved of the situation or not. Ambling to the counter Jock halted at the bench and resting his rifle butt on the customers' edge with its bore pointed to the open slabs of the tree-bark roofing, announced who he was to the expectant looking Zeb Bosshart in a mix of Scottish brogue and American accent.

"Howdy, lad… the name's Jock Robeson, Sheriff of Lawrence," He brushed open his cowhide vest and briefly showed the star pinned to his shirt pocket. He knew it would not serve his purpose to explain that he was on extended leave from his duties.

"H-howdy, Sheriff —" Zeb beamed at his prospective customer. "…That thar is my wife stoking the fire," he gestured in the direction of a heavy brood mare like woman of undermined age, in long skirts and bodice.

"Howdy, ma'am —" The Scotsman nodded in her direction and in exchange received a tight lipped smile as without pause she continued with her work. He could hear some kids playing vocally out in the backyard and knew he would catch up with them later before hitting the trail. Jock got down to business. "I'm looking fer a fellow who's carrying a badly burnt arm around with 'im… Anyone like that been through here, recently — about the past few weeks, ago?" He drew the palm of his goatskin glove over his jaw and felt the need for a shave and time to trim the length of his drooping moustache that had gotten out of hand since leaving Lawrence. "He's a sort of 'loner' an' could be going by a new name… He was known down my way on our Wanted Dodgers as Samuel or "Sam" Korda, though he may or may not have stuck with that name. I'd like ter run a few names by yuh and see if anyone of them come ter mind…?" He took in the trading folks with a passing sweep of his eyes; they in turn nodded, that they were prepared to hear him out, so he went on: "…Smith, Lithgow or mebbe, Bucksmith. He could even be traveling under a new name, these days." Jock leaned heavily on the counter awaiting their response, as they clearly appeared to be searching their minds. *The trouble is, if the wanted man had come by here he wouldn't have been dumb enough to use his own name and then even going by a fresh name might have realized someone might come after him and therefore he may have paid these folks to forget he ever passed through this way. I can't really trust what they tell me, but all the same it's worth a try.* He thought as he gave them plenty of time to search their braincells. *…before I push on I will check with the children, if Korda was here they might be more forth coming because of their innocents.*

While thinking how best to answer the lawman's question, Zeb poured the traveler a "Bosshart" whiskey/rum mixture that would kill off any would-be influenza hiding down there amongst yuh bone marrow.

"Ta," said the Scotsman as Bosshart placed the drink before him — ignorant of the fact that he should have said a few "Hail Mary's" before chucking it down his throat. ***Gawd Almighty!*** Breathed the Sheriff who had tried his fair share of powerful home brews since coming to America — tears welled in the eyes as if they were under attack from the gritty sand of a dust storm — "You should not dispense that brew without warnin', Bosshart! — Now, now w-what about — Christ that's got a ruddy after kick! Wh-what about some answers?"

Bosshart surmised that by now the trappers would have caught up with the feller that had the bandaged hand, and done their worst. So he saw no reason to deny the man had been through here. After all, there had been nothing in it for him. "Yeah…we did 'ave a feller through here wiv an injured hand. Kept it wrapped the whole time he was here and treated it like a newborn baby. Must've been painful though he didn't complain about it —"

"Perhaps he didn't want ter draw attention?" Jock suggested. Zeb nodded. "…Might be you is right about that now yuh come ter mention it. I let him have the lean-to out in the yard; he didn't wanna sleep here inside where it's warmer…"

Mrs. Bosshart suddenly came in on the conversation without warning. "He's the man yuh lookin' fer Sheriff, he lit out fer Canada, but he won't make it."

"What makes you think that?" Jock asked as he left the counter and crossed over to where the woman was working.

" 'Coz three of our regulars realized he might have money after playin' cards with 'im — with those three you don't let on much where money is concerned, do you Zeb?" she said, turning the heat on him.

Turning back to Zeb Bosshart, Jock said: "What's the story behind these three regulars?"

"Nuthin' special," Bosshart admitted from his point-of-view of them. "They've been trappin' around these mountains fer years — ever since we took over this place. They're two white guys and a breed of some sorts, they say he' a *Greek* — but I've always had my doubts."

"This place here, would be pretty lawless, wouldn't it?" said Robeson. Both the Bossharts nodded their heads. "Then if they set off to get the drop on him and succeeded — you reckon he would be a corpse by now, right?"

Zeb nodded again.

"If he gave 'em the slip he would be over the border, unless he were a-walking backwards. Whatever way it turned out we won't see those three trappers back here for a week, they do a lot of livin' off the land an' only come here mostly when they're low on ammunition," Zeb picked up the whiskey bottle and gestured it towards Jock Robeson who reneged with a gesture of his head. "He had shoulder length hair when we saw him last, all wif rattail ends and he called himself *Sam Cobb*."

The feral grizzly slobbered in anticipation of its next meal — Korda knew the bear had finally corned him and that its hour of stalking was at an end, and so well might be his life, if this bear gets its way. Everything was to its advantage, strength, speed and agility — it reared up with the razor sharp claws of its forelegs only yards away from him pawing at the air as its   growl became a threatening roar. He knew his six-gun didn't have the power to stop a bear as awesome as this in its tracks, unless he got a lucky shot and put a slug through the beast's eye and square into its brain; but he doubted he had steady enough nerves for that — yet as sure as a sow drops piglets, that was his only chance… the grizzly now raised to its full height on hind legs — its wide spread arms exposing its furry chest and the flea ridden community therein… The sharp claws thicker than a man's fingers were truly instruments of death and were as effective as any Bowie knife this side of The Alamo!

Yet while the bear teased its prey, Sam Korda wondered whether or not a bullet in the heart might be as good as a head shot, but at the same time Korda realized within his own skull he did not know where exactly the heart's position was; Center, left of center – or right of center? No, a head shot was his only chance…

The grizzly's snarl was bone chilling as it commenced to totter towards its cornered victim, Korda couldn't run or back-off, for he was already hard up against the trunk of a think pine — he went for his pistol and the animal dropped to all fours then charged forth, he got off two shots but the hot lead was ineffective as it only did superficial muscle damage to his intended killer — the bear's foul hot breadth was in his face and now his six-gun jammed — the bear swiped him aside with its powerful paw, the claws slashing a path through his clothes and flesh like a hot knife through butter — his prayer of a quick death was answered as his intestines spilled from his torso on to leaves, pineneedles and pine cones — he would never be aware of the mauling the brute of an animal dished out to him.

Jock congratulated himself on his tracking skills when he came upon what was left of the trappers' bodies after the scavenging forest animals had taken their fill of them. An inspection of the human remains proved that somehow, for the time being, Korda had escaped death or injury. Robeson had to perform the sickening job of a body-search, just in case they had somehow ended up with some of the spoils from the stagecoach robbery; the search was futile, Robeson left the dismembered cadavers where they were scattered and set off after his man, Sam Korda.

Some hours later he stumbled upon what was left of Korda's horse, it could have been brought down by either grizzlies or wolves, it was hard to tell; this established that wherever Sam Korda was, he was now afoot and in an endangered position. The man's saddlebags were intact and Robeson recovered all that was possible of Korda's stake from the Marbles' robbery – this made it possible for him to consider what would be gained by hounding the thief any farther. Sure, by giving up on the man he maybe allowing him to get away with his part in a double murder, but then lots of people in pioneering countries do get away with it in some form or another, it was all to do with the sign of the times and isolation. Besides, there was Matt Flynn still left to be accounted for and every day the ramrod's trail was growing colder and colder, so, he wheeled his mount about and made tracks back to the trading post where he informed Zeb Bosshart that three of his regulars wouldn't be patronizing his establishment in the future. By this, Zeb understood that Robeson must have over taken the trappers and Cobb, the four critters must have went down, for the count; the lawman had completed his task and rid the world of the mountain scum.

Bosshart had only been told what Robeson needed him to know, and would never know the full gist of the story this episode in the lawman's colorful life.

The last the Bossharts was to ever see of one Jock Robeson, was him headed off back in the direction of Rockwell; and as far as the trader and his woman knew, all this talk of gold might just as well have been an empty rumor fueled by an over active imagination and the wish that Cobb had gold in his possession.

15

STROUGHTON'S PARTY HAD to give up on the idea of getting through to Fort Hancock in the one day. It was now an accepted fact that they would spend the night on the side of the road, warming their butts by a fire fueled with tumbleweeds, deadwood and dry cow chips gathered from the plains. A few times during the night they had some unwelcome visitors when curiosity got the better of the odd coyote, that moved up to experience the campfire's warmth.

Don sent them scurrying on their way with a few hot slugs in the direction of their tails from his .38.

"—must you fire that damn thing? … Every time I nod off — **BANG,** you fire that gun!" Cotter growled in the lawyer's direction. "Don't tell me you're tryin' to sleep?"

Stroughton responded. "Even this crummy fire won't get you warm enough to let you drop off!"

"So be it, but is it necessary to set off a shot every ten goddamn minutes?!" Frank arose from the blanket they had thrown on the ground and threw a cow pad on the stinking fire to keep it burning and add to the established aroma that kept mosquitoes at bay.

"It is, if you don't want one of them coyotes comin' in and biting a chunk of flesh out of your ass!" said the Attorney. "— they're not too fussy yuh know."

Warner started coughing and kept it up until he had hawked up phlegm from his lungs and spat it in the fire, where it sizzled until it had evaporated. "…He is right, Frank — they're jist another form of the wolf strain; you never wanna be taken in by one of 'em, you'll pay fer it, believe me."

"What can we expect to do here all night? Wriggle our toes?" Cotter snarled for he had steadily been slipping in to a caustic mood because of his shoddy sleeping periods over the last forty-eight hour.

I guess we can allow for his mood swing, thought the lawyer. *He's no doubt missing his whiskey bottle.* Truthfully the Attorney told Cotter: "There is a valid reason for makin' this stop, Cotter. It's too dark ter travel in this light; it's only a quarter, moon — one of the horses might step in a hole and do in a leg … and there's the chance of getting lost by losing the road… You being and Easterner wouldn't understand this. So mebbe you ought to think about where you truly belong."

"Look, Don — I'm not leaving Junction City until I have exhausted being able to trace that fifth man at Lester's accident; so forget trying to elbow me from my course, I won't be shifted!"

The Counselor sight, "So yuh back on that again? Your persistence is wearing **us all** thin, you know?"

"And who exactly is **the** "us"?" Frank said, knowing full well who the concerned people were.

"The syndicate: Bevan, Dunne, Hill and me — of course!"

"Oh, **that** syndicate," He said sardonically. "Yeah, when you come to think about that, you have got yourselves a nice, neat parcel there." Frank squatted in the firelight and pushed his hat back so that he could scratch his scalp, then he resettled his Stetson.

"What d'you mean by that?" Don Stroughton's eyebrows rode up along with his case of suspicion. "I thought there was some folks in Junction City knew that Lester and Pearl Courtney had a thing going between them — meaning they were pretty close?"

"Where are you heading? You sure make it hard for me to follow you?" The look in the attorney's face was indicative of the man being one step ahead of the newspaperman.

"No where special, only I thought you friends of Lester's were all cozy pals — I'm surprised that none of you thought to bring Pearl in on the syndicate… I'd've thought on behalf of Lester's memory, this would have qualified her. It would have been a responsible gesture *I* would have thought…?"

Stroughton knew where Cotter was coming from now and was thankful that Warner had not clicked to the double-talk. "You miss the point, Frank. Miss Courtney's forte, is the stage — not the business arena. One would have thought *you* of all people would appreciate that?

"The formation of the syndicate was purely a business move and not acted upon for sentimental and emotional reasons. Those things just don't cut the mustard when it comes down to running a successful business venture."

Warner wasn't gripped by the conversation taking place between Don and Frank, during the dialog traveling back and forth between the two men, so he went on to do something constructive, and rolled the group a cigarette each for their enjoyment round the fire.

Cotter was done with squatting on his hams and after accepting a smoke off Jake Warner then sat down for comfort.

"All the same, she ought to have been included in the syndicate as a silent partner at the very least; regardless of her business sense," Then directly to Don he said bluntly: "You could have guided her business-wise by what I have seen of you in that media..." Cotter turned to the fire and selected a twig with a glowing ember and touched it to the tip of his fag while drawing a current of air through the cigarette's length that in turn stimulated the tobacco weed to smolder.

Meanwhile Donald Stroughton refused Jake's offer of a rolled smoke and brought a cheroot out of the inside pocket of his blazer — placed it between his lips and during the continued conversation between Cotter and Don, they exchanged the ember so that the lawyer could fire up his cigar: "I am as human as thet man (He puffed his cigar alight) "— I make mistakes... I do not wanna be the one accused of giving Miss Courtney bad business advice," said the lawyer. It was hard to define whether or not the mouthpiece was being up front or just covering his tracks, so the scribe left it at that.

As the morning sun edged over the uneven horizon to the east of where Frank and company had spent the night; it stirred the men from their light sleep. The lawyer rose and stretched his cramped legs then had a morning wet... The three men's eyes searched for the team that had not been able to wander far due to being hobbled; so it wasn't very long before they were under way. The men were hungry for that first and most important meal of the day, breakfast — but no one had anticipated that they might not make it through to the fort and had therefore not brought along enough provisions. So bearing their discomfort, they continued with their journey. They eventually reached Fort Hancock at 1300-hours, even though Stroughton had seen to it that Ma Kelly's team kept up a good clip.

The Fort's position had been well chosen and constructed on a flat hilltop; so those within its fortified walls had a commanding view of the surrounding country, as well might some Indian warring parties of the past would be able to ratify with the statistics of their dead.

The cavalry had never had it any better and were able to show the savages that the paleface warriors were near invincible. The outpost's walls consisted of thick conifer logs and parapets that comfortably stood up to the attacks of arrows, musket-shot and bullets from the hostiles of the region. The closely located field surrounding the fortress; showed a loss of prime forest tree-line for what had been left in its wake was a regimental of bollard stumps. The fort's double gates were wide enough to accommodate two Prairie Schooners and a Concord buggy side by side, and had been assembled from logs similar to those used in the construction of the stronghold's walls — these days, hostilities were all but nonexistent between the Army and the Redskins so the gates were open all day, this allowed the people from the outlying districts to come and go about their business at the fort, within its walls was a self-supporting community, corrals, stables, hay loft, smithy, quartermaster's store, mess halls, saddle and harness maker, administration building and living quarters for married men, a school-house, and a barracks for the enlisted and unmarried troopers of the Army stockade Two artillery cannons were positioned at the front of the Administration building facing down towards the fort's entrance, overlooking the parade ground which was bordered with whitewashed stones the size of garden pumpkins — the stockade cells, where Sheriff Boston was housed had two other boarders, a couple of AWOL blue bellies.

The surrey wheeled into view from round behind the masking palisade and slowed to almost walking pace as it passed under the overhead parapet that bridged the gap between the gateposts. Stroughton was aware they might be challenged by the sentries on guard duty, but instead were ignored and thus proceeded towards the administration building in the distance, taking a course up the empty quadrangle. On the way Don instructed Cotter to wait outside with the surrey while he and the Indian agent, Warner, met with the garrison's C.O., whom they both knew from previous dealings.

Cotter was not keen with the lawyer's idea about being left out of things but had no time to argue about it, as the surrey arrived out front of the main building and was soon parked parallel with the three tier lumber steps that rose up to and butted against the sidewalk beneath the porch. The newspaperman was sort of left holding the baby as it were — when Don passed the teams' reins to him. Frank did not allow himself to become bored with the responsibility. Instead he keenly surveyed his surroundings.

Meanwhile, General George Boulter's aide-de-camp escorted the Junction City duo in to an audience with the man himself. The General was only four weeks away from retirement but even with his grizzly hair and full beard he still looked every inch an officer. Boulter arose from behind his mahogany desk to greet the men as they came in under the fanlight. The general indicated that the high back chairs before his desk were there for their convenience. The threesome sat down after a round of salutations had run the course, through all this baloney, the General's aide stood at attention near the C.O.'s right hand. The "Good afternoon, gentlemen" from the general in no way betrayed the florid man's mood, so to win brownie points, Stroughton concentrated on not being the slightest way offensive to Boulter.

"I gather you have come to secure Sheriff Boston's release, and I take it that you are his legal representative?" The General boomed in his baritone voice.

The town lawyer edged slightly forward on his chair, while Warner sat stone-faced and ramrod straight as though he had a fire-poker running down the interior of his spine.

Stroughton began with a nod. "The mayor and town council are at a loss to understand what exactly the sheriff's being charged with by the Army, sir."

"I can assure you counselor that it's nothing personal,' intoned the General. He picked up a sheaf of cartridge paper which had arrived in the mail from Washington. The officer had no need to use his spectacles to read the document lying here on his desk— he'd read it at least three times to date but nonetheless for the benefit of the occasion he pretended to be going through it once more for the lawyer's good. "It's apparent that whoever Boston takes his orders from it seems according to Washington's view; that he's in their opinion — being misguided and that's placed him in a position right outside his charter. He arrested an' jailed Army personnel while they were in the act of doing their duty; Washington views this as a serious breach of his powers. And this has been viewed in the light that he ought to have been bendin' over backwards to assist these men—not hinder them…" With barely a pause, Boulter changed focus from the paper on the desk at hand across the desk at Stroughton.

"You can see Mr. Stroughton it would appear that your Sheriff has too many overseers… The local council is his employer, yet it is well known in certain circles that the Chairman of the Cattlemen's Association, Lazarus Rollo, also pulls his strings and it's fallen to me to find out just who it wuz got him to act so uppity—when he made that arrest of our men. Is there a third party somewhere in all this that Washington ought to know about? I need to know here and now counselor Stroughton, just who are you representing? … The town's Council or the Cattle Association in this affair?"

"I can sincerely assure you sir—I am here on the behalf of the Mayor and Aldermen of Junction City to secure the release of our town Sheriff. I'm certainly not hiding any cards up my sleeves in this case. However I shall admit, for it would be foolish of us not to appreciate that the Association is a powerful organization in these parts in all due respects—but believe me as far as I know—Mister Rollo has no vested interest to poke his fingers, or would want to interfere with Army business—after all, he's a patriot of the highest order.

"I know the reason why Captain Roscoe and his lieutenant were arrested, they simply broke the law and I was brought up to believe that the law applies to everyone, am I right, sir?"

Boulter slowly nodded and the thought crossed his mind that he best wait and see where this mouthpiece was coming from, but pointed out that in some circumstances the Army was above the law.

The lawyer continued on a little brashly: "The captain and lieutenant Briggs seemed to have taken their mission a bit too far in the way they handled a certain citizen of Junction City and it was this person who braced Sheriff Boston with proof that they'd actually assaulted him. Mind you, there were some people in the town who have had no reason to believe they were military men and in fact they came across as a couple of thugs, and at no time did they produce any documentation to Sheriff Boston to change his view of them being no more than a pair of saddle tramps. Even after Boston arrested them they didn't establish beyond any doubt who they were.

"Boston was just performing his duty as he saw it. Any verbal claims as to their identity had to be wisely ignored—after all they might've been a couple of phonies?" Attorney Stroughton allowed here at this point a pause as he took the time to try and gauge how he was fairing with the General. There was no doubt in the lawyer's mind that Boulter wasn't as stiff as he had appeared when they first entered the room.

"I would be lying if I was to come out and say I knew what these Washington officers were doing operating in my territory for whatever they've been conducting it has been without any of my knowledge; I'm not even sure whether by being here if they even come under my command, for as yet, I haven't had time to interview them to learn what their mission is and why it has had to have been carried out under such clandestine means …" General Boulter admitted: "So until I've at least heard all **sides** of these stories floating about; I'll just sit back and play things by ear."

"Excuse me for coming in here," said the Aide-de-camp. "But I took the liberty of talking with Captain Roscoe on your behalf, General. And from that talk I can say he was put in an awkward position by the assignment, we have to understand that he was after certain vital information from the citizen in question, and his endeavors were unduly obstructed by this thoroughly obnoxious, person. He felt he had to fight fire with fire. Mebbe he could have handled the situation on a more professional note, but then, we weren't there to be able to appreciate the officer's position."

Boulter nodded his thanks to the Aide and turned back to Stroughton. "Be warned Counselor, don't come here pleading leniency on behalf of the sheriff an' think you can sling aspersions against this man's Army—here, you aren't playing to a courtroom gallery."

Stroughton's face colored as too did Warner's. Antagonizing General Boulter had been the farthermost thing from the lawyer's mind—but then old habits die-hard. Now he realized he would have to work much harder to win back the ground he felt he held when they first came into the room. "…I understand, General. If I have offended you or the army in any way, then I apologize. It is just that this whole situation has pole axed us towns' folk—most of us are running about like stunned steers!" Don needed time to think and he gained this by making his Stetson fall from his lap to the floor and retrieving it, again.

"So what are the charges against, Boston, General?" the attorney asked humbly, knowing humility never went astray in the service world.

Boulder scratched at the whiskers of his right cheek, and then said: "...Obstructing the Army in its duty by arresting the Captain and Lieutenant when they were about a special assignment. That information comes to me via this here document." The General tapped the Washing directive lying before him on his desk with his index finger.

"Then can I be so bold as to suggest a way in which things might be resolved between Washington and the town Council?" Don asked. The puzzled Warner was wondering how the lawyer could manage such a thing.

"The hour's too late," General Boulder said. "We have a Federal Marshal headed this way with orders to relieve Boston of his authority."

"He's not here at the post, yet?"

The General nodded. "The Marshal's due here the day after tomorrow."

"That will ruin the Sheriff's record," Stroughton explained. "—Does Washington realize that even if Sheriff Boston is defrock, so to speak ... that the criminal charges a will still stand against the army officers and that they will have to be made available to answer them in Junction City's Courthouse, General?" Don Stroughton stated, "And they can't avoid the case even if the Army does try to spirit them away out of reach of the courts!"

"As you so aptly pointed out before, Counselor, "no one is above the law," said the general from under a pair of hooded eyes.

"If I could git Sheriff Boston ter drop, the charges against your men...would it work in Boston's favor?"

"It would go a long way in his favor, yes—might even be able to persuade Washington to reconsider their position on the sheriff losing his office..." General Boulter then looked from Stroughton to Warner and then back to Stroughton. "But tell me, gentlemen. Why are you so damn keen to get this Boston feller out of clink?"

"There is a bunch of folks in Junction City fixin' ter setup a lychin' party," said Jake Warner. "You knew 'bout my injuns wards hittin' the town, General?"

"We heard, and wired Washington for orders," said the Aide.

The General cut in: "I am awaiting their reply to the incident."

"Sheriff Boston has been gettin' right on to it—he wanted to try and save you and your men getting involved. He has already locked up the ringleader ter help keep a lid on it! " Warner lied.

Stroughton saw the lie as a chance of building up Boston's value to the town and played on it. "Without Boston back there in town there is no one else who can keep a lid on that explosive situation, General … The town, in fact the whole district, could go up in flames and then *you and your boys* **will really have yuh hands full!** I don't think the Pawnees at the reservation are gonna sit in contemplation of their navels, do you, General? Once one of their braves has had his neck stretched by a violent mob, it will be just the catalyst to make this land run once more with blood in open warfare!"

"The Sheriff's a cripple," General Boulter reminded them. "He wouldn't be able to do much about holding down a wild mob boiling with hate an' fire in their hearts!"

"You very much under estimate Sheriff Boston and his ability, General," Don Stroughton said. "If anyone can stop that this business boiling over, it's Klem Boston, and that's why the situation needs his calming hand—and fast!

"I know right now you see him as some sort of enemy to the Army by what he did to your Captain Roscoe and Lieutenant Briggs; but on this one you couldn't be more off target! He would've given them all the help they wanted but it seems to me that they were partly at fault by not taking him into their confidence, that's why I am sure he'll drop the charges against them—their Army service records will remain unsullied and no one outside this incident will know that they've ever been arrested…"

"And I c'n verify that," put in Warner. "It wasn't until after Boston arrested your men that` he begun ter think their side of the story might be worth lookin' at.

"I wuz there when yore men came fer him; only jist before they busted down the door of the jailhouse, he wuz toyin' wif the idea 'bout settin' the pair free!"

"I know he took it upon himself to ride out to the reservation and see things for himself, and that is when he got the inkling that the Captain and lieutenant might be telling the truth!" Stroughton added. "Think how it will affect both their careers in the army if these charges against them aren't expunged before they get a chance to surface. Surely you, with your authority can turn the tables on this chaos, General."

General Boulter thought hard about the problem, which they faced here. He did not need something like this hanging over his head this close to retirement with an unblemished service record.

"My hands are legally tied now until the Marshall gets to Hancock; you must appreciate that, Counselor?" He finally told the lawyer.

"Sir, you can make it happen, you are empowered to do it by virtue of your office! *…You must* stand aside Boston's arrest and let him have a free hand to put the lynch mob to bed — even if it is only for seventy-two hours, release the sheriff to me! *We do* need him back in Junction City now, today, not next week that won't check   these hot-heads planning ter stretch the neck of Warner's Indian — you have some responsibility to our cause, surely?"

"D'you *really think* Boston can do what you and this Indian agent claim?" Boulter said in a weakening voice. Was the General starting to bend in the lawyer's favor? The man arose from his chair — this pretty much signaled the end of round one as in a prizefight. Stroughton and Warner reluctantly rose to their feet, too.

"What you are suggesting to me is tantamount to me sticking out my neck so some unknown Washington bureaucrat can chop off a man's head…" General Boulter muttered.

"No, general — I promise you, I'll do all in my power ter see it doesn't happen. Promise!" said the Attorney; the look there in his eyes showed that he meant every word of what he said. But down deep inside it might really be a different story. The general decided to take a punt on Boston and Stroughton, and in essence on Junction City and the faith its citizens the mouthpiece seems to believe is in existence. He relented on the arrest of the Sheriff and took a quill from the inkwell and scratched out an order for the lawman's release. "…This is only temporary so that Boston can return to Junction City and thereby forestall the possibility of an all out Indian war through this lynching business. He's in your charge Counselor and must stay within the town boundaries until the Marshal relieves him and or Washington cancels his arrest warrant.

"Understand this Mr. Stroughton, I'm only granting him a parole, not a pardon, that's not in my power as much as you may think so — the Federal Marshal can sort it out with Washington and the Junction City Aldermen when he hits here. So right, go, go, go, before someone on my staff points out to me where I've gone wrong!"

"Oh, and one more thing, General —"

"Don't push your luck, Mr. Stroughton," murmured Boulter.

"No, this is only something minor — can we all grab a meal in the mess before we set off on our return journey, sir." General Boulter gave a grin to which he could only see the funny side of, and ordered his Aide to take Stroughton's party down to the officers' mess.

Sheriff Boston was brought from the stockade to the mess in manacles which were removed in the hall by the escorting staff sergeant. While the men ate their fill Klem Boston's horse was prepared for its homeward trek.

Boston was obviously glad to see them all except for Frank Cotter, for it was he, he held responsible for his loss of freedom. Especially when Warner explained to Klem; that his freedom was only temporary, that he had been paroled only into Stroughton's authority. And that his release had only been secured by lies and half truths, yet all the same he knew with the Williams brothers being in on the organizing and stirring up a lynch mob, he had a volcano on his hands and he doubted whether or not he was capable of weathering it, for as far as he knew or anyone else for that matter, he could wind up being out gunned by the two men he fears most in Junction City, Harry and Reg Williams.

During the meal, Donald Stroughton leant across the table to Cotter and said: "…Cotter, the reason I didn't want you in the General's office is because in my opinion – you are a Jonah. If I was you I should wait here for the stage bringing that Marshal and climb aboard once he's vacated his seat and get your hide out of the territory. I'll make sure the bank sends your account on and I'll git Pearl Courtney to pack up your gear and forward it to the next bar along the trail, for that is as far as I reckon you will last…!"

"— I'm not leaving town until I am good an' ready!" said the scribe.

Looking in Frank's direction, Klem asked Cotter: "What is Don whisperin' to you about, Cotter?"

"He wants me to pull out of Junction City," explained the victim of Roscoe and Briggs' wrath.

Chewing gristle from the army stew Klem nodded. "Sounds like good advice ter me. Do you realize that I now view you as a born troublemaker, Mister ... Well yuh have been since you hit *my* town. You know, as Sheriff, I could ask ya ter move on and now I think about it, I should have done it the moment you hit town and had no fixed address. When you git back ter J.C., I suggest you find the cost of a stage ticket outa town!"

Frank Cotter now realized that he was fast running out of friends. Thank God he had not set eyes on either Roscoe or Briggs in his travels about the fort. The Mess Stewart came back to their table and told them that General Boulter had arranged overnight lodgings for them as guests of the Army. The three surrey passengers agreed to stay the night, but Klem had had quiet enough of the fort's accommodation and was happy to collect his horse and set off for Junction City, there was little chance of him getting home before nightfall but this did not bother him, only the thought of bracing the Williams boys nagged at his mind — he departed right after filling his belly.

The bugler woke the whole fort from its nightly slumber with plenty of gusto. And the men set to return to Junction City, hightailed it out of Fort Hancock right after a hearty breakfast. But the tension between Cotter and Stroughton was such that there was no way Frank was going to ride up in the front seat of the surrey with the lawyer; he finished breakfast first and then hurried outside and commandeered the rear bench seat for himself.

The weather was telegraphing that it could not to be trusted as big, cumulus clouds in the east seemed to be magnetically attracted to each other, and they closed the gaps between themselves at an alarming rate of knots, by midday the clouds were massing as large as some islets of the Cayman Islands. No one mentioned it but they were all of one mind that the possibility of drenching rain could be on the table.

The atmospheric conditions changed to rain when Stroughton's party was two and a half hours out of Fort Hancock, daylight seemed more like dusk, due to the thickness of the cloud-bank which defused the sunlight like that of a canvas awning. The under belly of the cloud-bank had soon taken on a dark plumb coloring and within the folds could be seen angry gorges, valleys and canyons that looked as though they were made by the hand of Satan — the thunder and lightning displays once commenced, went on endlessly and looked and sounded more spectacular as the clouds in parts, became as black as mined coal. The fright injected in to Ma's Morgan's, made them break out in a sweat and Donald Stroughton warned those on board with him to be ready to jump for their lives if the team took it in to their heads to bolt — for in truth, he wasn't sure of his ability to hold them in check, but after a couple of minutes and the definite signs that a downpour was eminent the attorney brought the horses to a halt and held them on a tight rein while Jack Warner alighted and went round the vehicle, rolling down the weather shades for the onslaught of the threatening change heading their way.

Warner did one side of the vehicle first then the other side belting the shades into place with their small buckles and short straps at floor level, all the time the Morgan's were sniffing at the weather and pawing the ground beneath their hooves and snorting with eyes wide open. The agent avoided going anywhere near them and work around the surrey from the rear. Once the shades were secured he climbed back in beside Donald and the lawyer let the Morgan's have their heads each horse leant into its harness and the surrey was away. Cotter took available of the fact, which he could hunch down in line with Stroughton's body mass that acted as a shield against the heavy rain coming in from the open front of the vehicle. Warner and Stroughton's only protection from the weather were their dusters and they were soon wet right down their fronts —they would continue to get a drenching just so long as the rain-heavy clouds continued to drop their loads…

Entering the sopping town of Junction City was akin to coming across an abandoned ghost town—Main Street was fetlock deep in rushing, mud colored water. Loose flatiron sheeting banged in the gale force winds, business shingles on defiant link chains swung back and forth as though they were within inches of snapping apart and sending the sign flying dangerously through the atmosphere — where it might unleash more destruction… A wooden shutter banged away like a Gatling gun, now the Morgan horses were almost at the end of their tether and the rain that beat down on them was so heavy that no mud splatters clung to their hides anywhere above the fetlocks — the surrey's appearance could be mistaken for a vehicle that had been dredged up for the bottom of a lake-bed.

The team nosed up to the locked double doors of the livery and both seemed to let go an audible sigh that they'd now reached journey's end. Warner reckoned that it had to be after eleven at night. He jumped down on top of the raised level ground before the doors, so constructed to hold out the water flushing down the street, and engineering idea which had developed to ward off floodings of the past.

Jake pounded on the doors with both fists, the whitewash door palings now slick with rainwater; it was his endeavor to get the folks inside by the warm potbelly stove to come and open up. After a pause which suggested that maybe those inside had bedded down, thinking no one would be crazy to be out in these stormy conditions — folks with brains would be tucked up somewhere warm — not even a horny cowboy would be out searching for a cat-house. The wicket inside one of the high, broad doors swung open and was grabbed by the howling wind and slammed into the wet palings at the back of it.

Middle-aged Ben Wright thrust his head and shoulders out through the aperture left by the open wicket with a storm lantern in his hand, the wild wind whipped away his greasy hat — his bald head and upper body got a dousing during the time it took him to recognize the Indian agent…

"You want in…?" Wright bellowed over the noise of the storm.

"No," Warner retorted with an aggravated snarl. "—we're jist out here in this whirlpool fer the good of our health, idjit!" The astringency went over Ben's head, but nonetheless he disappeared from view while he got help from someone inside to drag open the doors that had been barred for the night. Jake stood aside, prepared to continue with being a target for the rain while Stroughton made the horses move forward across the threshold and down the aisle between the stalls occupied by boarded horses and mules.

Donald reined in the dead-tired team and they stood there with heads bowed and trembling with cold, rainwater drained off harness and hide onto the flagstone floor — which showed signs of very poor house-keeping, short straws, chaff and some dry manure the brooms and rakes had missed were clearly in evidence in the gloomy illumination and the background noise of the night's tempest.

The lawyer climbed down off the surrey and moved forward to un-harness the twin horses — while Wright and his cohort wrestled to get the main doors shut and barred, Jake moved down the other side of the Morgan's and begun assisting the attorney to free the horses from the vehicle.

Frank Cotter seemed to wake from his dummy sleep and he too alighted from the rear of the surrey and seemed suddenly awake as his boots touched terra firma. Wright's assistant, Bob Gordon, approached the scribe while Wright went off to lend lawyer Stroughton and Warner a hand with the horses.

"Step this way, sir..." said Gordon as he strode passed the newspaperman and led him along to where the livery staff has a brazier going to put some warmth into the barn-like interior. A flock of wild pigeons were roosting in the rafters and the cold blast of wind that had accompanied the entrance of the surrey and its horseflesh had disturbed them and they were now trying to resettle. "—Yore as wet as a trout and look colder than an Eskimo! This way..." Frank followed in the wake of Bob Gordon.

Donald Stroughton told Wright: "Ma Kelly's horses did a mighty job getting us from Fort Hancock in the one day in such foul weather — see yuh take fine care of them when you bed them down."

Holding his lantern at eyelevel, Wright gazed over the lawyer and Warner in its light, and saw they were tuckered out and as cold as brass monkeys in the middle of winter.

"Git yore selves back up there wif that tenderfoot, pal, in front of the brazier — Bob Gordon c'n help me wif these nags... None of yuh looks fit enough ter dance a polka...Bob, a hand if yuh will down here?" Wright hollered.

Gordon swung away from the heat of the brazier and headed in the direction of Wright, while Warner, eager to rid his bones of their chill, homed in on the burner like a moth to lamplight.

"Can you tidy up my surrey before I need to take it out again, Ben?" Don begged of Wright.

"Sure. I know she's yuh pride an' joy, Mr. Stroughton. I'll see it gits a good wax an' grease the axles, hubs, how's that sound?"

"That's good enough to earn you, a bonus!" Don Stroughton grinned in the man's direction then made his way up to spend some time in front of the burner until there was *a* break in the present squall so he could venture out and home to his bedroom above his chambers.

At the brazier Jake said to Cotter: "What has kept you down in the dumps all day, Mister? That tongue of yours got tied ter the roof of yuh mouth?" Frank stood there over the burner with both palms facedown and fingers splayed gathering all the heat he could. The ex-newsman made no move to answer the agent straightaway; he knew the man was closer to the attorney than he. Say the wrong thing and he knew he'd have another caustic soul against him and his case.

Finally Cotter said: "When a man knows he's not wanted, there is no point in making one's self a damn target for a venomous tongue! If there wasn't a shortage of transport I wouldn't have returned to town with Stroughton!"

"Whoa, I do not wanna buy into that one," Warner said wisely. Already light steam had begun to rise from the damp surface of their dusters. "But if you have those sentiments down there in yuh guts, why didn't you wait back at the fort and board the incoming stage it goes east?" Don arrived at the heater, removed his hat and shook the rain beads from his Stetson to the flagstone floor.

"Have you decided on what your next move is gonna be?" Stroughton said to Cotter without bothering to address him by name or focusing in his direction. The question was a continuance of their last conversation that had been having way back at Fort Hancock's Mess.

"Aw, go stick your head up a horse's ass!" This sudden retort was certainly out of character from what the folks of Junction City had come to expect from Cotter. The scribe twirled away from the burner and stormed off back down to the wicket in the big hefty door, tugged it open and stepped through the aperture out to the street — fighting to get the wicket closed after him.

Outside he used both hands to keep his Stetson in place, as the wind had not abated with the rain that was taking a moment's spell.

Cotter turned eastward and moved down the mouth of the alley which ran all the way through to Starr Street, the very same alley where he had been left in a shocking state by — Roscoe and Briggs, when they had wrung all they could out of him by filling his liver and kidneys with rot-gut, then left him for cowboys and stray dogs to wet on … tonight the alley had by now collected in to mud-pools in the alley's depressions, the aftermath of the storms. He jogged up the lane through the sloppy mud and near ankle deep pools, crossed muddy Starr Street and clumped along the wet boardwalk in the direction of the infamous street intersection where Lomax had met his death, in his trail he left the rain-washed sidewalk stained with the muddy print of his boots. He cut away from the walk and mounted the side stairway to the apartment and fumbled for the door key …Inside the dark apartment he paused with his back against the casing of the door to catch his breath.

Stroughton gazed deep into the red-hot coals of the burner. *Heat can be a mighty dangerous thing,* thought the Counselor. *Especially when it comes from the temper of man…*

"Mebbe it's not my place ter say this counselor —" Warner ventured in a husky voice across the brazier to the Attorney; it was a dead-set give away that Jake Warner was developing a throat infection from exposure to the weather. He continued when the Counselor made no move to still his tongue. "I'm wonderin' if you an' Sheriff Boston aren't bein' too hard on that Cotter feller?

"He came here full of expectations an' all he has got since bein' in Junction City is grief. I reckon he thought a lot of you in some respects — and err… looked upon yuh as someone ter replace the sudden loss of his pal, Doc. Lomax. Someone he could term it in his hour of need. Whaddya' think, Don …? I can't understand why you cast 'im aside like yuh did…? You were pretty harsh on 'im — I reckon?"

"Don't blame *me* fer that," Stroughton warned Warner. "…He did it to himself the first time he crawled down the neck of a bourbon bottle!"

Frank stood with his back against the door — it dawned on him that he was not alone in the dark of the apartment. Instinctively he balled his hands into fists. Was someone there in the dark planning another attack on him? Sweat began to leak through his pours. Suddenly the cat was at his shins and rubbing its fur flanks against the mud splattered legs of his trousers… he now knew he wasn't in danger but was receiving a show of affection by Lester's black cat for being locked up inside away from the ranting, raging weather, which had engulfed the town and the surrounding district.

The cat left him and in the camouflaged blackness of the parlor, it went off to explore the suite with the aid of its night-vision. Frank pushed himself away from the door and crossed confidently to the dinner table where he found the lamp in the middle of the tablecloth spread atop the table as the moon appeared through a cloud break. Moonlight glinted off the lamp's glass reservoir of kerosene… he fumbled for a saucer kept nearby where matches were kept, and ignited a match with the friction of its head on the coarse thread of the cloth and with his free hand, raised the lamp's chimney and lighted the kerosene soaked wick… the room's darkness rolled back as the illumination grew in strength. Frank decided, as he shook the match out — that the cat would have to be put outside where it could find cover and warmth in the wood stack under the staircase, for he did not want the feline wandering about in the apartment. He called the cat and crouched down alongside the table in its shadow and the cat trotted back across to him; he picked the furry pet up with both hands and turned towards the door which had slipped its catch and was slowly but surely being pushed open by the incoming draught. He moved towards the door and in so doing glanced down at the floor and saw two envelopes had been pushed through under the door at some stage in his absence; He gently set the cat down on the landing and collected the mail, then closed the door and this time made sure that the latch, caught. Then he strode across to the table with the envelopes — Cotter was not aware that Junction City had its own house to house mail delivery service until this.

One was a business size envelope and stamped, while the other was a small square homemade envelope without a stamp but smelt strongly of lilac and had been hand written, in a woman's script; He did not perceive the writing and it was this mystery that decided for him, which of the two letters he would open first. He tore open the side of the envelope he supposed that it might be from someone back east he owed money too, and that they had somehow found out where he was living. He shook out a folded sheet of writing paper onto the table, putting aside the enclosure in which it had arrived he unfolded the written sheet…the page was only half used and so before reading its contents he forced his attention to the signature at the end of the text. It was signed by ***Pearl Courtney***.

The note explained that she had left with Peter Kelly on that morning's stage for Kansas City. It seemed that a telegram had come from Peter's relatives in Chicago after they'd received news of his mother's murder and were prepared to have Peter come and live with them. Courtney had been toying with the idea of moving to Chicago in the hope of getting work in that city's theater district, and so coupled the escort duty of Peter Kelly, to that of her venture to the windy city. She did not know how long she would be away, but would definitely have to return to Junction City to tidy up her affairs in the not too distant future.

Frank read Pearl's letter twice. Then finished up by sniffing, the perfumed page, like some lovesick beau. Then he turned to the second letter and found that it was from **THE NEW YORK COURIER**, his article on the Pawnee attack against Junction City had been accepted and would be close to publication by the time he received this letter — included in with the letter was a check for ten-dollars!

The money was certainly going to help. And most exciting of all, was that the Courier also offered him the post of being their correspondent out west and were prepared to offer him a retainer of a $120-dollars per year, should he accept the offer.

Under normal circumstances Frank would have grabbed the offer with both hands, for he now found himself in a favorable position to tell folks back east about his experiences in the West — just to date; however Cotter realized in his opinion, Junction City stank as a town, he would be glad to see the last of it once he has secured a legal inquiry in to Lester's death and rooted out the missing witness, who surely must have something to hide, otherwise, why the disappearing act? He would write a scathing story for the Courier, and thus embarrass the citizens of "Junk City", as he would anoint the town, leaving a somewhat bitter stew for the town folks to swallow— however this wouldn't worry him, for when he left this town it would never see hide of him again in the rest of its existence. Leaving his mail on the table, he went in to the bedroom and turned down the covers — upon his return to the kitchenette he went ahead to stoke up the Franklin stove and put three kettles on the boil so that he might sponge himself down before slipping in to a neck to knee, nightshirt for bed.

16

THEN JUST BEFORE turning in, he padded in slippers back across to the dining table and sat down to re-read Pearl's note against the background of rain beating lightly on the windowpanes — Frank realized the night clouds had closed in again and resumed shedding their water. When he had finished with Pearl's note, Frank arose, broke out Lester's writing material from one of the drawer in the kitchen cabinet and upon returning to the table, spent a fruitful couple of hours working out on a truculent article for the New York paper... His analytical newspaper mind worked quickly on the line this special introduction feature to the readers would take, knowing full well that if he did not make a start on them before bed, he would have a restless night and above all, he felt within himself that tonight he wanted to sleep tight…

Eight hours later he awoke under the covers of Lester's double bed. He had written himself into a corner and had to finally surrender — succumbing to 'Writer's Block' and fatigue. He was so exhausted that his mind could not even generate his usual collection of tormenting dreams, or if it did, he could not remember anything about them. He had a dull headache and a crick in the neck, both he discovered the moment he tried to rise out of bed and resolved to put up with them until they had worked themselves out of his system of their own accord, which, from past experience he knew would happen.

The rain had gone and the sun's charter was set down for it to dry up the mud colored pools of water left lying about, which the parched soil hadn't already absorbed. The scribe prepared himself with a cold wake-up rinse and a change of wardrobe then in the kitchenette check the temperature of the water left in the cast-iron kettles — each was as cold as a Mother-in-law's kiss—he did not feel like stoking the Franklin up and instead headed off to the diner but before that, he was drawn to the table where his previous night's work lay and browsing through it; he gained the curious feeling that the correlation of the pages had been disturbed, they were certainly not how he had left them—it had happened again!

The papers were uncoordinated, strengthening his belief that there was too much prowling going on in this town than was logical to expect or tolerate. As he closed and locked the apartment door Frank wondered if his prowler might be one in the same person, the very sod responsible for Ma Kelly's death…he shivered involuntary at the thought that a killer might have been drifting in and out of the apartment while he slept. He had to alert the sheriff of this and maybe they could set-up a trap and catch the offender and thus solve what appears to be an unsolved murder — but that would be a problem, Klem Boston had made it clear back at Fort Hancock that he was washing his hands of Cotter … the point couldn't have been made any clearer than when Boston suggested that he ought to set his affairs in order and catch a stage out of town.

The woman cashier at the diner never failed to ask Frank Cotter to check in his firearms—every time he passed her station he had to remind her that he was unarmed. Frank was sick of the oft-repeated question; this morning with all his problems it was enough to push him over the edge. He tongue-lashed her so vehemently that the short order cook came out of the kitchen with a meat cleaver at the sound of the haranguing Cotter had given the poor, cowing woman—the cook had grown up tough and wild and was capable of quelling many a Mêlée — having been a chef on the gambling paddle ferries of the Mississippi and dens of inequity — where one had to fight with one's back to the wall if you claimed to be a professional chef. Curt Borchardt barrel-chested, Cotter from the premises along with the threat that he might bring his meat cleaver into play. It was a rather undignified exit to say the least and made worse when the scribe slipped over on the walk in front of the diner's doorway.

Frank had to pick himself up as though he had taken another one of his drunken falls of the past … he straightened his vest and dusted down his frockcoat and the knees of his trousers for the sidewalk was a haven for dust off the dirt road and spittle from male pedestrians. Then just as he was about to set off for another diner he realized that his Stetson had gone amiss, it had rolled over the edge of the walk and landed, near the water trough, the aqua of the vessel brimmed the utility that stood between the fascia board of the sidewalk and the tie-rack, were a couple of saddle horses stood hitched.

"Let that be a lesson to yuh …!" Borchardt snarled at him as he stood in the diner's door under the fanlight. "—don't come here again, or I'll have the law put onto you!" The short order cook stood blocking the doorway with his heavy baulk, in a contumaciously manner.

After Cotter located his hat and stepped down off the walk to retrieve it, he brushed it off and set it back where it belong—his body language clearly betraying his embarrassing exit from the café. He made no effort to hide the scowl he shot the cook as he made it back to the sidewalk and debated with himself that the nearby saloon might serve him a hot breakfast. As fate would have it, it was the very saloon Sheriff Boston and Robeson had made the arrest of Captain Roscoe and Lieutenant Briggs.

Here, Frank Cotter got a serving of four duck eggs delivered sunny side up and a tin mug of piping hot java, laced with goat's milk. In all, it was not a bad meal—the bar didn't smell too overpowering of stale grog from the night before, as fresh sawdust had been spread over the old dry blood spots and spit stained floor—the wear and tear of a short lived fist-fight and the result of plain ignorance in upbringing.

Two cowhands in from the range were holding up the bar and minding their own business. Frank mused into his coffee bean brew that Boston wouldn't have to worry about his re-election if he solved what seemed the unsolvable—Ma Kelly's murder… *Where, and whom is the mystery man from Lester's accident? Why is his existence being so vehemently denied?!*

"Do you want ground coffee or beans…?" asked the clerk at Macquarie Mercantile. The counter jumper had thick hair the color of a Palomino and more youth on his side than Cotter could account for. His clean-face glowed with health and he smelt like he had over experimented with a barber's shop after-shave lotion. Lomax's friend took in the white shop- bought shirt and string tie of the youth that was all of 5 ½ feet tall in his elevated city shoes. "Better make that ground, please," answered Cotter. "— I've no idea if Doctor Lomax has a coffee mill; I haven't seen one about the place…"

"Oh, I see yore Doctor Lomax friend frum back east?" Remarked the clerk, gaily.

"Yes. Guilty as sin on that charge," Frank admitted.

The counter clerk only had to reach down under the counter to get a paper bag of coffee grounds from the shelf, the coffee having been bagged a few days ago. Leaning slightly forward to place the bag on the counter, the friendly feller said: "—He was a very good man, was the doctor. Bytheway, better introduce myself—I'm Derrick Carter!"

"Did you have some professional dealings with Lester, Derrick?"

"I used to be one of his patients," the young man proclaimed proudly. "That was until he became too involved with his work for the Indians. Now, I see Doc Hallway —which, I'd've turned to anyway, seeing that the Doctor died. Dreadful business, gettin' bowled over by a wagon; still, you never know about these things, do ya? "

"No, that's for sure," said Cotter as he took in the price of the coffee penciled on the outer of the bag.

"Anything else you need in the grocery line ter make yore self comfortable, sir?"

"Not too much I hope," Cotter said, thoughtfully. "Having heard about the shocking news of Lester's death I've had to think seriously about returning to civilization. Hmm, but come to think of it, I might need a small side of bacon — oughta be able to make do with that until I bugger off." Cotter would not have dared use that phrase in the presence of female company.

"Fresh, Bacon on the way!" Derrick shipped out to another part of the store to fetch the swine, while Frank continued to hold up the counter and eye off two of Junction City's Womenfolk across at another counter, their eyes were on bolts of fabric resting on the counter-top. The material would certainly cut up into fine looking everyday dresses.

Derrick returned with the side of bacon sheathed in cheesecloth and placed it down on the counter next to the bag of coffee. "— How come yuh planning ter uproot yore self so soon? Why the paint ain't even dry on the walls!"

"Meaning?" said Frank as his eyes took in the clear glass jar of hard-rock candy. "I'll take a small bag of that there, candy, too."

"Got a sweet-tooth, have we?" Derrick asked with a smile as he collected a brown paper bag from a bunch of bags the same size, tied together with string looped through a hole punched in the left-hand corner of the bag and knotted, to a nail embedded in the edge of the counter on the clerk's side of the bench; the nail's gage was the thickness of a sewing needle.

"Occasionally; Say, what d'you mean by that paint business, Derrick?"

Derrick unscrewed the jar's lid and his hand dived in and clawed on to some candy, "You only jist hit town ... One would've thought you'd stay on a piece?"

"I was gonna stay. But the town sheriff and I don't see eye-to-eye over a few issues, so he has asked me to move on. One can't disobey the law — seeing as my late pal's business attorney agrees with him."

"Strange. I've not known Sheriff Boston to be so pushy, before. Still, there's no accountin' fer people is thar...?"

Frank judged that it would be unwise to run the sheriff down in public so ignored Derrick's question. "How much do I owe for these goods?"

"Three dollars will cover it nicely, sir!

Cotter thought the price was a bit steep but said naught and instead fished out the money from the pocket of his vest to cover it.

"I'll be with you in just a moment, ladies," Derrick called to the women who were evidently cross with him for fussing with the stranger in preference to the town's home-grown customers, even though they had entered the store after this male intruder of their domain.

Frank added: "— I would not be surprised of your good Sheriff having acquired a sneaky feeling that Ma Kelly's death is in some way connected to my presence in this town!"

Derrick frowned. "Why do you think that?"

"Because of something Ma Kelly told me about Lester's accident: Yet everyone seems to deny," Frank said.

"Yeah, is that right?" the clerk's eyebrows rode up and his brow went into ridgelines. "What did she have ter say?"

"According to Ma… the woman had a front-row seat to the accident from her upstairs window overlooking the intersection. She all but saw the wagon run the poor doctor down — though she barely just missed seeing the event, she did see folks come running to Lester's aid.

Ma Kelly saw the bloody mess Lester's head was in with the blood and grabbed some towels for it as he was attended too by the five men at the scene; who eventually lifted Lester off the road to the boardwalk under some shade.

"Now the accident's statements given to the local law officer, your sheriff Boston, no one outside of Ma Kelly will attest to there being a *fifth* man there, as only four witnesses made statements and legally that's the witness number but Ma, she reckons there was a fifth man in attendance, who it seems didn't make a statement to Boston — he's like a damn ghost and vanished with the same skill of one! You could liken his disappearance to that of a climbing young boy who vanishes in to thin air in those Indian rope tricks pulled in the squares of overseas bazaars!"

Derrick regarded the tenderfoot with a wary eye as he muttered: "…And now she's dead, there is no one left to confirm what she believed she saw?"

"That's the size of it. I want the sheriff to look more closely in to the doctor's accident, an' check if Ma's murder is linked in some way to all this business," Frank opened the bag of candy and helped himself to a sugar rock.

The youth looked at Cotter for a moment as if he was sitting in judgment of him from the prospect of a juror. Then his superior looked softened, as if the emotion which had created this inner light had toured to the end of the line so Carter then said: "Hmm… you know the feller driving that wagon was a friend of Doctor Lomax? A feller by the name of Sean Dunne and it's hit him very, very bad!"

"I know," Frank proffered the bag of rock candy to Derrick for now he caught the odor of decaying teeth from the youth before him and wanted to sweeten the feller's offensive breath. The clerk had no idea that his breath was offensive. Derrick waved the offer aside because he could not afford such luxuries on his small salary and did not want to acquire the habit. Cotter closed the bag but backed off a half step and the range between them made a great difference to the power of the odor. "— It is partly for his sake in a roundabout way why I should like to find our missing friend; maybe this fifth feller can throw a new light on the accident as an independent witness. But since he has disappeared — everyone involved swears that he never existed so no one's prepared to prove it one-way or the other…."

"And so now that Ma Kelly's dead, you've been left like a ship in dry-dock?"

"That's it, Derrick."

"But you still seriously wanna find this guy?"

"You bet! He might hold the key to this whole strange affair —"

"Look. I can vouch that what Ma Kelly said about that fifth guy helpin' out with the Doc's the truth…"

It touched Frank's water the confident way Derrick had spoken on the matter; it was quite plain that Derrick Carter might know something. "What makes you say that? You aren't this "missing man" by any chance?"

With by just a slight movement of his head, Derrick indicated he wasn't the missing mystery man the scribe could be seeking, for a brief second there he felt like a prospector, who had struck a long lost gold-vein after years of fruitless searching for the mother lode, but had to grimly accept that his find was only pyrite — "fool's gold"!

"I was coming down Starr Street from the uptown end of town towards the intersection of Starr and Bryant — on the same side as Ma Kelly's building. Like her, I didn't see the doctor get hit — but nearin' the corner I realized there had been an accident…I glanced across the intersection and saw five men gathered round someone or something down on the ground, I thought at first it might've been a hound rundown be the wagon. But no, I realized it was a person there in the dirt and the gatherin' was trying ter make up its mind about how best to move the accident victim off the road. That's when I could tell it was a person lying there and it was might upsettin' fer Mr. Dunne. Then it hits me that he must've been the guy drivin' the wagon. Then the five men lifted the badly injured feller up and carried him to the sidewalk under the veranda. Yes, there were five of 'em who lugged the Doctor away an' I know this 'coz with doing mental calculations all day in my job, I'm in the habit of instinctively makin' note of things. I thought I'd give 'em a hand but I was too far off to get involved, besides

I got the notion that there were enough folks there to handle one man, they oughta have been able to lift an Elephant, so I stayed back right out of it."

Suspiciously Frank asked: "I don't recall your name ever coming up as a witness to the accident?"

"No, it wouldn't. I was happy ter keep right out of it. After all, I didn't see that wagon collide with Doctor Lomax or even know how he comes to find himself under the hooves and wheels of the wagon ..."

"Hell," exclaimed Frank. Then in a slightly quieter voice said, "— *I do* wish you had made yourself known to Boston. A statement from you would help no end!"

"It's like this, sir. I have me reasons fer staying out of the limelight."

Frank looked at the counter jumper with narrowing eyes. "Why so? Surely you must realize you've a civic duty to come forward, no matter what reasons you have for holding back?"

"It is sumthin' very awkward for me to admit too and embarrassing. Mebbe if I explain to you my reasons for staying out of it, but you've got to be prepared ter keep it between you and me, sir. Gawd, if it gets out around town I'll wish I was dead and people will be laughin' me all the way out of town!"

"I can promise you, if this phobia's not related to Lester's accident, it will strictly be kept between you and me, right?"

Derrick nervously and unnecessarily brushed back his hair, licked his lips with the very tip of his tongue. "OK...here it is... I, I talk to myself when I'm out walking alone.

"I tell myself adventure stories like you read in books; I make 'em up as I go along. Sometimes I am so caught up in my imagination, that I ferget myself and start to answer aloud to some of the characters livin' in my head! Now does that make good sense fer a grown man ter be doin', does it, sir?"

Frank looked hard at the youth. "Are you on the level? You hear actual voices in your head?! ... How long has this been going on?"

"From the time I was about five or six."

"How old are you now?"

"I'm not sure exactly... nearly twenty," the clerk frowned.

"I see. I'll tell you this. Your secret's safe with me. But I must tell you here and now, I can't use your information. You're a romancer — you live in a world of fantasy, you're of no help to me unless … **unless** you know the identity of my wanted man — give me that, and we might be in business and able to track this feller down, that is of course, if he is a local!"

Derrick Carter shook his head and this displaced some of his flaxen hair. "When the men picked up the Doc from the dirt, the attorney positioned his own body so that it hid the identity of the man you'd be interested in, from even me."

This is disheartening, thought Cotter, then stated: "This mystery man seems to get all the breaks when it comes down to having his identity protected. Ma Kelly was at the wrong angle to get a good look at his face – she said his hat's brim was too wide and acted like a mask!"

"Most people who spend time in the outdoors have ter wear a suitable hat, sir…" Derrick Carter explained.

"Excuse me," called one of the two women still waiting over at the far counter, "but might we have some service Mr. Carter. One cannot devote all their time to the gentleman, surely?"

"Look this is embarrassing, but you'll have to excuse me — " The humble clerk said.

"— Go right ahead, Mr. Carter — we shall have ourselves another chat, later…" Cotter collected his meager purchases and turned away from the counter, doffing his hat in the direction of the ladies who looked as though they could be some of the local Church Committee's womenfolk, the woman gave him a couple of dark looks before turned away in a most truculent manner.

Stepping out of the shop onto the sidewalk, Cotter practically collided with Attorney Donald Stroughton.

"Sorry about that Stroughton!"

"…That's awright," Stroughton stopped and by the look on his face he seemed to be in a more amicable mood than when they were last in each other's company. "— been doing your shopping?"

Frank changed the bacon parcel across to his other hand. "Yes — Some gear for the larder."

"I shouldn't buy too much food, if I were you… Have you booked on the outgoing stage, yet?"

"You're pushy, Stroughton. It's almost like a disease spreading throughout this town. But 'fraid I'm going to be a thorn in your side for a while longer —"

"Oh, howzat?"

"I have been picked up as a correspondent for a New York newspaper and they want me to hang about here for a while — they are interested in what might come out of this raid the Pawnee bucks made on the town. So I'll be busy putting pen to paper. Oh, and I just got some interesting news which might foul yours and a few other folks anchor lines around here, too…"

"That, so?"

"I have unearthed a witness who can verify that there was *a fifth man* helping you Samaritans at the accident — what do you think about that?!"

"I hope your witness isn't that darn mule skinner, Burnacre?"

"I am not prepared to name names at the moment, but it will come out in good time."

"Well, if'n it's **Burnacre** I can tell you as a witness he's the most unreliable person in Junction City one can put their faith in."

"I am not saying. However it goes to prove that Ma Kelly's head count was correct and that you and your pals are just too damn eager to sweep her statement under the carpet!"

"Rubbish!"

"…I am beginning to think there is more to Lester's accident than meets the eye." Frank told him bluntly.

"The only people you can count on are the people who were there at the scene when it happened. Ma Kelly came along after the event and this so-called witness you say you've dug up, couldn't have been within a hog's breath of the scene 'coz *I was* there, an' I can account for the others being there!" The attorney still did not like the look buried there in Cotter's eye, even after what he had just said, it made the lawyer most uneasy but he set himself the task of hiding it.

Cotter ventured the councilor a sly grin then turned on his way.

Most of the pedestrians had taken to strolling the walk on the shady side of Main Street at this time of the day — even the saddle horses were hitched to the tie-racks for experience riders took advantage of avoiding hot leathers, it is no delight for a man's scrotum to feel as though it's been touched with a branding iron.

Sheriff Boston limped towards Cotter as he made his way uptown from somewhere down near Bryan Street's way. The scribe got the impression that the lawman was not even going to be bothered giving him the time of day, so Cotter deliberately blocked the officer's way. Annoyance flared in Boston's eyes at being made to check his rhythm.

"Are you loco?" Klem snapped, as he looked the tenderfoot up and down. "…try sumthin' like that again with me, an' I'll put a bullet in yuh foot, which'll hurt you for a lifetime!"

"Hold on, I've something for you!"

"I want nuthin' you've got, Cotter!"

"I have found someone else who c'n corroborate that Ma Kelly's head tally at Lester's accident was right…"

"I don't care. As far as I'm concerned, that man's accident has been dealt with to *my* satisfaction. It is over with. So shut the gate and git on wif life; finish off the job you've started which is pickling what's left of your brain!"

"You can't do this — yuh wrong, Klem!"

"I've been wrong before an' I am sure I c'n live wif it! …That all you've got ter say?"

"No."

Klem's brows went up like those of a ventriloquist's puppet. "Awright," He said like a tired old man, "let's have it, git it orf ya chest so I can sleep easy tonight."

"Someone's still getting into Lester's apartment to snoop around — I don't know what their motive would be or who they are, but I have had all this sneaking around I can stand, I've had it right up to my fuckin', gills!"

Klem regarded Cotter for a moment or two and could see that the man was sincere. ***Pacify the man*** was the command that came to light like a heliographic message in his head. "What makes you so sure of this? Last time you had unwelcomed guests it wuz the Army. They're out of the frame, so who d'you suspect now?

"Understand, you have caused me a great deal of trouble and I am not going ter get caught out again!"

"If I knew that, I wouldn't be wasting time trying to get you involved once more, would I?"

"I'm no professor. I'm not sure what you'd do today or tomorrow — frankly I'm not sure I even understand yuh."

"I have been engaged by a city newspaper to write follow up stories on the town since that Indian raid. Last night I wrote up part of a feature article that I intend sending out east for publication. This morning, when I was sorting through it I realized that the pages were out of sync in places, which means that someone had been sorting through it and got the pages out of correlation —"

Boston folded his arms across his chest and rocked back on the heels of his boots... "— and that's yore proof that you've had prowlers?"

"When I'm working and come to the end of workload I always leave it nice and orderly, I am fastidious with my work—" Cotter could see the look of doubt in the lawman's eyes "— drunk or sober I don't leave my writing in a mess, yes, someone was *there* prowling about. Believe me, if this business doesn't cease I'm gonna see *Yolson* about a gun and I swear, I'll shoot anyone pussyfooting about the surgery without good reason!"

"Don't waste yore time with that Russian gunsmith... He'll rip a city slicker like you orf."

"*I* don't think so. You are the only one here trying to fob me off!"

Boston shook his head, "Not me."

"Then believe what I am telling you! I know I haven't lost my marbles, yet. I know when my stuff has been moved. Maybe it is Ma Kelly's *real* murderer, we don't know?!

"If I bow to this latest request of yore's and it comes ter nuthin', will you git out of **my hair** and out of **my town** when my investigation's through?"

Inwardly Frank was most reluctant to wholly agree with Boston's demand, but it looks as though this is the price he'd have to pay to get the lawman's help, then he would pay it.

After all, he could always back track on his word; a result is what counts. There was no one in this town now that meant a hill of beans to him except Pearl Courtney, and who knew when she would get back to this town of contemporary buildings.

"That's fine then... We'll get together about this later..." Sheriff Boston started to edge by Cotter.

My God, Sheriff Boston is giving me the brush-off; I can feel it in my water! Cotter thought. He could feel his emotions getting the better of himself as he sensed that he was being handled like some senile old reprobate that ought to be hidden away from the public. To avert the likelihood of tears and making a fool of himself, he sent his eyes dancing about like billiard balls bouncing off the cushions of a pool table.

Boston saw the look in the newspaperman's face and knew that he had not pulled off the smooth brush-off, he thought. He decided he owed the poor fellow an explanation. "I know this isn't very satisfactory for you; but while I wuz bein' held in the stockade my problem here jist got bigger an' bigger; some folks still wanna wrap a rope round my Injun prisoner's neck — the situation is a festerin' boil on this man's ass. I'm gonna have me hands full cuttin' out that carbuncle a-for it gits outa control. Right, now, the men stirrin' the pot are the Williams boys — I've never been keen on the idea of standing up to either one of them, why? I don't know…mebbe they've got my name on one of their cartridges and sumthin' here is warning me 'bout it," (the Sheriff tapped his chest just over his heart's position) "I do not know, only wish I did. Let me sort this lynchin' business out and then I promise; we'll deal wiv yore problem — cross me 'earth an' hope ter die!"

"Sorry — I apologize," pouted Cotter.

"Right," Klem said as he moved away from Frank. "…A day or two is all I need then come an' see me." The Sheriff then continued on with what it was he was doing before Cotter had accosted him.

Farther up Main Street, the Sheriff came upon Lazarus Rollo strolling down the walk with his teenage bride, Brook. Lazarus has set tongues wagging when he married the lass before a preacher man — who had passed through Junction City, for none of the local preachers or a Judge would abide the marriage of a thirteen-year-old to a man of his age.

Rollo was dressed in one of his impeccable three-piece suits, which had become his trademark now that he was a big shot in the community. Lazarus opened up the conversation as the Sheriff limped heavily to within a yard of the couple.

"Howdy, Sheriff; Out an' about on your daily patrols, I see?" The President/Chairman of the Cattlemen's Association remarked.

The folks halted on the boardwalk in front of a weed strewn vacant block, squeezed between two buildings. Now the street awnings had petered out, Brook Rollo put up her parasol, for she had delicate skin which had yet to come to grips with the sun of these open skies; Brook's husband and the sheriff wore Stetson's against the sun's harsh rays but Brook preferred her bonnet and parasol.

"No, that's me deputies jobs. But it's to do wif business." Then the sheriff turned to Mrs. Rollo. "Afternoon Missus Rollo, look I'm sorry but I must borrow yuh husband fer a few minutes ter talk shop, that awright wif you, ma'am?" Klem waited for her permission, and then drew Lazarus aside.

"No need to apologize — I'll slip across the street to window-shop in Morton's jewelry for apiece…" She stepped lightly away from the men without awaiting her husband's approval and crossed the dirt road, holding the hem of her dress clear of the ground's surface. Brook was not alone when it came to admiring Morton's eye-catching baubles on the display trays he dressed the window display with, there were more than enough cowboys who had continually near empty pockets as a result of their female acquaintances, being bewitched by the bracelets and bangles of silver and gold brought in from afar. This was especially done if they were courting a damsel with honorable intentions.

Lazarus kept a patient eye on Brook until she was safely across the street on the opposite sidewalk. She lowered her parasol and furled it before settling down to viewing the rings and precious stones and semiprecious gems.

"And what business is it you think you have with me, Sheriff?" asked the Chairman.

"You would have ter be deaf, dumb and blind not ter know that there's rumors circulatin' town of a lynch mob gettin' ready ter string up *my* redskin without a trial. *I know* the Williams boys are behind it. So tell the brothers ter pull their horns in or they'll find 'emselves in a cell next to the Injun. **And *I mean it*** — even if it comes ter me as the Law, running them and their guns outa town!"

"Moving the brothers on Sheriff, is a pretty tall order." Rollo informed the lawman after taking a deep breath; he hooked his thumbs in the forward pockets of his burgundy vest.

"They're lawfully employed, so I can't see what grounds you could use to run 'em out of town, if'n either you or yore deputies could pull it off. Especially, if those boys were ter dig their heels in!"

The Sheriff shifted all his body weight on to his good leg and continued on in his official capacity. "They are yore men Mister Rollo and I always thought I could rely on you ter keep 'em in line; otherwise I'll have no choice but ter step in. After all, I always thought that wuz what you and the council paid me for, to head-off any likely stampedes headed our way! "

"C'mon sheriff, you sound like you've been taking advice from a lawyer?" Lazarus looked Boston over like he was inspecting a new breed line of Bull.

"In the past I rode both sides of the line for you an' the Association, and I didn't mind doing it. There wuz never ever any need ter bring those pair of gunslingers to town. They are a pair of vipers, no more and no less. Besides, no one wuz bucking you or yore authority, I saw ter that. We both know that there are some folks in this town reckon I have always been too close ter you fer my own good, and mebbe in the past they're right. But that Army arrestin' me has made me see the light. If you respect a man and what I've dun fer you in the past, you'll do what I'm askin'. What yuh say?"

"Rope me up like a hog if I'm wrong, but I think I detect a note of fear in yore voice when you talk of the Williams boys? That's not all bad; in fact it's the sort of thing I expect of folks 'round here while they ride fer me. Look, leave yore problem with me and I'll see where we get with a little talk to the brother's jis', fer you, right?"

"— By the way, sir, what you see in my eyes isn't what you think is *fear,* but *caution.* Bear in mind, if I have ter face that pair head-on, I'll make sure the odds are stacked in my favor — if you know what I mean, sir?"

"Yore not plannin' ter dry-gulch 'em?" Rollo's eyes narrowed.

Boston said no more, but dipped his Stetson to Rollo as an indication that their articulation was at an end. But upon the big man's departure, he added: "— be assured Sheriff, yore message will get through on that account … how much notice they'll take, I can't say. Good-day Sheriff, have a nice one."

Rollo crossed the street to collect Brook.

"— I'm sorry dear," Rollo said to Brook as she turned from the window display towards Lazarus. "Something's come up and I have to get back to the office," Rollo took Brook by her elbow and steered her away from the shop to the edge of the sidewalk into the glare of the sun.

"Oh Lazarus, does this mean our lunch date's off?" whined the girl/ bride.

"There'll be others; you'll see…"

Pouting with the sulks Brook said: "I knew I shouldn't have let you stop and talk with that Sheriff. Whenever something comes up he can't handle, he expects you to wave your magic wand and put it right. He gets paid to do a job and you should make sure he does it!

The cattle business and the running of this town are always going ter come between us like a wedge. I hate it — ***I really, really do!"*** she stamped a shoe on the walkway planks.

Gruffly Lazarus ordered his new bride to behave. "Don't you ***ever dare*** to stamp yore foot at me again, in public!!? …People are always watching me and I won't stand for it!"

"I don't care Lazarus, do you hear? **I don't care!"** (Her voice had that bitch-witch tone to it, and realized the spectacle she must be projecting to passersby, she lowered her voice — "Folks in this town expect too much from me!"

"Brook, you've gotta stop carrying on like a spoilt child! You'll force me to take a razor-strap on you like a parent treats any wayward child." Rollo exclaimed.

"Then in that case, this spoilt child shall leave you to get back to your precious office. I shall find my own way home, good-day!" Brook snapped at Rollo, and then flounced off on a course of her own.

The Williams brothers lounged with all the cockiness in the world on the Chesterfield in Rollo's office as they heard him out.

"…So that's the word frum Sheriff Boston. But regardless of what he says, it is *I* who want you two to easy up a little on this lynchin' business. It is an awkward time for Boston and this town. He has that business of his position with the Army yet, to face, he could end up being drummed out of the law game over the arrest and those two soldiers. If you stupid cusses dirty Boston's copybook with a hangin', it could be jist the excuse Washington needs ter send in the Army and put the town under Martial Law — which will clip everybody's wings in this town, the Association and the 'Masons!"

"Are you backin' out of the kitchen Mr. Rollo, 'cause things are gettin' a bit hot?" Reg Williams suggested as he dropped his right ankle off his left knee and hunched over slightly. "You wuz all fer seein' that our Pawnee friend got what's owed ter, 'im?"

"—We thought we wuz playing things jist like you wanted 'em, Mr. Rollo," Harry Williams said, as he brought one of his twin Colts from its holster and started toying with its chamber…but not to threaten or put any fear in to Lazarus Rollo, because he was too big for a cheap trick like that, but because, he liked the feel of each click's vibration passing from the weapon to his body and this felt grand and even interested him, more than Rollo's lecture: "In my book, it is worth the risk to have that brave kilt, and the safest way is having a mob run amuck an' do it. If we wait about fer the legal eagles ter do the job fer us, it could take years an' years of court's time, before this Injun gets his neck slipped through a noose — I fer one, think we should push it to the hilt…"

"And— I order you an' your brother ter nip it in the bud!" Rollo cut in. He opened the desktop cigar box and selected a longish thumb-thick Havana… "I thought I made it clear to you guys that the Cattlemen's Association rôle in all this business is that we put a halt to the Indian claim for grazing rights, for their government supply of cattle, to our land holdings — that's why I didn't butt in on Doc Lomax's snake medicine business with 'em, specially when I heard frum the Indian agent what effect it was having on some of 'em. The more it killed or crippled meant the less braves we might have ter tangle with, later if it comes down to doin' a little pushing an' shoving…"

Rollo paused while he circumcised the cigar's end with a clipper before placing it between his lips and torching it. Fumes from the phosphorus match head only had a short lifespan until the cigar became active. "The reason I encouraged you fellers ter get that jailbird's neck stretched, wuz ter knockout any more of them Pawnee braves gettin' more big ideas about grabbing hold of a Sharps or whatever and throwing hot lead down on us whites," Lazarus blew cigar smoke towards the ceiling. "That is why I wuz for yore idea at first, boys. But now another line of thought slips ter mind; if the Army takes over the running of the town, on behalf of Washington; they'll snatch whatever they deem necessary fer the Indian cattle and the Association will lose out…"

"So as long as the army is kept at arm's length, the argument fer land will be momentarily forgotten?" Reg said.

Rollo nodded.

"Hooray, now yuh using that thing God gave you on the top of your neck, Reg!" Lazarus told him and took another pull of tobacco leaf, smoke. Then went on: "With the Army held at bay, *we — the Association,* can control the grazing rights in the district as we have in the past..." He turned to Harry. "Do you get my drift?"

"OK," Harry said. "I'm beginnin' ter see the mark yer makin' in the sand. But it doesn't—look good fer Reg and me, 'Specially to the men we've been working up into a lather about this lynchin'. I don't know if we can stop the avalanche that's ready ter break loose.

"You brought us here ter ride roughshod over the Association's troublemakers and do yore dirty work and now you want us ter eat crow? That's gonna weaken our stance in this burgh and then we won't be the muscle-power you wanted us for."

"I'll have to concede you that point," Rollo tapped cigar ash in to the ashtray. "But sometimes to win ground you've got to back up a yard or two. I'd love the folks here abouts who have lost relatives in fights with the Indian to have their revenge on Clearwater —a hemp collar or a lead pill's justified, **hell** I know that ... But if'n we believe in civilization coming to Junction City then we've got ter let folks see that Law and Order works and this town is above mob rule!

"After all I have yuh ter keep people in line fer me... I hope I c'n depend on yuh pissing out the fire you've lit an' cool folks off. In fact I *know* I can count on you not to let me down, right? " Rollo stuck the cigar in his mouth and took a long pull and waited patiently for the cigar's smoke to have its desired effect.

"If that's the way you want it, sir.' Harry said as he rose from the davenport and shoved his pistol deep into his holster, "—Jist realize yuh might be diggin' yore own grave..." Harry, being the one nearest the clothes' tree, gathered his brother's Stetson and passed it on and then took charge of his own hat, which he clutched to his chest.

"Oh...and one more, thing —" Lazarus Rollo said as he came out from behind his desk in the brothers' direction. "— make sure it's done properly, leave no loose cannons on the prowl...it's always the loose cannon that's a danger to any venture; d'you get me, fellers?"

They nodded—their actions reminiscent of a couple of marionettes.

"Loud as a mission bell, Mr. Rollo…" Harry answered for the pair of them. Then he turned to Reg and went on sarcastically: "And jist how clear is that to you, brother?"

"Oh as clear as them fancy Paris chandeliers 'round the Theater Royal," Reg said, then to Lazarus added: "That clear to you, sir?" He said, blank-faced.

Rollo knew that the Williams boys were trying to take the Mickey out of him, so ignoring them and went on to say: "The lynching is off, right?"

"No worries," Reg said. Then he tapped himself on the temple with his forefinger; "It's built on a strong foundation in here…"

"And jist how strong is that, Reg?" Harry asked his sibling as they neared the door to the outer office—Reg wrenched open the portal and momentarily paused briefly to answer his brother' question.

"Strong— as a skunk's fart!"

Harry turned in Rollo's direction and added with a nod over his shoulder: "An' brother that's a mighty strong piece o' wind frum where yore standin'…"

"Very funny boys, very funny—that wit of yours wants hog-tyin' before it gets away and causes damage!" Rollo ushered the droll comedians from his office suite.

Later that day, in the back portion of the Blacksmith's establishment on Main, the Williams brothers had gathered together a small group of business men who had responded to the call to form a lynching party that was planning to take justice into its own hands, as far as the brave, Clearwater was concerned. They were attending the meeting the brothers had convened that had grown out of their meeting with Chairman Rollo. The quorum was made up from people who had a vested interest in a mob rule, theory. But alas it was a shocking surprise to their way of looking at things when it came home to roost, that they were being ordered to drop the whole idea of a necktie party and back off to leave Clearwater to face the justice of the courts.

"Bah, this is completely out of order," said the Smithy in his soiled work clothes. "You men are the driving force behind this hangin' business—now yuh says its orf!" The Smithy was all steamed up like a kettle on the boil.

"Hold on," bawled Reg to the audience before him and his brother.

"Hold on, nuthin'..." The Smithy hollered

"Keep yuh voices down," ordered Harry. "No one is s'posed ter know anythin' about this gathering... This is s'pose ter be *all* secret like—I know some of you is 'Masons and ought to know all about keeping, secrets!"

Wally Tourner tried again at a much softer level. "Every man here has g-g-g-good reasons to hate the Injuns; there's not a man here, who hasn't lost a relative at some time or the other in raids and, skirmishes." Then forgetting himself, roared: **"Our blood is high and by God we are gonna see it through!"**

By this, Harry Williams had climbed up atop of a couple kegs of furrier's nails and another one of iron horse-shoes which only need a bit of tailoring by the blacksmith to fit individual hoofs.

"Jist hold yuh 'orses a minute," Harry said sharply, his eyes boring into the faces of the assembly below him. "It must be understood, that it is not *us* doing the backing out—it is the unofficial mayor of Junction City, an' I know **you all know** who that is wiv out me naming names. So make it easier on all of us jist go crawl back down in yore gopher holes fer a spell!"

"So," said Lansky rising up from his seat on a roll of tarpaper, "— that's all been a waste of everyone's time and a lot of hot air!"

The storeroom was truly a crowd of mixed feelings at the moment, like that of a Caesar salad. The brother's scanned the faces in the mob to see if they could sight anyone here who had the look in their eyes that they might go it alone—back-shoot the damn Pawnee through the window of the cell, which faces alley. It was not easy to try and take on the role of a "seer" without any worthwhile experience at it.

Ike Rose? Nothing: *Wally Tourne,* nothing: *Luke Moore?* Nothing: *Jimmy Long?* Nothing: *Graham Greene?* Mebbe.... The brothers shared the same views of the bunch and without any confab decided that Greene was the man most likely to work cowardly under the shadow of darkness. They had to get him away from the others so the he can't sway anyone to join him. Harry said: "...I reckon you all know what Lazarus Rollo wants and if you know what's good for you, you'll play along with 'im. So I reckon this meetin's achieved all it's gonna achieve. Gentleman, let's call it a day..."

The meeting began to break-up but the blacksmith called for quiet.

"…Before you all leave like a herd of buffalo—a moment of yore time," Though the Smithy was a robust man he was not just all brawn and muscle. "We don't wanna attract attention as per usual; I suggest you leave one at a time out the back down Gibbs alley, for yuh homes."

"Good thinkin'," added Reg. "But mebbe we all shouldn't leave by the back. Someone on the street might've noticed a few of us come in here through the front, and it'll sure look darn peculiar if no one goes back out that a-way—so some, better mosey out by the front, right?"

"OK," said the Smithy to the brothers. "Then that better be you guys, yore a conspicuous pair." He picked up his leather apron and tied it back on, having removed it before the meeting. Harry took a head-count and he noticed that Graham Greene and Lansky had gravitated together and was carrying out a conversation of their own. Harry decided that he would like to know what they were discussing so he moved in on them.

"Mind my company fer a bit?" Williams asked.

His brother, Reg had cornered the blacksmith to arrange for his horse to have its shoes looked at.

"Not at all," said Lansky. "But you have to be prepared ter get a roasting."

"How, come?" He hooked both thumbs through the belt of his six-gun shells.

Graham Greene took over: "I and Lansky aren't happy to hear the change of heart that Mr. Rollo's had…"

"And what makes you think me and my brother are high on it? We only deliver Rollo's messages, don't mean ter say we agree wiv everything he says. We've got no love fer them redskins, they kilt off members of our family too, ya know?"

"It sticks in my gizzard the fact that all this has been fer nothing…" said Lansky. "Hell, look at the trouble my wife went to…" He produced a blue mask hood from the inside of his coat, it was hand stitched from two pieces of cloth with round eye-holes cut out for the wearer; it looked smart and a bit in line with the type of hoods wore by the Klu Klux Klan, the organization a good many folks knew about, though the Klan didn't have a chapter established in this part of the territory..

"Might, I…?" Greene says as he held his hand out for the mask—Lansky handed it to the fellow who went ahead and began a close examination of the item, as though looking for flaws.

"Bernice thought it would be a good idea if we all wore 'em or something like it. She didn't want any of us vigilantes, getting fingered as being in on the hanging" Lansky watched as Greene turned the mask inside out, then raised his brows in surprise at the craftsmanship, Lansky's wife had put into it. "Want a look?" Lansky asked Harry.

"—Bernice poured her heart into this, as you can see…" Graham Greene passed it across to Williams who turned it the right way out and poked his index finger through the aperture of an eye-hole.

"How many she make?" Graham asked Lansky, while looking at the mask in Harry's hands.

"Only the one; as a sample…she thought if everyone in the party wore a mask no one could be singled out later by Boston and his men." Lansky retrieved the mask from Williams and stood there toying with it in his hands. "She reckons the other womenfolk should help out making masks for their husbands, patterned on this one; but it's all gonna go by the boards, now I guess…"

"Why d'you say, that?" said Williams looking rather smug with himself.

"No one will buck Rollo in this town, you know that!" Graham said, "You brothers are his muscle."

"Aahh, but that's it…Who knows where a loose cannon lies hidden?" Williams started rolling himself a curly. "Rollo said in his own office only to-day, that the likelihood of loose cannon doing the wrong thing could ruin the town's business in more ways than one…" He rubbed the tobacco he had in the palm of his hand with that of the other, while closing his tobacco-pouch with the draw strings in his teeth and allowing it to dangle there, where it swung like a pendulum as he continued to talk through clenched teeth while manufacturing his smoke.

"Now if someone wuz ter take it into their own head to deal out a bit of punishment to that redskin while he wuz curled up nice and warm in his cell—who could blame some do-gooder? All it would take is fer some feller ter sneak down along the alley at the back of the jailhouse, and put a bullet in the brave as he sleeps. Why, the shooter might even go there wearing a mask so no one would know his identity... Boston can only blame himself if he hasn't got the brains ter close off an' set-up a guard in the lane behind the jail, now, ain't he...?

"BANG, BANG — all over in a flash!!" Harry said, then licked the gum-line on his cigarette paper and stuck it down and pocketed his tobacco pouch. "All it would take is a feller with a steady hand and be a bit swift on his feet. Take that mask yore holdin', Lansky, somethin' like that would save his skin. But you would need ter keep yore trap shut about it fer ever and a day, it's an act I guess would take a very special man ter pull orf, one who keeps it all locked away and never brags about it, not even to his best, friend ..."

"He would have ter be prepared to be a silent hero for ever and a day — that about the size of it, Harry?" asked Graham Greene.

"That's it! A "silent hero" — you've hit the nail right on the head, Graham, right on the head!" Harry fired up his curly and then shook out the unwanted match and tossed it away on the storeroom floor.

"If something like that happened, you wouldn't look too good in Rollo's eyes," Lansky pointed out to Harry.

"Why me ...?" Harry said.

"Well Mr. Rollo sent you down here to make sure this lynching caper got swept under the carpet. If the Indian gets murdered it will mean the end of Boston in this burgh, won't it?" Lansky questioned.

"Is that a big deal or somethin'? Who gives a rat's tit about Klem Boston? I would love ter pistol-whip him in a dark alley some night, but young Reg would out run a stampede ter beat me to the punch!"

"The Army marched Boston off outer here before, an' they'll sure do it again," Graham Greene said. "I bet if the Injun does buy it in Klem's cell, the Army will come down on Junction City like a ton of bricks, we might even find ourselves under Martial Law and Rollo and you boys won't like that!"

"That can't be helped," Harry said. "I, Reg and the law can't bolt down every loose cannon in the city."

"True. What will be, will be..." said Greene. "I'm going now — I'll go out the front way as you suggested, Harry. You two fellers take care of yourselves now!"

"Sure will," said Harry as both he and Lansky nodded. Graham Greene left. Lansky and Harry were then joined by Reg whom had wound up his conversation with the blacksmith.

"I saw you fellers having a good jaw-wag from over yonder. What wuz that all about?" Reg asked.

"Nuthin', much," Lansky told him in answer to Reg Williams' question. "Well, no point to hanging about here any longer — I am better off home with Bernice. Good-bye, you two!"

"See you about," Harry answered.

Once the brothers were by themselves, Harry told Reg that he hoped he had sewn the seed for either Lansky or Graham Greene to take matters into their own hands with regard to

Clearwater. Reg did not like it, he felt that Harry was double crossing Rollo but understood that his brother must have his motive for playing such a dangerous game, even though he could not see where his brother was coming from.

17

FOR THE SAKE of keeping the peace all rounds, Cotter tried out the diner in the uptown section of Starr Street — it was closer to home than his usual haunt. It served a different clientele and a plainer menu. In reality it was a "greasy spoon" that had simply migrated west for a quick dollar. Its popularity was tame in comparison to the place frequented by Sheriff Boston and the likes of Stroughton, Hill, Bevan et cetera, this could have been due to the fact that the building was only straight across the street from the Mortician's establishment: and perhaps the sight was unsettling to some people who didn't like being unconsciously reminded of their mortality status by its presence — the diner's counter was profile to the funeral parlor's front door and if the thought of the dead lying directly across the street numbed the appetite, avoidance of such a reminder could be had by gazing at the shelves of alcoholic liquor beyond the shoulder of the clerk, who had a ready pencil behind his ear and a scribble pad on hand to jot down your order for food or drink — all the cooking was done out in a back room located to the right of the customer at the counter — down the bottom of the enterprise, the food order was either served at the counter or delivered to one of the eight round-top tables that sat four apiece, scattered throughout the remainder of the diner's interior; like some of the town's saloons this diner's floor boards in the customer's area was generally covered with a carpet of sawdust was renewed every three days, its main purpose to absorb spit from the customers and soup or stew spillage and ward off breakages to crockery...an unsuspecting reward was that it keep the noise of tramping footwear down.

Frank made it a rule to stop off at the counter on the way through to leave his meal order, and then he would saunter over to where a vacant table located almost hard up against the east wall. Invariably he would choose the chair with its back to the street. Most of the folks who patronized the business were strangers to Cotter and he to them, there were a few who called in from time to time whom he knew by sight but he preferred to sit alone at the table of his choice.

Roland James, the stage clerk and the front of house funeral parlor staff were on nodding acquaintance with him but other than that, the rest who passed under the diner's lintel were foreigners.

Today Roland James entered from the street and ordered breakfast at the counter as too was his usual routine — he was more than likely on his way to work, thought Cotter. Even though the scribe practically owed the Englishman his life, he remained a bit distant to him, something he himself could not explain. It is sometimes like that with people, and yet there is no reason one can explain why.

James often saw the scribe at the table either waiting to be served or in the middle of a meal when their paths crossed. Cotter always reminded Roland James of a riverboat gambler, they way he sat with his back to the wall, ready to face up to a disgruntled looser looking to reclaim his losses from a card game that had not been played on the up'n'up. But this morning the Englishman was earlier than usual and surprised the scribe by approaching him and asking if he might share the scribe's table. Cotter had no reason to refuse the request and not only nodded his approval but pushed a chair directly across from him out with the toe of his boot.

"…Not at all," said Frank and he turned on the charm, which chased his morning blues off in to another corner of his mind, somewhere. *Maybe this is a good as way to break the ice,* thought the newspaperman.

James caught the eye of the counter jumper and signaled that he would be dinning with Cotter so the busboy would know where to bring his order. The short-order cook was also behind the counter collecting a tin of lard hidden away out of sight on the shelf under the bench-top—the counter jumper pointed out the new seating arrangement s at Cotter's table so that their meals wouldn't go astray.

"So how is Mr. Corbin these days?" Frank asked the limey by way of opening up their conversation.

"OK, when I last saw 'im yesterday," Roland answered as he settled himself at the table.

Because of the early hour the atmosphere in the street outside was caught up in morning mist which one could rightly assume would be burnt off as the morning sun gathered strength.

"I notice that you've become a regular here these days Mr. Cotter – I thought you frequented Werner's diner on main?" queried Roland.

Cotter hand no intentions of spilling out the real reason for his change of venue but came up with a lie which has a reasonable amount of gut to it to be acceptable. "I felt like a change—besides, this establishment is near to my apartment than Werner's." With that Frank picked up the local newspaper from the empty chair at their table—he himself had read the organ within eight minutes; he laid it on the table on the off chance that the limey might want a read of it. But Roland ignored it and Frank thought that maybe he too had already scanned it before calling in for breakfast.

"But there is no comparison of the two diners as far as cuisine goes," said Roland.

"That being the case," opined Cotter, "why don't you use Werner's? I've never seen you round there?"

"I board nearby—only use this place to catch breakfast. I'm a two meal a day, man…" he informed Frank, not that Frank was interested in the information. "So how do you keep yourself busy of a day?" asked Roland as he briefly scratched his upper lip— this drew Cotter's attention to the limey's newly growing moustache in the making.

"Why do you ask?" said Frank.

"It's just that I've heard the rumor buzzin' round town before you got here, as to why Doctor Lomax engaged you and brought you out West. But as the doctor's no longer with us—I was wonderin' where that's going to leave you?" Cotter could see that the Englishman was genuinely keen to know the answer. Not that it bothered Frank. Roland went on without awaiting the answer to his question. "Employment-wise there isn't a lot going on around Junction City at the moment for chaps with our skills – though we can expect things to liven up when the railroad gets here, they, the railway, will be wanting tally clerks, but." Roland lounged back against his chair's backrest. "They already have an employment agency here in town and I've been interviewed for a position."

"That, so—" Frank said, "I suspect that your current employer, Mr. Corbin— wouldn't like to hear you talking like that, Mr. James? That might be easily interrupted as putting down Butterfield."

"I owe no allegiance to Butterfield or them to me. I get work wherever I can snatch it." This made Frank begin to wonder whether there was more to this conversation than just two jokers chatting away at the diner's table. Roland James went on: "—I haven't been outa work for more than a couple of weeks since I arrived here from England. My first job was a lounge steward in a Gentlemen's club in New York. I should've liked to be still there, but after a few years I became unsettled and moved on to explore more of my new country. Even been down and worked the paddle steamers on the Mississippi."

"Huh, I wouldn't have thought you burly enough for that heavy work?" the expression on the scribe's face showed that he was not trying to put the feller down and Roland James knew it.

"Oh I didn't do the work of a slave, not that the South's s'pose to be holding any now…not since the war. I was a tally-clerk on the wharves but did get the chance to make a few trips up river an' see how the other half, lives. Saw a couple of gamblers tarred and feathered for using marked decks!" Customers at nearby tables also heard this information, too; for James wasn't talking exactly low-key in here.

"It's a wonder they weren't lynched," said Cotter. "So how did you ended up way out here working for the stage line?"

"Lung, trouble; Too much dampness in the air both back home in London, and on the river Mississippi. Doctors out here have said my lungs would never be any good unless I went and took up living in a place with dry air. I knew they were right, coz I worked that out for myself back there in ol' England, hence me settin' out for the New World."

Their breakfasts arrived together and as the busboy transferred them from his tray to the table Frank told Roland James that he also has weak lungs due of course to his prior indulgence with alcohol. But on a brighter note Cotter said: "I've had a bit of a windfall, actually. I've been appointed news-correspondent for a New York rag…" Cotter had been fobbed off with a soup spoon to eat the gruel the kitchen had given him which they sold as rolled oats – the two things you could say about the dinner's gruel is that it was cheap and most of all, filling. James had ordered eggs, sunny-side up and Hash Browns. "—since the attack on Hallway's surgery and my report on the incident it's created a need with some Easterners to want to know more; especially those planning to move West to try an' better themselves. This means I can earn enough money from the newspaper to keep me fed and clothed—

that's all I need at the moment. I haven't yet begun to start milking my experience of the robbery and murders I've witnessed coming out here to join Lomax. Then there's the mystery death of Ma Kelly, a very colorful character that woman was, so that all leaves me plenty of scope to write about!"

"It sure sounds like things have turned the corner for you, Mister Cotter. I expect you have heard the rumor, about the possibility of a lynching in this town pretty soon. Some damn people are out to get that redskin and hang him high! Now wouldn't that be a scoop for a newspaperman?

"The mob I saw tar an' feather a gambler, were like madmen and there was no stopping them by what I saw, so I'd imagine a lynching mob would be more hot headed an' dangerous? I heard tell, that the lawmen trying to protect their prisoners soon turn to piss and in cases join in with the mob!" James stopped talking here so that he could fork part of a Harsh Brown into his mouth and you could see that Roland was let down at the newspaperman's lack of response about news of the coming lynching. He tried something else on the doctor's friend. He told Cotter than he had news that Miss Pearl Courtney's name was on the passenger list they had received through Western Union. "—I should have thought she'd leave this hole for good, seeing she's made the break by escorting Peter Kelly away from this place."

"Well, her return will be like a breath of fresh air—" Frank said as he tilted his cereal bowl to get the last of the gruel in to his soup-spoon. "I'll make it a point to learn how young Kelly's new relatives reacted to the sight of him—Ma made herself quite a stash of lucre over the years and he gets the lot, stock an' barrel; I'd say it would make him quite acceptable to the family once they sight his bank balance, even though Ma had subject herself to a life of outlandish risks an' look sin in the eye."

"That's true," agreed James who wished he had only half of what Pete Kelly had. "But the heir apparent would have had his income servilely clipped when Ma's Lawyer shut down the theater and bordello—the bordello looked to me as it was pulling in more than Pearl Courtney's theater troupe did! I bet that fact always stuck in the craw of the town's do-gooders?" Frank laid down his spoon in the bowl and quickly got out his handkerchief—he was just in time to stifle a sneeze.

"You've not heard the story about the bordello, Mr. Cotter?"

Putting away his hanky Frank said: What's the story there?"

"The ladies of the night have been slipping customers in through the backdoor all along. The Attorney is playing dumb, but talk has it that he is making a packet on the side for himself. Some blokes in the town, reckon what he's making from those girls; won't ever get in to Pete Kelly's purse."

"Tsch—doesn't surprise me. If that's the case I can't allow Miss Courtney to stay on there when she returns. She'll have to share Lester's apartment with me—even if it means I have to sleep on the sofa until she can make other arrangements. If Lester were here, he'd have it no other way."

"Is that wise?"

"What do you mean, Roland?"

"Don't interpret this as me speaking out of turn," said the ticketing clerk. "But stayin' there with you in Doctor Lomax place without a chaperone won't do her rep' any good… I don't even think she will go for it—she's funny that way, I thought you'd noticed?"

Frank noted the limey's point. "Aahh, yes, I know what you mean—" Frank nodded. "Well I can counter those ideas of folks—I'll sleep downstairs in the unoccupied surgery, and all we'll just share is meals – surely that won't upset the status quo?"

"I'm sure that will go down much better with the biddies in this town…" said the man knowingly. When they finished breakfast they ambled out on to the sidewalk and together, they headed off in the direction of the intersection where Doctor Lomax ended up as just another road static.

Neither man commented about the accident; but Frank could not ever walk by the area, without glancing over the scene, and — then — his imagination would run wild as it conjured up what it might have been like at the time…*Why the Hell hasn't the mystery man come forth of his own volition, why?* The scribe thought to himself, diligently.

Pearl Courtney was pleased to see at least Cotter there waiting for her when she alighted from the dusty stage.

While waiting for Miss Courtney's trunk to be off loaded from the top of the stagecoach's turret, Frank pestered her with questions about how the Kelly family in Chicago had responded to Peter.

"Fine," she told him as she fanned herself with a wax paper Chinese fan in the Butterfield waiting room. "They made him very, welcome. He saw his first real steam train in Kansas and it frightened him—I honestly didn't think I would get him to ride in it to Chicago. But once he got used to its movement and the way it raced round curves in the line and roared across bridges, he was like a young kid! I'm sure he shall have a fine life in the big city with his relatives.

"By the way—any headway been made on Ma's murder?" Pearl wriggled uncomfortably in her corset and could not wait to get the irritating thing off.

"Nothing," reported Cotter. "Been some changes in relationships while you have been away..." He told Pearl about being estranged from Stroughton and Boston, all because of his stand on the Indian attack on Hallway's surgery.

Naturally Pearl was sorry to learn this. Then he put it to her about the bordello business and that he felt that out of respect for Lomax he couldn't allow her to move back in with a gaggle of girls who earned their living from prostitution.

"You come up with a better solution, then!" Pearl threw back at him.

He asked her to move in to the apartment above the surgery and he would make himself comfortable downstairs. Pearl was a bit wary about the idea but decided to give it a try. Then they arranged with Roland James to get a stage line lackey to trundle Miss Courtney's trunk to the Doctor's old place and the Englishman was glad to see that it was done.

They strolled up via the alley through to Starr Street and climbed the wooden stairs to the apartment, where Frank opened the door to the suite. Then they went down and opened up the surgery to let it air before Cotter moved in and she satisfied herself that he could be reasonably comfortable down there. They had to return upstairs when her luggage arrived and she insisted on a visit to The Royal, so that she could collect some personal belongings from her old room. It was while en route to the bordello that Pearl explained that she was only back here for a short time to get herself organized for a full move to Kansas City, Chicago or New York's theater district in search of work. She claimed that she had promising prospects with a booking agent by the name of Aaron Pentel, and a speedy return to the world of theater was in the wind. She was thrilled to bits...

The next three days were hectic ones. During the course of time Cotter explained to Pearl that he had had a short talk with Derrick Carter about the doctor's accident, and that like Ma Kelly, he didn't want to become involved but agreed that there was a man there at the accident who helped with Doctor Lomax's body and then vanished ... why? What reason was there for becoming a missing link, he didn't know, but he had his own reason why he wanted to stay clear of the growing turmoil that seemed to be gathering momentum, now that Cotter was in town and asking questions which seemed awkward for someone; who that someone is, is a question in itself.

Frank Cotter enjoyed having Pearl in close proximity to him and was prepared to put up with the discomfort it caused. Not that it caused any great drama. He did not tell her that sleeping down in the surgery was a nuisance and that he really had not thought just how much of a nuisance it would be. Every morning he woke up with stiff neck that took some disguising and never worked itself out until about two in the afternoon.

This morning after quietly rising he rinsed his hands and face in a surgical hand-bowel, in cold water, which was not far above freezing point. He just wanted to freshen up before he set off with a change of clothes to the bathhouse and then pay a visit to McBride, for a daily shave all in that order. While drying himself he heard movement coming from the overhead floorboards, and knew that Pearl was out of bed. He wonders whether or not she would like to join him in his trek to the Chinese—it was damn silly that they walked up and back separately just so as a certain majority of citizens would not have room for complaint.

Frank had discovered Doctor Lomax's safe but neither he nor Pearl could manage to open it. Pearl thought she knew the combination but it proved wrong and in the end they both agreed that the only answer to this was that Lester had changed the combination before the accident. Perhaps the town Smithy could force it. They learned from the blacksmith that he had a backlog of work lined up. The iron work on three Prairie Schooners awaited attention—the wagons had dropped out of a train that had passed through Junction City three weeks ago and their owners were anxious to get back on the trail to Dodge City, there, a land agent was holding lots for them, that had come onto the market when a big cattle spread went bust through bad management and was cut down to make smaller ranch-holdings.

Pearl arrived in the foyer of the bathhouse with a change of clothes just as Frank was paying the small childlike Chinese woman across the counter for today's ablutions. The cashier was all smiles and prattled on in Mandarin at Cotter as though he were a native.

"Good morning, Frank—sleep well?" Pearl inquired, ignoring the small flat chested cashier's chitchat, for both she and Cotter knew the woman could barely manage English.

"Like a body on a slab!" Frank lied as he took his change from the cashier, who looked out of sync being too cheerful this early in the morning. "—and yourself?" Pearl nodded. Then Frank stepped aside to allow her access to the cashier as he went over and opened the door out onto the sidewalk. Not far along Main Street he watched in amazement as he saw the scruffy robed mule-skinner known to one and all in the town, splashed the trough's suspect water on his face and through his hair, oblivious of the fact that horses and mules had been drinking from it— Cotter shuddered, he was close enough to be heard by the homeless feller, he bid the hatless man a "good morning". The muleskinner raised his head in Cotter's direction as he untied his bandanna to use for toweling purposes. "'Mornin', Sir... This is the weather I like!!" He called down along the street to Cotter. The old timer continued spreading his joyful cheer, "Yes, a right ol' day fer a swig—eh?" He stuffed the damp bandanna in the hip-pocket of his worn Levi's and picked up his battered hat that had a piece bitten from its brim at some stage by a revengeful Mule or something. Before settling it on his head he examined it either for fleas or lice, take your pick.

Frank set of for McBride's shop and as he drew near to the old Muleskinner the man began hawking up phlegm from deep within his lungs and spat it in the water of the trough where it floated like a wood-chip. Ahead lay the cross street of Bryan and then soon he was bearing down on the town butcher's shop. The butcher was grooming the sidewalk in front of his shop and looking serious about it too, they nodded in passing and then Frank turned in the entrance of the barber shop and found that he was not McBride's first customer for the day. A feller was in the chair lying back with a lush lather of shaving soap brushed deep down into his whiskers, as McBride strolled back from his butler-tray with an open razor in his hand; Frank noticed that there was another cowboy, a stranger to him, waiting for either a haircut or shave or maybe both.

The newspaperman went over and sat down on the bench seat against the wall alongside the cowhand who was trying to make-like he was reading the out dated city newspaper from Kansas. Why the illiterate fellow bothered with the paper was a mystery in itself, for he had it upside-down and therefore fooled no one. The man in the barber chair coughed to clear his throat, so both McBride and Cotter knew that the man wasn't taking time out for a snooze while getting his facial hair removed. McBride worked on without looking up to see who had entered for he was aware of what was going on in back of him.

Frank picked up the local newspaper which was only a weekly, and started to thumb through it, but dosed off and didn't register anything until the barber called him and he found that both the cowhands had gone and here he was alone with McBride in the shop.

"I saw you wos enjoyin' yer sleep, so I let you be until I wos free ter give you my full attention," McBride told him as the news-hound strolled toward the high chair and mounted it.

Cotter settled on the still warm leather of the upholstered barber's chair then the hairdresser drape him with a drop cloth. "You know what it's like. Sometimes no matter what you do, you just can't drop off to sleep. It's like a lodger trying to avoid his landlord's rent collector!"

"That's, true." McBride said from experience as he draped Cotter. "What will it be?"

"A quick shave without any loss of blood thank you," He thought it best to smile while saying that as the barber might not appreciate the hidden humor in it.

"And how are you and Miss Courtney going sharing the late doctor's apartment— not too crowded, is it?"

To Cotter it sounded like McBride was making a snide remark about the arrangement he and the actress had established and this bristled him, he did not like aspersions being cast about, especially as Cotter and Pearl had gone to the trouble of seeing no one got the wrong impression by leaving things suspect. After all he was the one suffering with cricks in the neck after a bad night's sleep.

"What are you driving at, Mr. McBride?" Frank said curtly to the candy strip shirt barber.

"Oh, please don't get me wrong, sir—" McBride quickly came to panic stations. "I wasn't in any way suggesting any impropriety existed in your arrangement with Miss Courtney!" He was in fear of losing a paying customer.

"For your information, *I moved* into the downstairs' surgery to preserve Miss Pearl Courtney's reputation..."

"Oh yes—yes I realize that Mr. Cotter and I'm sure, no one will interpret it any other way," McBride was sweating to try and find another subject to switch too... McBride made it his business to check the keen edge of the razor. "What is Miss Courtney going to do now that her show has been cancelled?"

"I don't rightly know her business ... I think she's going east looking for work in a new show..."

McBride interrupted. "Did you hear the latest? The Kansas Pacific Railway are gonna move a couple of track layin' crews out here ter establish a railhead. They will start laying tracks from both ends of the rail route as was dun by the Union Pacific, but not on such a grand scale. The first crew here will work on parts of the proposed route that engineers have predicted to be more likely flood prone. They'll be building high levees here an' there for the track to be laid on..." McBride paused for a breath.

"Sounds great—just what's wanted—but boy this Kansas line has had more than its share of delays. The war was no help and brought with it its share of sabotage..." Cotter reminded the barber.

"That's true, that's true." McBride agreed. "If what they say is true, then the excitement and action will liven up the old town. I hear them railway crews are a pretty rough bunch of critters an' don't mix in wif cowboys too much. Sean Dunne's in the box-seat to make a buck or two out of the cartage contract until they take over — I heard off this feller, that the lines been pushed another ten miles west of Kansas City already!"

"This is news to me, where did you learn your stuff?" Frank asked, toying with the idea he might make a note of it in his journal that he had begun to write up when he got back originally from Fort Hancock.

"I cut a Drummer's hair first up, this mornin'; he came right here off the coach. He is the one who seems ter know all about it…"

"What carpetbagger was that?"

"Guy by the name of Dragoon … Wasn't he the feller wuz aboard the stage you were on that got robbed?" (Cotter nodded in answer to the question) The barber went on: 'He hit town this morning and has a deal going with that Russian, Yolson. In fact he tells me he is rolled out his bed-roll down at the Yolson's home above the gunsmiths shop!"

Frank nodded and this annoyed McBride for it made it awkward not to nick him with the razor…"I'm surprised to learn he's back in town so soon."

"Dragoon and the gunsmith are starting up a gun club — they are gonna teach folks who can't shoot fer a hill of beans how to possibly protect themselves if the Pawnee make further attacks on the town or outer ranches…"

"Anyone, expecting that sort of thing…?" asked the concerned newspaper man. "I thought the folks at Fort Hancock would be first off the mark to can anything like that coming out of the reservation?"

"You're not wrong there. The trouble is those Indians who threw lead into Hallway's place have thrown a scare in to the whole neighborhood and that Jew an' Whitney Dragoon can see there's a buck ter be made by floggin' guns off to people… That's what's behind their little scheme — clever, hey? Folks'll buy guns they won't have any use fer once the whole thing cools down!"

McBride got a fresh hot towel and wiped the small islands of shaving lather from Cotter's jowls. "You know what part of this Indian trouble is, don't you …?"

"No."

"The Pawnees on that reservation don't come from around this area. They were uprooted by the Army and marched here to split up the tribes so as they lacked the strength in numbers to band together into any formidable force. It's the old rule, divide and conquer. Been part of European life for hundreds of years…" McBride dumped the soiled towel and splashed Cotter's newly shaved facial skin with Bay Rum…

18

PEARL COURTNEY CAME out of the stagecoach depot after booking her ticket on next week's coach and headed back to the apartment via the alley, mindful of course that the stage line's stables had gateways into and off their properties as access to their corrals. Back at the apartment she set about boiling up some spuds, cabbage and beef silverside. The vegetables she had purchased earlier in the day from the Chinese green grocers as with regard to the meat that came from the butcher shop in Main Street.

As Pearl walked home, she mused to herself how Starr Street, seemed to have lost all its life when Ma Kelly had been murdered. Now even at night no one was keen to be in that part of town, alone — and the Royal's closure didn't help. Cotter made his way to call on Carter at his place of work, in the hope that he, Cotter, might be able to enlist the shop-clerk's help in so far as, at least tell the Sheriff what he noticed at the scene of the accident — who knows, it might get Boston to set out and try to find this missing, ***fifth Man.*** Cotter came upon the Mexican beggar whom had heard singing about the town for over three months, he had been in residence before Cotter arrived on the scene — he was in good voice on the edge of the sidewalk, with his back to the road. Frank dropped a few coins in the busker's old cigar-box and noticed that he was a bit on the prosperous side these days he was now wearing a new pair of Peewee boots. Then Cotter caught sight of Sheriff Robeson coming along the street on foot from uptown, the lawman was leading a nag that was unfamiliar to the scribe, he had no idea it was the mare Matt Flynn had scored somewhere along his attempted escape route — it wore a Bar Z brand.

In recognition of one another, each man slowed their stride as they drew near. Talk was that Jock Robeson had taken leave from his post in Lawrence to take on the job of bounty hunter for Rollo and the Association.

"…Well my God what a sight to see — how are you?" Both men stopped to shake hands and beamed at each other with broad smiles. "What are you doing here in Junction City, Sheriff? — Last I knew of you, you had headed off with your deputy back in the direction of Lawrence? "

"That was trew. But you were aware that I was going ter try and pick up the trail of those fellows that knocked off the stage and was the cause of the death of two fine gentlemen…?" Robeson reminded the scribe.

Frank nodded, "How could one ever forget?"

"The Deputy, whom accompanied me here to visit Mr. Rollo, took over my position at Lawrence and that left me free ter pick up the trails of the highwaymen who hit the stage. Korda and his partner, Matt Flynn —"

"There was a third guy in with them, a Canadian, going by his accent?" interjected the scribe.

"Most people who spend time in the outdoors have ter wear a suitable hat, sir…" Derrick Carter explained.

"Excuse me," called one of the two women still waiting over at the far counter, "but might we have some service Mr. Carter. One cannot devote all their time to the gentleman, surely?"

"Trew… But one man would have to be some kind of Wizard to rope them all in, and one man on all their tails is spreading things a bit thin — but all a fellow can do is his best under the circumstances. I ran one of them to ground up near Canada just this side of the border. But Mother Nature had other ideas. He tangled with a darn cantankerous grizzly and come orf second best. I found his remains an' it weren't a pretty sight but what wuz left of his face was enough ter recognize by yer sketch. It was, Korda. Lucky for me, lad, the bear wasn't interested in man's riches."

"Korda…? That's strange, I thought it would've been Malthouse," blurted out the scribe. "There was no sign of him at all?" The Scot shook his head. Frank went on: "It's jist that when you spoke of Canada I naturally thought of the ex-Canadian. They were most likely traveling together, though. You don't reckon the bear got busy with one of the pair and the other feller took advantage of the situation and run out on his partner?"

"Nay; never saw his spoor anywhere. Maybe they split-up an' he found his own way across the border. I'll leave 'im to the Mounties."

"So you recovered the loot?" Frank asked.

"Only what Korda had in his saddlebags but it's a start to some form of recovery. My next part of this case will be the part bearing, Flynn's name. They split up weeks ago and only by a fluke did I cop Korda's trail first. So I went orf after the Sassenach — best to rope in one of the crim's and be sure of a part success, then trying ter do the impossible and wind up with none."

"Word never reached here that you nailed anyone! Truthfully, I never thought you would have any success. Still, I guess Mr. Rollo had to try to get the Associations riches back, or look as though he was..." Cotter stated, "So what happened next in this saga?" He leant with his should up against a veranda post and crossed his boots at the ankles.

"I held onto the Korda's stash to personally hand over to Rollo, and hope it would make 'im happy. But in the meantime I pick up on Flynn's spoor. The Lord blessed me there, but I had no idea if I was gunna be as successful with that feller. Still, one out of three would have to be judged as pretty successful, hey?"

Cotter nodded. *There is no denying that,* thought the scribe. *Now wouldn't this be a tale worth writing about!*

"Anything more exciting, occur?"

Robeson nodded. "I've got a prisoner stowed along up there in Klem's jailhouse," Jock changed the reins of the mare from one hand to the other. The horse stretched its neck out towards the nearby trough; Robeson gave the animal more rein. "...The prisoner is an acquaintance of yours."

"Mine?" the newspaperman's voice was incredulous. It brought a grin to the face of the Sheriff.

"Aye, a Laddie by the name of one, Matt Flynn."

"Are you goddamn serious?!" cried Cotter — Jock nodded. "You actually ended up getting two of them! ... This is fantastic!!"

"Yes. Much better than I ever hoped for —"

"*—you're amazing!* This will go down in history; do you realize that, Sheriff?"

"The thing is — it now makes it imperative that you stay here an' go State Witness against this Flynn fellow for the robbery and murders. Is it possible?" said Jock.

"I would be willing to stay around and go witness for you with all my heart. Only your pal, Sheriff Boston won't be too pleased. He has ordered me to pack up and move out… Much has happened in this place while you've been out stalking those road agents, Jock. As a result, Boston and a few other here, want me on my way."

This certainly puzzled Jock Robeson. "What d'you mean?"

"You wouldn't know that Washington had Boston arrested by the Army, they came over from Fort Hancock?"

Robeson shook his head.

"Look, it isn't right that you learn certain things from me… You and Boston better have a damn good talk, then, **you** make up your own mind that yore going to believe – then come and look me up if you feel so incline."

"I know I'm out of touch wif things. But what is it between you an' Klem?"

"I can't say. Like I said, you speak to him about me then make up your mind which way you are gonna, jump."

"OK… **so you and Klem** have your differences. Mebbe this news will change yuh mind a bit. The trial for the robbery and murder against this Flynn bloke," explained the Scotsman. "— won't be held here in this burgh … the crime didn't take place on paper in Klem's county, but mine."

Frank frowned at hearing this. "Everyone knows the crime happened in Boston's territory!"

"Originally, yes. But Washington has been busy. I called into Lawrence on me way out on the trail for Flynn. Washington's been playing round with county borders and for reasons of their own, they, Washington, have taken the creek where the crime took place, and moved it out of Boston's jurisdiction. So now, I take it you can appear in court against this Flynn fellow?"

"That certainly removes a hurdle or two. Yes, I'll make my way to Lawrence for the trial. That way I will be complying with Boston's order to leave town and he'll have no excuse to slam me in the clink."

"I've gotta tell you I'm not surprised you and Klem fell out. You were both gettin' a bit bitchy with one another because of how he was handling Doctor Lomax's accident. Weren't you thinking of playing detective or something? I know it was getting at Boston, he wuz seeing it as a reflection on his ability as Sheriff."

"In a way I am … but it's not as easy as I've begun to learn; it is an art-form of its own…"Cotter realized that he was admitting to his incompetence. As a change of subject he decided to enquire about how the Scot cottoned onto the robbers. "Sheriff Robeson, how come you brought your prisoner to Junction City and not Lawrence? I ask that question purely as a newspaperman."

Jock nodded. "Aye, a couple of reasons are built into that puzzle of yours, lad. Lazarus Rollo and company wanted the hides of the men who held up the stage, but they are only gunna have ter settle for one, whether they likes it or not. I'm orf to stable this nag down at the livery and then report to Rollo, I have only been in town around half an hour…" His travel weary clothes attested to that declaration. They were dusty, wrinkled and smelt of body-odor and horse sweat. "I run down the ramrod Flynn, completely by accident. I called into an isolated ranch to rest up and swap or buy a fresh horse, mine was fucked. And who should be working there as a cowhand, was yours truly! He had arrived two weeks before me — and was doin' likewise, resting up from the trail; only he was workin' there for his found.

"Naturally, we got involved in a lead slinging match and I winged him. His new found friends were even planning on lynching me from a tree! But before they hauled me to the open air gallows they made a search of my belongings and found my lawman's star from Lawrence …

"They worked things out for themselves and handed the wounded Flynn over to me and ordered us both orf the spread. Flynn wasn't in any fit state ter pull on a long draw all the way up to Lawrence, so I had to nurse him all the way here. That means, Rollo can get to see that I have been doing my job. I'm experienced enough to know that Flynn might still die on me from that lead embedded in him and that won't please Rollo, he's the type of man who likes ter get his pound of flesh and revenge; so I'm hoping Doc. Hallway can keep the bastard alive long enough to stand trial."

Cotter's brow corrugated. "…He's that bad?"

The ex-lawman, nodded.

Unfortunately their conversation was brought to a halt when the Williams brothers began to hassle the busker out of devilment, down the street a piece. In Robeson's eyes they were carrying things too far. Jock handed the reins of the cow pony to Cotter and swung up onto the walkway.

"Excuse me, Cotter — seems a lawman's work is never done!"

"Do you want me to get, Boston?"

He shook his head to that question, "Nah. I'll handle these creeps;" The brawny Scot went off in the direction of the ruckus while Cotter waited with the horse that now decided to let go its bladder. He had to keep pals with Robeson if he wanted the full story out of him of how he caught up with the desperadoes.

The brothers obviously had not noticed the Scotsman along the sidewalk from them when they began their "horseplay" with the poor Mexican, but were happy to yield to the ex-Pinkerton man's demands to lay off the busker. But the pair did not forget to tell Robeson that they were only bowing to his will, because he, like them, worked for Rollo.

When Frank joined Pearl for dinner he was spruced up like a city toff. He stood about awkwardly waiting while the actress checked out her cooking and served it from the cooking vessels onto the table. They both took a Windsor chair each at the table, then Pearl asked: "I want to ask you something about last night. You didn't for any reason come up here to the apartment, did you?"

"No, why do you ask?" Frank picked up his knife and fork, and then paused, looking at Pearl across the table. She could see that Frank wanted to know why she had asked such a question of him and was obliged to fill him in. "This must sound strange, but last night I woke up from a deep sleep..." She shook out her table napkin and placed it on her lap. "— and experienced the feeling that I wasn't alone here in the apartment, strange, really..." She took up her cutlery and with her knife commenced cutting up her few slices of silverside.

"Have you considered that you may not have woken up at all, and that it was partly a dream; it does happen. I take it for granted that you did lockup before going to bed?"

Pearl nodded that this was so. "...That is why when I thought I woke up, I thought you must have retained the key to the upstairs, and come in looking for something, like an extra blanket? I swear I could hear someone moving about out here in the parlor!"

"You've experienced a dream is all," said Frank, certain that this was all it was. "But there's that feeling it leaves you with after, the feeling of an invasion into your own private space it just simply won't go away until you have talked it over with someone, I'm all ears, Pearl…"

"There isn't a great deal to tell, really. I just came out of a sleep with my sixth sense, rife. The bedroom was as dark as a cave and yet my senses were most sensitive to my surrounding! I even thought of coming out here to accost you, but before I built up enough courage, I heard the door to the outside landing being carefully closed. I don't like being taken for granted — that's why I brought the matter up."

"It is most likely just a woman's imagination and don't forget, you are sleeping in strange surroundings," he pointed out — but it did remind him of the night he had been very sure that someone had gone through his dispatches which he had left out on the table, but he wasn't going to tell her about that.

Pearl shrugged and returned to her meal.

Toying with a small boiled potato Cotter thought: *I wonder what is going on here…? Something strange…someone will need to get to the bottom of it, what motive has this arcane prowler got with wanting to know what is going on inside this apartment? Heck, it might even be tied in with this missing-mystery guy…?*

An awkward silence prevailed for the next twenty minutes, then Pearl made mention of the fact that earlier that day she had gone to the stage depot and purchased her seat on one of the departing coach — due out of town next week. Frank did not tell Pearl that he had been ordered out of town, and now hoped they might be traveling companions, but he knew he could not leave just yet awhile — He also felt that at long last he could say that he had started to master the demon drink — a millstone round his neck. If he can keep his nose clean, it might be possible for him to declare his intentions to her; even though he knew what Pearl and Lester had meant to each other and certainly realized he wouldn't be able to fill Lester's shoes — she would most likely long for someone more promising than an ex-fly-by-night coot with a liver shot by having lived the highlife for far too long.

Pearl broke the silence by telling Frank that while in at the Butterfield stage office, she had met Donald Stroughton, he was there collecting a parcel from the east and Roland James was clearing the paperwork that had accompanied it. They engaged in a short conversation and she learned from it that Cotter and Stroughton had been trapped down inside the buried meteor, and that later when they went across to Fort Hancock to secure Sheriff Boston's freedom from the Army stockade, that he, Stroughton and Cotter, had become virtually estranged — not to mention the strained atmosphere that had emerged between Boston and Frank.

"…I didn't tell you about it Pearl, because I don't want to worry you about things that seem impossible to patch-up. But then who knows, next week we all might be buddies again? I'm thinking of maybe taking up residence in Lawrence to fulfill my obligation to my New York employer." Just as he finished saying this, there was creak from the timbers of the landing as Whitney Dragoon reached the apex of the stairs and come towards the half-glass and wooden door of their shared pad.

"Come in Whitney, the door's open!" Frank called as he pushed his chair back from the table and stepped the yard's distance across to the door and tugged it open. Whitney breezed in across the threshold and Cotter returned to his chair and waved the salesman into an empty chair at the table. "— sit yuh butt, on that!"

It was plain that Whitney Dragoon felt he was intruding on their privacy, but take the chair he did, sweeping off his hat, he settled with it on his lap in the spare Windsor chair. Pearl felt compelled to offer him a meal and rose to the occasion, but Dragoon tried to wave her back to her seat…

"No panic, Miss Courtney — the Yolson's have fed me up well," he instructed her; but by now Pearl was on her feet and so decided that they would share their coffee with him. She tracked down a cup and saucer for their unexpected visitor.

"You sure you don't want something to eat?" Pearl chimed while fetching him a clean coffee cup.

"Thanks fer the offer but this man is as full as a Grizzly prior to hibernation!" He turned to Frank. "Haven't you crossed paths with McBride — you look surprised to see me? He knew I wuz in town, told him ter let you know I'd be callin' on you…"

"If you care to look closer at my appearance you can see I've paid McBride a visit; yes, he not only told me you were in town — but also the business operation you an' Yolson hope to setup, here…"

Dragoon's face widened into an even broader mischievous grin as he explained. "…Are you jealous because someone else is making a buck out of the Indian attack on the Doctor's surgery, Frank? Your report on the troubles of Junction City has caused much concern back east when it wuz published. And Yolson has been inundated with small arms orders suitable for womenfolk, so we decided ter do something about it; no point in selling a gun ter someone who can't shoot for the goddamn life of 'em. So Yolson's wife came up with the idea we start a gun club and teach members ter shoot!" said Dragoon.

"Maybe *I* ought to join and get a few free lessons, seeing ***my yarn*** has fired up such interest?" Cotter put the question to Dragoon with tongue-in-cheek.

Pearl returned to the table with Dragoon's beverage. "— If you were going to make this part of the country home, I'd say: Yes!" Pearl looked as though she might be going to return to her meal for she armed herself with knife and fork, "I would go along with that, Frank," Then to Dragoon she said: "But like me, Frank is planning to depart town soon; so he just indicated to me before you arrived."

With the excitement still showing in his face Whitney nodded. "I knew this town wasn't ever gonna be home to you, Frank — it doesn't surprise me. Anyway, about this deal Yolson and I've got going — we're gonna make hay while the sun shines out of the interest in guns people are showing!

"Good for you," Cotter said. "As you realize I too am very much in the same boat now I am in position to furnish eastern papers with copy of life out here. Folks back east will be keen to get all the color in this part of the untamed west!"

"The west isn't as wild as it was before the war I hope you realize, Frank. I heard from the grapevine that Pearl escorted Pete Kelly to his Mom's relatives. How did they take to him?" asked the salesman.

"As good as one could expect for folks whom had distanced themselves from Ma for years — they had no idea how wealthy she had become and the value of the property she owns here in Junction City…" said Pearl as she gave up on her meal for the second time and decided to switch to her cup of java, waiting nearby.

As Dragoon prepared himself to take a sip of his lip scorching drink, he said: "…I thought they would've been fawning over him like he was the Prince of Baghdad, especially with the dowry he'll bring into their side of the family!"

"What I saw of them and their wealth — they didn't look desperate for money," Pearl confessed, "I guess money begets money!"

Dragoon nodded, as if he already knew the truth in that.

"Boston hasn't made any progress on the Kelly murder since you left, Whitney; and I don't reckon he will unless he's pushed, " Cotter mentioned by way of updating Dragoon.

Dragoon realized that he was staring to long at the delightful actress and that if he did not focus more on the scribe he might be asked to leave, so to throw Cotter off the track that he was attracted to her beauty, he said: "I was gonna ask you about that very same matter, Frank. I have also heard rumors that The Royal's back doing unofficial business?" Having said that, Dragoon wished he hadn't, as that sort of talk was not a subject one ought to discuss at a table, with a woman present. However, having started the ball rolling he went on, determined to avoid going into details of the whorehouse's activities. "—Lawyer Stroughton wouldn't be too happy about that?"

"Who are you kidding, Whitney? Lawyer Stroughton knows all about the back door. That's why I wouldn't allow Miss Courtney to return there to her old room. Can you imagine what living there would do to her reputation in this town, now Ma's not here to chaperone?"

"Right, Frank. Doctor Lomax would appreciate your concern for Miss Pearl Courtney. Oh, and by the way — I must commend you on yore coffee, Ma'am it's delicious…!" He gestured with his drinking vessel in Pearl's direction.

"Gracious," smiled Pearl back to him.

Going back to Frank Cotter, Dragoon asked: "Have you managed to get Sheriff Boston to agree to yore request of an open inquiry into Doc Lomax accident, or have you not had any joy in that direction?"

Cotter shook his head, "Frankly — no."

"That doesn't surprise me. I always thought you were chasin' moonbeams," Dragoon said, openly. The salesman knew the lapse of time and the fact that he and Cotter had been apart long enough for him to think the situation through — without being around Cotter so he wasn't influenced by the man's line of thinking and therefore developed his own point-of-view; maybe it was now the time to share it with the scribe.

Hearing the gun-salesman out, Cotter recognized that he was losing a convert to his view of the incident. But he believed that the announcement he would soon be making here in the parlor could well turn Dragoon's point-of-view about and that of Pearl's.

Frank said: "We all know I originally based my demand for the sheriff to set-up an inquiry in to Lester's accident because I thought his death was handled too blasé from the outset by all concerned. But ***our friend,*** the Sheriff, could not see the point to it. Later, after I'd met Ma Kelly — she mentioned in conversation that there was a mystery guy hanging around the scene of the accident and helped in carry the body to the sidewalk… By the time Sheriff Boston arrived this mystery man had slipped away and nobody but she could recall him being there. I personally thought that this might give me an edge into forcing Sheriff Boston to swing my way and re-screen the previous statements made by those whom were in attendance.

"I don't have anything to suggest that maybe to appease me that the Sheriff was gonna change his opinion, and follow through on Lester's case, but when Ma came to light with what she had witness, I thought I just might have had a show. Her evidence, would have given my argument strength; she was a strong willed woman, and *I* knew that people would listen to her. But Ma's murder put paid to that. So now there was no evidence that even what she claimed to have seen, existed.

"Well, believe it or not, I've found someone else who can substantiate that what Ma saw was a fact — and that the ***Mystery Man*** does exists … A young feller who works at the mercantile establishment on Main Street — a Derrick Carter!"

"Derrick Carter," said Pearl with her coffee cup held slightly clear of her rouge lips.

"Yes, do you know of him, Pearl?" Cotter said.

She shook her head as she lowered her cup to the saucer. "Not to talk to, other than across the shop counter — he has struck me in the past to be a little particular — what did he say that makes you feel as though he might have something important to add, Frank?"

"It turns out that he was on Starr Street near the intersection — Carter was on his way downtown and although he was otherwise preoccupied and didn't see the accident, he, more-or-less saw the aftermath…

"A gathering crowd went quickly to Lester's aid. And like Ma Kelly's version of events he can say unequivocally that the old gal was right about there being a fifth man assisting the folks carrying Lester's inert body off the dirt-road." Cotter paused to glance around at his puzzled audience.

Finally Whitney asked: "How is *this* gonna help you and yore cause?" He ended his question with a brow arched in the scribe's direction.

"If I can get him, Carter, on-side with me — we can troop off to Boston and make him reconsider his attitude towards an inquiry. Since you left town the Sheriff and *I* aren't the best of friends. He can barely bring himself to give me the time of day. The evidence of this young man may just force Boston's unwilling hand.

"Earlier today I was on my way to the store to see if he would come with me to the Sheriff after his work-day finished, but on the way I was delayed when I ran into Sheriff Robeson. When I finally did get to the Mercantile's, Derrick Carter had already left for the day; he was working a short shift — so I'll have to catch up with him later, maybe tomorrow sometime." Frank concluded.

"Sounds like this might be the breakthrough ***you need!***" Dragoon said.

But while Frank had been talking, Pearl had been digesting his words carefully, and had this to say on the subject: "Saying what you've stated about Derrick Carter is all true, Frank. I detect some feeling of reluctance there on Carter's part. Why didn't he come forward with his information before? Do you know why?"

Frank nodded in her direction. "…There *is* reluctance on his part to step up into the breech — and I know the reason why … but it has to remain a secret for now between Carter and myself." Cotter saw the look that began to engage the faces of Dragoon and Miss Courtney. "— don't doubt for one second that he is not a very anxious young man about his secret, and wants to do the right thing. But he's worried that whoever slit the old gal's throat, will come after him if what he knows gets out!" Frank picked up his cup and swirled the last of his coffee round in the bottom and swallowed it and the dregs down like one would skoal a nip of whiskey.

"Once Carter comes out of the shadows with what he saw an' its value analyzed in the light of day, Boston will have to open up an inquiry into Lomax's death and protect the youth," stated Whitney.

"You sure Mr. Carter needs protecting?" said Pearl.

The scribe nodded.

"Now we've got two people who can validate your belief that there was a fifth person —" voiced Dragoon.

"Not two," said Frank, "Ma's dead, remember!"

"She's unforgettable in my book, too. But now you've got to ask yourselves why did the Attorney and the others not subscribe to Ma Kelly's account of things, that's what I don't git?" Dragoon said as he placed his now empty cup in the middle of the table.

"If I must be forthright about those friends of Lester's, I reckon somewhere along the line they have something to cover up … And just what it is — remains to be seen!" Cotter said.

"You think so?" asked Whitney. "Then, mebbe you ought ter give more thought to that?"

"How, so..?"

It was Pearl who cottoned on to what Whitney Dragoon was suggesting.

"Lester, his lawyer, Hill an' co., Bevan — are all tied up with Lester in this medical discovery —" The gun-salesman came in over the top of Pearl, because he could see that Cotter wasn't, or didn't seem to be getting it.

"—the government reaction towards Lester and his business partners is one of an enemy digging in its toes in preparation for a fight. Mebbe Washington had this inkling about the tactics your friends were going to use in their battle with them and were out to quash 'em before you got here on board to drive their publicity machine? You've been tellin' me and anyone who would listen that you and Lester were gonna take the fight right up to 'em — mebbe fer all concerned, the Doc's accident was a godsend; whether the mishap wuz by design or accident, Lester dies and the investigation into each and every one of 'em dies with him."

Cotter said thoughtfully, "And my arrival on the scene asking for a judicial inquiry and instance that a ***fifth man*** was involved somewhere with the accident — doesn't help matters, any."

Whitney responded. "You need this shop clerk ter see the Sheriff — or the Sheriff ter see him; that way Boston can decide for himself whether this accident needs some more serious spade work."

Frank slid his cup and saucer in Pearl's direction, obviously desiring a refill. "Look, I'm gonna take a risk here with you folks. It's about the Carter feller. It's this. Derrick Carter has a damn embarrassing problem and that's the reason he's not keen to speak up ... If it comes up in court it could overshadow everything he says with a big question mark." Cotter relieved Pearl of his coffee. "It seems that Derrick goes about taking aloud to himself... imagine a judge putting a great deal of faith in the efficacy of anything he says in court, when and if – it came out?" Frank's question wasn't for anyone in particular.

Pearl took it upon herself to attempt an answer. "If it's not generally known, does anyone need to bring it up and humiliate the guy?"

"In the courtroom; everything's fair game. It only needs someone to know about it and expose the flaw then the man's character, and his testimony comes into question!" Cotter pointed out.

With a wry glint in his eye, Whitney said: "...If no one in the courtroom knows about it — and it isn't raised, I can't see the harm in it. No one here is concerned whether the feller believes in fairies ... And is talkin' to yore self such ***a crime?***"

"Only if you start answering yourself back I should think," smiled Miss Pearl Courtney.

"The thing is the young man is afraid it will become public via the court and he'll be ridiculed and made a laughing stock in the town. Unless he goes to Boston pretty much of his own free will, I can't shove him!" Frank stated.

"You're right... No one can push the young man," admitted Pearl.

"Did he get a better look at the guy in question than Ma Kelly?" asked Dragoon.

Cotter shook his head. "Apparently not; we can thank Donald Stroughton for that! He got his frame between Carter and our mystery man."

"That means he wouldn't know the man if he came and stood right in front of him?" Pearl asked.

"That's right. But that doesn't matter really. For once we have established that this guy was in fact there, and then it will fall to Boston and his deputies to trace the man down and put a face to him," Cotter said.

"That won't be easy," commented Pearl.

"Ghosts don't just vanish in a puff of smoke," said Frank.

"You're wrong there, Frank. It's Genies that use the smoke trick — Ghosts dissolve…" Pearl said with conviction.

"Sounds like Miss Courtney is an expert in the paranormal, Frank," Whitney told the scribe ruefully.

"Don't you believe in ghosts and the little people, Mr. Dragoon?" Pearl demanded of the man.

"I would be careful how I answer that Whitney…you could be putting a foot in the steel jaws of a bear-trap if you answer that wrong!"

"Ghosts … 'Little' people? Dunno — I haven't thought about m-m-my belief in those things fer years… You don't tell me you folks do, or have encountered sumthin' along those lines?"

Pearl shrugged. "…The other night I thought I had a visitation —"

"You don't believe in that rubbish, surely?" Dragoon sneered. "That kind of thing is for children and folks approaching senility!"

"Don't be so dogmatic about that, Whitney. Some people believe in the spirit world — even in today's climate…" Frank's bone china coffee cup had now been deposited on its saucer. "I've had an episode or two in my life which I couldn't explain —"

"— yeah," interrupted Whitney with a good-hearted grin, "but you'd be the first ter concede that *yore* experiences would have been ***whiskey induced!*** He dug out his fob watch and gave its winder a couple of twists before sighting the time and replacing it back on his person.

"In the past … yes. Just recently I've been beginning to doubt my eyes."

"You've had some experiences of late?" Pearl asked Frank.

He nodded, as it was clear that Whitney was becoming interested. "The difference is that I know where my "ghosts" are coming from," he told Pearl. "It has to be ***this place*** and its accessibility to attract prowlers and snoops. As for myself, I have not suffered any haunting effects since I have been down below in the surgery. Pearl was only checking with me today before you came over, whether I'd been 'sleep walking' up here in the middle of the night, with ulterior motives I suspect. But I think she may have been getting the same visitor I had who is prowling about. The snoop probably doesn't realize I've changed beds and thinks he's dropping in on me …"

Dragoon turned in Pearl's direction.

"Is that true, Miss Courtney?"

"So it would seem."

"Must be scary?" said Whitney Dragoon.

"It's weird. We all know it isn't uncommon for a lonely cowboy to wander in and out of the dark if some foolish girl's left the door to her boudoir off the latch, but I've always made sure I lock up after Frank goes down to the surgery, and before *you* ask, he hasn't a key for the upstairs. In some respects I don't feel threatened about the visitation — in my case it is like having a visit from a friendly ghost; I suppose that was because I thought it was Frank.

"I woke up with the feeling as though someone had been spying on me while I slept in Lester's bed. Then I lit the bedside candle and saw the room was empty, but then gained the feeling *that,* whoever had been watching me, had most likely moved out into the parlor. So I threw on a shawl and with a candle for light, came out here… but the room was empty. I felt a fool at first and thought I must've been dreaming   until I realized that the door to the landing had been left slightly ajar. Without thinking I went out onto the landing but the candle blew out, I paused at the top of the stairs and believed I saw a shadow hurry away from the newel out onto the street in the direction of the surgery; that is what made me think it was Frank creeping about. I was by then too afraid to say anything to the fleeing ghost whose shape was that of a man!"

"So what did you do, Miss Courtney?" Dragoon asked. Frank sat watching Pearl closely.

"I returned to the parlor and made sure I locked up the place and decided when the time was right, that I would challenge Frank about it —"

"Which I emphatically denied," Frank snapped, overlapping her.

"—but he said he had never left the surgery. So all I can now put it down too, was that I had a friendly visit from Lester's, spirit!"

Dragoon shrugged.

"Then how do you explain the experiences Frank has been having since moving in?" Pearl asked.

"Where did you first hear about them?" Dragoon was surprised that she had heard about them.

"Don't listen to her, Whitney… It's not the same thing, Pearl," Frank said with a dismissive wave of his hand. "Besides, lots of people do believe in ghosts and spirits, seriously. Take the church, the Catholic Faith — they believe in the Holy Trinity —

God, The Father— Jesus, the Son; and the Virgin Mary. Therefore if you are a religious person, you've gotta believe to a certain extent in the spirit world.

"Then on top of that — one cannot forget Warlocks an' Witches — you've got ex-slaves —believers in Black magic an' all that stuff's been slowly creeping into our society by the African slaves. No one in our world ever knew about the existence of Zombies — let alone explained or understand what they were all about. "

Whitney nodded. "The town of Salem's still got a lot ter live down, that I'll grant you!"

This all now brought the memory of the dead Priest appearing before Frank, in Bryan Street, but he resolved to keep that business to himself.

"You'll never guess who bailed me up on the way here, that old Muleskinner, Burnacre…" said the drummer. " — I felt sure he wuz gonna put the bite on me so I treated him pretty warily."

"I personally think he's just a harmless panhandler," Pearl said as she got up from her chair and began to tidy away the things off the table that belonged in the kitchen cabinet.

"He told me, as you said Frank, that the sheriff from Lawrence is back here wif a prisoner from that stage robbery — so looks like you and me will have a date to play witnesses before the court? Apparently the Scot brought old Burnacre the first decent meal he's had in a week at the diner up the road here in Starr Street opposite the funeral parlor—"

"— I know the one," interjected Cotter, "I too also eat there — I've been barred from Werner's." Both Pearl and Whitney looked at Cotter in surprise. "It's another story which I'll share with you both, later. But Miss Courtney's cooking now saves the lining of my stomach; But please, do go on Whitney…"

Dragoon nodded and continued. "So it turns out he caught up with this feller Flynn working on a ranch south of here. Robeson suspected the ranch wuz a stronghold for a bunch of cattle rustlers who run their purloined beef there ter fatten them up for market. Robeson only stopped off to rest up — but when he recognized Flynn from yore sketch he produced his manacles and of course they got in a shootout, with Flynn comin' out of it second best. Robeson wuz dead lucky the others at the ranch didn't come into it ter support their brother in crime. Mebbe they kept their noses clean because he played it dumb about them and their business from the start. Anyway, they let him take his wounded prisoner and leave, all acting "Mister Innocent".

"Maybe because he was carrying a badge, they didn't buy into it for fear he might have had a posse, nearby?" Frank offered.

"Who knows how the criminal mind works?" Pearl said as she packed the soiled crockery in a hand basin for washing.

"That old feller, Burnacre must have been a powder keg in his younger days — He helped Deputy Lexmon and that Roscoe feller sling lead at Clearwater and his pals outside Hallway's surgery!"

"That's common knowledge. In fact they are hinting that the white kid and his Mom who was hit with flying lead, caught the Muleskinner's stray slugs, there is doubt he hit his targets because of old eyes. I saw him in the street recently doing his morning ablutions in a trough on Main. Didn't think he was your type Whitney — how come you were mashing gums together?"

Dragoon said to both the newspaperman and the actress with a grin: You folks don't know me as well as you think you do. I'd talk to a darn deaf mule if it stood still long enough, when I'm in the mood fer conversation! " It was this gift that made him a natural salesman.

"Weren't there a couple of guys in on that stage robbery?" asked Pearl, then added: "Is this Flynn's partner gonna make good his escape?"

"Korda wuz the other man in it wif Flynn and some Canadian, Miss Courtney," Dragoon informed the actress. "This Sheriff Robeson is only one man, personally I reckon he was gonna need ter get lucky to catch up with anyone else in that piece of banditry. What do you reckon, Frank?"

"He was set an impossible task; that I'll grant you. The fact that he made any headway is a triumph. However, I happen to know that the other robber had fate stacked against him — according to Robeson, he nearly tracked this Korda feller through to Canada, but a wild Grizzly made a meal out of Korda in the interim. Lazarus Rollo is a damn lucky man I reckon, he might end up getting back almost everything that was riding in the strongbox." Frank told the pair of them.

"Gawd, the bottom certainly fell out of the bandits' cart." Dragoon exclaimed.

"Sure did. And as a writer I can't afford to let Sheriff Robeson off the hook about those tales — what exciting copies they will make on the daring-do of the West...'

Derrick Carter's drowning in a water-trough on Toby Street — between Starr Street and the schoolhouse, was bound to cause overwhelming distress especially to the pupils who discovered the body on their way to school, and as a newsworthy item it would become the lead story of the town's local press. The reporting of the incident spelled out that the street where the seeming mishap had occurred was so named after the Granddaughter of the Mayor of Junction City.

When found by children on their way to school, the shop-clerk was floating face up and of course was completely wet through for he had been submerged in the depth of the trough for hours. His flaxen hair waved back and forth like gossamer moss in a lazy breeze of willow trees, south in the Everglades.

It certainly was not the most convenient time for sheriff Boston and his deputies when summoned to the scene. For Doctor Hallway with the assistance of a personally tutored helper, were set-up to operate on Flynn's leg wound within the walls of the jailhouse, the ramrod was now gravely ill from the effects of Robeson's .44-45 slug, it was imperative that a sawbones with a good knowledge of gunshot wounds operate immediately, Dr. Hallway had cut his teeth years ago in that school of medicine and is more than capable to the task, also the man had full confidence in the Irish midwife, known locally as "Mother O'Grady" to assist him. She too had cut out her share of bullets before today.

Meanwhile the business of law and order would be conducted from the Mayor's office. Getting the prisoner into a state of unconsciousness so as they could do the painful surgery that awaited the ramrod, was easily achieved with the help of a bartender who was rumored to be able to mix this notorious Mickey Finn — that would drop an Elk within two strides.

The holding cell in which Clearwater sat nursing his fractured arm was masked off from proceedings with a tarpaulin tied to the barred divider separated the cells. The Pawnee's aloofness from the white man's world gave Hallway all the quiet he needed to devote himself to the operation without distractions. The amputation would take at the very least an hour of sawing and suturing, whether the patient survived the shock of having a limb removed was in the lap of the Gods.

Because Carter was deceased, there was no real hurry or need to get him hauled out of the trough, the post death urine and feces polluted water was Carter's own doing. Local street residences sealed off the thoroughfare and took it upon themselves, to send any further pupils about to enter the area away — the School Ma'am did not need to take advice in consenting to suspend school for the day.

When time permitted, Klem and his deputies went to the drowning in Toby Street with an ever growing procession following in their wake, for rumors of the dead youth's discovery had run from one end of town to the other and the unemployed came to gaze upon someone more unfortunate, than themselves.

The corpse's fixed open eyes were riveted on the azure sky but saw nothing, for these eyes were finished, life had long ago left their portals. Klem and his men removed the body from its watery grave and lowered it to the dry dirt about three feet from the trough. The street had no boardwalks, just dirt paths and the ground in general, was covered with wild grass and it soaked water up like an ink-blotter. Water drained from the soppy clothes like blood might from a busted open hogshead, but soon shortened to a mere trickle. Lexmon knelt down alongside the cadaver and attempted to close the eyes as he had seen mortician's do, but had no success, one eye kept fighting his efforts, so he removed his own bandanna and spread it out over the dead youth's face as though protecting its almost albino skin from sunburn.

The Mortician had been given word where the body could be found and had come to collect it like a rag an' bone man and would later prepare it for burial once he knew the funeral expenses would be covered. Boston sent a deputy along to the mercantile store to notify the youth's employer and collect any personal belongs and family information about Derrick Carter, for identification was never in question. As for he, Boston, knew who the private family was where Carter roomed and went to let them know the sad news. Here Klem learnt more of the youth's private life but most of it Boston already knew from town gossip. Carter was a known out-of-towner, it would now become the Sheriff's task, to put pen to paper and pass on the mournful news to the family of their son's, untimely death; for he now had the mailing address from Carter's landlord.

News of the death traveled fast but this did not surprise Klem, he had been the town's sheriff far too long for that. Before he got to the diner for a late lunch he had been stopped on the street by ten or so people; Men and women, all of whom claimed to have been served by him at one time or another, it was obvious that young Derrick Carter would be remembered as a nice effervescent type of individual. So much so, that one of his deputies had reported to the sheriff, that his employer would chip-in and cover the cost of burial if there was not enough money on hand for the job.

Frank Cotter learned of the tragedy from strangers on the street while out looking for the editor of the local rag to inform him that he was now the official correspondent for a New York daily. He had applied for a position with the local weekly paper but been passed over and it would give him a great deal of pleasure to rub the owner-editor's face in it. But that pleasure he had to forgo as he hurried back to the apartment to tell Pearl about the clerk's death. However, when he got to the apartment he found that Pearl had left him a note to the effect that she had gone down to **The Theater Royal** for more of her things. Already it had come to him that it was too much of a coincidence that the two people he knew who could state confidently that there was a **Fifth Man** at Lomax accident scene, were now deceased for there was now no proof.

Cotter finally tracked Pearl Courtney down and told her not only about the death of Carter but now, also about his theory that it was too much of a parallelism that Ma Kelly had been murdered and now Derrick Carter had drown!

Is it at all possible that Carter's drowning was no simple mishap but something more insidious? Maybe the sheriff could say whether or not by what he saw of the corpse, whether it too was a murder like that of

Ma Kelly's? He left Pearl and hurried uptown to the jailhouse, where like most everyone whom had a reason to call there today, found the written instructions pinned to the outside door that the sheriff's duties would be conducted out of the Mayoral office due to unforeseen circumstances until following notice. It did not state that prisoner Flynn was in recovery from an amputation and that the outcome still hung in the balance.

At the Town Council building Cotter was redirected to Werner's diner where Klem Boston and company were taking a late lunch break. Upon arrival outside the diner, Frank Cotter paused, not at all sure if he would be allowed over the threshold, then Pearl happened along the sidewalk and he quickly accosted her — apologized for rushing off like he had and asked her to fetch the sheriff from him. If the man protested or refused she had to explain that the matter was urgent and that at the present he, Cotter, was blackballed from the eatery...

The sheriff gave Pearl the courtesy of hearing her out and then got up from the debris of his meal and followed the actress out to where Cotter cooled his heels on the boardwalk.

The very thought that Derrick Carter was dead and he had now lost the only strong lead he had of forcing the law in this town to look deeper into the Lomax tragedy, made the newspaperman feel like a drink of something, stronger than java. But he saw the need for what it really was, a sure sign of alcoholic weakness and now wasn't the time for that sort of excuse to break out of his sworn ardent celibacy. Instead, he settled for a cigarette and reached for the makings in the left hand pocket of his trousers. The sincerity of Pearl's message to the sheriff from Cotter forced him to leave his meal with those in the diner and come to hear what couldn't wait to be said when the normal flow of things encouraged their paths to cross — Pearl had remained inside at the table on invitation of the other diners at the table while Klem made his journey outside.

LAZARUS ROLLO'S OFFICE SUITE ON THE SECOND-FLOOR OF THE CATTLEMEN'S ASSOCIATION BUILDING, OVERLOOKING MAIN STREET...

"—and that's all *you've recovered* of the ingots and banknotes?" Lazarus Rollo cried as he surveyed the recovered goods lying on top of his ink-blotter. The Chairman wore the expression of a man who might have lost a $20 banknote and picked up a lousy quarter in its place.

Jock Robeson nodded as he settled in the padded chair across the desk from Rollo, and thought: *What's with this ungrateful, Sassenach?! He is lucky I was able to recover any of the stolen property in one piece ...*

"I don't see my job as having been a dead loss." Robeson pointed out; "Flynn is in custody and I recovered his share of the stage hold-up, intact... I think yuh a lucky lad to have got as much as a red cent back, in my book!"

Rollo leaned back heavily in his chair. "What about Korda's cut, where's that? You *did* catch up with the man?"

"Nay. Well not exactly."

"Yore not trying to pull a quick one here an' tuck Korda's share away as bonus fer yore self I hope...?"

The moment those words left the chairman's mouth he had placed himself in jeopardy.

The Scotsman's blood pressure went skyward in a millionth of a second, and he was contemplating physical retribution against his employer. Robeson began on a soft and certainly an almost too quiet note. "You aren't serious about what you have just insinuated Mister Rollo... I mean it sounds to **this wee** Laddie that you're hintin' I've helped me self ter some cake from your party, right?"

"If the cap fits, wear it," said the Chairman, unfazed by Robeson's forceful reputation for being a hard task master, for in this town Rollo thought himself the cock of the walk, a man who held all the cards. The mistake was his! Robeson came up away from his chair in a flash; with a pistol clearing leather as fast as any would-be gunfighter could part company from iron and stiffened leather—the hard cold muzzle of his Colt rammed up into the chairman's face where it depressed flesh... it then slipped on the cold sweat which had broken out on Rollo's skin and rode up into the man's nostril!

Surprise and fear sent Rollo chalk white and his eyes bulged in the process. He recognized the strong possibility of a pistol-whipping or getting the top of his head blown off; the possibilities rocked the mighty man to the core.

"Jock Robeson is no crooked lawman, lad, an' don't suggest such — unless you're wearing a gun the size of a **cannon!**" Robeson left the gun in his face for a couple of beats, then eased away as he took the firearm off cock, and upon with drawing the end of the six-gun's barrel from Rollo's nostril, both men discovered it smeared with mucus and blood, Rollo's bleeding nose a paying tribute for the his own indiscretion…

Robeson produced a hanky from his person, and only after wiping off his gun did he throw it to the chairman, where it landed high on his chest, near his jowls. Rollo gathered it up and blew his nose while Jock went on to say: "—Now let's not hear any more of this business about me takin' a bonus fer myself," The Scot warned. "Korda got taken by a grizzly — he lost his horse and became easy meat fer our four-legged friends when he took to the forest on shank's pony. *I wasn't* about to try gutting the money or whatever out of slashed saddlebags. The lure for your loot wasn't worth it ter me! The bear or its hungry mate could've been still on the prowl for more fresh meat!"

Lazarus dabbed at the trickle of blood that ventured beyond the nostril as he continued to breathe heavily from the stress he had just endured.

The ex-Pinkerton moved back away from the Lazarus saying, "I wouldn't advise you trying for that pop-gun you keep in your drawer when my back's turned, my old chum…" He paused with his hand on the polished brass door-knob. "After you've settled your account with me, Rollo, I suggest there be no more dealings between us *unless* —" He wrenched open the door to the outer office where the Williams brothers lounged on-call. "— you have a pine box, handy…" He now spoke for the benefit of those in the outer room: "And don't send the brothers after me, Rollo. They aren't in my league. I'll be around until the prisoner recovers enough to travel, so don't you and your boys annoy me, huh?"

The Williams brother were on their feet and their paws hovered near the gun butts of their six-shooters, but held back going the full distance for they weren't sure what Lazarus Rollo wanted. The chairman came into view as he approached the open door from back near his desk; he looked shamefaced about something to the Williams brothers' mind of thinking, but all the same they held their stance and looked on.

"Relax, boys," said Rollo from below the lintel. "— the sheriff and I jist had a little misunderstanding, that's all. C'mon in, I wanna hear yore news…" Rollo stood aside, Robeson and the brothers exchanged watchful glances in passing, Rollo heeled the office door to, and Sheriff Robeson went off to learn how his prisoner had faired. The lawman was aware as he left the Association's building that his back was exposed and he felt nervous about it, for he was pretty sure that the brothers were not above back-shooting a man, any man. As long as he was going to be in town he vowed that he would always keep a wary eye out for them, they were lower down than the scales of a rattlesnake's underbelly.

Mother O'Grady helped Doctor Hallway bandage Flynn's stump, which more or less completed the operation save for the tidying up of the gory aftermath and the disposal of the severed limb. Had the Irish woman been asked whether or not the patient was likely to survive his ordeal she would have told one that in her limited opinion, she thought not. Flynn had done a lot of bleeding and the stump's bandage was so soaked, that the patient's blood tarnished the palm of her hand.

"…This isn't the best accommodation for an amputee to recover in, Doctor, if yuh don't think I'm speakin' above me station, sir." Mother O'Grady expressed as she gathered up the bloody cotton material from the cell floor.

"Agreed," Hallway said, "it could prove fatal ter move him to a new location before the next twenty-four hours have passed… It's here for the moment he has to stay and rest. I'm thinking of asking Don Stroughton if we can open up one of the upstairs rooms in The Royal, as a hospital room for the prisoner away from this environment."

"With the railway soon settin' up shop in town we'll need a real hospital — Industrial accidents come with heavy industry, my poor dad died back in England when he left Ireland ter work in the iron foundries. Even your surgery on Main Street is gonna prove too small an' pokie, to nurse anyone in who's as seriously sick as yore amputee," The informative Mother O'Grady added.

Still working away on his patient the sawbones mused: "I might try and push the council to seriously think about buying The Royal and turning it into a Hospital; the upstairs' rooms are quite spacious and would suit nicely…"

"I shan't ask how a gent' of your standin' would know about the room sizes in a bordello — that's yore business," said Mother O'Grady.

He looked deeply at the woman and felt he had to explain.

"Sometimes Ma's gals got careless and finished up in the family way. I jist accommodated her and her gals frum time to time, it goes with the territory for a bordello owner to keep a doctor on the payroll."

By now, due to Klem Boston's negotiation prowess his lunch table in Werner's diner, catered to the presence of Miss Pearl Courtney, Sheriff Robeson and Frank Cotter. It would seem that the newspaperman's association with the local law had gained him acceptance once more to the establishment. All four were so deep in conversation that none of them were aware of the passing pedestrian traffic on the boardwalk beyond the table's widow.

"...It could have put a new spin on things," suggested the ex-Pinkerton man.

"Like Ma Kelly, Derrick Carter did not want to get tangled up in anything which might draw attention to him," Cotter explained. "The youth was clearly a bit timid when *round* adults without a counter between him — he was afraid that no one would take him seriously. Also, in his eyes he believed he didn't see anything untoward happened. All he saw a group of men lift a body from the road over to the sidewalk and it wasn't until he heard gossip about the accident that he knew it was Doctor Lomax.

"Now the thing which strikes me strange about this, and I doubt that it's struck a chord with any of you, yet; is that now both folks who have as so much suggested that there was a *fifth* guy in attendance, are dead!

"Kelly had her throat slashed open and now this Carter youth drowns in — of all places, a water-trough! Hell, think about it? How in God's name does a young man just up and drown in a lousy trough of water...?" Cotter exclaimed as he slid back on his chair until his spine came to rest up against the back-support, then he removed his hat, wiped his brow and placed his Stetson on his lap. The others around the table had been captured by his spiel and were cogitating, the worth of his words.

Mebbe I haven't done the right thing by Doctor Lomax, thought Boston. *He did his best fer me that time back in Dodge an' never asked so much as a nickel fer his services. And, since this newspaper guy's hit town it seems ter be one thing after another. If there wuz ever a murder, Ma Kelly's death is one and now this Carter feller's, drowning …? Hell's bells — I ain't heard yet of anyone fallin' into a trough and drownin' — this feller might have somethin' here. Hell, even the actress girlfriend of Doc Lomax is all fired up about the possibility of there bein' a connection…Mebbe Jock Robeson has a worthwhile opinion wif all his experience, he might know which trail I should mosey down?*

"Whaddya reckon, Jock?" Boston questioned.

"Frankly, I thinking you have too much trouble in this burgh for one lawman and a couple of deputies, Klem." Robeson began ticking them off on his fingers. "…You've got the Kelly problem! The Indian matter – plus this store clerk's death to sort out; and now the Army ready ter yank away your star! Me? I don't envy yuh, Klem me boyo.

"This tenderfoot, an' Miss Pearl seem convinced this ain't no simple drowning yuh dealing with. Sorry Laddie — I'd rather stick to scything my own heather an' leave you to yuh own croft. Either way, things have gotta be sorted out into an orderly deck and that I'm afraid is gonna be your job, Klem," Robeson statement had a familiar ring to it and that was sounding, a little bit like the style of dear old Pilate.

Talking aloud Boston said as he mulled things over: "Toby Street peters out about fifty-yards beyond the school yard. It struck me a piece odd, that Carter should be in that neck of the woods — not a place you'd go wandering at night unless yuh wanted yore ankles bitten by stray dawgs, folks in that part of town have 'em as watch-dawgs ter keep out uninvited visitors …"

"Check and see if anyone heard any dogs yappin' down that way last night and what time? That might give you a fix on about when it happened," Jock told Klem.

"Yes, in my experience most dogs get on their guard around strangers and as night closes in," said the scribe, who knew what it was like to have a dog sink its fangs into his rump. "Was there any bruising on him to show that he might have been in a brawl — he's too big to simply fall into a trough and not find his way out! Was he facedown or what, when found?"

Boston shrugged. "He wuz face up when we hauled him out of the water —"

"No one just up and down without calling for help," the Scot stated. "Not in ***my*** book and ***not*** that close to cottages!"

By now Frank had produced a 6 X 4 writing-pad and a fancy new propelling pencil (this was really the last valuable item he had left from his professional days of being a scribe before the booze dominated that aspect of his life – he thought that it too had gone but found it tucked away in his luggage while Pearl Courtney was on her way to deliver Peter Kelly to his relatives in the big smoke) as he prepared to take notes. Neither lawmen objected, though they were in wonder of the newspaperman's writing gadget — an item new to this part of the world.

"Can you tell me what you've found out about Carter's private life, Sheriff Boston?" Cotter rolled the barrel of the metal pencil between his thumb and forefinger; the action caused the graphite core to extend slightly beyond the small barrel's bore, enough to bear the writing weight of the human's hand without snapping off, but only if the user gagged his or her weight to ensure such a catastrophe was not in the making.

"I tell you what I think you should know," Klem said as he signaled for the waitress hovering in the background to bring coffee for everyone. She went off to fill a coffeepot from the urn at the counter that was accessible via a toy-like faucet — "Though I can't figure how important it's gonna be…"

"Let me judge that," suggested Cotter with the tip of the graphite pencil poised over a fresh, pre-lines page of the writing pad. Klem went on, "Derrick Carter arrived in Junction City just after the end of the War to work at the merchant store where he worked behind the counter. He came from a place called Oliver's Ferry. It is believed his Pa wuz a casualty of the War an' Derrick sent most all of his earnin' home to help his Ma and siblings."

"That would be precious little," Cotter interjected, firmly.

Klem shrugged and continued: "He roomed with a family called Antsy towards the bottom end of Main Street – before the street cuts out.

"Tom Antsy is a cabinet-maker and his wife takes in washin' an' ironing fer some of the town bachelors and the like, who feel the urge of flashin' up apiece on Saturday nights. Derrick wuz a bit sweet on

Miss Sue Antsy, but the gal's parents didn't encourage it because the young hombre had hardly any cash ter call his own and bein' able ter sustaining a future wife wuz out of the question.

"However they were in the habit of going out for regular walks after supper, weather permittin' of course. Most times Miss Susan would be accompanied by her kid brother as chaperone.

"But not last night … Last night he went orf alone. By all accounts, he wuz in a cheerful frame of mind — according to the Anstys he had been so, for the past month…"

"Sounds like we can rule out **suicide,**" said Jock "Don't reckon that's the shape of a mind thinkin' of endin' things. People likely ter top 'emselves is usually melancholy."

Nodding her head, Pearl said: "The fact that he had responsibilities and was caring enough of his family back in Oliver's Ferry, doesn't sound like someone who would commit suicide…What d'you think, Sheriff Boston?"

Klem nodded over that mouthful. Boston realized that it was the newspaperman's suspicions on both killings, that had sent the man hunting him around town, and he would get no joy from the presence of the scribe who was like a saddle-bur to him.

Cotter looked across into the sheriff's eyes and he did not in any way try to hide his determination to press the cripple for a result that would be to his satisfaction, no more just this skimming over the surface. Finally Klem Boston muttered: "…I will do what I can but I can't promise much," and in that he was being honest.

"Just you establishing the fact that two people in this town are dead because they were connected by a common denominator will go along ways to setting things in their rightful place," said Cotter; "and we both know it's all connected to this missing witness which too many people are turning a blind-eye too — show the town and especially me, that this elaborate cover-up is finished and the murder is going to pay for his or her foul deeds!" While delivering his diatribe Cotter had continued scribbling out his notes on the top sheet of his writing tablet, the lawmen did nothing specific but look on.

Then Klem felt he had to say his piece, with a rippled brow he said: "That's easy fer you to say an' write — No one more'n me would like ter find Ma's cowardly killer. But the trail has gone dead cold, not that it were ever warm ter begin wiv. Oh, I could clear it orf the books, but that would mean blamin' her son, he wuz the only other person we knows of up there in the apartment besides, Ma. Yet as any damned fool in this town knows Pete ain't capable of it! There wuz nuthin' in the apartment he could have used ter do that mess ter her throat that were done —"

"Plus the lad would not have the brains in his noodle to know how to get rid of an instrument so we wouldn't find it; I searched the dwelling frum top to bottom!" rode in Jock Robinson, over Klem.

"— and now as fer as the murder goes, I'm at a dead-end," concluded Boston as he wiped each corner of his lip-line with his forefinger and thumb.

"Murder's a sly devious act an' it takes someone akin to the Devil to plan and pull it off," pointed out the Scot, who probably had more experience along these lines than anyone at the table.

Jock looked Frank Cotter in the eye and said, "How did you learn what Carter claims to have known about the Lomax accident?"

"Derrick told me when I went in for groceries — he also told me why he wasn't so forthcoming with what he knew to you, Sheriff Boston..."

Boston dropped his lip in the scribe's direction and interlocked his fingers of both hands on the tabletop.

Frank sighed. "I guess now that poor Carter's dead, there's no harm can come to his soul or him, if I tell you what his yoke of surfeit was... After all, Miss Pearl already knows. Derrick Carter was no doubt a lonely young man, and as you know, sheriff, spent a good bit of time alone walking the streets of town —" Boston nodded. "During these strolls he used to talk a loud to himself..." There Frank left it; folks could make what they will out of it.

Both lawmen gazed at each other as though they'd stumbled on someone who belonged in a sanatorium. Cotter could easily assume what the officers were thinking and decided he should say something in defense of the youth.

"Excuse me, gentlemen — but what you've begun to form there in your minds, is exactly what Derrick Carter feared, condemnation. He realized that if people knew about his eccentricity he would be looked down upon and lose all respect in the community, a community he'd dearly come to love. In fact he was petrified of folks thinking he didn't know where fantasy ends and reality begins! As long as his secret remained just his secrete he knew he was very much accepted as an equal, without that acceptance he was washed up in Junction City."

After a weighty pause, Boston spoke up. "It seems ter me, that going by what you've just told us 'bout this 'talking business', we can all understand why he kept himself to himself …" Then to Cotter he said: "You were privileged he admitted these private things to you my man!"

"I s'pose so … yes."

"Now I can say I understand the feller a bit more than I could before — but 'tis a pity he didn't involve himself more wiv life round him. Two folks knew there wuz this stranger at the thar Doc's accident and neither of them spoke up about our *fifth* feller. It would've supported your case Cotter, for an inquiry." Klem said doe-eyed.

"*And* don't I know it," Frank admitted with a degree of exhaustion in his voice, brought on by being forced to labor the point over and over, again.

"Who else knows about Carter's confession to you, other than this circle at the table?" asked Robeson. "*Think,* because it might be important?"

The newspaperman did not have to delve too deeply back into his memory to answer that. "Other than Pearl – and, and Whitney Dragoon — that's all I can think of. But someone else must've known something — hence his death …"

"You should have come straight ter me with it," growled Boston, "the moment you thought you had somethin'!"

"That is something Frank dearly wanted to do — but how could he speak sense to you after the debacle made over at Fort Hancock?" said Pearl. "You advised him to get out of town, and wouldn't give him the time of day. Trying to talk to you Mr. Boston might have ended up with him in one of *your* cells alongside your Indian buck!"

"Miss Pearl Courtney's right," Cotter told both lawmen, then directly to Boston, said: "— the moment I got Derrick's information I ran into you on the street in front of the mercantile and wanted to talk turkey with you, but you brushed me off until later. Had you heard me out there and then, the youth, Carter, might be still alive!"

"Hold it," said Klem as he raised a hand from the table in a halting gesture. "The time you caught me, I wuz up ter me eyes with tryin' ter divert a clandestine lynichin' party rearin' up on its hind legs, after all, that wuz why the Army let me out of their stockade, to hogtie those involved. Besides, when you stopped me on the sidewalk you never mentioned names — that's why I fobbed yuh orf, right?"

Frank nodded.

"When did you tell Miss Courtney and Dragoon about Carter?" asked Robeson.

"Yesterday afternoon — you can't imagine either one of those people could be a party to the young man's death?" It showed in Cotter's face the preposterousness of such a line of thought.

"The Pinkertons encouraged us agents ter come at things from more than one angle, lad. For instance, we've had men dress up and play the part of a woman to avoid detection — it's an onerous call to recognize a person's cut under yards of calico skirts and a veil, that's the sole purpose of the veil, to hide a five o'clock shadow…"

"I get your point," Cotter said as he returned to sheriff Boston. "Let us suppose Carter was murdered and didn't walking into that trough in the dark. Wouldn't it be possible that his killer might well be the one who slashed Ma's throat?"

Klem nodded. "Anything is possible. But unless *I was* on the spot when these things happen, such as the killin' of Ma and Carter — how c'n I prove it?"

"I'll tell you something, Sheriff. I would be almost ready to accept this youth's drowning *if* he had been found in a storage pond or a flooded creek, and was known like me, as a drinker. But we know he didn't drink because he had no spare money to fling down the neck of rye-whiskey bottles — his sobriety doesn't even come into question. I can't even dream up a reason for him to fall into a trough of water and drown. I might believe it of a guy like Burnacre, but not that kid! You sure he didn't look as though he had been in a fight of some sort?"

"I saw some bruises on his hands," said the sheriff, thoughtfully. "…I put that down ter 'im struggling ter try to git out of the water. I s'pose if'n you want ter look at it in the light of your lantern, they could've been the legacy of someone standin' over him and holding his head down under the water and him clawing the coarse sides of that wooden trough to break free of his attacker!"

A glint came in to Cotter's eyes as he said: "I've gotta admit that's plausible enough for me and in line with what comes to mind. Would it be stepping on anyone's toes if I called into the mortician's and had a look at Carter's body for myself?"

"Why?" Both Boston and Robeson asked.

"Unless you've had any experiences with stiffs, I can't see the point to it, Laddie?" Jock said with a frown.

"**We** don't need the corpse identified," added Klem Boston. "His employer offered ter take on that responsibility; though in this instance it will not be needed."

"I understand that. I just wanna view the body for my own satisfaction…"

Pearl looked at Cotter as though he were some kind of oddball. *Where is the pleasure one would get gazing at dead bodies?* The actress thought.

"If you can find some ghoulish pleasure in looking over the dead — then be my guest," said Boston, "Me and Jock'll sit a while and talk this out…"

Pearl left the diner with Cotter, out on the sidewalk the pair paused and Frank said to Pearl: "I don't expect you will wish to come round the mortician, so I suggest you go back to whatever it was you were doing before this drowning business reared up."

"Sure," she said and took Cotter by surprise, standing on the toes of her pumps and gave him a quick light kiss on the cheek. As she lower herself on to her heels, the surprised expression on Frank's face made her blush at her this impetuous gesture.

"What's **that** in aid of?" Frank's right-hand came involuntarily up to finger the area of skin on his cheek, her soft lips had caressed.

"Nothing special — I just feel you needed a reward of sorts for your persistence in all this. If ever I've seen a trout fighting its way upstream against the odds, then you're it, Frank Cotter. Keep up the good work!"

Turning, Pearl hurried off down along the walk and it was only then did Cotter realize he wasn't in a world of his own. He turned to locate the alleyway that cut through to the upper end of Starr Street, the very one Bevan and his friend had used the day he walked back from the cemetery with Lomax's backers. He knew he would exit just a few business premises up from the funeral parlor on the opposite side of the street.

Churcher, the mortician, and Frank were in the crypt under the premises of the funeral house, originally its purpose had been that of a cyclone cellar. Carter's body was laid out in a box of ice and sawdust with a sheet separating the deceased from the cooling material. There were another four corpses being preserved in the same way until either funeral arrangements had been confirmed or a coffin built to size.

The crypt was big enough to store a dozen bodies and also a workshop, where carpenter Hodder and his apprentice, labored away at a couple of coffins in various stages of completion; Light was admitted to the cellar from the crypt's ground level double doors which opened out into the overhead back yard where a shed was used to store two hearses, next to the shed was a tack-room and an enclosed stable for the team needed to haul the hearse from pillar to post when need be. A stable-hand-cum-groom was responsible for looking after the horses and a couple hearses. In all, the funeral house employed eight people.

"...There's not many people like to venture to his part of our establishment, Mr. Cotter...We keep the iceboxes down here in crypt as we call it, it sounds more up market than referring to it as a cyclone cellar; we find the ice doesn't melt so quickly if we cover it with common old sawdust and the cooler temperature of the cellar, though the people down at the ice works aren't too wrapped in knowing our use for their ice."

"I understand that. I just wanna view the body for my own satisfaction..." Cotter and Churcher stopped overlooking the icebox which held Carter's remains – the box resting on a couple of sawhorses, coffins and ice- boxes got the same treatment down here away from the publics' gaze; for when it was all said and done – it, after all, is a place of commerce.

Looking about the crypt, Frank said with a sigh: "So this is where my unlucky friend was parked before his burial."

Churcher ran his eyes around into every open corner of the cellar in search of something which one might deem offensive to the dead; he came up with a blank. Meanwhile Cotter stood there looking down at Derrick Carter's remains.

"No one has ever complained about our set-up before…do you find it offensive in some way, sir?"

"No," said Frank, which included a shake of his head. "I was just wondering how things work in your place, I expect in general all mortician houses operate much the same way. Was Doctor Lomax housed in a similar icebox before burial?"

Churcher nodded, "I understood that you've come here to view the decease, Mr. Derrick Carter. Have you seen sufficient, Mister Cotter?"

"No. I need to see more… Could I see the contact bruises the corpse got during the course of his death struggles, sir?"

"That is a rather odd request…"

"But nonetheless important — I assure you, Mr. Churcher."

Churcher exposed the face of the corpse first up. Now, whether it was due to the cold ice or not there was a bruise to the left-cheek and the right-eye gave the impression that it had commenced to swell but its action had become dormant once life had left the body.

Then without any sign of repulsion in his face, Cotter reached out and took the cadaver's right wrist and raised the deceased's hand up and inspected the abrasions on the knuckles … This surprised Churcher, for the scribe did it as casually as that of a person in the trade. Rigor mortise had left the body sometime ago now, so manipulation was not a problem. Clearly the newspaperman had seen all he wanted, so he replaced Carter's hand back on the cadaver's chest and stood aside for Churcher to lower the lid. Cotter and Churcher then adjourned to ground level of the funeral house.

"You seemed quite at ease with being around a corpse, Mister Cotter?" opined Churcher as they climbed the crypt's staircase back to ground level in single file.

"I was a news reporter on the front during the War — I had to sometimes check the casualty lists of the dead and missing against the actual bodies in the field…" The late Doctor Lomax's friend informed the Mortician.

They entered the showroom from behind a limp, powder blue curtain that hid the doorway to the cellar stairs.

"Who was it identified Doctor Lomax, Mr. Churcher, d'you recall?"

"Not off hand — give me a moment and I'll check our records, it'll be noted." Churcher went across to a wooden filing cabinet and opened one of its three drawers and traced down the information while chatting… "…Without seeking to be morbid in anyway, I can tell you that your friend was quite messed up. After all, he had been crushed under the wheels of a heavy-laden wagon…" He finally found the file and glanced over the paperwork. "Here we are. Hmm, it seems that no one actually did identify him *per se,* in the sense that he was so badly injured and disfigured. The way we did it was that the men who were with the doctor at the time of the accident, verified the body's identity and in turn each witnesses initialed my file, here, look for yourself — " Churcher handed the file to Cotter who took on the job with interest. But he learnt nothing he hadn't already suspected, Hill, Stroughton and Bevan, Doctor Hallway et cetera had all duly put their marks to the records.

"So I can take it from this file, there was no open coffin before the burial for anyone to view the body?" Cotter closed the file and handed it back to Churcher.

"That's correct," Churcher re-filed the folder. "…the body was in such a horrible state his lawyer — Stroughton forbad it — it was not something anyone would want to view."

"H'm. Now that puzzles me…"

"I don't follow?" said Churcher as he pushed the filing cabinet's drawer shut.

"OK — well according to people present at the accident, Doctor Lomax was conscious and talking prior to expiring. He was supposed to have been lucid enough to even issue instructions about my welfare… and that of Pearl Courtney. H'm, very strange…" The scribe's frown prompted Churcher to correct the man's thinking.

"Begging your pardon, sir… But I dealt with your friend and I can tell you quite honestly that he was not in any condition to have done any talking. The injuries to the body I saw — and bear in mind I am no sawbones, would have caused instant death — he was so busted up he could have been anyone other than Mr. Lomax, the only way I come to know who I was dealing with, was because I accepted Sheriff Boston and Doctor Hallway's word — they accompanied the body and verified his identity as did his friends…"

"I take it you knew Lester Lomax on a professional basis, Mr. Churcher?"

"Naturally — that's why we all were flabbergasted when we were made aware whom we were dealing with, Mr. Cotter. But I ought to have recognized the Doctor by his wardrobe; he had a distinctive way of dressing — slightly eccentric, one might say for this town."

"What was eccentric about my friend's attire?"

"He had the occasional habit of wearing spats. Doctor Lomax was a professional man and being a doctor he didn't go about like some down in the heel, cowboy. Show me a sawbones who would?"

"I used some pieces of Lester's wardrobe but I didn't see any spats amongst them?"

Churcher shook his head. "That's right — I saw to it that he wore them to the grave…" both men began to head towards the street doorway almost simultaneously, outside two of Ma Kelly's ladies of the night paraded on by on the lookout for a cowboy or any other males with time on their hands.

The scribe changed the subject. "How sharp are your eyes Mr. Churcher?" They halted; Frank on the walk across from the threshold and the Mortician balanced on the threshold directly beneath the fanlight of the establishment.

"Why do you ask?"

"Did you happen to notice the knuckles of Carter's hands? They were skin-barked…and err, his face looked to me as though he might have been in a fight, wouldn't you say?" He asked these questions quite out of the blue for just now they'd only been discussing the late doctor's situation. For a moment or two there, Churcher was lost and couldn't quite understand where Frank Cotter was coming from — then he realized that the man had switched subjects and gone back to the poor feller found drowned. He had noticed the damage to the knuckles but had accepted it as being all part of the deal of someone whom had injured themselves while struggling to get out of the trough, so nothing more need be attached to it."

"Yeah, I did notice that," his searching eyes also noticed a fruit stone on the walk near the edge of the boards, he came out and toed it over the edge down to the dirt, completing the act someone else ought to have done. "…folks struggling ter save themselves often do damage to their skin, hands and fingernails — " he returned to his position under the door lintel and leant with his right shoulder up against the frame at an angle with ankles crossed and arms folded.

"Derrick also had markings to his face — looked very much like he might have been in a physical altercation prior winding up in that tub, don't you think, sir?"

"Hard for one, ter say …. Like I said before, people in the act of trying to save themselves, *can* come through it and then to the untrained eye they look as though they've been brawling when, in actual fact — their fight has been, for their very life!"

"I s'pose … But he could have been struggling with someone who had him facedown in that trough against his will, submerged there until drowned; if that were the case, that would make it an act of murder, wouldn't it?"

Churcher considered what Frank Cotter had just said before answering. "If that were the case, yeah; But I've known of people to drown in six-inches of water and in the trough young Derrick was found in, there was a lick more than twenty inches deep, that's plenty enough fer a drowning!"

"I'd grant you that under normal circumstances. But I am a suspicious feller by nature and *I'm* seeing this as another of Junction City's climbing murder rate. I can't buy this as an accident or suicide — the Carter boy had too much to live for in responsibilities, alone. He was practically supporting his immediate family at some place called Oliver's Ferry. A guy with those sorts of liabilities isn't the kind of person who'd commit suicide in … I'm fast drawing the conclusion here that he was set upon by someone who battered him into semi-consciousness, and then forced him down under the water until he drowned; if that were the case, then that young feller got his abrasions as the poor wretch fought for his chance to live!"

"That can't be right. The way I heard it Carter was found lying face up in the water… If some damn coot had held him down to drown, how could he have ended up on his back? "

"Maybe the killer or killers rolled him over to satisfy themselves that the feller *was* indeed dead, and their work, accomplished?" Cotter suggested.

"I only knew the youth in passing — but he never struck me ter be the type of person who'd get on the wrong side of anyone. In fact I thought him rather timid…" Churcher pointed out. "So who would have any reason to do what yore hinting wuz done to him? No, to me, it is a simple case of suicide."

"That's a reasonable point of view to hold. Except that *he* shared some information with me about the Doctor Lomax accident, which wasn't common knowledge. and maybe to someone out there, if they suspected, **he** had this **information** and passed it on to me, certainly wouldn't approve of it — for it could raise some very poignant questions that will need answering before a court of inquiry. So whoever orchestrated this underhanded business would see their plans could be brought undone. That just might be an excuse for murder, don't you think?"

The mortician shrugged. "Sorry, but I can't help you there," said Churcher, "I only bury them as they come along."

"HOLY, HELL!" Cotter yelled, as a sudden thought erupted in the man's mind like that of Mt. Vesuvius — "you've given me an idea! Have you ever exhumed anyone,. Churcher?"

"Exhumed?"

"Reopen a grave!"

"I know what **exhume,** means," Churcher frowned in Cotter's direction, "…No, I've never been called upon for such a thing — mostly when someone's dead it's a case of gettin' 'em in the ground as quick as one can! What makes you raise such a question?"

"Something you said…" Cotter moved closer to the mortician. "You said when you laid eyes on Lester's features; they were in such a mess that if you hadn't been told who it was, you wouldn't have known it was the good doctor —"

Churcher nodded.

"—let's say just for argument's sake, that the body you buried wasn't the body of Doctor Lomax, but someone else?"

Scowling Churcher said: "You can't be serious to suggest an impossible thing as that?!"

"Oh, you can't know how serious this bod is, Mr. Churcher. It has happened before today where the wrong person has ended up in the wrong coffin or grave…"

"Impossible. It could only come about by design of a couple of conspirators for it to work!"

Shaking his head, Cotter said, "Conspiracy is not foreign to our way of life, stage magicians do it all the time in their line of work." The scribe gestured in a manner that indicated that the answer to Churches' question was, momentarily beyond him, but he would dearly love to know its answer. "Who knows? All one can do is speculate — maybe Lester found it necessary to disappear because things were getting too hot for him from another quarter, i.e., the authorities. Or maybe be realized the Pawnees were unhappy with his medicine and its results, as that of the government's, and had to make himself very scarce … maybe he realized it was eminent the settlement would be raided by a bunch of hot-headed Indians out after blood and revenge!"

"Don't you think this is a rather odd way to talk about your friend, Mr. Cotter?"

"No. What I've mentioned are all just possibilities — I'm speaking from an outsider's point-of-view, here. If Lester's grave was opened up it could settle the dust once and for all."

"And mebbe open up a whole new can of worms," Churcher said as he leaned up against the doorjamb, again. "— I told ya Doctor Lomax wuz unrecognizable. So how is digging up the body, gonna prove anything one way or the other? "

"True. But I know of one sure way of identifying Lester… He has a scare on his right palm, like this… " Cotter raised the palm of his left hand and showed Churcher his own scare. "We cut our palms like a couple of redskins and made ourselves "blood brothers" for life. If the body inside the coffin doesn't have a scare where I reckon it should be, then…?" The rest Cotter left unsaid with raised brows.

"Huh. Then I have news fer you. Unless Sheriff Boston is in on it, there'll be no unearthin' the Doc's box. And I can tell you, you'll be wasting yore time old feller."

This isn't a town I would recommend to folks back east, though the scribe as he raised his hat to Churcher in farewell and went off about his business. Churcher, was now puzzled by what the newsman had pointed out, he returned to the cyclone cellar and checked the body of young Carter out for himself and though not prepared to make a song and dance about it, he came to the conclusion that it was quite possible that someone had dragged the struggling lad to that trough and then held him under until he drowned, but if this were true, and, that was the way it had been done, then he was sure that it would have involved more than one person to accomplish what they had set out to do.

The gravedigger's shovel struck the coffin's wooden lid with a THUD even though there was at least three inches of soft soil still covering it. Convened at the opening of the grave were Sheriff Boston, Attorney Donald Stroughton, and Deputy Lexmon, Frank Cotter, Churcher and the cemetery's caretaker, every man jack of them were intently gazing down into the open grave.

The man doing the spade-work scrapped the remaining dirty spread over the casket's lid into a small neat hill and shoveled it up out of the hole onto the fresh oblong mound of soil alongside the grave, in all, it turned out to be three shovelful's of loam.

"Now comes the tough, part…" The grave-digger informed those about him at the edge of the grave, the man, clammy from his labor and already dreading the task ahead of reburial once the witnesses had moved out, so he threw aside his shovel and grabbed a wrecking bar and working with great care as he prized the lid open with very little damage as possible to the casket.

As the lid was raised, those standing round the edge of the grave expected to see the recently buried face of the doctor, but instead were meet by the corpse resting flat on its back within the coffin, a white silk bandanna had been draped over the cadaver's face to hide the horrific structural damage and because the sheriff did not find their task appealing in any shape or form, suggested that the bandanna be left in place and only the necessary palm of the body in question be examined. The gravedigger would not have a bar at touching the body so Churcher exchanged places with the man and climbed down into the grave and did the necessary. There on the deceased's palm was the telltale scare which compared almost exactly with the one on the scribe's own hand. From overhead the witnesses could see clearly down into the casket and each had his turn at sighting the scare to make it official. "I don't know why I let you talk me into this, Cotter…" Klem muttered bitterly to Frank. Churcher climbed out of the hole with Lexmon's help as everyone moved off save for the gravedigger, whose chore was now to close everything up.

Frank said: "At least we know we have the right man — I wanna sign the paper of identification Mr. Boston, shall I come back to your office for that?"

"Nah, we'll do it in the cemetery's tool shed down there," Boston said rather grouchily. "Anyone else need ter be a party to this, Mr. Attorney?" The sheriff looked around at the other witnesses before they began marching in the direction of the shed.

"Does this mean that my records are still in order Mr. Stroughton?" Churcher asked.

"I'm happy for them to stay as they are what about you, Klem?" asked the Attorney.

"Once Cotter signs my paperwork I'm all straight," announced the Sheriff.

Cotter strolled quietly downhill towards the tool shed a little apart from the others as he felt like a round peg in a square hole. Things were not going well for Frank Cotter these days as far as his relationships with people went. Pearl Courtney had been dead-set against Lester Lomax body being disturbed, and because of this and Cotter's insistence that it was all for the best, went a long ways towards cooling their relationship. Cotter knew that Pearl only remained in the apartment and did not return to the "Theater Royal" because he resided downstairs.

When Boston and Ben Lexmon got back to the jailhouse after their visit to Boot Hill, they were surprised to find the heavy breathing, sweaty horse of Jake Warner's hitched to the tie-rail on the street; inside waiting for them like a cat on hot bricks, was the Indian agent. Klem knew his visit could only mean one thing, trouble.

Klem and Ben removed their hats as they approached the sheriff's desk where Warner sat waiting. "Now what thar hell's your trouble?"

Boston snarled, for he had had enough of things for today and yet it wasn't even late afternoon.

Warner explained that he had received word that a number of the Pawnees were planning to come to town and break Clearwater out of his cell.

"Over my ***dead*** body," bawled the Sheriff.

"That there might be the end result," Jake Warner told him without any embellishment.

Ben Lexmon's gut tightened with fear. He never for one moment thought that earning a buck as a lawman was going to be so goddamn dangerous. He didn't reckon for a second that sorting out Indian troubles were in his charter, and believed that a chore such as keeping the Indians in check and in their place was the Army's job. Ben's actions showed that if he had questioned his boss — that is the answer he would get. Klem took off post-haste to the express office down town, and sent a wire off to Fort Hancock to alert the Army.

Fort Hancock received Boston's wire in its dot and dashes format — and when it had been translated by the signal's operator it was rushed to the Commander, who upon reading it, ordered instant action — this galvanized the Army post into full active service.

Fort Commandant ordered that Captain Roscoe and Lieutenant Briggs take command of the squad being raised to be sent off overland to the reservation and take charge of the situation. Their orders were to travel at the double as the crow flies.

The bugler sounded *Boots and Saddles* and the rush was on for the cavalry to ready themselves for the trek that lay ahead; it was truly organzied chaos, thoughts and doubts were there in the backs of the men's minds, as they rode out through the fort's gates, that some might be unlucky enough not to return.

Sheriff Boston met the town Mayor, Aldermen and Lazarus Rollo, Chairman of the Cattlemen's Association's, building. This time the town was not going to be taken by surprise as before. Everyone was expected to do his or her bit. The Williams brothers were ordered to gather a number of riders from the town and encourage them to head out in every compass direction, to warn as many ranchers as possible in the outlying reaches to prepare for an Indian war and or come to the safety of Junction City. The brothers put their heart and soul into the task before them, and rode their mounts like a couple of war-crazy Apaches from homestead to homestead just as the men they had ordered into the saddle did likewise, the only answer in the end was to swap mounts with the ranchers or hijack fresh horses from the ranch owners at gunpoint, but at least they got the job done.

In the brothers' wake, ranchers and dirt farmers bundled their families into buggies, covered wagons and headed for town.

The townspeople swung into action. Timber, hammers and nails became very short in supply as people boarded up windows and doors. In the beginning their preparations were somewhat helter-skelter and as things progressed, more thought was put into it, people realized that not all the buildings in town were in a position to be protected. Boston suggested that the main business district take priority over the rest of the settlement — it was his idea that they build formidable barricades inside the edge of the building line and everyone in the township would be herded together for their own well-being.

The construction of the barriers got made up with all manner of knick-knacks, anything that could hinder the progress of flying lead, was assembled on Bryan Street to the north, and to the south and east and west of Main Street. The east barrier on Main was constructed across the road from building front to building front, east of the express office, which also took in the entrance of the alleyway that ran through from Main Street to Starr Street.

The Russian gunsmith, Yolson, came to light with boodles of ammunition and a variety of guns and rifles began to see the light of day from his cyclone cellar, he had at times earned the wrath of his wife as she saw his purchasing of the civil war's surplus arms just a waste of hard earned cash at the time. But now like her husband was prepared to see that any man ready to defend the town, would be issued with whatever they had on hand— along with a promissory note from the town council of payment if the arms came to be used in the town's defense. Dragoon put himself to use by helping Mrs. Yolson keep the bookwork in order, for no matter how serious the situation the Jews couldn't afford to go out of pocket.

All the livestock such as horses and mules now in the confines of town were collected and corralled in the rear yards of all the saloons within the fortified area. The loose domestic dog menace came to the fore, dogs whom had long ago been abandoned on the streets of Junction City sensed the tension of the townspeople, and began making a general nuisance of themselves; by either chasing after folks as the citizens hurry about their chores or nipped at their heels or fought among them themselves.

Some armed cowboys here to lend a hand, started shooting the dogs, if harassed by them — and in the mix children's pet pooches ended up being the odd casualty. Ben Lexmon and his partner stalked the area for keyed up ranch hands and ordered them to save their lead for the Indians.

Yolson shut shop for lunch, and realized that the family had been too busy to organize a kosher meal in the kitchen of their living quarters, and decided to forgo it for an over the counter meal at the diner on Main Street as guests of Dragoon.

Upon them entering the eatery they met up with Frank Cotter on the sidewalk, the scribe was on his way down from the sheriff's office. Dragoon wanted Frank to join him and the Yolson family, but the newspaperman refused the invite as he wanted to tour the town and witness the ongoing preparations by the townspeople as they made ready for the proposed Pawnee attack, which as far as anyone knew could be anytime; even though Lazarus Rollo had sent riders north of Junction City out on the open prairie to watch for any sign of action coming from the reservation that would indicate the Indians were on the move; these guys would then need to ride hell-for-leather to town and sound the alarm.

Cotter finally decided to drop in around at Lester's apartment to try and mend the fence between him and Miss Pearl Courtney … plus he needed to take the weight off his feet after traipsing about inspecting the works of the town's fortifications.

He found Miss Courtney in the parlor on the sofa wringing her hands and giving her dainty handkerchief a torturous time of it, she was plainly pesky about something.

"What's wrong Miss Pearl?" Frank made straight for the Franklin stove where the coffeepot sat and tested both weight and the heat of the container to ascertain whether there was a ready brew on hand. It met both expectations and he then went to the kitchen cabinet for a couple of mugs…

Pearl spoke to Frank without the slightest bit of animosity, her voice was charged with anxiety. "Because of the Indian threat, the stage line had decided to bring the departure time of the stage forward — fearing the route will be cut off until the Army gets control of the situation… and no one's sure when that will be!"

"That's reasonable in the current situation," Frank said, "— it'll mean Butterfield will have your party well out of danger before the Pawnees look like hitting the town. The Indians haven't the numbers to cover every possible contingency." He poured coffee for the pair of them and brought Pearl hers. As Pearl took the offered brew from Frank, he could see that her prior temper towards him was more amicable than it had been after he had forced Boston to open up Lester's tomb. "How did things turn out at the cemetery?" she asked after having a taste of her beverage and then went on to dab at a tear welling in the corner of her left-eye with her linen hanky.

Frank had no doubt in his mind that it wasn't the suggestion of an early stage departure which had upset her, but the thought that the Doctor's remains were being disturbed. She had expressed her opinion at the outset that she was against Lester's grave being opened for any reason, and Cotter felt within himself that he was a bit of a prig, being so insistent at having his way and pushing Boston and Stroughton so hard for the exhumation — in the end he had been made look the fool. *But then we all make mistakes…* thought Frank, as he realized that he had been prone to a few since arriving in Junction City.

"It appears it was Lester, all right — the same identifying scare I showed you when I returned from Churcher's place." Cotter informed her, hoping hearing that, she would feel better about things towards him now knowing that Cotter was wrong.

"So you've come to accept that it is Lester in the ground?" She pouted at him as she lifted the mug once more to her lips.

"A man hasn't any choice — you'd hardly find a spare corpse a round with a scar identical to ours." He admitted to Pearl as much as to himself.

"I don't understand why you are looking so depressed about it, Frank? Knowing for certain that it is Lester up there ought to make accepting his accident for what it is. The passing of a great man," She placed her empty mug on the table.

Cotter sighed. "…Yes, I know to you and a few people that I must appear as though I lack any sensitivity. Perhaps you're the ones who are correct and I'm the odd one out.   If you feel I've done you and Lester any sort of injustice and showed any disrespect, then I am deeply sorry. I c'n see my mistake. Now I feel I shall have to accept things the way they are and lay off Sheriff Boston. Perhaps if a man had gone about this in some other way I might have achieved my aim." He paused to take a swallow of coffee.

"The way I see it, you were not after that inquiry for Lester's sake but your own. You're the one who felt guilty and I guess, let down by Lester's sudden death. The deaths of Ma Kelly and Carter just added to your convictions and I would have agree that your approach to the thing was off key…" Pearl Courtney was in fact agreeing with Cotter. "How did Lester's attorney feel about the exhumation?" Pearl said.

"He was an obstructionist, until he had no other choice but to accept the inevitable. But when like the rest of us there, he saw that scare — well, there was no doubt and he must have felt a million dollars! Huh. It certainly finished me in the eyes of Boston; my words in this town are as worthless as a plug nickel!" He shook his head from side to side then added — "So you all packed and ready for this coach?"

Pearl nodded.

"Then I'll help you round to the depot with your luggage…" He began to glance around the parlor for its whereabouts.

"It's in Lester's bedroom — you'll need someone from the stage depot to come round with a hand-trolley for the big wardrobe trunk…"

Young Private Anton Karas had been ordered to ride scout for Captain Roscoe's party, but found the pace they had been maintaining back a-ways behind him was such, that he was barely able to hold a lead of 200 yards on the company. Turning front he saw a cowpoke up ahead hazing a calf and its mother towards a distant barn and homestead.

The Private recognized the drover even from this distance, for he had been Karas' old boss before he was fool enough to be taken in by the glamour of being a uniformed member of the U.S. cavalry. He was proud of himself that he was able to recognize Adam Moore, though in point of fact one shouldn't have expected anyone other than Moore out here.

He rode to within hailing distance of the unsuspecting cattleman. Anton was filled with pride that he was kitted out like a genuine blue-belly; he wore his blue field uniform with a touch of self-esteem and gave his campaign hat with its crossed sabers over the front of the brim a confident tug, to ensure it wouldn't depart his head when he eventually put his boot-hooks to his mount's hide.

"Mister Moore — Mister Moore… " Hollered Anton at the top of his lungs.

The rancher twisted in his saddle to look back over his shoulder and saw the cavalry rider heading his way at a good clip. He drew rein and turned his horse to face the oncoming rider, letting the cow and calf continue on at their own pace. The excited rider was now close enough for Moore to recognize as he mustered up a warm grin, while back beyond the scout he could see the rest of Roscoe's company and then a gape back to two covered wagons, he knew instantly that something serious had to be up to call for an Army circus this size.

Moore's stake in the land was too far out from Junction City to be included in the Williams' brother's warnings.

"Anton …?" Adam Moore critically looked the Private over and had to admit to himself that the youth had improved his outward appearance now that he wore the nice sharp uniform of the Government. He would have looked poster perfect but already his clothing was showing signs of travel dust. It took Karas a moment to catch his breath so Moore continued: "…This is a darn surprise, and my, don't you look smart in that there cavalry get-up? Army life seems ter have done wonders fer you, son!"

"Thank you, sir." Anton responded in kind. The cavalry mount snorted to clear its nostrils of dust as the two horsemen were enveloped in the passing dust haze of Karas's trail dust.

"What are you fellers wantin' on my land, son? …Youse practicin' maneuvers?" Moore asked.

Karas shook his head — as the company continued at double-time towards the pair. Anton looked back behind Karas to the troop and then swung round to face his ex-boss. "We ain't here on maneuvers Mr. Moore. The Pawnees are gittin' troublesome. Hasn't anyone been out ter warn you?" Moore shook his head as the both horses began to nuzzle one another.

"I don't wanna alarm yuh, but I reckon you should be gittin' yore family ter town until it blows over. If'n yer reckon Junction City's too fer away, then git yuh family into the homestead cellar!"

The company was in range of yelling distance and Lieutenant Briggs bellowed to Private Karas. "You hit the road Private — I'll deal with this…"

Private Karas saluted the approaching officer and swung his mount away from Moore and returned to scouting ahead of the troop.

"What's this business about the Pawnees, Lieutenant?" Adam Moore asked as he rode towards Briggs.

"It seems they wanna taste of Army discipline — they're gettin' might uppity so mebbe you could warn yore neighbors huh, stay close to home until we've brought them to heel.

"We don't believe they'll bother you folks out here, but it pays ter be careful… Their beef seems to be with the folks at Junction City!" Briggs told the rancher. Moore nodded his thanks, back his mount up and then about faced to race back to the distant ranch house a couple of miles distant. He spurred his workhorse into life and ignoring the cow and calf — his priority now being the protection of his family back at the house, whether he had time to get involved with any neighbors was going to be a matter he'd need to decide.

The stage depot was crowded by those who wanted to witness the departure of the last stage out of Junction City before the place went into shutdown, this situation would remain until after the townspeople knew the outcome of the current Pawnee grumblings.

Reg, the clerk, and his work-team were busy readying the passengers and the outward freight for their journey. There was no discounting the fact that folks were nervy, it showed in their darting eyes and clipped speech, even though there was always a certain amount of danger when traveling west of Kansas City or Omaha. Sheriff Boston sent Deputy Ben Lexmon and Mrs. Yolson down to the depot before the stage departed to make sure that everyone on the stage was armed with a revolver, including the women passengers, just in case the cunning redskins decided to switch tactics and hit the stage, but with those on-board the vehicle now armed, there was the chance of giving as much back to the Indians as they got, and this could be the difference between life and death … anyway, folks all saw it as having a bit of an edge.

The feller riding shotgun was all prepared, he had a Henry repeater and a 17-shot level action Winchester and a Greener, all of which wouldn't leave a would-be attacker in good health after an encounter with either firearm. Tim Hackamore was vain of his arsenal and his prowess as being known as a good shot but couldn't quick-drawer a handgun for neither love nor money. But no one feared this fault because Hackamore never had any intentions of letting anyone get within pistol range of him and the stage.

The limey had trucked Pearl's trunk around from the apartment via the alleyway, which had unhealthy memories for Cotter. The Englishman had personally supervised its loading and secured it to the drop-down tailgate of the Concord's stage.

Standing almost toe-to-toe on the sidewalk outside the front door of the depot, Frank told Pearl: "Whatever you do Miss Pearl, don't be neglectful — I wanna be kept posted of your whereabouts…" Frank said sincerely, "The moment I can make a decent break from this area I'll come looking you up in either Kansas City or Chicago…"

"If you think that's a good idea."

"I'm sure it's a good idea! You just take care, that's all!" Frank gave her hand a gentle squeeze.

"Awright folks… let's have yuh," shouted the reins-man as he hauled himself up into the driving box alongside Hackamore. Settling on his seat he checked that his personal effects were where they ought to be, especially his chewing tobacco and added in a less vocal voice, "…time ter say yuh good-byes!"

The horse team sensed it was time for them to earn their chaff by the sound of Enoch Rawlins' voice; they pricked their ears in anticipation.

Even the two mules that made up the team number seem to pay attention. A gangplank had been placed from the boardwalk out to the open door of the coach so that the passengers might simply walk aboard. Enoch knew he had to be cautious at this point in time for if the eager teams were to lean into their harness collars of their own volition; the vehicle might be dragged forward while someone was on the gangplank and then without a doubt and accident would ensure. He grasped the reins and ordered the team to stand steady, repeating the instructions over and over again until he heard the plank removed from the vehicle and the door slammed shut, then he flicked the reins and the beasts of burden put their backs into getting the stagecoach rolling.

As the coach pulled away from the false front of the depot it was noted by those on board that already the barricade that would close off the street had left it a tight fit for the stage to pass through, this would be sealed the moment the Concord was away. A few heavy-hearted folks continued to wave out the departing coach even though those inside the Butterfield stage had already started to dismiss the folks left behind to face their unknown peril. But all the same the stage passengers weren't overwhelmed by the fact that they were guaranteed of make it through to the first rest-station without striking Indian trouble.

19

To save Sheriff Boston legs, for he was going to be called on to be almost everywhere, the mayor had loan the lawman his personal buggy so that he could move back and forth to check the progress of the barricades the town was putting together. The Sheriff had suggested that a barricade be established across the top of Main Street, 10 yards down town from the T-intersection of Main and Ridge Road. North on Bryan Street off the town's main intersection which headed out of Junction City in the direction of the Indian Reservation and south on Bryan Street, just back from the Starr Street intersection.

The alleyway connecting Main Street with Starr Street at either end of town were blocked off by tipping a couple of buggies over on their sides, so no raiding party could make it through to the business section of the town where all the townspeople had planned to make their stand. Having the mayor's vehicle for these patrols, was a Godsend for Klem Boston's gammy leg.

Sean Dunne contributed to the building of the town barriers by lending four of the company's long-bed freight wagons to the council. One was to be placed at the uptown and downtown ends of Main where they were set up across the thoroughfare and tipped over on their sides with axles and wheels on what would become the inside position of the impediments from which the town's militia would be shooting from in crouched or standing positions, if it came down to it — which was a pretty foregone conclusion — for it had been taken for granted that the thick floorboards of the wagon-beds would easily withstand the impact of bullets, arrows, and lances. For cover at either end of the overturned vehicles the space between it and the next part of the barricade was blocked off with anything folks thought capable of hindering the onslaught of flying lead, it mostly consisted of household furniture and bales of hay from the livery stable, their inflammability having not been taken into account.

More of Dunne's wagons were used at the north and south ends of Bryan Street; Again, when the final wagons were in position they were manhandled over onto their sides in the hope of getting the full benefit of their bulk as a buttress against the marauders should they hit the town from either or both directions — it was surely a busy time for Junction City as all prepared for the worst.

The business section of the town area began to fill with folks and traffic in general, coming in from nearby ranches for any protection the town might offer — it was quickly becoming dangerous for pedestrians as the congestion grew on the streets of horse-teams, wagons, buckboards, buggies et cetera. Now and then a horse or mule would bolt unexpectedly into the crowd of folks thronging back and forth across the thoroughfare like free ranging cattle — and it was becoming continually more difficult for Sheriff Boston to get around to the various barriers to see how construction was progressing. As an individual, he was under a good deal of pressure and this only added to his problems and left the man in a curt mood. He snarled at one mother for not keeping her children off the busy street and up on the sidewalk where they'd be safe under the buildings' awnings. Although a hundred percent right in what he said, it was the way he spoke to her that lost him her husband's vote next time the sheriff's job came up for reelection, sure her husband wasn't with her at the time and women didn't have any voting powers, but one could bet their bottom dollar that she could and would sway her man's vote come next election.

McBride sought out Doctor Hallway and offered his assistance to the medico in any capacity he felt him capable of filling, for the possibility of gunshot and arrow wounds were going to be too much for one man and his helper, the town's midwife. Hallway was most grateful of the barber's offer, and placed him on standby.

Don Stroughton went to the quiet of his office and drew up a list of names of the men he thought should be posted at the town's different barricades as overseers — something like this had to be done for without a controlling influence there was the strong likelihood that whatever barricade came under attack first, panic and chaos would ensure and ammunition wasted for no good reason, especially when every bullet would count as the town didn't have an unlimited supply of ammunition.

The attorney knew the importance marksmanship would play in the incident that was bearing down on the townsfolk if things deteriorated to the level of bloodshed; he hoped and prayed that the Indians might be open to negotiations right down to the wire. Donald knew he wasn't alone in this but preparations had to be made.

The Williams brothers loomed high on his list when it came to thinking about firepower, but together they would be loose cannons and to gain the best of their abilities would mean splitting them up, the bothers would best serve the town by being placed at different barricades. He, himself, would be prepared to oversee one of the barriers and judged that the most likely one to be hit first would be the north end of Bryan Street, but conceded that if the Pawnees rode round to the east, and hit from that direction also made sense to him, for the Indian knew all about using the sun to their advantage in battle and how important it was to have it in the eyes of your enemy as much as possible — then the downtown fortifications near the stage-depot would be the one to come under attack first…

There were just so many possibilities and that withstanding was why it was most imperative that they had ***thinking men*** as overseers at each and every barrier, not boneheads who only had cotton between their ears and a trigger finger. The way he saw it, Sheriff Klem Boston had to be freed-up from the responsibility of being anchored in one place so that he could move from point to point unhindered, and the only way for this could be done effectively was to be mobile, hence the vehicle. Folks who carried an authoritative figure had to be in charge at the fortifications to direct the fire-power, men like Lazarus Rollo, the Mayor and the Scotsman, Robeson, the ex-lawman of Lawrence. He wrote out the list quickly with his quill and then hurried off to the council chambers where he knew the Mayor could be found.

Cotter made his way down to the express office and asked if the telegraph line was still open — it was. The key operator had naturally alerted the garrison at Hancock of the town's Indian threat, and as far as he knew the Army was going to be as pro-active, as they could at this stage. But he fully expected that the town would lose contact with the outside world at any moment. The manager of Western Union's office had also wired Kansas City and points beyond for any help they could muster. Frank left to find the sheriff to offer his services, though he realized his weakness with a firearm didn't leave him much to offer a busy Klem Boston nor the townsfolk.

Mrs. Snowy Warner realized that her position here at the reservation was growing more precarious by the minute, especially if those getting ready to make war on the township of Junction City knew that her hubby, Jake wasn't about. The Pawnees would put two and two together and the idea would soon dawn on them that he had gone off to either warn Junction City residence, or alert the Army post at Fort Hancock.

She acted as though she suspected nothing of what the Indians were contriving, her act worked beautifully — they seemed to be doing nothing out of the ordinary but adhering to their regular routine; while on the side, she sneakily saddled the Indian pony which the tribe had presented her with a year back, her actions made it clear she was taking the horse for exercise, and clearly in the opposite compass direction to that of Junction City.

Once on the move she circled about until she was in a position to set a new course for the settlement and hopefully secure her own safety, for she had no trust in the hot-headed Indians, certainly not going by the atmosphere in the reservation that she could feel in her very bones.

Meanwhile Jake Warner had borrowed a buggy from the livery-stable and set off with a fresh horse in the hope of getting back to the reservation to weasel his wife off the grounds and head back to town, for he was sure that once the Pawnees rode down on Junction City he and his wife would be just another phial of spilt blood in the dirt. The only thing was, that Jake wasn't aware that "Snowy" had already commenced her getaway, and that within the next fifteen minutes they would be both heading in separate directions, one to town and the other to the reservation on separate routes, and in no way would their paths cross.

Deputy Ben Lexmon had sworn in a posse so that they could manage to control the crowds of people now filling the town to choking point. This action grew out of the fact that Klem realized after his run-in with the rancher's wife and children early on —it proved that he could not hope to keep a lid on everything; he was after all — only one goddamn man!

Part of the posse went round to Ma Kelly's whorehouse on Starr Street and rounded up the gals and shepherded them with their belongs to the waiting room at the stage depot, as a temporary billet. Glenn Corbin, the depot manager certainly didn't welcome his guests with open arms, but he was in no position to argue the matter. Reg James and his men had to shield the ladies of the night from the prying eyes of passersby out there on the street; he organized drops of tarpaulin from the inner ceiling of the baggage storage area at the back of the ticket counter. The reason this was called upon, was because the gals were careless in their dress and posture and not all of them were in the habit of wearing bloomers under their skirts, for it proved too much of a hindrance in some cases for any sexual foreplay — which was as much part of their business as the flashing of bare skin or the odd naked bust spilling out over the tops of their loose, broad necklines.

Matt Flynn had been transferred from the jailhouse to Ma Kelly's bordello, when Hallway felt the amputee was up to it as had been planned, for the doctor had persuaded the Aldermen that it ought to become the town's future hospital and a trial run was accepted by housing the recovering prisoner there under guard.

Since the removal of Flynn's limb it had not been an easy road for the ex-ranch foreman, turn holdup-man — he hovered at death's door longer than the doctor had hoped. Hallway put that down to the poison which had set in to the wound before he got the chance to work on it.

Living space was fast becoming a premium in the Junction and finding another place suitable to stand in for a hospital, was far from easy for now as things stood the **Theater Royal** was now in one of the town's danger zones. It fell to Deputy Lexmon to use the weight of the law to get the gravely ill prisoner in to a second story room of the self-same saloon, where Boston had arrested the Captain and Lieutenant Briggs for beating up Frank Cotter at Doc. Lomax's place.

Robeson's prisoner was now fortunately being housed within spitting distance of the ex-lawman — though neither man would be spending any time together, for Flynn was semiconscious most of the time and Robeson had his hands full, helping Boston and the townsfolk.

The nearsighted muleskinner, Burnacre, was one of the firsts to report to the gunsmith for a free supply of ammunition and to try and screw the Russian Jew for one of the seven-shot repeater rifles. He knew the gunsmith had in his gun-cabinets lining the walls of his business premises. Yolson had by now heard the talk going round the village, that the skinner's wild shooting may have taken the life of the young tiny-tot at the shoot-out in front of Doctor Hallway's surgery, Ivor was reluctant to hand over any cartridge shells to a man likely to be as much a danger to those behind the protective barriers, as the raiding Pawnees.

Burnacre went off in a huff to get someone in power to sanction him being issued with the ammunition he felt entitle too. Whether he would finally be issued with shells was something that remained to be seen.

Clearwater was taken in shackles down to the blacksmith's shop where he was chained to the Smithy's spare anvil — there was no hope of him being able to break free, nor any likelihood of his tribal brothers setting him free before he'd be smote from a shot by someone in the sheriff's posse, who had taken him there in the first instance — without consultation of Lexmon or Boston, which would become a pretty volatile situation once Sheriff Boston learned about the prisoner's transfer.

Stroughton went to the Mayor's office with his now completed list. The mayor welcomed the Attorney's unrequested input, and studied the suggestions put before him with an eagle eye. He was overwhelmed with the work the man had done and could not deny its value, implementing these suggestions the mayor could see that precious time would be saved and pressure eased from his burdened shoulders and that of Rollo and crew.

The mayor was in the midst of setting up a group of volunteer firefighters, so handed on the attorney's work to the capable hands of Alderman Playford, who got right onto it with relish. Meanwhile the mayor went ahead with his present chore planning the strategy of the firemen which would come into play as fires broke out behind the fortifications; these would be disastrous if they got out of hand. The lumber, buildings in the town's business section were mostly semidetached structures made of which once alight, could easily turn to a firestorm that would burn Junction City clear off the map.

Water would be the vital element needed to quell even the smallest of fires that if once out of control would be inviting a calamity. Without hesitation the Chinese management of the bathhouse offered the used bath water from their dam, to the firefighting service.

Tar lined wooden pales were being gathered from all over town and filled with the carbolic flavored bath-water and stored ready on the boardwalks for use in front of the commercial establishments. A few stray dogs discovered them and began to congregate in packs to lap up the liquid; they smartly found out that it wasn't to their taste nor smell as the liquid was laced with caustic soda from homemade bathing soap.

Captain Roscoe and his men now had the reservation in sight; the largest building structure on the lot was that of the hospital that could be seen from afar—the army was fast approaching with their two covered wagons lagging behind in the dust kicked up by the mounted troopers. The first wagon carried extra ammunition for the squad and a concealed, rapid firing Gatling gun, whose firepower alone would knock a foolhardy brave right out of his or her moccasins before the victim could shit themselves with fear, and to top things off, three kegs of black blasting powder; the second wagon carried food palatable to a white man's field diet for the troopers and oats for their mounts.

Acting on Roscoe's orders, Lieutenant Briggs ordered the column's bugler to recall the scout, for out there alone, the young recruit could easily be the first victim of this engagement and no one wanted that.

Both the Captain and his lieutenant rode stride for stride on the lookout for anything which might warn them they could be riding into an ambush, such as a column of smoke for it would certainly indicate that the Pawnees had already started their rampage and were destroying anything belonging to the white man and his way of life on the reservation. But alas, there did not appear to be any such indicator; though this did not stop the troopers feeling some growing anxiety with ever step their horses took in the direction of the government post. No one had to be told what to watch out for, as most of these troopers were seasoned campaigners save for the odd two or three fellers riding amidst the horse soldiers.

Still traveling at speed with the rattle of sabers in their scabbards the column, stormed into the reservation's compound ahead of their own dust and milled about chaotically in front of the administration office, where a sergeant's voice hollered above the din of their arrival for the Troopers to form up on their mounts facing the rustic log building, the Warner's home and supply store. Before the horses were wheeled left to face the building, there wasn't one mount that hadn't caught the smell of water from the well which they had been racing towards in a seeming stampede until checked by their masters.

Beyond the well on flat ground, about a furlong away stood a semicircle of thirty Indian dome shaped wickiups, near some of the openings to the structures were either gourd vessels or baked dry clay-pots, items used in the domestic life of the Pawnee tribe — had they been in residence. At the back of these wickiups stood an empty corral at least an acre and a half in circumference now denuded of any live stock — a windmill that had been sunk handy to the corral looked rather forlorn and out of place now, for there was no stock to water, its vanes barely turning a full circle in the current movement of air.

Roscoe and Briggs dismounted almost simultaneously with the reins of their mounts in hand, as the low rolling dust cloud trailing the wagons over took the milling horsemen and vehicles. The dust thinned out into a haze in its struggled to disperse.

To a man, the area appeared deserted of human souls and the place would have been entirely mute save for the cavalry's arrival; the windmill was too far away for the sounds of its mechanism to carry all the way back up to the quartermaster's store. The Captain and Lieutenant strode the yard and a half to the porch, a mongrel dog whose combined genes were dominated by that of its coyote dam's heritage, came out of hiding and dared to snap at the heels and ankles of lieutenant Briggs, but a well placed kick in its ribs by Captain Roscoe sent the animal off seeking a safer climate.

"...Don't appear as though anyone of significance is about, Sir —" Lt. Briggs suggested as the captain pushed open the door and stood in its frame to survey the interior. The room did not look in any way out of the ordinary; it was as he recalled it from their last visit here, though in Roscoe's case, a month ago.

"It looks lifeless to me, lieutenant — what d'you think?" Roscoe asked.

Briggs looked in the room from over the captain's shoulder and although he had to agree with the officer-in-charge, he paused long enough to complete his own inspection of the place, for he, had been the one whom had paid the building the most recent visit. Finally he added: "Yeah — thankfully it doesn't have the feeling of death about."

The two men moved further into the building, leaving the door open behind them while the sergeant's voice could be heard in the background outside, giving the troopers the command to dismount.

By now, still unseen by the cavalry soldiers because the infirmary was now to their rear, a handful of squaws whom had been attending to the ill and potential dead, gathered in the open doorway of the hospital, and mournfully eyed the horse soldiers. Not a female amongst them, did not know what the arrival of the Long Knives meant.

It was almost two minutes before anyone in the army column knew that the nursing squaws were in attendance, well not until they began to spill out of the infirmary, by now the two Army wagons had drawn up alongside one another almost parallel with the hospital. The wagon drivers tied off their reins on the brake poles and climbed down to stretch their legs, the Gatling's three man crew accompanying the concealed gun, climbed over the tailboard of their vehicle and dropped to the ground, meanwhile; a fleet-footed squaw slipped unseen from one of the hospital's far side windows to the powder-dust covered ground, making sure to keep the building between herself and the Long Knives, she was well aware that her moccasins would greatly aid her in a mute flight across the open ground and through the prickly pear patch — in her quest to carry the news of the army's arrival to her clan-folk in camp at Cedar Creek; this young squaw had the running speed of a prairie wolf and was known in her tribe for her running prowess. She would definitely alert the tribe's braves of what lay in store for them — should they returned to their village in blind ignorance of the Army making the reservation their headquarters at this time.

When Jake Warner arrived back at the reservation he breathed a sigh of relief to find the Calvary in residence, and setting up their camping site — they were well at home with some of their mounts unsaddled and corralled behind the wickiups where they were being fed and watered. Two-man tents were being erected, pegged out in military fashion , in straight lines between the well and the reservation's main building – the space separating the administration buildings by 75-yard, plus 30 yards from the administration's porch to the infirmary; Warner reined in his horse and rode the brake-lever until the borrowed vehicle had come to a halt. He alighted from his seat as his lower half of the body became enveloped in his passing trail dust. A Private on guard duty armed with a carbine outside the front door gave Warner a smart salute as he approached across the porch boards; the soldier opened the door for Jake as he neared his destination, Warner was known to the enlisted man by sight, though playing his military role right through to the letter he, looked right through the civilian, then came to attention as the man went ahead into the building.

In the interim, Jake removed his weathered Stetson as he passed under the lintel and found Captain Roscoe had taken over his office, the officer, sat hatless behind Warner's desk — the captain's gauntlets lay one on top of the other, on a pile of the reservation's paperwork that was of no real importance at the moment by the way things appeared to be developing.

"How long have you and yore men been here, Captain Roscoe?" Was the first question to spill from Jake's anxious lips as the officer rose, the backs of his cavalry boots shoved the wooden swivel chair back about six-inches from its present position on the waxed floorboards; the office section of the store was the only part of the otherwise undressed floorboards to have the extravagance of waxing.

"I'd say about an hour or so," Roscoe came round the side of Warner's desk as he fished in the side pocket of his tunic for a couple of cheroots and offered one to the Indian agent whom was looking quite agitated.

Briggs came in from the warehouse, which separated the front section of the building from that of the living-quarters; his eyes and face had the expression of a nonplus Moose as he came up the room to join Warner and Roscoe.

"…Is Snowy about — was she here when you arrived?! Jake looked apprehensively from the captain to the lieutenant and back to Roscoe.

"We found the reservation all but abandoned — save for the few squaws looking after what sick are in the infirmary," Roscoe told Warner. The captain knew whom Jake Warner had meant when he asked about "Snowy".

"Mrs. Warner seems to have left the place along with the Pawnees… Though I can vouch for the fact that she is not with them," He told Warner as he lit a match off the seat of his pants to ignite their cheroots. "How do you know that, Captain? — Mebbe they took it into their heads to slit her throat!?" He allowed the officer to torch the end of his cheroot and inhaled a good serve of tobacco smoke down into the bowels of his lungs.

"I think not," said Roscoe with raised eyebrows after lighting up his tightly rolled tobacco leaf. "I sent a couple of men off to follow the Indian pony tracks from the corral, and they led to Cedar creek. My Troopers observed an Indian village still under construction from a stand of trees and they reported back that there wasn't a sign of any white woman, even as a prisoner — I made it perfectly clear to the men, before they departed for the creek they were to watch out for any sign of her … alive or dead. I c'n confidently say that she isn't with them — willingly or unwillingly, Mr. Warner."

Jake's eyes were now smarting from the smoke of his cheroot, he wiped them and went on; "Mebbe they suspected I knew before hand about the plans of the rebel gang of braves, an' when I went missin' they put two and two together. M-mebbe they've butchered Snowy an' hid her body, somewhere?"

"If they did," Lt. Briggs pointed out, "They must've done it with a slight of hand — because there is no sign of anything out of the ordinary about the establishment. In the time we have been here I've given yore quarters and the surrounding grounds a thorough going over… The signs are that Mrs. Warner isn't here and it's probable she's come to no harm."

"— that's fine fer you to say, soldier — because Snowy isn't yore wife. What about the well? Have you made a search there for a body?" Jake's dilated eyes search both cavalrymen's faces.

"You're letting your imagination get the better of you, Warner —" said Roscoe. "— would we be drawing water from there before checking it would be safe…? Indians have been known to poison wells, Warner. It hasn't been used for anyone's grave. Show some sense, man!"

"Eighteen months ago the Indians made Snowy a present of a toffee colored cayuse — did you see it out the back in our stable? Snowy wouldn't go far wivout it if any ridin' wuz gonna be involved," Jake explained.

Roscoe looked at Briggs to supply the answer.

"…There's no stock or harness tack out there in yore stable, Warner, not when *I* inspected it. I'd say Missus Warner had hightailed it outa here for Junction City, especially if she sensed there might be trouble hovering in the background…"

"I never passed her on the way here — why's that, huh?" Warner thrust his chin forward like a man goading someone to whack him one.

"There's more than one way ter town. Hell, you pair have lived in these parts longer than I maybe she took a short-cut!" Captain Roscoe ended his assumption with a deep draw on his smoke and the expression on his face was challenging enough that it caused Warner to think along these lines.

Frank Cotter was not one to let opportunity pass by. He could writer quite a forceful article about Junction City preparing itself for a showdown with this, the threat of a second band of renegade Indians determined to descend on the town; but realized that the drama and graphics of the townsfolk were in danger of being sacrificed by these people, would be greatly enhanced if accompanied by 'on the spot' sketches executed with charcoal as they toiled to fortify the town— later for the sake of history these sketches could be turned into historical engravings if there were any survivors; for words covering the event just wouldn't be enough.

In an unguarded moment while hanging out at the down town barricade near the stage-depot, Cotter took to his heels and slipped up the alleyway through to Starr Street in the direction of Lomax's apartment in an endeavor to secure his art tools from the flat. As he covered the ground between the protective barrier and the apartment, he began to breakout in a sweat and felt queasy in the tummy — from past experience, he put these symptoms down to the fact, that it was another cross to bear for being on the wagon and the fact that he had been existing on irregular meals of late.

By the time he got to the flight of stairs that led up the landing of the apartment he was experiencing the shakes and decided to rest up, until he felt well enough to press on. He used the newel for support while his dickey legs settled down — looking up at the landing he had no doubts that the climb wasn't going to be easy for him, but he knew also that he couldn't afford to waste too much time down here as there was the likelihood that someone might be patrolling the neighborhood to check on the building to make sure they weren't occupied. He'd have trouble explaining himself to someone in authority about being in this part of town.

The black cat came out of hiding in the wood stack, but sensed that now wasn't the time to approach Cotter and returned to its snuggle. Frank pushed himself away from the newel and forced his protesting body towards the risers, he used the banister to drag himself upwards, hand over hand until he was finally on the landing face to face within a short distance to the building apartment's door… He fumbled with it for a few moments to get it open and knew that if he didn't make it inside soon, he would pass out before even getting across the threshold — as he felt the rising swell of unwanted companions, perspiration and nausea. Once through the door he staggered in the direction of the sofa and only just made it to his destination as his legs gave way from under him and he fell — face down on to a brocade cushion, he was so glad to have made it. The relief his tortured body felt at not having to support his very being was indescribable — even though he knew he was falling into unconsciousness he realized there would be no turning his inner body's action away from it, he had to accept the inevitable…

The wrap of a gloved hand against Warner's door was followed by it being thrust open an in the doorframe stood a breathless trooper being crowed on his heels by the guard posted outside, the same armed fellow had earlier led Jake Warner to his own front door; the trooper in the shadow of the low lintel was a clean faced private — he was a little on the excitable side for to him he was on a mission of dire straits. He snapped to attention and gave Roscoe a snappy salute that would have done a West Pointer, proud. The guard behind the trooper hovered in the doorway with his carbine to port.

Roscoe returned the salute.

"Private Croydon, sor! — message from Sergeant Major, Heath sor!"

Croydon had come to a halt and stood his piece of flooring like a human size statue attached to a plinth — his unblinking eyes focused straight ahead as if seeing nothing.

It was Lieutenant Briggs who stepped up alongside Captain Roscoe and addressed the Private.

"At ease — Private" Briggs said on behalf of his captain, the trooper's fame relaxed and in fact shortened his statue by almost two inches though his eyes still continued not to make eye-contact with anyone in the room.

"The Sergeant Major, has instructed me to report to the Captain, that a band of Pawnees — consisting of men, squaws and children are headed this way from the direction of Cedar Creek, Sor…!"

"… Have you witnessed the incoming Indians for yore self?" Roscoe asked of the Private. Roscoe glanced at Lt. Briggs to see if he was assessing the cavalryman's worth as that of being reliable. Briggs looked satisfied by the trooper's demeanor and Roscoe decided that he would go along with Brigg's judgment. He turned his attention back to Private Croydon.

"Do they look threatening, Private?"

"No, Sor. They didn't look like trouble, sor… Well, not ter me sor. In fact, they looked like they could do with some serious attention frum Mr. Warner's government stores, sor."

"Whoa — may I chip in?" Jake Warner cried as he closed in on the trio and aimed his attention at Private Croydon. "— Are you suggestin' that those Injins haven't been properly looked after by me, soldier?" Warner was most definitely on the defensive.

"No, sor, I am not!" He went on to make his position clear. "This soldier believes their condition is of their own makin' because they've been doin' it rough fer a while. Pardon me sayin' so, but they look beaten an' ready ter take things up frum where they left 'em…"

"Fair enough," said a pleased Roscoe and to Warner he delivered the man a curt nod. "We won't take issue with that — we are here to ensure this whole unsavory business ends here and now, peacefully. Lieutenant, return to the sergeant-major with trooper Croydon, see that the Indians are resettled and find out, as to why they moved away to the creek — and anything else you can learn you think can be of help to us and the brass at Fort Hancock."

Briggs, along with the trooper came to attention, and saluted Captain Roscoe as if being pulled by puppeteer strings. The captain returned their salutes.

"Carry on, men!" Roscoe muttered and turning to Warner, and said: "You c'n go on looking for your missing wife Mr. Warner—the Indians will be our worry for the time being."

"That's my intention. Captain Roscoe — Snowy is more concern ter me than a bunch of would-be tamed Injuns. I'll head off back ter Junction City by the back country an' see if I can pick up her trail. Whichever way it goes you won't see any more terday!"

"Fine," said Roscoe, "we will settle in and allay things with the Pawnee — you work at finding yore dear woman."

"You can count on that," Warner stated as he turned and went in the direction of the door that had already been shut by Briggs and company as they made their egress.

Frank woke up from his faint, his face still pressed in the cushion of the sofa; but sensed — before he had twisted himself about onto his back that he wasn't alone. His head felt thick as if it was stuffed up with a bad head cold. But somehow he knew he had to put his self-pity aside and give his attention to the broader picture… His focal point became that of Sean Dunne standing over him ready to pour water in his face from a vase empty of flowers. He tried to signal the teamster that the gesture he was considering wasn't necessary, but regardless of his message to the man, Dunne, still emptied the water all over his face with a snide grin, clearly he, was getting a kick out of soaking Frank's shirt -front.

Cotter could not do anything about it, water cascaded from the vase down into his face and washed away the stale stickiness of his perspiration, he managed to get his eyes shut in time for he knew the water would sting if any got into them. As he sat up and swung his legs off the sofa to the floor he wiped his face with his hands, Sean Dunne backed away but kept a hold of the vase for now empty it would make a formable weapon if the scribe dared to make a lunge at him.

"I hope that didn't make you feel any better…?" Sean told him in a husky voice.

Frank knew that Dunne meant what he said. Cotter shook his head vigorously to try and clear it and sent minute droplets of moister in all directions.

"Someone here wants a word with you, feller —" the teamster told him and glanced back somewhere behind Cotter. Frank twisted about on the sofa and saw over at the dining table Doctor Lester Lomax, bearing a mischievous smile. Cotter believed without much thought that he was having another hallucination, the kind he'd experienced when he saw the Priest in Bryan Street; He ignored the phantom and turned back to face Dunne, and would not have been surprised in the slightest if by this time he had vanished... for now he was certain he was in the goddamn middle of a throwback to his day's trapped with the DT's.

But Dunne had *not* been absorbed into nothingness, he still stood where Cotter had seen him last, holding the empty vase and continued to ignore Cotter as he went ahead to address the Doctor's apparition behind him. "You'd better say something' Doc. **He** thinkin' you is a ghost of his bloody imagination and pickled brain!"

Frank kept watching Dunne closely for something that might be give-a-way that he was definitely part of this hallucination. But no matter how hard he sought to find evidence of this, he simply and plainly could not.

Then the unmistakable voice of Cotter's old friend came across the room from almost behind him.

"You're not hallucinating, Frankie... I'm alive, in the flesh..."

Frank turned back in the direction of his mind's ghost and looked the Doctor, over; Cotter saw the image of Lomax but could not accept its reality. Lester did not believe that he would have any trouble convincing his old friend that he was not like Jesus Christ, returned from the grave.

"You can touch me if you so wish," Lomax said as he rose from the chair at the table and came around to the sofa where he stopped before the scribe and held forth his hand. "Go ahead — feel me, I'm as real as **you,** Frankie..."

Frank turned away and shook his head once more as if trying to clear his head of the cobwebs he believed were tangling his reasoning.

Fed up with Cotter's slow acceptance of the facts, Lomax grabbed his friend by the shirtfront, hauled him to his feet — and forced him to look him in the eyes. At this close quarter Frank's senses had no option but to accept the reality there before him, but it was too much for Cotter to comprehend in his present condition and he swooned away. The weight of his body caught Lomax by surprise as his newspaper friend fell unconscious down on the sofa – his loose-limb fall like a of a corpse…

"We've been here too long, Doc. Let's get outa here before someone notices the buckboard!" Dunne went over and replaced the vase on the drum table alongside the storks of flowers he had taken from the vase earlier, when he had hit on the idea of using the water to rouse the scribe. A couple of the flowers fell off the table to the floor, unnoticed by either of the men, not that it would have mattered to them. "…We've got what we came for. While we're here, is there anything you want me ter do about **him?**" He gestured in Cotter's direction.

"What are you driving, at?" Lomax asked.

"Leave 'im like he is and when he comes out of it, he'll spill the beans about us all over town; He's gotta be kept quiet, you can see that, surely?!"

"I know what you want done Sean — but this is not some drunk we can leave in a horse-trough; No, **he** comes with us to the hideout."

"Why?" Dunne couldn't believe that the doctor was serious. After all, they had only found the scribe here by accident. The teamster and the other members of the syndicate ought to be preparing to cut themselves free of Junction City and sailing to a free port.

"I owe it to him to have his chance to join us — we just can't leave him high an' dry. He comes with us until he has had the opportunity to decide his future for himself. You get the buckboard from the alley alongside The Royal – I'll bring Frankie downstairs…!"

The teamster shrugged. "OK, but it's **his** funeral if he doesn't make the right choice when you put it to 'im…!" Sean made for the outside landing with quick powerful strides, then, disappeared down stairs to fetch the buckboard. He and the doctor were hopeful that folks were too damn busy down the far end of the alley near Main Street, to notice the buckboard parked in the laneway, off Starr Street.

While Dunne was away, Lester thought of reviving Cotter but dismissed the notion as it dawned on him that conscious or even partly conscious the man might be a drawback; but fully unconscious he could be lugged about like a sleeping child and certainly be less troublesome.

Lomax went out onto the landing and waited until the teamster arrived back. Things were still working in the syndicate's favor for the fact that this section of town had been abandoned now meant that there was little chance of discovery by a stray citizen.

Dunne walked the horse from the alley out into Starr Street and down in front of the boardwalk in line with the staircase. The doctor saw him arrive with the buckboard and went inside to Cotter, who was still in a dead faint ... Lester pulled on the difficult aspect of hauling the unconscious scribe up across his shoulders and under the strain of the body on his back he made his way across the parlor and through the open door to the landing, taking extra care that he didn't knock Cotter about while passing under the lintel of the doorframe. By the time he had reached the top of the stairs, he found Dunne already on his way up to help him.

Down at the buckboard, Dunne and Lomax laid Cotter out on the floor and covered him with an Indian blanket; Lomax had gone back up into the apartment for a stash of cash which he had hidden on top of his bedroom wardrobe in a hatbox. There is no doubt that had Frank done a thorough inventory of the apartment as Lomax's attorney had requested he would have discovered the money! But Cotter had let the lawyer down in that respect. In the interim, Dunne had parked the vehicle facing east down, Starr Street. The moment Lomax was settled aboard the vehicle, the teamster quietly walked the horse down pass **The Theater Royal Hotel** for about the distance of four street lots, and then he whipped the horse up into full pace until they had run out of street and hit open country. There he set course for the meteor site, while every now and again Lomax kept a lookout back over their shoulders to see that no one from town had discovered their presence.

When Cotter regained consciousness he found himself lying prostrate on the hard rock floor of a cavern, but at first he had no idea where he was and certainly none of how he came to be here. Even though he did recognize that he had been placed atop of an Indian rug it did not do much to arrest the pressure of the rough surface biting into his flesh through the thickness of the woven fabric. Had he the inclination to lift portion of the blanket away from the floor to expose the stony hard lava-like surface — he would have found it branded with spider-like vein ridges in a pattern seemingly without rhyme or reason to it. But there would have been no point to such action for as he lie there trying to get his bearings, he was not helped much by the fact that the only light in this fake darkness was that of a campfire burning somewhere over to his right on the base of the floor, its flickering flames lighted the rough-cast cavern walls and the likewise overhead vault ceiling, which his eyes tried to focus on. With trepidation he attempted to sit up and found it not a problem, but he heard the ringing slap of a harness buckle somewhere at the back of him, so he twisted round in the direction of the sound — eight yards away, just barely in the illumination of the fire light — Cotter recognized Dunne in the act of freeing a horse from between the shafts of a buckboard, the Morgan horse, was already partially unharnessed.

Cotter rolled over onto hands and knees and struggled to his feet and stood with jelly like legs slightly apart without hardly any noise, due of course to the coarse woolen rug. He realized he was hatless under the canopy of overhead rock and tried to make sense of his surroundings — he had no idea where the deuce he was, but the sight of the vehicle over yonder gave him a very good idea as to how Dunne must have got him here.

Then his memory kicked in and he recalled how his inquisitive eyes had alighted on Lomax just across the parlor from him and his almost, tone deaf ears heard as his mind groped for and established the fact that what his eyes were seeing, wasn't just another drunken hallucination like that of the priest.

Sean Dunne led the roan mare round in a half circle from the buggy before he sighted Cotter's silhouette standing as still as a rock sentinel rooted to the rug. The teamster eased the horse to a halt, the beast of burden between him and the scribe.

Dunne spoke across the horse, "…So you have finally joined the masses?" Sean held the animal in check by the bridle and the horse began to chew noisily on the bit. The teamster dropped his right hand and hauled his Colt free of his low-slung holster and leveled the weapon at Frank across the mare's back. "I hope yore plannin' ter be a little liberal about past events, pal…" He went on acerbity as he lightly slapped the mare's neck in a signal for the horse to move out from between him and the scribe. The horse responded as Dunne had hoped it would. The teamster cocked the hammer of his revolver and directed the muzzle right at Frank's mid-section. Had the man a mind to shoot in Cotter's direction there was little doubt in both parties' minds, that the teamster might miss his intended target, although Dunne was no gun for hire — he could hold his own in a gun-duel and the unarmed scribe never doubted this for a moment.

"Where is Lester…?" Frank croaked — his throat dried out from the trail dust, which would have entered via his partially open lips.

Dunne moved forwards towards Cotter with measured steps and squinted eyes as he asked: "So yuh brain box ain't been affected by the gun-stroke? Where Lester is, ain't yore business." The bitter, surly looking man came to a stop just over arm's length back from the prisoner,

"My head's as well as can be expected. Look, I have quite a few questions he needs to answer for me; but in the meantime, have you got something I can quench my thirst with?"

"There's a canteen under the seat of the buckboard… **You** want it, **you** get it — I'm not yore nursemaid!" Dunne stepped aside so that his prisoner had a clear path up to the vehicle, but kept him covered with the Colt in his fist. Frank shrugged and went down to the buckboard and after a brief search, found the canteen. It wasn't a fancy receptacle with a screw cap but was fitted with a cork stopper.

He returned with the canteen to the blanket and as he approached he said: "You partial to some of this?" He proffered the canteen towards the teamster — Dunne backed away to maintain a safe distance between him and Cotter and warned Frank not to follow him up by raising the Colt's barrel and extra inch while still holding his aim. The gesture was not wasted, Frank paused and tugged the cork from the spout and took a healthy gulp of the liquid to wash his throat, and sate his thirst. Having had his fill, Frank replaced the cork and took hold of the vessel by the web-strapping, the length of the webbing allowed the canteen to dangle down as far as his calf.

"You sure you don't want any? There's plenty!"

"Don't waste yuh time tryin' ter curry favor with me, Cotter. Until me an' the Doc know where you stand in our river — I'm keepin' my distance — git it?!" Dunne looked as belligerent as he sounded.

After considering their position for a moment, Cotter said, "That's fair enough under the circumstances — but I should say you are cutting off your nose to despite your face. As I asked before, are you gonna tell me where the deuce Lester is or not, Sean?" He stood there and waited, he could see in the firelight the feller was struggling with his conscience. Cotter could not understand why the man continued to hold back for he knew his request was only reasonable giving the situation; Thankfully, it was at this moment that Lester Lomax seemed to appear from out of the very rock face of the wall, right behind that of Dunne but on second glance in the man's direction, who seemed to possess the ability to appear and disappear like some kind of will-o-the-wisp — Frank noticed the arched entrance of another tunnel — and it was that direction Lester could only have come from.

"What's the story here, Lester?" Frank demanded as Lomax moved up and stood at the back of Dunne, while Sean's eyes stayed fixed on Frank Cotter.

"I realize this has all been a shock to you, Frankie…" Lester said as he stepped round Dunne and came to a standstill alongside the man whom most everyone in and outside of Junction City — had come to believe had run the doctor down, in a so-called fatal accident.

"That, my dear friend, is the "understatement" of the goddamn century!"

Lomax's face broke into a grin. "— Yeah, I guess you could say that," Then he turned to Sean and asked him to stoke up the campfire, for by this time, it was starving to death for want of wood or dry brush.

"I'll have some of that water you offered, Sean… if you don't mind, Frankie?" The doctor asked with an outstretched hand.

Cotter swung the corked canteen up and Lester caught it with both hands on the swing; the wary newspaperman realized that his tricky friend was dressed in the clothing of a cattle drover and although clean shaven, he truly looked the part.

"So what is it Lester, am *I* gonna get the "real" story behind this almighty charade or am I to be left riding the same carousel as everyone else?"

As Doc Lomax drank his fill from the canteen he looked at his one-time friend with vacant eyes. There was no way of trying to read his thoughts for they were buried deep down inside him. It was soon evident that he had no further use of the canteen for his benefit and he corked the utensil — Dunne finished stoking the fire, the chore had necessitated him stowing his six-gun in its holster where it ought to have been housed from the beginning. He wandered over and sat down on the corner of the square rug with his back to the fire.

Lomax swung the canteen in the cartage contractor's direction and sent it flying through space, for the man to catch. He was pretty adept and caught the airborne container as easily as any circus trained juggler. This suggested to Cotter that Dunne had only been play acting at being a drunk. Dunne uncapped the canteen and swallowed his fill as Lomax and Cotter ambled over to join him. Both men settled down across the Indian blanked from Dunne and Frank turned in Lester's direction, the latter, and conscious of where he ought to place the sharp rowels of his spurs.

Frowning quizzically in Cotter's direction — Doctor Lester Lomax said, "...I expect you're full to the gills with unanswered questions, Frankie?"

Cotter nodded. "So where are you gonna start, Lester?"

"That's the conundrum... Where does **one** start?" He put the question more to himself than anyone of the men nearby as he gazed off into the darkness of the cavern as though in search of the right answer somewhere out there in the ether.

Cotter, the scribe, prompted Lomax. "Might I suggest you begin with how you engineered such a phony accident that was able to fool all and sundry...?" This ignited a spark there inside Doctor Lomax's gray cells.

Lomax's stare was exchanged to that of a serious appraisal of Cotter — it was noticeable in the depth of Lester's hazel eyes that he had arrived at a suitable starting point in his mind's eye. Cotter ached for the man to begin but Sean Dunne was pretty much indifferent to the situation on hand, Frank guessed that it was because of Dunne's, Irish extraction.

"Tell me," said the Doctor to his old friend, "did you sincerely believe that I was dead?"

"I had no reason to think otherwise..." Cotter admitted — "Especially, when I saw your grave and heard the stories of your accident from folks whom one would've thought were creditable witnesses."

"But still, from my observation, you went on to embrace a mantle of 'doubts' about things. Why, why, damn you did you take that tack?!" Lester's eyes glowed heatedly as he questioned his once close friend.

Dunne was equally keen to know why the piss-pot had not swallowed the news of Doctor Lomax's death as readily as he would down a shot of rye whiskey.

Cotter thought about this before answering. "I, I…decided to take up your job offer as proposed in your letter. I was in a painful state both physically and mentally, I guess… I never had so much as a plug nickel to bless myself with; no one, would stand me drinks — so against my will and my pickled brain I began a drying out process and in so doing, saw things in a different light… You see I blacked out an' woke in hospital; all I had of any worth on me was your letter which had served to identify me to the hospital authorities.

"Upon summing up my overall health, a group of doctors concluded that if I continued to live as I had been to date, I was on a one-way journey to the cemetery. My only chance of survival was to take up your offer and the stagecoach ticket you had enclosed. The doctors were one in the opinion that away from the temptations of city booze and women, the fresh country air might work miracles and with a bit of luck I might survive another decade.

"Where death's concerned I'm very much the coward. So once I recovered enough, I wrote to you I'd take up your offer and only just beat it out of town a couple of steps ahead of some cuckold spouse — he was after my balls with either a very sharp knife or a goddamn gun! None of which I was partial too.

"Then when I got here to Junction City — I learned what was supposed to have happened to you, and I saw my sandcastle of hope, crumple into dirt before my eyes. Selfishly, I cursed the fact that I'd placed all my eggs in the one basket and as a result, I was near broke and pretty much stranded in a town of strangers with no future, or so it seemed. Then out of mere curiosity I started asking questions of folks about town to try and get a picture of how fate had clearly dealt me a ***Dead man's hand…***

"You know how your landlady came to my aid?"

The Doctor nodded.

"…Yes, of course you would, you were almost right at hand, weren't you? Literally, lurking there in the shadows… It was you I threatened that night on Starr Street when I was on my way back to your apartment; wasn't it — it was you in that recessed shop doorway?"

Lester nodded as his face took on a grim dimension.

"It was Ma Kelly's story of how she viewed the aftermath of your so-called accident from her elevated point-of-view through her upstairs' window — which got me thinking that maybe …just maybe…there was something about this accident that wasn't, how we say it back east — kosher. The very thing which kept getting under my fingernails was that no one seemed keen on holding and official inquiry, not even Sheriff Boston; everyone wanted to accept it at face value and they wanted to sweep my questions away, under the carpet!"

"And that didn't satisfy you, did it?" Lester murmured.

"No way! Everyone was too laid back about it!"

"That's the way things are done out here in the west," Dunne pointed out.

"Here? Yes," continued Cotter as he went on addressing both men. "But not where I come from!"

Lester said, "Just think? If you had let things slide, gone along on their own way, this thing wouldn't have gotten as messy as it did! I never intended for any of this to happen."

"No, I suspect not. You just found yourself and your pals in a bog of quicksand, and if there was anyone whose ass was gonna get saved, it was gonna be yours, right, Lester?" Frank was determined to try and make Lester feel some remorse for the damage he had caused to the Pawnees, Ma Kelly and the counter-jumping clerk, from the mercantile store.

If he wasn't the one who had slashed Kelly's throat he knew who had done the deed, maybe because Lomax had sanctioned it? The same might well be applied to the drowning of the youth.

"I imagine you see me as a lowdown killer?" Lomax said as if reading Frank's mind. Frank made no move to agree or disagree with the man. "The only deaths I am prepared to shoulder are the people of the Pawnee tribe. I really made an effort there to better their lives and health — I fully believed that I had found the answer to the terrible inflictions they'd inherited from the white man! Such as cattle and chicken pox, influenza and pneumonia! I admit my elixir didn't live up to what I led myself and everyone to believe — in some cases it did more damage than good which was ***never my*** intention… I had full faith in my medicine in every drop the process churned out; otherwise I would've accepted its failure had the first lot of trials hadn't come through with flying colors!

"For it did knock over the diseases I expected it to combat, meant that it had to be potent stuff indeed; and it wasn't until after I had approached Washington with my medicine that things began to go wrong and we experienced those horrific side effects — "

"— I've seen these ***side effects*** myself," broke in Cotter with a face-masked that looked as though he had been forced to swallow a gallon of sour milk.

"—which appeared to me, that the samples I had sent to Washington for essaying by the Government scientists had been tampered with so that they would produce these ill-effects!" Lester removed his Stetson, his rage was coming to the fore and it began to make him hot under the collar.

While watching Lomax placed his hat on the blanket near his thigh, Cotter asked: "Did you know you were under investigation by the Bureau of Indian Affairs, when you offered me the job of being your publicist, Lester?"

"No. I've had that position in mind for you for a while, Frankie —I knew it was a job you could do blindfolded or with one hand tied behind your back! When you ended up in that hospital, it was sheer luck; some of the staff had been colleagues of mine from years, back."

Frank reminded Lomax, "Your letter said you needed me because the government was gonna run a campaign to force you to shut down everything to do involved with the production of your wonder drug? So that was all rotten, lies?" said Frank.

"It wasn't the truth when I first wrote, no. I had no idea it was gonna be so prophetic — as you surely must now realize?"

Nodding his head, Cotter asked: "And when did you realize your discovery was a failure and didn't perform to expectations?"

"About the same time I heard from a reliable source in Washington D.C., that *I* and the activities of our company had come under scrutiny, according to my informant, there was a clique in Washington's medical fraternity out to discredit our syndicate as a bunch of grifters…!"

At this point Lester paused and found himself a cheroot from the breast pocket of his range shirt; he fired it up from a match he ignited with the sharp edge of his thumbnail. This pause allowed Cotter to think back over what he knew from first hand; and it was those painful encounters he had with Captain Roscoe and Lieutenant Briggs, when their paths crossed — it was something he wasn't equipped to take in his stride.

Lomax continued without prompting once he had settled down with his Mexican cigar. "…I did everything I knew for the folks laid low by the medicine. I worked day an' night looking for an answer, something which would relieve their suffering —"

"The Doc worked himself to a standstill — an' collapsed, exhausted!" Dunne said. "No one could lend a hand because none of us knew the first thing about being a druggist."

"It was while thinking about you and your alcoholism, Frank," explained Lomax, "I got the idea that I might be able to ease their suffering by making them blind drunk and keep them that way until the hand of death touched their brow. The whiskey kept 'em oblivious of their agonized suffering — it was the only act of kindness I could do them."

"For all concerned it might've been best if you'd never meddled in something you knew nothing about!" Cotter told the Doctor.

"By taking things as they now stand, that's true…" nodded Lester as he exhaled cheroot smoke into the muggy air of the cavern, made so, by the nearby campfire as it embodied the cooking pot of a jackrabbit stew being readied for their coming supper.

"Back then, I was convinced I had the answers or I wouldn't have started down that path."

"OK. So how did Hill and Bevan come into the caper? …You know they've paired up like man and wife — I couldn't ever imagine them being your type of man?" The writer told Lomax with some indignation.

"Research costs money and, they sort of came knocking on my door with what seemed like endless billfolds of it without any questions. My only other source of income was what little gold dust I could cadge out of the Indians for my services.

"The War between, the States was a big financial drain on both sides — even though hostilities were very much over, the country as a whole ain't anywhere near as rich as it was — it'll take years for us to climb out of this economical depression it has brought down on, us!" Lester was on safe ground here, for he had stated something, which was very much common knowledge. "So what about this accident you and your pals concocted for everyone to swallow?"

"Huh … yes, **the accident.**" Lomax faltered as this question from Cotter forced him to reflect back over the incident Lester had orchestrated — the two murders, which in his eyes had re-sulted indirectly from Cotter's persistence to get to the truth of the matter; and thus force Sheriff Boston to get off his ass and delve into the unfortunate event that had befallen Lomax. The whole show couldn't have stood up to such perusal and would have brought the plan own like a house of cards. "— are you hinting at the *necessary* deaths of Ma Kelly and that counter-jumper, Carter? 'Coz if you are, Frankie, then their deaths are as much your blame as is mine!"

Frank narrowed his eyes…*Is he gonna try and ease his conscience by making me look the troublemaker?*

"How do you see that, Lester?" the scribe asked.

"You plowed the road right to their doors," answered Lomax with his half smoked cheroot clench between his teeth.

"But it was you or either Dunne who cut Ma's throat. And from the professional way it was executed, my money would be on you!"

Lomax removed his smoke as he sniggered at Cotter.

"And my next bet is that either **you** or both of **you** shoved Carter into that trough and held him under until he drowned!" The scribe's eyes were ablaze. "What did you expect? The madam's son, too get the blame for her death?"

Lomax shook his head slowly. "It wouldn't have been any great miscarriage of justice — Pete's gonna be lost without Ma to lean on, besides him being locked up in a mad house for the rest of his life, would be no loss to society.

"She and Carter had to be gotten rid of — thanks to your interference; that's why you're to blame for their demise! "

"Why don't you call it for what it is Lester — Murder?" Frank Cotter shouted in the sawbones' direction. "Done by your hands; the hands of a so-called, **healer!**"

Sean Dunne was himself, now halfway through building himself a cigarette, and said as he worked on the tobacco in the palm of his hand, "This powwow ain't goin' like you hoped, Doc…" he got out a rectangle piece of onion cigarette paper from a small tight pack of the same.

"Sean reckons I'm wastin' my breadth trying to talk you into seeing things our way," Lester explained. By now the teamster had commenced to form the once rectangle of cigarette paper into a cylinder of paper and tobacco.

"Dunne is right… I can't bring **myself** to see any virtue in what any of you have done in this whole circus of events," Cotter agreed but at the same time without pausing to think that he alone had just done himself a disservice and unwittingly put his life in danger by being too forthright; it would have been safer for him, if he had given himself time to think of the consequences and reworded what he had said — so that it wouldn't antagonize the enemy for that's whose camp he was now in.

"I brought you here hoping we could work things out," Lomax told Cotter.

"Just where is **here?**"

"You haven't guessed where you are?" Sean Dunne questioned.

Frank shook his head.

"You're down inside the meteor," said Lomax; "— you're here at my mercy… I've been using this place for a hideout ever since my unfortunate, accident; no one's gonna find us out here — why do you reckon I haven't hog-tied, you? You're not going anywhere without **my say so,** an' you won't travel far on "shank's pony" if by a freak of nature, you do get away."

"I see. Then humor me? Tell a drunken, ignorant fool, how you pulled off that street accident in broad daylight — of all things — that has to be a master stroke if ever there was one!"

"I can tell you this; it was a clever plan and was the best idea Donny Stroughton had in years," Lester said as he flicked ash from the end of his shrinking cheroot.

"I thought **he'd** somehow put an oar in it somewhere. I wanted to cotton onto him but there was always something holding me back!" Cotter confessed.

"It worked like this. When we knew from my spy in Washington that the Indian Affairs were sending a couple of officers to Junction

City after my hide, I knew I had to make myself scarce. The only way we were ever gonna get Washington off my case was for me to vanish. *We* knew that I'd be on their Wanted Posters for years and they'd never call off their hunt as long as someone up there in Washington thought I was live and breathing. But there is no point in hunting a dead man... so I ended up dead. But as Donny pointed out —"

"— He was always part of your mob?" threw in Frank.

Lomax nodded. "That's a very guttural word on your part, Frankie! *We* prefer to refer to it as a **syndicate...** It sounds much more businesslike. Anyhow, Stroughton pointed out that any investigation into our affairs would not end with just a report of one's death; we need something damn dramatic — whereby, folks either saw what they thought was true or what we wanted them to see. Either way, Lester Lomax would be dead in the eyes of the public..."

"So you staged managed your accident?"

"Yes. Just as any magician stages his tricks of illusion. It had to look real to the audience —"

"—that wouldn't have been an easy thing to do in the light of day? As you now realize Ma Kelly was more than a threat with what she thought she saw of the accident than a help." Frank reached over and took what remained of Lomax's cheroot from the man's fingers and took a pull on it before handing it back to Lester. "...That extra stranger she thought she saw at the scene of the accident, I take it, it was you?"

"That's about the size of it," Lester admitted as he flicked the remains of the small cigar in the direction of the campfire. "Donny arranged the set-up of the cast of players such as Hill, Bevan and himself. We knew our parts backwards, as they say in the theater."

"Was Pearl in on any of this?" Cotter wanted to know.

"No, she didn't have a clue. We had to have people caught up in the events that unfolded whom were not in any way savvy about the set-up. People like Klem Boston; the town deputies, and Doc Hallway, plus the folks at the funeral parlor."

"Where did you find the surrogate body to play your part in the con?" Cotter asked with a burning interest; for he had actually laid eyes, on the substitute being, when that coffin had been broken open.

"Now, that was a Godsend..." Lester said, "He was a saddle-tramp just passing through Junction City who took ill with guts pains at just the right moment. He collapsed at the bar and Ma Kelly sent for me as I was just down the street. When I got to the theater with my bag of tricks, Ma's staff had already lugged the sick man a round backstage and laid him out on a theater prop — a chaise lounge.

"On examination of the stranger I realized he had a fatal case of appendicitis, the color of his vomit that someone had caught in a spittoon before I got there told me that. I knew the opportunity **we,** the syndicate needed — was lying there before me. I told Ma and company of onlookers that I couldn't do much for the man here, backstage; that he ought to be taken to my surgery.

"Ma organized for the Williams brothers to stretcher the stranger on board the stage-prop he already occupied. When they got him to my place I sent everyone out — back to whatever it was they were doing before hand, and did a more detailed examination of the patient — it confirmed my suspicions. He later died without regaining consciousness." Lomax drew two more Mexican cheroots from his pocket and offered one to Frank who felt he needed it just as much as Lester.

Dunne crossed to the edge of the campfire and knelt down to collect a faggot protruding from the flames, his intention was to bring it back to his companions, so they might utilize it as a taper with which to light their cheroots.

"Ta," said Lester as he took the light from Dunne's hand and instead proffered the smoldering coal in Cotter's direction so the scribe could torch the tip of his small cigar, first.

With the cigar clenched between his teeth and lips Cotter began sucking on the rolled tobacco leaf so the cheroot might ignite between draws… "So — so n-n-now you … you had a body …but…but how were you going to go about giving it a similar scar, similar to what we share Lester… How, how about that? Dead men don't heal, even I know that!" Frank pointed out as he pulled back from the tip of the taper, now sure that his cigar would smolder and be on hand, as he require its supportive crutch.

"You're correct about the dead body; The scar you all witnessed was nothing more that stage make-up and grease paint," Lomax began to torch his cheroot, studying Frank through the flame of the taper. He began to shake it out now that he was happy with his light, then tossed the burnt out faggot across to the fire without making any adjustment to his sitting position.

"— OK, so now you've got the body with its obligatory scar to fool everyone so that there'd be no questions, asked. But you are not going to tell me that even you were callous enough to smash the poor guys face in so that it was unrecognizable with something?" Frank knew that the things he heard along with Dunne, was a horror story that was beyond most folk's imagination — he knew it was authentic for he had seen bodies in all their revolting horror during the war.

Lomax continued. "I got word to Donny Stroughton —"

Lester nodded, "— right…The tramp had a longhorn-like moustache, which I shaved off before Stroughton arrived. It was getting late, maybe about ten or eleven thirty at night by the time he got there.

"We sent Sean off to get one of his freight wagons and we loaded the cadaver aboard in the dark while no one was around — mean time, Don and I dressed the feller up in one of my best suits." Lester paused and looked across at Dunne, whom by this time had gone over and hunkered down in front of the fire to check on the stew. "You tell **our friend** how you handled things, Sean…" Lomax prodded.

Dunne pivoted around from the pot on the balls of his Peewee boots, in the direction of the scribe and Lester. He brushed his hat up higher on his forehead but his features were hardly discernible because of the backlighting from the fire. Sean Dunne took up the tale from where Lester had dropped it in his lap. "I took the dead feller back to the freight yard. The warehouse up there is big enough ter hide a whole company of soldiers; that's where I keep things in storage out of the weather.

"Don, came down ter lend a hand in riggin' up the wagon fer the accident we were in the process of plannin'. You see, Stroughton knew the accident would be best affective in broad daylight — but we had ter be the folks callin' the shots.

"In the course of my normal business, I'd picked up a couple of wire-mesh oblong hen coops fer transportin' fowls. The coop we picked fer the job had ter be able ter hold a man's body, and, that's where we stuffed him… that Don Stroughton's a damn genius; Yuh see he come up with the idea that we attach the hen's coop upside down under the bottom of the wagon bed with the body in it, with the lid of the coop so that it dropped open towards the ground and this would allow an object, such as the body ter fall down onto the road under the wagon. We rigged up this lever near my seat which when pulled, opened the lid… ”

Doctor Lomax took over. “— only thing was, by our own experiments in the warehouse we couldn't guarantee that when the body dropped onto the road that it would fall so as the wagon wheels would pass over it and inflict the damage to the body we required.”

“I suspect I know how you solved that problem?” Frank told the teamster.

“How?” asked Dunne as he turned back to the fire and the cooking.

“Must I go into it …?” said Frank.

Lomax shook his head and spoke the worse that had to be done to the corpse. “We had to damage the cadaver so it wasn't easy for anyone to know it wasn't —”

“The only problem was you went too far,” said Cotter. “You characters knocked the body around too much, you over did it — when a professional like the funeral director got hold of it, he knew that the victim couldn't have survived the accident long enough to say the things you s'pose were to have been said in the moments prior to death, true, Lester?”

Lester Lomax nodded.

“…So you had to have the body's identity established by the time it reached the mortician's. That's where Stroughton and Hill came in. Before Sheriff Boston got to the scene, they all verified it was Lester, and established the instructions you'd dreamed up. OK, I can see how the Sheriff was suckered; but what about Hallway? That man wouldn't have been have been fooled as easily as a layman, surely?”

“Some things went better than was planned or could be expected,” Lomax told his old friend as he suspected their association was dying. “My stand-in – the saddle-tramp, was as you know, dead by the time Hallway arrived and I was hiding nearby in my surgery spying out the scene – Hallway and Boston had no way of knowing the smashed about body wasn't me in that condition; it was academic that they'd established its identity before it reached the mortician's.

“That's where Stroughton, Bevan and Hill came in. Churcher had no reason or foundation to guess otherwise. Not with the sheriff of the town and *my own physician* identifying the corpse they escorted to the parlor; and that of course, saved the day.”

"Hallway was also in on the fraud?'

"Not that he knew about it. He was sure the body he came to the aid of was mine."

"I had the job of dropped the stiff right in the intersection where we wanted it," said Dunne as he stood up. "That jackrabbit's ready if you wanna put the nose-bags on!"

"We can leave it a while yet,' said Lomax, "it'll be too hot; let it cool." Dunne acted on the doctor's advice and took the time to stretch the kinks out of his body and came back to the blanket.

"Who was the cold bastard who made the body unrecognizable?"

"That was Sean's tasked — under my guidance."

"What did he use?"

"Do you have ter know every callous detail?" said Dunne.

"Humor my ghoulish tastes."

"If you must know, I used a goddamn iron bar — satisfied?"

"I never thought in a hundred year that you would end up in a Godforsaken mess like this, Lester. If it had been me, I'd've understood — but not you, how can you account for it? It looked to me as though you had the world at your feet?"

"And so I did," Lester confessed. "I thought I had it made. My business and medical end of things seemed to be thriving and I reckon that to some outsiders it looked as though I was going to knock poor Doctor Hallway off his perch. Then the plight of the Indians out there on the reservation being knocked over like flies by disease, as per us white folks — made me take a second look at things. I devoted my time and energy in trying to come up with something that might knock these scourges in the head, and turn the medical world on its ear and staunch the death rate of the Pawnees. They began paying me in gold dust that ran through my fingers like water. The cost of research you understand —"

"I've heard that part of the story from Hill," Frank said with a dismissal wave of his hand. "And how, you came to Dunne's aid with his transport business. You know it is clear that when the Indians began paying you in gold for this elixir they didn't understand the value of that dust in our white man's world? I suspect that when Washington heard that, it made folks back there jealous, and, that's why they started coming after you with a big stick, especially when the medicine you were producing was a crippling killer.

"You laid a trail of gunpowder leading to one gigantic powder keg and set the stuff on fire — heading with the speed of a runaway locomotive which no one looked able to stop; and that loco' comes in the guise of a bunch of hostile Pawnees charging down on Junction City where a fuckin' lot of innocent people are gonna die — how does that make you feel, Lester?!" Cotter queried.

"That was never my intention. But in this world one can only worry about number one!"

"What about Pearl?" Frank asked. "Your use of her was like that of a two bit whore, you're supposed death has rung her out emotionally —"

"She's much more resourceful than you realize. But then again, by what I've been able to observe — you and her seem to be growing closer than I would have expected?"

Dunne got up without warning and hoofed it off up to the buckboard where he got a couple of tin plates and some outdoors cutlery.

Cotter told Lomax. "If I had known you were alive, I'd have not showing my emotions. I didn't think I was so transparent?"

"At times, when she wasn't watching you — you looked upon her like a "love sick" bull. When this is all over and things have sorted themselves, you can have her if you want Frank — I've no use for her, she has served her purpose."

Dunne came back from the buckboard with their meal gear, as Frank said: "You can toss her aside just like that?"

"To her I'm a dead man, an' with luck I'll stay that way; especially once I've done my disappearing act with my share of the gold the syndicate's amassed…" Lester told Frank and somehow Cotter realized that for once the doctor was being truthful.

"Making that offer to me about Pearl means you hold her no higher than a slave to be sold to the highest bidder. What gives you the right to treat her like that?" Frank asked as he watched Dunne got to the Dutch oven, put the plates on the stone floor and remove the oven's lid, the stew's tasty aroma impregnated the air and made their mouths' water.

"Like I said before — you want her — you take her!" Lomax said magnanimously.

"If only I had something to offer her — yes, don't think for a minute I wouldn't. I can't even get two straps of jerky beef together and you know it, Lester."

"Then now's the time to use your brains. Thrown in with Dunne and me and come to Canada. It's a whole new country over the border and we will be safe there to start anew!"

"Is that the plan?" Frank asked no one in particular. Then he spoke directly to Dunne as he approached with a plate full to almost overflowing with 'rabbit stew. "What about the others, Bevan, Hill and lawyer Stroughton?" But Dunne didn't looked prepare to comment and so Frank turned to Lester, "…You're just gonna leave 'em for the authorities to be collected like storm debris?"

"They know the score," Dunne said as he handed a tin plate of stew to Lomax and started back towards the fire to load up another plate. "There are plenty of spoils ter go round fer everybody…" he began spooning stew onto the plate he would later pass to the scribe. "…Stroughton has been turnin' the syndicates gold in ter hard cash a long time, now." Dunne returned to the Indian rug and handed Cotter a hot plate of food. "— slow but sure, was the operation. His journeys ter Dodge an' other places here abouts, haven't always been fer court hearings an' clients, it's been ter cash in the Pawnee gold without anyone in Junction City bein' the wiser."

Sean could not help but grin when he saw that Mr. Frank Cotter was finally seeing the light; he swung away from the scribe and returned to the Dutch oven, to dish out his own serve of 'rabbit as the boozy scribe's eyes shifted back in the direction of the campfire. Lester allowed his hard-set face to lighten up as Cotter said to Dunne, "I got the idea long back that you're married? Are you just going to up and dump your responsibilities and shoot through to Canada or someplace — what about your wife?"

Dunne found the rabbit's hind-quarter amongst the gravy and vegetables and forked it onto his plate saying: "My duty is ter no one but *me* — she'll survive…" He rose from his haunches before the oven and made his way back to the blanket; he sat down facing the fire and took a tentative mouthful of hot stew. It was far too hot for the inside of his mouth and as his left-eye began to smart, a single tear coursed down his cheek; he spat the offending stew back onto his plate.

"That's rather crude," remarked Cotter in reference to Dunne's attitude to his marriage; but Dunne assumed that the scribe was referring to the fact that he spat a mouthful of food back on his plate and it irked him.

"What do you know about *me* an'— *my* married life?" He bawled in Frank's direction, each word of his dialog chased from his mouth by tiny spit-balls — Dunne wrapped up his tirade with a goggled eyed expression.

"Easy— easy, easy, easy, easy —" said Lomax, "Yelling like *that* is gonna rouse the Pawnee ghosts within these walls!" exclaimed the one time medic more concerned with calming his aroused partner in crime. He was on safe ground knowing that the scribe would take his cue from him and not turn it into a shouting match.

Dunne snarled like a dog on a chain in Lester's direction, "— then don't let **yuh** friend try poking his cock inter **my marriage!"**

Both Dunne and Lomax traded glares as black as carbon soot, eyes locked with one another. It was Lomax who broke the spell as he turned away from the riled Irishman and took up his own fork and plate of stew and forked some of the meal into his mouth and changed the subject by saying: "Hmm — you know this stew isn't half bad, c'mon forget the arguments and enjoy!" Lester poked at the air with the prongs of his now empty fork, dripping the juice of the stew off down into the body of the meal.

"So what is my future in all of this?" asked Frank with half a mouthful of stew. "Do I get to join the rest of you and go waltzing off into the sunset and leave the mess behind of your making?" Cotter did not realize that as far as Sean Dunne was concerned he had signed his own death certificate earlier, when he stated his views about the way Lomax intended to treat Pearl Courtney. He was going to play the upright gentleman to his detriment. He, Dunne, could easily put a bullet in the scribe's carcass without the slightest remorse! For he knew the doctor would likely be too sanctimonious to go through with it if things were reversed. But if anything, *I will be pleased to do the job,* thought Dunne.

"As far as the Indian uprising goes; unless you have a magic wand, it'll have to play out its, tune!" Lester said. "As for your own safety... I suggest you put yourself in our hands and hit the high road if you have any scintillation of sense in your skull — otherwise even *I can't* guarantee your safety."

"And if I don't hop into your pouch — I'm going to end up like Derrick, Ma and a few others, hey?"Lester just looked at his old friend unblinkingly; but in those eyes — the portals to man's inner soul, Frank could see that Lomax still warmed to their friendship, it also made Cotter realize that the Doctor would do what was ever necessary to ensure that he and his party would make a clean getaway even if he had to be the one to take Frank's life. "Look, I suggest you sleep on it tonight — then in the mornin' if your answer's agreeable you can look to a bright, new future…"

"But if yuh mind's thinkin' and ours don't coincide," interjected Dunne. "Then it'll be my please ter blow a hole through ya chest as per compliments of Mister Samuel Colt!" Sean

Dunne slapped the flat of his palm against his tied-down holster with meaning.

Lieutenant Briggs stepped out of the morning's sunlight up onto the plank floor of the porch, he'd realized while eating breakfast in the marquee earlier, that it was going to be a warm day for this time of the year, completely out of season and that later the shade cast by the sun's present angle to the awning as he approached the admin office of the reservation, would seem like a sanctuary. The armed private on picket duty saluted the lieutenant and Briggs responded and broke step slightly to allow the picket time to open the door of the building for him.

Briggs had come to collect Captain Roscoe for the Gatling-gun's demonstration that had been organized for the benefit of the tribal elders and any young hotheads who had the notion to become party or intended party, to the clandestine renegade mob that as yet had not shown its hand. Captain Roscoe had ordered the demonstration to take place this morning at precisely 0.830-hours.

Briggs pulled the door closed behind him and saluted his commanding officer that had once more taken over Jake Warner's desk.

Roscoe rose from the desk-chair, returned the Lieutenant's salute and collected his campaign hat.

"…The Pawnee that look like attending are assembling behind the hospital as requested, sir," Briggs announced. "The Gatling and crew are in position alongside the infirmary as per your instructions — the prickly-pear patch will serve as the targets for the purposes of our demo'."

Roscoe nodded his approval as he placed his hat on and joined Briggs on the other side of the desk.

The Army's covered wagon and team had been drawn up parallel with the outside windows of the hospital's sick-ward. Masking the window from which the Pawnee maiden has slipped out unnoticed, and ran like a doe-deer to the tribe at Cedar Creek.

The sun's current position was such that the hospital's shade spilled out over the canvas canopy of the wagon and the horses. The wagon was surrounded by a squad of armed Blue bellies with carbines at the ready. A group of interested tribal folk, mostly men, stood silently by — the gathering gave no impression of their ranking within the tribal structure and stood about as equals with hooded eyes.

Roscoe and Briggs marched in step round the corner of the hospital with a tinkle of spurs and the rattle of loose sabers and headed for the gun-wagon. A stocky staff sergeant standing quiet and relaxed was sneaking a quick smoke, he tossed his fag aside and came smartly to order, bellowed out as the officers came into view. "Squad… Attention!" The squad came to order on his command.

The stone-faced officers came up and haltered at the corner of the vehicle's tailgate — the wagon was broadside in the direction of the prickly pear patch. Roscoe removed his gauntlets as he glanced over the crowd of Indians. The size was down to what he had hoped for, but he did not let his disappointment register in his face or body language.

"It's not what you expected, is it sir?" Briggs spoke quietly so the nearby Pawnee would not hear.

"It's all show mister, on both sides;" said Roscoe. "They wanna show me that although they've returned to the fold, we aren't the masters of the situation we think we are…" The captain took one last look about to see if there were any stragglers en route, but alas there were none. "There are enough braves here to witness the awesome firepower of the machine-gun, I'm sure we can rely on them to spread the message to their hothead brothers and hopefully make 'em think twice about making the same mistake of Clearwater and braves whom had came in loaded with firewater. OK, let's not waste any more time — on with the demonstration!"

Nodding, Briggs turned to the covered wagon and nodded to one of the privates. The soldier shouldered arms and turned smartly to the right, marched the length of the wagon to where the wagon-master stood and nodded to the feller to unhitch the four horse team from the wagon-tongue. A safety measure, so that as soon as the Gatling was fired its noisy assault wouldn't startle the horses and embarrass the long knives by bolting off with the wagon and gun-crew.

The crew and their weapon had been kept under wraps since Roscoe's patrol had reached the reservation, no one outside of the Calvary knew what to expect with the element of surprise being taken for granted by the captain and his party — as being a very persuasive tool.

Suddenly the left side of the canvas canopy was hauled clear in a very showman like manner, this exposed to the Indian audience a shiny new Gatling-gun mounted on a tripod and point down range to the prickly pear patch. The gun's operator began cranking the weapon and the rifle-barrels started rotating into line with the gun's firing mechanism, it misfired on the first barrel which was sometimes a minor fault with the gun but never missed a beat on the rest. It spat hot-lead out in rapid succession in the direction of the prickly pears, something as never witnessed before by the reservation's natives — the hurling missiles chopped the plants to smithereens so fast the even portions of airborne pears were re-chopped while still in-flight from the ricocheting lead slugs that exploded on the hard earth after striking hidden bedrock. The Pawnees were awestruck by the impact of the Army's exhibition.

Never before had these people witnessed a gun with such firepower at its disposal — Roscoe and Briggs were pleased to see the effect, the demonstration had on those wide-eyed Indians at the showing, Roscoe took real pride in the fact that it all went well and that the Pawnees would surely realize that going up against that sort of equipment the white men had as a back stop, would be suicidal.

Upon realizing the demonstration for their benefit was over, the major portion of the natives drifted away back to their mix of wigwams too no doubt spread the word to those whom had been too obstinate to attend the show of strength — but the more adventurous and curious, made their way across to the war-wagon to have a closer look at the rife of many tongues, but found they weren't allowed too close and were forbidden to swarm all over the wagon as some natives were cheeky. The fusillade of shots had upset the wagon team and a trooper had been ordered to walk them about until they settled down before being hitched back up to the wagon. Others had gone down to the pear patch and were taking souvenirs of the plants and taking note of how the lead had broken up the soil and found they could even run the earth through their fingers.

Roscoe and Briggs returned the administration building to await developments from the Pawnee end of things, tensions were still running hot and cold between the parties and now it was a case of wait and see how things develop. Meanwhile the captain re-issued his previous orders to the troopers that every man had to keep his eyes on the Indians as the Pawnee wandered about their daily activities; this was on top of the Long knives attending to their own chores, routine maintenance and domestic duties of a troop in the field — for they had to be ready to swing into the saddle at a moment's notice.

It had also been pointed out to the recruits that their roving eyes had to be on the lookout for folks who seem to be casually drifting away from the hospital-cum-administration area of the reservation aboard their ponies — either singularly, in pairs or more; this fact had to be drawn to Lt. Briggs' notice, so that he could pass it along to the captain and or maybe send a couple of blue-coats out to arrest the would-be wanderers, whom would be slapped in chains, until interrogation established that his or her motives were purely of an innocent nature.

Naturally, if so invoked, this action would not rest easy on the shoulders of any red-blooded men in the encampment, and did nothing to ease the tension between the sides that simmered away like a hot pot of broth.

The night Cotter spent in the cave did little to encourage sleep. Lester gave the impression to Frank that he wasn't too bothered, but all the same, Cotter suspected that Lomax was awake most of the time. Dunne had rolled himself up in a spare horse-rug that smelt like briny horse-sweat, after allowing the fire to slowly burn low until it was a small mound of hot ash and glowing coals. Dunne bedded down somewhere between it and the mouth of the cave's passage, the same ingress from where Lomax had emerged when he made his entrance after Frank had begun to settle back into the world, from his bout of unconsciousness — Cotter had no idea whether the passage was the exit which ultimately led to freedom or if in fact, it went back deeper into the giant meteorite which had embedded itself in the earth's surface before man had come forth on the planet...

Without a storm lamp or firebrand in ones possession down in here you were surrounded in a black void that almost felt solid enough to touch, you felt that it was something tangible, and one's state of mind gave the misconception that the feather-like darkness was brushing against one's own sightless eyeballs, it was a screwy experience and when one comes to think about it, the imagined feel, made one slightly nauseous... It was now, that Frank realized that he was sitting erect and for the life of himself he could not tell how long he had been sitting there in the dark. He decided to lie down on the rug and stared off up to the rough rock ceiling that he could only imagine in his mind's eye, but it served a purpose, it settled his stomach and he brushed aside the sudden thought that came to mind that the jackrabbit stew might have been the cause of his upset stomach.

It was the sound of Dunne striking a match on an unknown surface which made Cotter aware that time had in fact been moving on and that perhaps he had found some sleep or sleep had found him after all... But there was no doubt in his mind that he was awake at this very moment. The teamster began to work at reviving the campfire and its wood smoke in the clearly began to irritate the man's lungs — his rough, ragged cough was like a poor soul stricken with tuberculosis, he hawked phlegm up from deep within his chest and spat it, into the fire's heart as he fumbled for more dry sticks from the pile of faggots near the fire's edge...

The barricades had been manned throughout the whole night by skeleton crews of armed citizens — those not on guard, slept as best they could in the vacant nearby buildings with their guns at their sides. It had been so silent throughout the township that night that men whom had seen action in the Civil War drew the analogy to the attention of non war veterans, that it was akin to lying in wait for the start of an upcoming battle. For there was no doubt that in the town-folks' minds, they could well be facing "The Battle of Junction City", and in fact, writing the pages of history with blood.

Klem Boston had not slept a wink all night and at first light began visiting the town's fortifications by buggy through the empty streets as the place had taken on the prospects of a ghost town. He had the company of his colleague, Jock Robeson. There was little they could do but give the men whom had drawn the short-straw to stand watch a moral boost, by showing them that someone else, was also losing sleep. By the time the sun was about to break the distant horizon line in the East, nearly every available kitchen stove in this region of town had been fired up, the womenfolk were preparing breakfast for one and all — most people feared that there could be a long time between meals if the Pawnee's threat to hit the town came to fruition. The business folk who ran diners and café outlets were glad of the extra help in coping with feeding the town's swollen population — demand for their services were astronomical and would soon empty their larders, for nothing was getting into town or out. The children freed from school were going to be an unforeseen nuisance no one had given any thought too.

A few of the late Ma Kelly's whores, whom were trying to nurse Matt Flynn through his ordeal were verbalized by the so-called "good-women" of town whenever they appeared on the sidewalks as they traversed between their temporary abode at the stage depot and the saloon, where their patient lay fighting for his life.

The prisoner's infection seemed to be settling and that in itself, gave Hallway hope, but the doctor knew the man had a long way to go before it could be considered that he was on the road to recovery.

A callous gambler, who hit town before Junction City had gone into shutdown from the rest of the country, was running a book on whether or not the ramrod would cheat the local grave diggers out of some pick an' shovel, work. Because of the mental stress folks found themselves in, their thirst for some sort of amusement which could ease the pressure a mite was outlandish; so no matter how sic it may sound, the local cowboys with change in their pockets placed the odd bet with the grifter. Even the Williams' brothers got in on the action. The existence of this bizarre game of chance reached the ears of the conservative folk of Junction City and thus, it gave the Preachers of the various faiths a foot in the door to they could preach about the sins of man on street corners or right outside the saloon doors; which the owners and managers strongly objected too.

Men at a loose end started guzzling the town liquor supplies as if there might be no tomorrow and some hotheads so eager for a fight, be it with the Pawnees or their fellow man, began bouncing their knuckled off the jaws of weaker fellers — but sometimes a bully came off second best when a combative drunk, sensing he was outweighed by his brawling opponent, felt the only course left for him, was to fill his paw with pig-iron, and put a quick slug through his antagonist or some unlucky, hapless bystander, depending upon how liquored-up the trigger man was at the time.

Most of this wild shooting only resulted in flesh-wounds — but nonetheless it was a serious irritant — and as a result, Boston's men were being run off their feet trying to control juiced up hot-heads; so much so, that the Mayor ordered the saloons shut until the current crisis was over. This made life easier for Boston and his deputized posse.

Dragoon, along with Yolson and his wife also got a rough night's sleep — but not so, the children. Their innocents gave them no room to appreciate the town's current emergency. The gun salesman arose and dressed quickly and quietly in the gunsmith's spare room the moment he hears the Jewish kids stir in their Queen-size bed next door to him. He fished out a fresh shirt and with a toilet travel bag in hand, crept out of the upstairs apartment and headed off up to the Chinese bathhouse. The walkway was busy, for with the saloons operating shorter hours folks got up and about to stretch their legs and see what the other half were up too. Because of the loss of revenue some of the entrepreneurs boldly set up their games of chance out on the sidewalks and snidely worked them illegally.

The bathhouse was not attracting much business this time of the morning so Dragoon got through with his ablutions in good time. Then he strolled with due care and caution across the busy street with his gear to catch breakfast with Cotter. He paused just inside the entrance and scanned the room in search of his pal. Werner's was busy and surprisingly enough most males in the diner were wearing holsters bearing various makes of pistols — although bearing arms in the diner was taboo, under the present circumstances this in-house rule, was being relaxed for good reason; no one knew whether or not when the town was going to be subjected to a raid and it would be bedlam if God forbid, one did occur; and folks had to scramble in search of their guns.

Whitney caught sight of Bevan and Hill in the early stages of eating breakfast at a table set for four, located deep within the diner. No one looked as though they were about to join them so Dragoon made his way over to their table; Bevan looked up from his plate of kidney beans and saw Whitney heading their way, he muttered something to Hill, who had his back to Dragoon.

"'Mornin' gents," Whitney addressed the pair. "Mind if I join ya?" Dragoon halted alongside their table and lowered his clutch bag of toiletries to the tabletop in front of a vacant chair and draped his soiled shirt over its back.

"…Yore welcome," said Hill as he turned his head slightly to look up in Whitney's direction.

Jonas Bevan nodded to one of the empty chairs. "Make yore choice."

Whitney left his possessions and went back to the cashier and gave his order and paid his bill then went down to the breakfast counter with his chit for the cook. One of the waitresses took his order written up by the cashier and passed it through an open hatch to the chef and then she took a soup bowl off the top of the stack on her side of the counter and ladled sticky oatmeal into it, and sprinkled it with raw sugar and doused it with hot cow's milk and drove a soup-spoon into the porridge mountain, then gave the lot to Dragoon, who meanwhile had poured himself a mug of black coffee from the urn. Dragoon, with both hands full returned to the table.

Bevan and Hill were tied up in conversation when Whitney joined them so he put both his bowl of oats and coffee on the table and tried to pick up on their intercourse. When there was a suitable break in their dialog he chipped in.

"Have any of you fellers been called on to work the graveyard shift on the barricades?" He worked his spoon through the milk and oats, blending the lot together and turning it more into gruel as far as its consistency went.

"Not as yet," Bevan told him.

"Jonas and I start out tour of duty after breakfast," Hill looked at his turnip pocket watch to check the time.

"Are you two, together on the same barricade?"

"Nope," answered Bevan who broke a cob of bread in half and started mopping up bean juice. "— I'm diagonally across from Doc. Lomax's surgery. Where did you draw?" He asked of Hill.

"I have been given a spot at the barricade down near the stage depot. You been fixed up with a place yet, Mr. Dragoon?"

"I've my hands full arming people from Yolson's store — that will keep me out of trouble. What's Frank Cotter doing for himself? I haven't clamped eyes on him since yesterday…"

Both the syndicate members shrugged their shoulders. "About somewhere I guess," stated Bevan.

"No doubt making a nuisance of himself — that's his rôle in life," Hill suggested.

"Don't you like Cotter, Mr. Hill," Whitney asked.

"Not particularly."

"Had things worked out differently, you could've been working side by side in Doctor Lomax set-up!" Dragoon pointed out.

"That's something we shall never know," Bevan stated as he chewed a piece of bread.

"True," Dragoon added. "I suppose you know that Cotter is officially covering the events of Junction City for an eastern newspaper. I thought he would be out an' about gather copy and sketching folks as the town prepares itself — he's clever with a pencil, when it comes to depicting everyday life… a bit like that feller, Leonardo Da Vinci!"

"Who is this Da Vinci?" Bevan questioned without really any interest, and it showed in his face.

Hill said wearily. "C'mon, pal — don't show ya ignorance…"

"I know who he means, ya idiot." Bevan sneered sarcastically. "— I jist wanted ter see if *he,* Dragoon, knew."

Whitney swallowed a spoonful of sweet, milky, gruel and then asked: "…So you haven't see Frank about?" *Boy how I would like to plant my knuckle on Bevan's jaw,* thought Dragoon.

Hill picked up a toothpick from a vessel in the middle of the table and prepared to mine his teeth as he said: "Not for a couple of days. You know he has taken a bit of a shine to Lomax's' lady friend; Miss Courtney…?"

"I probably know more about that than either of you two!" Dragoon snapped to convey the fact to the two men that he was riding Cotter's fence on that score. "He's not stepping on anyone's toes — Lomax is dead, remember!"

Hill and Bevan dropped their eyes to the table and blushed.

"After breakfast I'll take me a stroll round town ter see if I can find out, what he's up, too."

"Try Lomax place for a start. He might have shacked up there last night, though that part of town is out of bounds," Bevan suggested.

"Sounds a good place to start," Dragoon said.

Before going round to the apartment, Dragoon dropped into Yolson's and left his soiled clothes and toiletries, then hiked it up the alley through to Starr street. As that part of town had now been designated as a no-go zone, he hoofed it around there like some kind of sneak thief. He arrived at his destination without detection and soon found himself standing on the landing. He tried the door, expecting it to be locked, but to his surprise he found it hadn't been keyed. He admitted himself, this time openly, for he had hoped to find Frank in residence. But as he crossed the threshold he saw that the parlor had been disturbed and there was a feel to the room, that things did not feel quite right. He called Cotter's name just in case the feller was in the bedroom but got no response. So he continued through to the room and there, discovered that the bed had obviously not been slept in. He inspected the washing-stand and the ablution implements. A dry cake of soap lay in the soap-dish and through dehydration had cracked like a clay tablet. He made up his mind to seek the scribe elsewhere and prepared to leave, but just before doing so he ran his eyes once more over the parlor and damn it, there on the carpet square in front of the sofa was Frank Cotter's newfangled propelling pencil!

He crossed the room and knelt down on one knee to retrieve it; Whitney knew this was proof that Frank had recently been here for the last time he was with the man he saw the pencil-top protruding slightly above the man's frock-coat breast pocket.

Dragoon returned to the active sector of town without being sighted and made for McBride's; surely the man would have made a barber stop for a shave in the last couple of days. Mc Bride admitted, that he hadn't seen the man in the past forty-eight hours. This meant that surely he would be in before lunchtime for both men knew that Frank had no faith in his hands when it came to using a straight razor. Whitney put in another two fruitless hours looking for Cotter, but people he thought worthwhile asking about Cotter, just gave him a blank stare. He called back at the diner a couple of times but drew blanks until he caught up with Donald Stroughton taking brunch. Uninvited, the salesman took the spare empty chair at the attorney's table and quizzed the lawyer if he had seen Cotter in his travels. Stroughton shook his head. "…Can't say, I have. But *you do* know that we aren't too friendly, these days?"

"I heard."

The Attorney went on. "I thought him being a good friend of Lomax, we'd have hit it off; but it wasn't meant to be. However if I come across the feller, I'll tell him you're looking for him. So where is the best place for him to see you?"

"The gunsmith's …"

Reaching for a china mug of java, Stroughton said: "…I'll be sure to do that. See yuh," he said from behind the rim in a dismissive tone. Whitney got the message.

The mayor's buggy couldn't make any pace along Main because of the congestion involving pedestrians, horseflesh and vehicles. It was just as well, for when Whitney Dragoon bowled off the boardwalk into the oncoming vehicle's path, it made Klem rein in hard to avoid the roan knocking the salesman flat on his back on the dirt road…

"Are you mad, Dragoon?!" Sheriff Boston cried.

"Ye cannot be right in the skull doing a crazy thing like thart!" Jock said from his place alongside Klem and instantly saw that the gun-salesman was a worried man, which altered his approach.

"Sorry," said the crestfallen Dragoon from down near the head of the mare. "— but I've got a problem I need ter bring up with you, Sheriff!"

"Haven't *we* all got more than our share!" said Jock as Boston wrapped the reins round his hands to keep a tight grip on the mare. "But Laddie, no matter what ye problem is, it doesn't give you the r-r-r-right ter throw yerself down in front of a vehicle ter get attention!"

Both lawmen stepped down from the buggy and approached Whitney down either side of the mare until they were at its head. "Awright, what is yore problem, Mister?" asked Klem.

"I have been trying to find my friend, Cotter. He seems ter be missing from his usual, haunts."

"Well what do you expect of me? I've got my hands full with this town right at the moment *if* you haven't noticed!

"And besides, this Cotter feller is more your friend than he is mine!" Klem Boston pointed out. "In fact, he has been more a *pest* to a man than any form of salvation since he hit Junction City. OK. Let's have it, what makes you so concerned about this Frank Cotter?"

"Well now he's affiliated with an eastern newspaper and is busy writing a whole essay on how the town is pulling together as one, to survive the coming threat. You know he's very handy with a pen and pencil and —"

"— Get to the point, Laddie," Jock said from Dragoon's side.

Ignoring the Scotsman, Whitney Dragoon continued: "The point *is*, I can't seem to find him anywhere in town. I missed him this morning at breakfast in Werner's diner…I have been all over town and no one I know has seen him. It's not like him. I'm worried for his safety…I know he's been to Doctor Lomax apartment —" Whitney proffered Cotter's propelling pencil towards the sheriff.

"Here's proof — it's his newfangled pencil."

Klem took the pencil and toyed with it until the graphite tip appeared. He had seen the pencil before when Cotter was making notes.

"That doesn't mean much," Klem said as he passed the pencil back to the gun salesman.

"Judging by the angle of the sun, I'd say it is gettin' on to 3 p.m., and I've had no feedback from anyone nor has he put in an appearance. I reckon it is very, very strange."

"We can't be expected ter look into it now, lad," said Jock who knew in his own mind that for anyone to just disappear like Cotter seems to have managed, didn't figure right. "— but right now there's bigger fish to fry. Get back to us once the town had come out of this affair with the Pawnees!"

"Sheriff Robeson's right, Dragoon…" Klem said. "I've been wet-nursing' that man since he got inter my town; it'll have ter wait." Boston turned his attention to the ex-Pinkerton. "C'mon." Both men hurried aboard; already they were getting black looks from a guy in a covered wagon, waiting for them to move on.

Dragoon realized he had been dismissed and he stepped clear of the buggy right into a pile of flyblown manure.

Klem flicked the reins and the mare resumed her journey while Dragoon hobbled over to the edge of the walk where he could scrape the mess from his footwear.

20

L AZARUS ROLLO WAS in his private office trying to calm down the few ranchers whom had been forced at gunpoint to turn over fresh horses to the Williams brothers, when they, under orders from him had been sent out to warn the cattlemen at the nearby homesteads about the danger of some renegade Indians hitting their places and the possible harm it might bring to their kinfolk.

Even now, though they were in the comparative safety of Junction City their feelings of indignation warmed their blood and they gathered together and confronted the Association's, presidential chairman.

Naturally under the circumstances Rollo was pretty short tempered and gave them a real bawling out for being so negative at this point in time when everyone had their hands full as a community preparing for the Pawnee. In the end, they left his office feeling chastened and now duty-bound to join the town's militia.

The teenage wife of Lazarus Rollo had been sent by him, to see what use she could make of herself down at the Masonic Hall where the spouses of the town's Freemasons were gathering together and set about making the hall into a temporary hospital for any of the upcoming wounded; for no one had a crystal ball that would give them a glimpse into the future.

When the Butterfield stage reached Letts' way station — it was truly ready for a change of team as driver Rawlins had worked the horses hard. When the Concord rolled to a stop outside the station's major building, Enoch Rawlins, verbally lit a fire under the stable-hands as he demanded a quick switch to fresh horseflesh and made it clear to his passengers that their spell here was to be only treated as a hurried toilet

588

break, then they were bustled back on board the vehicle to endure more of the rock and sway of the concord, which would carry them through to his planned overnight stop at Otto Lehmann's station, in the hope they could consider themselves safe from the Pawnee.

Enoch gave Letts and his men an update as he understood it on the Indian situation; so those not engaged in working with the horses were ordered to start fortifying the establishment for the worst. No one on board enjoyed the rush stop but assumed that the experienced driver knew, what he was about and abided by his wishes; though Miss Pearl Courtney thought their driver was being driven very much by fear, and was not all that at easy with his job on this particular trip. But under the circumstances those being driven eastwards out of reach of the Indian danger readily accepted this.

Sheriff Robeson had been sharing a table in the crowded diner with Hill and Bevan and until this, hadn't really made their acquaintance. They seemed an amiable pair of fellows but it was clear to the ex-Pinkerton that they were a couple, and it wasn't just as business partners, **still...** thought the ex-Lawrence Law Officer that really was their affair.

Hill chewed his cud; in reality a morsel of rump steak — and a moment before swallowing tugged away his napkin, which he had tucked down his front-shirt and dried his lips on it. When he commenced to speak his voice was muffled by the table napkin... Bevan appeared to continue to pay attention to the meal of potatoes and bacon before him but Robeson knew that Hill's sidekick wasn't missing a word of what was being said: "So Sheriff Robeson, how's your prisoner making out?" Hill asked, though it was not colored with the intonation of one who was really interested in the health of Prisoner Flynn.

Robeson noticed this as he placed his cutlery down parallel across the china dinner plate stained with his finished meal, which had included brown gravy sauce.

"Trewfully, he's a bit of a concern to Doc. Hallway, Lazarus Rollo an' me," said the Scotsman. "...If he caves in on us then all our works has been fer naught and the Cattlemen's Association's jist sent crook money after bad by hiring me privately. This Flynn fellow is taken a lotta looking after; the sawbones don't know whether he'll yet make it, especially if an' when the town comes under attack and wounded start pouring in fer the Doc to spend any serious time with … if gangrene takes a hold of Matt Flynn it'll be the end of him."

"Waal when all is said and done," stated Bevan, "The guy's nuthin' more than a highway robbing, killer — so why the concern about his health when the chips are down? He didn't have any feelings fer his victims, did he?"

Robeson arose and collecting his weathered hat from the empty chair at the table set for four, and added: "It sure doesn't appear to look like it. Now if'n you gents will excuse me, I'll be on my way to see what help I can be ter Klem and the Mayor — afternoon, folks…"

"Afternoon, Sheriff …!" Chorused the two bed partners as Robeson headed towards the bustling sidewalk. The man carried his Stetson in his paw until he was outside the establishment where he paused to fit it to his crown, then turned and made his way for the downtown part of town in search of Klem and the Mayor.

Frank crouched in the dark cavern, as blind as a bat and as scared as any would-be being about to face death. For that, which he suspected now faced him – as it was purely by luck and not design that he had broken away from one of his executioners and was now being stalked by another. Frank maybe the novice here, but realized that his breathing was too loud and if he did not get it under control it would be the death of him. He made a special determined effort on his part, and it now began to look as though it might pay dividends — if only his luck would hold! Cotter knew he hadn't killed Dunne in the struggle over Dunne's pistol and regretted the outcome, for now Lomax and Dunne could share the task of running him to ground. He cursed himself further for being so dumb as to admit he wouldn't fall in with their bunch and dash off with them to Canada; this meant that his death was the syndicate's only chance of survival and he realized that the lives of five men and their future rested in his hands.

Looked at it in that light there was no option — close friendships don't count when your own life is on the line.

The weight of the revolver in his hand was still just as foreign to him as it was back at the scene of the stage robbery when he tried to guard the bodies against the hungry vultures — he felt awkward with a six-shooter in his hand, let alone have confidence in his ability to use it with any measure of success.

Sweat oozed from the pours of his body without restraint because of how highly-strung he was, but right now he knew he wasn't the only man sweating vital bodily fluids. Somewhere off in the darkness two men were sweating for other reasons... One from the pain of a bullet from the pistol in Cotter's hand, the twin to the one Dunne still posed — the pain he was already suffering was from a slug that had torn a path across the flesh of his thigh when Cotter shouldered him as he charged the short distance that separated them just as Sean Dunne swung the hand-piece up in line with his, Cotter's, torso — Cotter's heart was thumping so hard his blood pressure made his triceps ache, he didn't envy the job of cocking the weapon's hammer — they stood facing each other no more than an arm's length apart.

Cotter had ducked and dived all in the one action and caught the hard case before the man could squeeze off a shot which occurred when Dunne's other gun had been misdirected by their clash, and when he did manage a shot, the slug tore a furrow across the meat of Dunne's thigh; then the teamster's leg collapsed out from under him — and that was when Frank yanked the revolver from the others paw, and charged off into the sanctuary of the cavern's inky darkness ... he round a curve in the cavern's wall out of reach of the campfire's glow...

Instinctively the scribe realized two things were in his favor — the blackness could be as much an aid to his safety as a threat, his feet were at risk, he had no idea where to tread on the broken, uneven floor and he soon fulfilled the obvious when he went sprawling flat on his face — luckily he had not lost the grip on the pistol in the fall, but his heavy breathing echoed round the whole damn chamber like a locomotive inside a tunnel! He was desperate to stifle the sound of his breathing — he forced his free fist into his mouth and he felt as though he was on the edge of dry retching, he realized he had no other choice. Finally he came out on top — and got the measure of his breathing as best he was ever going too — yet he still felt it was still too loud.

Lomax was also crouched out there in the darkness somewhere with a handgun in his mitt. Sure, he would be doing a sweat but Lester felt down in here in this meteorite he held all the aces… Lomax knew that Dunne was gun-shot and really need help, but first he had to ensure that the crazy drunk did not have luck on his side that he would find the way out. Dunne was lying back there a few yards away on the floor, bleeding and in pain from his wound which might put finish to him being fit enough to ride to the Canadian border.

The stray bullet had ricocheted crazily off the rock walls of the chamber and mortally wounded their horse in the process. Lester moved farther away from the firelight and made sure by feel alone, that the revolver's hammer was cocked — ready for use.

Lomax was also worried about the noise factor just as that of Cotter — out there in the dark. Lomax knew that of the two men left standing, he was the one with the advantages and had to use them to their fullest — for the lay of this land was his private holding next to the Indians; he had made the interior of the meteor his baby. The doctor could tell by Dunne's breathing that he was not going to be much help in their present crisis — he had no idea how badly hurt the teamster was without a medical examination.

"…How yuh doing, Sean?" he asked in a stage whisper.

"No idea, Lester. I feel awright but can't see how bad a wound that gunshot brought me…" Dunne made no effort to keep his voice down, there was no point, not with the echo-chamber they were in. "— all I know is that my leg's gone numb frum the groin down n' by the feel of my hands I reckon a man is bleedin' like a stuck pig!"

"OK, friend … Well once I've taken care of business with Frankie, I'll see about patching you up," Lester told the teamster and edged cautiously forward in the direction Cotter had bolted with Dunne's pistol. He had no fear of being gunned down for he knew how useless the scribe was with a shooter. He'd just track him down like any bovine creature that didn't know its head from its hindquarters and then do what he'd never have dreamed of doing in a thousand years, take Frank Cotter's life.

Lomax thought of grabbing hold of a small log of wood from the fire, to use as a firebrand. But once the idea had bloomed, his judgment canceled it out - *such a light would only telegraph my position, like a heliograph and forewarn Cotter…* instead, Lester filled both hand with his pair of six-guns, making sure they were cocked… Rising to the balls of his feet, he moved on as quietly as any sidewinder crosses a sandy dune, he crept towards where the contour of the cave's rock wall bulged out like the pregnant belly of a Squaw — here, Lomax was in the last of the light produced by the fire — once he rounded the porous, balloon of rock, it was all up to him — for like Cotter — he'd be entering the world of the blind. Lester made sure that he had room in-which to move without anything on his person brushing the sandpaper texture of granite, for in the stillness such a noise would betray his position and the scribe would be praying for help along those lines…

Frank worked himself into a sitting position, and by now he had control of his rasping breadth, but the perspiration from his body was something he could not control, it ran down the contours of his skull-bone structure in rivulets from the hairline of his forehead to the ridges of his brow, where it divided in to two different routes — each rivulet chose a side-wards course for a matter of 2-inches before both sweat-beads commenced their individual downward trek as encouraged by gravity, where they merged into his sideburns and his hair-roots became yet another barrier and broke the size down of these beads into yet smaller particles of moister in their descent down his face. Some sweat tried to take over the surface of his neck, but this was impossible because here the fabric of his smelly shirt collar absorbed immediately it surfaced —

Lomax was lucky, as he made his move round the bulging wall; the wounded horse back in the cavern made plenty of noise in a desperate effort to regain its hooves. The clatter and din covered the fact that Lomax had scuffed his right foot against a free lump of rock the size of a pomegranate, this contact sent it rolling a short distance which terminated when its weight acted against itself as its own braking force.

In this darkness both men were like a couple of blindfold victims — they had no reference points; In Cotter's case he was devoid of direction and recalled from that of his last visit inside the guts of the buried meteorite the futility, and vulnerability of a world without illumination. He couldn't afford to risk moving from where he was now sitting, and yet at the same time he realized to stay anchored to this spot wasn't going to do him any favors … he had to do something other than just wait like some bullock in a slaughter yard.

Frank ran his free hand searchingly over the revolver in his fist to get an indelible picture of it in his mind's eye. He caressed the bulk of the rotatable bullet chamber and the protective finger-guard ... For no pacific reason at this point in time, Cotter dragged the hammer back to the cocked position by its spur with the pad of his thumb until it locked in place with an audible **CLICK** — as he made the move, the scribe could feel the chamber roll a fresh bullet loaded cylinder in-line with the striking-pin of the hammer; the spent useless cartridge shell was rolled aside, encased in the cylinder until remove — and replaced with a live round by the hand of man.

The sound of the revolver's workings gave Lomax a fix on his quarry's position. He was nearer his man, than he had suspected. He froze like a bronze casting — the whites of his eyes grew inside his orbs but darkness was his protection, there was no fear needed of being detected. Without making another move the doctor sensed that he was almost on top of Cotter and found he had been taking the precaution of holding his breath so it wouldn't give him away to his enemy. Lester Lomax quietly exhaled in the hope that he wouldn't created a sound audible enough to sell him out ... he had to take in air— all he could hope for was that by breathing as lightly as that of maybe a snake, the scribe's senses would be deaf to the action around him — a light went on in Lomax's head! He realized that he could discern Frankie's body-odor... a second careful intake of breadth confirmed his suspicions — he was standing right over **Cotter!**

Lester knew he could not risk a gunshot at this point, even though he was a hundred percent sure of the scribe's position; The slug stood an almost certain chance of going right through the feller's body mass or it could *still* miss its target and the wild missile had the possibility of traveling anywhere, even ricochet off a rock-face and perhaps come back and hit him, like the one earlier had done to their buckboard's horse ... it was very clear the animal had died not long after clambering to its legs like a newborn foal, as no more was heard from the mare after her bodyweight thumped back down on the cavern's floor — her life having expired.

Lomax decided the danger of a point blank shot outweighed the virtues; He quietly holstered his guns... *I'll take Cotter out with my bare-hands,* he thought.

Cotter's strained eardrums hear the brush of leather as the guns were returned to their holsters — the newsman realized that Lomax was towering over him …With both hands he held the cocked pistol hard against his sternum, the muzzle directed upwards into the void.

Lomax took a half step forward and the toe of his boot made contact with Frank Cotter's footwear — in a split second he knew the exact position of his intended victim — he pitched forward with both hands at the ready — determine to used Cotter as a padded landing surface — his body weight pinned the scribe hard against the abrasive rock floor, murderous fingers found Cotter's throat and locked tight with ample force to prevent loss of grip, he caught the throat in a torturous unforgiving grasp — his thumbs trapped Cotter's Adam's Apple, the doctor was confident that his medical knowledge and strength would allow him to throttle the life out of Cotter!

But the unexpected happened which hadn't even been taken into account by the doctor — that of the impact of their bodies. It discharged the pistol in Cotter's two-handed grip and with a flash of gunpowder and the muffled bark of a gunshot, Lester died an instant death as the hot lead of the gun's bullet seared right through the upper part of his body at a 45-degree angle with lightning speed — the same missile then struck the cave's roof, Cotter witnessed the slug's disintegration in a shower of orange sparks over the shoulder of his would-be killer.

The lingering after-effects were only to be experienced by the living — the rolling report of the weapon's discharge and the smell of singed cloth from the powder flash, which had scorched the cadaver's clothing. Cotter had disposed of his nemesis with much of the success due to the decease, himself.

Locked together as one, Cotter realized that he was pinned to the floor by the deadweight of Lester's body — he lay there unable to move with the warm revolver trapped between them. There was little doubt in Cotter's mind that death had certainly enveloped Lester Lomax this time and, it had been instantaneous.

It took Cotter a minute or two of bearing the weight of the corpse to finally find the strength to wriggle out from under and discover that his clothing was soaked with a combination of sweat, and gore — the perspiration his own, while that of the gore was from a man he had once called, friend. Still attached to the heavy gun in his right hand, he climbed awkwardly to his knees then with the aid of the tunnel's wall he rose slowly and shakily upright, and stood there breathing heavily with the effect of his legs indicating that they were not yet ready to enact their true function of producing, mobility. Then with the faint illumination of the struggling campfire he stumbled in the direction of the chamber where Dunne lay bleeding — the poor light allowed Frank to see the shock of surprise in the teamster's face at seeing him emerge from the dark beyond the bulging wall. Cotter's hand with the pistol clenched in it, now hung down limp beside him as though he had somehow broken or dislocated his collar bone, but he paid no heed to it.

He could see in the teamster's eyes that he was after answers but having just killed a man he had once called his friend, he did not feel up to it; He warned the bleeding man:

"Don't ask … Tsch, don't ask — just leave it at that."

Dunne nodded, but really had no idea how the scribe felt about taking a human life, let alone someone whom had been so close to him. Sure, Sean Dunne had killed his fellowmen in the past but it wasn't anything like Cotter had been forced into. Taking and giving life was God's realm, his period of playing God was back in the War and out of character for most men but he sure as hell learned that once you've performed the heinous act of taking a life you were never ever going to be the same; those cards that followed in the deck, were running through his head full of thoughts that the teamster went on to point out that they now shared a bleak future unless he, Cotter, pulled another extraordinary branding iron out of the fire: " We're not goin' anywhere…The hoss caught a stray slug, it's dead!"

This was something Frank never bargained for and its importance hadn't gone amiss — the tragic events of the day seemed destine to keep piling up… The pistol slipped from the scribe's loose grasp as if his hand had realized it were clasping the offspring of a guilty delinquent — the Colt clattered to the cave floor; Frank moved like a zombie over to take a look at the teamster's thigh, its flesh plowed open — exposing the hemorrhaging raw muscle in a furrow left by the trail of the .44-45's lead.

Even though he was no medical man he could see that the teamster's wound was going to act like a convict's ball and chain clamped to his limb — clearly he was going nowhere in this place unless given a shoulder to lean on.

"You realize you'll have to put your trust in me," Cotter explained to Dunne. "— I'll have to hike back to town and bring help."

"What makes ya think you'll find any town, standing? The Pawnees might've wiped it orf the map by now!"

"For your sake, you better pray they haven't…" The newspaperman took up the two water canteens not far from the campfire — by their combined weight he knew there was sufficient water in them for each man, especially if they were careful on how they were used. Cotter returned to Dunne and handed him one — the wounded man snatched the container from Frank as though it was a stash of gold and pried out its cork so he could sate his thirst — his thirst being a direct result of his blood loss.

"Wouldn't be too rash on how you use that; I've no idea how long I'll be!" Cotter reminded Dunne.

Sean Dunne took his mouth away from the vessel's chunky spout and wiped his lips with the back of his hand; both men could hear the water in the canteen sloshing about. "Then you might have ter move faster than yuh planned on those legs of yore's…" But all the same, he intended taking the tenderfoot's advice about conserving the water and resealed the canteen. "Can you give me a hand ter git over near the fire? I wanna keep it fed while you're away, Cotter."

"Sure. So long as you don't try to pull something smart …"

"— Am I in any shape fer sumthin' like that?" The wounded man reminded Frank. "I've no choice but ter plays it straight wif you, even though whichever way the screw turns, I'm gonna end me day's wearing a hemp collar…" Even in the gloomy light of the fire Cotter saw the degrees of honesty etched into Dunne's face, a pity his honesty came to him this late in his life, thought the scribe. Dunne offered his elbow so that the man might haul him upright. The teamster was foolish enough to try and take some weight on the injured leg but it collapsed and it was up to Cotter to half carry him to his destination. He lowered the teamster down alongside the fire which was in server need of fuel and both men set to the task of putting a couple of logs each on the hot coals, ash and a poor number of orange sparks and flickering flames hinted that the campfire might survive. Cotter then located the oven and checked on its contents; not that it had much to offer, but used sparingly — one person could make a meal or two of it he judged, and carried the food container over near the fire for the teamster, who groaned in pain for the first time in the last forty-five minutes.

"You've got water and food on hand, I'm sorry I can't do much about that pain; I'll take my share of the water and head off," Cotter said as he went over and collected the canteen.

"Hold it!" Dunne rasped. "It might be a good idea if you took the Colt —" Cotter looked at the wounded feller; Cotter's face had an unvoiced question stamped into, so Dunne explained. "— You might come across a bunch of hot-headed Pawnees in ya travels. It would be a quicker death to use a bullet on yuh self than let them toy wif you,"— his message got through to the scribe loud and clear. Nodding, Cotter picked up the six-gun and stuffed it under his waistband.

"Can I trust you not to shoot me in the back as I leave, Dunne?"

"Yore safe ... yore my only chance in *my* situation…"

"OK. So which way is it out of here?"

"Across the fire and follow the upwards slope of the floor — you'll hit the outside in less than the length of barn. Then follow the wheel tracks of the buckboard and you should hit the outskirts of Junction City in maybe two and one half-hours. Good luck."

"I hope you're not just selling me a bill of goods on this?"

With more pain showing in his face the teamster reached for a short log of wood the size of a man's shin and added it to the blaze.

"…JIST GO!"

It had been just a little under two hours since Cotter began dogging the buckboard's tracks; the sun was high and hot. He had lost his Stetson earlier back in the cavern in struggle for possession of the gun with Dunne, and had not thought to recover it too much was going on to bother about the whereabouts of one's hat. But now it was imperative he had shade. He removed his waistcoat and shirt. The latter he wore upon *his* head like a poor imitation of an Arab's headdress and the waistcoat took over from his shirt — however the city guy had no illusions that his bare arms which had barely seen sun before, would burn red within the hour and on this score the weather conditions did not fail him. He slung the canteen over his shoulder by its strap; the water vessel lightly tapped his hip with every stride. Flies, were a pest he had to endure for they were attracted to the front of his trousers and the waistcoat by the drying blood, an open invitation to the hungry mass; rivulets of salty perspiration traced pathways down either side of his face until they run out of surface and fell away from his lower jaw line onto the waistcoat, the sun dried them to salt deposits on the cloth.

Way out on the distant plain where Cotter was headed lay a shimmering horizon, yet between him and the same horizon were at least a dozen small pools of water — the writer wasn't fooled by their existence — he now knew a mirage when he saw it…Cotter avoided yet another gopher hole — having already twisted his ankle in one only twenty minutes from the exit of the cave, the rewarding limp had slowed him down considerably as he nursed himself along, he was conscious that he wasn't going to make Junction City, in the time Dunne had reckoned on — He was sure that he could almost double that time.

Sitting high and erect on their mounts, the Long Knives out of the Pawnee Reservation had a broad view out across the open land — the four troopers were under the command of Lt. Briggs whose mission was to carry the news to Junction City that Captain Roscoe had taken over the reservation's headquarters, and restricted the movements of all within its boundaries; no Pawnee could move freely about as long as the Long knives held the balance of power.

The imprisoned Indians were not happy but the horse soldiers held the upper-hand, for an armed cordon had been thrown around the Pawnee village and the native's knowledge of the gun that was capable of barking many times before reloading, had instilled a cautious respect in the braves whom were in awe of its capabilities.

Way ahead of the troopers, Briggs could see the form of what appeared to be a man making his way across the prairie in the direction of the town. He reined in, and those riding with him, did likewise. A trooper kneed his mount in alongside Briggs and without being asked, produced a set of field glasses and passed them to the officer who put them to his eyes and focused on the figure, clearly stumbling on some rough ground at the moment … through the glasses Briggs noticed that the man was favoring his ankle but had now settled back in his stride as the ground he traveled now flattened out. Finally adjusting the instrument so that its focus was keen, Briggs saw that the figure of the wandering soul was not having an easy task to toil — he lowered the glasses and handed them back to the Private without taking his eyes from the distant man.

"…The man out there needs help," Briggs turned to the trooper who was busy stowing the field glasses in their leather case. "— Gallop out to him and see how he is for water, and stay with him until we arrive. He'll have an interesting story no doubt, as to why he's in this fix; in the meant time prepare yore mount ter carry double… OK Trooper, Ride!" Hollered the Lieutenant who had twisted in his saddle and belted the trooper's mount, hard on the rump — the unsuspected gelding vaulted in to action and the trooper almost lost his campaign hat in the process, he recovered quickly as per his experience in the saddle dictated, and spurred his mount on — its hooves throwing up clods of earth in its wake until the speed made the animal light footed, from then it just began leaving trail-dust in its wake.

Briggs turned to the rest of the party and said, "— c'mon… let's ***make*** these bastards earn their oats!" He said in reference to their mounts and, the trio lopped off after the trooper. "Those folks in town will be tickled pink ter hear our news," exclaimed the Lieutenant.

By the time Briggs and party had caught up to the trooper, the Calvary man and the stranger had greeted one another and the trooper dismounted to adjust his saddle equipment to make it suitable to carry double.

Briggs was most surprised to find the wanderer was Frank Cotter and that he was clothed in a bloody dry pair of pants and a waistcoat with the shirt being used to ward off the sun, and thus prevent heatstroke in the style of an Arabian Bedouin, Briggs had come across this knowledge in his book learning' days. "What in God's name has happened to you, Cotter…?" He demanded as he reined in.

The bloody clothing and the pistol shoved beneath his waist was all out of character to the man Briggs thought he knew.

"Hell — never thought the day would dawn when I would be glad to see you, Briggs!" Cotter brushed a couple of flies from his vest and they made straight for the reservoir of liquid in the corner of his eyes.

"That's mutual," Briggs opined. "…So what's with all this gore an' shit all over you?" Briggs dismounted so that he might have a closer look at the news-hound from the same level. "Looks like you've been workin' in an abattoir as a slaughter man — that blood human?"

Cotter nodded and the officer noted that the man's blinking rate had gone up and as he ran his eye over the writer's frame he could see the man had begun to tremble. *I hope this guy isn't gonna swoon off on me like a love-struck woman?* The officer thought.

"Are you awright Cotter — you look ready ter pass out?"

"It is…I-err…I have to — well the truth of the matter is that you, your captain and the people in Washington were right about L-L-Lester Lomax. He, he, he played all of us for suckers — me an' his Indian friends included.

"I don't know how you are gonna put a halt to the attack on the town… But if you Army fellers can't get a stranglehold on the situation there will be a lot of dead white people out there on the plains…"

"We've corralled the Pawnee trouble makers at the reservation. The threat to the town's over; we're riding there now with the news for Lazarus Rollo and company …" Briggs told the tenderfoot, then he turned to his steed, found his stirrup-cup with his boot and with both hands, hauled himself up into the saddle, saying: "—Where did yore blood-soaked clothes come from?"

Frank Cotter closed in on Brigg's mount; then taking it by the bridle's bit-ring said, "You'll be surprised to know that this blood came from Doctor Lomax, it's **his blood.**"

"Can't be…" Briggs said with a shake of his head, "the man's been dead for weeks!"

The tenderfoot shook his head. "That might have been the general, consensus… But I can confirm — **he is now.** What everyone thought about Lester and the accident mendacity — because **I only killed** him awhile ago!" Cotter stepped back a pace from Brigg's horse and whipped the revolver from his waistband, the mare flinched and the lieutenant had to settle her. **"*That's* the weapon** I used!"

Cotter came forward and handed the pistol up to Briggs, butt first. "That's the last I wanna see it."

Leaning forward to take charge of the revolver, Briggs said: "W-where did all this happen?"

"I'll show you and the sheriff proof of everything, later. But right now, one of the men in Lomax charade is in serious need of Doctor Hallway's services…" Frank turned and approached the trooper with whom he knew he was expected to ride double.

"The Indian Affairs Department sure had Lomax pegged; but we're aware he wasn't the only nigger in the wood pile … wuz there anyone else in this con business besides the fellers known ter us, Bevan an' Hill?" Briggs asked as his party began moving in the direction of town.

"There's more than three in it with Lester. You can include that shyster, Donald Stroughton and the teamster, feller by the name of Dunne. He's the one back at the meteorite waiting to be patched up…"

"What about Sheriff Boston; He's surely part of it?" Briggs suggested.

"No, I don't think so; his only crime is that he lets Lazarus Rollo, and the Association has too to say in town affairs. Doctor Hallway is the one I'm not too sure about. But if you slap him in irons, who is gonna look out for the security of the town?"

"We better get these horses diggin' dirt," said Briggs, "otherwise that feller back yonder might skedaddle on us —"

"I doubt it. His leg's a mess… the same as my butt will be after riding double to town!" Cotter pointed out to Briggs as a reminder to the lieutenant of the occasion when they had all made up Sheriff Boston's posse, and gone out to view the horrific side-effects of Lomax's elixir.

The lieutenant was secretly pleased at the reminder of the painful way the newspaperman had had to pay his dues for his involvement in his dead friend's business. His mind went back to the pain of the saddle-sore ass he went through in his early riding days, but he never voiced it. Briggs looked at the scruffy scribe and wondered how he had the nerve to kill one man and wound another…he looked far from being the type of man who would cope with life in the west, let alone survive it.

"— So where did you find the guts and ability ter face down a couple of armed men? — Kill one and, wound another? "

"I don't know where I got the nerve… I guess a man's capable of almost anything when he's faced with a situation that threatens his own mortality. I simply did what I had to do to save myself."

Briggs knew this to be true of him and some good Army men he had served with.

The group of riders continued on pretty much in silence the rest of the way to Junction City.

Stroughton pause momentarily in front of his business premises. Stepping across the threshold he belched and realized that he had eaten a much too heavy meal… The reception room was stuffy and this was evidence that it had been shut up for too long; he went about the front and back of the suite, throwing open windows to allow air into the place. In his office he went to the low safe he had behind his desk up against the rear wall of the room, and squatting before it he went ahead, opened the object of his visit — he check the stack of banknotes he kept in store, money he always had on hand in case he had to make a quick getaway. There were two stacks of bills on the shelf alongside property deeds he held for clients and a double barrel over and under Derringer — he was just about to close up when he had second thoughts and picked up the small handgun, shoved it in the inside pocket of his coat, the opposite side to where he wore his shoulder-holster … then, using his free hand he grabbed up the stacks of money which filled his mitt to capacity … then standing over the flat top of the safe he dropped the two bundles on top of its cold steel top, and taking a bundle in each hand, he hide them in the side pockets of his frockcoat in relation to a specific hand. With a greater effort than he had anticipated, he kneed the heavy safe door partially shut and because of the irritating pain it caused, regretted the action.

Then he looked the office over as if bidding it *farewell* for the last time and went upstairs to the living quarters where he packed a carpetbag he kept stored under the bed, then it was back downstairs once more and out onto the sidewalk, he lowered the bag to the boardwalk and drew the door to the street closed and lock it, while all about him the folks of Junction City went about the foreign business of preparing for war. He hurried up the street to the Chinese bathhouse and left the carpetbag with them.

Harry Williams stood at the edge of the walk smoking a cigarette, casually leaning with his shoulder against the veranda support facing the passing traffic on Main Street. He was red-eyed through lack of sleep but when he saw Stroughton come out of the bathhouse without the carpetbag he had taken in, he asked by way of conversation. "You got the Chows doin' yore laundry these days, Mr. Attorney…?"

"What makes you ask, Williams?"

"I saw you lug a stuffed bag in there wif you a while ago — now you've come out empty handed!" Williams pushed himself off the post and stood firmly before the lawyer.

"That's being mighty observant. Why should my business interest you, Harry?" Stroughton's temper began to heat up toward Rollo's town spy.

"Jist curious, you wouldn't be plannin' ter give the town the ass in its hour of need?"

The Attorney's sharp court-room eyes drilled into the man. "…That's not even worth wastin' time to consider working up an insult over. Like the rest of the folks here — I'm willing to take my chances; but it's you and your brother who puzzle me, Harry, you really do."

"How, come?"

"You've let your position with the Association and Rollo goes too much to yore heads; it's not a good thing — you'll over step the mark one day and someone will hit you with a Lawsuit the size of our Freemason hall."

"Let 'em try. Mr. Rollo will take care of it for us with no sweat." Harry pitched the butt of his cigarette out onto the road as his brother joined them. He too looked as though lack of sleep was his bugbear.

"What's up?" Reg wanted to know.

"Nuthin', jist joust in' wiv the mouthpiece," Harry told his sibling. "—Stroughton jist paid the bathhouse a visit and left sumthin' behind which I thought looked a bit suspicious in this day an' age."

"What d'you mean?" Reg doffed his hat to Rollo's teenage wife as she went by. The lass gave her husband's employees a sick smile in return as she continued downtown in the direction of the Freemason's Building, now doubling as an ambulance station in-waiting.

"Our lawyer here looks like he's gettin' his laundry done in there by the Chows — I'd've thought at this time, laundry, would be the last thing on peoples' mind. What if he has paid a visit to the bank an' emptied his account and any others he's got control over? He could be gonna ter ride off in to the sunset wiv the money when nobody's watching? — jist a thought, that's struck me, is all…"

"Go on wif ya!" Reg said. "He's not that kind of lawyer…" But as Reg looked the attorney over he could not help notice that the mouthpiece was looking a bit pale on it. "Hey — what's up? …You looking a bit guilty 'bout sumthin'… Is it 'coz of Harry's line of thinking?"

"You and your brother have bats in yore head; there's nothing more wrong with me than a breakfast that isn't sitting square on my insides. Now if you gents will let me be on my way, I've got important work to do and no time for standing about chewing the fat… Good morning!" Stroughton stepped round the brothers and left the pair gazing after him. Stroughton wanted to wipe the perspiration from his brow, but assumed that it was a gesture that might make him look as guilty as he felt at this very moment, to the nosey brothers.

With his eyes still on the attorney's back, Reg said out the side of his mouth. "Yuh know brother, that lawyer thinks he's a smart cookie…"

"You c'n say that again…" Harry said thoughtfully, "we had 'im goin' there for a while."

"But ya know it mightn't hurt ter keep an eye on 'im. What did he take into the bathhouse anyway?"

"A carpetbag; It wuz a bit on the fat side too —"

"I see. You mosey orf and I'll ask the Chinese ter give me a look-see at the contents of the bag — the situation facing this town might make a feller do some strange things, it's too late ter try an' shut the gate after the hoss has bolted. Mebbe I should have a word in Mr. Rollo's ear, too."

The brothers split up — Harry going off after the lawyer to see what he was about. Reg turning into the bathhouse to try some stand-over tactics on the Chows.

Stroughton knew that he had Harry Williams sticking to him like a leech and that there was nothing illegal in that, it just annoyed him is all. He came upon Bevan and Hill in the street and they paused to one side on the plank sidewalk.

"And how are you gentlemen this morning?" Donald said by way of greeting them.

"Like everyone else I guess… Expecting the worse when the damn Pawnees hit town…" Hill said. "You …?"

"All we can do is take it in our, stride," Attorney Stroughton said with a slight nod.

"Look about you? We've got the numbers and the fortification; and they'll be attacking from out on the plains — I'd say we stand a pretty good chance of doing more damage to them than they to us. Also remember, the soldiers are on their way from Fort Hancock. I think when this is all over the Pawnee people will be a nation of has-beens — history!"

"I hope ya right. Have you had any word from Lomax, Stroughton?" Hill asked the question, for Jonas Bevan's benefit which was on both his and Bevan's minds.

Donald shook his head, "Generally, he leaves messages in a safe drop we have up at Boot Hill, which I collect, under cover of darkness. But I haven't been able ter get anywhere near the place with so many eagle-eyed folks spying… I'll try an' slip up there tonight and see if he's left anything." The attorney drew the carpetbaggers' attention to Harry Williams lurking back down along the sidewalk in the background without turning about. "You know the Williams brothers?"

Hill and Bevan nodded — there was hardly a soul in Junction City who didn't know Rollo's henchmen.

"—over my shoulder you'll see one of them pussyfooting down there outside the Milliner's shop behind me…" The pairs' eyes fell upon Harry then quickly looked elsewhere as they did not want the hound-dog realizing that he had been made. "— He's been trailing me like a damn wolf. He's got some idea that I'm up to no good — so I can't make a move while he's sniffin' about. Reckon I might play it safe now I think of it, and defer my Boot Hill visit another twenty-four hours…"

"That being the case, we best sit tight." Jonas Bevan pointed out. "You know Dunne slipped the noose and got away about twenty hours ago."

"That's understandable. Out of the lot of us, Dunne's had a very hard job, keeping up appearances around the place that he's distraught to the hilt about the accident that killed Lomax!" Stroughton muttered.

They nodded in agreement.

"I never knew how he managed to take on board so much liquor and play the role of a man rollin' over into becoming a drunken booze artist," Hill exclaimed. "We were lucky there."

"We were," Bevan admitted with arched brows.

"Right," said Stroughton, "Now is the time for me to do a little bit of confessing. How handy are you pair to your stash of lucre ? "

"Why?" Jonas Bevan carefully gave the attorney the once over.

"What are you getting at?" asked Hill.

"I've been getting this feeling that there's been something going on between Dunne and Doctor Lomax; it's something on a "need to know" basis... When Sean Dunne left town his action was meant to be a signal to me."

"I don't follow ..."said Hill with narrowing eyes.

"Nor do *I!*" Bevan said.

"His disappearing act was a signal from Lomax to me that we should be prepared to pull out of this burgh without delay and head for the Canadian border – we're to meet in a place called, Moose Jaw. He obviously thinks the Pawnee will burn the town to the ground and that if we wanna make good our escape rather than get caught up in an Indian War — then now's the time to grab our steak and high-tail it outa here...! "

Looking at the threesome from his point of view, Williams thought: *... Now I wonder what that little meetin' wos all about?*

The owner of the bathhouse looked on with expressionless eyes while Reg Williams went through Stroughton's bag and shrew its contents on the bare plank floor of the office. The Asian wasn't happy about the hard case barging in and demanding a look inside the Attorney's traveler, but he was not in a position to tell a man like Williams "*— to go take a slow boat to China... "*

Williams was not at all happy about finding nothing one could rate as suspicious amongst the Lawyer's shirts and underwear. He turned on his heels and marched out of the premises, leaving the Asian to pick up after him.

Meanwhile the syndicate members broke up their meeting on the sidewalk and Donald Stroughton continued on his way, while Hill and Bevan hurried back to the boarding house to recover their stash of money hidden behind a loose board in the wall of their lodgings. Then they intended to purloin a buggy and set off for Canada as pre-arranged and hope in the meanwhile they can avoid any Indian bands out on the prowl.

Lazarus Rollo sat in his office chair, watching folks moving back and forth on the boardwalk from his second floor office. The people moving along under the building's awnings were unaware that the man was counting heads and wondering just who among the town's folk would survive the expected attack on Junction City. He knew that the redskins on the reservation had been harboring a great deal of hatred over their treatment by the white-eyes... But suddenly his thought changed to other matters when he caught sight of his wife sashaying along the crowded walk with her furled parasol in her girl-like hand. Lazarus wished she'd stayed indoors where he knew she would be safe and he toyed with the idea of calling his clerk and sending him out with a message that she should either return to their house or accompany the clerk back to his office — an unexpected knock on the door panel over his shoulder brought Rollo about and he saw Harry Williams with the door partly open, standing under the fanlight – behind Harry was Reg, the pair had been thinking as one, and had arrived from their different assignments at the entrance of the Association's building as if answering a call put out by Chairman, Rollo.

"Sorry for disturbin' you sir — but I thought you should know that Lawyer Stroughton has started actin' a bit strange," Harry crossed the threshold of the office and closed the door after him, and then approached the heavy oak desk.

Lazarus edged the desk-chair up to the edge of his desk; puzzled by the intrusion. "I hope you aren't imagining things," Rollo suggested with a frown. "—after all, people in this town are under an awful lot of pressure and could be susceptible to some eccentric behavior."

"This mightn't be anythin' worth worrying about; but you always said that we brothers had ter keep an eye on folks — especially those with access to the association's money accounts..." Williams reminded his boss.

It took a beat before Lazarus Rollo responded, and by then Reg was beginning to wonder whether he ought to be bothering the chief about such a frivolous matter … maybe Harry wos cryin' wolf fer nuthin'.

"You might be doin' right," said Rollo. "I've always been a bit of an untrusting soul when it comes to employees having a free hand. Look how I recently got my fingers' burnt over that stage robbery? I know with yore other duties around town at the moment, that it's expecting a little too much to keep an eye on any particular person's whereabouts, but it's damn appreciated. You can never know too much about people. Maybe I ought to see that Boston stations Stroughton at the same barricade you've been assigned too? It can be done, you know?"

"I can't see it hurtin' Mr. Rollo."

"OK. Look, I've got another little job for you to do, too. I saw my wife from the window at the back of me, headed down the street towards the Masonic first aid station

… I've reconsidered her offer to help the women down there when trouble breaks out – I fear she's too young to be expected to cope with what they'll be asked to deal with; so trot down and give her my regards … then escort her home or bring her up here to the office — what-ever takes ya fancy!"

Williams nodded and departed the office suite to pick up Mrs. Rollo's trail – he opined that if he couldn't immediately find her down there on the street, he would catch her at the Masonic building.

Lieutenant Briggs and party caused quite a stir when they arrived outside the town's northern, barricade — asking to be admitted. One end of the barrier had to be partially dismantled for the purpose of their entrance, but just as quickly the men on hand reconstructed it once the last horse soldier had ridden in.

Briggs reined about an addressed the townsman who seemed in command of his fortification. "Who's running things here…?"

"The Mayor, Rollo and I guess the sheriff — Sheriff Boston!"

"Where will we find 'em?" Lieutenant Briggs demanded.

"Hard ter say, Soldier. They're runnin' things frum two joints… City Hall and, Cattlemen's boardroom."

"Then where do you suggest we call, City Hall or Rollo's, place?" said the scribe.

The man vacillated and it irritated Lt. Briggs and Cotter no end. "C'mon man!" Hollered Cotter filled to the brim with frustration. "— Stick your neck out and suggest an establishment, we're here on Army business!"

The man knew Cotter by sight and hadn't noticed him up there on the horse behind the Private, but when he did he was taken aback to see the feller and the state of his garments; he had never seen a tenderfoot in this state before. The poor feller was flabbergasted!

But eventually things sorted themselves and in less than an hour Briggs was addressing Sheriff Boston, the Mayor and the City Fathers along with Rollo; Frank Cotter stood by the lieutenant as if he was now part of the Army's operations, now in a change of clothes supplied by Lazarus Rollo from the closet in his office suite; the Cattlemen's Association having been taken over by the town council for the purpose of this gathering.

"Gentlemen," said Briggs as he stood at the head of the boardroom table with legs slightly apart ... " Captain Roscoe sends his respects an' wishes me to inform you that Junction City is no longer under threat of attack by the Pawnee nation!"

A roar of delight filled the boardroom.

"Quiet, please ... quiet please," Briggs called over the cheers of jubilation — when he had the silence he demanded, he continued. "Now some of you in this room will be aquatinted with Mr. Frank Cotter — standing here alongside me... He has something you've all gotta hear, so pay him the same courtesy you would give me. Meanwhile I shall have to take my leave of you and get down to the Express office, and get a telegram away to the Fort who'll be anxious for news from Captain Roscoe an' how things have worked out — good afternoon, gentlemen," he said and bowed out.

All eyes turned to Cotter who, although feeling self-conscious went on to tell his captive audience about the *real* death of the late Lester Lomax and his part in it.

Turning to Sheriff Boston Frank said: "...I reckon you can close your books on the murders of Ma Kelly and Derrick Carter. I'm certain the person who butchered the Kelly woman was Lomax ... And it was also the doctor or Dunne, who held Carter face down in the water until he drowned, either that, or the both of them did it! "

Boston made to interrupt; but the scribe waved for him to wait and listen to what he had left to say. "Up until very recently our Doctor Lomax was alive. He didn't die in any road accident, which will mystify a lot of people here in this room, not to mention the town. The whole business was a phony set-up from the beginning!"

Klem Boston finally got his way and cut in on Cotter. "— But all of us at the cemetery saw his body when we opened his grave… even you verified it wuz *him* by the scare?!"

"— I was duped right along with the rest of you! The scare *we saw* was as phony as too was the accident that was s'posed to have killed him; the scare was done with clever stage make-up. Though it doesn't seems as though I've been missed from town, I was kidnapped by Lomax and Sean Dunne — they spirited me off out to the meteorite … Lomax was gonna spare my life if I joined up with him and his friends on a quick trip to Canada; and the pair of them all but admitted their parts in the killings…"

"What was the purpose of all of it then?" asked Boston.

"If you mean the phony death of the doctor …?" Frank asked.

Boston nodded. "… And those other two, murders?"

"I think you mean **three murders,** don't forget the body they used and substituted for Lomax… he was an unexpected player in all this — The doctor knew what ailed the man when he suddenly fell sick, and although I can't prove it, I believe that Lomax might have allowed the man to die purposely, so that his body could be used for the illegal purposes they had in mind; All to throw Washington in a spin and get the investigation they were running into their gold scam, wound up.

"Doctor Lomax was Washington's main target; the way I see it, with Lester dead, Washington has nothing they could hang the fiddle on. So, end of story." Cotter shrugged.

"Does anyone know the name of the feller who played the substitute fer Lomax?" Klem asked Frank hopefully.

"I don't reckon anyone does but I know how it was done — but that's another story I can tell you about, later. First we've now gotta get this town back to looking like a town!"

Frowning, Robeson said to Boston: "We both saw Ma Kelly's throat. I reckon this city lad might be right; come ter think of it did look like whoever slashed her throat knew what they were doing. What do you reckon Klem?"

"Yeah ... Lomax was no dunce, when it came to using a surgeon's knife — I'm prepared ter go along with that; but I'm worried why Lomax thought that Ma and Carter, had ter die...?" asked the harassed sheriff.

"Because they knew about the existence of the missing witness and that witness was none other than Lomax in disguise." Frank pointed out.

"He's right," said Jock Robeson. "I'll bet my kilt on it!"

Boston shook his head. "It sounds pretty right. But someone had to have told the doctor what Carter and Kelly knew fer him to have 'em killed. That means there is a spy in the town who knew all along where the doctor was?"

"And kept him up to date on things," said Jock. "Anyone got any ideas who that might be?"

"My thought is, the spy was none other than, Donald Stroughton, but proving it won't be easy," exclaimed Cotter. "I wouldn't be too surprised if our friend has already flown the coop!"

As a result, the visiting Sheriff from Lawrence whom had been a great help to Boston and the people of Junction City said he was willing to lead a posse out to the meteorite to recover Doctor Lomax's body where the wounded teamster awaited in need of medical aid. This would allow Klem Boston to supervise the tearing down of the town's fortifications and thereby get the town back to normal.

Standing amongst the people whom had crowded into the boardroom to hear Cotter was Donald Stroughton, who only waited around long enough to hear about the death of Lomax and he was off like a mountain lion that had just had his hide shot at. Down on the street he patted down the pockets of his frockcoat and ascertained he had his money. Then he boldly strode to a nearby hitching rack and helped himself to a cow pony; the choice of horseflesh looked fleet of foot, and that is just what he needed at this very moment. He mounted and rode through the heavy crowded thoroughfare, somewhat on the dangerous side, and hauled up at the hitching rail outside the bank which had opened its doors for business when news had reached it, that the town was no longer under threat from the Indians.

Stroughton strode into the bank and demanded a fast withdrawal of substantial amounts of cash from those accounts he held the Power of Attorney over. The worried bank clerk and manager attempted to fill his unusual demands while he ran across to the livery stable and got the ostlers to make ready his surrey with Ma Kelly's splendid team of strong winded Morgan's. Then it was back to the bank, where the money he required had been locked up in a canvas mailbag fitted with leather collars and padlocks, as used by the express office and the stage lines. He carried the moneybag to the livery and was glad to see that already half the barricade at this end of town had been dismantled and traffic was starting to flow once more.

The fellers at the livery had his surrey ready and he slung the bag aboard and climbed on after it. He was growing anxious already that someone who knew he was wanted, might stumble upon him so when he drove the team out onto Main Street he flogged Ma Kelly's horses into action, throwing and caution to the wind, he headed east … leaving his partners, namely Hill and Bevan to their own fate — probably destined to face the town and its law.

An unsworn posse hunted down the two carpetbaggers whom Stroughton had abandoned. The irate mob — led by the Williams brothers, whom had worked the small crowd up into a gang hungry for blood, cornered the southerners in their lodgings, and tossed a couple of ropes round their necks and wanted to hang them from the highest point, handy. But before they had managed to drag them out and string them up; Boston and his deputies came along in time to throw cold water on the situation as the Williams brothers' plan to take the law into their own paws and stretch the pairs' necks … in some way this played into Harry William's hand and he did what he always wanted to do, he drew on Boston with a speed so fast that he had his pistol clearing leather before the sheriff's hand had slapped his own pistol-grips… Williams was amazed by his own lightning-like speed, but hesitated a fraction of a second before thumbing the hammer of his weapon back, but it didn't matter — his fate was sealed by a faulty cap and a misfired was in the cards — this gave the man of justice an edge he never knew he had — his hand now full of pig-iron cleared leather, the astonished Harry Williams, made another attempt to discharge his revolver in Boston's direction, but it was all much too late. Boston's six-gun fired right on cue and the discharge slug traveled the nine feet separating the two men — bring instant death to Reg Williams' brother…

Reg could do naught to support his sibling—he watched, dumbfounded, as the missile that ended his brother's life, tore through the man's solo plexus and out his back, carrying flesh and spine bone fragments with it… The Sheriff's men had drawn their guns by now and had the drop on the rest of the group; had any of them made a stupid move—the area would have become a bloodbath. No one was keen to join Harry up there before Saint Peter.

Harry lay sprawled on his back with his shirt tugged from the waistband of his Levis … the front of his garment appeared to be barely damaged while at the back where the lead-slug had made its exit, a hole the size of a cinch buckle; gravity drained blood from the lifeless body. No one dare to move a muscle for a whole five seconds; the air was heavy with human body odor mixed with saltpeter and gunpowder.

Reg Williams was a changed man from the moment he had lost his brother right there before his eye – he became numb inside and didn't desire to even consider taking revenge against Boston; all he wanted was to distance himself from the town, Lazarus Rollo, and everything the Cattlemen's Association stood for.

Bevan and his partner seemed to be momentarily forgotten by the sheriff's mob and slunk away without notice. They knew now, would be a good time to shake the dust from their boots if they were going to get away in one piece, while the posse were still overwhelmed by the shootout; They stole the first unattended Concord buggy they came upon, and hit the trail regardless of the fact that they looked a couple of square pegs in a round hole, and not dressed for the road—getting away was their main goal; but the freedom of the open road for them was only short lived. They stood out like a couple of moles at a Christening.

Clearwater sensed that the threatening cloud of doom, which had been a burden to Junction City for the last few days, had, somehow been swept aside—he could feel it in the air—a sort of gayety becoming the mood of the white man, his children and womenfolk. The Pawnee strained at the chains with his full strength, but realized he wasn't going to free himself from the anvil; there was no hope he might be able to slip his manacles! For in the excitement of the spreading word that the

Army had taken over the reservation and confine the Pawnees within its grounds, the condemned man; Clearwater, had to face facts, and short of gnawing through his limb like a wolf or bear when caught in a steel-jawed trap—there was no way he'd slip his anchor, even though for the moment he had been left unguarded by his keepers whom had gone off to join in the town's revelry.

The Indian knew that although the town might now have a future, there would be no future for him, he had to face the white man's justice and ignorant though he was, he understood that he was bound to hang in the end for his drunken gun-raid and those of his terrorist brethren.

The townsfolk went silly with relief and even became drunk with merriment—their actions were as wild as those experienced when hostilities between the North and South Armies came to an end—the saloon and gambling houses threw open their doors and the shelf-liquor ran free! But in the midst of all this revelry there were those who took time out to think and talk about serious matters, and when Lon Parker, the bank manager learned about Lawyer Donald Stroughton's part in the scheme of things with Lomax, he was furious for he realized his bank had just about been stripped of all its cash reserve. Parker ran in search of Boston to report the matter and insist that the Attorney be hunted down like the thief he was — however the sheriff was far too busy with the town and its problems to be tying himself and his men down to running off after one man. Hearing this, but by no means wanting to understand Boston's point of view, he returned to the bank, rounded up the male members of his staff and set off on horseback after the lawyer who had a head-start on them by a little over three-quarters of an hour.

Their desperate ride after the bank's cash was doomed to fail from the beginning and they returned to Junction City empty handed three days later — a group of men totally exhausted and saddle-sore, all worried whether or not the bank could trade itself out of its losses. In the meanwhile the body of Lomax had been recovered and now Dunne lay in the same saloon as Flynn — both patients of Doc Hallway's were being nursed by ladies of the night.

21

WHEN THE BUTTERFIELD stagecoach company resumed full services to the outside world, Frank Cotter made damn sure that he was on the second stage out of Junction City, he would have been on the first coach, but it was in great demand and seats on any of the next ten stagecoaches had all been booked in advance. Cotter was lucky that a seat cancellation became available at this time, and in the mean time the newspaperman settled up any debits he'd fostered since being in the town and really looked forward to kicking the dust of this godforsaken town from his boots. He thoroughly enjoyed the last bath at the Chinese place as he readied himself for the coming journey and turned the key in the lock of the apartment, which had been his home since arriving in the town. He returned the keys to sheriff Boston, and hoped to see Sheriff Robeson before he caught the stage, but the ex-Pinkerton had already left town to reclaim his job in Lawrence as prearranged. The scribe was disappointed in having missed Jock, and he hoped that they might catch-up back in Lawrence if luck would have it.

Robeson had no worry that Matt Flynn might escape, but the thought need not have crossed his mind, as the ramrod was darn lucky to have survived Hallway's operation — Jock or his deputy would return later when the amputee would be fit to journey onto Lawrence in a covered wagon, the Scotsman knew his prisoner would never sling a leg over the back of another horse — besides there was a hanging rope reserved for him; Flynn wouldn't live to see old age or have the worry of where his next meal would be coming from, for unlike most amputees, whether the result of an unfortunate accident or the results of War.

The stage journey from Junction City right through to Kansas City via Lawrence, was torture for Cotter. For him, the coach wheels couldn't turn quick enough and the switching over to fresh horse teams seem tedious, on all occasions to that of his first time over the same country. The only time he showed enthusiasm for the trip was when they reached the creek crossing, where the hold-up had taken place and he got his first taste of the real Wild West — and a glimpse of death that was part of its infrastructure.

Kansas City was a much more established than that of Junction City, there being no hint as to what the place would become if it survived into the far distant future, for no one could envisage what it would be like in the Twenty-first Century or if whether there would be a Twenty-first century for the world of today.

Cotter departed the stage depot with his baggage and from a billposter plastered to a veranda upright handy to the depot, he found directions to a rooming house where he took a shared room and a bath in that order. Then making sure not to leave anything of value in the obviously overcrowded room — for those already settled in the dormitory were absent, either at work or taking in the sights. In Cotter's case he was eager to find the whereabouts of Miss Pearl Courtney, he hoped her theatrical agent had found work for her here in the city, as from past experience he knew the burgh harbored two, maybe three theaters; but the call for some food under his belt had to take priority, so he made for **THE RIO NEGRO CAFÉ & RESTAURANT**, the place he had dined at when bound for Junction City.

This time of the day the café wasn't busy; the hour was maybe too early for some or too late for others. Once inside Frank found his way across to a row of booths separated from the street by a thin timber and picture window glass wall. The wall only really gave a suggestion to customers that they were cut off from the street, as one could easily hear the conversations of passersby's on the sidewalk through the flimsy structure. The establishment cheated further on the illusion of privacy, by hanging café-curtains on the lower half of the street window, which prevented pedestrians ogling in on one's table setting.

A comely waitress soon arrived at Frank's table with a pitcher of water plus a handwritten menu. Then she left him in peace to decide what he would like to enjoy — he noticed that the prices of the meals had remained static in his absence so this encouraged the scribe to enjoy the cuisine on offer. He settled only for the main course, a plate of boiled meat and potatoes.

While waiting for it to come, Frank's thoughts turned to Pearl and his feelings towards her — he recognized these as something more substantial than he'd held for any of the other women in his past decadent lifestyle. Sitting here in the restaurant, Frank's melancholia flowed through his veins like blood additive; it acted as a sort of projector which threw Pearl Courtney's image clear into his mind's eye ... a seriously sad face with her hair-pined up the way he especially liked, though Pearl wasn't aware of it.

Determined to save the moment, he brought his notepad out from the pocket of his frockcoat and flipped it open to a virgin page before dropping it face up on the plain white tablecloth, then he produced his propelling pencil which Dragoon had returned to him, and set about sketching the face of the woman he accepted as his one true love.

His hands were much steadier these days now that he'd managed to stop with the booze and thus within minutes the pencil lines on the surface of the page began to make sense as they merged and swirled across one another and overlapped, and took form ... In time the portrait of a young woman began to form there before him but at first lacked any significant identity or personality; he continued to improve on it, thus it soon took on the likeness of Pearl's appearance as it had burnt into his mind with the affection he felt for her and yet he knew, he was not entitle to feel like this about the woman — Frank completed the sketch to the best of his ability and satisfaction, and then with a blasé gesture added a cameo broach to the neckline of the dress.

The waitress arrived with his meal on a butler's wagon and began setting it out on the table of his booth. After completing his meal and paying the bill, Frank Cotter stepped out on to the boardwalk and realized it really was not too far from the time that folks who took an early supper at the local eating houses would start putting in an appearance ... he decided to take a stroll around the immediate precinct; he really hadn't had much of a look over Kansas City when he came through by train to link up with the stagecoach network headed farther west. All he had seen of the place was the railway terminal, stockyards and the adjacent housing area from the inside of a train carriage — what he had realized was clearly the poor part of town. On that visit his saloon room was not much more than a dump and that is why this time through Kansas City — he planned on taking better digs but this wasn't possible for the town was holding its annual rodeo with a purse of $800. The rodeo carnival had attracted cowhands from near and far, hence, Cotter was lucky to get a room at all — let alone be forced to share his quarters, as sharing sleeping digs in an all male dormitory is common out this neck-of-the-woods, brought about by a shortage of rooming houses.

He walked his meal down before returning to the rooming house to set-up his bed for the night. Upon letting himself into the room Cotter found a cowpoke lying stretched out, fully clothes on a cot — spurs and all — the boarder's holster and handgun had been draped over the iron foot-rail, the scribe had assumed on arrival which beds looked as though they were already taken, though the room was empty save for nine cots lined up so close together that they appeared as though they were attached, he took the cot which looked as though it were free because the stained kapok mattress was still rolled up and tied with twine, the bed blankets and stuffed pillow were piled on the bedsprings alongside it.

He had made the right choice and marked his territory by placing his carpetbag next to the mattress and blankets. The awkward part about sharing this room would mean the only way one could get into bed was to lean across the foot of the cot and crawl along its length to the head-stead.

The man lying on the bed was busy staring up at the unlined ceiling, showing no interest in the newspaperman, nor did he seem anxious to make his acquaintance. In Frank's case he was ready and willing to introduce himself, for it was just common etiquette — after all, sleeping together in the one room was as intimate as you could get.

Cotter approached the man with his hand out. "…Hello — I'm Frank Cotter, one of your rooming partners…" The ranch hand glanced down to the foot of his bed in Cotter's direction. He didn't look as though he was awash with friendliness.

"I take it you're in town for the rodeo?" said Cotter, feeling foolish standing there with his hand proffered towards cowboy. He got a picture of himself looking like a monkey begging for peanuts.

The man put himself out and sat up with a creak of bedsprings and leaned forward from the waist with his arm fully extended so that he might shake hands with this guy who was obviously a goddamn city slicker. They were now so close together that each could smell the others body-odor... The ranch-hand smelt like stale horse sweat and cigarette smoke, between his index and second finger of each hand he could see they were nicotine stained — a visit to a barber or bathhouse would have done wonders for him, thought Frank as they shared a firm handshake.

"I'm Ric Blane," a husky whiskey voice announced as it issued through a mouthful of teeth that had already seen their better days and yet he wasn't any more than twenty-five to thirty years old.   To the cowhand, Cotter's BO was that of toilet water and flour used for soda bread. His hands were soft to the touch like a woman's — this man had never known calluses or if he had it had been a long time ago.

"Yuh ... I'm chasin' after the rodeo purse – ain't had work fer a stretch." Ric said as he removed his Stetson and scratch his scalp through his uncombed mousy hair. *It's possible this ranch-hand has nits,* thought Cotter. *I hope he's not carrying, fleas too?*

"Care ter join a man fer supper, Frank ...?" He enquired, displaying a now warmer manner and scrambled awkwardly from the bed.

This feller said he was out of work; he might be after a patsy to buy him supper? Frank thought; so he said: "Thanks for the invite, Ric — but one's already eaten. I'm gonna make up my cot for later, then it's a stroll about town for some fresh air before turning in. The stage from Junction City wasn't a smooth ride and its jostling tuckered a man out...Maybe another time, Ric?"

"Suit ya' self," Ric Blane stepped round Frank's frame and headed for the door that opened out into the hallway, his spurs jingling away with him as he left Frank to his bed making chore. Frank noted that the cowboy had left his gun and holster behind, and wondered if he would make a goat of himself by calling after Blane about it. He let it pass, but thought it rather careless of the feller to go off leaving his beloved six-gun behind. Since coming west Cotter had learned that a man's hardware was as much part of himself as his horse. But Frank opted to mind his own business, get the bed made and go in yet another search for Pearl in the theatre district even though he wasn't certain that she was still in town. It was something he had to do even if it was a washout.

The theater marquee decorated with Chinese lanterns caught Frank's eye — for he was on the lookout it. He went over for a closer look and search the billboard outside near the ticket kiosk for Pearl's name but did not see her listed anywhere, then it struck him that she maybe too small time here to rate any billing. The kiosk wasn't yet open for business but a stocky woman wearing plenty of rouge and dressed in black taffeta was behind the grille sorting through receipts of an earlier performance. The interior of the kiosk was lighted by a lamp smelling heavily of kerosene. Cotter fronted the woman who scoured at his intrusion while she was busy with her own chores. The scribe wanted to know whom he would have to speak to about checking for the likelihood of work in the theater game. "That would be Mr. J.C. Cohen. But he ain't available right now it's far too early for 'im. Mebbe I can help with yuh enquiry – I know pretty much about the ins an' outs of what's afoot with the program and folks hooked up with the show."

"Fine, then maybe you can help. I'm looking for an actress friend of mine who might have recently joined the show here in Kansas City; I'm only playing a hunch I've no real details to go on..." Frank could see the woman mentally searching her mind. Then scratching the nap of her neck she said: "I fear you might be on the wrong trail, mister. This whole company came down direct from Chicago, lock stock an' barrel. But I do recall, there was a lass here after some performance work but all Mr. Cohan could offer her was a place in the costume department but as I recall she thought that beneath her status."

"I see," said Frank, "and you haven't seen her here about since then?"

The woman shook her head and with that Frank guessed that if it was Pearl then maybe by this she has pushed on up to Chicago in search of work, so he decided to call it quits and returned to the rooming house.

Upon his arrival back at the dorm night was rolling in and he guessed that he ought to make like most country folks and turn in early, after all, that stage trip had made his bones pretty weary; only two cots were in use at the moment of his arrival and their occupants were involved in a "snoring competition" — their cowboy boots gave off the smell of stale diarrhea that is peculiar to some types of sweat-stained leathers.

Frank disrobed and got into his nightshirt and decided that the only way he was going to have a hope of trying for get any sleep, was to pull the blanket up over his head and hopefully that would keep the noise of the snoring sleepers out and the odor of their boots… Ever since his confrontation with Lomax outside Junction City, Frank had difficulty settling down to sleep — the events of the shooting and killing of a man he once called "friend", was not easy for him to live with, it was a *nightly* worry, before allowing him to succumb to a light sleep; but tonight looked as though he was going to have additional problems. He searched for and found the offending boots and carried them out into the passage where their owners would find them with a little effort on their part, but the smell still lingered, they were that *high*. It turned out that besides Ric Blane sharing the room with Cotter there were two other drifters. They and the rest of the fellers sharing Cotter's room were all early risers who assumed that everyone west of Fort Wayne regularly arose with the break of day, but today was different to most days — for the local ranch-hands and town hanger-on's, stood a good chance of winning 800 dollars — big bucks in any ranch dud's language.

At the front of the house Frank found the parlor had been converted into a dining room where breakfast was eaten at the long dinner table which had been polished to a high gloss with place-mats laid out for the boarders — the breakfast servings, crockery and utensils were set out on a nearby buffet— one server held a batch of fried free range eggs served sunny-side-up, lying alongside the dish was a set of food tongs so one could pick up the number of eggs you felt might satisfy your fill; the second serving dish had crisp ham strips ready for the taking, cutlery had been laid on, next to eating irons were a stack of thick China dinner plates, coffee mugs and a couple of coffee-pots, heavy with piping hot java. Cotter brushed away a fly who was coming to make a landing on the eggs as he piled about six bacon rashes on his plate along with three eggs, then he grabbed a set of eating irons and brought it over to the table; here he hesitated, not sure where to sit as he didn't want to encroach on some regular boarder's space. A guy already at the table, was halfway through his meal had half a china mug of coffee-bean juice in front of him; he informed Frank he could put his butt on any vacant chair at the table. So he took one midway down the way and returned to the buffet where he poured himself a black coffee.

As he settled before his breakfast the feller who had acquainted Frank with the boarding houses "breakfast routine", said: "…you, going to the rodeo, stranger?"

"Yes — where exactly do I find it?"

"Down near the freight yards; alongside the railroad tracks. They use one of the stockyards for the event. They've put up a temporary settin' on either side of the bull yard and yore expected ter drop a five- cents donation in a can for a seat — the money goes towards the Catholic orphanage the 'pats built at the edge of town… Father O'Brien will be there with some of the inmates from the orphanage, no doubt."

"And do they charge something for entry to this rodeo?" Cotter asked.

The informant nodded. "The town council hits the spectators, a quarter for anyone passing through the rope walkway. But it's worth it, for the entertainment; they also issue yuh wiv a ticket so as you c'n attend the evening square dance an' see the winning rider collect his prize money!" Then suddenly the man seemed to realize he hadn't introduced himself to the stranger along the table and rectified that as he went on to apologize for his indiscretion.

It turned out the fellow was a Justice of the peace, and went by the name of Mervyn Tucker. Tucker invited the newspaperman to join him at the carnival but suggested he wear a hat as there was very little shade in the open area and he'd be a candidate for heatstroke going bare headed. Cotter told the feller he had a Stetson down in his room but someone whom had been sharing the room had taken a liking to his hat and purloined it, so he would have to buy a new one.

Ric Blane entered the parlor. He had found somewhere to shave and wash-up, but in the process had nicked himself on the cheek with the keen edge of his razor. The cut had stopped bleeding but the injury was noticeable. He served himself breakfast from the buffet and was clearly conscious of his facial cut for he dabbed at it a couple of times with the fistful of bandanna he had in his paw. He wore a smart dark-blue shirt with fancy white piping and a pair of stonewashed jeans. His Stetson was hooked over the butt of his six-gun that was protruding out of the top of his tooled holster and kept his left hand free to feed himself with his knife and fork. He obviously knew the JP; Blane came down to take a chair at the table across from Frank.

"Are you saddling up in the rodeo, this time round, Blane?" The JP inquired.

"Sure am, Mr. Tucker — this'll be my forth year at tryin' ter win that purse!" Blane began breaking down the crisp bacon rashes into small mouth size bits.

"As I recall," Mervyn Tucker announced to the table, which had inherited a few more male boarders. "You've been the runner up fer the last two years. You are slowly but surely getting there; this jist might be yore year!"

Ric spoke with a mouthful of ham and egg and ignored the trickle of blood that had begun to move down his face. "That depends on the standard of nags the council's got down at the stockyards. I'm broke as a rattler with a snapped spine; been outa work fer most of this spring, so I need the cash!"

"I heard tell they've got some pretty nasty critters in this year's bunch, so be warned," Tucker cautioned. "Yore not as young as you used ter be."

"I feel that this is gonna be **my year,** I feel it in me bones." Blane told his breakfast partner.

"You'd better be right — 'coz I'm putting my green backs on you with Red Sanford…" Tucker informed him.

"Didn't know he wuz back in town… Is he runnin' book again?" Ric asked.

Tucker nodded and picked up his drink. "There's five bookmakers have council approval ter cover the action…" The JP took a swallow of java.

Cotter looked at Blane and wondered if energy-wise the man was up to what Mr. Justice were expecting of him. Unfortunately no one could foretell what was ahead for Ric Blane; no one knew that he'd be dead before the day was over — the result of a broken neck when thrown by an outlaw bronco called "Lightning", so named only for that day's Wild West rodeo.

Cotter went shopping for a new hat before the heat of the day came down and had arranged, to meet Tucker out the front of the RIO NEGRO for a civilized midmorning coffee. The JP had some legal papers to sign off for the local lawman and was running a bit late.

Frank closely watching the passing pedestrians on the off chance he might sight Pearl among them. He assumed that if Pearl was out and about town, she could pass by from anywhere. *A man must remember to keep his eyes open at this rodeo, too. She might appear out of the blue,* thought Frank. *She will get a surprise to see me in Kansas City, I bet? Pearl will be thinking I am still back there in Junction City. I shall have to break the news to her about Lester's death — it will come as a surprise, for her to learn he didn't die under the wheels of any freight wagon like the whole town believed.*

How will she react to the fact that it was I who shot and killed Lester? What effect will it have on our relationship? Maybe it'll soften things if I explain to her that it was him, who sliced Ma Kelly's throat from ear to ear and was hoping young Pete got saddled with it! And then there was the death of Derrick Carter. Did Sean Dunne do the drowning alone on Lester's instructions; or did it take the pair of them to pull that off? No matter, the feller was certainly murdered, yet another victim of the Lomax business syndicate because they saw too much.

No. I can't destroy everything she loved about Lester. Not if I can expect our relationship to become something meaningful. But I shall never be able to keep the truth of the business from ever coming out.

"You look lost?" Mervyn Tucker's voice broke through his consciousness.

Cotter turned to find the JP standing at his elbow — he must have come along the sidewalk while Frank's attention was focused on the folks on the other side of the dusty street.

"Merv'?"

"Sorry I'm late. You looked miles away there in yore mind?" The JP added.

"I was thinking. OK, let's go inside and put some coffee in our bellies?"

As the two men turned to move inside the restaurant, Mervyn said: "I got waylaid by the Sheriff on the way here — he had me sign some court documents. Let's grab that free booth over yonder by the curtained windows, which overlooks the sidewalk?" He said as both he and Frank came in off the street.

"Sure, anywhere will do me — what time does this rodeo start, Merv?" asked Cotter as they homed in on the booth and sat down across the table from one another. The same waitress whom had served Frank on his previous visit appeared and took their order. She explained to the customers that they were now giving their clients the choice of having their coffees sweetened to taste by sugar lumps that would accompany their beverage in the cup's saucer. The lass asked the men how many lumps they thought they'd have to sample this new delight, plus, she added there were cream buns to go with their coffees.

The men decided to give it all a try and agreed it would be a new experience … creamy buns and sugared coffee, they discovered a whole new treat for themselves.

Upon being admitted to the rodeo, Tucker took Frank to where the horses and Longhorn steers were corralled in the pens. The animals seem to sense they were to be facing a stressful time — both horses and bulls showed signs of twitchiness and the wranglers were mindful of them as they sorted the beasts out.

All intending riders were gathered in a tent in an unruly queue where their names were being recorded on strips of paper and dropped in a hat. Another Stetson stood next to this hat, which already had the names of the wild broncos, and eventually a riders name was drawn from the hat and matched up horse and number. The fellers who thought themselves the most experienced riders, or could it be that they were less fearful of being hurt, put their names in to ride both horses and bulls — not all of them were destine to complete their ride, as being thrown and maybe stomped on by their breed of beasts would sort the men from the boys, but whether these thoughts entered their minds, it did not show on the surface as they were all displaying a jolly front to their colleagues.

The mounting chutes had been built onto the fencing of the stockyard but a square yard was out of the question so bales of hay had been arranged into a straw wall 3-feet or slightly more in height, to cut off the corners of the square so that the bucking broncos and the steers would be guided as they moved in the confines of the circle — thus giving the public in the two islands of bleachers a decent view of the action… The chutes were being tested without animals to ensure that they'd function right when the rodeo got underway. Once the rider was given his allotted mounts, he drifted off to check his gear as a broken cinch strap or stirrup leather coming at the wrong moment could put a rider out of the competition for the rest of the program, leaving one no chance at the big money, for it was the size of the purse that dragged in the rough riders.

There were folks putting the finishing touches to the tri-colored bunting and rosettes about the area. Two Army Mess tents, had been erected between the islands of bleachers, these sold refreshments, one tent for each of the areas of plank seats; So would-be riders determined not to be put out of the competition by aches and pains from an early fall, were fortifying and anesthetizing themselves with whiskey and locally made beer. Raspberry toffee apples on a stick were laid out on a table covered with white butcher's paper for sale to the cheerful children and ladies with a sweet tooth; a bored adult did her best to keep flies at bay while a lost wild bee alighting on the candy coating of the apples … two teenage boys practiced with ex-army bugles and a fat kid accompanied them on a kettle drum — these were definitely the musicians for today's events.

A steam locomotive hissed and puffed about the marshalling yard; shunting railway cars, trucks and vans about on various tracks and spur lines; the smoke and smell of steam and oil drifted on the breeze across to the bleachers where they seem to finally settle for keeps. There were folks in the growing crowd who were testy about the noise and smell of the working locomotive, their discomfort was being tolerated for it was hoped that the steam engineers' shift would be over by the time the rodeo got started. Tucker did not seem in any haste to get a seat and Cotter tagged along with the man wherever he wandered — it eventuated that JP was searching for the bookmakers, whom had set themselves up under a canvas annex attached to a gypsy style caravan.

True to his word, he placed eight bucks on Ric Blane and encouraged the newspaperman to follow suit.

Finally Tucker began to eye off the seating near where they were and Frank Cotter sighed with relief — *not before time,* he reframed from turning these thoughts into dialog for fear of losing touch with his new found acquaintance.

They climbed their way up through people whom had already claimed seats and settled on a plank on the sixth tier overlooking the arena. Frank mopped his brow with a hanky and ran it round under his shirt collar; the JP did likewise. Cotter caught sight of Blaine down the front, leaning with his back against the timber railing of the rodeo ring, seemingly surveying the spectators, Cotter pointed Ric out to Tucker.

"Blane looks relaxed enough…" The JP suggested. But Cotter was having doubts about the bet he had placed on the cowpuncher; sure it wasn't more than a dollar but again it wasn't a buck he could afford to throw away. He felt he had been stupid. In his opinion the ranch-hand looked as though he could have done with a better night's sleep.

"Time will tell, Merv," Cotter responded as he brought about the demise of a lazy, heavily pregnant blowfly, as it decide to take refuge near the inside edge of his nostril. It was then that Frank saw Pearl step around Blane as she made her way along the fence line of the arena — she carried a light blue parasol and wore a stiff straw bonnet in matching color in the style similar to the type adopted by William Booth's Salvation Army gals who wielded their tinny tambourines on high…He also noticed that she wore a bustle under her long skirts and looked every bit a Lady. "You'll need to excuse me for a moment, Mervyn!" He rose from the plank and instinctively brushed the seat of his pants before setting off after Pearl — he didn't want to lose sight of her in the crowd, though she seemed to be walking with a purpose.

Tucker frowned, "Where ya going, Frank?"

"Hold my seat!" He called over his shoulder as he hurried off after Pearl at which point the buglers and drummer struck up a tune, their rehearsal now over and it was down to business. Cotter battled his way through the crowd, leaving the odd angry person in his wake; He lost sight of Courtney when the crowd came to its feet and balked his progress as the Master Of Ceremonies stepped up with a loudhailer in his hands on the Judge's stand — he brought the instrument to his

mouth and began hollering out to the spectators through the horn: "…
Good afternoon ladies and gentlemen." He paused, not only for
effect but to allow the noise and voices of the audience to quiet down,
so that he might be heard across the arena.

"Now before we start I wanna thank yew for yore cooperation,
folks. We're jist about ready to start today's program and today' Judge
is our most honorable, Mayor, Roger Boone — whose decisions I
might remind you and our riders, will be final… Our timekeeper is the
honorable Deputy Mayor of our City, Mr. Paddy Mead. So, without
further ado let the Kansas City Rodeo of 1867, begin…! "

The crowd in the bleachers cheered like it was the Fourth of July
— the cowboy given the duty of being the first contestant, gradually
lowered himself down into the saddle's stirrups of the wild mustang
whose hooves pawed the broken ground of the chute, it threw its head
from side to side with warning snorts and slobber escaped from its snout
and mouth as its teeth bit down hard on the bit in its mouth, trapping
its tongue.

The emcee continued to enlighten the crowd through his red painted
tinhorn. "— Today's first rider is a well known town identity,
Mr. Tex Slye who's going up against "The Beast". C'mon now
boys let us see some action!"

The horse wranglers dropped to the ground on the outer side of
the chute as Slye's bat winged riding chaps were worked into place on
either side of the fierce animal and his boots found the stirrups … The
chute gate was thrown open and the horse vaulted sideways to land clear
of the chute out in the arena — the abrupt movement of the mustang
whipped Tex's head about on his neck and his Stetson was sent flying
end-over-end, slapping the timber planking of the stockyard's fence
and landed near a pile of fresh manure — a rodeo roustabout ignored
the chance to study the cowpoke's rough-riding style, which was only
ordinary, especially for a man who spent as much time in the saddle as
Tex Slye; it didn't take the bronco long to unseat Slye, the horse dump
him heavily on the center ground of the arena — the end result was
that Tex had been rewarded with a bruised, butt — while the stallion,
now free of its rider, turned all its anger towards trying to rid itself of
the saddle gear. As the ring's mounted wrangler spurred his cowpony
forward into roping range, the stallion crashed into the wall of straw

bales, a bale got caught up between its legs and brought the feral animal to ground with flailing hooves flying in all directions.

Cotter missed most of the action because he was engrossed with returning to his position up there in the bleachers alongside Mervyn Tucker. Later in the afternoon he and Tucker witnessed the fatal ride Ric Blane made, but on the surface it didn't seem as serious as it turned out, he was carried from the arena semiconscious and died later in a tent that was in fact a makeshift ambulance station, that some thoughtful person on the council had insisted on being established in the shade of one of the liquor bars. No one expected anything as drastic as a death to mar proceedings and the organizers made every effort to see that the outcome wasn't common knowledge until after the rodeo had closed, and then liken to an open floodgate the sad news raced through the streets of Kansas City as the topic of the day.

THE RIO NEGRO CAFÉ AND RESTAURANT

Cotter and Tucker had returned to the restaurant for a return round of cream buns and coffee, that was fast becoming some sort of addiction for the pair. Pearl Courtney came in the building on the arm of Donald Stroughton. The sight of the couple took the wind away from Frank's sails — they were led by a waitress across to a booth near the windows and seated. Neither Stroughton or Courtney caught sight of Frank as they passed close by Cotter and Tucker's table … this was understandable as they clearly only had eyes for each other.

Frank sat there hurt, his mouth agape — it was a couple of long seconds before he realized he was sitting there with a cream bun dusted with castor-sugar suspended in his hand over his plate.

"Frank? … You look like you've had someone walk over ya grave!" His new acquaintance, murmured. The question broke the spell that had engulfed Cotter.

"Hey? — oh, sorry," The scribe said, returning to Tucker. "…I was distracted. What were you saying?"

"I said I did my money cold when Blane got thrown."

"It's obvious he didn't put enough glue on the seat of his jeans…!" Frank said as he turned his head slightly to one side and sank his teeth into the soft texture of his bun — the bite squeezing a dollop of thick cream out from between the sandwiched layers of the dessert — it was streaked with veins of strawberry jelly as it fell to his dessert plate; his upper lip was left with a white powdered sugar moustache, that he paid no heed of as he chewed the tasty concoction of pastry. He glanced in Pearl's direction over Tucker's shoulder, it was clear even to him she was besotted by her escort and had no intentions of taking her eyes off the attorney, whom had removed his hat and placed it on the bench seat alongside him, between his right-thigh and the wall.

Frank wondered if the man was wearing his shoulder holster under his suit coat, not that it matted a hoot to Cotter. Donald Stroughton seem to sense he was the center of someone's attention, he began to glance about to locate who in here was sending out vibes his six sense had tuned into. Eventually Stroughton and Cotter locked eyes across the expanse that separated the men and the attorney's eye gave an involuntary start — Cotter would have been the last man he wanted to see and in fact he had thought that when the drunkard scribe had reached Kansas City, that he would have hightail it out of the burgh by the next train, East.

Stroughton did not want Pearl catching sight of Cotter, so he shifted position to block her view of the newspaperman and started another line of conversation with the out of work actress to keep her occupied.

Tucker was having a sip of coffee and perusing the menu left at their table; in fact he seemed momentarily to have forgotten Cotter — maybe he was worried about his heavy bet and was having some regrets?

I wonder what Stroughton has said to Pearl about me? Frank thought, *— has he told her that I was the one who shot Lomax? I can't recall whether he had heard that part of my story before he fled Junction City… One would have thought he would have gotten farther away from JC than this! After what he did this town is still too close for comfort to his crime scene. He will need to do something about me, because he knows that I could go to the Sheriff of this town and tell him all about what happened back in Junction City, and he will get a pair of irons clamped on his wrists…*

Cotter felt compelled to approach the couple and lay the cards on the table…

"Excuse me Merv — I have to call on someone — I'll be back," said Cotter as he pushed his chair away from their table.

"Yore a damn funny man, Cotter," said the JP. "You are always flying off somewhere — have I got body odor or somethin'?"

Cotter, now standing, continued, "No. No way, it's nothing like that, no, nothing personal…" he pushed his chair in. Then he gave JP

Tucker a smile and headed off in the direction of the window booth which Pearl and Stroughton occupied.

Pearl Courtney turned her face in Frank's direction as he homed in on them and her eyes widened — Stroughton had no choice but to follow Pearl's line of sight but knew Cotter was the only one in the room likely to be coming their way.

Both reacted surprised to see Cotter — but he knew that only one was acting and this time it wasn't just the actress. Pearl began to butter a slice of bread that had arrived at the booth pre-cut on a plate with four other slices; Stroughton poured out a couple of tumblers of water for Pearl and himself from the table carafe. The lawyer suspected like himself that their throats had dried.

"Who let you put down roots in this burgh?" asked the lawyer as Cotter stopped at the end of their table.

"You've got **that wrong,**" said Frank. "It's **you** who shouldn't be here—" then nodding in Miss Courtney's direction, continued: "Has this feller mentioned anything to you, Pearl, about fleeing Junction City and the cell they've got waiting for him back there?!"

Frank turned fully to Pearl. "He's only one step ahead of the law and I might make it my business to see the law here holds him for Captain Roscoe and his friends! I've got a Justice of the Peace handy back there!"

"Stop talking verbal diarrhea **you** drunken clown,' Snarled the Lawyer. Pearl stopped toying with the bread and slid along her bench seat to make room for Frank, bulldozing her furled parasol along the seat, until it ended up wedged between her and the wall. "I expect this must turn your guts, seeing me here squiring Miss Courtney on my arm?" Stroughton asked.

"Not really..." Frank lied. "You're not a bad mouthpiece for a country lawyer — so, what is it now, have you run out on your other friends — or were Bevan and Hill always going to take the fall for you?" Cotter asked as he sat down in the booth alongside Pearl and put both forearms on the table and rubbed his hands nervously together.

"How long have you been in Kansas City, Frank?" asked the actress.

"Does it matter Pearl?" Frank asked. Then, remembering the episode between him and the woman down at the theatre last evening, decided

to be bitterly cruel to her. ***"I know** you didn't get taken on by Cohen –
so what are you doing for a crust, working the streets!"*

Pearl was shocked to hear this come out of Frank's mouth. She
had no chance of covering up her reaction and Stroughton became as
tight as a drum as he had to fight the impulse to smash his fist into the
reporter's face.

The scribe continued without any significant pause. "So how come
you and Donald Stroughton are acting so cozy and friendly all of a
sudden?" Cotter asked.

"We're not exactly strangers," said the Attorney as he helped
himself to a toothpick from a vessel on the table. The movement
opened the front of his coat just slightly but it was enough for Cotter
to glimpse the man's concealed weapon. "Does it rile you to see us
together?"

"Why should it?"

"You know very well, why, don't act dumber than you already are.
People in Junction City aren't that blind — you weren't just showering
Pearl with brotherly love; you've got a soft spot pretty close to your heart
for her … Only trouble *is* pal — you don't appeal to the lady. Go ahead,
ask her! Pearl wants someone with class, not some whiskey soaked has-
been whose only claim is that he shot dead the man that meant anything
to Pearl until I came along," said the lawyer.

Frank turned to Pearl and found her giving him a look as cold as
any ice Ma Kelly's ice works ever produced.

"You know?" he asked Pearl with searching eyes.

"I know more than you realize —" she said.

"One thing you don't seem to get Cotter," said Stroughton; Frank
turned back to the shyster who then continued when he had the scribe's
full attention: *"We*…Lester, me and Pearl — we are all cut from the
same cloth, the one class… You were never in the hunt when it comes
down to winning Pearl's pelt. Tell him Pearl, you can see the guy
doesn't wanna believe a word I'm saying!"

Pearl Courtney cleared her throat as Frank Cotter's eyes turned back
to her sitting in the booth between him and the wall of the restaurant
— she was boxed in with nowhere to go, but who says she wants to go
anywhere?

"Don is right. You and me, we're no match —" Miss Courtney said.

Frank's eyeballs began to ache as the realization truly hit home and tears, long since dried out were attempting a rebirth.

*All of them, Lester, Pearl and Stroughton were out to fleece the Pawnees and the rest of mankind just as Washington suspected. I might have been a drunk and an Adulterer! But I **never** and **would never,** turn my hand to knowingly make and sell a concoction of empty dreams to poor unsuspecting souls in dire need of hope…*

Then suddenly he heard his name called from somewhere to his right, a voice laden with hopeless pain; Cotter twisted on his portion of the bench in the direction of *the* anguish voice, standing only eight feet away from him was a man from his dark past; this man now looked as if he had been through a living Hell — there in his fist was a Navy Colt; the threatening muzzle swept up and began to level with Cotter's head. Any escape from the inevitable seemed hopeless, Pearl lay between him and the pane of glass that faced the outside street, and the table between him and Stroughton, he saw only a slim chance and that was to dive under the table in the crowded booth, and pray that the gunman's aim was going to be way off target — his play was one of desperation — he heard gunshots exploding in rapid succession above him over the table and realized that if the table-top was the shooter's target that its timber wouldn't stop a bullet's missile, and he knew that one of those bullets surely had his name on it!

Hot lead was flying here, there, and everywhere about the restaurant! Cotter saw none of action though his presence here had triggered off — only the polished linoleum of the floor…

Cotter's would-be killer was a cuckold husband whom had been hunting for the scribe since the day he learned that the newspaper man had replaced him as his wife's lover!

When the shooting stopped and the RIO NEGRO had become exceptionally stilled, Frank Cotter crawled out from beneath the table to find that a lead slug in the volley of shots had grazed the shoulder pad of his coat and busted it wide open to expose the enclosed padding…

Cotter rose cautiously and looking about him, the deranged gunman lay sprawled dead on the floor with blood pooling out from the underbelly of the corpse — he was aware that there was no movement around and behind him… he turned in the direction of Stroughton who was now lying along the bench, a neat bullet-hole in his forehead and bulging eyes, his death mask, frozen surprise … then Cotter glanced to where Pearl's top half of her body had slumped across the table — a wild slug had caught her in the neck, it was evident that she would speak no more of Shakespeare's written words — folks, who like himself had escaped injury by ducking for cover began to risk moving, wounded began whimpering and folks who had lost loved-ones or a friend began to shed tears.

The shooting had appeared to on-lookers to have been between the lawyer and a bitter drunk, caused mainly because Stroughton had taken the gunman's action as being aimed at him personally, he pulled his concealed .38 and fired a fatal shot into the wild man's body-mass, in turn the impact of the slug had caused the gunman to fire at where the scribe had once been sitting — but now wasn't, for he had dived out of sight; the lead meant for him, struck Pearl in the throat, her destiny was to bleed away her life. But in his death throes Stroughton's trigger finger kept his handgun firing round after round, into the gunman's pirouetting body — whose own weapon also sent wild shots in the direction of the surrounding patrons.

Tucker, the JP, had caught a stray lead in the elbow but the most amazing thing was that Cotter — had somehow escaped without a scratch. And out of all this the scribe had this abstract notion, that within himself — he had the demon drink, under control, certainly a weird and unexplainable train of thought to have at a time such as this — but the brain is an unpredictable dynamo with a law unto itself and he had thus saved his own hide.

Frank Cotter felt comfortable about catching the next train east, for this was now where his future lay ahead of him, but if it had not been for the crazed feller who had come into the *Rio Negro* two days ago and filled the place with mayhem who knows where the chips would have fallen? In a sense, that man's actions had cleared the way forward for the has-been newspaperman in more ways than one. However, no one other Cotter could know how delighted and excited he was about the new position he had been offered in New York as the sub-editor of THE NEW YORK COURIER...

THE   END

Dear Reader,

Current work in progress in the Western Genera by Ronald Williams under the pen name of **_Ira Bex_** is the adventure, LEFT FOR DEAD.

When an out of control posse leaves a U.S. Marshal and that of an ex-Texas Ranger and a prisoner for dead at One Tree Hill, they neglected to make sure their human debris were wholesale corpses — nothing was more surer they'd be bound to regret it big time come the future.

The County seat of Nazareth had its checkered past and even in today's climate of 1870, still proves to be the gateway to heinous crimes of rape, incest, lynching's plus searing lies — which brands the innocent and guilty in their wake and exposes far more to the light of day than bargained for...